The Miasmic Mist
—Volume One

Sisters of Aphrodite

STEPHEN GRENFELL

BALBOA
PRESS
A DIVISION OF HAY HOUSE

Copyright © 2018 Stephen Grenfell.

All rights reserved. No part of this book may be used or reproduced by any means, graphic, electronic, or mechanical, including photocopying, recording, taping or by any information storage retrieval system without the written permission of the author except in the case of brief quotations embodied in critical articles and reviews.

Balboa Press books may be ordered through booksellers or by contacting:

Balboa Press
A Division of Hay House
1663 Liberty Drive
Bloomington, IN 47403
www.balboapress.com
1 (877) 407-4847

Because of the dynamic nature of the Internet, any web addresses or links contained in this book may have changed since publication and may no longer be valid. The views expressed in this work are solely those of the author and do not necessarily reflect the views of the publisher, and the publisher hereby disclaims any responsibility for them.

This is a work of fiction. All of the characters, names, incidents, organizations, and dialogue in this novel are either the products of the author's imagination or are used fictitiously.

The author of this book does not dispense medical advice or prescribe the use of any technique as a form of treatment for physical, emotional, or medical problems without the advice of a physician, either directly or indirectly. The intent of the author is only to offer information of a general nature to help you in your quest for emotional and spiritual well-being. In the event you use any of the information in this book for yourself, which is your constitutional right, the author and the publisher assume no responsibility for your actions.

Any people depicted in stock imagery provided by Getty Images are models, and such images are being used for illustrative purposes only.
Certain stock imagery © Getty Images.

Print information available on the last page.

ISBN: 978-1-9822-0403-7 (sc)
ISBN: 978-1-9822-0404-4 (hc)
ISBN: 978-1-9822-0402-0 (e)

Library of Congress Control Number: 2018905777

Balboa Press rev. date: 05/15/2018

This novel is dedicated to my wife Brenda for her unceasing encouragement and my son Simon who greatly assisted in bringing about the final realisation of the project. August 2017

Prologue

I feel a shiver. Perhaps a sensation of déjà vu somewhere amongst the myriad of faces, staring at me through a haze of alcohol induced fascination, deep in the psyche of the throng of babbling guests. I am momentarily lost in a maelstrom of emotions as I move to speak. I do not need to enlighten my guests, nay most of them will forget nigh all of my short presentation in the twenty minutes or so it will take to deliver but as my father announced to them all, "I'm paying the bill for this so you can at least humour my daughter----- and then you can get to the dance floor where you can grope your wives, or someone else's!"

This at least gave some standing to my chat, which should have been done years back at that much more sober juncture but I was too young. Paradoxically, on the day of my nuptials I have now to tell a tale that could never be adequately recounted in a mere twenty minutes. I shall show these folk some photographs on the overhead projector, a short movie, an actual, albeit fleeting, action film, which would make Bruce Willis look like an amateur. It will be really cool and may even have some gob smacked into the deepest realms of incredulity.

I still stare; pick up a glass of water to clear my throat prior to this monologue. I am so terrified and yet this homily was my idea and now it seems merely to be loosening my bowels.

I am, was, no different to the majority of young women my age. I wanted to go to school, then a gap year to see the world, university to study and try out a myriad of male arse, graduate, get a job, stay single for a few years then marry an intelligent hunk with a great career prospects. Well, I did all that, I think. But although I love my new husband dearly, he will always have to take a lower place to the other two great men in my life. Even to the ten most important women in my life and that figure excludes my numerous girlfriends. My husband, the dearest person you could meet, handsome, strong, energetic, compassionate, generous and kind still lies but third in the hierarchy of men that are most important to me. No, I can hear you thinking that I still retain a flame for some old beau and went to the altar on the rebound; well it is a fine line for the plot of a Mills and Boon but alas not here.

In this place I can see diaries, recall wondrous tales and evoke, with both pride and sadness, experiences I was party to. Strange happenings that appeared at the time to defy known science, were born of such knowledge albeit oft inexplicable, yet were true as I stand here, words such as Armageddon flash by, my mental faculties bring the pages and the stories to life as I clear my throat prior to commencing my oration. It is surreal, my mind is lost in a cacophony of memories and thoughts as I maintain a grip on the here and now but the wall of chronicles, semi legends and anecdotes finally breaks through with a completely selfish and rash fervour. Numerous recollections blend into a single amorphous field of energy that can transcend space and time. I begin my talk and slideshow but on another dimension I seem to be slipping through the net of existence to a place in the Cosmos long prior to my birth. Of course, it may merely be a product of my very fertile imagination. Who knows?

Chapter One

PHILIPPA AND JAMES, 1950

"Pip." The voice echoed gently from the foot of the thickly carpeted, oak staircase.

"Pippa, lunch is ready, darling."

"Coming, Mumma." The small auburn haired toddler was wearing a flowery dress, blue cardigan, white pinafore and black shoes. She carefully replaced the dolls in the small cot and slowly made her way down the long mezzanine.

A figure tiptoed behind the small form as she skilfully negotiated each little descent towards the entrance hallway. "Hello little munchkin," came from behind her. She was swept from her feet and lifted, giggling, high into the air.

"Daddy, lif' me high," Philippa implored, "Lif' me up sky."

Tom Marchant, all six feet, two inches of him, raised the small figure then lowered her. He rubbed his nose along her stomach which effected another bout of nigh hysterical chortling. In his pinstripe suit and swept back hair well-oiled with "Brylcreem" Tom made his way with the giggling bundle into the expanse of the Wye Hall kitchen.

A maid in her black dress and white pinafore was ladling soup into a bowl for the first course of luncheon before the watchful eyes of the mistress. Louise Marchant, a beautiful woman, golden haired, wearing a tartan skirt, white blouse and blue cardigan adorned with pearl ear rings and a pearl necklace, had decided to oversee the meal whilst utilising the substantive eating area of the kitchen. The dining room was, thankfully, being redecorated for the first time in decades.

"You spoil that child, Tom." Louise gently remonstrated with her husband.

"I know my dear," the earl took a seat and bounced Philippa up and down on his knee, "As is perfectly right and proper, I spoil our daughter. And as it should be, our son is the apple of your eye."

"James will not be a problem," she commented while motioning to Hodges, the butler, to pour some wine as the same youngster ambled into the kitchen.

The five year old had black tousled hair, wore black, corduroy short trousers and a formerly white shirt now blotched and smeared with a myriad of green and brown markings. James had obviously made recent ebullient descents from various trees. Blood and mud were also liberally bedecked across both of his knees although he had deigned to wash his hands prior to eating. "What problem will I not be? What's a problem?" The youngster innocently enquired as he dried his hands then unceremoniously plonked onto a chair as a bowl of soup was placed in front of him. "Nothing darling, despite your rather wild and somewhat uncouth, at times, playing habits, one day you will be the Earl of Wye and women will flock, vying to be your intended. You will be able to elect, as men always do, with some assistance from Mummy and Daddy, of course, which of your belles will make the most competent and eligible wife, the next Countess of Wye."

"I do not wish to get married, Mummy." James slurped on his soup. "I hate girls. They are boring and not much fun. They are weak and don't like fighting. Just want to play with dolls."

Thomas guffawed. "That's how it should be at your age, James, but perhaps you will feel differently when you get older. Now eat your lunch with some decorum."

"I truly hope so." Louise rolled her eyes and momentarily gawped. "But when the time is right, Daddy and I will give you every indication as to which of your lady friends will best be suited to be an ideal wife for you."

"Humph-," James was totally disinterested. The idea of getting married only happened to old people like his parents or in fairy stories, never to young warriors such as him.

So his outward persona asserted.

"Thank you, 'Becca." Philippa smiled at the maid as she scooped a ladle full of soup from the tureen and discharged it into the bowl in front of the two year old.

Rebecca smiled back briefly then, once all four had been served, made her way nervously towards the kitchen to await further instructions from Hodges.

"Please do not acknowledge the servants, darling," Louise Marchant directed as she squirmed in a semi-serious turn of phrase, "Apart from Hodges."

"Why Mumma?" Philippa lordly enquired.

"Because they are our servants and not our friends. We need to maintain a definitive line of division between them and us. We are their masters and mistresses."

"I like Rebecca," James opined as he looked up from his bowl, "She's fun and laughs lots. Not not like the smelly old people that come here."

"James! She may be blessed with mirth, but that does not mean she is the right type to be your friend. You will know when your type of friend comes along. And do not call our circle of friends smelly." "You're such a snob, darling," Tom briefly asserted, however the half-hearted smile somewhat relieved Louise.

"That's as maybe, darling, but we both have a duty to our children, as our parents had such obligations towards us."

"You mean they arranged our marriage." Tom sardonically smirked. "Made sure we were unable to choose any other, whether or not we approved."

"It was, is and always will be the way for the upper strata of society, duty and honour must always predicate our relationships. Anyway, would you not have chosen me come what may, that's what you used to say when you were a young Guards' officer on leave from the war? Or were you just after something else from me?"

"Of course, I'm still young and still stand by that avowal." Tom helped Philippa with her soup. "But I would still have appreciated a modicum of self-determination, to at least briefly scan the field for myself. And there is one thing you seem have forgotten, Louise, which is what transpired back in '46. I don't want some no-good bounder from our so called "type" for Philippa who only wants her for her money. I'd rather have a hard worker from elsewhere."

"Elsewhere, you mean the lower middle or even working classes. That is not how things work in our universe and you are as aware as I am. It cannot happen." Louise was adamant.

"Daddy and I always found your avant-garde liberal ideals so endearing darling, I always will, but we reside in the real world. Nonetheless, we have at least ten years to sort matters out, but I already have a few thoughts on Philippa's future."

"My dear, I think we can wait awhile before we arrange Philippa's nuptials."

After lunch, while his sister was taking a nap, James wandered back into his mystery land, his Spanish Main, North West Frontier and Red Indian hunting ground, namely the arboreal expanse, Wye Woods, that stretched for some distance commencing at the boundary of Wye Hall grounds to the family crypt and beyond. The damp smell of the decomposing flora that formed the carpet of his lair was as sweet as the finest eau de toilette to his young nostrils. It was here that strange creatures inhabited and dangerous foes were to be challenged and defeated.

The youngster was a little conscious of current events. He was also helping fight the dreaded communists and drive them from the British Empire, namely Malaya. He needed to scout his territory for the accursed enemies.

EMILY AND JAMES-1950

"I'm off for a walk in the woods, Mommy." Emily squeezed into her small sized Wellington boots and picked up her coat. The early summer in verdant, rural Oxfordshire normally was mild and dry. Nonetheless, it was always so prone to a rapid transition into cold, torrential rain.

"Emily," Mary Wilkinson called from the kitchen.

"Yes, Mommy?" Emily looked up awaiting the imminent bout of counsel.

"Your mother wants ye t' watch out an' keep away from strange men."

"Harvey!" The tone was one of a gentle rebuke. "Only one of us needs t' tell our daughter, if ya wish to, then I'll be quiet." "That'll be fine m'dear.

Time for me t' gets back to work anyways." "Emily, ya' just take cares out there, girl."

"Yes, Mommy." The blonde five year old replied. She was wearing blue dungarees and Wellington boots while slipping into her light summer coat, picked up her bag, opened the lower half of the stable style door and walked out. Soon she passed her father's blacksmith shop and then continued walking through the village of Alvescot.

She waved at her father, Harvey Wilkinson. The blacksmith was medium height with thick black hair that was betraying the very first hint of grey. He wore his work overalls while opening up his stone constructed work place. Emily hopped and skipped as she continued on towards the small wooded hillside that veered away to the north of the community.

The earth was still damp from recent heavy showers but this would not deter the tiny artiste from seeking out her favourite working spot from where she would write great yarns of young Lochinvars and Robin Hoods who would drive away the evil men and woo young maidens in their stone castles. After composing such accounts in illegible scrawl, she would illustrate her classic work with drawings in wax crayon.

Whilst in her private spot, the top of a wooded knoll that overlooked the greater expanse of woodland, Emily saw a brief image flash past her eyes.

It seemed, in the short time she had to view, like the outline of a man in black intermingled almost to obscurity by the green hue of the leaves and dark shades of the woody aspects. It moved furtively and with stealth towards the mansion house on the other side of the forest.

Her curiosity overcame her desire to write and she slowly sauntered down the hill. The phantasm appeared to be moving from tree to tree, watching each way as if to check whether or not opponents were proximate. The sprite flashed into the ether and out of view. Nevertheless, the intrepid young explorer continued to trail the spectre as it wove in and out of the shrubbery into the heart of the woodland, where she thought strange creatures dwelt.

The eyes were demonic, wide open and bereft of any compassion. There was simply a feral instinct to inflict pain and relieve desire, accompanied by an unseen yet equally galumphing and ignominious peccable entity of base malignant traits.

The saliva flushed around the mouth of decomposing teeth as he moved while tracking a quarry that meandered in and out of the interstices of the abundant arboreal sculptures. The groin was aching, he needed something forbidden but his soul would not rest. No matter how decadent or affront to any edict man, notwithstanding those of God, would subsequently be transgressed.

The breath was in uneven pants as a mixture of fear and apprehension flashed across his consciousness.

He would never be found out. He would perform his vile deed, drink his fill of the cup of such a prey then remove the small remains to where the police, or indeed anyone, would never suspect. Yes, yes, they would doubt him; they would deem him as guilty as Original Sin but would never prove it. The man laughed silently at the thought of outwitting the Oxfordshire Constabulary, sweet revenge for all the other times they had taken him away for questioning.

They had been wrong! Yes, yes, he had done that which they accused him of but they would never understand, what is so wrong?

Small children tease you on, they are equally as culpable but no one except he and his kind would ever appreciate or empathise such a premise.

"Normal", he grunted, "whatever that means, but normal men my age like women, some even crave men their own age but I, love, yes have a passion for, boys who are but a quarter of my own short span of years."

He had followed the chit, observed him for months, and now it was time to cash in the expanse of hours and effort he had invested in this sordid undertaking.

Time would exculpate him from his deeds; they must for they control the shadow; that never, never land that lays some place between the shores of a moment and the scent of a dream. We who can practise our arts with impunity, for who would believe a five-year-old boy against that of a grown man? Such imaginations or deceit do the young folk impart on the world and many actually believe their erroneous fables and misconstructions.

His breath was thick with halitosis, the stench of decomposing perspiration and filth oozed from the depths of his rarely laundered clothing. He could see the silhouette of a small figure, a child whom he knew would be heading in this direction, a prey so oblivious to his presence that the snatch would be a mere basic move in his arsenal of sadistic mischief.

"I have to investigate," Emily muttered to herself in a quasi-adult manner. She silently followed the dark silhouette now heading to the easterly edge of the woodland.

"The hide of Cochise." James' eyes opened wide with excitement as he scurried up the embankment to the rocky outcrop above. "Have to take great care." He noticed the many and varied loose rocks near the summit. "If I start an avalanche, the Apaches will hear and the trap will be useless."

The mind was agog with visions of hordes of Red Indian savages concealed in the undergrowth ready and waiting to pounce upon the intrepid troop of the Third US Cavalry led by the heroic Captain James Marchant. He was far away in 19th Century Arizona, prowling after the great chief Cochise and his braves in the forests that juxtaposed the hunting grounds of the ancestors.

"We have to be careful, Sergeant," the child called out in his most officer like voice, "Yes, we have sir, " he responded, doing his utmost to sound vaguely similar to Sergeant Major Michael O' Rourke. The Ward Bond character had featured recently in the Western film "Fort Apache", which he had recently viewed with his father at the local cinema. "Place is full of injuns, sir," the Ward Bond voice called. "Sergeant, take the men to the top and spread out," the officer voice commanded.

"Yes, sir," the O'Rourke character loudly acknowledged. James promptly ran up the escarpment to marshal his cavalry and prepare to repulse an Apache attack.

He knew that the Apaches were galloping from the reservation to the fort. James had to hold them or the garrison would be wiped out by Cochise and his savage hordes.

"The Third Cavalry will stop him." The boy grinned as he made the summit of Indian mountain just before the imaginary Apaches, whooping and a hollerin' made their attack.

"Charge," the officer voice called as in a pivotal instant James was thrown to the mushy ground then lifted high in the air before being dropped again.

The fetid, musty, foul smell made him retch.

"Little boy out playin'." A voice sneered through an onslaught of disgusting breath; James gasped for air and tried to scream.

"Little boy, naughty, shouldn't be 'ere, not 'ere." Tears welled as the youngster could feel a rough hand undoing his short trousers, this was not fun, it was frightening, and it was not part of the game. Macabre visions took over his mind as he could feel something touching his private area. "Keep quiet young Marchant, no one can 'hear ye."

His throat was then being crushed. All manner of strange colours and figures shot across the panorama of his weakening consciousness. James could still taste the pungent breath on him as darkness began to envelop his very being.

He could barely make out the sound of a thud when the figure at his throat suddenly relaxed the enormous pressure of his grip. The erstwhile assailant fell to the leaf festooned earth at the side of the barely conscious James.

"You little—," the man whimpered before a second crunching resonance of stone on bone exploded nearby.

James tried to look up but was only able to distinguish what he deemed to be a small figure. The outline of a little girl holding what seemed to be a large object above the moaning assailant then dropping it onto his head.

There was a small cry and the child proceeded to repeat the action which seemed to James as if it were counted in dozens.

The man lay still. Silent and still. No rank breath was exhaled from the bloody, stubble encircled mouth, no movement from the slim torso and limbs.

"Upsie". A little hand reached for him. "Up yo' get, th' bad man's asleep now."

James fastened his trousers. He looked up with disbelief as the prettiest girl he could ever have imagined helped him to his feet. "Who are you?"

"I 'm the blacksmith's daughter. Who be you?"

"I am James, who is the man?"

"He be the village idiot, Barry Frost."

"Who said he was the village idiot?"

"Me Dad. He said Barry Frost's the village idiot an' I should keep aways from 'im. What be a village idiot?"

"You talk funny." James sniffed the air.

"Y' talks posh, like Lord Snooty. D 'ya knows what a village idiot is?"

"Must be a stupid person that lives in a village." James puffed his chest to underscore his intellectual prowess. "And I do not talk like Lord Snooty."

Emily took James by the hand as they looked at the motionless figure of Barry Frost.

"At least his bad breath has stopped, is he dead?"

"No, he just sleepin'." Emily stood on one of the filthy hands. "Me Dad tells me that 'e'll hit me wiv his drivin' 'hammer t' gets me t' sleep if I stays awake at night. I hit 'im wiv a rock 'cause I don't 'ave a drivin' 'ammer. He's asleep. How d' ya know ya don't talks like Lord Snooty, 'ave ya 'eard 'im? He's in a comic. Th' Beano."

"I know he is in the Beano comic and no one has heard him talk. I wish I had a driving hammer or whatever you call it."

"Ya can see my dad's 'hammer," Emily suggested then smiled, "It's not far to my dad's shop. It's a blacksmith's 'ammer. "

"Your father is the blacksmith and farrier. He shoes the horses on my father's estate?"

"Yeah, 'e is. Harvey Wilkinson is 'is name. I'm Emily Wilkinson."

"Pleased to meet you, I'm James Marchant." He was in the midst of a bout of decorum when the previous confidence evaporated, reclaiming the full terror of the recent incident. It began to manifest as he started to shake uncontrollably and burst into tears. Emily put her arm around him. "Let's go t' my 'ouse. We can get a cup o' tea." After a while James regained composure and wiped the tears from his cheeks, sniffed then looked at Emily. "I would love a cup of tea, thank you. I think we should get married. You are very plucky for a girl. "

"I am an' I thinks we should be married too."

The little girl picked up her bag of papers and crayons, put on her coat and sauntered hand in hand with her newly betrothed towards the blacksmith's workshop.

⇢ Stephen Grenfell ⇠

THE DIARY OF DANIEL - PENNED IN 1966

What is reality? I, or someone I aspire to be or may be or may imagine, perpetually poses this immortal conundrum, ranking but second to that of the sages since time began; -Why? I feel yet it is not substantial, I see yet the light is opaque. This existential riddle may, nay will, never be fully probed and become implicit but in the realms of the miracle of being it lies within that which I believe to be the veritable psyche that stands on the shore of time striding betwixt that which transpires in the waking world and a hazy, esoteric universe, a replica, perhaps, of consciousness. Nonetheless who can say for certain when we dream, in dreams dream or are really in the substantial mode of life. From a very young age, long before I can recall, ergo I rely on the testimonies of others. I spoke with words and phrases unknown to my tender years augmented with total gobbledegook. Such verbalisations caused an amalgam of incredulity and intrigue to those actually listening. These included -"déjà-vu," "the Swinging 60s," "Aden and the emergency during the Summer of Love," "Vietnam war and the Battle of Hat Dich," "The Beatles," "Free love," "LSD", "Man on the Moon," "Punk Rock", "The Northern Ireland Troubles," "Abba", "Lib –Lab Pact," "Thatcher's Britain," "The Falklands war," "Prince Charles married Lady Di."

The list is almost infinite. I was two years old in 1950, I could barely talk let alone converse in such an almost intellectual manner, prognosticating about affairs that seem never to have occurred but were to in years yet to come. There were nice, nugatory, childish, words emitted such as "Dada off to work" intermingled with "In 1969 I shall be at war in a hot foreign land." These presages were initially ascribed to my photographic memory and repeating items I had heard until I chirped out in a baby voice in that the war in Korea would end in 1953 and be a stalemate. My doting parents were obfuscated. No war was being fought on the Korean peninsula, yet three weeks later when North Korea invaded South Korea they were mortified.

The news of such an invasion was bad enough, but they could form no rationale for my astonishing oracular faculties.

I can see plainly a figure, a man, perhaps in his early 60s. He maintains an astonishing level of physical fitness and muscular potency. This entity stations himself within a quadrant of the Cosmos connected to me by some ethereal thread and there is an exchange of energy across the strands of time and substance. I am convinced that man is me, or a version of me.

I have no means of proving my astounding hypothesis but I would like to believe that all time and matter choose many directions in which to navigate eternity. Perhaps, just maybe, identical persons travelling through this eternal road experience a cross of trails, a union of souls if you prefer, abstracting all knowledge and experience from one Universe, to another. Just perhaps, no one will ever truly know. Or will they? I can perceive that deep in my innermost cerebral mechanics, churning through a trillion, trillion, trillion neuron jumps, reaching from the innermost recesses of the coastline of my soul to the zenith of consciousness. I sense that man. Yes, it is a man, and it is a man with the same DNA, identical thought patterns and physical structure. Peradventure in a parallel Cosmos, we are one of the same. We may be divided and connected by the very composition of time itself. Not space as that lodges in the same sphere, but time, the enigmatic fourth dimension that Herbert George Wells so beautifully portrayed in his classic "The Time Machine" and has been ruthlessly plagiarised since.

However, proximate to this person I observe another being. This individual is not benign. He boasts a pallid face, swept back hair with a rapidly receding hairline boasting a mouth so replete with malfeasance it fills me with the coldest, primeval dread. I feel that my future will unfurl this mystery, one that has slept since the creation of existence itself, back before a chronological perception, before God.

DANIEL-1948

"Mister and Mrs. Gibson." A young physician approached them exuding an air of concern disturbing the already unsettled parents.

"What's wrong with my baby?" Daisy Gibson blurted, severing his intended verbal flow in midstream. She almost choked on the odour of strong, redolent disinfectant fumes prevalent in all hospitals of the new National Health Service. The maternity cottage hospital in Alnwick, Northumberland, Hillcrest, was no exception. .

"Not so much wrong, Mrs. Gibson." Doctor Robertson was measured in his response.

"Well why da 'ee wanna see us, Doctor? It's only two weeks since she gave birth."

"Your son is well, Mister Gibson. As far as we know, he is of normal size, with no surplus fat over and above what a baby should, yet he weighs 15 pounds. This would be fine after a few months but for a newly born it is very heavy yet we cannot explain it."

"Sounds like something's amiss t' me, Doctor."

"It may be that his muscle is more compact than other babies, Mister Gibson, but since he was born we have been monitoring him very closely and have drawn two fairly dramatic conclusions."

"An' they are?" Daisy was puzzled; she seemed to be floating in a maelstrom of uncertainty, unsure as to whether or not she should panic or bloat with pride.

"He has two things which we all aspire to. He will have great strength, and by that I mean that if he continues to develop at this rate he will be 20 times as strong as say a coal miner and have an extremely high level of intelligence, much higher than a university professor."

"What we gonna do about the wee bairn?" Daisy looked over the rolling landscape. Jackie drove them in an old Morris 8, dirty and unkempt but nonetheless mechanically sound, towards their property, Coquet Farm. It was located some nine miles from Alnwick along the densely wooded banks of the beautiful River Coquet.

"What the hell d' ye mean, woman?" Jackie sounded bemused by his wife's question.

"If the little bugger's as strong an' brainy as the doc says, he'll d' all the work on the farm soon as 'e leaves school."

"Aye, maybe Jackie Gibson but he can do all that after 'e comes back from university. That's if 'e wants."

"Alright lass. We can argue 'bout that in a few years or less. As long as 'e gets the chance t' work on the farm."

"If he wants to work on your farm, he can. After he's been t' university."

"Well Daisy, pet. At least he can learn judo an' karate likes I said. Ye cannot be against that? Th' doc says he'll be strong as an ox. Ten oxes!"

"Alright Jackie Gibson, ye can get that bloke t' teach 'im judo when he's older and that other thing, long as he gets to university!"

Daniel was placed in his wooden rocking cot. He energetically moved his arms and legs around whilst gazing intrigued and mesmerised by the long, gnarled branches swirling tantalisingly in the autumn breeze outside the old, draughty window frames. Images crossed through his small head, which meant absolutely nothing and totally everything to the infant.

One of the cats yawned then slumped lazily onto the mat next to the wooden crib.

The proximate log fire made this a prime resting spot for the luxury seeking feline.

The room suddenly became much lighter, the intensity turning it from deepest shadows of night to the radiance expected of mid-day in an instant. The illumination was fired by a raceme looking anomalous luminescent apparition which appeared seemed to glide from an expansive lustrous object hovering within. At once the cat shrieked out in terror and bolted from the room.

EMILY AND JAMES-1950

"Come on." Emily impatiently hastened James on as she carried her bag of writing materials in one hand and virtually pulled the small pallid figure of James in the other.

"Are you sure we need to say anything?"

"O'course ye silly boy. We'll tell m'dad that the village idiot is asleep in the woods."

The reverberating noise of steel against steel on the anvil echoed throughout that segment of the village.

"Emily," the voice of Harvey Wilkinson, village farrier cum blacksmith, sounded from the bowels of the smithy.

"Yes, Daddy."

"Yous is back early, girl."

"This 'ere is James, he was playin' in the woods when the village idiot tried t' take off 'is trousers so I put 'im to sleep with a rock."

The cross pein hammer fell to the floor.

"What 'appened, PC Ord? Is Barry Frost dead?"

"Aye, the doctor took a look at 'im in Wye Woods and e's as dead as a dodo."

"But what 'appended will they arrest Emily? Hang her?" Mister Wilkinson seemed on the verge of a nervous breakdown as he frantically quizzed the stout village policeman.

"Calm down, Harvey. She'll neither be arrested nor hanged. If for no other reason than she's well below age of what they call criminal responsibility," Ord evenly reassured the hysterical figure stood before him. They were in the small interview room of his village police house.

"The doctor has seen Master Marchant and little Emily. WPC Evans, luckily down from Witney, and me talked to James and your little Emily. Seems like Frost attacked young Marchant in the Wye Woods and your little girl, far from bein' a criminal is in fact a little heroine, she saved young Marchant—."

"What is going on officer? What has happened to my son?"

The figures of the Earl and Countess of Wye burst into the room. PC Ord was well over six feet tall yet the daunting figure of Thomas Marchant seemed to well overshadow him.

"My Lord, I shall inform you at once, sir."

"Terrible, just terrible, Ord." Marchant was visibly shaken by the traumatic revelations. "They be, My Lord. But could 'have been much worse if little Emily Wilkinson 'ad not been passing nearby."

The tear stained face of little James Marchant appeared, tightly holding the hand of the equally diminutive figure of Emily.

"Let Emily go, James," the quivering voice of Louise Marchant lightly resonated from behind her son.

"Will not! Will not! Will not! Emily stays with me!"

"Emily, let go of young Master Marchant's hand."

"Daddy, James not want me to let go."

"Let go of 'is hand!" Harvey Wilkinson intentionally sounded threatening as he moved slightly towards his daughter.

"If I may suggest," Thomas Marchant said, proffering a diplomatic interjection.

"Yes, M' Lord?"

"Mister Wilkinson. It would be no great trouble for your daughter to come and spend a little time with James at Wye House, if of course you agree, and perhaps it may also assist James as he appears very unsettled right now." "Are you sure, dear?" Louise was not totally at ease with the idea and cogitated momentarily. "Very well, Tom, my driver Biggs will take her home."

"Thank you, Louise, in these very strained and confused circumstances I am sure that it would do James more harm to have Emily torn away from him at this moment."

Activity was intense at Wye Hall, albeit subdued. The butler came into the entrance hall to meet the earl and the others. Lady Wye spoke out in her normal authoritative manner.

"Hodges. Master James had a terrifying experience so a young girl from the village is here to keep him company for this afternoon. Could you get cook to prepare them both high teas in half an hour? Fried chipped potatoes with something is what I believe young Miss Wilkinson would like?"

"Yes, My Lady." The tall former Coldstream guardsman assumed a rigid stance then marched briskly off to the kitchen.

"Mrs. Cromer!" The butler swept into the servants' wing. The dumpy, grey haired cook was busy stirring a massive bowl of seed cake mixture while Rebecca arduously scrubbed the marble worktops. "What's the news about little Master Marchant, Mister Hodges?"

"I understand from what the master said, quietly to me after her ladyship had taken young Master James to the nursery, that he is very badly shaken."

"What 'appened Mister Hodges?" Rebecca's eyes widened, beaming intensely with curiosity.

"In due course, Rebecca. Mrs Cromer, would you and Rebecca prepare high tea for Master James and his guest? Something like a nice plate of sausage, egg and chips with lemonade and bread and butter would be appropriate on this occasion."

"Who's the guest, Mister Hodges?" Mrs. Cromer wiped her hands of the gooey cake mixture and began to move crockery and cutlery onto the main kitchen table.

"I believe it is a young girl, name of Emily from the village---."

"Emily Wilkinson!" Rebecca was engrossed in the subject as she began to peel potatoes. Her red hair was falling over her brow while her long slim hands laboured at pace.

"Refrain from interrupting, Smart." Mister Hodges was irritated; Rebecca assumed a muted stance and continued to absorb the revelations emanating from her household manager.

"Rebecca's just a tad rash, she's young Mister Hodges, continue wiv your disclosures if y' would, please."

"Well. This discussion must not leave these four walls."

Rebecca and Mrs. Cromer both nodded. The remainder of the staff were out attending to their duties.

"Alright. Mister Biggs drove his lordship and the countess to the police house where young James had already been seen by the doctors. Young Emily and master James were being spoken to by PC Ord, our local constable, a very upright and compassionate man, and a WPC from somewhere other than Alvescot."

Hodges sat down and lit a Players Navy Cut cigarette as the women continued to prepare the meal.

"It appears," Hodges continued his narrative then drew deeply on the cigarette, "That Master James went walking, as he does almost every day, playing his games of soldiers in Wye Woods. And that very strange boy, the one that is retarded—."

"You means Barry Frost the village idiot." Mrs. Cromer was psychologically uplifted by the enjoyment of knowledge not yet possessed by the normally taciturn and dour Hodges. The events of the day had morphed the tall butler into a garrulous individual.

"That is precisely whom I mean. Apparently Frost had followed young master James into the woods--."

"He should never 'ave been let there by 'imself." Rebecca deigned to offer her opinion.

"That is by the by." Hodges frowned at the maid. "Nonetheless, it happened. Master James was playing in the woods when the poor young mite was assaulted. Frost tried to—em, you know what I mean?"

"What's that?" Rebecca was determined to remain inclusive.

"I'll tell you when you gets married. Now go on Mister Hodges."

"Humph," Rebecca silently griped.

"Well it transpires, according to Mister Biggs, that before that brat Frost could inflict any real physical harm, little Miss Wilkinson bashed him soundly over the head with a rock. Now he's dead."

"Ooh my Lord. We must make the master and 'is little saviour a banquet fit for a little king and 'is little queen and saviour. Let's move Rebecca, we've big helpings of sausage, egg and chips, lemonade and bread and butter to prepare."

Emily began to tuck into her large portion of high tea. The two tots looked even smaller in the huge, luxuriant, classic dining room being waited on by Rebecca and supervised by the lady of the house.

"Emily." James smiled at his new friend. "Would you mind if I showed you how we correctly hold our knives and forks when partaking in the eating of food?"

"That'd be nice, as you're to be me 'husband, I think it's right."

Rebecca giggled while Louise Marchant almost choked.

PHILIPPA-1950

Philippa tossed and turned. Her sleep was interrupted by the noise, the cacophony, of a distraught James having to say goodbye to his friend Emily. Philippa had deemed Emily to be so grown up and such a champion she had decided they would always be friends.

The staff had echoed her parents' praises for the little heroine who had saved the life of her darling elder brother although she was not totally sure what saving a life meant.

Daddy had put her to bed although Rebecca had first washed and changed her into her nightgown. The tiny eyes began to slowly slide shut when she could see a shimmering light hover from the window until it was circling the area next to her cot.

"'Ello," she looked at the spectre, sensing she should really be scared but instinctively discerned that there was nothing to instigate undue apprehension.

"Hello," a gentle voice spoke from the core of the translucent apparition.

"'Ho are you?" Philippa was intrigued, her eyes beaming at the glow.

"I am not sure, I'm either dreaming or I've gone mad. Are you Philippa Marchant?"

"Yes, is Phi'ipa. 'Ho are you?"

"I'm not sure whether I should tell you this, you are so young but I am your husband in the future."

"Weally, we's is married likes Mummy and Daddy?"

"Yes."

"Does we live happy?"

"You speak well for a two year old toddler, in due course all shall be revealed." The illumination was gone in an instant.

"Mama," Philippa tucked into her soft-boiled egg and buttered, toasted bread soldiers,

"Man, bright, like lights up there, came to my woom, said 'e would marry me."

"Louise, what did Philippa say, darling?" Thomas looked up from his Daily Telegraph.

"Our daughter has a very vivid imagination, she just said that a man made out of light came to her room and said he, or it, would marry her."

PC ORD-1950

The fallen leaves from autumn still lay putrefying. They lay on and around the drenched mud path that wound from the narrow country lane to the cottage where Violet Frost, widow of the Parish of Alvescot in Oxfordshire lived. Earlier in the day, Woman Police Constable, WPC, Katie Evans, on loan from Witney, had already broken the news to Violet that her son, Barry, was dead. This was ironic to the edge of dark humour as he had been slain by a five-year-old toddler.

A chill wind blew dispassionately down from the Cotswolds. Police Constable Stuart Ord was not yet overweight but could feel the onset of adiposity around his midriff. He stepped briskly over the pathway to the deteriorating cottage and knocked on the door.

"What's ye want?" The unmistakeable voice of Mrs. Frost bellowed out before the hapless police constable had even reached the paint peeling stable style door.

"I just wanted a quick word, Violet."

"Ye can go and stuff yerself, Stuart Ord. I remembers the days you went sniffin' after me crumpet." Ord eased passed the middle aged slapper and into the cottage kitchen.

"Ancient history Violet. More important things to chat 'bout."

"Yeah, like that little bitch that killed me boy. Are you gonna arrest 'er?"

"Barry was up t' no good."

"Whatcha mean?" Violet was even more incensed.

"WPC Evans told you, Violet, when she came to tell you 'bout what 'appened to Barry that she's only five. And WPC Evans also told you she can't be arrested for anything!"

"You's gotta arrest 'er." Violet was shaking with anger

"Can't, ye knows that Violet not 'til she's at least ten."

Violet was pulsating grief. "Stuart Ord, I think ye'd best go. We knows about the Wilkinson girl, an' God 'imself will judge her."

"That's right Violet, but if I was you an' your boy, I'd just 'ope that nothin' 'appens to little Miss Wilkinson and I don't need t' spell that out t' ye. Ye knows that from ya own kids, Violet. No criminal responsibility 'til a child's ten year old."

"Fuck that Mister Ord!" The small, dark haired, unwashed and unshaven figure of Jimmy Frost pranced in, his face bulging and distorted with acrimony

"What's ye mean?" "Just whats I says, Mister Ord!"

"I says. Whats ye mean Jimmy?" The police officer turned curt and officious.

"That little bitch, five she mays be but she killed me brother, our Barry, an' she 'as to pay."

"I knows you're upset Jimmy, but yer 'ave to stop makin' threats. Yer old enough for the gallows now ye be 18. I says I only came 'ere to see if ye was alright, I'm sorry 'bout Barry but 'e was up to no good."

"Whatcha mean?" Jimmy and Violet snarled in riled unison.

"Ye knows Barry was always followin' little boys, both of ye do. He's been in front of the magistrate enough times, well 'e was molesting young Merchant when little Emily bashed 'im with a rock. I'm sorry for ye Violet that Barry's dead but I think ye know what the truth be."

Ord glanced across the detritus cluttered kitchen, briefly at Violet Frost then left.

"Bastard," Violet gasped.

"We'll have our revenge mum." Jimmy maliciously scowled.

Chapter Two

NARRATOR

The words of the tale march boldly along. But what are words? Sounds, marks on paper? What is sweet, or sour? Do they taste the same to us all or do we each have a unique, personal sensation when it comes to colours, smells, touch taste and resonance? Perhaps. Perhaps not.

My brain is working at full throttle. I am feverishly articulating events, a history, lives, yet concurrently my subconscious mind seems to be regurgitating in a loquacious overdrive, the narrative in a few moments that which the weaver of life laboured for aeons to finalise.

Somewhere deep in the trillions of nerve endings housed within my cranium I can perceive, but slightly, a phenomenon, the way in which our highbrow, buoyant scientists speak of the Big Bang Theory. That is to say an entire Cosmos is born within millionths of the measurement of time we refer to as seconds. Not epochs, millennia, centuries, decades, years, months or even weeks, no, in millionths of a second for histories to be written, Biblical events to transpire and the rise and fall of many an empire. At least that is my extremely naïve understanding of the principle. In my private Big Bang I verbalise on one level to an audience that actually seems to be taking note, hanging on every syllable whilst my oh so slightly trembling voice imparts to all. I have heard many theories of life and the Cosmos and am sentient that my discourse with my semi-inebriated listeners has lasted but a few moments. It has barely begun in fact, whereas in my analogous, personal rendition, time, or the concept recognised as such, has speeded ahead a few short years and the foremost people in my life had aged accordingly.

→ Stephen Grenfell ←

REBECCA 1955

Rebecca April Smart, known only as Rebecca of course to those living upstairs in Wye Hall, had become loved by the children and appreciated by the adults for the undiminished enthusiasm and zeal she applied to her work. She held the position of nanny and maid in the household of the Earl of Wye and his family. Becky, as the other members of staff addressed her as well as the ten-year-old James and seven year old Philippa, perpetually thanked the gods of fate for the outstanding good fortune that had befallen her since commencing her position as a chambermaid with the Marchant household in Wye Hall.

Becky was like so many children of World War Two, those whose father never came home from the conflict. She had been 11 years old in late May 1944 when her beloved father kissed her goodbye and left forever. John Smart was in Three Commando of the Army when a few days later he died a hero on Sword Beach, Normandy.

John had been a conscientious, proud man who worked the farms man and boy, marrying his childhood sweetheart Margaret McGregor in the summer of 1930. They lived in a tithe cottage on the estate near Bampton and the work was regular. However, it was poorly paid by industrial standards although a few perquisites existed apart from working in the clean, fresh air. There was a weekly ration of a dozen eggs, two quarts of milk as well as the proceeds both financial and fare from the large kitchen garden attached to the cottage.

Becky was the first to be born in 1933, three years after the couple's nuptials, and a longish gap between marriage and the first birth by the norms of the 1930s working classes.

Somewhat paradoxically, from Becky's birth there was almost a production line of births. Margaret Smart once told her eldest "the kids were batched out yearly until 1940".

John Smart was blessed with a penchant for hard work. Accordingly, he ensured that his expanding family was never short and the farm labourer could easily have avoided military duty in the Second World War. The work he performed was designated a reserved occupation, i.e. essential to the war effort. In 1941 John enlisted with the Gloucester Regiment and after training, plus some active duty, was selected for the commando course at Achnacarry in the Highlands of Scotland, 15 miles north east of Fort William. This was followed by intense endurance tutoring at the Special Training Centre Loch Ailhort on the west coast of northern Scotland.

John Smart became one of the new elite commandos and took part in the Dieppe raid of August 1942, then saw action in Italy before returning home briefly for the invasion of Europe. As part of the 1st Special Service Brigade he was killed on the first assault ashore of D-Day on June 6th 1944. Rebecca was devastated by the loss of her father. Nonetheless, circumstances soon obliged the mature 11 year old to assume an adult role in the household, principally taking care of her younger siblings.

The owner of the farm, Ian Forsyth, made every effort to allow the family to stay in the modest, thatched cottage but inevitably it became essential to replace John. It was not long after that the family was forced to leave to a smaller property on the edge of the village of Clanfield.

Margaret applied herself to a variety of house cleaning jobs and worked as a bar maid in the Plough Hotel whilst Rebecca cooked and cleaned before and after school. The slightly built, smallish, red haired girl was rapidly turning into a beautiful young woman, a fact not missed by her mother's new beau, Peter Emms, a man of low reputation and exceptionally lazy. It was nonetheless a product of the times; Margaret Smart knew that eligible men were in short supply, especially for those women with large readymade families.

The wastrel Emms may have given Margaret Smart a little of the affection and comfort she desperately craved after being widowed but to the rank individual he viewed the situation from a somewhat obverse view. The small unshaven man had by some unknown means evaded service of any kind in both world wars. He now enjoyed the luxury of having two women to wait on him hand and foot and a war widow's pension plus Margaret's work wages to plunder for his own needs. The individual moved to seduce Rebecca one night when Margaret was working at the pub, only to be met with a robust and total rejection.

The young teenager duly informed her mother who simply replied that she was jealous and attempting to put a wedge between her and her "darling Peter."

The final showdown over, Margaret Smart unwittingly became the loser in this triangle as Rebecca immediately packed her bags after her stepfather had brazenly lied to her mother claiming Becky had "made it all up."

The youngster lived a rough, outdoors existence until an old school friend, anxious to help, had mentioned that nearby Wye Hall was seeking the services of a parlour maid.

The 14 year old knocked at the front door instead of using the tradesman's entrance as would have been deemed the only acceptable custom for such solicitations.

A stroke of fortune or destiny had befallen that day as the servants had all been given the day off and the only person to receive her was Thomas Marchant, the Earl of Wye himself.

Rebecca was duly invited inside where she nervously explained her dire predicament to Tom Marchant. Tom was duly impressed; her late father's proclivity for industry was widespread knowledge around Oxfordshire. The earl was also well aware of John Smart's impeccable war record and premature death on the beaches of Normandy. He had little hesitation in offering the vacant position to Rebecca with a salary commencing at £104 per annum. The work would be hard with long hours but to the resilient teenager, arduous labour was no stranger as she positively thrived in such an environment. Becky enjoyed the comforts of her own room, albeit very small, the use of a bathroom and flush toilet, three square meals a day plus assorted snacks, a uniform and the protection of a caring family. The young girl would take her mother ten shillings a week. This sum, along with the recently introduced Family Allowance, five shillings a week for the children except the eldest, was a great asset to Margaret Smart. In reality these small receipts became her income for the entire family as Emms continuously stole her widows' pension and wages to fund his excessive beer and cigarette consumption.

Margaret fell ill and the pub refused to give Emms her wages while the canny clerk at the Post Office declined to hand over the Family Allowance. In desperation he came up to Wye Hall and demanded to see Rebecca. When the young maid appeared he became abusive and menacing, insisting that she hand over her wages. The tense situation was short lived. The earl's driver, a former Royal Marines Commando called Fred Biggs, stepped in and during a brief fracas blackened Emms' eyes. It was later that day when Mister Biggs had several of his old troop comrades visit the same person for an unambiguous appraisal of his earlier less than gentlemanly exploits. These were augmented with a robust suggestion he ought not to repeat them including a few hints of the consequences if he just happened to be so reckless.

Emms left Margaret the next day, the resultant aftermath being the adolescent Rebecca was smitten, carrying a massive teenage crush for the tall, brown haired and brown-eyed muscular chauffeur.

PHILIPPA-1955

"Do you love Mister Biggs?" Philippa innocently enquired as Rebecca fondly brushed her long auburn hair. "Ooh, Lady Philippa. That's a little personal, is it not?"

"Yes, but I see you talk to him and when you do you giggle and turn red."

"Spect I does Lady Philippa, I giggles a lot, the master and mistress do not seem to mind and it gets hot in here, that's why I turns a bit rouge like. Anyway, enough of the chat, you're a big girl of seven now and we 'ave to get ye dressed an' ready for school."

Philippa quickly hugged Rebecca then made her way to where her clothes were neatly laid out ready for her.

"I can dress myself now, Becky." Philippa stuck her nose imperiously into the air.

"I'll still wait 'ere Lady Philippa, just in case you needs a hand."

The young girl managed to clothe herself in the blue infant school uniform, although Rebecca tidied up the edges before the pair gracefully stepped down to the breakfast room where Philippa's parents were already seated.

"Breakfast is the most important meal of the day, my little munchkin, and you eat plenty of it. Have less lunch and a small dinner though."

"Daddy means when you get older that's what you do, Philippa, at the moment you are attending school, you work hard and then play for hours to burn it off. Consequently you are at liberty to eat to satisfy all your appetite."

Somewhere on a nearby wireless set, a song called "Unchained Melody" by a new singer by the name of Jimmy Young was floating through the house.

Philippa loved the lyrics and began to hum it as she tucked into her hearty meal of eggs, bacon, sausages and toast.

"When is Emily coming?" The seven year old nonchalantly enquired. She was totally cognisant of the fact that it would initiate a response whereby her parents, specifically her mother, would stir uncomfortably in their lavish chairs.

"Philippa, it is time for Biggs to drive you to school." Louise could sense her daughter was being a tad mischievous and was in no mood to commence another family deliberation.

"I shall go and visit her on Friday evening when I return from school." James also sensed the current of raw emotions circumventing the room.

"Do you need to, darling?"

"Of course he has to, Mama," Philippa responded for her brother, "Emily and James will be married one day, he has to visit his betrothed."

"School, now!" The countess had lost all residue of patience for the morning.

"Off to school little sister." A snigger came from James.

"You too! Biggs has to take you all the way to Faringdon! See you on Friday!" Louise yelled at her son.

Philippa was drinking in the scenery on her short car ride from Wye Hall to Saint Peter's Infant School and fell deep into thought. The translucent entity from earlier times had continued to bumble into her dreams. Nevertheless she had no idea who or what it was let alone whether or not the apparition actually existed. Her one true confidante was the adorable Becky. To her mother the maid cum nanny was simply a member of staff, a highly appreciated employee but nonetheless a member of staff. However, in the eyes of the sensitive seven-year-old, Rebecca was an angel, a loving relative, like her Grandma Rathbone, Florence Rathbone named after the famous Crimean War nurse Florence Nightingale.

Philippa had told Becky of her future husband who took the form of an ethereal, verbalising swirling light. The nanny had simply smiled. "Nice t' know who ya husband's gonna be. Even if he's just a bright light in your dreams, Miss Philippa. I'm still waitin' to see mine."

"Mister Biggs will be your husband, Becca," Philippa confidently responded in her oft used mature tone, "And this light's not really my husband, don't think, not sure. It just said it was like a foot, from the future he said. Do you understand? He's like a spirit, you know what I mean? He's much, much older? He said lots of funny things, could not really know what he was talking about."

"Lady Philippa you speaks so intelligent like for a seven year old. You're a real brain box."

The musing over the very rare nocturnal illuminations soon ended as the car pulled up outside Saint Peter's Church of England School. "Your stop, Miss Philippa." Biggs bounded from the Rolls, jogged around and opened the back door. The youngster picked up her school bag, alighted from the vehicle and ran to meet her "best of best friends", Judith Parkhouse, Christine Vickers and Patricia Laidlaw.

"Pip!" The small girls all squealed in unison. Each of them was smiling with a massive beaming countenance. Everyone anxiously vying to be Lady Philippa Marchant's "best of best friends".

JAMES-1955

The black Rolls Royce Wraith stopped outside the gates of Saint Hughes Preparatory School at Faringdon. James took his case and bag and as Biggs opened the front passenger door, the young schoolboy rapidly departed with a succinct "Thank you" to the driver. The tallish, jet haired boy met his friend "Sniffer" Parkinson, shorter with sandy hair, at the entrance and together they ambled onto the schoolyard.

"What's up Marchant? How are things?"

"They are very good Parkinson, grading exam results today and mater and pater already trying to marry me off to someone." "Who do they have in mind this time?"

"Isabelle Napier-Fenning," James nonchalantly responded.

"God, she looks like a warthog, Marchant. Still better than the other one whose name I forget. Not like Emily though, she is pretty, eh? You're only ten years old though, too young for any marriage or what. Is Emily disliked by your mamma and papa?"

"Not disliked so much, just looked down on for not being of our class."

"Well she's not; she's a blacksmith's daughter, certainly not on your social level. Mama says you will never marry her, your mother would never allow it."

"She is a lot more interesting than many of the poltroons of our class, and don't you ever criticise her again, Sniffer Parkinson."

"Poltroon, you've been reading pirate stories again. Shan't criticise Emily again then Marchant, we have to stay friends." "Did your mama say that also?"

"Well, yes," Sniffer disclosed with more than a hint of embarrassment.

At the same time Anthony Bowman, a boy from the senior school approached.

"Marchant," the medium sized, spotty faced and fair-haired individual ominously encroached on James. "I hear your family want you to discard that little girl urchin from the common folk you seem to like so much," Bowman uttered in his most intimidating voice.

"Drop dead." James walked past the 12 year old who stepped back in front of him, his bravado increasing as more of his age group approached.

"Oh come on Marchant, your family just need to pay her off. It will be an inexpensive enough application for your father. After all he has plenty of money and they live in a little hut."

"You are a wicked person, Bowman. But if you want to be beastly then two can play that game."

James began to move on but found that his path was being ever so slightly impeded by the encroaching boys.

"What do you mean, Marchant? I said what do you mean?"

"Bowman, yes my father has plenty of money, as you said. Unlike your family who are almost bankrupt and you may have to leave this school."

James had obviously struck a raw nerve.

"You lying little insect!" Bowman grabbed James by the throat. In a microsecond his hand was thrust aside, complemented by the pain of two rapid boxing jabs to his chin bringing him crashing to the damp turf of the school yard. This ignominious tumble was accompanied by raucous laughter from the animated and boisterous schoolboys who had gathered close by.

James picked up his bags and walked with Sniffer through the school doors aware that Bowman would never deign to be friendly towards him, ever.

EMILY-1955

"Mummy, I'm off to school," Emily called out. The youngster slipped into her navy blue overcoat before skipping energetically out of the back door and into the crisp autumn sunshine.

The pretty little blonde haired figure ran to catch up with her two best friends, Kathleen Burton and Beryl Appleby.

"Emily, you look very nice." Kathleen complimented her friend through a continuous smile. "You always do, wish I was as nice-looking as you."

"Stop talking rot, Kathleen," Emily replied hugging her pig tailed and crooked teethed friend, "You're really pretty."

"Am I?" Beryl sounded a tad insecure.

"Of course," Emily responded to the petite round-faced schoolgirl.

"Is James coming to your house sometime?" Kathleen enquired with great interest.

"I think his parents are going to visit mine, I heard mum say something that she had received a note from Mister and Mrs. Marchant."

"That sounds nice." Beryl turned her head. The three girls walked along Church Lane and veered into the playground and solitary hall of the combined infant and junior school with its standard vibrating cacophony of small children at play.

The total roll of Saint Peter's Church of England School was a mere 19 pupils but still meant that this particular establishment was noisy. However, and thankfully for those concerned, the resident din was far less intense than many others of the same ilk within the county.

The staff consisted of only one teacher, Miss Fettis. An old lady, so the children thought. To the pupils she was aged anywhere between 40 and 400 years old. The schoolteacher was a small, plump, bespectacled and plain spinster of the parish with a frightening stare for misbehaving children. Nonetheless, she was also in possession of a warm empathy and total conviction to maintaining an optimal education for the young of Alvescot. The 55 year old as normal had her grey hair kept up in a bun and on this morning she had some news to give out to the older children in assembly.

"Quiet!" Miss Fettis called out once all had found their pre-designated places.

"I have an announcement to make."

The sense of anticipation swept through the older children. It was the call of destiny, especially for boys. Nonetheless, it was probably the single most life-changing event most would face; if they had passed the Eleven Plus, the grading examination. It would decide whether or not they would attend a grammar school, possibly university and, more so if male, look forward to a career in academia or the professions. Emily was almost shaking with acute nervousness as Miss Fettis stepped forward with a sheet of paper.

"Listen, children," Miss Fettis called out, "I want the following pupils to step forward; they have passed the Eleven Plus with an "A" pass and will not need any further selection examinations." The schoolmistress shuffled around with her sheet of paper.

"Dennis Tweddle." The small blond haired boy wearing circular frame National Health glasses moved to the front next to his teacher.

"Beryl Appleby." The small round-faced youngster stepped forward.

"And last of the "A" passes, Emily Wilkinson. Congratulations to you three. Kathleen Burton, you have been awarded a "B" pass and will need to take further selection tests at St Hughes School. Listen, children, out of six pupils from St Peter's School who sat the Eleven Plus exam three have passed outright and one needs to sit a further examination, an excellent achievement for us."

As was customary, children who had achieved "A" passes were allowed briefly return home and inform their, hopefully, overjoyed parents. As Emily tirelessly sprinted to the family cottage she noticed a large modern black saloon car parked on the road outside.

"Mummy!" She dashed into the cottage. There she came upon the Earl and Countess of Wye seated in the small sitting room taking tea with her parents. Emily was monetarily silenced. The golden locked ten year old, all of four feet ten inches tall, caught her breath. All eyes in the room fell upon her.

"Emily, why's 'e home?" Mary Wilkinson broke the silence.

"I passed Mummy, I passed the Eleven Plus with an "A" pass, I'm going to grammar school."

"Congratulations." Louise Marchant stood up and gave Emily a genuinely affectionate hug.

"Yes, James will hear his results today also, although his name is still down for Eton." Thomas Marchant had totally forgotten the day that the grading examination results were publicised.

"Emily, 'cause the earl and countess were so thankful that ye saved young Master James' life all those years ago, they said they'll show their appreciation."

"That's nice. How so?" Emily was nervous and intrigued.

"They's gonna send ye to Oxford High School, the best and poshest in the county."

"Yes, Emily." Louise grinned like a Cheshire cat then shuffled a little. "Of course it is a boarding school and you and James will not see so much of each other.

THE DIARY OF DANIEL 1955-PENNED IN 1966

"Daniel!" 11 years earlier I had heard a voice call out from somewhere. "Are you playing or not?"

I was drifting through a mental hiatus, as I recall a bright apparition. Was it a spectre or just a manifestation of my six-year-old mind? The opaque light that does not speak but imparts knowledge I was sore afraid to divulge to my parents. The being, the thing for want of a more suitable noun, telepathically, its words not mine, transferred data (sic?) from wherever in the order of things it lies to me in my bed. I had not to tell any of such matters. I always listened to mother and father and was so convinced that they would have had me sectioned and sent to Saint George's, the lunatic asylum at Morpeth. I was so swayed by this notion I remained unvoiced, quiet replete with secrecy while keeping normal as much as I could. Of course we have to know what normal really is. On that eve, the presages flew like bats out of hell, visions, like a cinema screen picture speeded up and not sound but emotions, each as diverse as the infinite array of snowflakes. It was a language, I think, I thought, my brain was stewed up, I had only walked this Earth for less than seven years and I felt as if it has been 60. The luminosity was talking about an unknown singer, called Elves or something, Priestly or a name quite similar, who would have a hit record next year. It also spoke of something bad happening in Hungary and a place called Suez, which I already knew was in Egypt. I could see soldiers, many jumping from the sky, but it was mainly a blur. The only thing I could be sure was that these events would transpire in 1956. In hindsight all prophesied occurrences were veritably quoted to the boundaries of inscrutability, genuineness and of a provenance I have yet to unearth. I am aware I have a design to fulfil.

DANIEL-1955

"Daniel!" Stuart Dawson called out yet once more. Stuart, from Morwick Road, Warkworth, was growing tired of repeating the same question. The two boys were making for the old stone infant/junior school next to the River Coquet along The Butts in the village.

"I can hear ya Stu." Daniel sounded irritable.

"I thought we'd play Japs and English while we cross th' field until we get t' the castle."

"Not today, Stu," Daniel responded. He was unusually subdued.

From the corner of his eye, Daniel caught the distinct outlines of Billy Hardy and Mick Foreman crossing the road to their right. They were strutting menacingly in their direction. The two local bullies now aged 11 had failed the grading examination. As a result, they would both be attending the secondary modern school at Amble, one and a half miles along the river. The small fishing town at the mouth of the Coquet. This would be after the summer break some eight months away but for the moment they remained on the register of the junior part of Warkworth Church of England School.

"Gibson! Dawson! What ye two homos up to?"

"What's a homo?" Stu looked at Daniel. He was more than a tad bemused by the unfamiliar noun and very uneasy about the oncoming "big" boys. Daniel simply shrugged his shoulders.

"We're just going to school," Daniel timidly responded.

"Oh yes, two little homos walkin' past the castle." The turgid remarks came from the figure of Billy Hardy, a tallish, for his age, slim and with black greasy locks almost swimming in a surfeit of "Brylcreem" hair oil. Hardy lived on a worker's cottage near Forsyth's farm, his father being a local labourer.

"Yes we are actually." Daniel appeared to be nervous, his speech wavering slightly.

"Ye two homos can 'ave a bit bum in the bushes before school." Foreman chuckled. He was in dress and appearance almost a doppelganger of Hardy and equally as minatory.

"No Hardy and Foreman." Daniel appeared to be shaking with trepidation. "We are simply going to school."

"Ye don't 'alf talk posh, Gibson." Hardy stood in front of the route Daniel and Stu were taking.

"I do indeed speak correctly, in that you are correct."

"I do speak correctly," Foreman mimicked Daniel.

"We are on our way to school; please get out of our way." Daniel sounded even more apprehensive whilst Stu was dumbstruck with fear.

"We's ganna beesh ya faces in!" Hardy announced somewhat boldly, ahead of Foreman to assert his superiority.

"From what you say, you are going to bash our faces in. Oh dear. You two are a real pain in the backside." Daniel was now less nervous and even smiled a little.

"Aye, that's what wu's gonna dee, you little homos!"

Daniel smiled and moved towards them, the grin widening making the greasy haired duo extremely uncomfortable. In a precise set of movements and with extreme dextrous rapidity Daniel took a hold of Foreman, threw the lank individual easily over his shoulder followed immediately by Hardy. The pair lay prostrate on the long, rich grass of the meadow that led to the old medieval stone castle; both were transfixed in a state of total disbelief.

"The next time you persons pick on us I shall bloody your noses. Come, Stu, we'll be late for school."

"How d' you manage t' do that, Daniel?"

"I told you Stu, but you don't always listen or understand. My Dad was a Royal Air Force pilot in the Far East fighting the Japs and took a liking to the Oriental martial arts, mainly judo and karate. He was very keen to have me skilled in those. So, ever since I was three years old I have been tutored in judo and boxing and am now a judo Black Belt. I'm now studying karate and by the time I'm 13 I hope to be a tenth degree Black Belt, Seventh Dan I believe. It's good fun, especially good to beat bullies with."

PROFESSOR DANESH GIDEON AND DOCTOR KELLY ARESTI

"Professor!" The voice called from the cold passageway that ran the perimeter of the considerable Hartfordshire University laboratory complex. Doctor Kelly Aresti made her way towards the scientist in his remote, white painted brick working area.

"Yes, Kelly. I thought you would be tucked in bed with your boyfriend at this godless hour."

"I may have been."

The young flaming haired medical doctor and PhD shuffled uneasily in her tight green skirt, white overall jacket and black patent leather high heels.

"Professor Gideon." Kelly looked at the wad of notes in her right hand. "According to this account of your experiments, it sounds more like stalking than science to me."

"Such a nice, competent specialist of the medical variety, Doctor Aresti. You are extremely attractive, five feet two with red hair and a great figure. When one combines these superlative physical attributes with such immense intelligence you must be sought by all males in the kingdom with an IQ above that of a peanut. It is even more commendable when one sees that you interrupted a great career as an accident and emergency consultan, to devote a year or so to a great passion of yours here in my laboratory. So far medicine's temporary loss is physics' temporary gain."

"Professor!" Kelly was clearly embarrassed by the brief encomium. They trundled over the polished wooden floor of the long, glazed green and white brick corridor. "Cease the salacious remarks. You are discomfiting me and could easily be construed as harassment. I repeat! These notes make no sense. They sound more like a Peeping Tom than a scientist. What the hell have you been doing going into a child's bedroom?"

"I was directed there, not by choice. It was the fabric and mechanics of the more intricate aspects of the formula that I believe navigated the machine. The infant seemed to have some potency that attracted the guiding system. Nevertheless, it was a blatant error and I immediately departed. Even so, I was still veritably absorbed by the rationale of the machine directing me to that precise locus. Anyway, Doctor Aresti, if you demur with such compelling vigour pray inform me of the basis of your current attendance?"

"I am intrigued, Professor. This thesis, these opinions, formulae, conclusions are surely in the realms of science fiction not fact. I appreciate that quantum physics is but a side-line for me yet possessing an inquisitive mind I deem sections of your report to be fascinating."

The professor was a six foot tall, a grey haired academic and a child of the 60s. He could boast of having seen The Beatles, Roy Orbison and Gerry and the Pacemakers performing live on June the eighth 1963 at Newcastle City Hall. A hippy in 1967, he was vehemently against British, Australian and American involvement in Vietnam. With no lack of irony he secretly wished he could partake. Professor Danesh Gideon was grammar school and Oxford educated and frequently regretted never enlisting in the armed forces or police service. He turned to his novice.

"Doctor. Have you ever read the" Chronicles of Narnia" by C.S. Lewis or Jorge Luis Borges' "El Jardin De Senderos Que Se Birfurcan", in English "The Garden of Forking Paths"? Or more recently John Wyndham and his short story "Random Quest"?"

"Professor. You quote literary works but I fail to see the relevance bar that I passed "A" level English Literature on my way to University. But, this work that you allowed me to view is science, much theoretical and some vague, nonetheless science. Based on the plethora of solid evidence you have thus far presented I do not believe that it is not some fictional yarn."

"You obviously are not conversant with the books I quoted. Yes. We are discussing not only the theory of parallel universes, as the novels I quoted expound in variant ways, but the practice of travelling between them. This concept to date remains solely in a quasi-virtual reality form."

"You can not only prove the existence of parallel universes but you can travel in them? At least view them! Professor I wish to go!"

"Easy, young lady." Gideon grinned warmly at his most recent charge. In his opinion Kelly was certainly most attractive to date. "The notes you have are from my observations when I travelled. It can only be the basic draft of a massive legend that is yet to be penned. I would prefer it if we went over to the lounge of the Black Bull where I could enjoy a pint and smoke my pipe whilst you can partake in a Balkan Sobrani cigarette with a port and lemon."

Kelly accepted the invitation despite the working notes proving somewhat worrisome.

The 27 year old from Stevenage in Hartfordshire had never suspected the professor of being anything other than a zany but genius scientist. She had witnessed his positive, genuine and warm reaction when Gideon's daughter in law had brought two of his seven grandchildren to pay a brief visit. Nonetheless, the contents of the written comments were a little unsettling. Gideon turned out the lights and bade goodnight to the security guard at his desk.

Kelly Aresti admired the professor and in more than a professional capacity. He was still physically fit and although deep into middle age had a countenance and presence of a man decades younger. Danesh was totally void of the cadaverous and wan features of many of his chronological contemporaries. The young doctor was the daughter of an Italian father from Turin, Roberto Aresti, whose own parents had been amongst many from that land who came to Hartfordshire after World War Two. Roberto was a market gardener who had met and fallen in love with Kelly's mother, Catherine Adamson, the Countess of Dun Eideann, a Scottish aristocrat from Arbroath. The young Miss Adamson had been working as a trainee accountant in north London shortly after graduating from the University of Edinburgh with a BSc in Economics.

The two had met in the Glam Rock days of the mid 1970s and eventually married on Saturday the 19th of June 1982, two days before the birth of Prince William and five days after the end of the Falklands War. Kelly was born three years later.

The pair took a seat in the corner from where although the jukebox was clearly audible it was neither deafening nor uncomfortable.

"Cheers," Professor Gideon said as he touched his pint glass of Greene King IPA with that of Kelly's Cockburn's and lemon.

Once they had both ignited their smoking paraphernalia, the sound of the up to date "Part of Me" performed by Katie Perry was to be heard.

"As you seem to be au fait with my work, Kelly, I suggest we talk about taking our research to the next level."

"I want to know everything, Professor. If it takes all night, then so be it."

LOUISE AND THOMAS 1955

"I'm not so sure I can accept y' kind offer. M'Lord and M'Lady. Don't likes charity."

"I understand Mister Wilkinson, please do not regard this suggestion as charity. Your daughter saved our son five years ago and now we wish to recognise that by investing in her future. You can repay us if you so wish but no demand will be made."

"Thank you. M'Lady," Mary Wilkinson interjected. She smiled at a very smartly attired Louise Marchant then glared at Harvey. "Me husband is a tad hasty. We'll discuss this an' get back to you immediately."

"That sounds splendid," Tom finally spoke up, "but we shall need to know very soon. I have pulled a few strings to reserve Emily a place and Miss Stack the headmistress is already oversubscribed."

"We shall be in touch forthwith," Mary did her best to articulate with a polished inflection

The second the Marchants had left the relatively humble surroundings of the blacksmith's cottage, Emily crept out of her room. It was the same instant that Mary turned on her husband.

"What ye playin' at Harvey? D' ya not want what's best f 'ya daughter?"

"Bloody posh folk! Bad enough Emily talks like 'em! I'm not takin' their bloody charity and that's that!"

"It's not for you, you daft old git! It's f' our Emily!"

"She's already got a scholarship to the local grammar school, that'll do!"

"This's Oxford High School, a private school where she'll get the best education, like we never had, with a great lady in charge, Mrs. Stack. It'll help our Emily move up in the world. And, it's not f' ya Harvey, it's f'

Emily and if 'e canna giver her this chance then I'll pack me bags and me and Emily'll go back to me mother's place."

"No mum," Emily cried out as she ambled into the room. The young girl was sighing, conveying an air of complete dejection. "I'll just go to the local school then come and work for dad in the smithy."

"No!" Harvey could tell he was in for months of no bedroom acrobatics if he failed to concede. The rugged blacksmith was not a stupid man and even through his dented pride he could see the benefits on offer. Naturally he would ensure that the Earl and Countess of Wye were repaid in due course. Their son was alive due to his daughter's actions; it was a concession not charity he pragmatically deduced.

"No to what?" Mary was and sounded totally bemused.

"No to ya packin' ya bags. Emily can go to the high school in Oxford. I'll take her there Monday mornings and pick 'er up on Friday afternoons once she starts."

Mary kissed him on the cheek and whispered, "Early night tonight Harvey."

Tom Marchant drove the Bentley R Type Continental the short drive from the smithy at Alvescot to the expansive, tree enveloped, Georgian built Wye Hall.

"Do you think Mister Wilkinson will accept our offer?" He turned briefly towards Louise whilst driving along the serene, verdant country lane. The earl then lit a Players Navy Cut cigarette.

"Of course, darling. Mrs. Wilkinson rules that place. No bedroom delights if he does not accede."

"Sounds like us; if you are after something you just drop your drawers."

"Naturally, darling, the best weapon in a woman's armoury is under her skirt."

"Emily will only be away during the week," Tom quietly cautioned.

"I very aware of same, darling. However, as she gets older that will give her time to see other boys and lose interest in James. It would be no advantage to forbid James from seeing Emily, as he would merely hate us. Next would follow secret liaisons. Trust me, he would never forget. This way she can gradually get to know other boys and soon our son will fade from her memory."

"I see where you are going but two things seem to have been missed from your calculations." Tom drew on his Navy Cut.

"They are?"

"Emily is going to an all-girls private school, no boys. Secondly, James and her are, to quote the Bard, a pair of star crossed lovers. From opposite sides of the fence and are madly in love."

"He's only ten years old. He does not know what love is. And even if he did there is more than ample time to fall out of love with the little blacksmith's daughter. In answer to your comment on girls' schools, trust me. Once the pubic hair is in place and you are getting your monthlies, and into stockings instead of socks then it is like musk. Boys find you or you find them. It's in the hormones. Darling, I know, I was at an all-girls school."

"Yes, then who do you have in mind for James, is it still that Napier-Fenning girl?"

"I think so, is there a problem darling? Problems with the Marquis of Donnington, his daughter would be ideal for James."

"Louise. I know you are partial towards the family, they are veritable blue bloods. However, rumour has it Eli Napier-Fenning has cash flow problems with that new company he formed recently.

Eli has made an appointment to see me in the London office next week. I think he will be asking for a loan to bail him and Cecil Bowman out. Poor Cecil is almost on the verge of a nervous breakdown. He is nearly consigned to the workhouse because he is so badly in debt."

"Oh gosh, Tom. Is that a bad sign? The Marquis asking for a loan I mean."

"Might not be. Short term cash flow problems are common. I am just wondering if he is up to his eyeballs in debt and the bank will not loan him anymore."

Tom parked the Bentley outside the house whereupon Fred Biggs chauffeured the limousine into the garage. The earl and countess strode into the ornate entrance foyer where Hodges the butler was stood awaiting instructions.

"Will you and Her Ladyship be partaking in luncheon, My Lord?"

"Lady Wye will be, Hodges. I am shooting off to London and will be staying in the Sloane Square house. The property needs a little more professional domestic application. Could you possibly spare one of the servants for a couple of days to help spruce the old place up?"

"Of course, My Lord. May it please you if I enquired if there are any hindrances afoot in the selection and recruitment of suitable domestic staff at your London property, My Lord?"

"As you are aware, Hodges, I have four staff in London, Hodges. Notwithstanding, the social season will start in a couple of months, at Easter as per usual. I wish the property to be spring cleaned in time. I do not hold a preference for which of the staff will assist but have her, I assume it will be one of the girls, packed and ready to go in an hour."

"Of course, My Lord. I crave your indulgence for my lack of comportment. I think Smart will be available my Lord." The butler sounded a mite crestfallen.

"Relax, Hodges. We'll be back on Wednesday night and Rebecca will be taken good care of." "Of course, My Lord."

"Eli," Thomas Marchant stood up from behind his desk and shook hands with Elijah Napier Fenning, the Marquis of Donnington.

"Whiskey?" Thomas grabbed the crystal decanter from a table near his desk.

"Yes, can we cut to the chase, Tom? I really need an answer rather rapidly."

The earl did not respond immediately, merely poured a generous nip of Scotch and handed the tumbler to his friend.

"Cheers." They touched glasses then both sat down in the massive leather bound armchairs, which stood in the centre of the luxuriant office. The medium height, moustached and bespectacled Napier Fenning fumbled for words.

The earl found the nervousness of Eli embarrassing so elected to speak first. "How much?"

"60 thousand. A fortune I know, Tom, but Cecil and I have had a bad run. We just need some cash to tie us over the next few months----."

"I agree. My terms are ten per cent per annum interest until the loan is completely settled plus ten per cent in perpetuity of gross profit."

"I agree. That is amazing, Tom. Thank you."

"You may not feel so disposed when your company is profitable. I require that half the profit share accrued will be paid bi-annually and be held in trust for family members and others whom I shall name when appropriate. I shall instruct my lawyers draft up the agreement. I hope it will stop Cecil from having his breakdown. Also the Duke of Surrey, Crispian Lee Watersby is in your partnership, is he not? He'll be relieved also?"

"We all will. Tom. I don't know what to say."

"Come and I'll treat you to lunch at my club. This afternoon we'll sign the agreement and a cheque should be in your possession before the banks close. As I said Eli, it's ten percent of gross profit, not net profit. And if you become, as I am sure you will, the head of a hugely profitable corporation then I shall be the winner by far."

"No one else had faith in these calculating machines, the Yanks call them computers. We got the idea from all that hush hush stuff at Bletchley Park in Bucks during the war."

"Eli, you say these computers, is that what you call them, are the future?"

"Yes. At the moment they are pretty basic but at a company called IBM, International Business Machines, the Americans are developing a calculator that will soon be able to play drafts. Not too long afterwards they hope that it will be competent at chess. The idea is to speed up the work done in offices. Of course that state of affairs is well and truly far into the future."

Good idea, Eli. When I see the amount of clerks I employ for pretty repetitive stuff, it would save a fortune if I could cut that number down. That of course would also be well in the future. If it happens at all."

"How is Louise?""

"She's fine, thank you. Excited and apprehensive that James will soon be at Eton. He easily passed the Eleven Plus exam so we know he's intelligent enough. It will dent the pocket a little though. A lot in fact. "

"He'll do fine, Tom. We did well after our time at the Old School." Eli smiled displaying no small measure of relief.

Rebecca had been extremely busy. The large property in Sloane Square,

Belgravia, London, town house of the Wye family required much arduous attention. The significant residence required dusting, the carpets and curtains cleaning and all surfaces, floors, cutlery, crockery and glassware necessitated rigorous polishing. The 25 year old was busy giving the stairs a final brush when a voice behind her whispered, "Well hello little beauty. Who the devil are you?"

A grey haired and bearded, tall but mature man in a Saville Row morning suit stood over her. "I'm Rebecca, the maid from Wye Hall. I'm here to help out, sir."

"I'm Professor----."

"He's Professor Peregrine Marchant, my uncle! Uncle Perry come into the parlour for refreshments, I want a chat. Jenkins!" Tom Marchant ushered his relative into the wood panelled and lavish drawing room.

"Yes, My Lord," the London butler dutifully responded.

"Bring us the decanter of Scotch and a soda siphon, also a bucket of ice."

"At once, My Lord."

The act of being removed so rapidly from the company of Rebecca had somewhat miffed Peregrine.

"You were a tad hasty to break up my getting to know your delightful little maid. There's life in the old dog yet."

"Uncle Perry, you'd best give the servants, at least the attractive females, a wide berth. Louise would metaphorically remove my manhood if any of them, especially Rebecca, ended up in the family way due to your lascivious and Epicurean tendencies."

Jenkins entered with the whiskey and relevant accoutrements. The earl charged two tumblers and handed one to his uncle.

"Now, Thomas. Just what is the veritable basis for my unexpected, but much welcomed, invite to Wye Hall?"

"It is to do with Philippa, Uncle, and no mention to Louise."

"What about your daughter?"

"I know I can trust you with her, Uncle Perry. At least if I can't I'll set Louise on you which you would certainly not hail. But as you are a Harley Street surgeon, I would be in your debt if you were able to allocate some of your valuable time to give Philippa a basic schooling on doing your job. It seems daft for a girl but she wants to be a doctor after university."

"Young women should know their place. Being a doctor is a man's job."

"I think my daughter is made out of sterner stuff. So will you tutor her? There will be an appropriate stipend."

"Of course I will, dear boy. No fee necessary. It will be a pleasure. Just a lavish dinner or two. I shall come down to Oxfordshire at the weekends."

Chapter Three

NARRATOR

The blanket of esotericism is woven upon what seems like a sea of faces in a Dali canvas, engrossed yet somehow disconnected from reality. I continue my narrative, short in real time, years in the outer measurements, from the scabrous depths of the psyche of the Cosmos, acidulous yet full of harmony and connectivity. The chronicle remains as a tempestuous spirit upon the waves, crashing incessantly on the banks of the shores of time and matter.

I gaze at the face of my relatives and friends sitting at the reception tables, some have achieved more in less than one human lifetime than most could pack into several.

At least they are all still awake and appear to be listening.

PHILIPPA-1959

"Good evening. It has been a long time," Philippa articulated. She was now a mature 11-year-old and exceptionally advanced for her years. The young girl was no longer startled by the emergence of the conversing, translucent radiance, missing from her bedroom for the previous two years.

"Hello." The irresolute shape behind the hazy glow spoke. "Where am I? What is the date?"

"You ask that each time you come. Although it has been a long time since you were last here. It is December the second, 1959, and I am sitting my Eleven Plus examination tomorrow."

"You must be Philippa, and you pass the examination."

"I am Philippa and you also always say that I'm your future wife, it's getting boring. I am confident I will pass anyway. Are we still getting married or are you calling off the wedding?" "No, have patience. I think there has been a miscalculation. Are you same girl I met previously?"

"I am the same Lady Philippa Marchant. Of course I am. Are you some kind of idiot?"

"It should only be 1957 now, are you sure it is 1959?"

"Absolutely. Now unless you have something important, you'd best go as I need to get some sleep for my examination tomorrow. I wish to be a doctor by 1972."

"If it is 1959 then you are not my future wife but what you are is a crucial element in the structure of the Cosmos. Accordingly I have tidings."

"Am I meant to be impressed?" Philippa sounded more than a little irked.

"It is of no consequence whether or not you are amazed or otherwise. However, I am deigned to be a harbinger. The bringer of a despatch from the Nucleus of the Dimensions to you. My counsel asserts that you pay heed."

"I do not have any idea what a harbinger or a despatch is. I am 11 years old and we do not use such words. Just say what you have to and be gone!"

"A harbinger is a herald or messenger. And you are one of an inimitable group of individuals.

A unique sect that exists in every universe, you refer to them as parallel universes, and in every time frame and each decade and century back to the beginning. Your world entitles it The Big Bang Theory. You and your ilk span all across the infinite universes and are termed The Aphrodite Strain."

Philippa smiled at the glowing phantasm like apparition.

"I am named after the Greek goddess of love?"

"The Greek goddess of love was named after your race, not the reverse. In order that the crucial balance of the Cosmos is retained it is essential that you mate with a member of another line known to those of sapience and import as The Hercules Strain."

"Now you confuse the issue by using a Roman name. The Greek equivalent is something else. I can only marry one of those people?"

"Yes and no and Heracles is the Greek version but that is of nil import.

The caveat that accompanies your great ride through the Universes is a teller of evil. Not the evil replete horror stories or religious tales from the great tomes. Nonetheless, he or it is an execration whose sole destiny is to eradicate the Aphrodite species. That singular line is the nourishment upon which is vital and fundamental to his very continuation. His base stratagem be to hold dominion over the all the universes in the entire Cosmos. To prevail in this diabolical design he must slay the Aphrodite and defeat the Hercules. You and your sisterhood must be prepared for the coming of this creature and hunt him and countervail his ghastly forays until his final and sempiternal demise. Failure belongs elsewhere, lest he will dine on your souls. I have concluded my remit, now I must depart!"

EMILY -1959

The gramophone in the dormitory for the fourth year pupils of the Oxford High School for Girls was playing Cliff Richard and the Shadows recording of "Travellin' Light". This current hit song was followed immediately by the new release from Adam Faith, "What Do You Want?"

Emily sat down on her bed and hitched up her skirt before rolling on a pair of stockings.

"God, I could do with a cigarette, anyone want to go for a walk up to the town?"

"You amaze me Emily." Kathleen Burton sighed. She was slim, almost too slim, with spectacles and black hair and gazed adoringly at her 14-year-old friend. Emily boasted an hour glass figure, blonde locks, film star looks and a seemingly boundless well of stamina and intelligence.

"How so, Kath?"

"You always look great, Emily. You have all the boys crowding around you. You passed the grading exam without trying. You got a scholarship to come here, and you'll pass your GCE "O" Levels all without any effort. I did not even pass the Eleven Plus straight away, I had to try again with my "B" pass and my Dad dug deep into his wallet to send me here. I don't have any boys look at me."

"Shut up Burton!" The sensual figure of a fifth former entered the dorm. It was five feet two inches tall, 16-year-old brunette, Penelope

Whitehead. She was accompanied by Jennifer Hislop, her ever present, equally as attractive and mousey haired side kick.

"Get lost, Whitehead." Emily began to brush her long flaxen mane.

"You too, blacksmith's daughter, you're only here because of a benefactor. It's not because your wretched parents have any money. The crime is imitating someone who actually is rich. At least Burton's family has money, unlike yours."

Emily totally ignored Penelope and continued to attend to her golden locks.

"Kath, could you change the record and put on Bobby Darin singing "Dream Lover?"

"Nothing to say, Wilkinson?" Penelope remained trenchant as the music altered. "You did not get a scholarship, your fees were paid."

"That's my business, Whitehead, not yours. But I think your problem is not that I am with fewer funds than you seem to be alluding to. I imagine that it is more like Mick Wilson, the "I want to be Elvis Presley" guy, is gagging to get into my knickers and not yours. Best move with haste though, Penelope, as Her Majesty has called him up for National Service. He is due to go into the Army any day. Also, he's not eligible to attend our Christmas dance."

"You whore!" Penelope bawled, her face turning crimson.

"Let's leave her, Penelope," Jennifer tensely advised.

"Yes, I would if I were you. I am not merely a blacksmith's daughter but I can also fight like one!" Emily glared menacingly at the senior girls. "You all know I killed a grown man when I was only five years old, you two would be no problem."

The older pair grunted and began to move away at pace.

"And Whitehead," Emily added.

"Yes!" came the confrontationally charged response.

"I have no interest at all in that halfwit Wilson, you're welcome to him."

Once Penelope and Jennifer had left the room, Kath walked back up to Emily and sat on her bed. "You are so great, Emily, you've looked after me since we came here."

"Take it easy Kath, that's what friends do. I know this is a girls' school but I am not a denizen of the island of Lesbos."

The head girl and prefect confidently entered the sparsely furnished and decorated living accommodation. She was 18 years old Naomi Schwarz, from Golders Green in London. Naomi was about five feet seven inches tall with black hair and jet piercing eyes. Even in her school uniform she looked like a fashion model. Positively radiating a classic beauty that Emily imagined the great Egyptian, Queen Cleopatra, must have possessed.

"Wilkinson, Burton, I take it you two are going to the school Christmas dance?"

"As fourth formers I believe we qualify." Kath sounded overly sure of herself. In response she received an icy rebuking glare from Naomi.

"Yes, you are but on two conditions."

Naomi sounded like the headmistress, Ann Hancock ME. Emily noticed that detail but remained mentally adrift rolling on her stockings.

"Wilkinson, are you listening?"

"Yes, head girl." Emily looked up from her labours.

"You will go with a chaperon to the boy's school. That chaperon will be me. You will dress modestly, school uniform and stockings only. None of this trad fad jazz type stuff."

"Sounds great, head girl," Kathleen re-joined the discourse.

"I did not say this but if you want a crafty smoke, hide well out of sight. Do not let me or any prefect or even worse one of the teachers, certainly not Miss Hancock, catch you in the act."

DANIEL-1959

"Mum!" Daniel had sprinted the one and a half miles from Warkworth elementary school to the farm house. The effort to his frame was minimal although his breathing was marginally more rapid than the norm. "What are ye doin' here? Why's ye not at school?"

"Miss Clark gave us the Eleven Plus results, Mum. I got an "A" pass, so did Stuart."

"Daniel, that's really great." Daisy Gibson tightly hugged her son. "Yer dad'll be so pleased. He's out on the tractor, pet, but he'll be back soon for his dinner."

"I have to get back, Mum. I'll be at the Duke's Grammar School in

September. That'll be great and I can play rugby as well as do my martial arts."

THOMAS AND LOUISE-1959

"The Honourable Crispian Lee-Watersby and the Honourable Lady Barbara Lee-Watersby are ready to be received, My Lord," Hodges graciously informed Thomas Marchant.

"Show them in, Hodges."

"Yes, My Lord."

Hodges announced the tall and very stout Crispian Lee-Watersby and his equally lofty and plump spouse, Barbara.

"Crispian." Tom shook the hand of his male guest then kissed Barbara on the cheek

"Barbara." Louise kissed her female visitor then Crispian.

"So nice to see you both, Louise and I are glad you could come." Tom ushered them to the drawing room sofas.

"Hodges, whiskey and soda for the men and whatever the ladies want."

"Yes, My Lord." "And Hodges," Tom added.

"Yes, My Lord."

"I want the footman to remain to attend to the guests. You will be far too busy ergo inform Shearer to assume those duties."

Once Hodges had served the desired refreshments he took his leave.

A few moments later, the young and dark haired Andrew Shearer entered the drawing room.

The house footman was only a few months out of the army following his two years National Service. Young Andy, medium height and build and in morning dress stood erect by the door, awaiting orders from the master, mistress and guests.

"Cheers!" They all touched glasses then sat down.

"Good grief Mister Hodges," Andy gasped with incredulity. The footman had finally been dismissed from the task of serving drinks and snacks to the earl and countess and guests.

"What's the matter Andrew, you 'ave a slight hint of discontent 'bout you?"

"'E always looks a bit narked, Mister Hodges." Mrs. Cromer grinned at the butler while stirring a bowl of cake mix. "Even worse when Rebecca's up in London."

"Mister Biggs was even more annoyed, Mrs Cromer." Rebecca smiled at the chauffeur who turned red when the butler noticed the intimate body language.

"No, Mister Hodges, it's the master and mistress. They're already arranging Lady Philippa's wedding, to some Julian Lee Watersby. She's but the sprite of a girl, not even at high school yet. It's like talkin' about selling a bullock or heifer."

"It's the way in upper class families, Andrew." Peter Hodges philosophically shook his grey locked pate.

"I can't see my Lady Philippa bein' handed over to some idiot, she'd just run away," Rebecca dryly commented while still smiling at Biggs.

"Aye but I doubts if she'll have any choice. I've seen a lot of ladies married off t' lads they didna like."

"Yes, Mrs. Cromer," Rebecca interjected while beaming a perceptive grin, "But I knows my little Lady Philippa. She passed 'er Eleven Plus exam now so she'll do as she wants, not what they thinks she should 'ave."

JAMES-1959

James put on his black tail morning coat, false collar and waistcoat with pinstripe trousers. The 14 year old enjoyed a room in Godolphin House, a beautiful brick constructed residence and part of the highly elitist Eton College. His good friend Ronald "Sniffer" Parkinson knocked briefly then entered. They were both of a similar age albeit Ronald was slightly built and far less lofty than James.

"It's just the start of Michaelmas Half and I'm homesick already."

"Me too, Sniffer." James was graciously empathetic. "Whatever, we must be resilient and keep our nose to the grindstone."

"Shall we go to Bekynton for some breakfast?"

"Yes, I fancy some scrambled eggs and toast."

"Marchant!" Anthony Bowman called out from the corridor. "Wish you could be my fag."

"I'm too old Bowman. Such a pity as you would like to own a fag as in the American use of the word. I would never do anything for you, Bowman, no matter how many beatings I got."

"Wish I could give you a beating, Marchant."

"I'm sure you do, Bowman!" James snarled threateningly, "But you know I would put you in hospital for a month. Not good to impress the old Mater and Pater."

"Mister Bowman." Doctor Baily, the house master, cautiously entered. The forty-year-old geography master and rugby union fanatic viewed Bowman with suspicion. "Should you not be with your own Walpole House students this early?"

"Yes, sir," Bowman meekly nodded and took his leave.

"You boys should get along, unless you need to see the dame."

"No, Doctor Bailey, we will be off now, sir." James replied.

Sniffer and James walked out into the nippy but sunny September morning.

"Bit of rum luck Bowman coming to Eton, I thought his parents were bankrupt."

"They were, Sniffer, but his company got a huge loan from Papa's businesses. So I overheard, and now they are making lots of money. So Papa says. The family of Lee-Watersby who were with them in this venture are equally as fortunate." James took a deep breath of the crisp autumn air.

"Sniffer. It's just as well you are now five feet four inches tall. Or you would still have to wear a bum freezer jacket."

"I know, Marchant. You are so lucky to be tall. All the local girls yearn for you."

"I don't care; I only have eyes for Emily. She is getting very grown up now. She wants to pass ten "O" levels, three "A" levels then study law at university and be a Queen's Counsel, As well as writing novels and painting pictures."

"She is very ambitious for a girl, wanting to be a QC. I saw her in the summer hols; she looked like a young version of Doris Day. It's a pity you don't have a sister that's old enough, Marchant."

"Well I don't, Sniffer, so there."

"Does she ever have flashbacks to the time she killed Frost?"

There was a heavy pregnant, silent hiatus. James turned red and yelled at Sniffer,

"How dare you, you stupid arse! Come out with stuff like that again and I'll give you such a dashed good beating!"

DANESH AND KELLY

"Those are my findings to date." Danesh Gideon sipped on his third pint of Greene King India Pale Ale. The professor then sucked on his pipe, full of some sweet smelling tobacco by the trade name of Drum Shag. Kelly was moved to a clipped period of hush as she took a mouthful of port and lemon then lit a Balkan Sobrani Black Russian cigarette.

"I am trying to get my head around this, it sounds more like something from Isaac Asimov than factuality," Kelly mumbled then drew on her Sobrani.

"Mathematics is the key, Doctor Aresti," Professor Gideon muttered through a cloud of tobacco smoke, "The explanations for all such matters, apart from the question, "Is there a God?" reside in the magic of the numbers. We do not have to delve back far into the past to find when it was even considered once to be a form of black magic. The use of numbers to reveal facts, or supposed facts, is a fact. The calculations are indeed enormous and takes even one of those giant IBM machines several hours to process and compute into a definitive resolution. "

"Mathematics, especially the world of algebra and complex quadratic equations, Professor, is neither my area of expertise nor any source of interest to me." Kelly was noticeably irritated, on the border of a full blown fulmination with Gideon but managed to wisely hold her tongue.

"She is a brilliant medical doctor," the scientist silently deliberated, "With great perspicacity and a propensity to absorb the minutia down to the most basic constituent of any project or problem."

The young woman was completely engrossed in Gideon's project. If proven, it seemed to be a novel approach to the peripatetic. It was not travel in the conventional sense but the means to voyage through space, time and the esoteric fabric of other dimensions. His narrative was even worlds beyond the comprehension of the current most erudite and apt astronomical physicists and other people of science. The professor was undoubtedly a trailblazer across these enigmatic, uncharted paths to places which lie far beyond the realms of any chronicled course. Let alone understanding.

She remained infuriated. To Danesh, she appeared even more pulchritudinous when her hackles were raised. Nonetheless, she had a profound, extremely deep craving to understand the very concept. The challenge was gnawing away at her soul despite the cerebrally eroding mathematics. She was determined to prepare for and when ready make the journey into that land beyond the veil of current scientific intellectual capacity.

"Doctor Aresti." Gideon was aware he had led Kelly into a quagmire of detail for which she held in the lowest basement of import.

"Yes, Professor."

"Questions?"

"If you travel, when you travel, do you go as yourself or is your image distorted in the inter-dimensional termini within your landing area?"

"Doctor, I must confess, that is certainly an overtly atypical question. I believe that when I depart on my expeditions, I am travelling through a gap in the framework of the Cosmos. I set out to a place similar to the chronology of Earth but not specifically matching. Thus far it has been like looking through very opaque glass. As if I am enveloped in a massive cloak of a malleable cloth through which light passes but inefficiently."

"How do you know wherein and when you have reached this counter dimension?"

"Calculations and observations, Doctor Aresti. In my craft I can see items during the daylight hours of my incursions when I appear to be almost invisible to the residents of that dimension. As I have stated, it is similar to trying to view through the glass window on the wall of a shower. However of course, during the darkness hours matters are somewhat altered. Breaking beyond the dense ectoplasm is a problem I shall presently resolve. Before long I intend to walk within that parallel world as one of them, mingle I suppose. I shall not discern these matters until I attempt such a venture. Nonetheless, I can make out newspaper headlines although not small print, like being pretty long sighted. I look at newspapers and other items, which give me some idea and listen to the radio. Things are identical with a few almost insignificant minutiae. These details one could only distinguish if one was in possession of a great local knowledge and an in depth understanding of current affairs, our current affairs. One minor variation is the portrait on a packet of exclusive cigarettes. But there is one problem which is not quite so minor."

"Enlighten me."

"It is a blip, probably caused in the first, miniscule tiniest micro seconds of the Universe. This infinitesimal epoch is when all current scientists agree space, time and now I believe other dimensions were probably created. These alternate worlds are very, very similar to each other but like identical twins, there are marginal differences. In the grand scheme of the Universe such variations are negligible and began as nothing more than a minute, the tiniest possible of hitches. But over millions of millennia they have grown, albeit remain extremely diminutive. I shall elucidate. It appears to be that I am not actually but only appear to be, travelling through the fourth dimension. That is of course H G Wells' great topic. Time. I merely journey sideways to where events are actually almost identical to this world but are 40 to 50 years behind our dimension. I have to verify the differential."

"So you are not travelling through time per se, but to a place in the Cosmos identical to Earth only 40 years behind us. So it is like travelling back in time."

"No Kelly. Well, yes and no. At least the tests I have done so far have proved it not to be so. I always come to the same places. I have several landing sites and period no matter how much I adjust my calculations; I can veritably prove that I am not travelling in time. This other world is identical to us and exists alongside us. The fact remains it is 40 years younger."

"So what do you hope to achieve?"

"The people that inhabit this world are, as far as I can see, the same as we were 40 years back. I intend to take a leap into other, possibly preternatural, realms. I will conduct numerous laboratory experiments to examine one mystery that has remained elusive since the days of the ancients. That is to accurately deduce whether one's life has been preordained by some great Weaver of the Cosmos and is in tablets of stone or if fate, destiny, can be changed. Imagine if you, well not you, you are too young, but let us take for example your father. Let us hypothesise that he was given all the correct answers to the problems we all endure through our lives. These are naturally extremely numerous and some very insignificant but nonetheless life changing. This mega list will contain gargantuan inventories of girlfriends, chance liaisons, careers, friends, where to go, what to study and so on and then decisions were made accordingly. Of these life's poses, some we happen upon we find agreeable, in some cases extremely so, but to many of us huge swathes are total disasters. The catastrophes of our life's journey. All of us are aware of the most beneficial path and all necessary solutions once we have access to that wonderful benefit known as hindsight. Would this artificial hindsight alter his life or would it merely travel the path it would have devoid of such comprehension? I would love to offer my doppelganger in this alternate place the wisdom of my worldly experience. Then I could assess as to whether some divine or scientific entity rules our navigation through life, whether it is random and if we can alter our path of destiny."

"Professor, that is amazing. I want even more to partake."

"That may be difficult—."

"I'm sure we can reach some accommodation." Kelly was not to be derailed from her burgeoning agenda. "Invite me to your flat and we can talk in detail."

"That is called being a tad forward, Professor. A touch of solecism there and what would your third wife say about that?"

"You win, Doctor Aresti. If you have time, tomorrow night in my lab. There will be lab technicians present also so don't worry, you will be safe."

"I'm not scared of you Professor. I'm a black belt in karate and I did not decline. I merely said you were a little forward and asked what your third wife would say."

EMILY 1959

The music from Saint Mary's church hall was comfortably loud. A local band from Oxford was playing some crooning old songs from the 1940s. The musicians suddenly bounced onto the current scene with a reasonable rendition of the Cliff Richard and the Drifters' song, "Living Doll". The venue on Magdelan Street was acceptable enough. It was a sizable hall with wooden chairs around the edging and a stage large enough to accommodate the musical quintet. The building stood close by the world famous and oft featured in films the Randolph Hotel. Emily and Kathleen had gone outside and up a nearby alley to smoke a Woodbine Tipped cigarette each. They ignited their tobacco sticks and loudly inhaled.

"We'll have to be quick," Kath commented with some concern whilst looking towards the main road.

"Naomi saw us come out. The head girl knows we're coming for a quick smoke. Let's get back, there may be some boys worth making out with," Emily naughtily suggested.

"I thought you only had eyes for James."

"I do Kathleen but he's not here. I'm not going to let anyone take my bra off or even worse get into my knickers but a little exchange of mouth fluids would be in order."

The girls, both in their navy blue school uniforms with dark stockings, sauntered back towards the church hall.

"Hello darlings." A heavy Oxfordshire inflection echoed behind them.

They turned around to see the tall, dark figure of Mick Wilson. He was shadowed by his ever present sidekick, the shorter and less aesthetically pleasing Geordie Angus.

Emily turned around to face the young men.

"Yes, Mister Wilson, what are you up to?" Emily was drawn towards the tall dark haired figure. Her teenage hormones began to kick into over drive. Nonetheless, she fought desperately to contain the potency of these organic compounds and for the moment at least she enjoyed a modicum of success.

"We're off t' the Royal Marines in a couple of days, Emily. Do ya fancy comin' for a quick walk with me, in case I get killed in Malaya? Kath can go with Geordie."

"Only to outside the church hall and for ten minutes only."

"Emily," Wilson sounded boringly importuning.

"No, ten minutes or nothing and don't try anything. Kath, would you like to go with Geordie for a few minutes?"

"We have to get back, Emily." Kathleen seemed uncomfortable at the prospect.

"Ten minutes, Kath, then we'll get back."

"Alright Emily, ten minutes only." That was the signal for Geordie to take Kathleen by the hand and walk off.

Wilson took Emily by the hand and swept her up the foreboding dark jaws of a further alley and towards an area of tree lined open land.

"No!" Emily stopped. "This is far enough. I said ten minutes only."

"Alright," Wilson agreed then eased her against a shadow enveloped wall. The night was still as he gently kissed her with a wide-open mouth, the warmth of his breath was stimulating Emily towards a place she knew she wanted to be yet resisted entering. Her young adolescent groin felt as if it were about to boil and a flowing sensation began to emanate from the most restricted and secret parts of her anatomy. She could feel his hands easing around her back. One slipped into her blouse and grasped her right breast, went inside her bra and began to squeeze the nipple.

This delicate action ignited a spark which rapidly evolved into a furnace within her young loins. The other hand then crept under the hem of her skirt, passed the tops of her stockings and to the edge of the gusset of her briefs. Emily was swaying and purring in the zenith of ecstasy. Wilson then began to slip his hand inside her underwear when a scream came from nearby. She pulled away from the very aroused figure.

"Stay here," he sternly ordered. She ignored him as her friend yelled for help.

"That's Kath! I'm going to see what's up. She sounds distressed."

Wilson grabbed Emily tightly by the arm. "You stay here. We've started somethin' and we're gonna finish. It's just your friend and Geordie havin' fun."

"Get your hands off me; I'm going to check on Kath."

"You'll stay here 'til I'm finished."

Wilson pushed her back against the wall and tried to kiss her. Once again he slipped his hand up her skirt. That continued for a mere second when a piercing, agonising pain burnt through his testicles. He screamed out in synchrony with the thudding impact of a knee crashing into in the same area. The lank figure was bent double with hurting when a further crack of bone against bone echoed. This was the sound of an elbow flying into his back with lightning rapidity. Wilson slumped to the ground before painfully looking up at a defiant Emily.

"What the fuck?" he grunted agonisingly. Wilson was lying in the prostrate position, face into the cobbled surface.

"Never, ever, ever try and tell me what to do, Wilson! If you ever do again you'll really get hurt! You have no idea what you're messing with!"

The slight but curvaceous form ran off in the direction from the shrill cries came.

She raced passed a wooden gate and into a patch of dense shrubbery where in the dim light she found Angus on top of her friend. The aroused youth was desperately trying to pull her briefs down her thighs. Emily was by now seething with wroth and grabbed him viciously by the hair, threw him to the ground and stamped down hard on his face.

He lay shocked and groaning in pain on the musty, damp earth.

"Kath." She grabbed her friend and they made off back towards the church hall. "Let's get to the dance; we'll be deep in the poo if we don't move with some celerity."

Kath adjusted her distorted clothing and then burst into tears.

"Why did you ask me to go with that maniac? He nearly raped me!"

"Sorry. I had the same problem with Wilson."

"Are you alright, Emily? Did he hurt you?"

"No, I'm really fine, Kath. Wilson has sore balls and groin but I'm top hole."

The two girls soon arrived back at the church hall. The band was playing the Sam Cooke classic, recently covered by Craig Douglas, "Only Sixteen".

"Wilkinson!" The voice of Penelope Whitehead was as cutting as it was annoying.

Penelope and Jennifer Hislop walked into Magdelan Street from the hall.

"What is it Penny? You appear to be a little lost."

"Have you been seeing Mick? You'd better not have been, Wilkinson!"

"Your somewhat nice but dim beau? Ah, yes, I believe I did bump into him. He tried to shag me so I kneed him in the balls. He should be all right in two or three days. He won't be any good for a strumpet like you tonight though; his tackle is still in some physical distress."

"You little ---!" Whitehead made towards Emily until Naomi appeared from the dance hall. "Whitehead, any problems?" The older girl cynically enquired.

"No, head girl," Penelope responded and walked back into the dance with her friend.

"Burton, are you feeling well? You look as if you've been crying."

Naomi glanced over at the two remaining pupils.

"A boy called her names." Emily smiled as she offered the explanation. The ebony locked head girl seemed, at least superficially, to accept the elucidation.

"What did you do about it, Wilkinson?"

"I stamped on his face, head girl." Emily cheekily grinned.

"Of course you did." This time Naomi sounded unconvinced which totally suited Emily.

Chapter Four

NARRATOR

Yes, one microsecond all seems revealed then a mephitic haze seems to throttle the existentialism, the lifeblood, the very essence of all that has been and will be. Do they emanate from the depths of the pit or from the highest zenith of virtuosity? I am not versed in much; I have studied yes, comprehensively, naturally. Nevertheless, to date I have merely scratched at the surface. A magnitude of validations vibrate and I am able to communicate with ease and clarity ergo all are suitably enlightened one could assume. However, a massive subtext surfaces from the inner sanctum of a long gone chronicle, an amalgam of myth, science and legend. All such issues lie deep within the bounds of veracity yet so profound only those with the wisdom could attest to their accuracy. They are still with me, yet awake and deeply engrossed in my encomium. They are sitting agog at the revelations and reaching for their glasses when a humorous or tragic portion is recounted and emoted accordingly.

Time is of the essence. Or is it?

EMILY-1961

The new Ford Anglia 105E turned off Belbroughton Road and into the grounds of the Oxford High School for Girls. Harvey Wilkinson pulled up near the entrance where Emily and Kathleen stood waiting. The girls were dressed in their dark seniors' school uniforms holding suitcases that had been packed for hours. They were raring to be away. The final term of this academic year was over. It was time to return home for the summer holidays. The 16-year olds were bouncing with joy as the General Certificate of Education Ordinary Level examinations were finally completed. A year of nose to the grindstone swatting, perspiration, trepidation, anxiety and uncertainty was concluded. Temporarily at least. That would be until the results were announced in two months. The elation of completing them all, staying the course and a massive wave of confidence relating to perceived success was still fresh in their very beings.

Harvey and Mary leapt from the car brand new car and hugged both the girls.

"I expects ya hungry girls, we'll get ye home and I'll get fish an' chips on the way."

"That's great mum, I'll be starving by the time we get back to Alvescot."

Emily was in good spirits.

The girls sat in the back, sighs of relief as the car accelerated along the A4165 along the Wolvercote area of Oxford, onto the A40 and west on the direction of Burford.

"Did ya enjoy your exams, girls?" Mary was anxious to strike up a conversation.

"Mum, schoolgirls enjoy exams in the same way other people enjoy having their teeth pulled out."

"I like your new car Mrs. Wilkinson," Kathleen chirped in.

"Yes, as Emily was at a posh school Harvey got a new car. Not a posh car but a new one."

"Ye two girls will be out tonight?" Harvey enquired as he increased speed on the rural A40 outside of the city of Oxford.

"I'll be." Kath pointed a perceptive grin at Emily. "I think Emm will be visiting James."

"The countess was in the village shop this week," Mary interjected, "James's already finished 'is summer half she called it and 'e's back home. She told me an old family friend was at the hall--."

"Isabelle Napier-Fenning." Emily cut her mother's vocal flow in mid stream. "And yes, I am conversant with the fact that the Countess of Wye has for at least two years been grooming that young debutante with a view to her being James' future spouse."

"Doesn't it bother ye?" Harvey looked at Emily through the rear view mirror.

"Of course not. If James wants to do as his parents wish he can. But of course but he won't."

DANIEL-1961

The British Broadcasting Corporation Home Service announcer was telling his wireless listeners that the United States of America had sent its first man into space. This pioneer was called an astronaut, stellar sailor, and his craft was a space vehicle called Freedom 7, part of what the BBC had termed Project Mercury. The name of this ground breaking astronaut was reported as being Alan Shepard. However, the feat had been accomplished less than a month after the Soviet Union had successfully propelled into orbit and returned to Earth, Yuri Gagarin. This space explorer had been described by the BBC as a cosmonaut, the Soviet name for an astronaut. .

Jackie Gibson had been up since five in the morning milking his small herd of Jersey dairy cattle. The brawny farmer was busy tucking into his massive breakfast of eggs, bacon, sausage, tomatoes, fried bread and tea. The eldest offspring had a somewhat less hefty serving of cornflakes followed by a bacon sandwich and a mug of tea. .

"Funny things them Yanks sending funny things up t' space, it'll ruin our weather. And maybe that's why it's bin rainin' so much lately. I see funny lights, yellow lights, near the house at night." Jackie both speculated and commented as the newsreader moved on to inform all that the following day would see an FA Cup Final between Tottenham Hotspur and Leicester City.

"Of course it won't affect the weather, Dad. Those lights may just be from the fighter aircraft at the Royal Air Force station at Acklington." Daniel disagreed with his father on what was fast becoming a regular basis. The grammar school student was already in his grey school shirt, slim "junior tie" for those in forms one to three, a black blazer with the Duke's School badge and the mandatory black school cap in his pocket. Failure to wear the cap outside the school bounds or produce one on demand by the form master, Mister Rodway, would probably result in a caning.

"And if the Russians are sending men up into space the Americans will have to, it's part of the Cold War. Only America can afford to develop such an expensive programme and maintain huge armed forces."

"I think 'e knows too much for a lad of 12 and a half, Daniel Gibson. Ye talks like an old man at times," Daisy Gibson opined as she came into the kitchen with a basketful of dirty washing followed closely by five year old Debbie.

The little blonde hair and blue-eyed daughter was all prepared for her father to take her to the village school in Warkworth. "Little" Jackie had already left for the same school; he preferred to walk. The younger son was ostensibly preparing to sit the Eleven Plus the following year.

"Mother, it's the wonderful grammar school education you wanted for me! I'm not old! You and Dad are old and Grannie Gibson down at Amble is very old."

"Daniel Gibson, ye's a right cheeky lad. I'm not auld. Noo had away off to school."

DANESH AND KELLY

"Time to get up, Prof." Kelly rolled out of the luxurious king sized divan and wandered over to the en-suite bathroom.

"Must we?" Danesh called through the closed door over the echoing sound of running water from within.

"Yes. We must. Professor." Kelly's voice resonated with a grim determination after which she commenced brushing her teeth. "I have been screwing you for two years. At the same time I am supposed to be engaged. I know you're not bad looking, Prof, for a guy in his 50s or early 60s. Also, you're also in good physical condition. But I already have a fiancé, been engaged for a year. You and I have been practising and rehearsing parallel universe travel for two years and I am impatient, worse I am tired. I have sat in that electron colliding chamber dozens of times. We have been over the procedures hundreds of times. For God's sake Danesh, it must be easier to fly one of those Typhoon fighter planes or a space shuttle than all that technical stuff you have me do. You said I can try it out today so today we will. Or I'm gone."

"Do you screw your fiancé?"

"None of your business Prof and if anyone finds out about our illicit liaisons your testicles will no longer be attached to your torso."

The tall bearded figure of Professor Gideon managed finally to expend sufficient energy for him to arise from the large double bed he had been sharing with Kelly for what to her seemed to him to have been several epochs.

"I've missed you since you left my project and returned to Lister Hospital, Beautiful Doctor Aresti. And I never imagined you would go into the urological department. Do you like shoving your finger up the backsides of old men with prostate problems? Any chance we can go without the condom the next time? You're on the pill!"

Kelly slipped effortlessly into her bra and briefs then rolled on a pair of tights.

"Whether I am on the pill or not is also none of your concern. You bear a sordid reputation. Since your wife kicked you out they, that is all who claim to be your friend or acquaintance, contend that you are frequenting with escort hostesses. I don't want to catch any STDs. Thank you very much. You ought to be happy you're getting anything. If my Royal Navy officer fiancé was here instead of shooting insurgents far, far way, you would get nothing. At least not from me and he would shoot you. And as far as leaving your lab, there was nothing tangible to show my health trust so they withdrew support."

"Alright, I understand but as far as your beau is concerned, I thought he was a doctor in the Navy?"

"He is." Kelly slipped into her light summer dress and zipped it up. "He can still shoot and has completed the commando course. Something you missed out on. Now let's get into the kitchen and make some breakfast. I'm starving and we have a busy day today. I either travel in a parallel universe this morning or by lunchtime you and I will be history!"

EMILY AND JAMES-1961

The green livery Ford Anglia pulled up outside Wye Hall as several Rolls Royce and Bentley cars were doing likewise.

"Ye looks like a million quid." Harvey Wilkinson was beaming with pride at Emily. He and his wife had always thought their daughter was beautiful. Now they were totally convinced after her appearance in a chiffon, cape and ball gown with a décolletage accompanied by a bouffant Jacqueline Kennedy style hairdo. The final touches of the magnum opus were an application of, bright red Marilyn Monroe lipstick and a black leather patent clutch bag. This accessory exactly complemented her gleaming shoes hidden well beneath her petticoats.

"I think perchance you may be erring on the side of extreme bias, Dad." Emily smiled as she opened the passenger side door.

"Sometimes Ah think ye've swallowed a dictionary, 'ave a good time."

"I will." Emily kissed her father on the cheek then slid from the Anglia.

The silhouetted figure slowly and nervously walked to the main entrance steps that led into the massive countryseat of the Earl of Wye.

Mister Hodges was at the door verifying the invitations before nodding to Andy Shearer to usher guests inside to where Rebecca was collecting various outer items of clothing.

"I know you have an invitation, Miss, please go in." Hodges smiled at Emily.

"Thank you."

"Emily!" James ran forward and kissed her briefly on the lips. "You look fabulous; you have to be the belle of this ball."

"You are biased dear James, and you look great in your dinner jacket and black bow tie." She took his hand and walked towards the cloakroom after saying "Hello" to Rebecca as the maid took her cape.

All eyes were on the voluptuous student from Oxford High School. The 16-year-old could easily have been mistaken for a blonde version of David Bailey's girlfriend, Jean Shrimpton. The top photographer's belle was a model gracing both the covers and insides of all major fashion magazines including the major publications of Vogue and Vanity Fair.

As Emily sauntered by the assembled groups of debutantes and future top-drawer professionals the girls turned green with envy while the boys openly panted with lust. "My God." A voice gasped to Nigel Farnborough. "I see what they mean about Marchant's filly. She's a knock-out!"

"Good evening, Emily." Louise greeted her in the reception room with a cold, piercing gaze that Emily felt had sliced through her very soul.

"Good evening, Lady Wye. You look, as you always do, remarkable."

"Thank you, Emily, and you look, er ---."

"She looks fabulous mother. As well you can see," James hurriedly interjected.

"James, I hope you don't corner Emily all night. Your father and I have invited many of our friends' children to your ball, and I am sure many of the boys will be dying to speak to a charming young lady like Emily."

"Mama, fear not. I shall do my best not to upset anyone. However, I cannot guarantee it."

"What do you mean?"

"Mama, I jest. Excuse us as we mingle."

"Mad Marchant!" A voice came from the far side of the reception room.

"Good Lord, it's that little homo Sniffer Parkinson. What're you up to you hound dog, bog, bog."

"You load of logs, bog, bog, dog, monkey dog."

Emily screwed her face as the two 16-year-old boys made strange animal like noises and jumped around emulating orang-utans.

"Hi, Ronald." Emily attempted a smile as the two descended into a set of screeching noises which had everyone bar her laughing in encouragement and sycophantism.

"James, you stay with Ronald, I'm going for a glass of orange juice."

Emily lifted up her gown from the floor and ambled past her antagonists, Penelope Whitehead and Jennifer Hislop. The two stood alongside her potential arch nemesis, the Lady Isabelle Napier-Fenning.

"Nice dress Emily, where did you buy it, or were you donated it from a charity shop?"

Penelope snarled in a deliberately undignified tone.

"Oh no." Emily brought her hand to her mouth in a facetious posture. "Oh, dear Penelope, I did far worse than that. I made discreet enquiries to find where you bought yours and I certainly did not follow suit. Fortuitously as mine actually looks like a gown, not like a bag of horse manure tied in the middle, you chose unwisely."

"God you are such a scarab, Wilkinson," Penelope was becoming crimson with fury.

"Emily," Isabelle scornfully cut in, "you are not one of us. Why don't you get back into your cheap little car and drive down to your cheap little hovel."

A wry smile flashed over the face before Isabelle. A million emotions fired, epic tales were written in a microsecond. It became akin to some great revelation, a prophecy from beyond the veil that had been transformed from legend, hearsay or myth into veracity. The megaton of fury which bordered on release was skilfully contained.

Emily could feel she was checkmated and nodded then began to move.

She then turned in an instant to Isabelle. "You are of course so precise in the sheer astuteness of your clinical observations. However, I bear a major caveat. I will always be amongst you and your kind as I will always have James. You never will."

Isabelle dropped her glass of fruit punch.

PHILIPPA-1961

The Bush gramophone was playing "You're Driving Me Crazy" by The Temperance Seven. The girls and boys at the end of term party danced to acceptably loud music emanating from the single speaker.

Philippa was trying to look adult as she moved to the Vaudeville style recording with Judith Parkhouse, Christine Vickers and Patricia Laidlaw all dancing close by. The trio had been good friends of Philippa since before they had all commenced Oxford High School for girls the previous year.

The girls had been deemed much too young for the end of term celebration at Wye Hall. However, they had been had been given permission for a chaperoned party the venue being the house of Judith's parents.

"Those boys are stupid," Pat Laidlaw commented whilst eying up one of them, "All they do is make strange noises and belch and fart."

"Do you like Julian?" Christine innocently enquired.

"Why? Do You?" Philippa sounded a tad barbed.

"Christine, Pat." Judith beamed like a glowing beacon. "Don't you two know that our Philippa has been fixed up to get married to Julian farty arse Watersby by her parents, once she has finished university?"

"Is that true?" Christine and Pat responded in unison as if choreographed.

"I heard that's what they want," Philippa reluctantly conceded in an unhurried air, "But personally I think the boy is about as nice as a sweat ridden armpit, just look at how stupid and idiotic he is. I would rather be at home in a pair of slacks or jeans playing with my dolls' house instead of wearing this uncomfortable dress, suspender belt and stockings and for what? To look good for that boy so my mother says. I think he's an idiot."

"They all are," Judith groaned, "Just look at how they blow their lemonade up their noses and see who can belch the loudest."

The boys were giggling; looking briefly towards the girls, laughing and ascertaining how much lemonade they could consume in one go. Julian was making the most noise.

"Your future husband, Pippa." Christine giggled mischievously.

"Yes, well I hope not, he's such a bottom hole." Philippa squirmed and went to change the record from Jimmy Shand to Del Shannon singing the recent hit song "Runaway".

In the more silent hiatus between the choices of music, the podgy figure of Julian meandered slowly away from his kindred pack of immature boys and approached Philippa.

"Why were you laughing at us?" Julian sounded very malicious to the 13-year-old. "Because you act stupidly," Philippa responded as the strains of Del Shannon echoed across the large dining room.

"You are impudent and need to be taught a lesson."

The stout 14-year-old then stamped on Philippa's foot. A move which had her scream out in agony before bursting loudly into tears. Christine, Pat and Judith immediately sprinted over to sobbing figure.

"You beast!" Judith glared at Julian who merely stuck his nose in the air and walked away. "Are you going to apologise?"

"Of course not. She is already on the way to being my betrothed. Her parents told mine. She should consider herself lucky that I am in agreement."

"You cad," Pat snapped, "Let's get Philippa away from this person."

"You rotter!" Philippa began to hit the reprobate on the arm. This reaction merely instigated the youth to hit Philippa with some measure of force across the face. She ran screaming out of the room.

Julian Lee Watersby merely returned smirking to his sycophantic group of friends.

The Miasmic Mist —Volume One

DANESH AND KELLY

"Professor. I am now suitably fed and watered and am now in great need to be introduced to your technology. Or has it all been two years of bullshit? Whatever, no ride to the parallel universe, no more rides with me in bed. That's final!"

"I hope you don't mind but we will need to go to my laboratory cum observatory deep in the countryside near Stanstead Abbotts." Danesh put on his long dark coat and picked up his large leather Gladstone bag.

"No problem wherever, whatever. However, let us make haste for in the classic words of the legend that is Captain Kirk of Star Trek, I am sorely anxious to boldly go where no woman has gone before."

They briskly stepped out of the Professor Gideon's relatively out-of-the-way brick-built cottage in Nazeing, jumped into the Mercedes Benz C Class saloon on the pink gravel drive. With Danesh at the wheel they headed in the direction of the town called Hoddesdon some five miles from the county town of Hartford in Hartfordshire. Within 20 minutes the professor had turned off the main road and up what seemed to Kelly to be a farm track leading well away from civilisation.

"Professor, I was unaware you had a property in such a remote spot."

"I bought it many years ago. As a young university lecturer back in the 70s. It was going for a song, a couple of thousand, although it was derelict and overgrown. I spent years renovating it then decided to conduct my more discreet experiments here."

The dirt road finally went passed a few cottages then down a long and winding hill to where it branched off onto a metal thoroughfare.

The secluded road continued on towards a distant farm while they turned left along the floor of a wide valley several miles to the south of the town of Ware. It was only half a mile further along the ash and dirt track when a large detached house appeared, as if in a latter-day horror yarn or a fairy tale.

Danesh jumped from the Mercedes Benz and opened the farm style gate. He returned to the car and drove through the opening, leapt back out of the Mercedes and closed the gate.

The professor next took the vehicle the 100 metres to the drive way of the large building. This edifice was literally, or seemed to be, in the middle of nowhere.

The large brick-built property seemed utterly out of place amongst the adjacent shadowy, dense woodland that crept up to, almost touching, the sizable windows.

"Very spooky." Kelly slid from the passenger seat and gaped in awe at the picturesque surroundings.

"Very private," the professor robustly emphasised, "I am a scientist. Ergo I leave all this supernatural bullshit to the charlatans and the folk naïve enough to believe them."

"Well said, Professor. You are certainly veracious about it being private. But how is it we've never been here before?"

Danesh picked up the Gladstone bag and walked towards the red painted double entrance doors sunk into a stone made portico.

"The experiments we have partaken in to date have been pretty much at the elementary aspect of my research spectrum. The intricate electronic equipment I have constructed within is far more highly developed than anything the Institute of Quantum Physics Research can boast. Even afford."

"Will I travel to a PU today?"

"If my computer deals out the right numbers prior to any trans portal crossing then, Doctor, you may well journey to a sister universe or dimension. Although you will still require the suit that bends light. It will keep you nigh invisible though. However, rather than pontificating thereon, Doctor Aresti, let us fire up the proverbial engines. There will be several hours of sustained labour before she is ready to embark!"

DANIEL 1961

Daniel and Stuart walked from the Duke's School rear gate; they were discussing the Latin homework.

"Puffs, netty nuffs, puffs." Alistair Clark barged passed them, grabbed Daniel's school satchel then belched and broke wind almost simultaneously.

The overt intimidation unleashed by the fellow pupil on Daniel had been exponentially growing in regularity and intensity over the previous months.

"Give that back Clark," Daniel called out. The taller 13-year-old merely pranced around, singing some strange shanty about Latin loving homosexuals.

"Fuck you. You're a fart and like boys too!"

"Give it back." Stuart supported his friend.

"Fuck you too. Two little puffs who like Latin too!" sang Clark in response then belched again. His school cap was perched precariously on the pinnacle of his thick mop of curly brown hair.

Clark then opened Daniel's satchel and emptied his books onto the pavement much to the amusement of Clark's toadies nearby.

"You're an arsehole, Clark," Daniel snarled defiantly as he stuffed his books back into the school bag.

"If ya call me that you poof. I'll kick the shit out of ye."

Daniel ignored the threat and to the dismay of Stuart simply walked away.

A figure nearby smiled contentedly. The white face, irregular hairline and blood red lips were oozing with absolute fulfilment.

REBECCA, EMILY, JAMES AND PHILIPPA-1961

"Emily, you appear a trifle irked. Are there any mêlées of which I am not acquainted?"

"No, Lady Wye, I am just a mite flushed. It must be the heat."

"Ah Yes." Louise cast a captious, knowing smirk. "Of course statements are uttered oft without malice aforethought which upon the deepest of reflections may just echo with a timbre of veracity."

"Lady Wye, I take that to convey that you consider me an unsuitable belle for your son?"

"Your words not mine, dear Emily. However, I am aware of what you did for him and we shall always be grateful as manifested by our support of your education. Nonetheless, at the end of the glorious day, I must reluctantly deduce that I am without the ability to disagree with the gist of your statement."

"With all due respect, Lady Wye, you employ a very convoluted means to convey an extremely simple message. I shall bid you goodnight, My Lady."

"Goodnight, Emily." Louise smirked then turned away to oversee the party.

Emily almost sprinted downstairs to where the footman, Andrew Shearer, was standing. "May I have my cape Mister Shearer please?"

"Of course Miss Wilkinson, I shall get it for you immediately."

Hodges entered the flurried atmosphere of the kitchen as Rebecca was devotedly preparing vol-au-vents and Biggs was shining his work shoes. They immediately looked up at the butler.

"Mister Biggs, I have just been given instructions by the earl after he received a telephonic call. Would you and Miss Smart be so kind as to drive to the residence of the Parkhouse family and collect Lady Philippa? She sounds a little distressed and urgently requests transportation back home."

"Is she alright, Mister Hodges? She told me this morning she didn't want to go, some boy would be there she wanted to avoid?" Rebecca was genuinely disquieted as she grabbed her coat.

"None of our concern, Rebecca. However, as a precaution I think you ought to go with Mister Biggs on the chance Lady Philippa may require some female reassurance."

The Bentley was soon off along the expanse of driveway that led from Wye Hall. As Biggs turned left and drove towards Alvescot, a young man whom he recognised as earlier being at the party, was staggering towards the hall. Nigel Farnborough had a slither of blood trickling down his face and was wearing a dejected, traumatised countenance.

"That's one of the guests, Mister Biggs; I think it is Mister Farnborough."

Biggs brought the car to a halt next to the obviously shocked and bruised young man.

Rebecca lowered the passenger window. "Are you alright, Mister Farnborough? Do you need some help?"

"I'm fine!" Farnborough came to within a hair's breadth of a scream as he responded.

"Very well, sir." Rebecca closed the window. Biggs slammed in the gear and sped off towards the village.

"Someone's given that snotty nose git what 'e deserves, Mister Biggs."

"In my opinion, Miss Smart, and between you and me, they didn't hit him hard enough. And whoever it was, good on them. I saw him eyein' up Miss Wilkinson when young Mister Marchant was busy chattin' to his friends. The young man should keep 'is eyes open."

"Between you and me, Mister Biggs, I think the lady of the house would be 'appy if they did splits up. You knows what I mean?"

When Fred turned onto the country lane that weaved its way to Alvescot, the silhouette of a young woman came into his headlights.

"Miss Emily." Rebecca opened the window once again. "Is you alright m' dear? Would ye like a lift?"

Emily appeared to have been weeping. She straightened herself, sniffed then turned towards the passenger door. "Yes, that would be nice, thank you."

James had been engrossed in chatting to his friends for over an hour. It suddenly dawned on his consciousness that he had not spoken to his belle for some time. Certainly far more than she would deem appropriate.

"Has anyone seen Emily?" He asked as a general enquiry and all shook their heads.

The young man bounded impatiently about the house as if stung by some waspish insect.

"Mama!" James marched imperiously into the drawing room, "Have you seen Emily?"

"My dear." Louise approached her son, smiling in a way that James sensed in a nanosecond denoted some variation of subterfuge and intrigue. "I think it may be better for all if you direct your attentions towards Isabelle. I am of the opinion that perhaps Emily has finally at last come to realise a fundamental truism. This being that we are of such a different background to her that it would probably be greatly advantageous for all if she took her leave."

"Better for you, not me! You like Isabelle that much mother you spend time with her!"

"Do not talk to your mother in such a vulgar manner."

James barely heard the words as he turned and ran out of the door and towards the village.

Philippa came forward to meet the car. She jumped into the front seat beside Rebecca and began to wail loudly.

The maid threw her arms around the young teenager.

"That's alright, Lady Philippa, you 'as a good cry. Mister Biggs will have you home soon."

"I don't want to go home yet. Is there somewhere we can go for a while?"

"Come to my place," Emily suggested from the back seat.

"Emily!" Philippa turned her head. "You should be at the party."

"I think perhaps my days of attending balls and parties at Wye Hall, or anywhere else, are in the past. I am not of your stock, Philippa."

"That is tommyrot Emily and you know it." Philippa overcame her own distress.

"Why are you so obviously upset young Philippa?"

"That bounder Lee-Watersby hit me."

"What? Do you want me to thump him?"

"No Emily, he's a boy and you're a girl. You can't thump him."

"That's what Nigel la dee da Farnborough thought when he tried it on tonight. I gave him sore testicles and a bloody nose. He thought that I would just succumb to his so called manly charms. I think boys are such idiots. Except James of course."

"You hit Mister Farnborough, Emily? Good for you girl!" Rebecca smiled in jubilation and Biggs nodded in concurrence as he pulled the car over outside the blacksmith's cottage.

"My parents are out at some local barn dance. Come in and I'll make us all a cup of tea and give Pip suffice time to recover to go home. I think I will have to sort Mister Lee-Watersby."

"I think not, let us leave it. But a cup of tea would be welcome." Philippa's voice continued to betray the bitter chagrin bubbling within.

A few minutes later they were all sat around the glowing, radiant fire enjoying a cup of tea and a cigarette except for Philippa. She was intently listening to a 45 rpm recording of the Shadows with their recent hit "The Frightened City" whilst drinking orange juice. A bang came on the door and Emily could see through the small glass windowpane that it was James. She pensively opened the door.

"Yes?" Emily glared at the diffident expression that sculpted James' face.

"Where did you go?" "Your mother virtually announced to the world I am not of your bloodstock. She deems me unfit to be with her son."

"That's absolute claptrap! I want you to come back to the party, please." James eased his way inside to see his sister, Biggs and Rebecca drinking tea. The bow tie so meticulously fastened earlier now hung loose on his chest.

"Looks like a better party here than at the house," James sardonically beamed then glanced at Philippa. "What are you doing here little sister?"

"Emily invited me. Rebecca and Mister Biggs came to collect me as I wanted away from my party."

"Your friend, that back passage called Lee-Watersby, hit your sister. I hope you will uphold her honour." Emily remained incensed by the harm inflicted on Philippa.

"And Emily gave your friend, another anal piece called Farnborough, a beating when he tried it on with her. I hope he is in pain," Philippa muttered whilst standing and pointing with a sisterly deference.

"Lord James, sir." Rebecca was a little supplicatory. "I'm sorry. Mister Biggs and me are here and not attending to duties at the party. We was just sent to collect Lady Philippa and so we'll get right back."

"Becky, Mister Biggs." James seemed dumbfounded. "I would never suspect you of doing anything untoward. Stay here, Miss Wilkinson does not mind and neither do I. All those cads and snobs can survive without you for a short while and I'm sure Mister Hodges has all under control."

He then turned to Emily. "Did you really whack Farnborough?"

"Forget that! A disgusting piece of excreta has hit your sister and you have to sort the bounder out! And before you start snivelling your way back to me, your mother already has you lined up to walk down the aisle with Isabelle. I think we should call it a day."

"Not on your life," Philippa now joined in the conversation heralding a cringing frown to visit James' youthful visage, "I really do not relish that nasty, turgid Isabelle as a sister in law. I wish for Emily to be my sister. She and Becky are like my big sisters already."

"I think you have been at the dictionaries again, Emm and I need to talk---."

The rhythm of the speech was sliced by an appearance seemingly from thin air. The spectre was an opaque ghostly shaped haze, a portentous profile of viridescent plasma. Initially the entity was totally without lineament. It then altered in form from humanoid to a flat star fish like creature transforming into the shape of a small motor driven vehicle.

The two males in the room were frozen into a fear driven hush. Philippa was completely undaunted by the presence of the entity while Emily and Rebecca seemed not to be unduly affected. Albeit very minor, their trauma was nonetheless at a greater degree than the apparently stoic 14-year-old. It was an unconcerned Philippa who stood up from the couch and slowly sauntered towards the presence. "You terrible being! You're back again! What are you seeking this time?"

"It's another this time. Are you Philippa?" A crusty female voice rattled as if from a deep wooden box.

"You know I am her and you sound like a woman. Where is my future husband?"

"I know not of that to which you enquire. Notwithstanding, you and I are cosmologically entwined."

"How so?" "I shall, hopefully, return with a more comprehensive rejoinder to your uncertainty. But there is one certitude in this matter and it is you and I are very similar, identical even."

The voice from behind the ectoplasm like matter reverberated gently and within half a second the entire extra-ordinary mass had dissipated into the ether. For a few bizarre moments all bar Philippa were in a stunned, tacit trance. Without any forewarning the conversations recommenced as if the phantasmagoria had never deigned to make such an implausible entrance.

It was fortuitous, yet uncanny, that all except Philippa were apparently without the capacity to recall such a nigh preternatural experience. Some years later Philippa would more than suspect that under the right conditions, Emily and Rebecca would be able to recount the curious incident.

Chapter Five

NARRATOR

The river of time flows on an uneven course on its dissonant journey to the bourne all of us must reach, the terminus of our allotted span. It is the eternal sea by the shore of the never ending or subsiding, unwieldy void that absorbs our psyche and welcomes with soothing radiance our transference into immortality. I trust that the Almighty does not yet have designs on my post deceased being as yet although I as recite more of my saga, the few small minutes feel like decades, the living seem closer and the departed feel in my presence. It is as if I am in a movie about a life, several lives. I can see the dead clearly and the old are young once more. Faded old photographs, phantasms of the legions of the sepulchre dance and smile at me, beckon me to come forth. I am fortunate or ill-fated to enjoy esoteric ownership of sapience that envelopes a multitude of truths and if disclosed, these essentials could probably render me liable to be locked away somewhere dark, far away from public view. Bereft of same I would believe that my mind had long since degenerated into mush possibly instigated by mysterious and recondite knowledge only imparted in a galaxy of minutia, rationed out over the years of my existence in this Universe, or others. My guests are still awake and attentive so the oration may be imparting that for which it was intended.

EMILY -1963

The two senior girls strutted along the corridor of Oxford High School for girls. Emily and Kathleen were inane to a point of boisterousness, bubbling over at the utter relief of completing their three General Certificate of Education Advanced Level examinations and were now university bound.

A young second form pupil from Oxford called Rachel Plumber ran around the corner and nearly collided with Emily. The small figure expected a summary excoriation only to be told by the almost giggling individual, "Plumber, do not run in the corridor. Or at least unless you know who is there. You may run into Miss Hancock, you know her, the headmistress."

"Yes, head girl," Rachel nervously stuttered.

"Then be along with you, quietly young lady," Emily modestly directed.

"Yes, head girl." After which the 13-year-old, red with embarrassment, briskly walked off.

"You are such a soft ball, old girl," Kathleen said jokingly, "A dumb blonde letting off the little insects without even a mild rebuke. She should have licked the head girl's shoes."

"Plumber is no different than we were back in the second form. It seems like light years ago now and you seemed to have failed to recall."

"Of course I do." Kathleen chuckled. "Back then no man had touched your stocking tops and even your bra let alone pulled your draws down."

"Well only one has to date and back then you were very au natural, not the lesbo you are now." "Back then I was confused." Kathleen showed a brief hiatus of sober honesty. "Now I am sure. I prefer the female body to the male."

"Each to his or her own. So, now I can't ask you who your favourite Beatle is. Can I?"

"If I was a normal girlie sort I think Paul. He seems to be the nicest."

"No!" Emily barked. "John by far, he is a real man. I love that new song of theirs, "She Loves You"; will not be released for a few weeks though."

"They were on tour a few weeks back with Gerry and the Pacemakers and Roy Orbison and some twit from that TV programme Coronation Street, Christopher Sandford," Kathleen briskly imparted.

"I know, I saw them up in Bristol. You could not hear them, too much screaming. But it was nice just to watch them," Emily revealed then changed the subject. "Come now we have to move!"

"Where are we off to my becoming head girl?"

"We are to enjoy a fleeting fond farewell and sherry with the headmistress. After that the whole of the upper sixth is having a final leaving party, meeting at the Randolph at eight. Daddy will pick us both up early tomorrow morning. No doubt we will all be suffering from gale force hangovers."

"What next for you dearest Emily, I mean before uni? Will your beloved actually get down on one knee?"

"The family has a hunky new gardener but James is hunkier. There's no rush. I just like the smell of him and his strength. I love him just being around me, listening to music. We love walking in the rain and breathing in the heavenly petrichor."

"Ah, I know, the fresh smell after rain. However, a new gardener will be a man so no interest for me. You are such a romantic Emily Wilkinson. What do you like most about him? James I mean, not the gardener."

"I like that too Kathleen, my lesbian friend. We are off again to his other private cottage, up near Chedworth Woods on the way to Cheltenham. It will be for a dirty weekend with lots and lots of hot sex in every room in the house. When we first meet after being apart he cannot even wait for me to undress, just pushes me on the couch, flicks up my skirt, pulls down my knickers and he's away like a rabbit. After he first rolls on a French letter of course as I do not want to end up like Beryl Appleby. That is married with a baby before I'm 20. I am adamant to be an artist, a QC and a writer, But I still love James getting on top of me."

"You are such a naughty head girl." Kathleen impishly chuckled. "And I 'm so glad that James' mother came to see sense."

"Trust me my little old friend from Lesbos, I am very naughty. However, the Countess of Wye no more wants me as a daughter in law than she would the Bride of Frankenstein. So, no, she has not come to her senses. More veritable is that James now virtually ignores her."

"I knew about that." Kathleen grinned obtusely. "Your champion of a man stood his ground.

Are you rushing off immediately to your love nest when you get home tomorrow?"

"No." Emily smirked. "Following our shindig, our leaving school party, tomorrow, we, you and I, are going home for a long chat and to meet up with old friends. Once we have talked, smoked, drank and listened to music to our fill then James will collect me and we shall drive to Gloucestershire."

"Sounds spiffing." Kathleen impishly beamed. "I have arranged to meet up with my new true love. This is the one. At least until the next one."

"You are such a strumpet and slattern, Kath. At least I only have one man. You have a different girl or woman every fortnight."

"I plead guilty to all charges, my darling head girl. Now let us make with alacrity. We have to see the headmistress and partake in the first and last sherry we shall ever have from her personal cabinet."

JAMES-1963

"Would you like a scotch and soda?" Tom Merchant looked up at his son. James seemed to be criss-crossing the room and wearing out the luxurious patterned Axminster whilst staring at the floor. "James, is Emily in the family way?"

"Good God no," he spluttered, "And yes, I shall have a whiskey. Thank you, Papa."

"Hodges, pour Lord James a whiskey."

The dutiful butler brought forward a glass of Scotch resting on a silver salver.

"Are you about to announce your engagement? After that serious spat with Mama two years back I think it would be wise to wait for another few years. There is an outside chance she may just about be over it by then."

"It has nothing to do with that Papa. And I have to say that with all due respect, you and I both know that Mama will never accept Emily. Emily and I have both agreed that if and when we do make an announcement it shall be some time after university. Not before."

Tom was quietly relieved.

"Well, boy. Forgive me, young man, what great revelation are you about to disclose?"

"I know you wished for me to join the family business after university." James shuffled then sipped at his Scotch.

"I hoped, the choice would always have been yours." Tom looked up as Louise entered the drawing room. She was wearing a brown tight pencil skirt and golden silk blouse, which matched her sunburst shade of hair

"Oh, is this men only talk?" The countess enquired with no intention of taking her leave.

"It's alright Mama," James sighed, "I was only telling papa about my plans after university."

"We have already agreed upon this matter." Louise was becoming seriously aggrieved. Her various arrangements for the future of her offspring were severely digressing well variant to the order of the template. "James, you attend Oxford and graduate in Economics. Papa arranges for a job in the City, possibly an articled clerk. You then work for a few years towards becoming a chartered accountant. Then you join the company as the general manager of the UK operations. Naturally we will opt for the metal and food processing plants as they are the most lucrative as well as challenging. And eventually, when your Papa feels he wants to spend more time at his club or on the golf course, then you shall assume the full reins of his business empire."

"Sorry, Mama, I have ambitions of my own." James' face tightened with determination.

"Oh no! Are you telling me that Emily has tampered with your future?"

"Leave her out of this. She is not aware herself of my plans."

"And your plans are, James?" Tom was a tad tetchy over his wife's interference.

"I shall read and receive my BSc in Economics. Then I intend to apply for a commission in the Royal Marines. This should last for 12 years after which I shall sort out a career in business or writing."

"No you can't!" Louise was stunned.

"Yes, I can, Mama. Please do not regurgitate that rubbish about being disinherited because I simply do not care. Like Papa, I shall plough my own furrow and make mine own fortune. Otherwise, I can see you two, especially Mama, supported as always by Papa, telling me "I would never be anything without your assistance" which somehow lodges in my gut."

"Why the Royal Marines? If you want a military career, which I consider to be of great esteem, then accept a commission in the Guards. I am close friends with the Major General who commands the Household Division. We frequently share a round of golf."

"Papa, that is exactly why I want to join the Royal Marines. I am sure your influence with them, especially as a former Guards officer, is very scant if at all. I want to achieve goals by merit and mine own endeavours and endurance, and not by being the Honourable James Marchant."

Tom shrugged his shoulders whilst Louise remained frozen with astonishment.

"And, if and when Emily and I wish to make an announcement it shall not be until I am well bedded down in my military career. Therefore Mama, you have at least until 1969 before you need to start panicking again. Unless of course you are now concerned about who Philippa may take as a husband?"

Louise gave a sickly smirk while maintaining her silence.

"Your mater and pater were hunky dory, what ho? I mean about your desire to be a manly Royal Marine. A person of such physical prowess, animal magnetism and unadulterated sexual attraction he makes the pupils of Charles Atlas look like blubbering little wimps. Like little fags from a junior school second form."

"Sniffer, you always sound such a homo. If I had not seen you with your hand up Beryl Appleby's skirt before she ended up with a bun in the oven and had to get married, rapidly, I would have deemed you to be irrefutably a puff." James slowly drank his pint of beer in the saloon bar of the local village pub, The Plough Inn.

"Well she got married to a wanker called Furtack. He's a total knob head with the IQ of an earwig. It might have been my seed that germinated in her lovely body. But we'll never know."

"Sniffer, you never told me you had ridden the lovely Beryl. I am a tad jealous." James finished off his beer then lit a Capstan cigarette. "It's your round Sniffer. Mine is an IPA."

"In a mo, the Honourable Mister James Marchant. Are you really going to be one of these Battler Britton type Marine people that shoot anyone and anything that moves?"

"Of course, Sniffer. I shall be an officer of the highest calibre and fight the Communist peril wherever it rears its obnoxious, execration of a head." James smiled and drew upon his plain cigarette.

"Alright Colonel Blimp, I only mention the fact to congratulate you on winning over the parents. A pretty neat piece of brinkmanship if I may say so. Mumsy and dadsy can be a smidgeon leaning on the awkward side when such a yearning grasps them. Mine would never have given the say so, yo ho."

"You are such a materialistic navel gazer." James chuckled then pointed at his empty glass. "Keeping one eye on your impending inheritance, Sniffer, you do not want to scupper that."

"Of course not, have now finished my congrats but not the speech old boy." Sniffer was attired in a conservative tweed jacket and corduroy trousers. He moved his lank figure a little uncomfortably, tossing back the extended blond hair that normally fell across his forehead. "I thought I'd divulge, best I thought I would instead of some ass—."

"Sniffer, hurry up and get the beer in. I'm dying of thirst. After which I think we shall drive to the Chinese at Didcot for a good lunch. Emily is coming home from school tomorrow so will have no time then, nudge, nudge, wink, wink."

"Dear James, I know you are dying to shag the arse off your lovely Emily. I mean you have not set eyes on the gorgeous filly for all of four days. But before we fly off to our Chinkie meal best thought I would let you know something. That mass debater, your sworn enemy, Bowman, that tedious wanker, well he has joined the Royal Navy or Marines as an officer. He dropped out of Oxford and is now somewhere in Devon. I forgot the name. Learning how to be a trained killer commando or something of that ilk."

"Oh fuck," James grunted.

"Yes. He will be a general or a colonel or something by the time you get in, old boy."

DANIEL 1963

The two friends walked along the road, adjacent to the River Coquet that ran from Warkworth to the fishing village of Amble on the coast.

They were off to buy a fish and chip lunch then wander around the place scouting for any talent.

This consisted of any female form, preferably their age and even better Carol Green. The actuality being that almost any girl old enough to wear stockings would suffice for them. This sport by instinct would be enacted only once they had watched a film at the local cinema. Stuart carried a transistor radio, which was playing the Beatles recent hit "From Me to You".

"Stu, do Ya think kids our age should make a plan for their lives?"

Stuart Dawson looked up at his best friend. He was always transported into a realm of sheer incredulity each time Daniel spoke.

"Dan, what the hell d' we want t' make a plan for? We is just youngsters."

"Of course Stu, but I was thinking, should I say an idea popped into me head last night--."

"The only idea that popped into your head was when can ya shag Carol Green. Well it's never Danny Boy because she fancies lads a lot older than us. So, let's try to find some talent more like we can get. Not just those we like but those that likes us as well. Ah don't want to dream of a lass. I wanna feel one, kiss one. Ya knows what I mean?"

"No, I had an epiphany last night--."

"A fuckin' what? Danny I knows we's is Duke's School boys but some of the words ye comes oot with is a little bit weird."

"Stu, ya should do more readin'. Why it's only two years until we sit our "O" Levels. You'll never pass English Language or English Lit unless ya get a better vocabulary. Epiphany only means I had, or believe I had, a supernatural experience and Ah think I was given divine knowledge. A figure, an object, has been guiding me for years and this creature, or apparition, is now saying I need a plan."

"Bloody bollocks," Stu riposted then spat before loudly farting. "Best move away from that Danny Boy, it stinks. It's got shit behind it."

"Anyway, if ya can have these divine things then maybe ye can find us a lass each," Stu suggested once the pungent aroma of methane had abated. This was coincident with their approaching Amble. The two friends strolled up the steep bank called the Wynd before making for Gino's fish and chip shop.

"Cod and chips lunch twice, please, Gino," Daniel requested from the small, bald, friendly Italian. Gino Conti was the proprietor of his favourite eating-place in all the county of Northumberland.

"Another Saturday in Amble, boys?" Gino enjoyed the custom of the young lads from Warkworth.

"Aye, Gino, we're down for the afternoon and tonight we're off to the flicks to see a film called "The Birds"," Daniel enthusiastically imparted.

"Ah yes." Gino smiled as he poured salt and vinegar onto the portions of cod and chips. "I believe Alfred Hitchcock directed it. It stars Rod Taylor and a new actress called Tippi Hedren. A bit frightening, they say."

"I guess so," Stuart interjected, "It's an "X" rating but now we look old enough to get into the cinema to watch them."

"Two and sixpence please Daniel." Gino handed the wrapped fish and chips to Daniel who paid for them with a half crown coin. The music of the transistor had changed from "Wipe Out" by the Surfaris to "I Like It" by Gerry and the Pacemakers.

"See ya Gino," the boys spoke in unison. They crossed the road, passed Amble dole office, officially known as the Labour Exchange and down Bede Street until they arrived at the top end of Church Street. From that junction they would cross over to Queen Street, which was the idea until the appearance of Alistair "Bowk" Clark, Chris Wrigglesworth and Bobby "Boxer" Beadle.

"Hey, it's the puffs, rubbadub dub nettie nuffs from Warkworth," Bowk Clark called out as the three Amble boys moved towards Daniel and Stuart.

"It's the puffs," Beadle echoed. Clark then belched loudly.

The tall dangly figure of Bowk, with thick bushy curly hair, almost bow legs, in very tight jeans and a leather jacket came towards Daniel. The 15-year-old was about three inches shorter than his arch-rival but when Clark punched Daniel's fish and chips out of his hand and across Bede Street he transformed into a nemesis.

"I've worked all week for the money for that Clark," Daniel growled.

"Hard luck you little puff, you nettie nuff, ain't that tough?" Clark sang back to the tune of "I Like It" which was still playing on the small radio.

A voice boomed within the head of Daniel, a sound, which echoed across time, history and infinite chasms of vacuum emptiness, "Hit him!"

A force swept through his body, a great dynamic that propelled every muscle, tissue and sinew in his frame to divert raw energy from the distant receptacles of his psyche into unadulterated revenge, sweet, clinical and with impetus.

The right hand of Daniel slammed into the stomach of Clark with the force of a Hawker Hunter jet fighter. He grabbed the groaning schoolboy and twisted the right hand up his back before frog marching the despondent figure to the side door of the Bede Street Club. The wooden structure provided an excellent medium for Daniel to bounce his opponent's head off, several times. The youth then unceremoniously grabbed Clark and screamed directly into his ear, "Ya bastard!" This coincided with "Boxer" Beadle taking an opportunistic swing at his head.

The purported pugilist seemed light years unpunctual as a right hook punch crashed into his nose sending blood and mucous spurting in all directions. As Beadle was hitting the pavement with a whining moan, Daniel grabbed Clark by his thick wavy mop of hair. He sent an equally as destructive left hook onto the nose of the groaning teenager.

"Clark!" Daniel screamed once again directly into the ear of the dejected mass. "You ever piss me off again and I'll rip your balls off! D' ya know what ah mean?"

"Ugh, yeah," Clark was too traumatised for further conflict. Daniel dropped him to the pavement. The victor stood on the moaning Beadle then deliberately walked into Wrigglesworth' This caused the ginger locked chum of the two defeated bullies to fall against the adjacent stone wall of the terrace of house that stood near Gino's.

Daniel walked back to Clark and removed a shilling and a threepenny piece from his pocket. He snarled at him once more. "Ye owed me that for the fish and chips. Ye can have the cod and chips on the road."

He walked passed Stuart who was beaming with satisfaction. A new release by a group called The Searchers entitled "Sweets for My Sweet" was announced by David Jacobs on the radio.

"I believe mine honour hath been restored," Daniel declared in a pseudo "BBC accent".

"Yes, this day the ruffians have been taught a stiff lesson! And your victuals are replenished," Stuart articulated, mimicking Daniel's temporary inflection.

PHILIPPA -1963

"And that covers in basic terms the circulatory system. Any questions?"

"Very good Uncle Peregrine. I am aware of the principles. However, when I was invited by Daddy to study with you the basics of anatomy, to assist in my becoming a doctor, I did not know the anatomy would be mine."

"How so my little juicy fruit? I have not alluded to your fine physique in any way shape or form," Peregrine responded with an air of innocence. This rejoinder seemed aptly highlighted by his blue blazer and white shirt, trimmed moustache, swept back grey hair and mauve cravat. The underscore was further enhanced in emphasis by his smoking a cigarette using a long holder.

He grinned, reminding his student intensely of the comedian Terry Thomas starring in the current film "Mouse on the Moon."

"Not so much today, Uncle. Normally you are craftily looking at my chest or trying to see up my skirt. That is when you think I would not notice. Still you are teaching me a lot."

"A man has a duty to admire a pretty lady, Philippa."

"Perhaps." She smiled and packed up her books. The teenager looked very becoming in her Lesley Gore hairstyle. This look was enhanced by her wardrobe of a tight pencil skirt and brown stockings, flat shoes, blue blouse and golden hued cardigan. "But Uncle, I am 15 years old and you are 68. I love the Beatles and you listen to who is it, Al Martino? Billy Cotton? Also, I think you are a tad on the mature side for me. By that I mean you are old. Nonetheless, dear Uncle, I am grateful for your assistance."

"My pleasure you young beauty. You exude a wisdom far beyond your tender years. I shall see you next week for several hours more nose to the grindstone."

"Yes, of course. And as always no hint to Mama. Daddy's orders. She believes you are just on a social call while visiting some femme fatale in Bristol. It's my ambition to practice medicine." Peregrine packed away his notes and equipment, gave Philippa a quick kiss on the cheek then took his leave. She warily vacated the hall. It was ornately decorated with old masters of which many of the subjects seemed to be casting critical glances. Philippa hesitated for a second then assiduously headed in the direction of the kitchen.

As the young teenager passed by the study she could discern the countess conversing with someone male. It was not her father. Philippa had thought this unusual. She had been given to understand that her mother was visiting her Grandmama Rathbone in Weston-Super-Mare. As the study was not a private room, she opened the door and marched steadfastly in. Inside stood her mother and a strange man. It appeared to Philippa that only seconds before they were getting extremely close. Almost intimate. And had jolted apart with some rapidity. Louise was crimson with obvious embarrassment and stumbled for words.

"Mama, so sorry to disturb you." Philippa grinned meaningfully and then turned to the man. He was 40 to 50 years old with black hair greying at the sides, tallish and dressed in a blue pinstripe suit and tie. "My name is Philippa Marchant, the Lady Philippa Marchant. I do not believe we have been formally introduced."

"I beg your sufferance, Lady Philippa. I am Charles De'ath, an old friend of your mother."

"Yes." Philippa cast a smile but held the expression on the verge of transforming into a full-blown smirk. She lightly shook hands with De'ath. "It is so nice to make your acquaintance, Mister De'ath. However, I must take my leave. I have tedious school homework to complete and notes to update."

Philippa stepped smartly to the door. She turned left and sprinted along the corridor. The next manoeuvre was to rapidly cross the entrance lobby and hurry down the rear staircase into the busy kitchen. Rebecca was feverishly working on the night's dinner menu whilst Mrs Cromer stood nearby looking pale and exhausted.

"Lady Philippa!" Rebecca exclaimed upon which Maggie jumped into activity.

"What brings you to the kitchen?"

"I just wanted to see you, Becky. I'll put the kettle on." The youthful figure picked up the gleaming copper vessel and made towards the taps.

"That is no work for young ladies of high standing, My Lady." Mrs Cromer relieved Philippa of the kettle. This was the clear signal for the young debutante to take a seat at the massive marble topped kitchen table.

"Who is that new gardener chappie?" Philippa opened the biscuit tin. She carefully removed a "Rebecca made" chocolate-topped brownie then wolfed it down.

Mrs. Cromer was noticeably slowing in pace. Once the indefatigable sole creator of the culinary delights that emanated from the kitchen the previous few years had seen Rebecca assume more responsibility. Maggie

Cromer remained overseeing the operation and offering guidance where she deemed appropriate.

"Young Jim Parnell," Rebecca responded whilst stirring a Yorkshire pudding mix. "And e's 23. He did 'is National Service in Cyprus and now wants a steady outside job. And he's too old even if 'e was of suitable breeding for you, My Lady."

"Of course, he's too old." Philippa slipped from the chair and walked over to the radio. "But I can window shop even if I am not buying the goods. And he is dishy, very dishy."

"That's so cheeky, Lady Philippa." Rebecca smiled at the feisty 15-year-old unceremoniously demolishing another of Rebecca's homemade biscuits.

"Mrs. Cromer. Who is that man visiting mother? I 've never set eyes on him before."

"That's Mister De'ath, My Lady. Spelled like death but with a thing in the middle. He's an old friend from her ladyship's early days as a debutante in about 1940. It was just 'fore she went to university. Such a nice man. A Battle of Britain Spitfire pilot and hero who won the DFC."

"They seemed very good, I mean very good friends." Philippa became a trace too much on the honest side for the total comfort of the servants.

"Her ladyship is a wonderful mother. As you know Lady Philippa. I'm sure she was just talking about old times, like old friends do." Maggie Cromer handed the teenager a mug of hot sweet, tea to accompany the chocolate brownies.

"I suppose so, Mrs Cromer." Philippa quietly mumbled in concession.

"How is school, Lady Philippa? No boys to disturb your studying?"

"School is great, Becky. Judith, Christine and Pat all love it but as far as boys go, there is a gorgeous 16-year-old in Oxford. A grammar school boy called Miles and the son of some artisan so I doubt if mama would approve of him. That other boy, Julian Lee Watersby, is my mother's preferred choice for me."

"Her ladyship is a normal parent, Lady Philippa," Maggie interjected, "She just wants what's best for you, My Lady."

"Hmm." the youngster sardonically grinned. "I have to concentrate on my "O" levels, then "A" levels, then university and medical school. I shall have no time for boys until I am about 26."

"Of course, ye will. The boy of your dreams 'll come along, sometime soon I'm sure." Rebecca gave a reassuring smile which effected a reciprocal beam from Philippa.

"Becky. When are you and Mister Biggs tying the knot?"

"We shall have to ask his lordship first of course but we hope to be wed next year."

"That is wonderful!" Philippa clapped her hands with joy.

DANESH AND KELLY

"Good grief!" Kelly shrieked as she stepped from the cockpit of the Particle Accelerator Driven Inter-Dimensional Transporter. This apparatus was known to Professor Gideon as PADIT and was a four-metre-long object that resembled a large racing car minus the wheels.

She was shaking uncontrollably as she ambled across the red tiled laboratory floor. Danesh swiftly poured her a whiskey and soda.

"I take it you enjoyed your sojourn into another dimension and world?"

"It was amazing Professor! Amazing! Amazing! So many things to tell! So many questions to ask! What next?"

"Take your drink. We shall retire to the lounge where you shall sit comfortably. Then we shall tape our discussion and I shall type it up for our record. Next, I shall upload the data from the PADIT computer. We will record your experience and search diligently for variations from the information and statistics collated to date. Let's move out of here."

"It was like journeying through a dream, Professor." Kelly spoke into the microphone, recalling the details of her singular expedition. "I sat in the cockpit, spoke to you. Then I was fired across a sky that was all colours and no colours. There were galaxies that seemed to melt, oceans rose and fell, and mountains erupted from plains. All these phenomena reached for the heavens then were swept away as sandcastles on some cosmic beach."

"It corroborates my travels, Doctor." Danesh stuffed tobacco into his pipe. "My observations conclude that it has effected an enormous impact on you. It may yet be premature, a tad early to enquire but I shall nonetheless. What substantiation arose to affirm that you were without doubt physically travelling within a parallel universe?"

Kelly knocked back her whiskey then lit a Dunhill luxury cigarette.

"I followed your instructions to the most minute detail. I input and followed the co-ordinates as you had loaded them into the PADIT onboard computer then set off. The eventual destination seemed identical to my own home town. I duly parked up the machine. The sights were the same and even people I swore I recognised were walking around. I stopped PADIT a couple of times and cautiously stepped outside. Naturally I wore the special suit we have which makes one appear to be totally invisible. I suppose it may scare people if they see you. However, although in daylight one seems to be totally imperceptible, inside buildings your outline can be pretty much distinguished."

"I am aware of such a flaw and all concurs with mine own experiences. I am working to dispense with the suit as soon it may not be needed." The Professor puffed on his pipe.

"Have you always smoked that disgusting mix? It smells like an old dustbin on fire."

"I have, Doctor Aresti. I would suggest since before you were born. I love the mix of baccy. I always was under the impression you approved of the aroma--."

"Professor. You are indeed a handsome man. But why do you think I ask you to vigorously brush your teeth before you sleep with me? The redolence is fine in the open air but not in the confines of your lounge."

"Your cigarette smoke is equally repugnant to me. Doctor, can you get on with your debriefing please?"

"I made for the countryside where I lived when I was young. PADIT flies like a jet that can be speeded and slowed to a stop in a microsecond."

"It is not observing the laws of physics exactly as they are on this world. It appears that between different universes there is a bending of the principles. I suppose fracturing them instead of breaking as Eddie Murphy commented in the movie "Beverley Hills Cop." It allows for amazing tricks of time and motion. However, there is a lot more research I need to perform."

"I'll have to take your word for that, Professor." Kelly poured herself another whiskey. "But I did travel to the village I lived in when young. You say one does not travel in time, merely across to another dimension to a universe like our own."

"That is my hypothesis to date."

"Well, I did see people that seemed familiar, although very much younger. I followed the path to a house that I recognised as living in when I was young, but I did not see the girl who lived there. Although whoever did, did not have my name. I passed other people that I once knew only they were much younger than I recall. It was like traversing the line of a dream. I saw a newspaper in the local shop. A tabloid red top, a national newspaper called the "Daily Provider". To my knowledge no such national paper has existed in this country."

"Interesting. What else did you discern?" Professor Gideon was hanging on every word.

"I saw on the reverse of the paper and noticed the date as being the 23rd of May 1963. It related to the 1962-1963 football season. Soccer that is, not rugby, Prof. I know you hate football. In this paper Everton were crowned champions of Division One, which nowadays we would call the Premier League. Instinctively I checked it on the PADIT computer. It is fortuitous that it contains a mega amount of info. It transpires that in our country and universe Everton were then actually in the old Third Division. What nowadays we would refer to as League One."

"Not earth shattering, but certainly interesting," Danesh conceded, "It may be you travelled several universes away instead of one. When is your fiancé due back from sea?"

"I am trying to carry out a proper debriefing, Professor. You know he is out in Libya. His father served with the Royal Navy's contribution to the British Expeditionary Force in Vietnam during the1960s and his grandfather served on some ship or other fighting the Russians in World War Two. It might have been off the coast of Africa. The Navy is in his blood, which is fine for some women, but I don't think that I'm suited to the lifestyle of a naval spouse. I like regular sex. I sometimes think that these men who join the Navy and so on and leave their wives and girlfriends are really closet gays."

"I doubt it. However, you get the regular sex from me--," Danesh boasted only to be cut off in mid flow.

"Only until he returns! We agreed, Professor. I got into bed with you as I wanted to travel to PUs. But it can't happen once he's back. Sub Lieutenant Jeremy Morton may not be too happy."

"Kelly, he's not back yet. Do you want to travel more?"

"Of course, I do. Don't worry Danesh, I'll sleep with you and yes, we can have sex, for the time being anyway. Please allow me to continue my narrative."

"Very well." He moved uncomfortably on the couch.

"You are jealous. I can't help that, live with it Prof! The other thing I saw were the cars. I am no expert, but it was mid-1963 and the models were from much later in our universe. The one that I did know was the Triumph 2000 which did not appear in our world until 1968. Also, the song by Billy J. Kramer and the Dakotas, "Bad to Me", was playing although it was not a hit song here until 1966. I took special note of the styles in fashion. Skirts were much longer than our world at that point in the 1960s. There was one other matter. As I drifted, almost invisibly through the village, I ran into my mother. I am certain of it. At least it was her double. My mother's doppelganger only of course. This woman was younger, only a little, but there was no mistaking her. I am certain of that. The high class and pulchritudinous mien, I look like her.

My mother always was a beauty. And still is. But the guy she was with I am certain was not my father. That is despite the fact I had seen photos of someone identical to him who was married to this woman, my alter mother. Well, I think she was, I'm certain she was."

"Anything else worthy of note?"

"Now you mention it, there was. I was so upset I must have jammed it from my thoughts."

Kelly disdainfully squirmed.

"And?" Danesh pressed.

"I was in my light bending suit and ostensibly invisible to all. I passed folk who were certainly not aware of me even though I was but inches from them. However, there was one repulsive, balding, greasy haired short man who seemed to be ogling me."

"What happened, Doctor?"

"Well this nauseating person looked directly at me despite being supposedly invisible. He ominously snarled. I quote him verbatim, "You are in the wrong world Doctor Aresti. I suggest you leave as this is a dangerous place for you and your kind!" I was shocked, stunned so badly

I made my way instantly back to PADIT. He may have been talking on a mobile phone. But I am sure they were not around at that chronological point and how did he know my name? He was so ugly and looked so menacing, I was really disconcerted. He sounded very, very threatening."

Chapter Six

NARRATOR

This glowing saga brings forth back the season of spring for many are now deep into the autumn of their allotted span. Inveterate truisms are promulgated and those here to listen on this day recall a munificence of love and affection. They rest alongside some material matters that stand on the pinnacle of life's great fabric and are so grand that even the many near illuminati sat before me would toil and labour for unknown aeons to elucidate.

I feel as if I am in some eerie offspring. A chimera of the eve of battle speech in Shakespeare's "Henry V". Perhaps some over loquacious politician in the House of Commons seeking a purpose to the tenure of her esteemed office. Tis no ghost of Banquo that shall be the spectre at the feast, at least that is my wish but who knows what the runes have in store for us? I can but sense the glow of spirits of the long and not so long gone. It is the summer, the season of youth for many. The performers within my tale, the glorious heroes and heroines confidently sit largely in the third stage of the Bard's Seven Seasons of Man. My receptive audience however seem predominantly of the final three stages of that glorious septet. I am aware of a gigantic story that rests between the many lines of the yarn I reveal. It is so bizarre I would recount matters until the dawn of the next ice age before I could summon sufficient pluck to divulge extra to my predetermined vocalisations. Those close to my heart look and listen with a pride that almost bursts at the seams. Nonetheless, the road travelled to this great juncture has not been void of trials and tribulations, and tragedy, along the winding, rocky way.

→ Stephen Grenfell ←

EMILY-1964

Lady Isabelle Napier-Fenning puffed nervously on her cigarette whilst listening to a record of the Kinks playing "You Really Got Me". She was being driven by hormones, anger, jealousy and a gamut of other emotions that had shredded her nerves. The internal maelstrom weaved a caustic path through her very being. The pulsating ire finally drove her into on to act. She lifted the handset and turned the dials on the red GPO 706 Modern Telephone. A voice slowly responded at the other end of the line. Isabelle breathed sensually into the mouthpiece.

"Hello, I would appreciate a favour from you. If you do that favour I shall be very, I mean very, grateful."

"Emily, we should be out playing hockey on this lovely summer's day."

The dedicated student responded by turning from her law book and looking up to view the hourglass shape. The shadowy outline was Emily's beautiful friend, Gloria van der Stay. She was a blonde, of medium height and blue-eyed, half Dutch under graduate at Cambridge University. The elite historical seat of learning where the flaxen haired pair were reading law. Gloria and Emily studied at the women's college of Newnham along with their other new friend, Jacqui Rosenthal. Jacqui was dark and slightly podgy, tallish and brown eyed and seen by some as less becoming. Nevertheless, she was a fun-loving individual whom Emily and Gloria deemed to be a "right bundle of laughs". A Jewish girl that somewhat ironically loved bacon and eggs and ham and cheese sandwiches, preferably washed down with a few lagers and lime. Certainly not kosher.

Gloria hailed from a wealthy City of London stockbroking family that lived in Hertfordshire. Jacqui's parents owned several bespoke tailor's shops and resided in Golders Green, part of the London Borough of Barnet.

"Gloria, my head is buzzing. When does Time Immemorial begin? What were the early Anglo-Saxon courts called? Does a contract need offer and acceptance, intent and consideration?" Emily lit a Woodbine Tipped cigarette.

"You know all those, Emily. I think it was the during the reign of Good King Richard, July the sixth 1189 and before. The second bit, can't remember but I think they were called the Hundreds and the last bit is yes, yes, you are right. Now get yourself dressed, Miss Wilkinson, you need to get out of this room, rapidly. You've been working too hard. We'll play some hockey to work up an appetite and a thirst. Then later you, Jacqui and I will all go to the pub and eat and drink like Anglo Saxon wenches. We merry band of undergraduates have to blow a few cobwebs away."

"Bollocks, Gloria, I have too much work to do, I do actually want to receive my Bachelors of Law."

"You'll pass with flying colours my little gentile beauty," Jacqui brusquely interrupted, "You are not through your first year yet and you can debate with the lecturers on an equal footing."

"Only with Mister Vallis, the Professor of Legal History," Emily riposted acidly,

"And he is a man, enough said. An old man, he must be at least 50. Nonetheless, a man."

Jacqui was determined to remain inclusive to the discourse.

"My little country girl, of course men are men, Professor Rudyard Vallis included. Apart from the homos, they all want to lay you down in a bright meadow and have their wicked way." Gloria picked out Emily's hockey kit from the wardrobe of her rooms and tossed it unceremoniously on the chair next to her. "There, take off your clothes and put on your sports kit. You'll easily get your legum baccalaureus, and be called to the bar then be appointed a QC. It's much easier for us women since Rose Heilbron and and dear Helena Normanton took silk in 1939. Easier but of course it's still a man's world. They still have the power and that is a fact. Now get changed as we need to build up a sweat, shower, into glad rags then off."

"Good grief Gloria, you're such a know it all and pain in the arse."

"I know but I have a nice arse. Now get changed, Miss Sword Edge."

"Ha ha!" shrieked Jacqui, "I got that one, Wilkinson Sword Edge razor blades."

"And there is more Jacqui, if you were any sharper you'd cut yourself."

"Very good!" She squealed again.

JAMES-1964

"Champagne?" Peregrine Walker-Thorpe called over to James.

"I'll have a flute," Toby Flynn called out, "Although Irish whiskey would be better."

"You've been a bit on the tight side, Flynn. Peeling an orange in your pocket, as they say, type."

"That's below the belt, Marchant," Toby protested loudly in his Northern Irish brogue.

This Oxford undergraduate made no attempt to mimic the latest 1960s' fashion trends of his stylish colleagues. Instead he was dressed in an old corduroy jacket, dirty pullover and crumpled pair of slacks. Toby was bearded and short with thick flaming red hair and ruddy, plain round face to match. Nonetheless he was endowed with some charisma and bright but fickle sense of humour. "If you can afford to drink champers, you should pay for it." James broke away from his letter writing.

The rooms in the Waynflete Building were Spartan but adequate. They were always enhanced when Peregrine came visiting along with his seemingly interminable supply of vintage Dom Perignon. It had become a nigh daily ritual.

"Sorry, but I don't have the rich parentage you two enjoy. Therefore, belonging to the proletariat, the masses. Consider it your civil duty to redistribute a tiny element of your exorbitant wealth."

"That's alright, Tob. Just light me a Players Navy Cut and you can have three flutes of Dom. I like helping the wage earners. A little."

"For one of the landed gentry, you're pretty fab, Perry. When the revolution comes, you'll be alright. Unlike you, Marchant." Toby winked at James.

"You do talk out of your arse, Toby. You have no money, so you say, but I never see you doing work of any description. Furthermore, I thought you Irish all went to university in Trinity College, Dublin and not Magdalen College at Oxford in England."

James was genuinely intrigued.

"He's a Catholic from Northern Ireland." Peregrine handed both a flowing glass. "And he lives over here." Walker-Thorpe was bedecked in a beige pair of trousers and white frilly shirt of the "Kinks" ilk, a blue cravat and navy-blue blazer. He was 19 years old, tall and slim, brown haired and deemed by most to be reasonably handsome.

"Cheers!" They declared in unison.

"Still Irish," James muttered. He was feeling decidedly under dressed in comparison to Peregrine. Young Marchant was wearing jeans with an out of date polo neck sweater and leather "John Lennon" style cap.

"James the Honourable Marchant." Peregrine rushed to Toby's defence. "Just in case it missed your history learning, Northern Ireland is part of the United Kingdom. That makes Toby as British as you or me."

"I know, I just like to annoy him because he's a dashed socialist."

"That I am the Honourable James whatever. Also, I believe that your young lady is as well. At least she's not from the friggin' silver spoon brigade like you. Perry also."

"Toby reckons that the British should sod off out of Ulster and let Ireland be one country. All 32 counties united." Perry poured more champagne.

"I certainly do," Toby agreed.

"Sounds fine to me." James grinned. "Let the Irish have their own land. Now I must finish my letter to Emm. After that we can drink and chat. But before that, I will procure one of your Players cigarettes, Toby. That is while you still have some and before you start sponging smokes from me."

"Is the becoming Emily joining you this week end?" Toby was interested, Perry less so. The Northern Irishman grabbed the leather cap from James' head and placed it on his own pate.

"I have to ring to confirm." James took a cigarette from Toby, lit it then grabbed his cap back from Toby's. He replaced it accordingly before recommencing his letter to Emily. "I also have to write to her, tell her what a load of moronic wankers I have as friends and room-mates. Especially that anal sphincter from the British part of Ireland, Paddy Flynn the socialist!"

"Yeah, yeah, very funny. You'll also have to tell her you want to serve Her Majesty as well. That's two timing. You don't know the Queen and you've known Emily 14 years." Toby laughed, walked over to the champagne bottle and cheekily refilled his flute.

"James, do you still want to be a Royal Marines' officer in a couple of years?" Peregrine drew on his cigarette then sat on the small couch near Toby.

"I certainly am still doing that, Perry. Of course, after I have graduated with my degree in economics."

"An Audie fucking Murphy." Toby sarcastically laughed. "I'll take good care of Emily while you're away fighting the foreign foe. She'll need a man, a big man with nine inches."

"Then you won't do! Not with your two inches," James retorted, "There are times when I think you're a puff."

"That's not what Emily said the last time she was here." Toby chuckled. "She was very happy." "Yes, happy to get away from you."

The telephone rang, and Peregrine picked it up. "James old boy, someone for you."

DANIEL-1964

The physical education and geography master of the Duke's Grammar School, Alnwick, Ray "Raffie" Watson, was known to the pupils as "Tarzan". The 35-year-old well-built and sandy haired rugby union player hailed from the Lake District in Cumberland. He was quietly reading an exam paper in the school staff room when a knock came on the door.

"Yes!" Watson gruffly bellowed.

"Sir." The 15-year-old Daniel nervously stepped forward. "I was told by Mister Dodds you were here, and I would like a word with you, please. That's if you have time, sir."

Watson had a free hour and was brimming with interest. He was itching to ascertain as to why the young fourth form pupil would want a tête-à-tête with a master, something unheard of in the normal day to day school time table. The masters, the designation by which grammar school teachers were almost always referred, would summon the boys. That would usually be for punishment, normally strokes of the cane, but a boy never asked to chat with a master. It was just not the done thing.

"Yes, young Gibson, what can I do for you?"

"What did Tarzan have to say?" Dougie Veitch, Peter Tyson and Stuart Dawson crowded around Daniel as he emerged from his meeting with Mister Watson.

"He said it would depend on how I did in th' mock exams. If I did ok, they'd give me the text books t' read over the summer hols and then I would be tested when I got back t' school."

"I still canna understand whys 'e wants to take your "A" levels a year early." Stuart was always sluggish in understanding a point.

"He's told you Stu," the slightly overweight and girlish faced Dougie responded for his friend, "Daniel wants to be an airman or something and serve in Aden. He wants to fight in battle. Serve for three years as a soldier type. We know, at least the man on the BBC News said, that we, the British, will be leaving Aden in 1968. So, to get his enlistment and serve and fight in Aden then go to university he'll need to take his "A" Levels in 1966. A year early. That's why he went to see Tarzan. To see if that was possible. He'll then join some military service or other for a short service enlistment, three years I hear. Then he'll go to university to study, politics, economics, business studies and journalism."

"Shit, Dougie." Daniel was more than a little agog. "Ya knows more about me than Ah do!"

"Your Northumbrian accent has grown stronger since you first came, Dan." The tall, dark and slim Peter contributed to the discourse. He then continued to trumpet his own intellectual prowess. "I read in the paper that a Roman Catholic monk had burned himself to death in Saigon, South Vietnam. There could be trouble brewing there."

"Very good, Dougie, Dan an' Pete. Your infinite knowledge numbs my brain to speechlessness." Stuart had long since become bored with the conversation. There was only one topic retained his attention span more than a second. "Come on, bloody Latin now, yuk. After school Ah wanna get to the stone cross in the bus station next to the Shambles. Ah want t' see if Ah can see Carol Green's stockin' tops while she sits on the steps. The whites of 'er thighs 's more interestin' than friggin' Latin."

"Ya disgustin', Stu, an' such a peasant." Daniel laughed. The others chuckled in agreement and then all four boys sped off to the form room of Mister Dodds and his double period of Latin.

"Dougie." Stu looked up. "Do ya thinks we is just tiny parts in a huge tin box in another universe?"

"Could well be." the budding physicist nodded.

PHILIPPA-1964

Philippa and her three school friends were all engrossed in the Beatle's latest album, "A Hard Day's Night". The quartet of young girls was singing along loudly to "If I Fell" whilst applying as much make-up as the after-hours rules of Oxford High School for girls would allow. Those deigned appropriate by the headmistress, Ann Hancock M.Ed.

"Pip, can you get a move on?" Judith Parkhouse called out.

"Judy, a mo. I have to make sure I am perfect."

"Perfect for whom?" Pat Laidler gave her friend a light dig in the side.

"I give her all--." Christine began to sing the Beatles song "And I Love Her". She was staring into the dressing table mirror at the reflection of Philippa applying a little mascara.

"You all know, stop teasing me," Philippa snapped.

"Come on Pip, don't be so obstreperous." Judith smiled. "You know we're all jealous. You have a very intelligent boyfriend. He's working class which is so in, and you tell us he looks like a younger George Harrison. We all want to meet Miles Benton. How fab and groovy can things be? And tonight we shall see him, yeah!"

Pat put on the single "Not Fade Away" by a more risqué group, The Rolling Stones.

"You're such a Bohemian beatnik, Pat," Judith commented on the musical preference with the other three nodding in concurrence.

"Come on you lot, my parents now like the Beatles. When that happens girls, time to move on." Pat scanned through the pile of 45 rpm records.

"Anyway, Phil." Pat rose up in her own defence. "You're en route to be a quack. You'll have to spend years at university, then years at a teaching hospital. You'll have to listen to music to keep awake while you drink and smoke and shag in your spare time. It will have to be music with soul, like the Animals, the Kinks, The Pretty Things or the Moody Blues. The style of music to thrust and gasp by!"

"Pat, you're filthy! No sex until I'm married," Philippa forcefully expounded.

"Is that dirty old uncle still trying to get his hands on you?" Judith enquired.

"Uncle Perry did try it on, but I said I would tell Daddy if he tried again. Daddy would shoot him. He is of course a great asset in my preparation to be a doctor. Also, I intend to stay a virgin until I'm married."

"That's crap." Pat put another Rolling Stones single on the record player, this one being "It's All Over Now."

"Philippa you look like a film star, gorgeous looks and figure. The contraceptive pill will soon be available to all **w**omen, so we can finally take control of our own bodies. We can have careers and children when we want."

Pat walked over to Philippa as she remained seated on the bedroom stool and stroked the auburn locks.

"You only need the right man and you will fall head over heels then fuck him."

"You can be so vulgar at times, Pat," Christine elected to join in.

"I plead guilty." Pat moved away. "When you do lie down for Mister Benton, the lovely Mister Miles Benton, before you pull your knickers down just make sure either you are on the pill or he is wearing a Durex."

"I want to see this boy that darling Pippa has kept hidden way," Judith gasped with excitement, then began to sing the Beatles song "This Boy".

"He said he could bring three friends, if you are up to that I can ring him now, best do it outside the school though," Philippa nonchalantly mentioned.

"Come on girls, I'm 15, by the time you lot get going I'll be 50." Pat impatiently egged them along.

"There he is," squealed an excited Philippa whilst running towards the boy at the head of a quartet of youths standing in the centre of Oxford.

The nearest youngster was tall, very good-looking, blond, slim and with long hair.

"You brought your friends." Philippa threw herself at the teenager.

EMILY-1964

The hockey club showers ran in torrents of searing steam and breath-stealing chasms of extruding, cathartic, pleasurable cleansing.

"Great game, we absolutely thrashed them ladies!" Gloria called out to her hockey team as they moved in and out of the spray.

Emily came out of the cascading fountains and into the changing area where she dried herself with some assiduousness before putting on her pre-socialising attire.

"You were fabulous, Emily." Jacqui plonked her naked frame down on the bench next to her exquisitely attractive colleague. "You can move like lightning."

"You were good too Jacqui and you have a great swing." Emily, as always, returned a sincere compliment.

"Come on wenches!" Gloria wandered around the changing room drying herself. "Time to hit Cambridge. The food and sack. Sack the drink that is, or both!"

The three young women quickly dressed. They dashed back to their rooms in Newnham College, changed into suitable attire which was flowing summer dresses and cardigans, not formal and not too casual. Once in their socialising gear they then quickly applied an adequate measure of makeup before proceeding at pace to their favourite watering hole, The Hare and Hounds.

"Evening ladies," Bruce Sumpner, the landlord, greeted them as they entered the lounge bar, "you're all looking beautiful, nice legs and bosoms, if I were 20 years--."

"I still wouldn't fancy you Bruce." Gloria sliced his heated flow in midstream. "Now be a good man and give us a pint of lager and lime each, please."

"Comin' up you gorgeous lady." Sumpner poured a dash of lime into three snifters and then pulled draft lager, the increasingly popular drink amongst many students.

"Three shillings and nine pence, or I'll let you off, wink, wink." The sandy haired, balding and bespectacled man grinned.

"No thank you Mister Sumpner, I could get a much better offer than that any day." Gloria cast a wan smirk and then handed Emily and Jacqui a glass each.

The girls took a seat next to the window of the bar.

"Cheers," Emily lifted her glass, which signalled the others to follow suit.

"Great game, nice early summer evening, what else could we want?" Jacqui pondered then put some coins into the jukebox, the first record being "Dancing in the Street" by Martha and the Vandellas.

"Sex!" Gloria giggled then offered her packet of Embassy tipped cigarettes to Jacqui and Emily who both accepted one. Emily flicked on the flame of her Ronson and offered the other two a light.

As if by some mystical direction three young men entered the lounge and took to the bar where they ordered drinks. The first observing. "Talent,

12 o'clock." The tallest of the trio quietly nodded to the others. "Three bits of crumpet. Two gorgeous birds, one acceptable, a three pinter I'd say."

The young men, all dressed in brown shoes, pressed trousers, blazers and open necked shirts approached the girls and the lead figure, a tall, dark and good-looking man spoke first. "I'm Nigel, Nigel Doncaster, this is John Simpson." He pointed at a slightly rotund, round faced figure in glasses. Doncaster then turned to a taller individual with chiselled features, certainly not lacking looks and possessing some modicum of charm. "And this is David, David Nilsen and I'm sure you lovely, lovely young ladies will just yearn for us to buy you a drink."

"You're My World" by Cilla Black came on the jukebox. "We may allow you to join us." Gloria indicated for them to sit down.

Sometime later, all three men were hobbling along the pavement, nursing head wounds and clutching their aching groins.

Doncaster made for the nearest telephone box. He irascibly placed some penny coins in the box, rang a number, pressed the button "A" and painfully gasped into the mouthpiece.

"You bitch, you didn't tell me she was a fucking animal! A fucking judo or expert or something! Next time you want to set someone up to get at the bloke you want to shag, leave me out of it!"

The three buoyant females were bouncing along the highway in the opposite direction.

"Emily!" Gloria beamed. "I'm going to enter you in the British karate team for the Olympics in Tokyo in October. You've one hell of a swipe and kick on you girl."

"Ever since that incident with the man when I was young. I told you about it, my Dad insisted that I learn karate and judo." Emily smiled, satisfied in the knowledge her would be assailant and or agent provocateur was now in agony.

"Why did you hit him? Why did you hit all of them?" Jacqui was still in a limbo land of incredulity. "Mine had not even tried to kiss me! At least you could have waited until he'd had a kiss and felt my fanny."

"Jacqui, you need to grab a cucumber and relieve yourself. "Gloria giggled. "Better not too get worked up by boys. But Emily, why did you clout those guys? I fancied a quick grope, nothing more but a long, juicy, all tongues in throats kiss!"

"Sorry, I have a boyfriend and I get all the shags I need from him. The one with intentions on getting his hands into my pants I recognised straight away. He accordingly his size 12 foot in it. I'd seen him recently with a friend at my arch enemy's house. I was there only as James had been invited although he did not see me. I remained very, very deep in the background," Emily rapidly explained, her breathing still a little hastened.

Gloria was still a tad miffed as Emily continued. "He denied knowing her, where she lives or anyone she knew. Well he lives in Didcot, everyone knows my arch enemy, yuk, so I would have known he was lying just by that!"

"So what?" Gloria was unimpressed, nonetheless remained simmering from her involuntary lack of a sensual encounter.

"So what! I called him a lying bastard and he tried to hit me!" Emily further elucidated. "So I kneed him in the balls and chopped him across the neck. That was when his amigos attempted to come to his rescue. They received the same. Two sore testicles and a stiff neck. That's all that will be stiff on their anatomy for a day or two."

DANIEL-1964

The bell for end of the school day had sounded per normal at 20 minutes before four o' clock in the afternoon. Dougie and Peter veered off to their respective homes in Alnwick whilst Stuart and Daniel made their way to the old bus station next to the town hall to catch the private school coach to Warkworth.

"Ah just wanna see Carol Green," Stuart repeated for the tenth time that day.

"What the hell's up with ye, ya like a bloody horny little bastard." Daniel laughed loudly. "Mind ya, Ah think that all the lads in the county would wanna get their hands inside her blouse. Ah think ya need a dose of bromide to keep ya cock soft."

"Look whose talkin'," Stu rapidly riposted, "Ya one of those dirty buggers that's after Carol, and 'ave been for ages."

The two 15-year olds headed along the main street of Alnwick, across the cobbled area opposite the Swan Hotel then moved on towards the Shambles, the walkway that circumnavigated the town hall. As they crossed the road again from F W Woolworth towards the old bus station, three girls from the Duchess School ran frenetically and in a state of obvious panic towards Daniel. They wore the standard uniform of blue blazer with narrow gold stripes, berets, white blouses and blue skirts. Lesley Armstrong, a pretty brunette, tallish for a girl, Ann Simmons, another brunette who was smaller and a little on the heavier side and Vicki Henderson, ebony hair, tall, very slim and plain, all charged up to Daniel. Leslie trembled as she gasped, "Dan, Eric Roberts and two of his bully friends' says he's gonna hit Carol. Can ya? can ya---?"

Daniel was momentarily stunned. This was due to a long-held tradition that 15-year-old girls would never normally liaise with 15-year-old boys unless they looked much older than their chronological years. Daniel and Stu certainly appeared no more than their ages. In reality they could have easily been mistaken for a year or two younger than they actually were. However, Daniel would always qualify statements regarding age by adding that he would become 16 in October.

"What's the matter Dan, the cat got your tongue? Are you gonna help her or not?"

Round-faced Ann Simmons was never in a mood for procrastination.

"Err, err, ok, take me to her, come on Stu," the youngster finally responded and followed the three girls at a fast jogging pace.

They made for the Shambles, near the public toilets and on the old bus station side of the town hall. Nearby, three youths, all with greasy hair slapped down with "Brylcreem" surrounded a frightened and crying Carol Green.

The figures of Eric Roberts, Geordie Marshall and Alex Harris were viciously at the terrified young girl while a small greasy haired middle aged looking man seemed to be observing matters from close by.

"Ye fuckin' bitch!" Roberts uttered as Daniel approached the group.

"Ya one bloody hero, three bloody heroes, pickin' on one little girl."

"Fuck off, Gibson! This is none of your business!"

"Roberts!" Daniel sounded much older than his 15 years. "You're so uncouth. Ah want ya and ya two gorillas t' go away an' leave this lass alone!"

"Or what?" The dark haired, tall, spotty faced 19-year-old sidled up to Daniel.

"Or Ah'll do what Ah did to a lot of your friends on Saturday; put ya in the hospital with a broken arm."

The girls gasped. Stu started to silently pray while more gathered to watch including Alistair Clark, Bobby Beadle and David Crackett who were anxious to see Daniel have his potent capabilities pruned following their recent clash.

They had all listened avidly to the rumours of his "sorting out" a huge swathe of the Alnwick hard men, thugs and general criminals two days before, over the weekend. It was a fact that the Accident and Emergency department at Alnwick hospital could not cope with the amount of men being admitted. All suffered severe concussion and broken noses, crushed hands and badly bruised testicles. Many had been referred to Ashington Hospital. These reports did have many tongues wagging but most deemed it to be merely exaggerated gossip.

Before Daniel could blink, Marshall and Harris came at him fists up, ready to strike.

It was at a pace almost too brisk for the eye to perceive when two lightning jabs flew out from young Gibson. These blows sent the leather jacketed duo ricocheting off the stone wall of the Shambles walk way.

He picked up the two feckless and stunned youths by their greasy hair as if they had the weight of a kitten. With no seeming physical effort whatsoever, Daniel then simultaneously and loudly, banged their foreheads several times on the wooden door of an empty storage warehouse. Part of the town hall complex. They dropped groaning onto the stone paved passageway as if pole-axed, lying among the clay like dirt and old newspapers.

Stuart, never ceased to be amazed at the combative skills of his erstwhile docile friend. He was totally agog by the exploits as were Carol, Lesley, Ann and Vicki.

The gathering was soon augmented by other Duke and Duchess School pupils along with general onlookers from the town.

Daniel's doughty face betrayed much determination as he turned towards the stunned and terrified Eric Roberts. In a second movement equally as invisible as the first, Roberts found his right arm being twisted up his back with Daniel squeezing his hand. A manoeuvre that effected squeals of agony from the semi toothless mouth of the local thug.

"Now Roberts." Daniel was as cool as a cucumber and in a very cogent position as he imperiously grinned. "Ya'll say ya sorry to the lady or Ah'll tear ya fingers off one by one."

"Sorry," the 19 year old stammered, his hand burning in agony.

"Not good enough." Daniel maintained in his broad Northumbrian inflection. "Tell the lady properly."

"Ah'm really sorry," Roberts gasped at which point the hold was released only for an instant to allow sufficient space Daniel to grab the older youth and also batter his head off the same wooden door for a brace of thunderous impacts. The three lay together in the windswept detritus of the Shambles. Daniel stepped over the dazed figures, nodded to Stu, picked up his school bag and calmly walked over to a yet shaking Carol Green.

"It's none o' me business, Carol, but If Ah were ya, Ah'd keep away from the likes of Roberts and his chums. They're poison."

The school coach was already parked near the entrance to the former bus station when Daniel and Stu, hastily making their way to the double seat they had long since claimed three rows ahead of the rear. Alistair "Berk" Clark looked over and called out.

"Dan, can ya teach me all that fancy fightin' stuff?"

Daniel merely snarled at Clark who looked away and sat down.

"Juliet" by the Four Pennies was playing on the coach radio followed by the equally as depressing "It's Over" and the distinctive singing voice of Roy Orbison. Daniel turned for advice on Latin to Peter "Horlicks" Hall, a young man from the Lower Sixth form.

"You're not going to hit me if I can't help?" Peter Hall was only semi jocular.

"Course not," Daniel almost snapped, "I want a bit of advice on the declension of irregular verbs in the future imperfect tense."

At the front of the coach Carol stared at Daniel. The youth was too engrossed in his Latin verbs to notice her amorous, admiring glances.

"Stop staring Carol, you said boys your own age were immature." Ann Simmons sounded annoyed.

"I know but I have grown up. Young Lochinvar, Rob Roy down the bus came to my liberation and salvation. That young hero rode to my rescue, I feel hot and stimulated."

"This morning you would not have even acknowledged him. You haven't since you were 11 so why the sudden flush of desire?" Lesley was also curious

"This morning was an epoch ago, as far removed as the next ice age is to us," Carol sighed, "I have met my Romeo, my Robin Hood; I shall seduce him when we get off the bus."

"Carol, what's the matter with you? Only an hour ago you were singing the praises of that disgusting Eric Roberts, saying how lovely he is, a real man, so intelligent and full of feelings for a woman! Yes, that's how you described him yourself, before he almost beat you black and blue." Ann's voice quivered with antagonism.

"If it had not been for us Carol---."

"Carol is right." Vicki Henderson entered the discussion cutting off Ann mid-sentence. "We did look for Daniel. She did not fancy him before but now she does., that's what young girls do, head for the best talent. She knows what she wants."

"Vicki, you astound me." Lesley shook her head. "Carol is in one piece because we knew how good Dan is at beating up thugs like Roberts. She would never have thought of him if you'd given her a century to dwell on the matter. She may be intelligent but she's an air head."

"Of course I'm an air head, so are all the great women film stars. But I have a warm moist sensation in my knickers--."

"Quiet!" Ann whispered very loudly. "There are first formers only a few feet away who should not listen to your slutty filth."

"Relax, darling Ann." Carol cruelly smirked. "Someday a boy will fancy you. Perhaps, someday."

The coach stopped in the old market square of Warkworth. Carol, Stu and Daniel jumped down the few steps at the exit door and onto the pavement of Castle Street.

Carol normally, religiously, ignored the two boys and made off without any acknowledgement. She would stride along to the Butts on the banks of the River Coquet to her parents' up market, six bed roomed detached house. Today was different.

"Daniel," she called over as the boys were crossing the road.

"Yes." The voice warbled with nerves, his legs seemed to turn to jelly.

"Stuart, would you mind leaving us alone please? Daniel will see you tomorrow."

Daniel gave a half-hearted nod to Stu. Carole took his arm and they began to amble through the walkway standing within and under the row of shops. The narrow access conduit led to the River Coquet path and in the direction of his father's farm.

"Ya goin' the wrong way. Are ye not?" Daniel almost stuttered the words.

"No." Carol smiled. "Well yes, I am, for home, but not for what I have in mind."

They walked along the path that straddled the Coquet and then Carol changed their direction into a thickly wooded area. This tree replete thicket overlooked the famous and historical site of the Hermitage, an old cave dwelling place that sat on the opposite bank of the central Northumbrian river. Once in amongst the densely leafed arboreal sculptures that formed a natural barrier betwixt the flowing river and the farmland of the south bank, Carol stood against a large, ancient oak. Daniel, in his bewildered frame of mind, assumed it could have been the worship site of Druids. She brazenly opened his grey trousers, unzipped them and pulled out his male organ. The cylindrical shape rapidly grew, becoming solid.

"Be prepared say the Girl Guides, or is it the Boy Scouts?" Carol breathed deeply on Daniel as she took a Durex Featherlite from her bag and removed the outer wrapping.

"What ya doin'?" He tremblingly gasped.

"I'm putting a Johnny on you. I may like a shag but I don't want to be a mother for a long time yet."

The condom was unrolled to cover the erect penis upon which she lifted up her skirt and eased her briefs down her thighs.

Before Daniel could utter a syllable she had dragged his midriff towards her upon which she took a gentle hold of his turgid protuberant male appendage. Using the precision of an engineering Venus standing in her provocative state of dishabille, she rammed the solid mass deep inside her.

"Move!" She commanded. "Move! I want to feel it!"

Daniel grabbed the space between her waist and the tops of her stockings and began to thrust with the vigour of a young lion and pressed his mouth hard against hers. All he could see was her flowing brown hair, closed eyes and gasps of ecstasy reverberating from the soft, quivering mouth.

Daniel had never been anywhere near as proximate to a female in his young life span, let alone one in such sexual abandonment. The young man had never felt so complete as his youthful emotions and adolescent nervous system blasted into supersonic overdrive sending messages from the zenith of gratification to his overcharging brain. The resulting explosion, the breaching of a heavenly dam emptying a torrent, came like a jet engine or the apex of a bomb blast, floating wildly across a newly unearthed base, sensual landscape. Both his head and loins pulsated. He drew howls of elation which echoed across the Coquet valley and into Warkworth. Nonetheless, Daniel was momentarily terrified of what physical damage may have been done during his end of virginity rite.

"That was beautiful, Dan, you've popped your cherry." Carol licked his face as she removed the Durex, pulled her knickers back up and let her skirt fall down. "I'll give you the blob. This thing here, to get rid of as it is full of your male baby juice. Kiss me once more then I must go home, but I want us to go steady. Not to get in the way of you and Stu as I have girl friends to see also but would you like to go steady?"

Daniel inattentively took the used condom. He was still floating somewhere in the stratosphere.

"Yes, ok. I'll see you tomorrow on the bus."

"No, not on the bus. You stick with the boys and me the girls. But on Friday night we can go to Amble dance, the Board Draggers are playing. . And after that we can walk along the shore for shag, if you want. You'll have to supply the Durex. No condom, no sex. I do know that they are three and nine pence for three."

The soon to be released single by the Kinks, "You Really Got Me", floated from a radio in a nearby cottage. Daniel relived the act of losing his virginity over and over and over whilst making his way home. During his victory march he proudly dumped the semen packed sheath into a waste paper bin on Morwick Road.

DANESH AND KELLY

The house was already brimming with academics from all fields of science. Each was chattering feverishly, virtually cross-examining Danesh Gideon.

Doctor Kelly Aresti entered somewhat warily. The young woman had not been informed by the illustrious scientific version of Ferdinand Magellan that he was inviting select people from the sciences, academia and politics to his country retreat.

For this Kelly was slightly miffed. She preferred the company of the middle-aged genius to herself. This yearning had become even further pronounced following the scuppering of her engagement to the Royal Navy surgeon flinging her back into single woman mode.

"Here is Doctor Kelly Aresti. She is one of my supporters and assistants. The doctor has witnessed the photographic studies prior to a video journey across a dimension and a parallel universe." Danesh seemed to introduce Kelly to a circle of intense scientists. "And now we need to re-examine. We need to explore to ascertain if one day we can photograph before assessing whether or not it will ever, yes ever, be possible to physically transport a human being from one dimension or universe to another."

"Why is he talking such bollocks?" Kelly thought whilst giving watery smiles in recognition of the many admiring glances she was enjoying. "Either I am in the wrong universe or he is spinning some version of top level hyperbole. Who are these folk?"

"Doctor Aresti." A medium sized, rotund man with red hair and glasses, probably in his early 60s was gawping at her. The figure was alternating glances between her chest and face.

"Yes!" Kelly grimaced, turning to the Professor and glaring the proverbial daggers in his direction.

"Is it true that you were instrumental in developing this planned photographic journey into a parallel universe and you may one day be the test pilot that will actually physically travel there?"

"Err-excuse me, I just have to have a quick word with Professor Gideon."

Kelly dashed across the spacious lounge. She made for the nook between a marble bust of Sir Isaac Newton and a massive bookshelf where Danesh stood. The gifted scientist was sipping on a large gin and tonic whilst engaged in deep discourse with a portion of his exclusive gathering.

"I beg your pardon, Professor Gideon," she interrupted in an extremely gracious manner, "If I may be so bold as to petition a minute in private with your good self. At your convenience of course."

"Excuse me." Danesh offered his apologies. He circumspectly withdrew to join Kelly in the small drawing room that lay adjacent to the lounge and opposite the kitchen.

The area contained merely a desk upon which a drinks tray stood and a single chair. Once the door was closed Kelly rounded on the professor.

"What the fuck is going on? Who the fuck are these people and how much have you told them?"

"Take it easy Kelly." He quietly motioned. "I have to tread with care. Have you any idea how many agencies and or government organisations, let alone criminal gangs, would pounce if they knew how far we have actually come? Trust me; we would be mere pawns in an international and very dangerous game of chess. It could be dangerous for both of us, so I'm now playing a game of bluff."

"Professor! I am always attracted to your avant-garde, totally and mind blowingly, eccentric, unconventional attitude towards work and life. However, this I must confess I find a tad disconcerting. Please enlighten me."

Kelly walked over to the silver salver where a decanter of whiskey and soda siphon stood.

She looked very chic in a light green woollen trouser suit with cream blouse, black high heel shoes and with her red hair up on the top of her head.

"Do you want a Scotch?"

"I will," Danesh sheepishly replied, "And I have to say Kelly you look very becoming."

"Stop that bullshit, Prof. I want to know what the fuck you are up to and I want to know it now."

She briefly opened the door to ensure no one was listening.

The professor shuffled in his tweed jacket and corduroy trousers and then accepted yet another drink to mix with the wine and gin and tonics he had already consumed.

"I received a visit from top civil servants in the Department of Education, Home Office and Ministry of Defence. I had been drawn to their attention by an MoD scientist who had read with great interest a research paper I had written. That particular work proposed the hypothesis that travelling between universes was not merely a pipe dream of over excitable and slightly nutty physicists. It was in fact, mathematically at least, extremely possible, possible in theory."

Danesh stuffed his briar pipe with Drum Shag tobacco then lit the top of the bowl.

"Prof, we both know it is more than possible as we have both travelled there and back! Is it for safety reasons that you are feigning ignorance of your discoveries?"

"Kelly, it's why I always kept it to myself, scientists bullshit a lot and are extremely envious, competitive, at times bitchy and even worse outright dangerous."

"Like any group of highly motivated individuals," Kelly smiled and lit a cigarette.

"Yes, my dear. However, my seniority in years, and the great erudition bestowed so liberally on me by my late father, meant that I would not share any of many discoveries with anyone. That is of course with the exception of your pulchritudinous self."

"And that was only to spread my legs." Kelly blew him a kiss. "Now proceed, we cannot be too long away from the revelry, your distinguished guests will suspect mischief is afoot."

"I shall cover merely the bare bones as time is of the essence. Nonetheless, it is safe to conclude that I have not, and will not, divulge my discoveries. The rationale standing prominent being that apart from any other motivation, the government will blatantly purloin them."

"It still sounds like hokum, Prof. So why the fuck are you entertaining, wining and feeding these trenchermen, obvious parasites and bullshit artists if you are not intending to divulge anything?"

"Oh my beautiful young doctor; I adore your infantile mannerisms. You are so bright yet at times a little naïve."

"Then enlighten me!" Kelly was becoming visibly frustrated.

"I paid from my own pocket the development costs of this project. Nonetheless, it amounted to well short of a fortune. I did at irregular intervals enjoy access to facilities from Hartfordshire University but that was minimal. Now these people folk we are entertaining are not just scientists. There are present some very senior civil servants one of whom reports directly to the Home Secretary and another to the Secretary of State for Defence. They are here to examine the potential viability of my thesis."

"Wow, what are they fishing for?"

"They want me to develop the theoretical and mathematical concept of inter dimensional travel or viewing. Their coffers appear to be brimming so accordingly they seem overwhelmingly confident about awarding me a substantial research and development, R and D, grant for that purpose."

"But you've done the research. You've both tested the theories and brought back video and sound pictures from another universe. To cap it all we have both physically travelled there although I have not been outside PADIT yet without a light bending suit. Are you telling me now you old rogue that you are going to charge HM's government for work you did free gratis and for your own benefit?"

"No, I am going to take retrospectively, reimbursement for my labours. Naturally I shall divulge very little of actual achievements. Just suffice to attest credibility with progress and warrant a substantial claim for recompense. I shall never tell them the full extent of my discoveries. We shall be paid a fat fee for work I have long since fulfilled but only you and I will be privy to such unbridled veracity. Accordingly, and presently, we shall be very, very affluent."

"That sounds very innovative. However, one thing I noticed on my last sortie to the parallel place, and that was that the time difference had shrunk a little."

"Interesting," Danesh commented while puffing on his pipe, "By years, months or what?"

"It started with a gap of around 40 years, now it seems a lot less. Are you sure you're sending me to the same universe each trip?"

"Of course, at least I believe it to be. To affirm I shall check my calculations. Now let us return to my guests, they are going to be a great source of income generation for us both. Of course you and I will be sleeping here tonight."

"Of course, I only came here tonight for a ride in PADIT and a fuck. I shall light up a Balkan Sobrani cigarette before we go and join the esteemed company. I fear many of them smell terribly, as if they need a damned good wash."

"They probably do." Danesh laughed as they vacated the room.

PHILIPPA-1964

"Come, "Miles beckoned Philippa then her friends to follow him.

Three other boys sauntered along behind them and began chatting to Judith, Patricia and Christine.

"The boys seem talkative." Philippa thought when Miles took her by the hand. He then greatly upped the walking pace as they moved briskly through the historic streets of Oxford. Judith, raven-haired, a slim, almost thin, young lady had already chosen the tall brown haired boy who was dressed in the latest Mod jacket, shirt and trousers with Cuban heel boots.

Christine, curvaceous, auburn and bubbly had almost grabbed the other of the tall figures. A boy in tight jeans, leather jacket and patterned shirt. Only Pat remained ostensibly unattached. A brunette, average height slightly plain but nonetheless full of joie de vivre, Pat was an extremely intelligent female Mod. She gravitated towards the remaining member of the male group. A smallish and slightly overweight, dark haired young man endowed with good looks. He was attired in jeans and old leather jacket under which he wore a white t-shirt, a "Rocker".

They paced through the town and across some open ground. Miles led them turned onto a piece of land fenced off from the rest of the area. In this pocket stood a very large wooden shed with sizable windows. "What's this?" Philippa sounded a little apprehensive.

"You'll see." Miles took a key from his pocket and opened the door. The long haired young man then flicked on a couple of light switches illuminating the large expanse. The construct was obviously bespoke for a brass band in which to rehearse. Sheet music and numerous other support stands were scattered around the skirting board of the structure. In the centre of the massive floor area stood a green "Premier" make drum kit and three large amplifiers against each was propped an electric guitar.

"This is a Fender Stratocaster." Miles picked up a red bodied electric guitar. He swiftly plugged the thick spiral wire lead into the socket of the instrument and one of the amplifiers. Moving at haste he turned on the Vox AC 30. Within seconds he was running nimble fingers up and down the fret board playing riffs from famous blues numbers. The most recognisable piece for the girls was the intro for the Rolling Stones cover song "Not Fade Away".

"You never said you were in a group!" Philippa shrieked with excitement as the others came into the band practice shed.

"The one with your friend Judith." Miles nonchalantly pointed to the young man picking up the other guitar, a Gibson ES-335 semi acoustic model. "He's our lead vocalist and rhythm guitar player and is called, Judith take note, Ray Hooker. The Mod with Christine is Bob Hetherington, he plays the violin very well but for us he plays the drums even better. The little scoundrel that Pat was wrapped around, the fat one, is our great bass guitarist. He plays a Fender bass and our vocal harmoniser. The baby of the group, Johnny Allen."

Ray, Johnny and Miles tuned in their instruments whilst Bob bashed the various parts of his drum kit, tightening the skins where he deemed necessary.

"Can you play any hits?" Judith was bubbling with excitement.

"Of course," Ray responded with a typical macho adolescent nonchalance, "But we prefer blues." "Beatles?" Philippa was anxious to stamp her mark.

"No, they're not groovy. They're out of time, yesterday's music. We play the Rolling Stones material," Ray answered before the others had an opportunity to even open their mouths.

"However." Miles was not about to upset his hot date. "For you, we can do both. Play a Rolling Stones song that was written by the Beatles."

"I Wanna Be Your Man!" Pat squealed and all the girls jumped up and down as the boys launched loudly into the song followed by John lee Hooker's "Dimples" and many more such earthy numbers.

Philippa knew she had found the one, that special one. Her young heart had been taken, stolen, and for the first time she was now madly in love.

Chapter Seven

NARRATOR

Somewhere I hear a song. It is an old song that echoes down the passages and caverns of our minds in which the concept of time is brooked. Within the precincts of some unknown desire, perhaps some minor misdemeanour, some little crime. Possibly only de facto recognition as such given by the overly sensitive and compassionate reflections on how we would have preferred things to have manifested themselves and not the oft diverging way the book of life was veritably transcribed. I am not yet a character in that great tome. The aspects of life that determine whom or what makes me whom or what I am is one of the still great mysteries that continually evade the searching minds of scientists and philosophers alike. Why am I me? I know my father posed that same riddle many times during the Summer of Love and as a human being.

An idealistic youth with great intelligence and like so many of his like questioned every conceivable matter. He and his ilk were perpetually challenging, renouncing, denouncing, reforming, rebuilding and reposing. Daddy asked a million times, is the sperm life? Is the egg of the woman life? If not, at what stage when they combine are they life and why do I feel? Why am I me? Why do I see? Is a red rose red to a man who is blind? Is green, green to you or is it yellow? Why am I in this body feeling things, and not someone else? Why do I emote? If God made everything then who or what made God? My mother was equally deeply into examining the reasons for the Cosmos. A condition endemic amongst intelligent youth. They think, they challenge and rebel. My mother was the professional, my father the adventurer and both were children of the 60s. I can feel them both so close, the security and strength of one, the warmth and comfort of the other.

I extol their many virtues and the moistening eyes smile in acknowledgement and recollection. I hold every nanosecond of their consciousness, I shall not betray that beautiful trust.

JAMES AND EMILY-1965

In the early dusk a scattered peppering of snow was falling. It was light and barely noticeable although sufficient to have the TV commentators frantically speculating on the prospects of a White Christmas.

James was wearing a thick trench coat and fedora with galoshes. He walked hand in hand with Emily. She was garbed in a thick woollen hat, woollen patterned trench coat, black stockings and high calf leather boots. They strode along Main Street towards the local pub, the Plough Inn, the hostelry of the village of Alvescot.

Some 100 metres before the pub entrance, a smelly, dishevelled figure appeared. This person sported very long hair and a beard. He was dressed in rubber Wellington boots and an old duffel coat. He faced James and Emily.

"Got a couple o' bob, Mister Marchant, for the poor o' the parish."

"Jimmy Frost, what are you doing begging?" Emily seemed unsettled by the appearance of the man.

"I'd get the train an' leave but it's three years since the station closed. It's a big miss."

It suddenly dawned on James to who this man was. It still haunted the undergraduate. The day the Frost's elder sibling had attacked him in Wye Woods almost 15 years earlier.

"There're no trains anymore, Frost. Thanks to Doctor Beeching, but there are plenty of buses if you want to get out of the village. Here's ten shillings. A lot of money I know but it will get you a few small things for Christmas."

"I thank ye, sir." Frost touched his forelock then rammed the monetary note into his pocket. "And as for ye, Emily Wilkinson, best take care, best take very good care."

James pushed Frost who fell onto the small burgeoning piles of snow forming on the pavement.

"And if you ever threaten her again, I shall pound your head into mush."

"Oh, Mister Marchant, she ain't your class. The world knows, ye knows. She killed my brother and Bible says, "an eye for an eye, a tooth for a tooth."

"As I said, Frost, your brother Barry was the criminal. Not Miss Wilkinson. So, if you want to keep out of gaol I suggest you piss off now and drop the matter for good."

Jimmie Frost glared at Emily as he took off in the direction of the Royal Air Force station at Brize Norton. However, neither Emily nor James believed for an instant the RAF aerodrome was his ultimate destination.

"Let's get to the pub." James took hold of Emily once again and together they negotiated the final steps to the Plough Inn.

"Pint of bitter and a lager and lime please Mister Thompson," James asked as they walked into the lounge bar with its lavish décor.

"Coming up Mister Marchant and a good evening to you, sir." The tall former guardsman greeted the couple. Hank Thompson was a tall man of some 50 plus years, sandy hair that was very marginally receding boasting the apposite disposition crucial for any professional landlord.

Within a minute James carried the drinks over to where Emily was sat. He took a spot next to her on the cushioned bench seat. They had much catching up to do. Regular telephone calls had been somewhat impeded due to a plethora of work which could not be shelved. The couple were both now in their third and final year at university. The chronological juncture where deferring academic matters in favour of socialising and partying was no longer an option That was if the student was serious about attaining at least a second-class honours degree.

"Cheers." James gave Emily a quick kiss. "Cheers." she touched his glass with her own.

"Well, what's new?" James smiled and offered her a Benson and Hedges cigarette, which she accepted. He graciously lit hers first. The distinctive and thoroughly contemporary sound of the jukebox playing the new Beatles single, "Day Tripper", floated in from the public bar.

"I am finally up to date with all my coursework, projects and reading.

I'm going round the bend with case law right now. How about you darling, are you up to date?"

"But of course, economics is really a jaw-jaw bullshit subject. My main tutor says we have to be able to cite specific examples, argue for a course of action but without showing any underlining political preference."

Emily smiled. "I'd think that would be nigh impossible. My university crowd talks all the time about politics. How evil the capitalist system is and how the United States is out to take the world over and only our friends in the Soviet Union can save us."

"Yes, heap of shit of course and they'll all be voting Conservative in a few years. What do you say to them?"

"I ignore them, of course." Emily took a sip of her lager. "But nevertheless, there could be some elements of truth in all the crap that flies around. It's alright for a rich aristo like you, sweetheart, not to worry about the future, but harder for the rest of us."

"Yes, but I'm going into the Royal Marines. Then I'll make my own fortune. You'll see."

Emily leaned her head on his shoulder. "You are an aristo, but you are a darling, darling. I'll love you forever no matter what you did."

"When we get married you'll be an aristocrat."

"That could be many years; never if your dear mama has any say. So, don't insult my immense intelligence by inferring that she has given up the ghost. I can tell by the way Isabelle Napier-Fenning looks at me she assumes one day you'll be hers."

The jukebox sprang back to life with the distinguishing guitar riff and drums of "Get Off My Cloud" by the Rolling Stones.

"It's difficult." James drew on his cigarette. Outside the snow seemed to be falling with a greater density. "I am having to walk a tight line with my family."

"That's total shit, darling! You're scared of dear Mummy and I don't blame you."

"No I'm not!"

"No you're not what?" Philippa entered with her friends Judith, Christine and Pat. All were dressed alike, resembling a set of teenage quadruplets. They were all attired in black leather caps, leather coats and mauve skirts. These kilt style arrays were nowhere near as short as Mary

Quant's recently introduced miniskirts, instead hung very slightly above the knee.

"Little sister, what brings you here?" James enquired before ordering the girls some drinks.

"I want a party at Wye Hall over Christmas, and I want my boyfriend's group to play."

"Why are you telling me, Pip?" James offered his packet of cigarettes to all present and all accepted.

"Come on James. "Emily slapped him lightly on the arm. "She's not my sister--."

"I wish you were, you will be someday."

"Thank you Pip. James, Philippa is asking you as you are the key. She wants to know, from you, if your parents are in an approachable temperament. If so you can then pose the question as they will say yes to you. At least your mother will, she still thinks Pip is 12. She seems to be completely blind to her adolescence."

"Thank you, Emily, I really love you. You know me better than anyone." James then turned to Philippa. "Alright, little sister, I shall approach Mama and Papa, together. That will be to preclude the necessity of recapitulation. I am sure, Pip, your pop singer boyfriend will have a booking at the party. Is our dirty old Uncle still tutoring you in medicine?"

"Uncle Perry is and thank you James. However, Miles is not a pop singer, he's an A level student who happens to play in a group. You will be very impressed by them."

Hank brought them their drinks as Toby Flynn and Peregrine Walker ambled into the lounge.

"Drink up quickly Pip, and your friends, two lecherous sods have just walked in and they will wish to try to have their wicked way with any females. Perhaps even with you lot."

"Sorry, boys, not a prayer," Pat spoke before the others could even digest the comment by James, "As we have really hot men to keep us warm. And they are in a group."

"That'd be ok me darling.'" Toby lasciviously grinned. "If ya ever wants a real man, just come an' see me. The Belfast stallion will be at your service."

"Alright, girls." Philippa was already tired of the new arrivals. "Let's drink these and leave James and Emily to the esteemed company they have just acquired."

DANIEL-1965

Daniel was exceedingly happy. His exhilaration was not attributable to Tom Jones singing his number one hit of a month earlier, "It's Not Unusual", which he could perceive coming from a wireless somewhere. It was not as a result of the great weather, April could be such a contrary month, nor was it even to the great sex that he and Carol had enjoyed. This carnal act had been performed at Carol's house whilst her parents were away at some fundraising dance. The elation was also not effected by the knowledge that he had sent three of the local thugs to hospital over the week-end. Each suffered broken noses, shattered right hands and severe concussion along with badly bruised testicles. This particular accomplishment certainly evoked a sense of extreme satisfaction but accounted not for his euphoria. This high fulfilment rating lay in the fact that he had attained pass levels in all ten of the mock General Certificate of Education, GCE, Ordinary level he had taken and would now be sitting 11 of the actual examinations in the summer. General Science would be added as a considered easy option. This would add one more subject to the green Oxford Examination Board certificate. This was the result that Mister Watson would require before he could petition Frank Mosby MA, headmaster, with the suggestion that Daniel could telescope his three GCE Advanced Level subjects into one year. The proposition had already been considered and readily accepted by Mosby. Unbeknown to all, the headmaster had served as an Army commando officer during World War 2.

TOM AND REBECCA-1965

"Rebecca." Tom Marchant, wandered downstairs to the servant's quarters.

"She's out at the village with Mister Biggs, My Lord," Hodges the butler graciously advised.

"Of course, she's out with her husband." The earl appeared to be a little disappointed, a reaction which failed to go un-noticed.

"Yes My Lord, Rebecca is out with Mister Biggs. They are in Oxford shopping for the dinner party tonight. The countess gave her a long list of ingredients she wanted Mrs Cromer to supplement the entrée. "

"Oh I see." The earl turned to walk upstairs when a commotion came from the side door. Rebecca could be heard saying, "Keep your 'ands off the stuff, you useless no good--."

She immediately silenced herself on seeing Tom Marchant standing in the kitchen.

"My Lord." Rebecca courteously smiled. "Mister Biggs and me 'ave been to Oxford. Her ladyship asked for some special items for me to add to the courses of dinner, she wanted them spiced up a tad."

"Thank you. The countess will be delighted you were able to find all the products for which she requested. But as Mister Hodges and Mister Biggs are together, I should like to ask a favour of them. And you also, Rebecca."

"Of course, My Lord," Hodges responded per protocol.

"As you know, her ladyship is holding a private dinner party for some personal friends from her book club plus neighbours and old colleagues from university."

"That she is, My Lord," Hodges affirmed.

"I have to go to London to host a business gathering. Unfortunately the staffing level there is short due to illness and a vacancy. I was wondering if I may borrow Rebecca. It will only be for a couple of nights. I really need to put on the most lavish culinary presentation and I know she will be more than capable of rising to the challenge. I shall pay three days extra salary over and above her normal wage to compensate for such short notice, so close to Christmas."

"I think we can cope, My Lord." Hodges almost seemed relieved. "No one on the staff at Wye Hall is indispensable. I assume Mister Biggs has nothing to add."

Tom deemed those remarks somewhat bizarre nonetheless elected to ignore them.

"Very good then. So Mister Biggs, I assume you are comfortable with your wife being away for two nights plus tonight at the house in Sloane

Square. Your services will be required at Wye Hall as I am certain you will be called upon to ferry guests."

"That is what I expected, My Lord." The tall figure of the chauffeur managed to successfully masque his discontent.

"Good. Then Rebecca, would you please meet me in the entrance hall with your bag and enough spare clothing for three nights? I shall be driving us to London in the Rolls. Mister Biggs will need use of the Bentley here at Wye Hall."

"I shall be ready in ten minutes, My Lord." Rebecca gave a small curtsey.

Once the earl had returned upstairs, Biggs turned to Hodges.

"Bit of a liberty Mister Hodges, takin' me wife away for what'll be three days."

"Perhaps, Mister Biggs. But both you and Rebecca are employees. His lordship has every right to use the services of the staff where and when 'e needs them. After all, unlike many other employers, 'e'll be rewarding her handsomely by paying her double for the time she'll be away. Not to be sniffed at. Now we all have work to do."

William Jenkins the butler stood at the door to welcome the Earl of Wye and Rebecca into the Sloane Square town house. The three hour drive from Oxfordshire had passed rapidly and void of undue incident.

"Mister Jenkins. I have brought Rebecca from Alvescot to assist. You intimated in your telephone conversation that the workload was well in excess of with what the available staff could reasonably be expected to cope. I am sure she will be a boon to you."

The elderly yet physically active butler took Tom's hat and coat. The grey haired figure smiled with obvious relief at the sight of Rebecca. "We can certainly use your talents Mrs. Biggs. I really was at a loss."

"Good, then Rebecca will go with you. I have to retire to my study to sort out the papers for this meeting. I shall take a brandy in ten minutes, Mister Jenkins."

"Of course, My Lord. And thank you for bringing us assistance."

"Thank Rebecca. She was the one who had to make the effort."

It was a long, demanding and hectic night. A herculean amount of preparation and cooking of many and varied ingredients together with setting of tables was required to serve each of the numerous courses. Once each gastronomic masterpiece had been consumed there followed a rapid turnabout of dishes, replacing and removing used crockery to be washed.

By 2.30 in the morning the final guests had taken their leave and the last piece of cutlery and china had been washed, dried and replaced in its respective cabinet.

The butler unlocked a sideboard and removed a bottle of single malt Scotch and five glasses.

The staff all took a seat around the kitchen table and lit cigarettes. Mister Jenkins, a family employee since he had returned from the Great War in 1918, poured each of them a large measure. The veteran butler handed out the glasses then said, "Cheers, this drink and smoke we have truly earned. Thank you all for your magnificent and stalwart efforts."

After Rebecca had finished both her whiskey and cigarette, she stood up. "I will retire now Mister Jenkins, unless Ya need me for anythin' else."

"No, Mrs Biggs. You have been marvellous as you always are when you visit us. You enjoy a good night's rest. However, you'll have to be up at six I'm afraid for the breakfast. The master likes a full English with kidneys and kippers for starters."

"Yes, Mister Jenkins, but with respect, I know what the master likes in the mornin' and he'll not be discontented. Good night to all of ya."

Jenkins together with the single footman and two maids responded in kind.

Rebecca dashed upstairs to her quarters. Then, without changing she paid a brief visit to the bathroom before tiptoeing up the back stairs. The maid moved towards the polished oak door of the room farthest from hers. She knocked lightly then walked in.

"Rebecca." Tom warmly smiled although he seemed to be tad surprised.

"Why did you knock? You don't have to."

"But I do, My Lord, I didn't know if ya were asleep or not, My Lord. I wanted to know if ya required anything."

The earl sat up in bed as the maid deferentially entered the chamber.

"Pour me a whiskey if you must do something and bring it to me."

"Of course, My Lord." Rebecca graciously nodded. She then removed the top from a crystal decanter and poured a large measure of single malt into a gleaming Glencairn whiskey glass.

She delicately placed the drink on a shining silver salver before handing it to Tom. He received it with one hand then with the other gently nudged her beside him.

"My Lord, pray what art thou undertaking?"

"You are such a great actress, Rebecca. Will you marry me?"

"That is, My Lord, totally out of the question and ya knows it. Ya guests were gone long before I expected. I didn't expect to get t' bed 'fore four in the mornin'."

"Oh, my dear Becky. I invited, they accepted and you all entertained them. They have now agreed to my business proposal and will sign all documents tomorrow. At that juncture I feigned a slight malady to arrest any opportunity they may exploit to remain late. They were by and large Japanese, hence the Oriental menu. Although the proceedings were not hastened, and all necessary protocols were strictly adhered to, I ensured they were gone by half past midnight. This was to allow you and the others to finalise the clearing away and for you attend to your lover. Will you marry me?" He knocked back the Scotch.

Tom unzipped Rebecca's dress, which she duly slipped out of, removed her bra, panties, stockings and suspender belt before slipping into bed next to Tom.

"I adores ya children, admire ya lovely wife and would do nothing to upset your happy marriage. I knows the aristocracy 'ave mistresses and I'm yours. I've loved ya, My Lord, since the day ya employed that young girl in the rain. I was so desperate for work, and you took her into ya 'ome. Nonetheless, My Lord, I'm a servant, you're the master and that's the way it is and always'll be.

I'm 'appy with that. I cannot and would not marry ya. Ya not thinking through your head but some appendage on your fine physique. It'd never work and ya would be a lot worse off."

Tom turned over Rebecca and faced her, running his hands through her thick locks of flaming red hair.

"You're such a marvellous woman, Becky. You of course speak with such erudition, something I am aware that I am oft bereft. My wife is having an affair but of course you will know that. He's an old flame from the War, Charles De'ath." His hands moved over her naked body. She turned onto her back and drew him onto her.

"What her ladyship does is none of my business, My Lord. But enough of this tête-à-tête, My Lord. I've to be up t' attend to ya needs in but four hours. So, if ya wants some hanky panky then start now as time is pretty short."

Their mouths met in a long, moist and lingering kiss as Rebecca guided his manhood into her before commencing a feverish paced bout of lovemaking.

A few minutes later the earl was fast asleep.

"I love you," she sensually whispered to the slumbering figure before smoking her final cigarette of the day.

Once the Balkan Sobrani had been stubbed, she quickly dressed. Rebecca listened to ensure that no one was about. She then slowly and silently made her way along the creaking oak floor of the dark passage back to her servant's chamber.

DANESH AND KELLY

Kelly flicked the velocity button on the control stick and sent PADIT soaring like a bizarre game of pinball through some interdimensional gateway. A pulsating oval portal enveloped in a staggering array of shapes and colours. The navigation of the racing car like machine was pre-programmed into the onboard computer system. However, due to anomalies which were mainly variations between one world and the sister dimension and in some cases could be excessive there was a manual overdrive for to fine tune the final descent when one was almost at the target area. The craft was invisible to the naked eye as it travelled when near the destination. It existed at that juncture within a molecular state in which time was speeded up by twice the norm until the engine was cut.

Kelly could see from the monitor and through the observation panels that she had arrived at the Lisher Hospital, Stevenage in Hertfordshire. The only difference thus far she had noticed was that the 17th Century spelling had been retained. In her dimension it had been altered to Hartfordshire from Hertfordshire sometime between the 17th and 19th Centuries.

PADIT hovered a while above the car park and then whilst still imperceptible dropped into a vacant space. Once on the ground and static, PADIT's doppelganger computer program immediately adjusted the shape of the frame to that which Kelly had selected. On this occasion she had chosen an outline identical to a small vehicle in the corner of the tarmac area. The onboard engineering system then duplicated every detail of this car bar the number plate. This was reported on the screen as being that of a doctor living on the Channel Islands who had never been to Stevenage. Once PADIT had finally altered shape, Kelly checked around her and put the print of her index finger into the keypad. The control panel displayed the narrative, "Recognised, Kelly Aresti." The various dials confirmed the precise location of and on the planet. That the atmosphere was carbon based, life sustaining and would be safe to venture without.

She flicked open the door, adjusted her tight skirt and then stepped out into the fresh air for the first time. The heart beneath her white blouse was beating rapidly. The young doctor was nervous and excited. It was her first time walking in another dimension, on the ground and breathing the air. Kelly had flown, the method of transportation as utilised in the very detailed manual constructed by Danesh. PADIT did fly although it was not technically an aircraft. She had journeyed numerous times to this strange place. A world almost indistinguishable yet not identical by some measure to her own. However, Kelly noticed even the differences she had recorded in a minutia within her own personal journal of such travels seem to have altered again.

These diversities were small to the untrained eye but to the probing mind of a physician, disparities betwixt and between the dimensions were numerous. As she walked around the hospital grounds she decided to look inside the reception area of the hospital, almost a duplicate of the establishment in which she worked some distance or no distance from there. The most glaring difference was nondescript. In the placing within the grand weaver's wheel barely significant namely the hospital sign entitled "Accident and Emergency" within Kelly's world was labelled "Emergency and Accident" in this outlook.

"Good morning Doctor Marston." An adolescent looking nurse smiled at her.

"Good morning," she responded. Kelly was nervous as she bizarrely recognised the face, but the name had completely slipped from her consciousness.

"I am called Doctor Marston here. Have I married in this universe?" Kelly thought as she walked towards the entrance of the Lisher Hospital. The young woman abruptly had cold feet; many possible ramifications and complications flashed through her mind. She promptly determined to institute a rapid return to the PADIT.

As she was going through the motions of turning about, a voice called out to her, "Doctor!"

Kelly turned. For a nanosecond that could have been an epoch she swore she was looking in a mirror. Standing before her was a person that was identical to her in height, looks, dress, build and the thick red hair was even in an identical style. The only perceivable difference between the two figures was the colour of their nail varnish. "Y—es." Kelly was dumbstruck.

"I tend to think you are in the wrong place, Doctor. My name is Doctor Keely Marston, Doctor. How are you known in your universe?"

Danesh Gideon could make out the distinctive purring sound that the PADIT 1 produced when it returned to the laboratory. He sat in his study enjoying a Scotch and after supper pipe. Kelly entered via the connecting door between the study and take-off/ landing area.

"Shit Prof, pour me a stiff one while I light a cigarette. I have mega amounts to impart from my latest mission to the parallel universe."

Gideon removed the cap from a decanter of whiskey and let a large measure of the clear golden liquid cascade into a crystal tumbler. Once Kelly was settled, although still positively trembling with excitement, the scientist then waited until what he determined to be the most appropriate and opportune moment before he posed the obvious question. "Well, what have you to tell me?"

"Oh Prof," Kelly nervously gasped, "I walked on the ground, breathed the air, drank café, ate a sandwich with another name, an odd one. But most, most of all I talked to my respective alter ego in the PU. A Doctor Keely Marston."

"The first funds from the government came today, but more important, was all as you expected?"

"For God's sake Prof, listen to me! My doppelganger in the PU was identical to me. She even articulated with my accent. It was like talking to a real live hologram of me only she was real. Really real."

"Pray expand upon that statement."

"Oh Professor, she is identical in every facet. A doctor at a hospital, called the Lisher which is identical to the Lister at Stevenage. We were even dressed in the same clothes! The only difference I could see, I did not check out her underwear, was the shade of nail varnish. Hers was red, mine blue. She saw me in the car park and we went into the hospital cafeteria for a coffee. When the woman behind the counter remarked we were identical she merely said I was her twin sister visiting from Australasia. Well, we chatted a lot. She too has a mentor, a Professor David Garside. He is obviously your doppelganger. She also has an ex-boyfriend who is Navy officer, Lieutenant Jerry Moreton. My ex is Lieutenant Jeremy Morton. Apart from minor details--."

"These may not be so minor in the great scheme of things, there may be more," Danesh carelessly interjected.

"Perhaps Professor, but in the ambience and excitement of such a ground breaking journey, the most important since a man first landed on the Moon in September 1969, and I could not tell anyone! Have you walked on the soil of a sister universe?"

"Only briefly so you were not the first. But that fact must never be disclosed Kelly. I mean it, all kinds of shit could befall us. That is something you must never mention."

"I will not, Prof. You know that I am the acme of discretion but there is so much I must reveal. Doctor Marston told me of all the things that were happening in her universe from the threat of global warming to religious terrorism. So, her world closely resembles our world apart from details. These on first consideration seem somewhat minor but to you are of great import. Her fiancé went off to fight abroad. Although she would have stayed with him, he was wounded and ended up being married to a doctor who treated him in the hospital in Australasia."

"A lot of minutia, Kelly." Danesh removed his personal DVD recorder from its box and picked up a note pad and pen. "I need to record it all then input into the computer when we can compare with previous data."

"Alright, there is so much, so much. I was switched on suffice to bring a few books and magazines from this parallel universe. They are in the cockpit of the PADIT, I will collect them in a sec. Firstly, before anything else, Professor, you must know this. Doctor Keely Marston, my doppelganger in the PU, told me that she is also travelling cross dimensionally. We both have concluded from our conversation that there is not only one PU but there are probably many and people are already travelling across them from one to not just another. Some to countless ones!"

Chapter Eight

JAMES-1966

The beers flowed in copious quantities in the lounge bar of the Oxpens pub in the city of Oxford. James, Peregrine and Toby along with a throng of other young people were well into the throes of their graduation party. "Paint It Black" by the Rolling Stones was booming from the jukebox.

"Hey Battler Britton, when ya fuckin' joinin' the fuckin' Army?" Toby was already inebriated. "Labour won the election, Lord Snooty!"

"You—u drunken Paddy," James slurred almost coherently.

"Toby you can be a real wanker when it takes your fancy." Peregrine Walker knocked back yet another pint of cider and although still vertical, swayed in a manner that suggested this would not endure for much more alcohol consumption. "James, our James finished his BSc in Economics and is to join Her Majesty's Royal Marines. Not the fucking Army, you Paddy scoundrel."

"Ho, ho, ho. The fuckin' aristocracy keepin' the workers in their place." Toby belched.

"Lord Snooty and Earl Puffy, a couple of arsehole bandits."

"Hey! Toby." A voice rich with a Northern Irish inflection called from across the lounge.

"Come here and tell us about the struggles against the English."

"Yeah Toby! An English name for an Irishman." James cheekily smirked. "Go and tell your pinko socialists they can never take over 'cause I'll soon be an officer in the Royal Marines. I can kick your arse. All your arses."

"Come over to the north of Ireland and we'll give ya a good Irish welcome. That's after I've shagged Emily, again." Toby laughed then staggered over to his fellow countrymen.

The telephone rang, cajoling a very unwell James to struggle from his bedroom into the hall of their flat in Oxford.

"Get the phone, Lord Snooty," Toby Flynn called out from his room while a moaning sound emanated from beneath the bed sheets.

"Fuck you, you Irish communist git from County O'Mally Bejesas," James irreverently responded, "And tell the woman in your bed, breakfast is not free."

"It is t' her," Flynn yelled back in a semi jocular tone, "I've had payment in full!"

"Oxford four one six two."

"James, it's me here." The distinct resonance of his mother's voice exacerbated the throbbing ache in his skull.

"Yes, Mama. Why are you ringing so early?"

"James, it's ten thirty in the morning, hardly the crack of dawn."

"We had a big night last night, Mama. Lots of beer, wine and whiskey. It's very early and I feel terrible. Can I ring you back?"

"No, it's just a quick call darling. You know you asked me to open any letters from the Admiralty?"

"Yes, Mama."

"Well one came for you this morning from the Royal Navy's Admiralty Interview Board at HMS Sultan at Gosport in Hampshire. They say you may attend there for several days of selection tests and interviews for a commission in the Royal Marines beginning on Monday the fourth of July through to Thursday the seventh of July. Just to let you know that if you must be an officer in the Army then leave these days clear as they need to assess you first for suitability. I am sure you will pass darling."

"Thank you, Mama." James' head felt as if a small man with a huge hammer was lodging inside his cranium and beating his brains to pulp.

"Get better soon darling and don't forget to be at Sloane Square on Friday. That's the seventh of June and Philippa is having a party there with this boy in the pop group."

EMILY-1966

The sound of the new single release by the Kinks, "Sunny Afternoon", drifted gently from the Bush transistor radio across the large kitchen. Mary Wilkinson was cheerfully singing as she prepared breakfast for her husband and daughter. Emily sipped her coffee whilst attempting to croon along with Ray Davies as she began to open her morning mail.

"Oh Mum, I have an interview for that law firm in London. For a trainee barrister."

"Oh my, my little Emily's off to be a big lawyer in London. What if ya don't pass ya LLB?"

"Of course, our little girl will pass this L bloody B thing." Harvey Wilkinson grinned at his daughter from behind the Daily Express newspaper. "She's the best."

"Dad, if I told you I could walk on water you'd agree."

"Well can't you?" He loudly guffawed.

"When's ya interview? What's James gonna think 'bout you goin' to London?" Mary was cogitating on behalf of her daughter.

"Mum, in a week's time James has an interview to be an officer in the Marines. Down near Portsmouth. He'll going to God knows where, if he gets a commission of course. While he's learning how to be an officer and a gentlemen and how to shoot the Queen's enemies he'll be near Deal in Kent or Exeter in Devon. Either he can come up from there or I can jump on a train from Waterloo or Paddington and spend the week end where he may be."

"You should be married before you spends the weekends together." Harvey attempted a mild rebuke on his daughter.

"Daddy, we've been sleeping together since I was 16. I'm now 20, pushing 21. The age that you two were when you got married. Neither of us wants children for a long time yet. I bet you and Mum didn't wait until your wedding night."

"Yes we did," Harvey grunted while Mary shook her head behind his back.

"Tell us about ya interview, Emily." Mary was fast losing patience.

"It's for a student barrister at the Honourable Society of Lincoln's Inn which is in Holborn, London. It's with a Mister Gerald Crawley, QC."

"Why? Women never get jobs in places like that," Harvey muttered while Mary pushed a plate of fried breakfast in front of him then a smaller one for Emily.

"Dad, I know being a woman is like being handicapped if you want a career. Nonetheless, I shall do my best and hope opportunities come my way."

"Aye but watch those buggers in London. They' ll be out to trip ya up, and not be like gentlemen." Emily beamed at her father. "Dad, it's just as well you had me learn all that karate, judo and stuff that you used when you were a Royal Marine on D-Day and after. I'll not have any boy trying it on with me, except James of course. I often wondered why James singled out the Royal Marines to serve in."

"Pretty Flamingo" by Manfred Mann came on the radio.

PHILIPPA-1966

"Good grief, Pip." Judith Parkhouse sipped her glass of punch as William Jenkins, the long serving butler passed by them. He was supervising the staff as they attended to the guests at the party in the Sloane Square townhouse.

"What is it?" Philippa sighed, gazing adoringly at her beau. Miles Benton, along with Ray Hooker, Bob Hetherington and Johnny Allen, were setting up their PA system, amplifiers and drum kit before doing a sound test for their group, "The Outcaste".

"You might as well talk to the wall when Miles is near, Judith." Christine Vickers shook her head then stared equally as moonstruck at Bob the drummer.

"Yes! But isn't Ray gorgeous. He looks like Stevie Winwood?" Judith was also smitten. The girls were in almost identical garbs. White calf length boots and similar massive plastic earrings, plastic caps, various coloured Fabiani blouses with pronounced ruff and Dior skirts that were about two inches above the knee.

"Johnny is lovely." Pat Laidlaw, the normally level headed and plainest of the female quartet was also head over heels with infatuation.

"I love these new tights, but Miles says he prefers stockings still." Philippa waved over at her adoring suitor as he and the other guitarists began to tune in their instruments using the piano in the massive lounge room as a tonal guide.

"Philippa, Miles would love you if you wore a potato sack. But apparently most boys prefer stockings to tights," Judith commented.

"Then they should wear them if they like them that much," Pat icily interjected.

"Christ!" Philippa suddenly looked over to the other end of the lounge where a large contingent of guests were arriving and having their coats hung by the staff.

"What is it?" The others gasped with bewilderment.

"Mama is such an ass at times. But you have to give her credit for not giving up."

"Pip, what is it?" Judith spoke for the others.

"See! I think you lot need to wear spectacles. In the entrance lobby, mingled in with a load of other guests is none other than Isabelle Napier Fenning. Mama still has designs on her marrying James."

"Still?" Christine was amazed.

"Yes, still. After all these years. But with James wanting to be some sort of soldier and Emily off to London, Mama thinks this is their chance."

"Your intended is here also." Judith giggled. "The Honourable Julian Lee Watersby."

"Yes, Mama, also thinks that Miles is just a phase and I shall be soon looking for a real man to become my husband."

"But you are studying to be a doctor, Philippa," Pat groaned, "Julian would not only stop you doing that he would tell you not to go to university."

"I know, he thinks women should not be educated, at least not too much. Their place is to be at home and take care of the household."

Some minutes later, the first strokes of the C chord at the introduction of "Daydream' were strummed. The Outcaste professionally performed John Sebastian's composition for his group The Lovin' Spoonful. Julian Lee Watersby skulked over the floor, drew Philippa away from her friends and began to do a variation of a waltz with her.

"It will soon be time for us to talk, Philippa. Your Mama is getting very impatient."

"Well Julian, my mater is very attractive for an old woman of 43. If you like doing what she says, marry her."

"Be serious." Julian persisted.

"I am," she curtly riposted.

"That boy, Miles, is not for you. You know it, I know it and your mother knows it."

"Whatever he may or may not be, Julian, he will always be better than you."

"Come now, now you are simply being childish."

The band concluded "Daydream" and stopped momentarily before commencing the next piece. James and Emily entered the massive lounge.

"Excuse me." Philippa dashed across the room and first hugged Emily then James. "God, I'm so pleased to see you both!"

"Is that due to the attendance of a certain Honourable Julian Lee-Watersby?" Emily could not fail to have noticed his presence nor that of her own arch adversary, Isabelle Napier-Fenning.

"Mama just does not listen. Both she and Julian and his family, want me to get my "A" levels. After that I leave school and take up some sinecure of a position until I am 21 then get married to that buffoon."

"Tell Papa, little sister. He appears totally oblivious to the level of scheming that Mama exudes nurturing her clandestine little matchmaking plots."

The Outcaste burst into the Troggs song, "Wild Thing".

"I 'm off to dance with the girls, I love this song." Philippa skipped back to her friends, passed Julian. The young man did not fail to notice the threatening glare on James' face. He deduced that the present was an inopportune time to educate the younger Marchant on the ways of the world. The voice from behind him certainly contended such.

The music changed to the recent Beach Boys' hit, "Sloop John B."

DANIEL-1966

The car drew to a halt outside Gunner House, standing opposite the Central Station in Newcastle-Upon-Tyne. It was the recruitment office of the Royal Navy, Royal Marines and Women's Royal Naval Service for Northumberland, Newcastle-Upon-Tyne and north Durham.

"I'll park the car." Jackie Gibson looked up at the Royal Marine on duty in the small entrance lobby. "Ye just hop in and tell the blokes what yer after."

Daniel felt very much a part of the adult world in his dark suit, white shirt, blue tie and black chisel toe shoes. He nervously entered Gunner House and came face to face with a uniformed figure wearing a green beret, Lovat uniform, khaki shirt, slim ochre tie, red drill sash across his right shoulder and a face that could terrify the boldest.

"Yes, young man. I'm Colour Sergeant Jock McKinley and what can I do for you?"

"I want to be a Marine," Daniel responded to the tall Scot, stoically concealing the almost overpowering force of his trepidation.

Some two hours later he came out perfect in every section of the medical examinations and was passed "fit for military service" by another of the plethora of Royal Navy petty officers who worked within Gunner House. He was ushered into an interview room where a Royal Marines officer sat at a desk. He wore jersey pullover order and held the rank of captain.

As Daniel took a seat, his father was invited into the nearby common area. Jackie relaxed in a leather-backed armchair being handed a hot cup of tea by one of the RN ratings.

"Well young Gibson, I'm Captain Patterson of the Royal Marines." The dark-haired officer smiled as he lit a Senior Service cigarette. "You seem to possess all the qualities required of a subaltern in the Corps and I'm sure you may well pass the Admiralty Interview Board. But that's when the hard work really starts so even if you are successful we'll find out pretty darn quick if you're truly officer material. You will be commissioned on your day of entry. However, so many blue beret officers drop out long before completing the commando course for their green beret. Also, young man, one bit of advice. If you pass and go to Deal then Lympstone, socialise only with fellow officers or their ilk, when away from home. It makes life easier, understand? Any questions?"

'Substitute" by The Who played on the radio in the farmhouse kitchen as Jackie and Daniel walked back in after their day out to Newcastle.

"How did ye get on?" Daisy Gibson was anxious to hear all the news.

"Our Daniel's gonna be an officer in the Marines," Jackie proudly blustered, "Ah had a word with a Captain Patterson. He said that our Danny's got all the things officers' needs."

DANESH AND KELLY

The sound of the PADIT returning was music to the ears of Danesh as he checked a superfluity of intricate mathematical formulae. Dressed in a tight black jump suit, Kelly eventually appeared from the landing zone sited in the outer area of the laboratory.

"I hope you lock the PADIT and make sure you always keep it in eye sight." The professor cast an icy glance as the young doctor ambled across the office floor.

"Of course," she tetchily responded, "I don't want to be stranded in an alien dimension. As I am fully aware, it would take a long time, if not forever, for you to trace me and make a rescue journey." "Good. Was your journey fruitful?"

"Very much." Kelly poured herself a drink then lit a cigarette. "I met up again with my doppelganger, Keely. Your alter self in this dimension, David Garside, also sleeps with her only he is still married."

"I do not permit you to travel to these areas of the inner Cosmos to collect snippets I could find by watching soap operas on the PU vision/sound system. Did you ascertain any facts of veritable significance?"

"I discovered significantly, the connections between the dimensions are near or removed. It seems to depend on how close you investigate. Keely told me that there is a difference betwixt and between all the dimensions which modulates in space and time. We can age say five years, but due to an anomaly in the Quantum Links they, in the parallel universe, may age 20 years and this can then reverse during a cycle until the opposite is the case."

"I suspected that fact and am still working on the maths to prove it. Anything else?"

"Yes, Professor. We spoke in length as I sampled her universe's moccachino with a dash of rum and it transpires that you have not been on the level with me, Prof."

"And what be that my beautiful young physician?"

"You can travel in time and you can change events."

"We received today a massive imbursement, part of our enormous grant, from the Ministry of Science and Technology. This was in return for a small amount of bullshit data, very basic stuff but they deemed it revolutionary and part of same I will utilise for bona fide research. This work will partly entail the concept of actual time travel. Not those incongruities that hampered our early attempts, but an actual state of capacity to voyage through the complexities that when combined become that esoteric phenomena we refer to as the fourth dimension. However, my sexy young laboratory goddess, the future, meaning anything beyond our precise chronological juncture, can be altered. Nonetheless, my computations strongly suggest that although we may be able to travel to the past, we may, and it is a very, very big may I hasten to add, we cannot alter it."

"Perhaps you are correct. Keely informed me that you can travel back in time only if the portal into the parallel universe is on a cycle that is behind your own dimension's relative chronology. That is not the same as travelling through time in your own world. What she did say, emphatically I hasten to add Professor, was that her own version of you, Garside, has already completed plans for time travel but only to the future as the past cannot be altered."

Danesh smirked. "What else about this Garside chap?"

"Yes, it would be interesting for me to fuck your doppelganger. My darling Danesh. Sadly, it would be the same as laying you. That is apart from his past. Garside is almost a dead ringer for you except he served as a soldier in Indo-China after completing his degree in physics. He did two years national service as a lieutenant, was highly decorated, and then began to work as a government research physicist. He is your double! I saw his photo, Keely had it tucked away in her handbag. Now to bed before much more work!"

NARRATOR

As Winston Leonard Spencer-Churchill remarked after the Battle of El Alamein in 1942; -"This is not the end, not even the beginning of the end, but the end of the beginning."

I can see the wine flowing, the audience applauding and boisterously cheering after each item of which they are aware of or can identify with clarity and accuracy.

I look for a brief instant at the men who have been most important in my life to date. My new husband has not yet ascended to that illustrious podium although no doubt he will soon. I expect him to anyway. When I was young, my father used to play me songs from his own youth. A late 1965 album by the Beatles called Rubber Soul was one. There was a particular song entitled "In My Life" which had been written by the late John Lennon. The lyrics for this recording are full of emotion, aspiration, love, life and death.

As I narrate more of my tale I can recall one line from the song, which was "some are dead, and some are living". An equivalence with mine own narrative. I look at the faces of those present and can see shadows, ethereal opaque and ghostly manifestations of those who should be present but are barred due to lack of existence.

I see three great men, strong and valiant. I perceive several women some beautiful, all compassionate and affectionate. I observe within the spectres of those present and those gone forever, the history, annals of not only several families, but it could be a nation. It may indeed be a replication of the story of mankind itself. Courage, drive, determination, love, trials, tribulations, victories, defeats, elation, sorrow, celebration, tragedy, birth, marriage and the ultimate terminus for us all. This is the story of the several families whose histories are combined into such a saga. I see them all plus invited friends and feel honoured to be able to recount this tale. I must proceed, like Chorus in Shakespeare's Henry V, there is much to impart.

PHILIPPA -1966

"Becky, if I didn't know you better I would think you fancied my dad."

"Lady Philippa." Rebecca swallowed with unease. "You shouldn't joke about such things. Beggin' your pardon, My Lady."

"Of course I'm joking, Becky." Philippa helped herself to one of Rebecca's homemade scones, with copious amounts of farm clotted cream and thick newly prepared strawberry jam. "But you always blush when he comes into a room and he likes you. I can tell that when he talks to you. But I am talking in jest. My father, is pretty dishy for an old man, well a man of 45. I know most of the women in Oxfordshire and London fancy him. I think your husband may object if you showed it too much. And my mother may also."

"His lordship is a real gentleman, My Lady." The aging and ailing cook joined in the parlance. "Of course, Mrs. Cromer, but plenty of ladies still flirt with him." Philippa poured herself a cup of tea to augment the scones.

"What are you up to this week end, My Lady?" Rebecca was as always interested in all such current news.

"I'm hoping to get over to Oxford to see my boyfriend. He's really nice. Do you like him Becky?"

"Of course I likes him, Lady Philippa. Mister Miles is a nice young gentleman, very polite, well-mannered and intelligent. I hope you and he stays together."

Philippa kissed Rebecca on the cheek.

"I love chatting to you Becky, you are so understanding."

"Beggin' your pardon, Lady Philippa." Biggs came into the kitchen.

"Yes, Mister Biggs, what is it? I was just chatting to your lovely wife."

"Yes, Lady Philippa. Her ladyship was enquiring about your whereabouts. It seems like there was a telephone call and she has an urgent message to pass on to you."

"Thank you, Mister Biggs, I shall go up to Mama as soon as I have finished these lovely scones and my tea."

"Yes, Mama, what is it?" James came into the drawing room.

"Philippa, come with me. Your friend Miles is in hospital. The renal unit of Churchill Hospital in Oxford, and I think we should go and visit him."

"Wh-wh-ats happened, Mama, what's happened?"

"Dear Philippa." Louise hugged her daughter. "I received a phone call from Miles' mother. He has been taken to hospital she said it would be better if you went to see him sooner rather than later. Of course, all may be well, but James will drive you as Daddy is in London today."

"Come on Pip." James motioned. "Grab your coat, bag and anything else you may need, and we'll be off."

The elapse of only half an hour, which seemed like an eternity to Philippa, had taken place when James came onto Old Road in Oxford. Minutes later he drove into the car park of the Churchill Hospital. He looked blankly at the sign, which informed all that the building was erected in 1940 and named after Clementine Churchill, the wife of the Prime Minister of the day.

Philippa was pale, her expression was sunken as entered the hospital reception area.

"Renal unit," James snapped at the visibly overworked receptionist.

"First floor, sir."

"Come Pip, let's find out what the situation is with your chap, Miles."

They turned sharp left and virtually ran up the staircase onto the ward. There, at the entrance a prematurely grey-haired woman stood. Freda Benson was certainly not ugly nor was she a beauty. She stood about five feet two inches in height displaying an extremely gloomy and despondent countenance. Freda, dressed in an old raincoat burst into tears as she made towards Philippa and tightly hugged her.

"What is it, Mrs Benson?"

"It's Miles, My Lady." Freda loudly sniffed.

"What about Miles?" Philippa almost screamed while. shaking uncontrollably.

"He died last night, Lady Philippa. Died of somethin' they called diabetes mellitus. I'm so, so sorry, my dear."

"Oh my God, James, James, what am I to do?" Philippa bawled and let go of Mrs Benson and wrapped her arms around her brother.

"Sorry, sir," sobbed Mrs. Benson.

"You have nothing to be sorry for Mrs Benson." James smiled at her as the other members of the Miles' music group, "The Outcaste", Ray, Bob and Johnny came through the entrance door.

The boys hugged Freda and then Philippa. It was Bob Hetherington who deigned to speak first during which he assumed a forced smile.

"Sorry, Pip it was so sudden. He's had kidney problems all his life."

James approached Bob and whispered, "Do you know when and where the funeral will be?"

"No, but as soon as I find out I'll ring you or Pip. I'll ask Mrs. Benson when she is in a better frame of mind."

Three hours later and James and Philippa were back at Wye Hall after a poignant, tacit and solemn drive from Oxford.

James pulled onto the gravel driveway at the front of the house. He had only just applied the brakes to come to a halt on the pink gravel drive when Philippa threw open the passenger door of the Austin Mini. She ran into the house, making her way directly to the kitchen.

"My lady, 'ave yer told her ladyship yet?" Rebecca whispered.

A short while later Philippa responded.

"No, I came here first."

"I thinks that's a great honour, Lady Philippa. But yer should tells your mum first. She's yer mum after all."

James had informed his parents of the tragedy. Tom and Louise were in the drawing room partaking in an after-dinner brandy. The young man had then took his leave to visit Emily.

Louise drew nervously on a Dunhill cigarette.

"Our daughter went to tell the maid before she told us! What the hell is up?"

"She loves Rebecca, she finds she can talk to her," Tom Marchant quietly replied.

"I'm her mother, she should tell me first! We'll have to dismiss Rebecca!"

"We will not. I'll have no talk of that. Our children love Rebecca and she has been a hard-working loyal employee for many years. I agree Philippa should have come to you first, but it's a tragedy, her personal tragedy. Philippa is totally distraught, let's not make it worse by scolding her for crying to Rebecca first."

"You would say that, she has you around her little finger. I know about her learning medicine from your Uncle Perry. And I think you are fucking Rebecca. You take her to London a lot."

"Twice in two years is hardly a lot. And I am no more fucking Rebecca than you are Charles De'ath."

Silence fell as Philippa entered the room. The young woman made her way to Louise and hugged her tightly. She then turned to her father at which point she began to cry. Again.

DANIEL-1966

"All or Nothing" by the Small Faces was playing as Daniel checked through his bags and pockets. He was leaving for Alnmouth station to catch the London train en route to Portsmouth.

"'Ave ye got eveythin'?" Daisy Gibson was shaking with anxiety.

"Mum, Ah'm goin' to Portsmouth for an interview. Ah'm not goin' to war."

"Aye, Ah heard that from the young lads in 1939. A few months later they'd all bin sent overseas to fight in France an' Egypt."

"'Ave yer got all ya stuff?" Jackie Dixon echoed his wife and Debbie giggled.

"Rail warrant, money, suit, three shirts, three sets of underpants, three sets of socks, tie, wash and shavin' kit, books to read and newspapers. What else?"

"They're officers." Jackie grinned. "Bullshit baffles brains when ya gets to be a sergeant but not in an interview for an officer. Be respectful; call them all "sir." Sit to attention and 'ave good answers for all th' questions Captain Patterson said ye'd be asked."

"Yes, Dad," Daniel impatiently sighed, "Let's get t' Alnmouth station, the Edinburgh to London train stops there at ten o'clock. Sunday service. It'll take about five hours t' get to Kings Cross. Then Ah've got t'take the London Underground to Waterloo. Then a train t' Portsmouth Harbour on the south coast. Ah'm rarin' to go!"

"Alright. Say bye to your mother, brother and sister and let's be off. Have yer got a packed lunch?"

"Yes, Dad. Mother give me a breakfast big enough t' last a week an' enough food t' last 'til Christmas. Ah'll be alright so let's go!"

JAMES-1966

"Glad to finally get off, Papa." James shook his father's hand then jumped into the passenger side of Emily's Ford Anglia. It was somewhat fortuitous that it was available to be borrowed from Harvey Wilkinson. She waved energetically at Tom and Louise then sped off towards Shipton. The small town that since 1964 had boasted the closest passenger railway station in the area.

"Are you nervous?" Emily mischievously enquired as she watched James take five minutes to remove the cellophane wrapping from a packet of cigarettes.

"Of course I'm bloody nervous," James snapped back, "I paid five shillings for this pack of Passing Clouds cigarettes."

"Consider yourself lucky you can afford to pay five shillings for 20 cigarettes. Anyway sweetheart, you can light one up for me as I am driving you to the station. No clandestine or furtive fucks down at this Navy place. I've heard that women who join the services only do it for the cock!"

"Emily. I'll have no time. Even if I had the dashed inclination." "Summer in the City" by the Lovin' Spoonful came on the radio. Emily sang along with John Sebastian while James lit the cigarettes.

"You wouldn't find someone who you could fuck in synchronisation like me. But I start my own work next week and I may find a stud." She impishly smirked and accepted a Passing Cloud.

"I'll probably not find a shag like you. You'd best put your foot down, Emm, the Paddington train leaves at noon from Shipton. There're only two a day."

"We have plenty of time. You'll be in London soon. You can hail a taxi to Waterloo and hop on a train for Portsmouth Harbour. You'll be fine. You'll get to HMS whatever in time for dinner. In two months you'll be Second Lieutenant Marchant of the whatever it is. You did say they start you as an officer?"

"Yes. If I'm successful, I'll receive the princely annual salary of 700 pounds and a bit per annum. About 1100 less than you'll get. About the same as a married enlisted Royal Marine at the lowest end of the pay scale."

"Of course, you'll pass. You're not joining for the money. With your father's connections and a degree in Economics you could make a fortune in the City."

"I know." James drew on his cigarette as "Get Away" by Georgie Fame and the Blue Flames came on the radio. "But I don't want Papa's influence to help. I want to do my own thing, be in my own scene, not his."

"I know darling James. Do you fancy a quick fuck before I drop you off? The back seat is just right for shagging and we're only a minute from Shipton station."

"Alright, but we'll have to be quick.

EMILY-1966

"Emily." Harvey Wilkinson was surveying the decent sized London West End flat. The property that his daughter was purchasing was situated in Red Lion Street. It came courtesy of a massive loan from him. Naturally the middle-aged blacksmith would never expect repayment.

It would be her first home. An initial step to begin her professional life as a student barrister.

"Yes, Dad," she answered whilst excitedly unpacking clothes and pieces of crockery from wooden boxes. She was ably assisted with due diligence by her watchful mother as "Out of Time" by Chris Farlowe came on the small transistor radio.

"A lot of small jobs t' do on this 'ere place, me dear, just as well Oy brought me tool box."

"Dad." Emily squirmed uneasily. "You've already paid my deposit and mortgage for a quarter. You brought enough furniture down in the horse box for a mansion, paid my electric and gas bills. Paid them for the next few months and given me money for food for months. For that generous gesture I will certainly repay you. There's no need to do all the DIY as well on this flat." "It'll take me no time t' do these few jobs. You and your mother can put the kettle on while Oy gets me tools from the car."

Harvey cheerfully set about the self-designated tasks in hand.

She was dressed conservatively in a dark pin stripe suit of a skirt which came to mid knee, jacket, light blue blouse, dark tights and black shoes. Emily nervously made her way into the building of the Honourable Society of Lincoln's Inn. At reception a plump middle-aged woman sat imperiously behind the desk and eyed her suspiciously. It was a Miss Fiona Derby, according to the nameplate near the switchboard apparatus.

"Not the one here on the day of my interview." She thought to herself.

"Yes," the woman abruptly addressed Emily.

"My name is Miss Emily Wilkinson. I am a student barrister and have an appointment with Mister Gerald Crawley QC at nine o'clock."

"Take a seat. The head of chambers will be out as soon as he is available."

Emily with some decorum sat down on an Ottoman, looked around for some time at the relatively ornate surroundings and noticed that the receptionist had not yet made any call.

As she waited, two young men skirted past, looked at her legs, chest and then spoke to each other about the "Nice bit of crumpet in reception."

"Excuse me, Miss." Emily returned to the reception desk. "It is after nine o'clock. I assume you made Mister Crawley aware of my presence."

"I know my job, Miss. I shall inform Mister Crawley as soon as I have time."

"How long does it take to dial three numbers?"

"Well," Miss Derby sighed in response.

A tall man, in his mid to late 40s briskly approached Emily. Frowning.

He was quite handsome with swept back, thick black hair which was greying a little at the sides. The figure was dressed in a dark suit, double tabbed linen banded shirt and a pair of gleaming Lord John shoes. A trendy brand to compliment mainly orthodox fashion attire.

"Mister Crawley." Emily leapt to her feet and shook his hand.

"Miss Wilkinson. I thought you had not turned up."

"I have been here for some time. The lady on reception must have been busy."

"Yes, quite." Crawley glared at Miss Derby who turned noticeably red.

"Come with me. I want a chat with you before I take you to your work area."

Crawley walked Emily into his spacious, sumptuous office. The QC sat behind his large oak desk and invited Emily to sit in the armchair opposite.

"Your interview and qualifications were exemplary Miss Wilkinson. May I call you Emily?" The head of chambers stood up and walked to look out of the window at the view of Lincoln's Inn Fields. "Of course, Mister Crawley."

"You have a lot to offer, an enormous amount. You are gifted, very attractive and ambitious. The qualities in a woman that are more often than not derided, scorned and diminished, by the male establishment. You will have to face that, and it could at times be quite ugly! But if you wish to succeed you will need to take it head on. Hence your generous starting salary of 18 hundred per annum"

"Sir, with due respect." Emily suppressed her annoyance. "I am not some straw in the ears wench from the country. I'm not stupid and will not be bullied by a few non-entities of boys."

Crawley smiled and turned his gaze from the window over towards Emily.

"I'm sure you'll not. And I certainly don't believe you will be walked over nor easily intimidated. But I wanted to ensure you are fully aware of the real dog eat dog world, especially in this profession that you have entered. It is very political in the work sense and your opponents could as easily be the women as much as the male student barristers and others. Many are jealous of a female who has the guts to aim for the top. There will be very few Madame Justice Rose Heilbrons for a very long time. Even in the enlightened 60s very few women make it in the workplace and even less in the legal profession. I cannot stop the backstabbing, the sexual banter and innuendos. I can really only interfere if they attempt unwanted and inappropriate physical advances."

"Mister Crawley, have you had a change of heart and wish that you had not offered me the position?"

"Absolutely not."

"Then you want me to fail. To use as a pretext not to employ women in the future?"

"Couldn't be further from the truth. I am willing you to succeed, but you need to know exactly how difficult it will be. Not merely for you, but for any woman."

"I'm completely aware that it will take at least until the 1990s before the Neanderthals that run our economy will concede to women in the workplace as the norm. Why do you want me to succeed so much? You are a male in a dominant position?"

"Simple, Emily, I have two daughters who want to be QCs. In the five and eight years respectively it will take, I want to play my part in reforming the profession. You Miss Wilkinson can be my pioneer for a better tomorrow."

DANESH AND KELLY

"I see Prof." Kelly drove into Nazeing in Hartfordshire and headed for the turning that would

take her to Gideon's remote laboratory. "Well I'm almost at your place. I am so pleased HM government deigned to sponsor you so lavishly. I hope our hard-working tax payers never get to be aware of this. I shall be there in a sec, see you then."

She switched off the hands-free car telephone and took a sharp right along a country lane. After unlocking and opening the gate, Kelly drove through. She stopped, closed and locked the wooden five bar before jumping back into her Ford Focus. From there it was an easy mile drive to the large, secluded country house. James Blunt sang "Stay the Night" on the car radio.

Danesh was already waiting on the gravel drive as she turned the Focus off the narrow metal road.

"Darling!" He ran over to Kelly and hugged her as soon as she was out of the car. "Such great tidings. We have two mill in grants. And much, much more to come. All for a load of bullshit with a tiny amount of actual bona fide results hidden within. And there is more!"

"Prof, save it until I have had one of your huge bacon sandwiches and a cup of percolated coffee. I'm starving. Then while we have a smoke afterwards, you can tell me all, before we go to bed."

Once Kelly had eaten and sipped all her coffee she lit a cigarette and turned to Danesh.

"Lovely sandwich, Prof." The young doctor gently drew on the Marlborough. "Now, what's up?" "So exciting darling, so exciting! I have been ensconced in the lab and on the computer for three weeks now. I feel like the narrator of H.G. Wells' book, "The Time Machine"!"

"For goodness sake, Prof, spill the beans!"

"Well, two things."

"Get to the point!"

"Alright Doctor Aresti, I shall reveal all."

The professor poured out two generous measures of whiskey into crystal tumblers.

"Kelly. I strongly believe, that I can prove the existence of not one parallel universe. We already have done and travelled to one. Accordingly, and based on your findings, I revisited many, many formulae. I now believe that numerous, possibly unlimited PUs may exist, and soon we should be able to view them."

"How do we know where our universe lies in relation to others?" Kelly was more than a little intrigued.

"The string theory tells it indirectly, but they lie next to each other. I would prefer to use the name railway sleeper theory. Just imagine that our universe is a sleeper on the tracks of an infinite railway. It may not be advisable, but I believe we can travel not only two ways, so far, we have only done one, say to the left, we could also turn right with a small adjustment. You have a left and right if you like of the sleeper we are on, but I am certain I can connect to the railway line itself. We will be able to travel, at least in theory, to any parallel universe."

"Oh Prof. You are so brilliant. That must be worth at least two shags. Let's get to the bedroom!"

"Finish your drink and cigarette first. I have not yet concluded my imparting."

"Come on then as I'm all ears."

"I was able to do this very detailed research thanks to our generous taxpayers, so I did divulge a small amount, very small, to the government. Just suffice to spice their bland dispositions to get them excited and have the Home Office boffins beside themselves with exhilaration."

"And? Prof, you take years to get to the punch line."

"HM Government will increase our grant, which is good. The data I supplied them with, the mainly insignificant results, came from work which I did aeons ago free gratis. The crux of the matter, Kelly, is simple, Whilst I was farting around with a myriad of statistics, formulae and computer programmes, like Archimedes in the bath, I had my Eureka moment."

"Tell me!"

"Kelly, I think I have discovered the formulae to enable time travel. It is a very long shot and may only be to the past and back. Nonetheless will not just be via fluctuations on the straight line inter universe passage, but within our dimension."

PHILIPPA-1966

"Ashes to ashes---." The vicar tossed some dirt onto the coffin of Miles Benson, resting six feet below in the open grave. He then solemnly concluded the funeral service. From behind a yew tree in the graveyard, the sallow, iniquitous face of a man with black receding hair smirked in satisfaction. That cool Thursday, the subsequent private wake of light reflection and remembrance at the house of Mrs Benson became the last time they would all be together again under the same roof. The girls were all from the same area. They had attended junior and senior school collectively and in just over a year would sit their A levels together. Then would remain friends.

Their respective relationships with the boys were now doomed. Miles, the glue that held them altogether in their pairs, was now no longer around to oversee such a burdensome duty.

Everyday occurrences that transpired would never be replicated even beyond the conclusion of time itself. But it was something with a much greater intensity of melancholy and poignancy that became sagacious within the intellect of Philippa. She tenderly sipped on red wine in between nibbling on cheddar and pineapple sticks. Philippa stood with Judith, Christine, Pat, Ray, Bob Sand John contemplating and making many an unsuccessful attempt to rationalise the universe and life.

"Must be the way the cookie crumbles," the 18-year-old mumbled whilst taking a cigarette out of a battered packet. She was given a light by Ray.

"What is that Pip?" Judith also lit a cigarette as Mrs Benson put some of Miles favourite songs on the gramophone starting with the Rolling Stones' "19th Nervous Breakdown".

"I want to be with Miles. He's on the astral plane now with all the other dead heroes like Buddy Holly."

"Pip, that's just shit," Ray grunted, "He's dead, dead, dead!"

"Shut up!" John interjected. "This is supposed to be a celebration of Miles' life and not an argument about whether there is a God or not."

"I think he's right." Pat decided to talk. "If there were a God young people would not die. It's bad enough in that disgusting Vietnam War but just to die when you were so fit."

"I agree!" Ray recommenced his chunter. "If there is a God then he has a funny way of doing things. See that old cunt we passed on the way to the church. He must have been 70 and pretty fit for an old fart. He's alive while Miles is dead. Any God thing would have a bit more logic. The old cunt would be dead, Miles would be here."

"Yes, why do we have life just to have it taken away? Makes no sense so I think God is an idiot!" Christine decided to join in then immediately turned to Bob, "I've had enough of this, do you fancy getting away? My parents are away until Tuesday. I have the house to myself if you drive me."

"Sorry Chris, I have things to do."

"Go and shove yourself up your backside then."

Philippa saw her father's Rolls Royce Silver Cloud III driven by Mister Biggs come onto the drive.

"Our lift home is here girls." Philippa turned to her friends. "I'm going to say goodbye to Mrs Benson, then I'm off. If anyone wants a ride. " Judith, Christine and Pat needed no time to debate the matter. They left without a bye, leave or goodbye kiss for the boys, hastily pursuing Philippa to the parked limousine.

In less than an hour Biggs' skilful aptitudes behind the wheel brought the four girls to Wye Hall.

They had all been dressed in black all day and were eager to be let loose on Philippa's extremely extensive and continually expanding wardrobe.

"Down to the kitchen, we need to feed on some real food." Philippa wanted a viable detour both to see Becky and avoid her mother.

"Philippa, are you alright?" Judith the ever-cautious one was concerned at the pace her friend's grief for Miles had seemingly evaporated.

"Judith, you are a mother hen and I love it. I have cried since the night Miles died. I'm all cried out, life must go on. Miles would have wanted that."

"How do you know?" the cynical Pat posed as they walked through the main entrance door to be met by Mister Hodges and Rebecca who duly took their coats.

"His mother told me," Philippa replied then smiled at the aging butler, "Mister Hodges, would it be in order if my friends and I popped into the kitchen for some of Rebecca's afternoon tea?"

"That will be perfectly in order, Lady Philippa," The 68-year-old replied.

"Thank you."

"Philippa!" Louise appeared from the study. "Julian is here, and he would like to spend some time with you."

"I'm sure he would, Mama. He can join us in the kitchen for tea and scones."

"Philippa, I think he would prefer a private audience with you. He is concerned about your recent upset"

"Of course, he is, Mama. Ask him to come back sometime but give me ample, really ample warning."

"Philippa, I think you have been mixing irregularly. You are becoming insubordinate."

"That's alright Pip." Christine and the others could see the direction of this latest mother and daughter spat. "We'll go. Give us a ring when you want, or we'll see you back at school next week."

Moments later Philippa walked into the drawing room, still in her black funeral suit.

Julian stood up. He stood six feet tall with longish brown hair and had thick lips. He was wearing a trendy mod jacket, bright orange shirt, yellow cravat, Cuban heel boots and bell-bottom trousers. "Julian, I am here to placate my mother. Whatever you have to say, make it quick."

"I want to start courting you with a view to engagement and then marriage."

Philippa felt nauseated.

JAMES-1966

James was travelling on the British Rail Intercity Waterloo to Portsmouth Harbour service. He was on the way to the Admiralty Interview Board at Gosport in Hampshire. He thought deeply, very deeply. In fact James was almost in a trance with the intensity of his contemplations.

Unlike his sister, James was not one to naval gaze and attempt to get his head around the meaning of life. Although one deep enigma did continually rise up from the inner most depths of his young mind. This deep cerebral riddle had relegated any nervousness of his impending rigours to not even warrant more than a flashing connectivity of nerve impulses. This mystery so tantalised him and within his mindset was as existential as any posed by philosophers of old.

"How was it possible Emily could make every fuck, even in the back of her father's Anglia, so erotic, fantastically mind blowing and always different? How come she knows my passion points and slides her hand with such ecstasy and precision? How does she move her inside muscles until my entire frame jolts with her? Just as well she's on the pill!"

James was mentally deep inside Emily until nudged back to reality. This transpired the moment a distorted, crackling British Rail loudspeaker with a Hampshire accent bellowed out, "Portsmouth Harbour, this is Portsmouth Harbour!" He grabbed his overnight bag and alighted onto the rail platform. The entire terminus stood on a wooden pier, a point that he noted with no small degree of interest. James briskly walked outside onto a thoroughfare called "The Hard" which once again evoked some mirth within the young man.

"Taxi!" a driver enquired as he walked away from the station.

"No thanks, I'm getting the ferry to Gosport".

DANIEL-1966

The train journey from Alnmouth station to Kings Cross seemed to have lasted an eternity. This voyage of near purgatory was followed by a ride on the London Underground railway to Waterloo station. The final leg of train travel was another British Rail journey terminating at Portsmouth

Harbour station. The July weather was summery and fine as he came out of the station and looked around the southern coastal city.

Once he had confirmed directions with a passer-by, Daniel set off along "The Hard" towards the small ferry port close by. The standard vessel was called Ferry Princess and the teenager patiently waited for the queue along the boarding ramp, named the Portsmouth Pontoon, to embark. He was a soon to be candidate for a commission in the Royal Marines and naturally wore conservative attire. This was a pair of shining black shoes, black socks, a navy-blue suit with a white shirt and a black tie. Daniel was simultaneously brimming with absolute confidence whilst standing on the verge of an involuntary evacuation of the bowels.

He had absorbed thoroughly the brochures and literature sent with his application forms and was totally conversant that the Royal Navy establishment of HMS Sultan was on Military Road. He was also cognisant that it was not a huge distance away from the ferry. Nonetheless, it seemed to be prudent to grab a cab, and it could not be very expensive, he thought.

The taxi ride was very short and cost three shillings. A sum Daniel deemed to be the extortionate. Nonetheless, he did not wish to appear miserly as he was attending an interview to be considered for a commission in Her Majesty's Royal Marines. Acting the refined gentleman, he handed the driver two half crowns and told him to keep the change.

"Thank you, sir," he said before driving off in his Vauxhall Cresta.

Jackie Gibson had ensured his son would not be short of cash during his three days away. This had partially prompted the sudden, albeit temporary, bout of generosity.

He walked through the gates passed the Arabic looking carved wooden figurehead and that in days hence had graced the bows of one of England's "heart of oak" ships.

The 17-year-old marched sprightly along the path juxtaposed to the large brick-built establishment from where Daniel could hear the Beatles record of "Paperback Writer" somewhere in the distance. He stepped into HMS Sultan's reception foyer. It was a thickly carpeted, ornately stained wooden panel decorated hallway. Here he was almost pounced on by a Royal Navy leading rating in a blue 1A uniform minus the familiar white cap.

"Name?" The sailor officiously snapped.

"Er, I'm Daniel Gibson." The response attempted to conceal the Northumbrian accent.

"You're in cabin three. That's a room to you civilians. Straight up the stairs and to the left. Dinner is at 19. 00 hours. That's seven pm, It's in the dining room, not the officers, the candidates' mess."

He picked up his suitcase then energetically moved up the staircase and turned left, bypassing the first door and onto the second which was marked with a metal "3".

Inside were two other young men in smart suits and appearing as nervous as Daniel felt that second. The first, dressed in a very expensive pin stripe suit, tall and good looking. Daniel gauged him to be over six feet, well in excess of his own five feet ten inches. He wore a gleaming white shirt, golden tie pin and golden cufflinks. This individual made Daniel feel that he was dressed a tad unkemptly.

The thick black hair had a pronounced large curl at the front on the brow.

The other person was aged about 20 and roughly five feet nine inches tall. This candidate was wearing a light brown well pressed suit and well ironed fawn shirt, brown tie. He was quite handsome, with a determined look, thin nose and wearing short but thick blond hair.

The young man in the pinstripe stepped forward with a reached-out hand.

"Hello, I'm James Marchant, from Oxfordshire. I'm applying for the Royal Marines, are you here for the Navy or the Marines?"

"I'm Daniel Gibson from Northumberland and Ah'm here to try to get a commission in the Royal Marines." The two men shook hands as the other applicant stepped forward.

"I'm David, David A. Moir, from Scotland. I've just finished a graduate course at Saint Andrews." The Scots accent was very pronounced. "Ah read History. I'm down in England t' apply fer the Royal Marines too."

"We can all have a beer at the Cocked Hat pub tonight," Marchant suggested.

"Downstairs, gentleman!" The naval rating called out as he came into the cabin,

"One of the officers will give you a quick briefing in the mess in five minutes. It's 'bout the next three days before dinner and before ya go off to the Cocked Hat."

EMILY-1966

"Excuse me, Miss Wilkinson." The tall figure of Bryan Villano approached Emily. She was sat at her desk in the main office of the Crawley and Partners Chambers. The small, bespectacled, balding fair haired and quite rotund figure placed a folder in front of her.

"Yes, Mister Villano." She deferentially looked up at the chief clerk of the chambers.

"Mister Crawley wants you to look at this. It may be a bit hard for a woman though."

He handed her a brown envelope file marked Regina v Cooper.

"Mister Villano." Emily civilly. "I am sure that even a weak and feeble woman like me may at least be able to have a stab at it. Would you not think so, Mister Villano?"

"Yeah." Ben Dooley, the 25-year-old clerk piped up. "After you've made us all a cuppa cha. That's what women is for." A small junior clerk in the corner laughed.

Emily walked over to the kettle and switched it on. "I shall make you all a cup of tea. But I think you Mister Dooley can make the next one."

"On yer bike! Blokes don't make the tea. That's for women."

"What subject is your university degree in?" Emily impishly grinned.

"Ain't got one but you're a bird so you 'ave to make the tea."

"Like I said, I'll be glad to make this one. You can do the next."

"Miss Wilkinson!" Villano cast Emily a sickly smirk. "I'm the chief clerk. I'll tells ya when ya makes the tea and when ya does other stuff. Understand?"

"Too true Mister Villano. Keep these birds in their right place." Dooley was encouraged.

"I do Mister Villano," Emily calmly responded, "I perfectly understand your point."

The skinny, narrow faced Dooley was in the heights of a psychological maelstrom. It was a place that he and Villano had rarely visited.

"If you was my woman I'd give you a back 'ander 'cross your bloody mouth," Dooley warbled, the latent anger boiling just below the surface.

"I'm sure you would." Emily merely generated a Cheshire cat grin. She then poured boiling water from the Russell Hobbs kettle into the rather antique looking tea pot.

Once she had allowed the tea sufficient time to brew she poured it into cups. Crawley stepped into the general office.

"Emily!" He glared at Villano and Dooley. "Please remember I have much for you to do. Dooley and Mister Villano can share in any such tea making duties."

The dumbstruck look on their faces unravelled an encyclopaedia of unanticipated emotions emanating from a bewildering circumstance.

"But Mister Crawley, women makes the tea. I'm the chief clerk," Villano protested.

"Yes, Mister Villano. I concede that you should be exempt from such duties. However, Miss Wilkinson will only make the tea, if Dooley and Hopper, I think your junior clerk is called Hopper, if they do as well. If they want any that is. I do not take anyone on with a first class Legum Baccalaureus Latin, LLB to you lot, to be a full time charlady. Emily, once you have sorted out the refreshments, bring the file of the Cooper case that Mister Villano has just handed to you. I want you to visit the client, Mister Cooper, in person." "Yes, Mister Crawley."

Villano offered no response.

PHILIPPA-1966

The summer breeze fondled the delicate ivy that hung like some majestic sentinel over the walls of the house. It gently swayed outside the bedroom of Judith Parkhouse. Inside the large country residence, the quartet of teenagers chatted away. They were trying on a multitude of Judith's seemingly infinite collection of resplendent outfits while discussing the main topic. Boys.

"I am going to live at the Sloane Square house," Philippa announced.

"You mean for the ball season, Pip, or all the time?" Pat unzipped and removed her mini skirt.

"Won't your intended, and your Mama of course, attempt to thwart such a bold expedition?" Judith interjected before Philippa could respond. She was squeezing into a party dress, one of many Judith's spacious, luxuriant boudoir.

"I have checked when Julian is out of the country. He is off to Australia for a year on August the sixth. The dashed man wanted me to talk about our future before he left but I refused. I said it would need to be after this trip, which is to groom him to be a future captain of industry in something or other. Thank God he will be out of the way. Mama was a teasy bit miffed. However, I said to Daddy, if he likes me that much he will wait. Then we'll both see how keen we are when he comes back. Which, hopefully, will be a very long time."

"I take it the earl was on your side?" Christine bolted into life. She then changed the record from the old hit of earlier in the year, "Groovy Kind of Love" by the Mindbenders to a brand-new release by the barefooted girl singer, Sandie Shaw and her song, "Nothing Comes Easy."

"Of course, Daddy always sides with me but then he always gives in to Mama."

"At least you'll have a year, time to complete your A levels and have selected a university before he has chance to throw a proverbial spanner in the works," Pat remarked then recommenced singing along with Sandie Shaw.

"I thought Julian wanted you to complete your A levels then get a little volunteer WI type job until you get married?" Judith commented then handed around her packet of Dunhill cigarettes. The girls took one each, lit them then continued the conversation.

"I'm going to Oxford medical college. I have Daddy's support and I shall see other boys while that person is well away in Australia."

"Good for you old girl," Pat chortled then placed The Kinks record of "Sunny Afternoon" on the small gramophone.

"Well all you have to worry about is Julian Farty Arse." Judith sounded forceful. "My parents want me to stop listening to pop music and concentrate on classical stuff. Practising the violin. They don't even know I smoke."

"How boring." Christine put her cigarette in the ashtray then stood in front of the full-length mirror. She was next to the massive wardrobe trying on a two-piece flared trouser suit.

"Pip, your brother is going to be a sailor or something. Is he not?"

"Christine, that outfit is absolutely you! And yes, James is having an interview to be an officer in something to do with the Royal Navy. Why?"

"I think we should all go to stay at your London house and when James brings his friends from the Navy to visit then we can shag them."

"That's so terrible, Christine. And James is already too heavy with that delightful Emily so that reduces the number immediately by one." Pat rolled on a new pair of tights to match the skirt she was modelling with her cigarette still in her mouth. "Pip, do you let Julian have his wicked way?"

"Of course not, Pat." Philippa removed her dress and selected another from the wardrobe.

"Are you still a virgin?" Judith enquired bringing the others to pay great heed.

"No!" Philippa impishly grinned. "But it was nothing to do with sphincter Julian."

"You did it with Miles? You little strumpet!" Pat shrieked then placed on the record player the flip side of "Paperback Writer" by the Beatles, a song entitled "Rain".

"Yes, I loved Miles, I always said I would save it for a boy I loved so I did. The only problem is I need to fall in--." Philippa began to weep.

All the young women flocked around her to comfort her.

"There, there Pippa Longstocking, you'll be fine." Pat stroked her friend's head.

"You are my dearest friends. We shall all go to Sloane Square for the ball season and have a jolly good time." Philippa hugged each one in turn. "And we will all meet lots of eligible boys!"

DANIEL 1966

Daniel knocked and when he heard "Come in" deigned to enter this sanctum. The shrine was only for those blessed, he thought. Individuals who sat with the gods and the muses, only such singular beings were worthy of entrance through this mystical ingress. An access to a revered spot reserved for the alumni of the highest echelons of life.

Daniel was with his new friends, his roommates. James Marchant from Oxfordshire, David Moir from Scotland and Evan Morgan from somewhere in Wales. They had all, with others, endured a day of the officer selection course at HMS Sultan at Gosport in the county of Hampshire.

Daniel had never dreamt England was so big. It had seemed like the width of the Cosmos from Alnmouth station in mid Northumberland to Portsmouth Harbour on the south coast of England and now he was about to face the pivotal point within the course, the Interview.

Day One had been challenging enough. He had been academically searched for his competency within intellectual and practical abilities. The young man from the North East of England had been grilled by examiners on a broad range of tests. which had included reasoning both verbal and written, speed and accuracy in numerical skills and theoretical orientation across a notional territory. He had written an essay for 45 minutes on the role of the Royal Marines once the United Kingdom had abandoned all commitments east of Suez.

Immediately that this task had been completed, he had then been sent to the gymnasium with the others. They had been placed into nominated groups where each person had to plan the solution to various objectives. These included the conveying all six members of his team across an obstacle course which was a simulate valley or river using only the props the examining team allowed. This Daniel had completed with ease using less than a quarter of the allocated time.

He opened the door and marched smartly in to be faced by a long narrow table at which four uniformed officers minus headwear were sat. He noticed there was also a plain clothes man in a lounge suit propped on a leather couch, some 20 feet to his right. This person appeared to be engrossed in a pile of paperwork. Daniel sat facing this array of senior members and could recite all the rank titles of both the Royal Navy and Royal Marines. The man seated directly opposite him was wearing an olive-green number two, an officers' Lovat uniform, and held the rank of a full colonel in the Royal Marines.

To the left of him was a lieutenant commander in the Royal Navy in his navy-blue attire and white shirt. On the right hand side of the colonel was sat a major in the Royal Marines and next to the major was a captain, also of the Royal Marines.

The entire room was ornate with very polished dark wood furniture, a mainly red and blue patterned carpet and a shining table. On the table in front of where the candidate would sit a long magic wand looking cylindrical piece had been strategically placed.

"Sit down Mister Gibson," the colonel cordially invited, "Now tell us why you wish to be an officer in Her Majesty's Royal Marines?"

JAMES-1966

His innards seemed to be self-destructing. The pit of his stomach was wallowing at the back of his throat, acid flowed as the anticipation and apprehension had long since formed an unholy alliance within the outer boundaries of his psyche. They were unashamedly swirling in a gargantuan vortex on the shoreline of his consciousness. James was on the verge of a serious accident in his trousers. The self-confidence, which he had held for so long in such high esteem, seemed to be under siege in this battle of wills. James drew deeply on his expensive Passing Cloud cigarette whilst awaiting Daniel to complete his formal interview with this panel of the Admiralty Interview Board.

He was the Honourable James Marchant, the next Earl of Wye. A member of the aristocracy albeit the middle echelons of that privileged club. Nonetheless, the 21-year-old candidate was by far the oldest of the group. James was totally aware that the maximum age for commissioned service stood at 23 years on the date of entry into the Corps.

The young man brushed with a phenomenon that he had not experienced since he was five. The momentous day when Emily had saved his life by bashing in the brains of the village pervert Barry Frost. The concept he experienced was simple envy, discomfort at others' abilities. James had first seen young Evan Morgan, the son of a coal miner from south Wales; go through the grinding actions of the examination treadmill. He mentally analysed the opposition.

Evan had stuttered a little in the first test, but improvements were on a rising curve until he appeared a natural part of the officer class. Next came the Scottish candidate, the cheerful David Moir from Edinburgh. Like his Welsh counterpart was grammar school educated but from a middle-class family, his father being an Advocate north of the border. Moir had stumbled a couple of times during the first phases of testing but had grown as the hours passed and now displayed the demeanour and confidence of a commissioned man.

The one contender that had literally taken all applicants by surprise was the Northumbrian lad, Daniel Gibson. The rich but strong accent had initially imparted to James of someone from a very working-class family. He had even felt surprised initially that Daniel had not applied to be in the enlisted ranks, in James' mind he had seemed to naturally belong within that fraternity.

However, within a matter of no more than two hours, the lyrical north-eastern inflection had refined. This now stood at a juncture whereby although the regional burr was retained, it was articulated with no small hint of authority, determination and faculty.

All of his friends would pass, James was sure, but he might not.

As he meandered deeper into his thoughts the petty officer shouted across the waiting room, "Mister Marchant, your turn next." It was the "crunch", time to face the men who would decide yeah or nay to a particular course of the path of his life. At least for the next 12 years and would have a direct bearing on the remainder of his allotted span on this world. He thought of the love of his life then walked forward.

EMILY-1966

Emily hopped out of the British Rail train at Hackney Downs station and followed the directions given her by Mister Crawley. These were to the "offices" of a client of dubious background. John Arthur Cooper, currently awaiting trial for offences which included theft and handling stolen goods. She circumspectly walked across Dalston Road, to Bodney Road and headed for Downs Park Road that straddled the actual Hackney Downs fields in London E8.

On the short train journey from Liverpool Street to Hackney Downs station Emily had scanned the notes and was reasonably conversant with the bulk of the case. The young lawyer moved along the main road before making a right turn. At that juncture she staggered into the very untidy shambles of a concrete paved yard. This area was stacked with old appliances, parts of vehicles and a plethora of bric-a-brac such as ornaments, broken toys and so forth. The clutter and disorder almost entirely covered the zone of Artie Cooper.

Over in the far southerly corner of this detritus bloated quadrangle stood a red brick building with a standard vermillion tiled roof. It was similar in size to her father's smithy back in Alvescot. Juxtaposed with this aesthetic, seemingly adventitious structure, were several much larger crumbling wooden edifices adorned with peeling paint. The 21-year-old guessed these were probably warehouses.

She was modestly attired in a very conservative blue suit with a knee length skirt and respectable jacket. To accompany this mode, she had donned a white modest blouse, dark brown stockings and almost flat heeled black shoes which matched her black brief case and hand bag.

The naturally golden hair was tied up on top of her head as she warily negotiated through the chaos about her. Emily prayed that she would not stand on any of the multitude of mounds of dogs' mess dispersed around the yard. A canine barked loudly followed a second later a medium sized man. The figure was aged about 45 and wore an old, filthy trilby hat with greasy unwashed grey hair protruding from it. His dress manner also included a grubby shirt with an even dirtier cravat around his neck and old brown corduroy trousers coupled with an equally as depreciated tweed jacket. The butt end of a "roll your own" cigarette dangled from his bottom lip

"Piss off!" The man grunted menacingly. "Whatever 'tis ya sellin' we don't want nothin'! Unless o' course it's what yer sit on."

"Excuse me! That is an insult!" Emily was equally as acerbic; "I have an appointment with Mister Cooper, Mister John Arthur Cooper. Could you please show me where he is?"

"Never 'eard of 'im," the unkempt man responded, "Now shove off."

"Listen." Emily persisted. "I have been sent here by Mister Gerald Crawley on a matter of extreme urgency. I need to see him, now can you fetch him, please!"

"Is that Mister Crawley the lawyer man?"

"The same one."

"Well Artie asked for the best guy 'e could get and yous is a fuckin' bird. Excuse me ma'am, but you is a woman so ya cannot be for Mister Crawley."

"Will you fucking well show me to him? Please!" Emily shouted, her fortitude having rapidly dissipated.

"Alright, keep yer 'air on Miss. I'm 'is site manager, Billy, Billy Parkins. I'll just go an' see if Mister Cooper is available."

Parkins opened the small green entrance door of the brick office and entered into the space beyond. In less than a minute he had reappeared and called over to Emily,

"Mister Cooper will see ya, Miss."

She skipped through the door of the brown brick and red roofed construction into a small vacant reception area. There stood a small polished walnut desk, secretarial swivel chair, a General Post Office telephone board and several grey standard metal filing cabinets each clearly labelled.

The oak door with gleaming brass handles opened into a spacious office with a recent and well vacuumed red patterned carpet, a large dark mahogany desk upon which stood a telephone and blotting pad. The office view, instead of facing the disorder of the outside yard looked onto the green expanse of Hackney Downs. The man sitting in the large leather armchair behind the desk was also, Emily deduced, about 45 but unlike Parkins was obviously someone who bathed and shaved daily. He was wearing an immaculate white shirt, spring armbands on the upper arm sleeve and dark blue tie with a golden tie pin, dark pinstripe trousers. The jacket to the suit was on a hangar on the wall behind his seat. The hair was well-groomed, brown, oiled and swept back with a hint of silver at the edges. Several portraits hung above the oak panelling affixed around the impressive room up to chest height, above which the walls had been painted with thick cream emulsion. The entire décor and tidiness of this office hit Emily in an instant; it was the complete antithesis of the debacle of filth and non-uniformity that was the exterior.

"I'm Artie Cooper, my man tells me ya 'ere t' 'elp me."

"I hope so, Mister Cooper. I'm Emily Wilkinson, a trainee barrister. Mister Crawley tells me we may have a good chance with your case and on reading the notes I tend to concur with his views. But before we talk, I am so curious. Why does your yard look like it has just been bombed and yet this office is absolutely spick and span?"

Artie loudly chuckled. "Yes Miss Wilkinson. The thing is, the yard's run by Billy. He couldn't organise a piss up in a brewery if ya excuses me

French, Miss. This little office, fact the whole place's looked after at times by me daughter, Dorothy. She's like 'er late mum was, tidy an' organised like. Dot works f' me part time. She's at school right now. But less o' this Miss, would ya likes a fag?"

The neat figure stood up, offered Emily an Embassy tipped cigarette from a packet on the desk, lit it for her then sat back down.

"Alright Mister Cooper--."

"Call me Artie, Miss, an' I'll call ya Emily. Now Janice, Janice McCready, me assistant, she's out at the shops right now; we'll 'ave a coffee when she gets back. Right now, ain't never seen a girl, beg ya pardon, a young lady, bein' a lawyer and it's a bit weird but long as ya does the job, ain't no difference to me. Alright?"

"That is perfectly alright Mister Cooper. Shall we discuss your case as it is only two weeks until the trial starts?"

PHILIPPA-1966

Rebecca rolled out of the king size double bed in which Tom Marchant was dozing.

"Becky, why the rush to get up? It's still very early."

"Lady Philippa an' her best pals is comin' down for the summer ball season, My Lord. So, no more hanky panky 'til she goes back to Wye Hall. It's no good us doin' it anywhere else."

Tom sat up in bed and accepted a cup of tea Becky had just brewed and then lit a Capstan full strength cigarette.

"Beck." The earl adopted a hang dog-pleading face.

"No, My Lord, Lady Philippa will know. She's not daft and 'as already asked me if I fancies you."

"Really?" Tom grinned and sat up even further as Rebecca washed in the adjoining bathroom.

"It's no laughin' matter, My Lord." Rebecca scowled as she rolled on her stockings. "I'll keep out of ya way, and the Lady Philippa will 'opefully be none the wiser."

"I'm sure she would never guess."

"My Lord, ya 'ave no idea what a bright girl she is, she'd know, and it might slip out to 'er ladyship. If that 'appened I'd be out of a job 'long with me 'husband. Her ladyship 'as the last word, My Lord, and you knows that too."

No reply came, merely a wry smile indicating consensus. Rebecca slipped into her black dress uniform and white pinafore and then fastened the white lace trim onto her head.

"I'm off now, My Lord. Lady Philippa will be 'ere soon and Mister Jenkins will be expectin' me to 'elp with the breakfasts."

She kissed Tom momentarily on the lips then doubled off before anyone was in the area.

The Austin Mini pulled into the very exclusive mews behind the Sloane Square house.

The newly qualified driver, Philippa, had brought with her Judith Parkhouse and Pat Laidlaw.

She turned off the engine as Christine, driving a Bentley T1, and her father, Nile Vickers, came to a stop immediately afterwards outside the main entrance. Nile, tall, slim and middle aged, had been coerced into driving up to London as the many bags and suitcases of clothing, shoes and makeup for the four teenage girls would never have fitted into Philippa's Mini Car.

Rebecca and Mister Jenkins were followed by the bespectacled brown-haired footman, Mark Lowney, and the small, plump new maid, Barbara Elliot.

"Lady Philippa," Rebecca called out as they all advanced on the Bentley to retrieve a veritable mountain of suitcases, gown holders, hat boxes, shoe boxes and an assortment of other storage trunks and cartons, "I see you've passed ya drivin' test."

Philippa gave Rebecca a huge hug and before replying.

"Yes, I did. I told the examiner I was Lady Philippa Marchant and smiled at the old boy. I think that's why he passed me."

"No, you's a great driver, Lady Philippa."

"Lady Philippa, to where would you wish your luggage and accoutrements be conveyed?" Jenkins was not about to have his authority diminished by a female servant, even one with a flawless pedigree as Rebecca.

"Mister Jenkins, I apologise. Would you and your staff take them to the main upstairs suite? Thank you."

Philippa next ran to and hugged her father. Tom followed by extending an invitation to Niles to join him for lunch at his club.

"Daddy, we are here for a few weeks. Will you be staying?"

"Only for a few days, Pip. Then Rebecca and I will have to return to Oxfordshire. As you are fully aware, Mama is not that tolerant. Now you and the girls get settled in, Mister Jenkins and the staff will give you a good lunch once you are ready. Meanwhile I am stepping out over to the club with Mister Vickers."

"That's fine, Daddy. We may see you later. We are off to the Duchess of Nottingham's party tonight, so we shall need to prepare."

The girls walked into the house chatting away as the servants, overtly at least, followed them stoically and cheerfully with the various items of luggage.

Philippa was sipping her flute of champagne trying to catch up with the London gossip, rife at this society ball. Christine, Pat and Judith had taken off on a mission to charm some boys with whom they had taken a shine. Philippa offered to pass on this expedition, as there were the only three cute dudes still available.

In reality the young men that her best friends were hoping to make out with stood well below acceptability on Philippa's personal benchmark. Her own personal gold standard when it came to fraternisation with the opposite sex. Both Philippa and James owned their own houses in secluded areas of the Vale of White Horse to the south of Wye Hall. A boy without his own property under normal circumstances was not worth even being introduced to. Nonetheless, there were exceptions but the debutante esteemed on this occasion no such grounds were in situ.

Julian owned such an abode. He also possessed a sports car, a massive wardrobe and boasted a personal bank balance of well over 2000 pounds.

However, and thankfully, Philippa mused, Julian was not present. He was in Brisbane or somewhere working in the Australian civil service having been seconded from the United Kingdom Commonwealth Office. He was procuring something or other for the Australian Army in South Vietnam.

Philippa was elegantly attired. She donned a gold lame full length dress, black handbag with her dark flame hued hair hanging down in a long Christine Shrimpton style. Around her neck was placed a string of pearls that Grandmama Rathbone had bequeathed to her when she had turned 12. The beautiful socialite was only 18 yet had already, like so many of her aristocratic friends, regularly frequented the pages of "Vogue", "Vanity Fair" and "Woman's Own". All such publications had wildly speculated over the distinct possibility that the Earl and Countess of Wye may soon be announcing the engagement of their daughter. A possible suitor regularly mentioned was the Honourable Julian Lee-Watersby. The young woman knocked back her glass of champagne, took another from the tray of a passing maid. She lit a cigarette.

Philippa could feel the glow of the alcohol gliding through her system.

Lady Elmira Bernard, eldest daughter of the Duke and Duchess of Nottingham approached the area at the foot of the stairs where Philippa stood. She was attired in an amethyst coloured, backless evening gown.

In the adjoining ballroom, the master of ceremonies with the performing group had just announced that they would next play a song written by Mick Jagger and Keith Richards, now a hit for Chris Farlowe, "Out of Time".

"Philippa." Elmira kissed her on the cheeks.

"Elmira." Philippa drew on her cigarette. "Such a great ball, such a gas."

"Of course, it is darling. Only the great and the good, well perhaps not always the good, but the crème de la crème of society, come to my parties. Philippa, you look a little as if you have been discarded into the dumps. Pray what irks you?"

Philippa drew thoughtfully on her cigarette.

"To be quite honest with you, Elmira, I do not want to get married to Julian. I am looking for a substitute, as the Who would say, for him."

"Julian is as interesting as a dry piece of cardboard. I suggest we take care of your needs."

"That sounds exciting Elmira, how do you effect such a strategy?"

A pair of young women approached from the proximate kitchen where the temporary bar was situated. Philippa was well acquainted with both trendy, well-heeled females. The girl to the left was Lady Kinsey Maple. She stood five feet three inches tall and wore a silver green Normal Hartnell creation. Kinsey was the becoming, red headed daughter of the Earl and Countess of Sawbridgeworth. She was accompanied by, almost attached to Philippa pondered, the blonde, maroon decked Lady Caroline Feversham. Caroline's parents being the very rich and influential Earl and Countess of Bamburgh.

The band began to play the haunting, Eastern influenced, recent hit by the Yardbirds, "Over Under Sideways Down".

"You see Philippa." Elmira smirked, the other two grinned in unison. "We can help you with your problem. However, one small, very tiny caveat. You have to lose those so-called friends you brought with you. They are not with due standing to belong within our circle. I take it you and I understand each other?"

JAMES-1966

The day seemed like a normal, fine, summer's morning. The fields and woods around Wye Hall appeared to buzz with a greater intensity of life and activity. A gentle, dazzling sun stroked the cornfields and cattle ruminating in the rolling, verdant meadows. The gold and black forms of nectar seeking bees added their own genre of nature's music to the idyllic scene.

James was in a positive frame of outlook as he entered the dining room. This soon reverted to the mild attacks of anxiety the young man had experienced of late.

Thankfully, he thought, Rebecca was back from the London house. It was a venue to which she seemed to have been seconded on a regular basis. Accordingly, why had his father not appointed a full-time maid in London? This action would spare his most revered servant of all time from bearing the aggravation of perpetually being separated from her husband to assist the staff in Sloane Square. Nonetheless, Becky had returned and naturally the kitchen fare was once again top of the range. That was in no way meant to demean Mrs. Cromer, James mused. Nonetheless, her culinary creativity had somewhat flat lined over the last decade. Now she was 71 it lacked a certain zing, blitheness and ebullience, a little zest, something more than slightly above school lunch standard. The charming elderly lady was reluctant to retire and his father would never coerce Mrs Cromer out of the door.

In the dining room, James smiled as he helped himself to the brilliant breakfast menu. The choices that day were devilled kidneys, local smoked bacon, grilled farm sausages, sautéed tomatoes, baked mushrooms, poached eggs, toast, orange juice and that wondrous percolated coffee that even American guests to Wye Hall commented positively on. Emily was doing well in her job as a trainee barrister in London and James missed her. He desperately yearned for sex but other matters at that exact point in time held even more prominence than intimacy with his adored lover. She would be home for the weekend on Friday night but even this great anticipatory event did not capitalise his concentration. At least not every second of it. The young aristocrat had to find something to do, a respectable activity that would generate an acceptable level of income. It was well over two weeks since he had bidden farewell to his roommates at HMS Sultan. The laughing Scot with a baby face, David Moir, the garrulous Welsh lad from the Valleys, Evan Morgan, and that serious but extremely competent Northumbrian, Daniel Gibson. The young graduate had forged a bond, albeit for a short expanse of time. This connection was formed of mutual respect. It was a support group that even at this stage in his life he was convinced could never be replicated in a run of the mill job or even a high-flying career.

"I must have failed." James stared at his father who was totally immersed in the Daily Telegraph. "How so?" Tom Marchant looked up briefly, sipped his breakfast cup of tea then turned back to his newspaper.

"I've not heard from the Admiralty about the results of my AIB interview."

"It's the Royal Navy, James, not a business corporation. Would you like me to ring them and find out for you? They do not dash out appointment letters. Not hearing for a while could mean the precise opposite to your postulation."

"No thank you, Papa. If I do not hear from them today I shall ring them myself."

"Lord Marchant, sir." Hodges the butler came into the dining room and addressed James.

"Yes, Hodges, what is it?"

"There is a telephone call for Your Lordship. A Scottish gentleman by the name of Mister Moir." James immediately bolted from his seat and ran into the entrance hallway were the telephone table stood.

"Yes, David," he nervously enquired into the telephone mouthpiece.

"I passed," the accented voice at the other end of the phone almost shouted, "I just received the letter. Have ye passed James?"

"Not received any letter," James divulged almost embarrassingly, "Have any of the others passed?"

"I haven't rung any of them yet. Let me know when you get your offer letter."

"If I do," James sulked.

"Ye will ye silly bugger. You, Evan the Taffy and Dan the Man are naturals, we all could tell. Must rush Jimmy boy. I'll speak to ye soon. Bye for now."

"Bye," James sheepishly responded and instantly David was gone.

As James lightly replaced the receiver Hodges the butler walked over to him carrying a silver salver upon which a white envelope addressed to him was placed.

"For you, Your Lordship."

"Thank you, Mister Hodges." James nervously took the letter and returned to the dining room, placed the slim packet on the table nearby then recommenced eating his breakfast.

"Well?" Louise Marchant looked over to James as Rebecca poured her coffee.

"Well what, Mama?"

"Don't act like a poltroon, James." Louise pointed at the envelope. "Open it and let us know. It was after all your career choice. It was not one that I would have preferred for you so at least you can enlighten us as to the result of your interview."

James apprehensively took hold of the piece of stationery, nervously sliced the envelope, withdrew the correspondence. He stared vacantly for a moment before beaming jubilantly.

DANIEL-1966

Jackie, "Little" Jackie and Daniel Gibson, all ably assisted by ten-year-old Debbie Gibson, had been labouring on the farm since the early hours.

The multitude of tasks included milking the herd of Jersey cows, delivering the subsequent churns to the pickup point of the Milk Marketing Board and repairing brickwork and a gate in the byre while afterwards collecting all the hen's eggs from the laying boxes in the chicken coop.

They sat at the large table on the kitchen where Daisy Gibson poured them each a huge mug of tea and served out large portions of fried eggs, bacon, sausage, fried bread and fried tomatoes.

Daisy had heard the daily sound of the red van pulling up outside the farmhouse, so she walked outside to collect the post. One item she knew would be the daily newspaper, the Newcastle Journal, which Jackie had sent by mail to save him having to drive to the village.

"Alreet Alfie." She greeted the Royal Mail van driver, the short and plump Alfie Allen.

"Aye Daisy, Ah've got Jackie's paper here an' there's two letters for ya boy."

"Which one, Alfie?" She took the envelopes, looked at the name then smiled at the postman.

"See ya tomorra Alfie."

"Dan!" Daisy walked back into the kitchen. The sound of the van driving off was still audible.

"Yes, Mum," Daniel grunted as he stuffed his face with a whole rasher of bacon.

"There's two letters for ya! One hand written and one from the Navy."

Daniel opened the envelope that had blue ink script on the address side.

"Oh crap!" Daniel exclaimed, "Seems like Evan Morgan didn't get a commission in the Royal Marines. Says he's gonna try the Army, the Parachute Regiment."

"Well did ye, Daniel Gibson? Ya shootin' ya mooth off aboot other folks. How did you do?" Daisy handed her son the metal letter opener kept permanently on the sideboard in the kitchen for her husband to tidily open letters. With a single slice the envelope was slashed and the official missive within carefully removed.

Daniel glanced over it and for 30 seconds or so said nothing.

"Well! Dan 'ave ye got in or not?"

"Yes, Ah've got in!" Daniel yelled out then cheered as did Little Jackie and a bemused but excited Debbie. "When d'ya go?" Jackie pressed.

"Ah've been offered a commission and Ah'll start as a second lieutenant. Ah have to report to somewhere called the Royal Marines Barracks at Deal which is down in Kent. That'll be on the first of October where Ah'll go through four weeks basic trainin' of drill and gym.

Providin' Ah'm successful wi' that then Ah'll go to somewhere called the Commando Trainin' Centre at Lympstone in Devon for six months tactical and officer trainin'."

"Best get down to Carol an' give 'er th' good news," Jackie winked at Daniel.

"Congratulations my brave warrior, my Lochinvar, Prince of Light, slayer of evil foes and defender of damsels in distress. Especially those in heat and in dire need of a fuck. Like me."

"Carol." Daniel squeezed her hand as they walked along the "big" shore at Amble in the semi light of a late summer's evening. "You're incorrigible."

"What am I supposed to do while you are away serving Her Majesty? How often can you come home?"

"Six times a year that they'll pay for a first-class rail warrant to come home. Anymore, if Ah've got permission, Ah'll have t' pay for me self."

"You'll have a wonderful time in the officers' mess, drinking pink gins and port. You will of course have to speak correct English. Just like when you had first returned from your interview but soon descended back into your broad Northumbrian twang. It's nice and quiet here and dark so I am going to take off my knickers and we can have a celebratory shag."

EMILY-1966

The entire courtroom had their eyes fixed on Emily. The black gown and the wig combined with a beautiful countenance formed a vision that would have stood its own against any of the current glamour models as well as female pop and movie stars of 1966.

Regina versus Cooper was being held in Courtroom Number 14. It was one of 18 such palaces of justice within the awe inspiring Central

Criminal Court of England and Wales better known to most as The Old Bailey. The stern looking judge, Mister Justice Worsthorne, was wearing the obligatory red gown and white horsehair wig. The pale face seemed to be permanently immersed in his notes until he discerned something that grabbed his attention.

The team for the Crown Prosecution Service of three lawyers was led by Mister Rodney Pope QC who had brought two trainees to act as assistants. Pope, a small, ugly, ruddy faced serious looking individual was perpetually scowling at Emily. This was a minor irritation and certainly deliberate provocation that she wisely chose to totally ignore.

Mister Gerald Crawley QC headed the two-person team for the defence along with his assistant, Emily Wilkinson LLB. The court clerk, a tall distinguished figure by the name of Thomas Arkwright LLB, from Yorkshire, sat in front of the judge. Arkwright was next to the usher and court stenographer who was busy typing every word uttered in that brown oak panelled chamber.

The figures of each of the legal personnel were at their allocated tables, all being attired in black gowns and smaller sized wigs. The eleven men and one woman of the jury, all being obligatory property owners, sat in their box. Their eyes moving between the judge, the accused in the dock, John Arthur Cooper, and the figure of Emily who had begun to cross examine Detective Constable Neil Heathcock. The prosecution through Pope had objected to her initial line of questioning, the judge appeared to agree then advised Emily to "Carry on."

The charges were handling stolen goods and attempting to gain money by menaces.

The 28-year-old sallow looking police officer was dressed in a crumpled green suit, which looked to Emily as if it had come from a charity shop. The cream shirt had not been washed or ironed for some time and the red tie was not colour co-ordinated. The detective constable's eyes were pink as if he had consumed a large amount of alcohol the previous night. The greasy brown hair was badly combed, and he held his notes in an unsteady fashion.

"Detective Constable Heathcock." Emily looked uneasily at Crawley who smiled reassuringly then nodded for her to continue. "May I remind you that you are under oath?"

"Of course, I know that."

"Then are you satisfied that you and DC Baxter did a thorough and true investigation of the allegations made against my client?"

"What on earth d'ya think we did?"

"Just answer the question, detective constable. Are all details a true and accurate record of the findings of your investigation?"

Heathcock began to squirm on his wooden witness box chair. "I've told ya that they are."

"I have a copy of your account of the search of my clients residence and also that of DC Baxter whom Mister Crawley has already cross examined under oath so I ask you again, are you satisfied that your dated and signed notes of my client are a true and accurate ---?"

"My Lord, I object." Pope jumped up which startled the judge. "Miss Wilkinson is covering ground already done by her senior."

"I am not sure what is irking you, Mister Pope. Nonetheless, I tend to agree it is being laboured a tad. Miss Wilkinson, please get to the point. It is already after two in the afternoon and we need to press on. Do you not agree?"

"I am about to reach the crux of the matter if that pleases My Lord." Emily bowed slightly to Judge Worsthorne who nodded in response.

"Very well, but waste no time, Miss Wilkinson. Time is money in this profession."

"I understand, My Lord." Emily turned again to DC Heathcock. "Detective, I have studied in detail both the testimony of DC Baxter and the notes you offered as evidence against my client. And you agree that your statement and that of DC Baxter are a true representation of the facts relevant to the case against my client?"

"I've already said so." The policeman on the witness stand was becoming visibly and increasingly aggravated.

"Then Detective Constable Heathcock, I shall make some observations from your joint testimonies if I may, bearing in mind you have already stated under oath that these bodies of evidence are totally and irrefutably veritable in all aspects."

Emily casually flicked through some pages of her notes, resting on the polished table.

"Detective Constable, let me draw your attention to page three of your case notes, you and the jury have a copy. In the second paragraph, relating to the search of my client's residence, where you say and I quote; "we checked through the sideboard in Mister Cooper's lounge and in the left hand top draw we found a note giving details of individuals Mister Cooper was extorting money from with the threat of violence. In the lower draw we found jewellery, a Kodak camera, a Sekonda watch, and various other items taken from a house the previous week. That is accurate, as you have stated. Yes?"

"My Lord, the counsel for the defence is unduly harassing the witness." Rodney Pope was also becoming nervous.

"It is the adversarial nature of our judicial system, Mister Pope. Miss Wilkinson please continue with a small eye on the time."

"Thank you, My Lord. Detective Constable, I shall move to the point forthwith. The details you have provided, relating to a note, which anyone could have written, and the items you claim to have found do not correspond with those of your colleague, Detective Constable Baxter. He mentions a sheet of paper, but it relates to items allegedly stolen, and the alleged stolen goods he claims were in the lower drawer of the same sideboard and the watch was an Omega, he stated, not a Sekonda. The camera DC Baxter had down as a Canon not a Kodak as you stated. I can recite all the discrepancies in your statements. However, even with these examples it is blatantly obvious, Detective Constable, that you two are so incompetent that you could not even get your stories to correlate even when they were pure fiction! I put it to you DC Heathcock that you are a corrupt policeman and had been harassing my client for some years as he had not joined in your little club of likeminded folk who oversee the East End. I put it to you that you planted the items in my clients house being told that a female trainee would be on the defence team so it will be a pushover, no need to cross the eyes and dot the tees. I put it to the jury that this is an amateur attempt to frame my client for personal revenge and gain. How do you respond detective?"

"You lyin' bitch, it's not true. We didn't stitch up Artie Cooper."

"Detective Heathcock!" Mister Justice Worsthorne intervened, "You will reply to counsel's question, any further such outbursts and I shall hold you in contempt of court, judging by the apparent revelations recently unearthed by Miss Wilkinson I would suggest that that may be the least of your worries."

"No further questions, My Lord."

"Foreman of the jury, have you reached a verdict?" The solid intonations of Mister Arkwright boomed across Courtroom number fourteen.

"We have, My Lord," the spokesman for the jurors responded. The usher of the court took the paper upon which the verdict was written. He handed the slip to the judge who remained poker face as he opened the sheet. "And are you all agreed?"

"We are, My Lord."

"In the first count, one of attempting to extort money by menaces, how do you find, guilty or not guilty?"

"Not guilty, My Lord," the foreman of the jury stood erect and motionless as a gasp of incredulity radiated around the court.

"In the second count, handling stolen goods, how do you find?"

There was a pregnant silence, which lasted but two seconds.

"Not guilty, My Lord."

The court erupted into a cacophony of cheering and the judge brought his gavel down shouting, "Order! Order!" after which silence returned to the courtroom.

"Mister Cooper, you have been found innocent by a jury of your peers and are therefore free to go. Miss Wilkinson, congratulations on a successful defence of your client."

"Thank you, My Lord."

Gerald, Emily and Artie Cooper returned to the chambers to finalise the all administrative matters appertaining to the case.

Emily went to her desk while in Gerald's opulent office, a whiskey was handed to Artie and he sat a leather-bound chair smoking a Capstan Full Strength cigarette.

"Thanks, Mister Crawley. I'll only be a minute, I'm expected at th' Three Sisters pub soon for celebrations. You're both cordially invited of course, but I wanted a chat away from th' boys.

A bit private away from th' family, ya know like. I'll get on the old dog and bone when I wants 'em to pick me up."

"That's fine Artie. Thank you for the invitation." Gerald lit up a Benson and Hedges cigarette. "But I think Emily and I will have to pass on your invite. We both have a lot of work to do."

"I understands Mister Crawley," Artie shuffled in his pocket and handed an envelope to an intrigued Gerald. The lawyer gawped in amazement at the size of the cheque therein.

"Artie, this is way more than the fee we agreed. After the verdict Artie, everyone will be keeping an eye on you, including the Inland Revenue. And the Metropolitan Police will be watching every single thing you do from now on. Especially after those two cops were arrested."

"I knows Mister Crawley. All you have to do is type me out another invoice an' we'll be strictly legit."

"This is 9,000 pounds Artie. Twice what we agreed."

"I know Mister Crawley, but we never expected t' get a not guilty. Did we?"

"We knew it would be hard, Artie." Gerald confessed. "But there was always hope."

"Beggin' ya pardon, Mister Crawley, but that's shit, ya knows it, we all knows it. It took the eyes an' brains of a wet behind the ears little girl lawyer to upset the stitch up. I got off, and a lot of work'll be comin' your way Mister Crawley, thanks to that little girl you 'ad defendin' me. One part of that, a grand, that's for Miss Wilkinson. A bonus, extra to 'er pay and more. I'll keep your chambers in work, good work, for ten years or more."

"That's good of you Artie, Emily will have to pay tax on the 1000 but even my accounts knowledge is good enough to get her a grand bonus, all of it, into her salary cheque."

"Good, if ya don't mind Mister Crawley, I'd like a quick word wiv Emily. Just a quick thank you. You and me knows it wuz 'er what swayed the jury, just like you an' me 'll 'ave to take care of 'er, Mister Crawley. A lot o' filth out there 'll be after 'er hide. She's family now, she kept me on the outside of Brixton nick. I'd 'ave got 15 years at least. That means a lot, she's gonna needs watchin'. She's a girl and a girl that upset the filth; she'll need lots o' watchin'."

"I'd love to tutor your daughter, Mister Cooper." Emily smiled endearingly. "English Law is an interesting subject, it would be no trouble. She'll need to get three good A level passes, all at least at grade B."

"We knows that Miss, an' I'll pay ya five quid an hour."

"You could get a university professor for less than that, Mister Cooper."

"Don't want one, want you, Miss. And worry not, it'll all be on the books, strictly legit."

Chapter Nine

NARRATOR

The journey of any tale is strewn with the detritus of lost loves, broken dreams, promises cast asunder and a general yet regular discomfort in the manner in which the universe oft tends to treat our lives so shabbily. Was it not in the Bible, the Old Testament, perhaps? "There is a time for everything-And a season for everything" The evolution of our heroes and heroines gains momentum and I recall the tales my father would recount of adventures, incidents and love long before I made an appearance into this world. Perhaps some of my relatives, close and distant may have the faculty to corroborate these tales. None would dispute they are true, many stranger than fiction, as authentic and genuine as any recounted. The cast of my tale are like the lyrics of that stirring melody, my father's old school song, "I Vow to Thee My Country"- "her shining bounds increase," and so they do. Some enter the stage whilst others exit. Some leave forever but nonetheless they have graced its confines. They listen, affixed to the monologue and thus far all have remained awake, that in itself is no mean achievement.

DANESH AND KELLY

"Doctor Marston, Keely." Kelly looked up at the woman from the other dimension as they sat enjoying tea in the Lisher Hospital cafeteria. As per the norm it seemed somewhat odd. The sensation was as if she was gazing into a mirror. They were dressed in identical attire, even down to the same blue cotton blouses, woollen navy skirts and golden silk shawls.

"Yes."

"Have you travelled yet to my universe? You 've done a lot of this inter-dimensional exploring yet I have never seen you back in my own world."

"Dear Kelly, you and I are not merely doubles, doppelgangers, so much so I have told the nurses in E and A that you are my twin sister. But to respond to your question, no. We can only travel one way, so far as Professor Garside has concluded in his tests. Rather like a set of doors on a huge corridor on the left and right of where you are standing. Because of the mechanics of the Cosmos we can only go through those on the left, all of us. Unfortunately, as your world is to the right of that road, so to speak, I am unable to go there."

"Such a pity." Kelly sipped her tea. It tasted the identical to that on her own world. "Are we the same, I mean DNA. Do we have the same DNA? Do you have the results of the blood sample I gave you on my last visit?"

"Yes. And in the world I can travel to, Professor Garside and I have studied our alter egos but as yet have not made contact. Therefore, the results I can share relate only to two separate parallel worlds. But there is nothing to suggest it may differ elsewhere."

"Keely, you are worse than Professor Gideon for being discursive and voluble. Did you test our respective blood samples?"

Doctor Marston raked through her handbag and withdrew an official looking sheet of paper. She handed it to Kelly.

"See, you do not need to be a doctor to conclude that according to that deoxyribonucleic acid test--."

"No need to be a smart arse, Keely, we all know what DNA stands for. Now tell me the result."

"We are not merely related, we are more than identical twins. Our respective DNAs are an exact match."

"And we have another sister, probably with the same DNA, in the universe you can access?"

"Doctor Aresti, Kelly, it is more than being a sister or an identical twin. For all intents and purposes, we are the same people."

"When do you intend to make contact with our other being in the world you visit?"

"There are some timing differences in that world, Garside is working on them."

Kelly was more than a little intrigued.

Keely sipped her tea, gazed around the near empty cafeteria before completing her statement.

"Our other sister, if you like, she has not yet qualified as a doctor. At least not in the time my version of your PADIT can transport me there. That is supposed to be a constant. The time I mean. Although the time continuum does not line up exactly, it is proximate but not exact."

"Keely, according to my professor, there could be differences of up to 40 years."

"I think not, Kelly. In adjoining universes, the mathematics indicates only a few years, five or six at the most. If your machine computer manages such a large overlap then you are not merely travelling through one dimension to another, but two at least. You are also a Cosmonaut in time. I would love to compare notes, can we?"

"Despite the Laws of Physics that may deter, has the idea of travelling to my universe ever taken your fancy?"

"Of course. How could it not?"

"Well Keely, I shall return to my indefatigable professor and see if he can resolve this Cosmological conundrum."

Danesh was in the laboratory. The professor was smoking a Capstan Full Strength cigarette instead of his normal briar pipe. The second PADIT machine, a far more advanced version than the prototype, was under construction. This vehicle was much larger. It had an internal volume equivalent to an RV or campervan as opposed to a sports car. It was still capable of reshaping into an object with a much less bulky capacity. The logic behind such a project was simple. Danesh wished to transport objects or people willing to travel from their own universes to his own to compare and enhance the already substantial relevant knowledge he boasted.

The whirring sound of PADIT 1 was heard in the landing area adjacent to the lab.

A few minutes later, Kelly marched buoyantly into the lab.

"Doctor Aresti, have you enjoyed your cosmic travel?"

She threw her arms around the older man's neck.

"Yes, but I have a riddle for you. If you solve it you will have a double fucks ration for the next month."

"That sounds intriguing. What is it?"

"Professor, your counterpart in the parallel world to which I travel to maintains that we, the humans, irrespective of our means of conveyance, can only voyage to the next dimension down from us. Those living on those worlds are unable to journey to our world. Can you resolve?"

"There are terrible potential dangers therein, many. Notwithstanding, I believe I may have found a prudent course to navigate these stormy waters."

PHILIPPA-JANUARY 1967

"I'm sorry," the voice at the other end of the phone assertively uttered, "You are not on the guest list and Lady Philippa is not available to speak to you. Good day."

"The bitch," Judith sighed almost in tears, "All the years we've supported that cow, now that she is going to Cambridge in September to do her medical thing--."

"An MB BChir," Pat interjected.

"Whatever, she doesn't want anything to do with us. The bitch."

"Ever since that party in London! Lady snotty nosed Barnard starting chatting to her and we are suddenly beneath her social standing." Christine put on the single, "I'm A Believer" by the Monkees.

"I have no idea why you two are so grumpy about this." Pat lit a cigarette than sat on Judith's bed. "We get invited to loads of parties. We're all going to the same university, the same one as Lady Philippa the snob and we'll all meet nice new folks. What's the big deal? If you recall we left Pip on her own and went off chasing those nice bits of talent at the party."

"It's so not nice though. It's pretty grotty to do that to her friends." Judith was obviously vexed.

"We were her friends, and now we're not. Live with it ladies. We'll have many new chums at Oxford and medicine is a subject full of hunky men." Pat inhaled before changing the record to "Night of Fear" by The Move.

"It's still a beastly thing to do." Christine gazed at herself in the mirror. "Do you think I need my hair styled, like Twiggy?"

"All I can say is no to your hair, and someday, I think Pip will want us back as friends."

"Why Pat?" Judith looked up.

"Lady snotty nose Elmira, she is claiming to be looking for a beau for Philippa. The truth is, so my grapevine tells me, she is in cahoots with Julian farty arse. What Lady Elmira "I wear no knickers" Barnard is actually up to is monkey business. This may or may not include that upwardly mobile and certainly not handsome twat, Lee-Watersby. Currently away in the antipodes."

"Ye gods." The others sharply inhaled.

"Such an exquisite party you have organised, Philippa." Louise Marchant smiled with overtly unabashed approval.

Wye Hall was buzzing; it was THE place to be. Where all the "In" folk from London and the Home Counties would consider committing murder simply to acquire an invitation.

The feverish vogue was enhanced to an even loftier tier of dizzy heights and addictive potency when the "Woman's Own", "Cosmopolitan" and "Vanity Fair" magazines were reporting almost weekly the exploits and gossip relating to Lady Philippa Marchant. These reports always included her three, albeit recent, close friends, Lady Elmira Barnard, Lady Kinsey Maple and Lady Caroline Feversham.

The band began to play the Tom Jones hit, "The Green Green Grass of home."

"Yes, Mama, these are cool and trendy folk. Of course, with the appropriate pedigrees."

"I knew you would learn eventually. Your rebellious traits were a normal part of growing up."

"I am sure you are correct, Mama, Elmira, Kinsey and Caroline are superlative company. We really have a ball together."

"Yes, darling, but remember you can have fun but be very discreet. Do nothing that will ruin your chances with Julian. He will return in the summer."

"Mama, I think Julian may want me to either leave university or take another degree course. That I do not want to do."

"You are a woman Philippa. The man takes the lead, you must follow."

Stephen Grenfell

JAMES-JANUARY 1967

The historical Old Red Lion pub on High Holborn in the West End was lively. Although so soon after New Year's Eve the clientele was probably still a tad the worse for wear. The establishment was not only relatively luxuriant but also an historical hostelry. It was claimed to be where the exhumed body bodies of Oliver Cromwell, Henry Ireton and John Bradshaw had been put on display back in the 17th Century after the English Civil War.

The weather was cold and miserable outside as three young women and three almost analogous young men sat and conversed.

James and Emily sat very close, holding hands. He was in his olive Royal Marines Lovat uniform, she wore a red miniskirt, dark brown tights, black leather coat and black boots.

Second Lieutenant David Moir from Edinburgh was attempting to strike up a close relationship with Gloria Van der Staay. The tall, blonde half Dutch beauty. Gloria was one of two old university friends of Emily who were present. The two seemed to be enjoying good chemistry as Gloria's dark tights, short blue skirt, tight woollen cardigan and black shoes were playing havoc with the raging hormones of the young Royal Marines' officer. The other young woman was Jacqui Rosenthal. A 21-year-old lawyer from Golders Green in north London who appeared to be suffering from a severe bout of ennui. Jacquie was not in the least interested in or attracted to the self-invited Northern Irishman, Toby Flynn. He was downing pints of Guinness as if the drink was about to be abolished, in between clumsily attempting to enrapture and woo the recent graduate.

"Hey General Marchant," Toby grunted in a slurry Northern Irish brogue.

"Yes you Paddy git?" James responded before giving Emily a snap kiss.

"When are ye off to subjugate th' poor oppressed Catholics of north of the border in Ireland."

"Well," James smiled, "I'm sure as soon as you lot start being a nuisance again we'll have to put you well and truly in your place."

"We'll have to put you in your place," Toby mimicked the accent that defined the Marchant family, "Well, I'll tell ya somethin' ya posh English prat. The day Lord Fauntleroy, you, an' Davie the posh bagpiper come to sort out the Republicans of Ireland will be the day you'll regret. We'll kick the shit out of ye all, Marines included."

"Aye, Toby, ye 're sufficiently well-read to know the Frances Hodgson Burnett character, but I think the Guinness is burning' oot ya brain cells because ya talking a load of bollocks." David was long since bored with Toby. "I'd keep oot of politics and try an' impress Jacqui. She looks pretty bored to me."

"I'm tired." Jacqui stood up and slipped on her coat. She kissed Emily and Gloria on the cheek. "I'll see you girls tomorrow night at your flat Emm. You have volumes to impart about your recent case and part time job working for a shady character. Goodnight James, goodnight David and goodnight, er-you."

She cast Toby an icy glance then marched off out of the pub, hailed a taxi and was promptly off back to Golders Green. The others stood up.

"We're off, Toby," James announced assisting Emily into her overcoat before putting on his RM issue topcoat, "I'll give you a ring next time we're in town. Or we might be posted to Belfast. There are a lot of garrisons in the province."

"Come over General, we Irish will show ya a thing or two. That's a promise."

Gloria slipped her hand into David's and the foursome began to leave.

"I look forward to it Toby, try to stay sober the next time we meet up."

"Fuck you, Lord Fuck Face and fuck you ye fuckin' Scottish twat, lettin' the Celtic brotherhood down."

"Toby, you were such a comedian at university. Now you are becoming such a drag," James grinned and left Flynn to down his Guinness.

"Ah'll show ye Lord Fucking Arsehole, Ah will, just ye wait an' see."

A small, pale figure in the shadows was well content with the evening thus far.

"I think your pal was a wee bit intoxicated." The irony was prominent in David's voice as the four of them walked briskly towards Red Lion Street and Emily's, hopefully, warm flat.

"He was such a laugh at Oxford, now he's just a piss head, " James dryly commented, "He could, and probably still can if he wants to, mix in with all people, He's no duck egg, has an MA in political science but he can be such a nincompoop when he chooses and that seems to be most of the time."

"He can actually be a gentleman when the mood takes him," Emily joined in as they picked up the walking pace, "a charming guy, full of the Irish blarney as they say. I would certainly never wish to make an enemy of him."

"This is such a cool pad you have, Emm," Gloria was admiring the décor of the single bedroom flat, "It's so well done out and you have such tasteful furniture."

James opened a bottle of claret as they all sat around the coal gas fire in the lounge. David and Gloria shared an armchair, she on his knee, whilst James and Emily took the small couch.

"Yes, " Emily handed over two full glasses of the red wine which David placed on coasters, situated on the nearby coffee table, "It helps to have a doting father who loves DIY and wants an excuse to visit. He decorated the place, tiled the bathroom and kitchen and fitted the kitchen cupboards."

"So chic, I see you have a brand new cooker, washing machine, TV, radio/record player and Hoover. They must pay you well or did you rob a bank?" James was curious as he offered his packet of cigarettes around, all accepted then he lit each one with the large lighter on the mahogany coffee table.

"Yes," Emily enlighten all, "Mister Crawley pays me exceptionally well as he wants to retain my services. "Or get your knickers off." James invidiously laughed upon which Emily gently nudged him in the side.

"There are many, many bosses in London who would do that. But I believe Mister Crawley is devoted to his wife and daughters, he wants them to be lawyers and I am his well-paid female pioneer to make the path easier for them."

"Still a lot of money spent here Emm, even on your lavish salary. I see you have new ornaments, paintings, a new bed, a lot of money has been invested in this place," James remained uncomfortably and curious.

"And a new car, an "E" reg Ford Cortina from next week. Well James, if you would talk about other things when you ring or write, other than sex and what you are going to do to me, tonight and soon I hope, you would know that not only did my first pay cheque give me my contracted monthly salary with deductions but a massive bonus of a 1340 pounds less tax and NIC of course. That was for winning my Cooper case. The bonus was courtesy of the client. 1130 pounds net salary, more than most earn in a year. So yes, I did spoil myself. And I still have 500 pounds left which is in the bank of course. You should have taken law instead of being a soldier boy."

"My god! Emm you are so lucky." Gloria was anxious to alter the flow of the conversation. "So rich. But to business, where are David and I sleeping. I'm half Dutch and we like more than picking tulips."

"I shall get you a mattress. I also have two sleeping bags you can zip together but not too loud while you are shagging. I don't want my elderly neighbours to get a bout of high blood pressure."

Fred Biggs had collected the two young blue beret officers from Shipton station. They drove up to Wye Hall where Mister Hodges had met them. The loyal and rugged employee picked up their suitcases from the boot of the car.

"That's alright, Mister Biggs." James took the case from the surprised driver,

"I'm an officer in the Royal Marines under training. I can manage to carry that. But thank you."

"James!" Philippa in casual jeans and blouse ran forward and hugged her brother. "I did not expect you."

"Mama told me you were having a ball and more. She asked me to attend. You know what her "ask" is? Well anyway, here I am. Mama says there will be lots of eligible young women.

That's why I brought a brother officer under training. Pip; this is David Moir, Second Lieutenant Moir from Bonnie Scotland."

"Hi, later I will be introducing you to a lovely lady. A golden blonde beauty called Lady Caroline Feversham; she is just your type!" Philippa smiled impishly at David, and then abruptly turned back towards the house, passing the earl as he walked down the short stone stairway that led from the drive to the main entrance door of Wye Hall.

"James." Tom Marchant bounded forward and shook the hand of his son.

"Papa." James pointed towards the young officer standing nervously in the doorway. "This young man is my friend from the Royal Marines. David, Second Lieutenant David Moir."

"Pleased to meet you, David." Tom tightly shook hands with the young subaltern.

"And I you, sir" Moir responded.

"Let's get inside. Mister Hodges, could you come to the study? We, that is the two officers and I require some refreshments?"

"Surely, sir." The butler smiled graciously at the two uniformed men then almost ran off onto the house.

A swirling cone of light appeared, hovered momentarily outside the front entrance, in an instant it had disappeared into the firmament.

DANIEL-DECEMBER 1966/JANUARY 1967

The sound of "Good Vibrations" by the Beach Boys was coming from the radio in the kitchen as the car pulled up outside the farmhouse.

Daisy Gibson took a roast chicken from the oven as Debbie Gibson laid the kitchen table. The figure of Jackie Gibson walked in with his son. Daniel was attired in his dark navy blue beret, the headgear for all Royal Marines under training whether enlisted or commissioned. He was also in a green jersey pullover with the single Bath Star better known as the "pip" of a second lieutenant on each epaulette, a light khaki tactical shirt with the collar over the top of his jumper, olive green "OG" trousers, puttees and a pair of gleaming black boots. Debbie Gibson enthusiastically hugged her eldest brother.

The recent hit by the late singer, Jim Reeves, "Distant Drums" came on the radio.

"The Australians is sendin' more men to Vietnam, it said so on the telly," Little Jackie commented being anxious to impress his elder brother.

"You're well informed young Jackie but that's one place I'll not be going to. Except perhaps for a holiday in the far distant future. Our Prime Minister, Harold Wilson, rejected President Johnson's attempts to cajole him into partaking in the Vietnam conflict." Daniel smiled at his younger brother. "But you never know where we might end up fighting in the future."

The music group, The Board Draggers, was playing their version of the Cat Stevens new release "Matthew and Son". The five-man combo, three guitars, drummer and vocalist, was both local and very popular. Nonetheless, the dance hall in Amble was always busy on a Friday night and with the newly record label signed and even trendier group from Ashington, Shades of Blue, topping the bill. Consequently, the venue was even more teeming than the norm.

Daniel walked inside hand in hand with Carol. The group of young men chatting just inside the hall noticed the young officer and immediately moved out of his way. They were unaware of the fact that he would never jeopardise his fledgling short service commission in the Royal Marines by being embroiled in any bawdy, common, after dance punch up.

The young subaltern was dressed in red corduroy jacket and pair of grey "hipster" trousers, white shirt newly ironed by his mother and a pair of black suede Cuban heel, pointed toe boots.

Carol was attired in a mauve, wrap around kilt skirt, with a white polo neck jumper, a new brown leather coat and black high heeled shoes and dark brown stockings. She had not spoken to Daniel for some while. Not since he had mentioned that girls in London, though not yet Devon, wore miniskirts and tights, not knee length skirts and stockings anymore.

The veritable fact that he had gleaned all this information from fellow blue beret officers at Lympstone and having done no personal research on the matter did not wash with Carol. She was annoyed and may have been anyway as she told him no sex for two days as "the decorators were in." They sauntered up the stairs to the balcony where he bought a bottle of Coca for each of them.

"Why don't we go to the pub?" She irritably snapped, "You're 18 now, you can drink, legally."

"No but you're not 18. I'm not risking it," Daniel quietly responded despite having precious little actual knowledge of English licensing laws.

"Humph." Carol sat sown on one of the bench seats of the large balcony area. She looked at the Board Draggers completing that part of the evening with a rousing version of the recent Four Tops hit "Reach Out –I'll Be There".

"I'm going for a leak," Daniel announced then skipped quickly down the mezzanine staircase.

Seconds later Daniel walked back up the stairs. This time his hair was slightly different, it looked dyed black and he appeared to be much older. Carol dismissed that illusion as being due to the bad lighting in the dance hall balcony area. Apart from those bemusing aspects, he was wearing a jacket in dark blue hue instead of maroon and a pair of charcoal black bell-bottom trousers.

"Dan," she yelled, "What have you done to your hair? Why have you got someone else's jacket on?"

The Daniel looking figure appeared startled and ran back downstairs away from Carol's view.

30 seconds later he re-appeared from the staircase looking his usual baby faced 18 years of age and normal non-greasy, thick chestnut hair and a red jacket.

"What are you playing at?"

"I've no idea what the hell you're talking about," Daniel replied as the now on stage Shades of Blue were performing the latest Troggs' hit, "I Can't Control Myself."

"Daniel, I've just seen you, in a blue jacket and with swept back greasy hair. Are you trying to wind me up!"

"Carol, I think you're a bit illusory. No way could I have changed like that. All I did was have a pee and chat to Alistair Clark, my old school chum. He's joining the Royal Navy."

"Daniel, I'm not stupid, it was you!"

"I'm not winding you up, I was not here."

Alistair Clark then came towards Daniel. He came forward in a manner that had held sway for years with all young men when approaching the elder Gibson; both obsequiously and tentatively.

"Dan," Alistair deferentially enquired, "have ye got a twin brother? Ah've just passed a bloke that was the spittin' image o' you."

"What! Did he say what he was called?"

"Actually he did, Dan, he said he was called David Garlight. That's what it sounded like anyway. But 'e looked exactly the same as ye."

Seconds later, another of his old friends and former adversary from school, Christopher Wrigglesworth, ran up the stairs. He stood, out of breath, panting and speechless for a few seconds. The Shades of Blue began to play "Gimme Some Lovin'", the current hit by The Spencer Davis Group.

"Dan, Ali, Ah followed that man that looked like Daniel into the Station pub car park."

Wrigglesworth stopped again for breath; he had obviously run into the dance hall from The Station only about 50 metres away.

"What did you see, Chris?" Daniel assertively enquired. .

The young man looked up. "Ah'm not drunk, not touched a drop but Ah swear to God, on me mother's life, we watched Daniel's double. Ah swear to God Ah'm not lyin'"

"For God's sake Chris, what did you see?" Daniel snapped.

"There was a car, funny lookin' thing, so it looked in the dark, parked over in the far corner, next to the drive up to the railway station. He said he was lookin' for a Dan Gideon or somethin' and he'd be back to find him! This dude got into the car then the car just disappeared into thin air!"

EMILY-JANUARY 1967

The Oxfordshire countryside was beautiful. Emily thought as she gazed onto the rolling farm and woodland that flowed away from the back garden of James' private dwelling near the tiny hamlet of Hatford. It lay peacefully in the beautiful Vale of White Horse, some ten miles south of Wye Hall. It was Sunday January 1st 1967. She gazed adoringly at James. He was still sleeping in the huge double bed so she donned a dressing gown then ventured to the kitchen to brew a pot of coffee. They had missed Christmas together so exchanged gifts on New Year's Eve instead. Unlike Philippa, James, much to his personal relief, barely got a mention in the trendy magazines. This scenario also suited Emily even though they had much more interesting tales to recount. The magazines and other gossip columns were totally fixated on her lover's younger sister.

She carried the coffee from the kitchen to the bedroom and nudged James to draw him gently from his deep slumber. They had stayed drinking at the Fox and Hounds in the village of Uffington with David Moir, Lady Caroline Feversham and a number of others. David and Lady Caroline had left early and gone to her personal cottage. A residence that stood even deeper into the Vale of White Horse. The rest of the party remained in the pub until the small hours then took off to their respective points of lodging.

Fortuitously for James, Emily had consumed only a small glass of wine and was therefore more than capable of safely driving them to Hatford.

"Darling." She poked James who groaned then slowly opened his eyes. "Here is some coffee. Her Majesty may have given you leave until Wednesday but I have to be back to work tomorrow. It's New Year's Day today. If we lived in Scotland it would be a Bank Holiday tomorrow but alas we do not so I have to get ready."

"Ugh, my head feels like there's a man in there with a hammer." James sat up, took the mug of coffee from Emily before lighting a cigarette.

"If you want to sleep with me tonight and tomorrow before you return to Devon to serve Her Majesty, you'd best get ready and come with me to London. I'm driving today while the traffic will still be light. You can catch the train from Paddington or Waterloo to Exeter late Tuesday or early Wednesday."

"Sounds good. Where's David?"

"James, you know he's probably asleep or shagging the arse off Lady Caroline. They hit it off like a house on fire thanks to your sister. Caroline seemed to be one randy chick so give him a ring if you want. However, I think that you and he will be travelling back separately to wherever you play soldiers."

"Ok babe, I'll get ready and come with you to London. I can't keep away from that gorgeous arse of yours any more than I must. Get back into bed with it"

Even the erstwhile dour, plump and middle-aged Miss Fiona Derby was effervescent.

"Good morning Miss Wilkinson," she chirped as the young lawyer came through the entrance lobby of chambers.

"Emily," Gerald Crawley hailed her into his office as she walked in the door.

"Yes, Mister Crawley, and a Happy New Year." Emily energetically skipped over to the head of chambers.

"Happy New Year, and come in Emily, I have someone for you to meet."

There inside the luxuriant interior stood a man of about average height and thick black hair. The individual was wearing a dark mod style jacket, red silk shirt with a beige pullover tied by the sleeves around his neck, dark hipsters, and brown desert boots, sporting dark glasses and smoking a cigarette.

"Emily, this is Mister Dean Sinclair, an American as you'll tell by his accent. Dean works for a magazine called Cosmopolitan and he wants a few words with you."

"Thank you, Mister Crawley." Sinclair removed his dark glasses and looked at Emily held out his hand and shook hers.

"One hot broad and I'm Dean Sinclair, but call me Dean. May I call you Emily?"

"I suppose so, er Dean, as long as you don't refer to me as a broad. What can I do for you?"

"That's the kind of woman I like. Decisive, no BS, straight to the point. No chewing around the edges."

"Would you care for coffee, Mister Sinclair?" Gerald politely offered.

"Not your Limey coffee, excuse the dig. You English are great at fashion, music, art, design and so on. You name it, you're great at it, except for coffee it stinks. However, I will have a small Scotch if there's one."

"A little early for us but certainly you partake in one." Crawley buzzed Karen.

"Yes, Mister Crawley." The voice came over the speaker link.

"Two coffees please, Miss Finch."

Once all the relevant beverages had been sorted Dean resumed his chat.

"Right, Emily. As you may know, in 1965 our New York based magazine changed from being a literary publication to one focused on women. The modern woman. Our editor, Helen Gurley Brown, is a real trendsetter. She wants to bring the young modern woman to the fore, not have them tied to the kitchen sink."

"I don't think Emily would fit into that category, Dean," Gerald interjected.

"Precisely, man." Dean drank his Scotch then lit up another cigarette after offering his pack to Emily and Gerald who both politely declined then Emily had a change of heart and accepted one of his "full flavour" Marlboros.

"I'm here on the direct orders of Helen. She wrote a book back in 1961, I suggest you have a read. It's called "Sex and the Single Girl". Helen knows where she's coming from and where she wants to be. One really groovy lady."

"I'm not a pin up girl, Mister Sinclair. And I will not pose half naked for your magazine--."

"Please Emily, just hear me out. I can see you're not in love with the concept. That's 'cause you ain't heard it all yet."

"Then enlighten me, Dean." Emily's tone stood firmly in the no man's land between sarcasm and authenticity. She had to restrain herself from mimicking the New York accent.

"Well, Helen was in London a few months back, during the summer of last year. She read in the paper of how a beautiful, newly graduated lawyer had turned an impossible case around. This sparked all kinds of corruption investigations into the London Bobbies."

"I think there may be a little journalistic licence involved around that, Dean."

"No matter, Emily. It's as Helen read it. That was in your Daily Telegraph, hardly a gutter tabloid. She then wanted to feature you in the next edition of the magazine."

"There must be hundreds of glamour girls, people far more suited to your magazine."

"Helen wants you for this edition," Dean swiftly responded,

"With photographs of you in your work attire. The gowns and wigs and the like with skirts short but not too short. Just above the knee, no more. A woman looking sexy yet still professional. Not a sex object in her words. She wants role models, women that are "get up and go". They are ambitious, attractive, of the moment, young and fashionable. And you'll be paid very well."

"How well?" Emily wasted no time.

"As you're well known in England, not yet in the States, she'll offer you 2500 dollars for the interview. And a further 500 for five photographs."

"US dollars?" Gerald piped in.

"Sorry, sorry, pounds, British pounds sterling."

"Fine," Emily acquiesced, "Provided you add a further 200 pounds to be paid to the Chambers as a fee for my services and you mention them in full in the publication."

Dean smiled; his errand had proved a success.

"Agreed, I'll have a contract drawn up today by our lawyers. And being lawyers yourselves, I doubt if you'll find anything not fully kosher."

She knocked on the door of the detached house in Hackney. It stood in a quiet cul-de-sac in a highly desirable area. Artie Cooper opened the massive, thick oak structure.

"Miss Wilkinson, Ah was expectin' ya. Dorothy's through in the study. Ah'll 'ave some coffee brought through. "

"Thank you, Mister Cooper. I'm sorry I'm late."

"No worries Miss Wilkinson."

Emily paced into the study. Inside the dark haired, slightly built, bespectacled, plain looking 17-year-old was scanning her law books. She was eager to commence the evening's tutoring.

"Hello, Miss Wilkinson." Dorothy stood up.

"Oh please, Dot, sit down. And please call me Emily. I'm barely older than you."

"That'll be great, Emily. Dad wants me to take "A" level in law. He said 'e'll pay for it if the school cannot fit it in the exam timetable. What do ya think?"

"Are you hoping to sit four "A" levels or two from the school syllabus plus law?"

"I was wanting to take four. I'm pretty au fait with English Lit, History and Geography. I'm sure, with ya 'elp, I could pass Law as well."

"If you want to go to Cambridge, and I'm sure you can, you may wish to concentrate on your current subjects. University places at the top educational institutions are really competitive. They are open to all based on ability and the interview. However, you will be at a distinct advantage if you have three "A" Levels at A passes instead of three "A" levels at B or lower passes.

Dorothy looked a little disenchanted momentarily to Emily.

"However," Emily resumed, "I know friends who can get me some old exam papers and the relevant answers. We could give it a try and see how you do."

"That would be great. What are we doing tonight?"

"We are going back to that old chestnut the English law of contracts. This dates back to the Roman, Pacta sunt servanda, which means agreements must be kept."

Emily opened her textbook on English Law then turned to Dorothy,

"What elements in English law must a contract have?"

Dorothy refrained from even looking at her notes and replied,

"Offer and acceptances by competent persons having legal capacity who exchange consideration to create mutuality of obligation."

"Excellent." Emily smiled with delight.

"I have a great teacher. You are so beautiful Emily; I wished I looked like you."

"Nonsense, Dorothy. You are a unique person, a lovely girl."

"Dad doesn't want me goin' out wi' the local boys, especially they that works for 'im."

"Your Dad is just like all fathers. He wants the best for his daughter. You get your "A" levels then go to university and you'll find a boy even your Dad would like."

Dorothy smiled. "My Mum would 'ave been so proud."

"She certainly would. Now let's get on with the night's work; we certainly have a lot to do."

Billy Parkins knocked on the back door. Artie was busy preparing mugs of coffee to go with the plate of biscuits he sorted for Emily and his daughter.

"What th' fuck is ya doin' 'ere, Billy? Dorothy 'as 'er lessons tonight wiv Miss Wilkinson."

"It's Miss Wilkinson Ah wanted t' talk t' yer about, boss." Billy lit a "roll your own" cigarette which was dangling from his mouth.

"Well spit th' fuck out, Billy."

"I 'ad a word in th' shell of one o' the boys wiv contacts in the Filth, Scotland Yard actually. They says that two bent coppers--."

"Fuckin' Heathcock an' Baxter." Artie placed the biscuits and mugs of coffee on a tray.

"How d' ya know that?" Parkins was both impressed and bemused.

"Educated fuckin' guess. Now wait 'ere, Billy. Ah'll just take this tray to the ladies an' than ya can tell me all o' it."

Artie took the refreshments to the grateful young ladies. He then returned to the kitchen where the nervous figure still uneasily paced around.

"Sit down!" Artie pointed to a chair the relit his cigar. "Now, what th' fucks up?"

"I hears that those two bent filth, the ones that tried to stitch you up 'as got a contract out on Miss Wilkinson. A gunman from south o' the river, Old Kent Road Ah thinks."

Artie rubbed his chin in concentration.

"Any chance of getting' it lifted, Billy?"

"No, Artie. Word is it's fixed."

"That case Ah want a shooter near that gal all th' time. Watchin' out for 'er. A permanent minder. Take care of 'er. OK Billy! Understand? She's family. No word to 'er or my Dorothy either."

"There's more about Miss Wilkinson, Artie."

Cooper poured out two glasses of Scotch and handed one to Billy.

"Ah'm listenin'" Artie knocked the entire glass of spirit back.

"Another geezer, Artie, don't know who. A stranger, a small little shit, but they say e's approached the Richardson mob. The word is this chappie wants Miss Wilkinson done away wiv as well."

"Well Billy, we ain't gonna let that 'appen, are we?"

Chapter Ten

DANESH AND KELLY

"It really works?" Kelly gazed in awe at the newly completed Particle Accelerator Driven Inter-dimensional Transporter Mark Two. The PADIT 2.

"It really works. Our updated PADIT can carry two people comfortably and four without effort. Along with a minimum of 100 kilos of equipment and supplies should they be required," Danesh divulged whilst admiring his latest creation.

The research and development of the blue coloured RV sized vehicle had been funded almost entirely by HM Government via the Department of Scientific Research. They remained totally oblivious in relation to the minimal amount of detail that had been imparted to them for their generous stipend.

"Well Doctor Aresti, while you have been patching up your patients at the Lister Hospital, I have been very hard at work."

"You certainly have Prof," Kelly concurred. Danesh thought she looked stunning in her green trouser suit, yellow blouse and black hat just covering her flaming red locks along with black high heeled shoes. Professor Gideon was more mundanely garbed in blue overalls, cream shirt, black trousers and buff coloured desert boots. Kelly stared into the cockpit of PADIT 2. She was excited to shaking level by the unravelling implications.

"It can easily carry four passengers, Prof. But according to your alternate ego in our adjacent universe, we can travel to his cosmos, but he cannot come here. Something about the directional flow of dark matter and the gaps in between electrons and the fabric of time."

Kelly had tried her best to recall the technical details that Keely had recited to her.

"Doctor Aresti." Danesh tightened up bolts on the instrument panel with an electric wrench. "You stick to patching up accident and emergency patients or old men's prostates, I forget which you do now, and I shall guide us safely through this remarkable world we have discovered. And then to yet another place. That location, until we discovered this amazing locus, lay between the bounds of science fiction and extreme theoretical quantum physics."

The professor removed his overalls then slipped into his tweed jacket.

"It is possible. But we have to utilise anti-matter when we travel against the cosmic currents and tides. It is something akin to that which we now believe forms the basis of black holes."

"Can we bring Keely and Professor Garside back here? Garside claims we cannot."

"Then I shall have to prove him incorrect. Hop in Kelly, we are going for a short test run. From there we shall visit our doppelgangers to the left of our PU, Keely that is. Sometime after that, I would like to try travelling, after due testing, to the right of our universe. It is actually far more complex than that and I would need a mathematical formula the size of an hotel to explain."

"Don't bother Prof." Kelly slid back the entrance door of the PADIT 2. "I would never understand it anyway. It would simply consume precious time. Now jump in and let's go, we have a lunch date in another universe."

The car park seemed identical, yet different in subtle ways. This perception advanced a notion of surrealism, a spasm of uncertainty aligned with sheer apprehension on several levels.

All these emotions flowed frenetically around the psyche of Danesh as, guided by the instruments fed from the onboard computer, he landed the PADIT 2.

The physicist and Kelly had travelled through a blinding kaleidoscope of starbursts. It was a veritable whirling wall of colours and shapes. Speeding through and along a tunnel and celestial tundra. This segment of the remarkable expedition was followed by enclosure, for perhaps an eternity, within a mountain hued from the matter that forms each universe. They were now somewhere in sunshine. It was bounded on one aspect by trees and fields whilst the converse faced a large, modern, stone and concrete hospital complex.

"We must be early." Kelly looked at her mechanical wristwatch.

"Early," gasped Danesh, "We have journeyed through a dimension of neither space nor time. An expedition for which only a tiny, tiny percentage of the population of our world has the cerebral faculty to even begin to grasp the basic concept of. We have landed at a zenith point in the 14 billion years since the gargantuan explosion that lead to the creation of life, time and space. You consider us early!" "You're nervous Prof. It makes you irritable." Kelly smiled as PADIT 2 came to a halt. Danesh flicked the control to transform the vehicle from its travelling cucumber shape back in an instant to the Range Rover looking car. The mind bending concept being still remained an esoteric miracle to Kelly. She still marvelled at the phenomenon that but 15 minutes of real time earlier they had departed a geographical, planetary provenance that was yet entrenched in the mists of a theoretical nebulous science.

"Professor, you are about to meet our alter egos of this world for the first time and I am about to meet yours for the first time."

A man walked along the concrete path that bordered the tarmac surfaced car park. He stood as tall as Danesh and could easily have been mistaken for him. That was apart from the darker brown tweed jacket and his head of thick greying hair still had a few inklings of the original black. The professor also looked more mature; his doppelganger still boasted some youthful aspects. Nonetheless, they could still have easily been mistaken for each other. The distinctive outline of Keely sauntered alongside the much older figure. Kelly leapt from PADIT 2 and made towards a youthful looking Keely. She was sporting a scarf which covered most of her long flaming hair. The parallel universe doctor also donned a tight knee length green skirt, white blouse, high heels and a small light azure jacket.

"Keely." She kissed her inter dimensional twin on the cheek. "This is Professor Danesh Gideon. The scientist who developed the concept of PU travel and also the inventor and test pilot of PADIT and PADIT 2"

Keely smiled and warmly shook hands with Danesh then turned to his doppelganger. "This is Professor David Garside. The scientist who developed the concept of PU travel and also the inventor and test pilot of the Transporter Inter-dimensional Driven by a Particle Accelerator, TIDPA."

Garside tightly pressed the hand of Danesh.

"I trust, Professor, that back in your dimension you drink beer. There is an excellent hostelry, The Pig in a Poke, across the road which serves a great pint of John Smith's bitter. I understand you have a resolution to the conundrum of the "one way system, two stop syndrome" which is the basis of mine own parallel universe travel."

"I am firmly convinced, Professor Garside, that after a beer or two, I shall have suitably enlightened you on the solution to your restricted PU travel. But it comes with a major caveat which you must; I repeat must, factor into every co-ordinate and test well before you lift off."

"I look forward to it, Professor Gideon. Ladies, shall we go?"

PHILIPPA-MARCH 1967

The sound of "Strawberry Fields Forever" by the Beatles echoed gently across the stables. The girls took the reins of their horses and led the animals as they majestically negotiated each step over the grey cobbled stones. They moved with a paced gait into the sunlight of the early spring morning. Lady Philippa Marchant, Lady Elmira Barnard, Lady Caroline Faversham and Lady Kinsey Maple were off to exercise three of the young fillies and a gelding from the stables of the Earl of Wye.

The animals were very ably cared for by the former footman, now heading the family stables. Andrew Shearer was discovered to have a penchant for equine care by Tom Marchant. The earl discovered this flair after Andrew had commenced at Wye Hall following military service as a corporal of horse. This enlistment had been in The Blues and Royals of the Household Cavalry.

The four young ladies were all similarly dressed. The equestrian attire being jodhpurs, riding boots, polo neck sweaters and green Tweed hacking jackets and obligatory black riding hats.

"Come on girls." Philippa breathed in the crisp country air as the small radio they brought with them then began to play "Release me" by Engelbert Humperdinck. As Andrew approached, she put a foot in a stirrup and climbed easily into the saddle.

"Beautiful job, Shearer. Candy, Peggy, Dawn and Pixie are all in tip top condition. We are off for a cross country ride." Philippa smiled as the others mounted up.

"It's a pleasure, My Lady," the tall, moustached figure responded, "They's a joy to work with."

Philippa turned the head of Candy, her chestnut mare. A beautiful animal that stood at 12 hands. She began to trot out of the stables area and onto the rustic country track immediately north of Wye Hall, moving steadily along the rain pool laden way. The other young women followed immediately behind Philippa. The quartet rode with seemingly instinctive trepidation by the haunting yet ornate Wye family crypt. The mausoleum was cherubim statue replete, constructed of granite and appeared to be of very Gothic architecture. Elmira was perched on the grey, 10 hands, filly, Peggy. Caroline sat on the other chestnut mare of 12 hands, Dawn. Kinsey was riding the only gelding, a 10 hands pie bald, Pixie.

They alternated between trotting and cantering as they moved uphill across the blooming daffodil strewn slopes of the extensive Wye Family estate. They stopped at the highest point in the area, which stood between the hamlet of Shilton and the A361.

"Beautiful view, Pip." Elmira pulled Peggy to a steady halt.

"Your family must be very rich, to own all this beautiful land." The blonde Caroline drew Dawn close to Philippa.

"Really, Caroline. One would think that the Earl of Bamburgh was on the verge of destitution the way you are talking."

"Of course not, Pip. But your estate seems to cover a great chunk of Oxfordshire, almost to Gloucestershire. A tad more than our 2000 acres."

"Caroline." Elmira smirked. "You're trying to sound so avant-garde. Just so trendy and proletariat but farming is a mere hobby to your father."

"Let's talk about something of more interest," the normally taciturn Kinsey piped up.

"Ohh." Philippa giggled. "Let's canter down the valley. To that copse by the bank of the stream where the horses can graze and drink. And we can talk about what Kinsey wants."

"A big muscular Marine like Caroline has! With a big you know what to make her smile at night." Elmira too chirped up. They all turned the heads of their mounts and rode down the valley. "You can be so common." Caroline scowled.

They moved down into the dale and jumped from their saddles. The girls rapidly secured the horses to a nearby wooden fence then sat on a patch of thick, verdant, dry grass near the bubbling stream. The clear, shallow waters that sliced through the centre of the local topography.

The four figures lit cigarettes then began to gossip.

"Philippa, I have a great young man. Just right for you. And he's coming to my ball tomorrow." Elmira simpered.

"Fab." A sardonic groan was exhaled. "Your selections really leave a lot to be desired, Elmira. The last disaster you tried to pair me up with was half blind, stuttered and had terrible halitosis."

"He had an excellent pedigree."

"That's how people talk about dogs." Kinsey cheerfully contributed.

"He was a dog. However, as long as he was from the right back ground Elmira is happy. That is as long as she does not have to follow the same rules," Philippa opined.

There was a short period of silence as the girls drew on their cigarettes.

"Philippa." Elmira shuffled with a slight discomfort. "You're becoming so cynical since you decided to go to university. I do like gorgeous men for a night, even if from the lower echelons. But purely for sex. Anything more and they have to be much higher up the scale. I know that may sound so snobbish in these liberal socialist days but class, the knowledge of one's correct place in the order of things, is the keystone to a contented, orderly society."

"I agree in part. However, I would prefer to decide for myself with whom I wish to spend my life." Philippa smiled at Elmira. Her raven hair was flowing wildly in the gentle breeze that swept along the floor of the valley.

"David is not from the upper tier. But his father worked hard and became an advocate, a Scottish lawyer. David went to grammar school, then the University of Edinburgh. He is now an officer in the Royal Marines. Even papa likes him." Caroline exhaled. She sighed at the mere thought of her young lover.

"Your papa will rapidly alter his opinion if he actually proposes marriage." Elmira sounded extremely spiteful. The comment was hurtful even by her base standards. She had visibly offended Caroline who surprisingly had offered no riposte.

"Philippa." Kinsey was anxious to impart her enquiry. "We all know your brother is tall dark and handsome. And despite affirmations made by your Mama to the contrary, we know that Miss Emily Wilkinson LLB someday will be his lady wife. And of course David has eyes only for Caroline."

"And?" Philippa glared with anticipation at Kinsey.

"My brother told me that only army officers from something called the Household Division, whatever that is, are suitable for true ladies of birth. However, darling Philippa, I have also heard that these Marines type soldiers are the roughest and toughest. Is James thinking of inviting anymore such officer types from them to visit?"

"You want a tough guy, Kinsey. However, I doubt that my brother will bring one to stay at Wye Hall just to satisfy your lust for one night."

"Why not?" Elmira returned to the discourse. "Kinsey has been secretly eyeing up James for ages. She craves a man with a rock hard body, rock hard all over.

She yearns for a muscular male to make passionate love to her all night long. She's utterly in heat! Caroline, you have the trannie. Tune it to your namesake, Radio Caroline."

She acceded to Elmira's request and "Here Comes My Baby" by the Tremeloes was heard from the small speaker in the transistor radio.

"I shall ask my James to bring a hard, not just hard you know what, soldier type officer home with him. That will be just for you Kinsey, your own little bit of rough. Although one can hardly describe officers as a bit of rough and apart from James I find all military types so boring. They are so plastic. I shall liaise only with non soldiers."

Near Oxford, the seat of the Earl and Countess of Bamburgh was vibrating. A local group was performing. They were the newly reformed Outcaste who had finally found a replacement for Miles. Elmira was deep in conversation with Frederick Byatt as the group played the Jimi Hendrix Experience hit, "Hey Joe." The tall young man had hair that was on the cusp of turning from the shorter coiffures of the early 1960s to a longer style. One of such would become iconic in the latter years of the momentous decade.

"Fred." Elmira looked stunning in her long black dress and wrap. "You are a groovy guy. You can charm the ladies. You charm Lady Philippa; make her fall in love with you."

"What things turn groovy and I fall in love with her?"

"Don't be so wet Fred," Elmira flagrantly snapped, "I know where your true preferences lie. That's why I am enlisting your support. I need someone who will not do that."

"I have no idea to what you are alluding, Elmira." Byatt appeared at once as if the very wind had been kicked out of his sails.

"Yes, you do, Fred, and relax; I shall keep it well and truly under wraps. But there is nothing to fear. That is apart from your wholesome reputation of course, as by July this year it will be legal. That is providing both are consenting adults aged 21 or over. That age you will have reached by the time the bill becomes law."

"Why do you want me to carry out this charade?"

"Fred, it is in mine, and my family's financial interests to ensure that Lady Philippa stays with and eventually marries the Honourable Julian Lee-Watersby. You shall keep her romantically occupied. It will entail thespian qualities of that I am more than a little aware. Notwithstanding, it will only be until the summer when Julian returns from a stint in the Civil Service working for the Governor General of Australia. He is a charming friend of the family called Sir Edric Montague Bastyan. It will be well worth your while financially. And naturally your reputation shall remain untarnished, as no one will learn of your predilection. You charm her; make her love you, than spurn the lovesick wench. That will be just prior to the date Julian comes home and she will run into his arms. The engagement will be officially announced and published in The Times. After all such steps have been successfully negotiated; a large sum will change hands. "

"We understand each other, Elmira. Just point me towards the chick and I shall groovily sweep her off her feet. I should be awarded an Oscar in advance for the film star level dramatics I shall be forced to partake in."

Stephen Grenfell

DANIEL-MARCH 1967

The wind blew cold with a savage bite. It gusted intensely from over the Exe estuary and across Woodbury Common. A much-reduced troop of 15 young "yoyos", blue beret officers, had stopped to briefly catch their breath. This short break had followed the extremely arduous Endurance Course coupled with several unarmed combat exercises. The batch of second lieutenants under training was doing their six-mile "yomp". They were overseen and tutored by three veteran non-commissioned officers. The NCOs were led by Sergeant Tony Helm from Plymouth in the county of Devon. Helm was of medium height, an almost flat pugilist face and receding brown hair. The Royal Marine was blessed with an almost inexhaustible supply of strength and energy. Sergeant Helm was a seasoned veteran of several campaigns and looked forward with relish to his imminent posting to Aden at the tip of the Arabia peninsula. .

Sergeant Andy Diggle hailed from the banks of the River Wear near Sunderland in County Durham. Andy was 24 years of age, tall with wavy brown hair with the physique of a human mountain. Diggle had served in Sarawak and was en route with his friend Tony Helm to be posted to one of the last outposts of the British Empire. That would transpire once this bunch of "nancy officers", as he called them, had finally earned their green berets.

The third NCO, and also the awaiting active service in the British Crown Colony of Aden was 24 year old Corporal Eddie McGrath from Edinburgh in Scotland. McGrath was smaller but well-built and blessed with thick black hair.

"Gentlemen!" Helm's voice boomed out. "We've had a lot of guys, sissies, quit the trainin'. Those left, you've progressed wi' ya tactical commando training' as well as ya officer and leadership skills development. It's now nearly time for the last big test, the 30 mile march.

However, before that, Corporal McGrath wants to sharpen your unarmed combat skills, Corporal McGrath can ye take over please?"

The instructors' private office near the sergeant's mess was full of smoke and banter.

Sergeants Helm and Diggle had been joined by Corporal Eddie

McGrath along with another non-commissioned officer, Gunnery Sergeant Neil Schwartz. The 30 year old "gunny" was on secondment from the United States Marine Corps. A small wiry character, Schwartz had thinning black hair, a strong Roman nose and smoked Marlboro full flavour cigarettes at every opportunity. This Marine came from a town called Hackensack in New Jersey on the east coast of the USA and had the misfortune to have had both his kneecaps shot off. This major setback had occurred whilst he had been partaking in Operation Hastings, during July 1966, in Quang Tri Province of South Vietnam. Neil was also the odd one out in the room. He had recently fought in a war and unlike all the others was a United States citizen and therefore not eligible to serve in Aden.

At the other side of the table to the NCOs, sat two officers, a Major and a Lieutenant Colonel. These men were also earmarked for imminent service in the Middle East.

The more senior of these spoke first. A tall figure with greying hair, aged in his mid-40s.

"Gentleman. Just in case you are unaware, I am Lieutenant Colonel John Owen and I am the next CO of 45 Commando currently deployed in Little Aden, Aden. This is Captain Peter Adams who from next week will be Major Adams. Mister Adams is also going to Aden to command X-Ray Company of 45. I am also totally conversant with the fact that you, Sergeant Helm, you Sergeant Diggle and also Corporal McGrath will all be flying out to the Middle East.

In fact, apart from Gunnery Sergeant Schwartz, we are all Aden bound. We will spend up to a year there, depending on our illustrious prime minister. At that juncture we hand the place back to the wogs."

Sergeant Helm and the others were more than a little curious. At this juncture it was normal for senior instructors to make their final assessments of the officers under training before suggesting any further tutoring if it was deemed to be required. It was certainly not standard procedure to have the CO of a commando involved in such relatively minor deliberations.

"I can see you are bemused, gentleman and I do have a reason for being here. It is simply that we require three of the latest batch of subalterns for immediate posting to Aden. I am going to have a cigarette, please enlighten us on in your opinion as to who the most suitable three to deploy are."

The three Royal Marines instructors offered their selections with accompanying rationale of the best and brightest subalterns of the current intake.

"Gunny, who would you choose?" Owen glared at the American.

"Well sir, no disrespect to my Royal Marines colleagues but they's way off the target.

I agree with choosing Mister Gibson. He's by far the best of the officer intake of 1966 stroke 1967. He'll get the Sword of Honour, made by Wilkinson I 'm told. Mister Gibson will make a great troop leader and be well respected by his men. If needed, they'll take a bullet for him and he would for them. He's a potential general. I can't speak too highly of Second Lieutenant Gibson, sir. But most of the other blue beret officers still need some training before going into combat."

"Ha, I agree, Gunny." Owen ironically laughed. "Alas, with respect to Mister Gibson becoming a general there is a slight snag. Second Lieutenant Gibson is on a short service commission. They are only three years in total and he's already served seven months. He actually resigns his commission before he reaches the age of 21. He will of course have to be on the Reserve List for a further five years. Nevertheless, it is probable that the highest rank he may attain is a full lieutenant."

"That's a pity, sir. I wished we'd had more officers like him in the 'Nam."

"Alright Gunnery Sergeant, who are the other two that you would choose?" Owen was anxious to glean the opinion of the highly respected Vietnam War veteran.

"Well sir, forget about those guys with names I can barely pronounce."

"Brackenshaw and Browolsky." Tony Helm assisted his American colleague.

"Yeah, those two, forget about 'em. They're okay but not ready yet, if they ever will be. Mister Moir chats a lot and I knows he likes the ladies but he'll make a pretty good subaltern. Mister Marchant may be from some kinda privileged background, some titled family and went to that classy school but he's pretty good too. He's nearly as good as Mister Gibson but nowhere near as tough. Still very good though. So I'd say Moir, Marchant and Gibson. Mister Gibson did his endurance course today in well under 45 minutes. As you know, sir, blue beret officers are allowed 71 to pass this part of their training. The fittest blue beret officer, in fact the fittest officer of any kind, sir, I've seen in my life."

"Thank you Gunny. I shall bear that in mind when we finally make our selections." The lieutenant colonel nodded with appreciation.

Daniel thought he was on the verge of a physical breakdown.

The 18 -year-old officer had pushed his body to the limits over the last few days.

He had overcome the rigours of a nine-mile speed march, the Tarzan assault course and the six-mile endurance march. He had negotiated "Peter's Pool", crawling through waist deep freezing water and storm drain sized tunnels. The troop was crossing the wilderness of Dartmoor. The incredibly athletic and burly young warriors were 29 miles into the 30 mile cross-country march. The subalterns were had almost reached the small bridge that signalled the final sprint. Daniel's entire frame was now screaming back at him, cloaked in gushing sweat and enveloped within seething physical agony. He was virtually in a state of an out of body experience. The 18 year old pushed, and drove himself to the outer limits of human fortitude and stamina. Daniel at once felt isolated and alone. A mirage, a shape, an almost human entity materialised to his left, or deep in his imagination and called to him. It seemed like the haunting sensation that accompanies the awareness of déjà vu. Something akin to a voice echoing along the passages of time, familiar yet alien. A light shone as the words stroked his senses. Another smaller figure with a sallow face appeared then ran into some ethereal forest.

"Go back and bring them all in with you." Daniel looked behind him and the remainder of his comrades were far to his rear, specks on the horizon.

The young man inhaled deeply, and then doubled back to the column. Within ten minutes he had urged, cajoled and bullied the entire column over the finish line, all a surfeit of time to spare.

For some time the subalterns caught their breath then finally formed up into three ranks. Several senior officers were in attendance, the most notable being John Owen. He automatically assumed the responsibility of distributing the coveted green berets to the new commandos.

"Congratulations, Mister Gibson." the new CO of 45 Commando shook Daniel's hand. He then presented him with his "green lid" which the young subaltern immediately placed it on his head. "And also congratulations. You are to be awarded the Sword of Honour at your passing out parade."

"Thank you, sir."

Once all formalities had been concluded, and the entire troop of officers was in appropriate headgear, Owen called over, Daniel, James and David.

"The Three Musketeers, Mister Gibson, Mister Marchant and Mister Moir." The Lieutenant Colonel made an attempt at mirth. "I understand you three are a team."

The trio of new commando officers merely responded with a muted, "Yes, sir."

"Just as well." The middle aged Owen dryly smiled, "You are to be troop commanders in X-Ray Company under Captain Adams who will soon be Major Adams. I think you all met him. He and I were on the panel of the Admiralty Interview Board last July. We interviewed you all although it may feel like a century ago now. Well, I have your plane tickets in my office. You three, along with other officers, NCOs and enlisted guys are flying to RAF Khormaksar in Aden. You will travel there via Bahrein from London Heathrow on Monday the tenth of April. You have to be at Heathrow by ten hundred hours so plan your schedule accordingly. After the pass out parade tomorrow, I understand all your parents will be present; you'll all be on leave for nine days. Enjoy it and I know you will not let the good name of the Corps down. You will soon be on active service in the Middle East, with real shooting, and it could be for up to a year."

JAMES/DAVID/DANIEL -APRIL 1967

The three young second lieutenants stood in the buffet car of the British Rail Great Western train heading for Didcot, due to depart Exeter Saint Davids at any moment.

They had decided not to imbibe excessively as much more revelry was planned for later that evening.

"Tell me, Jimmy." Daniel looked at James as the steward behind the bar handed them each a pint glass of Newcastle Exhibition beer. "Just remind me. How come I've got an invite to your place? I think it's 'cause no one else talks t' you. Just Davy and me. No one else likes you."

David grinned at the comments then drank his beer. The trio took their seats. They were watching the verdant rural landscape of Devon come into view as the train pulled out of Exeter and made towards Bristol. "Danny Boy, the pipes the pipes are calling. Okay brother, I'll not give up my day job. But Dan, Jimmy doesn't need anyone else to talk to. He's got a fab looking girl, I mean that this lass looks like a film star. She is the double of that model, a blonde Chrissie Shrimpton. She's a high-powered lawyer type. He also has a gorgeous sister. You'd like her Danny, but she doesn't like soldiers, so you can forget about her. Apart from that he has every hot bird in Oxfordshire lusting after him. So, he doesn't need Royal Marines officer types as friends. He has chicks as friends, all wanting to take sack out with him."

"David, you sure can talk a lot and don't be so vulgar." James scowled a little.

"Jimmy, you can be such a knob head when it takes your fancy." Daniel laughed and they all lit up cigarettes. "We're off to war in a week. Imagine, off to put our lives on the line for Queen and Country and you're whinging about being such a sex symbol."

"Don't call me Jimmy at my place. My name is James."

"Ohh, Mama and Papa will be so displeased.," David mimicked the accent.

"Why did you ask me? Does your sister need a Marine?" Daniel momentarily became earnest. "My little sister doesn't know what she wants and my parents do not help. Nonetheless, she asked me to bring a dashing young officer. Not David as Lady Caroline Feversham has already claimed him but another of the same ilk. Philippa does not like soldiers, but she has a friend, Lady Kinsey Maple, a charming lady who seems to be yearning for a brawny male. Naturally, she specified a Royal Marines' officer."

"I have a girlfriend already," Daniel mentioned as he collected the empty beer glasses and began to walk to the bar for refills.

"Crap, Gibson." David punched Daniel lightly on the arm. "You're 18 years old, not 80. We're all off to war next week. You're not engaged so get your leg over here in Wye Hall, it'll be outta sight. Then if you're lucky you can get it again in a couple of days when you go home. Up to that funny place where the Geordies live. And we'll have the same drinks again."

"Does your girlfriend wear stockings or tights?" David enquired as Daniel returned with three more pints of Newcastle Exhibition.

"Stockings," Daniel replied, "At least she did when I was last on leave. Skirts are not as short up there as around London. Not yet."

"I like stockings better, the piece of flesh between the stocking top and the thigh. Caroline wears them just for me. She would normally wear tights," David bragged.

"Emily wears stockings because she prefers them." James sipped his beer then lit another cigarette. "As well as for me. She has to wear such heavy clothes in court, she reckons stockings keep her cooler than tights."

Two and a half hours after leaving Exeter Saint Davids, the Delta class diesel locomotive and British Rail livery carriages pulled into Didcot station.

The young officers fastened their Lovat jackets, carefully placed on their new, hard earned, green berets and picked up their suitcases.

They speedily descended from the carriage and briskly walked along the platform. Once having presented their first-class rail warrants to the ticket collector at the exit gate, the young men marched purposefully and directly onto Station Road. Outside stood a beautiful, medium height, fair-haired young woman. She was bedecked in an expensive frilly blouse, wide blue hat, purple mini skirt from Mary Quant's Bazaar boutique and blue tights. She approached the trio of young men with an air of total self-confidence accentuated by a sensual smile.

"Hello, Caroline," James greeted her.

"Hello, darling." David kissed the young woman briefly on the lips. "Ye know James of course but this is our fellow Royal Marines Commandos officer. He was top boy of our class. The swat won the Sword of Honour. He's from Northumberland, close to Scotland, Second Lieutenant Daniel Gibson."

"Hi, I'm Caroline, so pleased to meet you. You have to excuse David, being Scottish makes him very garrulous."

"The pleasure is all mine, Caroline, I'm Daniel." They shook hands then she briefly scanned Daniel's puissant physique.

"I'm sure you will be well received at Wye Hall, Second Lieutenant."

She interlocked her arm with David's and they began to walk towards the station car park. "Good old British Rail at least got you here on time. I have my car, or should I say Daddy's car, the Bentley S III. My own little mini would fit us all in but not the luggage as well. Come with me." They walked towards a massive silver car, parked at the far end of the lot.

"Jump in boys." Caroline beckoned with a smile. "David in the front. I'm dropping James and Daniel off at Wye Hall. After which David and I are going to my own little pad in the countryside near Shifford. Standing on the banks of the Isis. Aren't we darling?"

David merely nodded in restrained anticipation.

The car pulled up half an hour later near a road with a sign reading "Wye Hall Only-Private."

"James, darling." Caroline looked at him through the rear-view mirror of the Bentley. "I do not wish at this juncture to drive up to the house. It is only half a mile. I'm sure two roughie toughie Marine types like you and Daniel can walk such a miniscule distance."

"That's fine, Caroline." James smiled meaningfully as he and Daniel exited the limousine. "We shall yomp the last few hundred yards. David, I shall see you a week on Monday at Heathrow Airport."

The Bentley drove off leaving Daniel and James to make their own way along the remote road.

The early April breeze stroked the rough grassland that covered the meadows behind a stout, dry stonewall on either side of the narrow road.

After about five minutes a massive stone built country house came into view, with castle like edifices, balconies, rose gardens, spiral towers and a large clock tower above the main entrance door."Wye Hall," James proudly pointed.

DAVID/CAROLINE-APRIL 1967

The isolated cottage was near the tiny hamlet of Shifford that stood on the banks of the River Isis, the name given to the Thames above Iffley Lock. There was picturesque, unblemished countryside rolling away as far as the eye could see.

David and Caroline lay naked in the giant king-sized bed of her 17th century cottage, an ornate long-standing structure tucked away in a very remote part of Oxfordshire. They were both smoking a Benson and Hedges cigarette after making love for the fifth time.

"I like Marines." Caroline smiled contentedly. "They are strong, tough with bodies to die for.

I hate the modern men's skinny look. When you go all the way Marines can shag you all day."

"Only if we have lots of time separate from each other to recharge my batteries." David slipped from under the covers and walked naked to the bedroom window. "Great view you've got here. Is this your place?"

"Yes, Daddy bought it for my 18th birthday, last September. Do you fancy me only for my money? Are you a lounge lizard gold digger? A financial predator?"

"If you had a face like a dog and a figure like a sack of spuds one may think that but you don't. You're a friggin' gorgeous blonde, with a Greek goddess figure. The fact ye have a place of your own is good as we can have sex in private. Emily's place in London is nice but not secluded like this."

"With whom did you have sex with at Emily's place?" Caroline abruptly snapped.

"I didn't." David had to rapidly unravel convincingly from the untruth. "But James and Emily did, four times in a night. I could nay get to sleep until she was satisfied. Not James, Emily. Just as well that lady has a Marine for a boyfriend, no one else could cope."

"Emily is beautiful, don't you think so?"

"Of course. She's out of this world." David turned on the radio and the sound of the Hollies playing "On a Carousel" came through the speakers.

"Am I not?" Caroline cast a suspicious eye on the young Scot.

"Of course, all ye ladies are."

"Don't forget we have to go to Elmira's party later. Emily should come to the balls and parties. She is always invited but always declines."

"Why?" David gazed at the stunning rustic scenery. "It Takes Two" by Marvin Gaye and Kim Weston came on the radio.

"Because the Countess of Wye, James' mother, still clings to the hope that her son will marry Isabelle Napier-Fenning. Louise Marchant makes it obvious she prefers Isabelle to Emily.

Consequently, Emily keeps away, which by the way also suits James. She was in Cosmopolitan recently. The photos made her look like a lawyer Raquel Welch. Rumour has it that she has been offered a job in New York as a legal columnist for the magazine. We all want to emulate her. Emily is a very successful lawyer in a man's world and we hear she is making an absolute fortune in London. She's selling her flat. It's totally paid for and is buying a huge house out in Hertfordshire."

Caroline slipped from bed, took a gentle hold of David's erect manhood and gently led him back to the bed. She sat on top of him.

"Before you do the business." Caroline gazed pleadingly at the Scot. Her eyes were soon flowing.

"What? You're sad, full of lamentation. Why?" David looked at her somewhat bemused.

"I had a dream," Caroline tearfully confessed, "I had a dream that you were in a place. A hot, dusty, smelly place. One day, you and another man went out and something bad happened.

It was very scary. Please, David, I want us to do something before you go. I'm so scared for you. I want us to do something. Now. Well tomorrow but I want it done."

"Och, Okay, but I'll be fine. And if not, I'll come back and apologise to ye personally from the other side. I'll return to tell you I love ye."

JAMES/DANIEL-APRIL 1967

James and Daniel marched with a seeming purpose into the entrance hall of Wye Hall. They were met by Hodges in the Greek style vestibule.

"Lord Marchant." The butler made an attempt to assist the two men but James waved him away.

"Yes, Mister Hodges."

"Sir, Miss Wilkinson called you on the telephone. She wishes to inform you that the good lady is home from London for the week end and would appreciate a telephone call from you, sir. That is the message she requested I convey to you."

"Thank you, Mister Hodges. Could you ask one of the staff to show Mister Gibson to his room?"

"Surely, sir." Hodges deferentially nodded at the precise moment

Philippa strode over to greet James. The sibling was sporting a short "Twiggy" style haircut. She was dressed in a pink mini skirt from Yves Saint Laurent's Riva Gauche chain, a plain white blouse, short sleeved pullover and light pink tights. "James, darling." She kissed him on the cheek. "I see you're wearing a different colour hat. Green is so "in" right now."

"It's a beret. Not a hat. I had to sweat blood for that." James was not enamoured by Philippa's seemingly flippant remark. "And this is Second Lieutenant Daniel Gibson from Northumberland. He and I passed out together."

"Yes." Philippa smiled impishly. In her mind's eye she had a brief vision of James passing out by fainting onto the parade ground along with Daniel. She deliberately refrained from looking at Daniel then added. "Daddy is away at London. Naturally he has taken Rebecca, again. They'll be back tomorrow. Are you and Emily coming to the party tonight?"

"Philippa, you know I'm not coming. Please do not embarrass me. Let Daniel introduce himself." Eventually the 18-year-old student deigned to turn around and face the subaltern. .

A giant spark seemed to envelope her psyche. For a few seconds that seemed like an eternity, her entire female frame washed with an overdose of desire charged hormones. The young woman was facing the most perfect male she had ever seen. Daniel was even more handsome than her brother and father and certainly more so than David. This young officer boasted a physique and looks that would have made Adonis proud, standing so confident, strong and gentle simultaneously. Philippa's internal furnace was burning at white heat.

"Hi, I'm Daniel Gibson. I'm a friend of James. We serve together in the Royal Marines."

The sound of the record, "I Was Kaiser Bill's Batman" by Whistling Jack Smith floated from deep inside the enormous building.

Philippa stood muted for a second.

"Hi," she stuttered then dashed inside the house.

"You'll have to excuse my sister; she's a bit scatter-brained and ill mannered."

"She's beautiful." Daniel exhaled with passion. "I've never seen anything so gorgeous in my entire life."

"I thought you had a girlfriend." James smirked then beckoned him into the house.

"I do, I think," Daniel responded whilst following James inside. The 72-year-old Mrs Cromer hobbled forward.

"Mrs. Cromer." James placed an affectionate arm around Maggie. "Would you be so kind as to take Mister Gibson to whatever guest room is ready. Please."

"Of course, Lord Marchant, sir. I'll do that right away."

"Daniel, dinner is at seven sharp. Dinner jacket and bow tie both mandatory I'm afraid."

"I have all the necessary, James. Will you be dining?"

"Yes, I shall be. However, unlike you, I shall not be attending the party at Lady Elmira's house. Rather I shall be keeping my young lady company."

"Lucky you." Daniel cast a perceptive grin. "I'm catching the train to Northumberland tomorrow. But as you requested, I 'll attend this party of your sister."

"That's fine," James stated, I owe you a favour. Now let's change for dinner. I apologise for bugging out on you. To be honest Philippa's old friends were a good laugh, the friends from school that is. However, her new circle, the ones whom she believes reflect her social standing, are a pain in the arse. Even a bigger pain in the arse since my sister began to be reported in and photographed for the gossip magazines, starting with Woman's Own."

James stopped the car outside the secluded cottage in the Oxfordshire countryside.

"Well old boy." He smirked at Daniel. "Now is the time to earn that champagne dinner that I shall buy you for this favour. Mama would not approve of me leaving but you are more than capable of going up to and beyond the call of duty. Sorry but Philippa does not like soldiers, so she is out of contention. I believe it is Lady Kinsey Maple, another red head who wishes to sample some military male prowess. Kinsey is the daughter of the Earl and Countess of Sawbridgeworth. She is a stunner and a gas, Danny. But whatever you do, don't fall for her. She'll treat you like shit if you do. Just have a ball then get back to your girl up north."

"I'll not let the side down."

"Do you have any guilt or whatever? I mean about going out with another girl?"

"James," Daniel emphatically replied, "We're off to war in a week. It's a little war, yes, but soldiers are still being killed there. I, we, might not come back. Ergo, I want to live as much as I can before I go. Now bugger off and see Emily."

Daniel sauntered at an easy pace towards the large cottage. He knocked on the black painted wooden door. From inside he could hear a record player vibrating with the vocals of Reg Presley and the Troggs with their current hit "Give It to Me."

A stunning woman with long raven hair opened the door. She was quickly joined by another with auburn locks. "Hi, I'm Elmira." The dark haired young woman in a fashionable sea blue long evening dress held out her hand. "And you must be Daniel. You're the second young officer from your lot. I think your colleague David is here somewhere, probably in a bedroom on top of Caroline."

"Yes, I'm Daniel." He shook her hand. The young man had been slightly taken aback by Elmira's almost dismissive, nonchalant remark.

"I'm Kinsey." Yet another hand was thrust towards Daniel. This one was attached to a beautiful woman with flaming locks fastened up. She was garbed in a black strapless evening gown. "And you are even more of a hunk and dishier than Philippa described."

"Thank you, I'm Daniel." He smiled at her as they pressed hands.

"Come in, Daniel and grab a drink." Elmira invited as the music changed to The Seekers recording of "Georgy Girl".

Daniel wandered along the corridor then noticed Philippa in a golden dress. A garment that perfectly matched her short auburn hair. She was talking to another trendily dressed young woman.

"Hello." Daniel looked at her but the chemistry of earlier had dissipated. She peered up. There was no attempt to even deign to acknowledge his presence. Philippa simply resumed her conversation. Daniel felt more than a little awkward. He waited for a few moments then moved into the kitchen where Kinsey had already poured him a glass of beer.

"James told me you officer types like a small beer to start with then pink gins or wine." She handed the glass to Daniel.

"Thanks, I prefer a few beers then Irish whiskey or gin and tonic though."

"Would you like to go into the garden? The house is very crowded?"

"I never refuse an offer like that from a beautiful lady." Daniel took Kinsey's hand and they wandered onto the patio just outside the lounge.

He placed his beer on the garden table and took out his packet of Embassy cigarettes.

"Listen," he whispered gently in her ear then offered her a cigarette. Kinsey took one which Daniel lit it then continued. "You're a beautiful woman, very sexy. We could spend all night chit chatting about everything from the diameter of a perfect navel to how far is it to yesterday. All that heavy stuff would be very interesting but also--."

She placed her finger on his lips as the music from the inside changed to "Ruby Tuesday" by the Rolling Stones. "Shhhh." Kinsey quietly indicated. "I did not ask Philippa, to request her brother to bring a fellow officer here so I could listen to military history. Nor the war in Vietnam serious as that is to some. Or even if James' young lady will appear again in Cosmopolitan even though she graces that magazine with verve. I have only just met you but I have already decided. I do not normally screw men on the first date, I'm not a slut. However, as you are going home tomorrow and to war next week, I can make an exception. We can skip the boring small talk and slip into bed. Elmira has already set aside a room for us while she keeps an eye on Philippa."

"One woman that will not be unattended for long," Daniel mentioned as she took him again by the hand. They walked back into the house and up the staircase unnoticed by all except Philippa.

The room was very small. Apart from an armchair, the double bed occupied almost the entire floor area. The sole illumination was a single bedside lamp. Daniel sat on the bed nearest the flower-patterned chair and removed his shoes.

"Unzip my dress," Kinsey requested in a soft, seductive purr and lightly kissed Daniel on the lips. She was wearing a perfume called "Intimate" which fanned the flames of Daniel's growing desire for the shapely figure. The young man immediately conformed, lowered the zip until the expensive black garment fell to the floor. Kinsey was now dressed only in bra, panties, suspender belt and black stockings. The debutante walked over her Harrods' gown as if it were a rag. The retail price was three month's salary for the average British worker. She undid his trousers and unzipped his fly. They fell to the floor.

"You take mine off and I'll do the same to you," she quietly suggested, "But before we go any further, do not even consider using a condom. I'm so avant-garde, I'm on the pill so just fire away. No jumping off right at the good bit, let your insides fly into mine."

He kissed her then undid her bra strap after which she removed the black bow tie, unbuttoned his shirt then removed it.

"Let's Spend the Night Together" by the Rolling Stones began to play from downstairs where things were getting into full party mode.

Daniel removed his own socks then Kinsey's briefs, sliding them all the way to floor, gasping with anticipation as he looked up at her nakedness.

Kinsey was about to undo the button on her suspender belt and remove her stockings when Daniel looked up.

"Leave them on, they look really sexy."

"Means you'll come fast." She withdrew the covers and pointed at the bed. "Caroline boasts that her Royal Marines officer can shag her four times in a night. Accordingly, I will require at least five fucks. If leaving my stockings on can make you do that then I'll be more than happy to oblige." He leapt into the king size bed and she swiftly followed him.

Within 30 seconds they were making loud, passionate and very athletic love. The first of seven times of such activity during the night.

EMILY-APRIL 1967

Emily drank her coffee and gazed from the window of James' house. Then the writhing impatience within her burst to the fore. She ran up the upstairs to the master bedroom where James remained slumbering in the large divan. The sheet and blanket were slung back. James jerked forward, instantly wide-awake.

"What the hell's up Emm? We had sex five times last night. You can't be horny."

"No, not at all, well just a little. My Royal Marines officer duly satisfied most of my lustful desires. You must get up and drive Daniel and David to Bristol Temple Meads station in time to catch the Penzance to Edinburgh train. I have to see Mum and Dad and I 'm going to catch up with some case notes at home. You need to see your Mama and Papa, and your wonderful sister. It's difficult enough to get into your mater's good books without her thinking I'm keeping you away from them. Get up and have a shower. You need one, and I'll make you some breakfast."

"When can we get together? For sex I mean."

"It's all you think about. Tonight, either here or we can travel to my flat in Holborn today. Whatever, I have to be back at work on Wednesday. Mister Crawley nearly died when I told him I needed a long week end. I explained that you were going off to fight in that place in the Middle-East and I needed to spend time with you."

"I suggest we go to London." James lit a cigarette. "We'll go in your Cortina. Eat on the way and stay at your flat."

"I have to be at work in two days, you might get bored."

"Not in London, Emm. Besides I can cook your supper. Becky taught both Pip and me the culinary arts."

"We'll talk about that, whether we eat in or out. We need to discuss what we are going to do when you come home."

"In what respect?"

"James, do I have to spell it out? I have an extremely lucrative career, which is on the rise. I am being bombarded by life choices. Sometime, in the not too distant future, we shall have to formalise our intentions. I need structure between us."

"Emm, I proposed to you when I was five. That was over 16 years ago. You can be assured that when I come back from active service, we shall make an announcement."

"Good, I'm getting dressed then driving to Alvescot. I shall see you back here at five o' clock this afternoon. If you cherish your testicles you'd better not be late."

It was a beautiful, sunny spring day in the sleepy village of Alvescot. Emily pulled in her car into a spot near the main thoroughfare. A Short Belfast transport aircraft flew overhead towards the nearby Royal Air Force station of Brize Norton. She got out of her Ford Cortina as Philippa appeared from her Austin Mini. She waved at Emily.

"Pip!" She dashed over and hugged Philippa.

"Emily, what are you doing here? I thought you were in London making a fortune as a high powered lawyer and an intellectual model for Cosmopolitan?"

"I'm here to see James before he flies overseas and to visit my parents. I have been a tad naughty and not been around for a couple of months. It's so great to see you. Let's have a coffee in the Plough and catch up on some gossip. I've missed our regular sisterly chats."

"I have found new friends." Philippa sipped her coffee then lit a cigarette.

"Good, but was there something wrong with your other friends? I always thought that Pat, Christine and Judith were jolly good fun. The four of you were always laughing and joking."

"They were fun, are fun. Nonetheless, as I am to be engaged in the autumn, I needed to widen my circle. I need to brush with a more eclectic mix of folk."

"Of course." Emily smiled, totally unconvinced. "It is completely your own business with whom you make friendships."

"But?" Philippa sensed a caveat in the tone of Emily's voice.

"You seem to be in a vortex of total confusion, I have known you for years and you have always been loyal to your friends and family, especially your brother--."

"Well the times they are changing, as Dylan said!" Philippa snarled at Emily, which startled her.

"Pip, tell me what's the matter. I've known you for all these years. This is totally out of character?"

"Everything is out of character. I'm under pressure all the time to do things I don't want. Even to marry a man who will forbid me from even going to university. And he would never allow me to be a doctor. Allow me! Should I need to ask permission? My nutty mother thinks he is a Greek god. James allows you to do what you want. Why can't he let me be a doctor then I could feel a little more disposed towards him? I'm screwed up, my life's screwed up and the only bits of sanity I have, James, is going off to war in Aden. And you, but you're in London now. I feel like screaming off the roof tops about James going off to that silly war. You should stop him! He would listen to you? I need my life sorted!"

Philippa shook a little whilst she lit another cigarette.

Emily sipped her coffee than slowly and calmly lit a Benson and Hedges.

"You really are a crazy mixed up young lady." Emily empathetically smiled,

"But you're 18. It goes with the manor. And much as I love your brother he does not give me permission for anything. I do not ask anyone's permission. I know that is a hard concept for you to grasp. In your world, and most people's, women have their place and never move out of it. Find yourself a man who'll do the same for you, Philippa. If a boy or a man is dictating your life before you're even engaged, then what kind of white slavery will your marriage be?"

"Julian is not all bad. He can be a laugh. Sometimes. But it is James, you are just letting him go! He may die!"

"Pip, we are both affected by James going off to fight in the Middle East. Nonetheless, he is a man. Legally. He is 21 years old and he chose this career path. I was neither for nor against his decision. It was his and his alone to make. I merely conveyed to him that once he had made his mind up I would support him and that's what I'll do. I love him more than anything, but I'll not even think about chaining his spirit. And Julian is a total wanker. Can you not find someone, er, a little normal?"

"There was a boy. James invited him for Kinsey although why I have no idea. Kinsey only wanted an officer because Caroline is having so much fun with David. But I think he is a flirt, David I mean."

"He is, but he's a man. I think my friend Gloria from uni had a brief romantic encounter with him," Emily cautiously divulged then added, "Is this officer called Daniel?"

"Yes, do you know him?"

"I met him very, very briefly when James passed out at Lympstone. James was always singing his praises. He once told me that Daniel was so physically fit; he was in better shape before he started his commando course than the others were in after they had completed it. What about him? I bet Kinsey has already bedded him."

"She has, and I stupidly ignored him before she had completed our introductions." Philippa sounded a little vexed.

"Philippa, that was very short-sighted of you. As I relish acting the role of your big sister I shall offer a few words of what I consider sound counsel."

"And they are?"

"You must end your mother's control of your future. You must find a boy like Daniel. Someone who is perfect for you. Also, you must realise your ambition to be a doctor."

"Emily." Gerald Crawley sauntered into the general office of the chambers.

"Yes, Mister Crawley." She looked up from her desk. It was a brief hiatus from arduously ploughing through a mountain of paperwork.

"I see you are busy but can you spare me a minute please?"

Emily was in typical work attire, one her conservative navy-blue suits. She duly tailed her employer into his office and closed the door.

"How is our new lawyer doing?"

"Excellently, Mister Crawley. Gill is a great help with all the workload."

"You haven't even met most of the male barristers. This will ensue soon enough. They were all too busy and now their workloads are easing although not by any means drying up."

"So one or both of the women will get the push to make way for them?" Emily turned red as soon as she had spoken,

"Of course not. And if I was stupid enough to go against you, Artie Cooper would take away the work he sources for us. He would simply drop it elsewhere. However, I have two matters to discuss with you."

"I apologise for my inappropriate riposte."

"No need at all to apologise Emily. I wanted to inform you that I am putting your case to the Home Office to have your elevation to the Silk speeded up. By a lot."

"How?"

"With the support of a woman much like you." Gerald grinned then pressed the intercom button to Karen Finch at the desk outside. "Miss Finch, coffees for Miss Wilkinson and me. Please."

He then lit a cigarette and sat down motioning for Emily to sit.

"Your reputation for being a feisty no nonsense lawyer has travelled far and wide. It has spread among the legal profession and to no less a distinguished person than Madame Justice Rose Heilbron."

Emily's jaw dropped.

"Yes. The campaigning lady sees that which she wishes for all her ilk. And with the Labour government things are beginning to change although a little more celerity would be advantageous. Ergo, the esteemed Madame Justice wants to chat with you. And, if she likes what she hears she may recommend that you be appointed a Queen's Counsel. Yes, she may personally lobby on your behalf the Right Honourable Roy Jenkins, our Home Secretary."

Karen brought in the tray of coffee then left.

"That interview with Madame Justice Heilbron will be on Friday, in her private chambers, at three in the afternoon."

"My god." Emily enthusiastically exhaled. "Just to meet her will be such an honour, one of the first women KCs."

DANIEL-APRIL 1967

David Moir waved briefly from the carriage. The sky blue and gold liveried Deltic diesel locomotive drew the azure and white carriages out of Alnmouth station whilst Daniel stood on the platform. The train had travelled from Penzance on its way to Edinburgh. The young officer looked at the local green hued connection train to Alnwick that was leaving from the adjacent platform. Daniel carefully adjusted his green beret. He then bounded up the steps of the footbridge through the exit to where his father was waiting in the station car park.

"Hi Dad," he called out while striding passed the ticket office and onto Curley Lane.

"Alreet kidda. Ah thought ya leave started on Friday night."

"It did Dad. But I went to visit a friend. You know James Marchant from Oxfordshire."

"Aye, the posh lad. We met his parents at your passing out parade. They were very nice. At least they said "hello". I liked the young lad from Scotland."

"David, he was on the train with me. We caught it at Bristol Temple Meads."

Daniel placed his suitcase and bag in the back of the Morris. Jackie

Gibson got into the driver's seat. Within a minute they had turned onto the A1068, the main coast road, and were heading south towards Warkworth.

"Dan." Jackie lit an Embassy cigarette. "Ah don't know why ye didn't choose the air force." "Dad. I told you before. I couldn't do three years in anything' other than the Royal Marines."

"Well, I was a sergeant pilot in fighters in the Far East. One thing Ah never did was to give your grannie even an inkling of what it was really like out there. Women worry, mothers worry. You do the same in Aden--."

"It's alright dad, I'll tell little white lies if I have to. Mother will never know the truth. That's of course if there's anything to hide in the first place. Is everything alright at home?"

"Aye, fine and dandy. Little Jackie leaves school in the summer. He'll work with me on Coquet Farm. Debbie's off to the Duchess School in September. It's good she passed her Eleven Plus." "What!" Daniel exclaimed, "She's off to the Duchess School in the autumn. Of course, time flies. I forgot!"

"Ah think we forgot to mention it, sorry. She's really happy, so is your mother. Of course, a good education's wasted on girls. They leave school. A couple of years later get married and start havin' kids."

"Don't underestimate your daughter, Dad." Daniel lit a Benson and Hedges king size. "She's got a mind of her own and a powerful brain. None of the duck eggs around here'll be any good for her. She'll need to go to university, not marry some thick local twat. She needs a man with some grey matter."

"That's what ya mother says. She's good on the farm but o' course Jackie's a lad. Mind ya, not all the local lads is thick twats. A lot are though. Anyways, let's have a quick pint. Ya mother said the tea can keep until seven. We can go into the Black Bull. That's unless you need t' get away." "As long as it's just one pint," Daniel smirked suspiciously. Jack turned on the radio to The Move performing "I Can Hear the Grass Grow".

Carol pushed her tongue as far down Daniel's throat as far as was physically possible. The car was parked down an overgrown farm track well back from the road. The trail itself was used at most only three or four times during an entire day.

On the back seat, Carol's skirt was already above her waist and her panties slipped to below the level of her stocking tops. "Daniel, stick it in as far as ye can."

"Yes, darling." He placed on the condom then slipped into Carol. "And when I come home from war we can talk about when we get married."

Chapter Eleven

NARRATOR

There is no doubt of the existence of a propinquity between mine own narration and that of others. Both near to and far from the spot in the Cosmos on which I stand at that precise moment in the development of time, space and ulterior dimensions. The specific facets may have diverged from the original template, nonetheless suffice concordance lies to provoke visions of déjà vu, an echo. Perhaps, a reflection stored of some small past deed or future undertaking.

The faces have formed and ought now to be familiar although a tome is yet to impart. I reach out to them. Somewhere deep in the darkest recesses of my cerebral assets perhaps there winds a river of energy. Upon this mighty flow may exist the volumes of our kin and ancestors, perhaps descendants. It may be perfectly transcribed in some evolution, or not, of hieroglyphics and may be readily accessed by those who have a penchant to deduce such things. I know not. The singular aspect that harnesses all my brainpower and mental and physical energies now enlightens this crowd. A gathering of mainly semi inebriated guests. Nonetheless, I appear to be in possession of their attention. I shall resume.

DANESH AND KELLY

In a remote area proximate to Nazeing, PADIT 2 transformed in seconds. It altered from an opaque, monochrome illusion into a solid vehicle on the floor of Danesh's hangar. This construction stood alongside his laboratory. A complex straddling the borders of Hartfordshire and Essex.

Once the onboard computer had verified that all was safe to disembark, the four doors slid forward, beckoning the outside atmosphere.

Professors Gideon and Garside and Doctors Aresti and Marston slid boisterously onto the transportation departure/arrivals area. This was a large concrete base surrounded by a circular, green glass panel and roof that entirely enveloped the proximate surroundings.

Garside was obviously ecstatic that they had travelled into the opposite parallel universe direction. A feat that until recently had been deemed impossible. Garside and Keely pinched their bodies to ensure they were still physically solid and had retained all their mental faculties. "Danesh, you are a genius. Not only of your own universe, and on one tiny planet but possibly trillions of similar compositions. Also, the innumerable parallel universes. We cannot even begin to calculate how many PUs there are. We have no means, no way to gauge that in all of the other universes that form time and space."

"The air is the same. We must explore, absorb like intellectual sponges as many facets of this world of yours as is possible. Or at least practical," Keely advocated. She then followed Danesh out of the landing area via a thick door. They all moved into the main hangar of the laboratory, through the research areas and into the lavish, spacious living quarters beyond.

"Keely, Professor." Danesh invited them into the lounge. "There are rooms through there with en suite facilities. Ideal, should you wish to change and freshen up. We can either dine out or in. The choice belongs to our guests from another universe."

"I would like to check out my room and change." Keely sounded emphatic. "I do not wish to be aesthetically outshone by my PU doppelganger."

At "The Fish and Eels" pub at Dobbs Weir near Hoddesdon, all had dined. They were relaxing, chatting and enjoying after dinner drinks. "In our world this place is called "The Eel and the Fish". "Garside took another swig of his beer. "And this brew tastes identical to our own ales."

"I have been trawling through your libraries and internet." Keely looked somewhat smug. "And I have deduced one thing that Kelly and I totally missed when we first met. Understandable though." "Pray enlighten us." Danesh sat back and lit his pipe.

They were sat on the luxurious armchairs which graced the wooden deck of the outside area. This overhang backed onto and overlooked the picturesque Lee Navigation. A steady flotilla of narrow houseboats glided by. They floated gracefully by on the two centuries old man-made waterway. All were bound for the river lock a mere half-mile downstream.

"Only things you would already know, Professor Gideon," Kelly interjected.

"Such as?" Garside breathed in the tranquil of view of river and meadows rolling away from the platform.

"Detail, the devil is in the detail. Are you sure that we are the most contiguous parallel universe to yours?" Keely enquired while taking video shots with her iphone. She surprisingly added. "Kelly and I have the same DNA. For all intents and purposes, we are identical. That is but for one small detail. An almost insignificant factor makes us dissimilar in a way I did not initially suspect."

"Keely, you deemed Kelly to be two years your junior?"

"Yes, Professor Gideon. How did you know?"

"From my copious calculations. All universes were created at the Big Bang from precisely the same provenance. Like circles in a pond when you throw a stone in. They are identical but slightly apart. The variations at first inspection are minor. Notwithstanding, when expanded over many thousands of parallel universes could indeed be exceedingly substantial."

"Danesh, I too have calculated this." Garside also lit his pipe. Apart from hairstyle and clothes he was identical to his other world persona. "But the PU s are not circular but more oval. As Danesh has already deduced, it is not that Kelly is two years younger than you, Keely. It is simply that a blip in the formation of the Cosmos made this world two years younger than ours. We have proved this by checking news items from two years ago on our world which are almost, almost, identical to this dimension."

"Is everything preordained?" Keely looked at the professors.

"Scientifically, almost certainly, yes." Danesh sucked on his pipe. "Infinite amounts of chemical reactions, the laws of physics, chemistry and biology intertwined in a massive singular motion. A momentum that encompasses the Cosmos and travels according to cause and effect down to sub atomic level within those laws. I know not and would never speculate as to whether these phenomena were initiated by some supernatural or divine entity. However, we can calculate and predict with no small degree of accuracy what will happen in the future. After all we do it currently with weather forecasts."

"Professor, what I am saying is, can we alter that which is already written on this scientific tapestry? Are we with the potential to change the future? Or the past?"

Garside stepped into the discourse. He held a beer glass in one hand and his pipe in the other. "That we have yet to determine. But one singularity we have investigated is the existence of UFOs."

"Unidentified flying objects from deep space?" Kelly gawped.

"Yes," Danesh spoke next, "However, I, we, are of the opinion, and it is backed by robust research, that UFOs do not come from the farthest parts of space in a universe, any universe. Instead, have been for several thousand years, merely visitors. At least so far, we assume they are just visiting. They come from parallel universes. These aliens are not from light years away. Those distances are impossible to cover without time travel unless you talk in terms of epochs. The close encounters as we call them are with fundamentally identical beings from parallel worlds. Their universes are a little older than ours. It is these beings we must seek out and compare notes."

PHILIPPA-JUNE 1967

"Becky, you bake such wonderful savoury snacks." Philippa tucked into a Cornish pasty. She had purloined it from a batch that Rebecca had only just removed from the oven.

"Lady Philippa, you are such a little glutton. You'll eat anything."

"No. I have tried to emulate your culinary masterpieces. Although mine have a reasonable taste, they are not in the same league as your Magna Opera. So yes, Becky. I will eat anything but only if you have prepared it. I do not get so many opportunities now as you spend so much time up at Sloane Square helping Daddy and his staff there."

Rebecca blushed profusely.

"Lady Philippa." Hodges somewhat deferentially entered the kitchen.

"I beg your pardon, My Lady. But the ladies Elmira, Caroline and Kinsey are in the drawing room awaiting your presence."

"Thank you, Mister Hodges." Philippa took a serviette and wiped the residual crumbs from her mouth. "Becky, I shall have a glass of champagne with the ladies. Would you be so kind as to bring some of those adorably delicious pasties up to us? Please. You are such a treasure. I love you so much."

"I'll get so embarrassed, Lady Philippa." Rebecca turned almost crimson. "Of course I shall bring you a plate of pasties up to you. Would you like something with them? Chips, cheese or chutney." "Some cheese and pickle would be nice, thank you."

Philippa skipped from the kitchen along to the hazel decor of the opulent drawing room. Inside, Elmira, Caroline and Kinsey stood alongside a tall young man. This figure boasted longish chestnut locks. He was dapperly dressed in a leather jacket and low hipster chequered trousers with a frilly white shirt. She recognised him as Elmira's friend, Fred Byatt, who belonged to a very affluent and influential family. The girls were all dressed in stylishly casual wearing beige trousers, pink blouses and blue silk scarves.

"Pip." Elmira refrained from smirking. "We invited Fred. Those two are besotted with officers serving somewhere in a foreign field and fighting the foreign foe. I am already claimed. I jest of course, I am still waiting for the right man. So to make the numbers up we brought Fred. Have you met Fred?"

"Yes, he and I have been introduced." Philippa sighed and placed a cigarette in her mouth. She then proceeded to place some 45s on the record player. The "play' lever was flicked, heralding The Mamas and Papas singing "Dedicated to the One I Love". The song seemed to emotionally affect Caroline.

Rebecca and Mrs Cromer knocked and entered. They were both bearing large silver trays of Cornish pasties garnished with a sumptuous variety of cheeses, pickles and salads.

"Thank you, Becky and Mrs Cromer." Philippa acknowledged the pair who returned the smile and took their leave.

"I was wondering if we could have dinner tonight." Fred nonchalantly posed whilst lighting the desuetude cigarette dangling from Philippa's lips.

Caroline and Kinsey gasped with astonishment. The music changed to The Kinks and "Waterloo Sunset".

Philippa smiled then looked up at the tall figure, their eyes affixed for some moments.

"Why not?"

"Good. Shall I pick you up at say seven? We can enjoy cocktails first. Afterwards head for Didcot."

Philippa was painstakingly completing the application of her makeup. A new release by The Youngbloods, "Get Together", was playing on Radio Caroline as she made her way down to the foot of the opulent oak staircase. The debutante had decided not to opt for hippie clothes, her latest wardrobe additions. Instead she elected to go with a more a conservative look. This being a Pierre Cardin mini skirt, cardigan, pink tights, sky blue leather jacket and scarf.

The clock in the entrance hall was striking seven when it the sound of a car pulling up outside Wye Hall was audible. odges bid Fred enter. Philippa kissed him on the cheek.

"Would you like a cocktail before we go?" Philippa dispassionately enquired.

"No thank you. Perhaps at the restaurant. I have booked the table for eight so shall we be off?"

Louise brusquely appeared from the study.

"Philippa! Are you going out with Mister Byatt?"

"Yes, Mama. I am having a drink with Fred and then I shall be staying the night with Elmira."

Louise was fuming but restrained herself. "Well have a good night."

"Thank you, Mama. Come on, let's go."

Philippa ushered Fred out of the door and to his green Jaguar E type. It was parked outside on the gravel topped drive.

"Let's be off while we can keep the roof down in this." Fred opened the door for Philippa. He stepped into the driving seat and switched on the radio.

"Silence Is Golden" by the Tremeloes was playing.

"Is this your motor car?" Philippa was suitably impressed.

"Goodness me, no, I could never afford even the insurance. Although Papa gives me almost permanent dominion over it and he pays for the maintenance, tax and insurance. Also bequeaths me a very healthy allowance. I want to work but papa says work is for horses and gentlemen take on some sinecure. This he says he will find for me but alas, or otherwise, he's still searching. I think no one wants to employ me."

Philippi giggled a little and gazed momentarily at the beautiful views flying passed as they sped across the Oxfordshire countryside.

"Where are you taking me?"

"The Chequers Arms at Aston Tirrold. Do you know it? It's south of Didcot in north Berkshire." Fred turned out of the drive and headed south for the B417 road.

"Of course I know it. I'm not a Philistine. It does a dashed good pate foie gras, and also scallops and chorizo. I'm starving so I hope your wallet is bulging."

The wind flowed through Philippa's hair as the DJ announced the next song current his as being "Pictures of Lily" The Who.

The waiter took their coats then showed them to the table. It was a window view looking out onto the Berkshire downs. The décor was stained oak panelling, padded oak chairs, matching tables and a thick green carpet.

"What would you like to drink? Champers?"

"Yes, but first I shall give you my order. I'll have pearl barley soup, and the scallops and chorizo. They have it on the menu! I shall choose for my main course the roast beef, medium rare, with celery and spears of asparagus with sauté potatoes. To accompany the meat I should like a bottle of Chianti, for the other courses I shall stick to Champagne."

"You are a positive woman, Lady Philippa Marchant." Fred deliberately raised his voice a little for the benefit of the prying clientele. Several diners looked around then began to gossip behind their hands.

"And you Mister Byatt are a trouble maker."

"Well, I want all to know that I am dining with Lady Philippa Marchant, a renowned socialite, debutante and main subject of all the women's magazines and fashion rags. The unofficial head of the "In Crowd" and a magnet for all society chat. Allow me to bask in some of enhanced scene the kudos of this will do for me."

The waiter approached. "Would you like to order drinks, sir?"

"Yes. I'll have a '63 Dom Perignon and a '62 Tenuta Fontodi Chianti Classico to go with the meat course. Also I'll have a gin and tonic for starters."

With the meal over, Philippa lit a cigarette as the waiter served coffee and brandy.

"You are such a catch, Lady Philippa. When are you marrying that Julian guy?"

"The Honourable Julian Lee Watersby." She inhaled and almost spat out the name. She then whispered. "Fred, everyone in this place is glued to our conversation. Some things I have no problem with accidentally on purpose divulging. However, this matter I would prefer to discuss away from prying ears. You settle the bill. I'll go and powder my nose and then we'll move on."

The darkness was enveloping the rustic scenery as Fred and Philippa stepped into the E-Type.

"Where to? "He turned the ignition and the radio burst into life with Sandie Shaw singing her Eurovision entry "Puppet on a String."

"I have a house, my own place in the Vale of White Horse. I'll direct you."

Philippa took Fred into the comfortable lounge of her property. This construct stood near the small Berkshire village of Goosey in the famous Vale of the White Horse. It was a medium sized cottage in a remote location. The vista overlooked seemingly endless acres of idyllic rural landscape. The room was furnished in good taste Edwardian style. A large aspidistra stood in a corner aside an Ottoman, two armchairs and a coffee table. There was a dry stone fire place with a large iron fender and spacious tiled hearth. Inside a huge wire basket were with a vast amount of thick logs. Within the fireside stood a well-stocked magazine rack upon which, looking somewhat out of place, perched a Dansette record player. The numerous singles and albums were stored in a wall of racks nearby.

"There's a bottle of claret in the sideboard." Philippa pointed at the oak cabinet. "Could you open it? There should be a cork screw next to it?"

"Now we can talk. Despite the quotes in magazines, some say your mother actually made them. I get the impression that you are not as much in love with Julian as the publications seem to think you are."

"I love music." Philippa sardonically grinned. She commenced playing a stack of 45 rpm records from the current charts, the first being "The Wind Cries Mary" by the Jimi Hendrix Experience.

"So do I. And I just love your hip collection, very groovy and right in my scene. But you did not respond to my pointed statement. Do you have a penchant for muscular officer types who serve Her Majesty and are willing to lay down, their lives I mean, for her?"

She walked up to Fred and ran her hand up and down his chest.

"Caroline is madly in love with her Marines' officer, David. She can't wait until he gets back from Aden. She'll go to university while starting to plan their future together. I hope to God he comes home alright from that war. If not it will totally destroy her. Kinsey is not in love. She really likes her soldier but claims not to love him. Anyway, he has a chick up north. My personal opinion is that Kinsey only wanted a soldier because Caroline had one. She's jealous of how happy the groovy smitten little kitten is."

"So?"

"I quite fancy him, Daniel I mean. He's very dishy, modest, latently powerful and very, very sharp. But I really do not have a penchant for military men, even as handsome as him. Of course you look pretty groovy as well."

Fred poured a glass of Bordeaux and handed it to Philippa.

"You have not yet commented on Julian."

Philippa lit another cigarette. Fred took an ashtray from the sideboard and placed it on the table beside her.

"Fred, you know the score as well as I do. If I had any feelings for him at all I would have brought him into the conversation. I did not, you did. He's not boss, just plastic. And I do not want to bring any scandal to the family so I obey my mother. Life is always easier when one placates the old mater lady."

Philippa drank her wine. "Let's take the bottle upstairs. There you can undress me then see if you can shag me as many times as a Royal Marine is supposed to be able to. So I am reliably informed. I do not wish to be left out of the fucking stakes."

"Philippa, is that a letter from Julian?" Louise came from the study into the foyer.
"Yes, Mama."
"You sound quite happy. May I enquire as to the basis of your felicity?"
"Oh Mama. I am not abundant with exhilaration. It is to masque my disappointment that Julian will not be back here until almost Christmas."
"Of course." Louise was not convinced despite Philippa sounding believable. However, she decided against pursuing the matter.
"I have to go, Mama. I need to do a little revision for the "A" levels I am sitting next week."

The 18-year-old ran through to the kitchen and poured herself a cup of tea.
"Lady Philippa." Rebecca removed the lid from a tin of freshly baked cakes. She placed some on a bone china side plate and handed them to Philippa. A huge smile beamed from ear to ear. "Just why 'ave ya got a grin likes a Cheshire cat?"
"Oh, dear Becky, I have news. Mister Julian has been detained in Australia. It appears thus that their civil service is very busy due to the war in Vietnam. Consequently, he is unable to return until late December. I am so sad."
Philippa burst out laughing. "It's so sad."
Rebecca gently laughed. "I think ya bein' a little sarcastic, Lady Philippa."
"Moi." The young woman sounded even more facetious.
"I'm sure Mister Julian is a really nice man."
"Becky, he's a stiff. A plastic cut out excuse for a man who's old before his time. Not groovy, very square and a dip stick to boot. I do my "A" levels over the next few days. After that I'll be off to university to study medicine. Long before he comes home. Put the radio on please, Becky."
Rebecca switched on the Bush transistor tuned into Radio Caroline. It soon had Philippa singing along to "The Boat That I Row" by Lulu.

"Becky, what did you think of that friend of James, Second Lieutenant Gibson, from up in Northumberland?" "He's at war. Is he not?"

"Yes, he is, but what was your opinion of him? You know how I value your wisdom."

"To be honest, Lady Philippa, he's everything a lady should want in a gentleman. He's young, strong an' handsome. He's intelligent, dashing, well mannered, well-educated an' he's goin' to university after his service. He's only doin' three years in the Marines. A great catch, even for someone. Well someone not too unlike a young lady not far from me."

"Really." Philippa was surprised by Rebecca's panegyric. "You think he's that good?"

"First Cut Is the Deepest", written by Cat Stevens and sung by PP Arnold, came on the radio.

"Lady Philippa you're too young. Ya only sees the looks or other things."

"Go on, Becky," Philippa sipped her tea.

"I've come across some stinkers of men in my life. Me mum was wi' one. I can spot a no good a mile away. Mister Gibson is the kind of man who'd be faithful, love you and take care of you. And, for you especially, I could never see him pushin' a woman around. He'd always discuss things wiv ya, see what ya thought. I thinks anyways. You asked me, My Lady, I told you."

"Yes, but I think maybe my friend Lady Kinsey has designs on him. I ignored him at the party. I told you Becky, I was a real bitch."

"Miss Kinsey's not serious. You invite 'im back 'ere. Be interested, My Lady, but not too much though. I'm sure you'll get him. Of course, after Mister Julian's been resolved."

EMILY-JUNE 1967

The bespectacled, plain looking clerk showed Emily through to the private chambers. The lawyer was simultaneously excited and apprehensive. She strode purposefully along the lavishly carpeted, sunlit and amply windowed corridor adjacent to the suite of offices. The 22- year- old had been meticulous and patient during the selection of the most apposite attire for her pre Silk interview chat with Madame Justice Rose Heilbron.

The young clerk knocked on the door and announced, "Miss Emily Wilkinson, Madame Justice."

The conservatively dressed, dark haired and elegant 53-year-old was reading the Cosmopolitan magazine. It was edition in which the article relating to Emily was featured. She turned to the assistant, also attired in a dark conventional suit, and requested courteously, "Miss Stokes, would you be so kind as to bring us a tray of coffee. And not that instant rubbish?"

"Of course, Madame Justice."

The woman departed closing the door to the well-lit and luxuriant office.

"Miss Wilkinson." Rose warmly shook Emily's hand. "My, my, you are just as beautiful in the flesh as your picture in Cosmopolitan magazine. Please, take a seat"

"Thank you Madame Justice." Emily nervously sat opposite the veteran QC.

"I apologise for having to postpone this little chat a couple of times. There were pressing matters at court that required my consideration. Yes, I did enjoy your article in Cosmopolitan.

It bestowed the virtues of women professionals without demeaning them. In this world, run totally by men and that hopefully will change, I have observed a few crucial truisms. If an attractive woman does well in their career, which seems to be rare, their peers will say she slept with the boss. If she is well known, the press will want to know all about her love life and not professional achievements. The photographs were sexy. How could they not be with a girl, sorry young lady, as attractive as you? And yet they were shot with you dressed almost as you are now. In a very low-key style with the skirt on the knee and not a yard above as seems to be the current fashion."

Rose picked up a packet of cigarettes and offered one to Emily who accepted.

"Madame Justice, the editor, Helen Gurley Brown, is anxious to tell the world about professional women. Not to present them as brainless sex objects for the gratification of men but people with potential. Those who can make a massive contribution to any organisation up to the top echelons."

Christina Stokes returned with a tray of percolated coffee and chocolate digestives. . .

"Miss Brown sounds like a woman after my own heart. Would you like a sherry as well as coffee?"

"That would be lovely, My Lady."

Rose poured from a decanter sherry into two large schooners then handed one to Emily.

"Cheers." They touched glasses, and each took a sip of sherry.

"Now Emily, you are entering a world where the odds will always be stacked against us Portias, female lawyers. If you make an error, no matter how slight, you will be adjudged a "stupid woman". This is exacerbated when the woman is blonde. Even blondes as intelligent as you are. Should you have the audacity to raise your voice by even a tiny volume you will be deemed to be either sexually frustrated or having your periods. And if you have the temerity to attain promotion the political gossip will maintain that you will have been having sex with someone who wields influence. But I am sure you are well aware of these personal experiences of mine. I am the daughter of Jewish immigrants who made it their mission to ensure that I was educated to the highest possible level. I was only 25 when called to the bar. If successful, you could even be younger when taking Silk. Now my dear Emily, I want to know all about you."

"Hello, Miss Wilkinson speaking."

"Emily, it's Dean here. Dean Sinclair." Boomed the voice at the other end of the telephone line.

"Yes, Dean. How can I help you? I'm very busy with a backlog of cases so I can't stay on the line for long."

"How are you fixed for lunch? My treat."

"No can do, Dean. Like I said, I have a back log the size of a mountain. However, I shall have no qualms if you want to treat me to a lavish after work dinner. I thought you were back in the Big Apple."

"I was but your article was a real blast Stateside. A lot of people want to find out more about you. What time should I have a cab outside your chambers?"

"To be realistic, Dean, I would say eight thirty. I shall dash home, shower and change and be back here, starving. Is this business or pleasure?"

"Well, maybe it's a touch of both. See you at 8.30."

Emily replaced the telephone receiver. She bounded out of the general office, up to the reception desk.

"Karen. Is Mister Crawley available?"

"Miss Wilkinson. He is. And unless he was entertaining Her Majesty, I think that Mister Crawley would always have time for you. Just go in."

"Thank you." Emily smiled, knocked then entered.

"Emily, what can I do for you? That article you did in Cosmopolitan was excellent. There was not only the huge fee we received but a swathe of free advertising. Consequently, the work is flooding in. You really have the Midas touch."

"Thank you, Mister Crawley. I am just letting you know that Dean Sinclair from Cosmopolitan is buying me dinner tonight. I shall let you know tomorrow what it is all about. Also, I have a shoot with Vanity Fair next week., they want photos as well."

"Of course, enjoy your evening with Mister Sinclair."

"What would you like to drink?" Dean looked up after scanning the menu.

"I'll just have a tonic water with ice and lemon. Perhaps some wine with the main course," Emily responded.

"Waiter," he called out, "Scotch on the rocks and a tonic water for the lady."

"Let's slice through the small chat, Dean." Emily lit a cigarette. "What is the real reason you asked me out to dinner?"

"I shall not pretend Emily. You're a delicious looking broad--."

"I would prefer you called me a woman, Dean. Broad sounds very common."

"Your wish is my command. You are a great looking woman. And I do have ulterior motives. Yes, I would like to go to bed with you."

"I have to admire you for your unambiguous approach. Alas, I am not available. With war between Israel and Egypt imminent and my boyfriend risking his life in Aden, I deem myself capable of the facility to abstain from sex for a few weeks."

"Fair enough." Dean grinned. He conceded defeat, at least at this juncture. "Then I do have a business proposal to present. Direct from Helen."

"Fire away, Dean." Emily picked up her drink.

The restaurant was very avant-garde. A luxuriously decorated new establishment called "The Old Dutch". The name sounded Cockney to many but was so entitled as it served Dutch food. Mainly sweet and savoury pancakes. The sound of Jeff Beck singing "Hi Ho Silver Lining" drifted around the place.

"Well Emily." Dean swigged his whiskey. "Helen read your article and absolutely loved it. She doesn't want the Sandy Posey "Single Girl" type. The sort who have ambition but give way to men's demands. She wants a trailblazer and someone who will carry the flag for a female revolution. She's working on the idea of a woman judge carrying out cases and decisions on a TV show. In her name of course. Also writing for women with legal problems in the magazine."

"Jesus, Dean. I know from university that American law is based on English law, but I have no idea of the details. I would not know where to begin. Nor do I know anything about television."

"A Whiter Shade of Pale" by Procol Harem came over the PA system in the restaurant.

"Relax." Dean cast a reassuring glance. "Helen is aware of all that. If you took the job now she'd have you tutored by the best law experts in New York State. She'd make sure you passed the bar exam. However, she kinda guessed you'd say that. Helen's a person who plans for the long term. She draws the big picture and works towards that. Helen will wait for when you're ready because that's how much faith she has in you. She'll hang on for ya for two or even three years. You're buying a house outright in somewhere near London."

"On Mill Lane in Broxbourne, Hertfordshire," Emily warily imparted.

"Well I can tell ya. You take this job up and with the pay cheque she would give ya, you'd soon be able to buy the whole town. You're pushing the ripe old age of 23. You could soon be paid as much as the top men in industry. Just think about it."

"Very tempting." Emily smiled as the waiter came to take their order. "Very tempting indeed."

Emily was dashing into her office as there was a mountain of work she had to read. The bulk being cases that Artie Cooper had directed to the chambers.

"Miss Wilkinson," Karen called out, "Mister Crawley wants to see you the minute you arrived. Please go straight in." She dropped her bag by her desk then knocked and entered.

Gerald Crawley looked up from behind his desk. "Emily, how did your recent Silk interview go?"

"It seemed to go very well, sir. But even I am versant with the fact that it would take much more than a good interview to make me a QC. One, because of my youth and two, because I am a woman."

"Have you heard of Roy Jenkins?"

"Of course, Mister Crawley. In our profession and beyond everyone knows the name of the Home Secretary."

"Mister Jenkins listened to the good counsel of Rose Heilbron. They both concluded it would be in order to call you to the bar, given Silk. Congratulations Miss Emily Wilkinson, Queen's Counsel."

"That's wonderful, Mister Crawley. I'm dumbstruck and so honoured."

"And you deserve such an honour. We will celebrate your elevation soon. Although it was back in 1939, Rose Heilbron was but 25 when she was made a KC as they then were. You are a mere 22. On business matters, we have appointed another QC. He's Mark Carlisle, and he'll head up the other team alongside yours. Artie Cooper was as good as his word. I trust he does not expect any "off the record" favours for all the business he has thrust our way."

"The only caveat I am aware of, sir." Emily smiled, her spirits were in the stratosphere. "Is that should he require it, we defend him."

"He means you defend him, Emily." Gerald lit a Senior Service. "There is a lot of bad blood in gangland. It is more than ironic but I suspect we have more to fear from the purported upholders of law and order than we have from the alleged criminals. I have spent a lot of time with both the police and villains. To be brutally frank, I would trust a known gangster like Artie more than I would some of the coppers I've worked with."

"I am aware, sir, those police officers, Baxter and Heathcock, were charged. They have been dismissed the service."

"Emily, I am cognisant of the fact that you are a black belt in karate.

Nonetheless, be just a little careful when outside of work. Those men have a lot of influence and long memories."

"I will, sir."

Emily briskly stepped back to her office, perused the check list she had of cases then turned to the young clerk, Eddie Hopper. One of two clerks allocated to both her and Bryan Villano.

"Could you please get me the papers from the filing room for that new case? Thomas versus Regina?"

"I have work to do for Mister Villano," Hopper curtly responded.

Emily glared. "Do you not even have a minute to collect some papers?"

"No, I have this job for Mister Villano." Hopper's position remained trenchant.

"I told 'im, he works for me." Villano entered the room and scowled at Emily. "You'll 'ave to wait. Until well after you've made the tea."

"Very amusing Mister Villano. I have far too many cases to go through--."

"After you've made the tea. Women make the tea."

Emily looked up, breathed in then nodded. "It appears to be the case. However, I do not have the time. I must go and collect some papers. It seems as though we will need a new clerk for this work soon." Emily strutted to the filing room whilst the two men grinned and chortled.

She was impatiently rifling through wads of paper when Villano entered.

"Mister Villano, this filing is in shit order. Can you get it sorted? Please."

"Good enough for ya. We does our best, Miss Wilkinson. We ain't all got the contacts like you 'ave. Shootin' from a trainee to blue eyed girl in months. Droppin' yer naffin' drawers eh! Lettin' those influential folk slip it in."

"How dare you make such allegations? Also, I am a barrister. I have brought business to the chambers and I don't expect to do my own filing."

"Too good for ya, too good for a woman. Well I'll tell ya, ya a woman! Ya makes the tea and flashes your legs to keep the men 'appy! Understand?"

"Villano, I wouldn't do anything to please you if you were the last man in the world! Understand?"

"Ya bitch; ya think it was ya that brought in the bacon here. Ah'll tell ya, it was me!"

Villano lunged at Emily. He grabbed her knee and attempted to slide his hand up her skirt. The clerk rapidly found himself pressed against a filing. The offending arm twisted up his back.

"Oops, Mister Villano. I never told you. I'm a black belt in karate!"

As Emily released his arm Fiona Derby and Karen Finch charged into the room.

"Miss Wilkinson, are you alright?" Karen glowered at Villano.

"We heard everything. Mister Villano, Mister Crawley wants to see you in his office. Immediately."

It was mid-afternoon. The sun was still high in the early summer heavens. Billy Parkins came into the kitchen of Artie's residence. He found Artie preparing the evening meal for him and his daughter.

"Billy, what's up?"

"Where's Miss Wilkinson, boss?"

"She's wiv Dot, givin' er law lessons. She wants to do it at university. Why?"

"The word is, Artie, that the office manager or whatever he was--."

"Villano," Artie interjected.

"Yeah, that's 'im."

"What about 'im, Billy?"

"After 'e got the sack for tryin' it on wiv Miss Wilkinson the other day, 'e went to see the bent coppers under investigation. The two Miss Wilkinson caught at ya trial. I hear e's put 'is two penneth. They'll now be workin' togewer. They is a team, I hears. Word is they's plannin' mischief and fucking no good stuff."

"Sounds like they's up to no good. Wouldn't trust any of 'em. What's the name of that copper we know. The straight one. An honest fella?" Artie asked.

"Johnny Robinson. From up north. He's an honest copper. He keeps away from the bent bastards. Robinson can't be bought There's lots don't like 'im for that."

"Not too many o' those coppers nowadays, Billy. Honest ones. Ah want ya to arrange a meet wiv 'im. Whose 'is snout?" Artie enquired. He removed a tray of lamb chops from the cooker.

""Totter" McCloud is the one we fink 'e uses, Artie. Ah'll check and see if we can arrange a meet."

"Yeah, 'cause Ah wants 'im t' look after Miss Wilkinson. On the QT o' course. In return we'll scratch 'is back wiv info. Even more on the QT. Check if any of our rivals been up t' villainy recently, Billy? If 'e looks arter our lady lawyer we'll look arter 'im, but straight. No fuckin' deals or spondulicks. You get my drift?"

"I think we have to close for the day. I have an appointment with my bank manager."

"How did Ah do?" Dorothy anxiously enquired.

"On the Local Government Act of 1966, you need to read a bit more. But on items like the Murder (Abolition of the death penalty) Act of 1965 you were excellent. Keep it up and you can come and work with me," Emily finished writing comments on the test paper of her pupil.

"Really?" The 17-year-old beamed. "I'd love that."

"Pass your exams first, then we can talk. Bye, I'll see you next week."

Emily walked into the branch of the Midland Bank at 210, High Holborn in the West End. She informed the receptionist of her appointment with the branch manager, a Mister Martin Greaves. "Come in, Miss Wilkinson." The lanky, grey haired Greaves pointed at a leather-padded chair in front of his desk.

"You are a very affluent person. Especially for someone so young." The manager cast an envious smirk.

"That, Mister Greaves, is my business. Yours is to take care of my money and if you deem yourself wanting in that task I shall take my business elsewhere."

Greaves seemed mentally thrown by the blunt riposte.

"Miss Wilkinson, please accept my apologies. I meant no ill will. I asked to see you as I may be the harbinger of some good news."

"It must be something of note to use words like harbinger, Mister Greaves."

"Yes." He smiled again. "I studied the classics."

"Bully for you, Mister Greaves. Please inform me of the reason for my summoning."

"Well, Miss Wilkinson, I am sure that you are aware of a company called Fenbow?"

"Never heard of them."

"Well someone in your family has. In 1955, a clause was made in a loan to a company that a portion of the annual gross profit was to be paid in perpetuity to several named persons. That organisation is now trading as Fenbow. I only know that you are one of those persons named. Your share was held, invested and in trust. That was until now, or should I say since you turned 21. I have now received the first cheque to pay into your account. Of course, I can put you onto investors, Miss Wilkinson. Your custom is considered paramount to my branch. There are many matters we can discuss, if you need a lawyer--."

"I am a lawyer, a QC, Mister Greaves. Are you saying that this company has paid me a substantial dividend? What do they trade in?"

"I believe they are called computers. They are very advanced business machines for offices."

"You sound as if the dividend was generous. Precisely how generous is it?"

"Miss Wilkinson, I received a crossed cheque payable only into your bank account, first post this morning. It was from Fenbow and is for seven million, 253, 417 pounds, 14 shillings and sixpence."

Emily was silent for several moments.

"Wow, that's a huge amount of money. Put it immediately into my deposit account. In a few days I shall return to you with investment instructions."

NARRATOR

We have arrived at a notable milestone. A pivotal moment in this saga. My tale of a journey, across time and elsewhere. It negotiates triumphs, disasters, elation and heartache. It replicates, perhaps, the passage of any soul from the cradle to the ultimate destination we all share.

As a young child both my mother and father would talk incessantly about the "Summer of Love". The heady days of mid to late 1967. Of course, as my father oft reminded me. If one happened to be a British serviceman in Aden, or an American, Australian, New Zealander, South Korean, South Vietnamese or other of the Allied Nations' soldiers in South Vietnam it was by no means a "Summer of Love". Daddy always mentioned, sometimes still does, the music of "Flower Power". Songs laden with "San Francisco" in their titles such as San Francisco (Be Sure to Wear Flowers in Your Hair), San Franciscan Nights and Let's Go To San Francisco.

All the singers and musicians had long hair. They wore long flowing, flowery garbs and were called Scott or Eric or something. Some were taking LSD and other stuff while ostensibly practising "free love." My mother never thought free love was so good. She always reckoned it was to keep guys happy but only served to keep young chicks under the thumbs of sex starved dudes. Nonetheless, I never asked either of them how well they did for sex during all that time of "free love". Apart from being embarrassing to me, my parents were not physically together. Daddy was off somewhere in a foreign land while mummy was hard at work back in this country. As I would expect, my adorable grandparents paint a valiant picture. Both working and serving, duty and family. It was almost written in the stars.

Whatever, it was an important juncture for them both. Daddy once said that when he first encountered mortal danger; it was the last day of his youth. His untainted and secure childhood was sent scattering deep into the darkest recesses of his consciousness.

JAMES-JUNE 1967

Second Lieutenant James Marchant threw his kit onto a chair in the officers' accommodation area, a room he shared with Daniel. He was the commander of 5 Troop, X-Ray Company, 45 Commando, Royal Marines, British Petroleum Camp, Little Aden, Aden Colony. James sat on the cot bed and began to remove his boots. The dust from the long patrol, hours in the blistering middle-eastern summer sun, lodged in every part of his body, clothing and psyche. It made him nauseated. His troop of young Royal Marines had patrolled a geographical arc, which ran from Silent Valley cemetery across to the Federation's Secretariat area in the village of al-Ittihad. This zone lay between 45 Commando's barracks in Little Aden and the highly volatile area of Sheik Othman. Here were their arch rivals, 1 Para, the First Battalion of the Parachute Regiment. This force was commanded by Lieutenant Colonel Walsh. It had been waging an almost private, some entitled it unholy, war with the NLF. The National Liberation Front, the main terrorist organisation in Aden. The paratroopers' observation posts were under attack daily.

Each day seemed to be surreal to the 22-year-old officer. The Royal Marines were part of the Aden garrison whose mission was to uphold law and order and the Queen's Peace as the colony approached independence. This break from HM Government was expected in the spring of the following year. James reflected on the six weeks he had spent in this, one of the last colonies of the once mighty British Empire.

The small region, situated at the southern tip of the Arabian Peninsula, had been subjugated by the British in 1839. Following its annexation, it been principally maintained as a refuelling port for ships bound for the Far East. Nonetheless, with the certainty of British withdrawal from all bases east of Suez, except Hong Kong and Brunei, the function of Aden would soon be redundant. The role of the circa 3500 infantry soldiers, supported by armour, artillery and the impressive Hawker Hunter FGA 9 fighter bombers of the Royal Air Force was to contain the insurgents. To defend British lives and interests until the last United Kingdom personnel had been safely withdrawn from this, barren, dry, rocky, searing, pungent place. He recalled the stirring talk Lieutenant Colonel Owen had given all the newly arrived men. James had looked and could not believe the sky could be so blue or the cragged hills so awe inspiring. He was less impressed by the capacity of the dry heat and dust to reach so far down the back of his throat. James forced himself into a level of activity by sitting on the chair in his small, private area within the officer's quarters. He stripped down his Browning nine-millimetre pistol. The bronzed subaltern adhered to normal practice insofar as carrying this weapon. In line with other officers, James also drew a Fabrique Nationale 7.62 calibre self-loading rifle, the SLR. This weapon had already been returned to the armoury. James had decided he would clean and oil his pistol. Following this he would shower and change then go to the officer's club for a drink.

"Mister Marchant," James' troop sergeant, Andy Diggle, called out. Diggle then knocked on the thin wall. "Yes, Sergeant Diggle."

"Sorry t' bother you, sir, but the CO wants all officers, warrant officers and troop sergeants in the officers' mess, sir. He said it was urgent."

"I'll come with you, Sergeant. I trust it will not go on for too long. I'm starving. At least the guys got their scran. They needed it. Didn't they?"

"Yes, sir, they did. It was a long patrol, sir."

"A long, fucking boring one, Sergeant. I didn't take the Queen's shilling to piss about like a school boy. Looking aimlessly at the rocks, hills and roads, and of course the BP oil refinery. It adds some dimension to the landscape, don't you think?"

"If you say so, sir. Oy never really looked with ya academic eyes."

"You're late, Second Lieutenant Marchant," Lieutenant Tony Bowman nastily scowled.

"Yes, I am, Mister Bowman." James walked on into the officers' mess where all summoned by the commanding officer had duly congregated.

"You call me "sir", Marchant, I am the senior officer."

"Bollocks," James responded.

"I think we can dispense with such formalities, Mister Bowman." Captain Bob Lowes, the company second in command came forward. "James, glad to see you back. I want to chat on some of the items in your debrief."

"Yes, sir."

"Peter," Lieutenant Colonel Owen approached Major Adams. Adams was standing close to his X-Ray company troop officers. David, Daniel, James, Tony Bowman and Dubliner Niall Quinn.

"Yes, sir," Adams deferentially responded.

"Are your chaps all here?"

"Yes, sir. All my officers and senior NCOs are present."

"Good, I think we have all six companies here." John Owen, CO of 45 Commando, made his way to the centre of the mess.

"Gentlemen," Owen commenced his oration, "As you may or may not be aware, you ought to be if not, on May the 22nd just gone, President Nasser of Egypt closed the Straits of Tiran to Israel. Three days later he expelled the United Nations observers from the Sinai. This is an act of war as they are international waters. Since then Egypt, Jordan and Syria have all mobilised. Despite having 20,000 troops in Yemen, just over the border from the British Protectorate of Southern Arabia, there are at least 100,000 Egyptian troops in the Sinai Desert." Owen looked up at the youthful faces around him then continued. "It is almost certain that war between Israel and her Arab neighbours will soon commence. Other Arab states, Iraq certainly, will join in any fray. Her Majesty's Government is officially neutral, but we have already placed two aircraft carriers, HMS Centaur and HMS Eagle at each end of the Suez Canal to prevent closure of the waterway. HMS Albion is on standby with 40 Commando. The British garrisons in Near East Command and British Forces Arabian Peninsular have all been placed on alert. This is to provide a contribution to any task force that we, along with our American and other NATO allies, may require assisting the State of Israel. That is of course should our government deem it politic and possible to do so. Here are the contingency plans, in case. If the balloon does go up, those involved will have to have their kit packed and ready to deploy three hours after the order comes. It will be that tight gentlemen."

Once James and Sergeant Diggle had outlined the contingency plans to their men they marched to their respective dining areas.

The young subaltern made for the officers' mess for a pre-dinner pink gin. The sun was still blazing with intensity. Nevertheless, it was much reduced in potency compared to earlier in the day. This cooler ambience allowed James to thoughtfully gaze across towards the houses on Marine Drive leading to the BP Oil Refinery, the beach and the terminal berthing area of Little Aden. The lines of tented accommodation looked almost life like as he hastened towards the officers' club close by the parade ground.

Inside David, Daniel, Niall and Tony were chatting to Captain Bob Lowes. Major Peter Adams and James entered almost together.

"James, come chaps, let's have a quick pre-dinner wet." Major Adams walked them all towards the crowded bar. From somewhere, the hit song of the day, "San Francisco (Be Sure to Wear Flowers in Your Hair)" by Scott Mackenzie was drifting over the oil terminal juxtaposed base. After dinner the CO, John Ivor Headon Owen, with his 28-year-old Commando Adjutant, Captain Ben Vickery, completed the requisite rounds of the six companies under his command. These were represented by the troop officers in the mess. Owen then drew his company commanders with their seconds in command to the far end of the bar, away from the ears of the subalterns.

Daniel, James, Niall, David and Tony were left looking at their empty glasses as the distant music changed to the Turtles and "Happy Together."

"I want to get to my pit." James yawned. "I'm totally fucked. I've been up since before dawn crawling across this God forsaken shit hole to watch sand, rocks and a few nice places. It's Sunday the 4th of June 1967. I've been here for six weeks and haven't fired a shot yet."

"It's the areas of responsibility." Tony Bowman acidly cut in. "You'll get your chance to shoot."

"All I've done so far is get bored to death." James continued his carping. "Ser'nt Diggle and I smoke like chimneys. Not out of fear but boredom."

"Jimmy, you're getting tedious," David deigned to speak up, "Either get back to your pit and have a wank about your gorgeous lady then sleep. Alternatively, inflate your mess bill and buy us all a drink."

"I'll have a drink, a shower, a wank then a gonk. I'm exhausted," James wearily imparted.

"Anyway, Davy boy." Daniel for a change offered his packet of Capstan Full Strength to the group. "On the subject of gorgeous ladies, are you decided which of the fillies who are in constant heat for you will you choose?"

"No choice." Niall took one of Daniel's cigarettes. "And I think we should report it in the Globe and Laurel magazine that Second Lieutenant Daniel Gibson offered his smokes without being cajoled."

"Piss off, you Irish reprobate." Daniel laughed and picked up his gin and tonic from the bar.

"Let's hear who Rudolph Valentino Moir wants to slip into the sack with as soon as he gets back to Blighty." James lit his cigarette as two Hawker Hunter FGA9 jets from RAF Khormaksar flew across the bay then banked north.

"I listen to him, Scotty Moir," Niall cheekily disclosed, "I listen to him as he gonks in my area and the randy bastard talks in his sleep. Yes, while he's gonking he chats away. And all it is, is "Caroline this, Caroline, that."

You can hoodwink other folk, Davy, but we know she's your lady. The subject of your fantasies. "Ohh Caroline, you have such lovely tits, and a lovely arse. I love you!" That's what I hear every night."

"So, it is the delectable Lady Caroline Feversham our Scottish warrior loves."

James was genuinely interested.

As his concentration had been on the mission since arrival in the Crown Colony of Aden, James had barely cast a thought about matters other than military until then.

"Of course, Jimmy. The curvaceous, gorgeous, Lady Caroline hath eyes only for our Scots officer." Daniel grinned at James who appeared to have returned to a different planet. That was until the sound of an explosion in the vicinity rocked the mess tent.

"Incoming! Take cover!" Sergeant Helm bellowed across the camp.

Royal Marines moved around the Little Aden base. As best they could, all measures had been taken to protect the area in the event of a frontal assault. The early afternoon June sun continued to beat down on the rocky peninsular. The "stand down" was finally ordered upon which troops of soldiers gathered for further instructions. Major Adams approached his subalterns.

"What happened, sir?" James came forward first. Much to the obvious annoyance of his former school colleague, Tony Bowman.

"Listen up chaps," Adams addressed his officers, "Seems like our friends the Israelis hit Egypt at 07.45 hours this morning and details are very sketchy. However, Royal Navy Intelligence reports that they flew out into the Med, away from Egyptian radar and hit the Egyptian Air Force on the ground. We have two carriers nearby, so the top brass thinks that this attack on the base was related to the Israelis. I do not have to remind officers to stay switched. Carry on."

DANIEL-JUNE 1967

Daniel was stretched on his bunk writing a letter. It was one of the three per week he mailed home. One was to his parents and two for Carol Green.

It was barely eight days since the end of the very short war. Six days in total between Israel and Egypt, Syria and Jordan which had left the tiny Jewish state overwhelming victors. She was now in control of territory which had seen her overall size enhanced by a factor of three. The British and other forces in the Middle East and Arabian Peninsular had not been called upon. Despite this undeniable fact, Cairo radio had blamed the Royal Navy for assisting Israel in the destruction of its air force. Naturally, such an inaccurate allegation was strenuously refuted by Whitehall.

The 18-year-old had only just returned from a long patrol with his 6 Troop. That being 30 Royal Marines plus Sergeant Helm. The small force had travelled to the border between Aden Colony and the sheikdom of Aqrabi, one of many such territories that formed the British Protectorate of Southern Arabia. The men had been mounted in Saracens, other armoured personnel carriers known as Pigs and escorted by Saladins of the 4/7 Dragoon Guards. They had traversed through the flat, arid, lapidary dust bowl that lay wedged beside the British Protectorate of Southern Arabia. The soldiers had dutifully reconnoitred for Egyptian sympathisers covertly entering the British territory. Daniel had ordered two section strength foot patrols into the desert. The 20 Royal Marines marched from the temporary base of laagered Saracens to watch for such incursions although none had been spotted. The NLF, together with their less aggressive allies/opponents, Front for the Liberation of Occupied South Yemen, FLOSY, had evolved, with Egyptian and Soviet assistance, into effective guerrilla fighting organisations.

These groups had to be contained. This was paramount despite the proximity, even at the most pessimistic estimate, as being no more than nine months to the British withdrawal.

Daniel had already cleaned and oiled his self-loading rifle before locking it securely away with the rest of his valuables.

As always, he had taken his Browning pistol with him to the shower. Once thoroughly washed and shaved the subaltern donned a fresh, clean shirt and socks, vest and underpants.

Daniel took no undue risks. Even on the base, the pistol was never more than two feet away from his grasp and always kept within view.

As the patrol had been returning from the borderlands he had noticed the locals, the Arabs, had seemed more than usual disinclined to make eye contact? It may of course have been a figment of an overactive imagination fuelled by a scorching, hostile environment

A riddle crossed his shrewd consciousness. Did they know something? Or had all the recent terror incidents in the colony pushed perception to the outer limits of sensitivity?

Like all those serving in Aden, Daniel had read the newly published hand-written warning notices posted across the extent of the territory. These notifications informed all service personnel to be extra vigilant and watch with care for booby trapped items. The communication had informed all concerned that many such devices may have been posted in buff manila envelopes marked "On Her Majesty's Service" or simply "OHMS".

The summer weather had been vicious, not cooled by the Gulf of Aden or the Indian Ocean. This weather gave rise to a salt laden humidity, which tended to rust metal with extreme alacrity.

The southern tip of the Arabian Peninsula sweltered in the intense heat as Daniel could hear "Something Stupid" by Frank and Nancy Sinatra coming from the OR's mess. Vehicles, weapons and soldiers alike needed constant maintenance. Once cleaned up, he lay on his bunk. He began to write profusely.

The teenaged officer lit an Embassy tipped cigarette then ceased putting pen to paper. Instead he revisited and re-read the missives received the day before. These correspondences had been studiously penned back in England by his mother and sweetheart.

June 6th 1967
Warkworth
Northumberland

Dear Danny,

I hope you're all right over there. News here has all been about the war in Israel.

Stephen Grenfell

We heard a lot of folk got killed but luckily it didn't last long, which is good.

The weather is good here, has been very sunny. Your dad moans about our Prime Minister Harold Wilson all the time. He complains about how much tax he has to pay.

Debbie will be off school for six weeks soon. She's going to stay with a friend's granny up at Beadnell before she goes to grammar school in September. Little Jackie says he's leaving school and wants to work on the farm with your dad. I'd be happier if he stayed at school.

But once you're out of the Marines you'll be going to university so if you and Debbie do that, Little Jackie can do what he wants. He loves working with your dad. He loves driving the tractor and clarting around with the engine.

I was talking to Fiona Green. You'll already have letters from Carol, so you'll know, but she says Carol is on her way to university down at Exeter in Devon. Isn't that where you were? Mrs. Green says Carol is missing you a lot. She says you two are serious and will be engaged when you leave the Marines in 1969 and married after you leave university. Once you have a job of course, in 1972 she says. Well that would be lovely. We all guessed that you and Carol would tie the knot.

Dad is busy putting new fences up around the top and the ford fields.

Now Danny I want you to look after yourself. Eat lots of good food.

Love from Mam and Dad and Little Jackie and Debbie

"Life goes on as usual back home, it's the 19th of June 1967 and I'm out here in this stink hole. It's like being in the furnace of Dante's Hell," Daniel muttered before lighting another cigarette and reading the letter from Carol.

June 7ʰ 1967
The Butts
Warkworth
Northumberland

Hello Darling,

How is my precious little warrior doing in the far off battlefields?

I'm busy listening to "Good Times" by Eric Burdon and the Animals. Wow! What a great group they are, and Eric is still a Geordie Boy. Warkworth is the usual, all the townies and their tarts going to the caravan site and the village pubs are full up.

I have to tell you my little soldier boy that I am in dire need of you. I told my mother we would be married in about 1972 and she thought it was a long time away but I told her you have to finish your army service, like dad did in the war. And then you have to go to attend university then get a top job, so I can stay at home and bring up the children.

Oh Daniel I'm so looking forward to being your wife. I shall have a degree but women don't have careers once they are married and I want to get married ASAP as I miss you and I want you between the sheets getting stuck in.

Oh, I'm being so naughty, I dream at night my pillows are you. I am listening all the time to the Beatles new album, Sergeant Pepper's Lonely Hearts Club Band. I love the tracks Lucy In the Sky with Diamonds, With A Little Help from My Friends and A Day in The Life.

I'm so randy thinking about you and I sprayed some perfume on this letter and kissed the bottom so you can kiss me even though we are thousands of miles apart. I dream of you, and even more so as I listen to Dedicated to The One I Love by the Mamas and The Papas. There's a great new song called A Whiter Shade of Pale by a group called Procol Harem, it is fab, really, hip and groovy. Cop a listen to it if you get the chance out in the desert.

I dream about you all day and everyday my baby, I love, love, love you to bits.

I want you to touch me, run your hand up to my naughty parts and make me squeal.

I will not even wear any knickers when you come back from out there.

I miss you loads and want you home so I can have a life of ecstasy and loads and loads of fucks. You look after yourself you little stud and keep your hands off those lovely belly dancers. Want you hot inside me. I need you inside me.

Love you, Love you, Love you a trillion zillion times.
Your randy girl
Carol

xxxxxxxxxxxxxxxxxxxxxx

Daniel pushed his feet into his black DMS, directly moulded sole boots. The next job was to wrap the long roll of his khaki puttees around the tops of the boots and fasten the bottom of each trouser leg to his lower calf. He had decided against writing anymore today. Instead he would make his way passed the barracks areas to the officers' mess and enjoy a few aperitifs before dinner. Soon after that he planned to hit the sack and sleep, gonk in his new vernacular.

He passed Niall Quinn.

"Hey Paddy," Daniel called to his fellow subaltern, "Do you fancy a quick wet, the sun is over the yardarm?"

"If you put it on your tab, ya Geordie fella." Niall smiled in agreement. What sounded like gunfire came from the direction of the Crater district of the city of Aden.

The two had only just entered the club when Major Adams followed them.

The company commander was in an obvious state of disquiet. "Daniel, Niall. Get put your guys on ready to move!"

"Sir, we've only just returned from the border." Daniel lightly protested.

"I can't help that, Second Lieutenant. Something big has kicked off. A lot of shooting, on Champion Lines. The Royal Northumberland Fusiliers and the East Anglians are involved, I believe. We don't know for sure. And Lieutenant Bowman and his troop are patrolling around Madinat al-Ittihad. Word is he may be in the drink. If so, we'll have to extricate him as all other companies in the Commando are on standby. So, put your chaps on prepare to move as we'll only get a couple of minutes to be ready when the whistle goes off!"

PHILIPPA-JUNE 1967

The day was fine. A slight breeze from the west stroked the cherry blossom trees nearby. The gentle gust had a shower of pink petals float gently onto the ebony hued thoroughfare.

Philippa parked her new "F" registration Austin Mini near Jesus College in Oxford. She began to walk in the direction of The Randolph Hotel situated on Beaumont Street.

It was the era of great music she mused as the sound of Cat Stevens singing "I'm Gonna Get Me A Gun" came from the direction of Worcester Street. Probably some new avant-garde wine bar or upper echelon café as pop music was "hip" and no place was "cool" without good vibrations echoing throughout. She deliberated and mulled over many matters. These happened to include the fact that she had completed her "A" Levels and was bound for the School of Medicine at Oxford University in only three months. An actuality that she still found surreal.

This situation had arisen totally void of her mother's blessing. The parental support for this aspiration was delivered solely by the Earl of Wye. It was he who had covertly and actively encouraged his daughter to realise her childhood ambition. However, and unsurprisingly, the acid test remained. This caveat was in the form of whether the Honourable Julian Lee-Watersby could accept his future wife going to university for what he had once described as "a complete waste of a few years."

"Well, Miss Snobby Face."

Philippa looked around to see her former school friends Judith Parkhouse, Christine Vickers and Pat Laidlaw coming in her direction.

"Judith, Christine, Pat, so nice to see you. How are you?" Philippa was momentarily psychologically unbalanced.

"We are all well, Philippa. As if you could care less," Christine responded first.

"Yes. Of course, we are not good enough to be the friends of Lady Philippa Marchant." Judith was the second to speak.

"It has to be Lady Elmira Barnard, Lady Kinsey Maple or Lady Caroline Feversham."

Pat brought up the rear. "And, of course we are not ladies of standing. We are of course but not that kind of lady."

"I'm sorry, but I have moved on. Now I must go. So nice to see you all again."

"Oh, you will see us." Judith impishly smirked. "We're all going to Oxford University to study medicine. So, you will certainly see us. That is as long as your quirky fiancé allows you to be a doctor. You're a real snob, Philippa. But even you could not stop us being doctors. And we have no nutty boyfriends to demand we leave our higher education."

"That is such a cheap shot, Judith. Of course, I 'll be a doctor. Now good day. I have an appointment." Philippa strutted off in the direction of The Randolph.

She walked into the lounge as Fred came to his feet and kissed her on the cheek.

"What would you like?" He smiled before offering her a cigarette.

"Just a Riesling. Make sure it's well chilled, Fred." He lit her cigarette then his own.

She placed her bag on the extended, rose patterned and cushioned chaise longue. It was by the window overlooking Beaumont Street. removed her vanity case prior to applying a small application to refresh her lipstick.

"What's up?" Fred returned with the drinks.

"Nothing more than any other dysfunctional family. Daddy spends most of his time in London. He claims it is for business, but his head office is near here in Oxford."

Philippa sat in her pastel pink trouser suit, with medium length hair and dark glasses. She drew on her cigarette then took a sip of white wine.

"What do you think your father is up to?"

"I have no idea. But I do know that Becky, our cook cum nanny cum maid, who is very attractive by the way, turns bright red every time he comes near her. She also seems to spend a lot of time at the Sloane Square house."

"Sounds perfectly normal to me, Pip. Our servants are old and craggy. Well they're over 40. Yet my father still has a little flirt with them. How is Julian?"

"Still in Australia, in their civil service. His father wangled him a cushy job in the Department of Defence based in Canberra. He works for the big man himself. The Defence whatever he is, some old fart called Sir Edwin Hicks who runs the show. He, Julian, buys, or procures to use his expression, equipment and stuff for the Australian troops in Vietnam. I wish he'd go there himself. He writes to me every other day and I reply once a fortnight. I tell him I'm very busy."

"Pip, you can be such a cow when it takes your fancy. What does your mother think about that?"

"I never ask her. She is determined I marry the bounder, inferring that the heavens will fall if I refuse. Continually blabbing on about the family name. Daddy does not even give a jot and he is the one that saved the family, name and fortune."

The jukebox began to play "Then I Kissed Her" by the Beach Boys.

"How is James? Do you still fancy that dishy officer type from up near Scotland?"

"I really hear a lot from James. Although he divulges less than my cat about what's really going on or what he's doing. If I believed all that he writes he's only taking jolly rides out into the blissful desert then drinking afternoon pink gins, having dinner, then more pink gins. I actually listen to the television and radio news and there is no way can he be doing that. Yes, I do think about Daniel. He is muscular and handsome and has brains too. The trouble is, I think Kinsey wants him. At least she claims to. I do know that Caroline is hot, very hot, for David. She's already starting to look at wedding gowns and they're not even formally engaged. Anyway, Freddie Byatt, I fancy you. I wanted to get away from the house and visit my cottage. I was wondering if you would like to join me for the night. I'm feeling very randy!"

Fred shuffled uneasily on the chaise longue before responding. Philippa believed for a second that he had spotted someone walking down the street outside. "I think tonight is out Pip. But give me a ring. I should be available soon."

"Is something wrong? Are you peeved with me? I thought we were groovy."

"A bummer but I have a tight schedule, Philippa. I shall ring you. But now I must go."

Fred kissed her lightly on the mouth then moved off at pace. He turned right out of the hotel. Fred was striding away when Philippa deemed he had grabbed a smallish man by the hand. This bond ended in an instant. However, she noticed that the face of the other person was pale, and the oily hair was swept back. The pair seemed excited as they walked off.

"Shit," she despondently muttered, "At this rate I shall definitely be marrying Julian the bottom hole."

It was less than an hour later when Philippa turned off the Alvescot road. She drove onto the long access lane that led to Wye Hall. The debutante parked up the Mini feeling not a little down and dejected. She walked around the spacious and nurtured garden, admiring the late June flowers. The daffodils and tulips had gone. Cherry blossoms were shedding their cerise spring blooms, nonetheless she recognised White Daisies. Further along were pink Granny's Bonnets in the expansive flower adjacent to the hedges of the maze that lay proximate to the tennis courts.

The sun was hot but not sweltering. Philippa took some time to admire the flora of the well-tended grounds that ran westerly from the house outwards to the paddocks.

The 18-year-old debutante was caught in a storm. She was riding a whirlwind, a tornado of cascading and competing emotions, desires and ambitions. The hormones within her becoming frame were raging as she stepped towards the small but impressive folly. It was an imitation Chinese pagoda, built between the tennis courts and the stables. She lit a cigarette and began to sob quietly.

Over near the stables a radio was playing "Ha Ha Said the Clown" by Manfred Mann. Philippa breathed in the air, the smell of freshly cut grass drifted around. The figure of the gardener, Jim Parnell, stripped to the waist and perspiring profusely, walked from behind one of the privet hedges. He almost collided with Philippa.

"Excuse me, M'Lady. Ay didn't see ye there."

Philippa made no immediate response. Instead she unhurriedly scanned the dripping torso with her craving fired youthful eyes. The muscular frame, bulging biceps and equally pronounced pair of blue jeans stoked an already rampant wildfire within.

"Mister Parnell, I believe there is a small piece of maintenance work that requires attention within the folly. Could spare a moment to look at it? Please."

The music from the stables changed to The New Vaudeville Band performing "Finchley Central".

"Of course, M' lady." Jim sounded self-confident although there was still a hint of circumspection. "Good. Then follow me."

She sauntered lazily. The curvaceous figure complimented by the cerise trouser suit did not miss the attention of 27-year-old Parnell.

They were soon at the folly. Philippa guardedly opened the French doors and entered the comfortable but not pretentious interior. There was a gramophone onto which the rubicund locked teenager placed "Silence Is Golden" by the Tremeloes.

"This has to be you, Jim." She pointed at the turntable as Chip Hawkins did his small solo vocal in the chorus, "but my eyes still see". "Silence must indeed be golden as the maintenance needed is me. I need a rogering. But before we get down to it, no pun intended, I will say this with all seriousness. If you want me, I'm willing as I'm on fire. However, a word of warning. I'm sure you have a sufficiently high IQ to know I mean what I say."

"Ay fancies ye M' Lady. Course Ay does."

"Then listen carefully. You must tell no one and I mean no one."

"Ay'll not tell a soul, M'Lady. Cross me heart. Ah'll do just what 'e says."

"It will probably only be the once Jim so enjoy and trust me, I'm no little servant girl, remember that."

"Ay understands M'Lady."

"Then take off your jeans and underpants. I want to see if the lower half of you is as good as the upper bit."

Within a paucity of time Jim was on top of Philippa on the large couch inside the building. She squealed with delight at the thrusting. The love making ended with a long shrill cry of ecstasy and the song changing to "I Got Rhythm" by the Happenings.

"God! Oh My God! Ah! Ah!!" She was engulfed in a floating, heat induced mental and physical frenzy. The searing flurry left her entire body convulsing from neck to toes.

The young woman lay on the couch, naked, gasping for breath. She was still simmering with elation when she reached for her cigarettes.

"Go away, Jim. Get back before someone misses you. I must say though, that was quite nice."

"It was 'eaven for me, M'Lady."

"Remember what I said. I was not joking."

"Will ye want to again, M'Lady?"

"I'm not Lady Chatterley and you're not Oliver Mellors. However, one never knows. Keep it to ourselves and you never know. I'll call for you if I have a need."

EMILY-JUNE 1967

The workload had been stupendous in both volume and intricacy. Emily and her team were battling through an exponential increase in cases. A deluge pushing both responsible managers to the limit of fortitude. Mark Carlisle, a new QC, was manager over Gill McMenemy, a barrister who lodged with Emily during the week. John Arthur was also a newly recruited trainee barrister along with two new clerks. Lester Freeman aged 21, tall and ginger haired, together with Paul Yankow. He was a

45-year-old Royal Air Force veteran of World War Two and tall with grey, receding hair.

Mark was five years older than Emily. The 28-year-old had missed out on National Service. He had been at university when his call up papers arrived, and conscription had been abolished by the Conservative government by the time of graduation.

Mark had swept back black hair with "Brylcreem" added. To date Emily had never heard him utter a single derogatory comment about women. Gill worked for Mark although he was as likely to make the coffee as she was. Karen, the receptionist would often take on refreshment duty when the jobs became too hectic. Emily soon perceived that Mark would never showed any animosity towards her, in fact the reverse. She became concerned that he might make an indiscreet move until Fiona quietly whispered in her ear that the new QC was homosexual.

Emily also employed two QCs in her team, Team A as it had been officially entitled. Old hand William Potter, a trendy 35-year-old and newcomer Roy Friarhouse, a chubby 29-year-old.

The dismissal of Bryan Villano had meant that the two incumbent clerks, Eddie Hopper and Ben Dooley, had come under the direct control of Emily. A situation that she relished. When the pace of work eased she would deliberately instruct that they make coffees for all.

"Emily." Gill walked into the general office of Team A. The young QC was feverishly writing up notes. "I was on the way out. Do you need any help? I was going to the house."

Emily tiredly looked up from her desk.

"No, Gill. I'll not be long. I did forget to prepare any dinner. If you are passing the Chinese near the station at Broxbourne could you get me sweet and sour pork, bean shoots, egg fried rice and a portion of chips and keep it for me? I'll heat it up in the oven when I get home. Thanks."

"I will. I'll pay for it and a bottle of wine. You've bought the last three takeaways. Also, I shall give you a cheque for the rent tomorrow."

"No rush, Gill. I'll just finish this case and I shall go straight over to Liverpool Street and get the next train."

"Alright, I'll see you later. Before I go, did you know there's a "World in Action Special" tonight on ITV? It's about the British in Aden so you may be interested?"

"Thanks Gill. But I hear all I need to about Aden. I'll see you later, I won't be long."

Emily completed the few small jobs, nonetheless essential to the case in hand. She visited the ladies room where she dabbed on a fresh layer of lipstick. Once her coat was on, she picked up her handbag and black leather brief case, turned out the lights and made for the exit.

Gerald Crawley opened his office door.

"Great progress today Emily. There's a lot of work to do so have a restful night."

"I shall Mister Crawley. Goodnight." She smiled then walked through the entrance lobby onto Lincoln's Inn Fields. Turning onto Remnant Street she headed for Holborn Underground station and the Central Line for Liverpool Street.

The young QC seemed to sense a presence close by. However, as it was London in the now entitled "Swinging Sixties" there would always be someone nearby in the West End. The capital city never slept. The Tube carriage was quiet, she lit up a cigarette then glanced at the Law Journal. Soon afterwards the train pulled into Liverpool Street.

Emily stepped smartly from the platform to the barrier where her ticket was checked. then up into the main hallway of Liverpool Street station. To her dismay she had narrowly missed the 19.20 train for Hertford East and would have to wait for the next one that would stop at Broxbourne. That departure was the 19.55 to Cambridge from platform five.

"Damn." Emily groaned and then decided on the spur of the moment to have a quick walk over to Spitalfields Market. The voluptuous barrister crossed Bishopsgate and headed up Artillery Lane. As Emily she came near to where Artillery Lane connected with Sandy Row she thought she noticed a bizarre spectacle. This appeared to be a revolving cone of golden light pursued by a distinct sensation of terror. From out of the illumination four figures menacingly encroached. They moved to her front and tail.

"Fuckin' bitch!" The first man grabbed at Emily her. He was garbed in a red corduroy jacket and boasted greasy, swept back hair. The thin face was unshaven displaying a thickly stubbled chin.

Emily responded by viciously kicking out then belting him across the chest with her elbow. The second assailant, a smaller man in a black leather jacket was poked in the eyes which such force he screamed and fell back onto the pavement. As she was aiming at a third attacker, a fourth struck her forcefully on the head with the handle of a pistol. Emily slipped painfully into unconsciousness.

A face materialised as her eyes focused on a man. He was about 45 years old, shining a light in her eyes.

"Who the hell are you?" Emily shrieked.

"Take it easy, Emm." Dorothy Cooper stood behind the man and the torch. "This is Doctor Les Sinson. You 'ad a bad bang on the head. He's just checking ya out."

"You seem to be fine." Sinson concluded. "However, Miss Wilkinson, I'll give you some painkillers and I strongly suggest that you pay a visit to your GP in a few days. Much earlier if you feel dizzy or get unexpected headaches. Just to make sure all is well." The doctor packed away his medical equipment then departed.

"Where am I?" Emily sat up and recognised she was in Artie Cooper's house. "What happened?"

Dorothy brought a cup of tea.

"Here, drink this, Emm. Ya was set on by three geezers. Ya gave two a right hidin'."

"Obviously not all of them. I recall trying to hit the third when something hit the back of my head. Dorothy, was it your dad that arranged the attack on me.?"

"Course not, Emily. It was 'is blokes that 'ave bin watchin' ya girl. They even followed ya on the Tube and chased the buggers off."

"Watching me? Why?"

Artie entered the room with a tall, handsome man, about six feet in height. He had black hair that was short yet in a modern style. He was wearing a smart, but not upmarket, blue suit.

"Miss Wilkinson, are ya alright? My boys 'ave been watchin' ya an' they stopped the villains takin' ya away. But just too late to stop 'em giving ya a crack on the bonce. We hopes yer alright."

"I'm fine Mister Cooper. A sore head but fine. How did I get here?"

"One of me boys from near Liverpool Street. He brought ya here in his motor car. Made sure we collected your brief case an' 'and bag. No one's bin through 'em. We got the for Doc Sinson. Thought it was safer for ya to get ya 'ere."

"Safer from whom?" Emily picked up her handbag, took out her cigarettes and lit one.

"Some nasty villains, Miss Wilkinson. Not just criminals but the Filth, sorry." Artie looked at the dark-haired stranger who just grinned. "The police. Some bent coppers 'ave been followin' ya."

"Why?"

"Because you more than ruffled their feathers in a recent court case, Miss Wilkinson," the dark haired man spoke up.

"And you are?" Emily glared.

"Sorry, Ma'am. I'm Detective Sergeant John, most call me Johnny, Robinson. I come from Newcastle on Tyne but moved down here and work for the Flying Squad."

"Your Geordie accent is very refined Sergeant. I am still bemused by why I was assaulted."

"We suspect, in fact know why, but cannot as yet prove it. You've upset some bad, very bad people," Robinson explained, "It must have been serious for Artie Cooper to contact me. As a rule, he would normally run a mile when I appear. Now it's like he's converted to the side of the angels. Artie has been watching, guarding you. Right, Artie?"

"Why the fuss?" Emily remained confused.

"It could soon get as high as the Met Commissioner, Sir Joseph Simpson, Ma'am. There could be soon a real drive to root out corruption in the Force. There'll be a huge increase in business for lawyers like you as every bent copper arrested will bring in a mass of appeals from the criminals they got convicted. These characters will waste no time in having the convicting jurys' decisions overturned and claiming massive amounts in compensation. It'll upset the balance between the criminal and police fraternity. It looks like they want you out of the way as you seem to be very successful in defending cases, especially where the police evidence is somewhat spurious and that's why you were targeted. They all want you silenced. Both the police and the villains. It's no exaggeration, Ma'am. If this anti-corruption drive is only a fraction successful, then there'll be mayhem. The villains don't want incorruptible cops as they like them in their pocket. We also have some feedback from abroad that it may also involve international organised crime. You've kicked a right hornet's nest."

Emily took a sip of her tea then turned first to Dorothy. "This is why you have to pass your LLB at university Dorothy. Mister Cooper, I shall need a lift to the nearest over ground station if anyone is available."

"My Dad'll get someone t' drive ya." Dorothy gazed towards her father.

"Yeah, yeah, sure. Ah'll 'ave Billy take ya to the station. Dot, go an' tell Billy to bring the Rover around an' drive Miss Wilkinson t' Hackney Downs station. Better still, ask Billy if 'e can takes 'er all the way t' Broxbourne."

"OK, Dad." Dorothy nodded and began to move off.

"That's alright, Artie. I'll drive Miss Wilkinson all the way to Broxbourne," Sergeant Robinson graciously offered.

"That is very nice of you Mister Robinson." The impish expression seemed to suggest that Emily was recovering from her ordeal. "I have a house I share with another lady lawyer. I also have a boyfriend who is an officer in the Royal Marines serving in Aden. So there will be no elongated night caps."

There then followed a pregnant pause in which Robinson shuffled with embarrassment. Although it lasted but a couple of seconds, to the policeman it seemed like an eternity.

"I had no such expectations, Miss Wilkinson. I merely deduced that after your tribulation, you'd appreciate a ride to your door in safety." Johnny was adept at being economical with the truth. He believed that he had masked his true intent. "Then let's go, Sergeant. We ought to be there in about three quarters of an hour taking the A1170. Then onto the Great Cambridge Road."

"Nice house," Robinson stared at the impressive large, detached property in Mill Lane, Broxbourne. The famous 17th century New River lay at the bottom of its garden and boasted a picturesque vista. This was of lush pastures and woodland rolling towards the London to Cambridge railway line some quarter of a mile in the distance.

"Thank you." Emily beamed and picked up her brief case from the floor of the passenger side. "I think you deserve a cup of coffee. If my housemate has done as she promised there should be some Chinese food. That is if you like foreign cuisine."

Sergeant Robinson merely grinned then nodded with eager anticipation.

Inside the house Gill saw Emily coming along the path and quickly dialled a number on the telephone.

Yeah," a voice answered at the other end.

"You failed. She's back."

JAMES AND DANIEL-JUNE 1967

It was early morning. Major Adams had gathered his all troop commanders in the briefing room for an "O" group. The second in command of X-Ray Company stood next to the major. The blond haired, longish side burned, of robust physique and medium height, Captain Bob Lowes. Located before them were four of Adams' five troop commanders. The grimly determined figures of second lieutenants Gibson, Marchant, Moir and Quinn.

The quartet of sergeants was noticeably absent. The senior NCOs were feverishly readying their men and equipment for an immediate sortie into the recently constructed town of al-Ittihad.

Opened only six years earlier in 1961 by a young Princess Alexandra, al-Ittihad lay across the bridge near Wedge Hill that connected the Royal Marines' BP Camp to the imposingly rouge hued desert. This tract of land lay between that area and the main trunk of the colony and on towards Sheikh Othman. The arterial road to the town hugged the coast along the bay to Aden and beyond, all making that day even more of a tribulation for Adams. The 26-year-old company OC was inwardly churning although his address was so cool it could have been delivered at a kindergarten party.

"Gents. The crap is hitting the fan." Adams lit a cigarette. "It's 06.00 hours on the 20th of June 1967, a date which may be written with infamy in the annals of British military history. We now know that Mister Bowman is definitely pinned down in the square at al-Ittihad. Intelligence reports that everywhere else in the colony, hostile forces are preparing to attack. Are we all ready to go into al-Ittihad?"

"Yes, sir," the four troop officers responded in unison.

"Right, this will have to be quick," Adams brought forward a blackboard with a rough map of the target area scrawled on it.

Daniel ran out to where Sergeant Helm was waiting by the Saracen armoured personnel carriers. The wily NCO handed Daniel his SLR. "Just thought you'd prefer this rifle to that pea shooter of a pistol, sir."

"You remembered where I told you the key was Sergeant. But did you also draw ammo and bomb up my mags?"

"Sir, I'm a professional Royal Marine. Ah could never forget my troop officer's ammo."

"Enough sarcasm for one day, Sergeant Helm. And thanks. We've a big op on, is everyone mounted up? Do the vehicle commanders know the grid reference and location of the objective?"

"Yes, sir," Helm respectfully responded.

"Then let's go!" Daniel called out as he and his sergeant jumped into a Ferret scout car. The second lieutenant took the lead at the head of the three Saracen armoured personnel carriers, APCs, that housed his troop. He and Helm then embarked at a fierce, expeditious pace.

Daniel was behind the lead Saracen. The APC whined to a noisy halt. They were at the road junction immediately prior to the thoroughfare leading directly to the contact area and extraction point, the town square of al-Ittihad.

The Marines dismounted from the APC. Two of the Saracens veered left and right respectively at the cross roads on the cusp of the built-up areas just beyond. The vehicles from the 4/7 Dragoons were guarding the open ground that faced towards the main highway and causeway across the bay and Aden port. The Ferret scout car was parked next to these vehicles.

"Sergeant Helm," Daniel called once all three sections of his troop had disembarked.

"Sir," Helm replied.

"Make weapons ready, safety catches on. Lance -Corporal Foster to remain with the two static Saracens, with four of his rifleman. The other riflemen and gunner will come with us. Foster will cover our rear. Corporal Greenham will take the left axis of our advance and he'll cover buildings to our right flank. The machine gun will face forward. Corporal Ely will be on the right, covering the left houses with the gun forward. We'll yomp ahead of the third Saracen. Tell the commander to follow our advance and to bring down covering fire immediately an enemy is spotted. It will be in the way if in front of us and block our view. Once we make the opening to the square all three gunners will fire at their arcs. They'll be supported by the 30 cal on the APC and the rest of Lance Corporal Foster's guys."

"What about rules of engagement sir?" Helm cast a slightly roguish grin.

"Sergeant Helm, I'm fully aware of the contents of the blue card. We, our troop, goes in to get Mister Bowman's troop out. That is our mission. Understood?" Daniel donned his green beret.

"Yes, sir." Helm gave an empathetic nod, his balding pate shining in the sunlight.

"Then let's go, Sergeant! We've pissed around here too long!"

PHILIPPA-JUNE 1967

The song by the trio sized group called Cream, "Strange Brew", was playing on the radio in the kitchen as Rebecca was busy preparing lunch. She was assisted a little by Mrs. Cromer. Maggie Cromer was aging. She was now 72 years old and deep into senescence.

Jim Parnell walked into the kitchen whistling. "What time's dinner?"

"When it's ready," Mrs Cromer snapped, "12.30 as usual."

"Why you so 'appy?" Rebecca looked at Jim. "Ya looks like the cat that got the cream. You've been like that for a few days."

"Nuthin', Mrs Biggs." The gardener smirked.

"Come on. You've got somethin' to tell us."

"Nope. Just nice to be admired by the ladies." Parnell continued to beam.

"Good fer ya." Rebecca lost interest. "Who's the lucky lady?"

The music changed to "1941 New York Mining Disaster" by the Bee Gees.

"That'd be tellin' Mrs. Biggs. But she's only one of many."

"Thinks 'e's Chip Hawkes from the Tremeloes," Rebecca facetiously remarked.

The Miasmic Mist —Volume One

As Mrs Cromer began to lay the servant's table, Rebecca checked on the upstairs meal sizzling in the oven.

"Is the luncheon on time, Mrs Biggs?" Mister Hodges was his usual pernickety self.

"Yes, Mister Hodges," Rebecca responded, "Today the earl and his family, plus guests, will have poached salmon mousseline. That'll be followed by Beef Wellington with sauté potatoes, mixed summer vegetables an' Peach Melba for dessert. Our fare is somewhat less exotic. It is tomato soup, pork chops, peas and mash then a jam topped steam pudding and custard. The family're are lunching at one, Mister Hodges. I'd suggest we eat now."

Rebecca had begun to pass the servant's china plates to Mrs Cromer as Philippa entered the kitchen. She was dressed in a pink mini skirt, white tights, and chiffon blouse with a light orange silk scarf wrapped over the top of her head.

"Hi." Jim Parnell smirked.

"Er, hello. Kindly address me as "My Lady", Mister Parnell. Becky, something smells great. What is on the menu today?"

"I did tell the master, Lady Philippa. It's salmon, beef and Peach Melba."

"Mama says lunch will be at one today. There are some ghastly people visiting Daddy. I must attend of course, but after the midday meal I want to dabble in the garden. I would like Mister Parnell to assist me. I know so little about plants and am anxious to be educated."

"I'm sure Mister Parnell can spare some time," Hodges stated, "But Mister Biggs is also an expert horticulturalist. Perhaps he may come too or instead of Mister Parnell."

"Oh no. Mister Biggs may be called upon to partake in driving duties. I shall not keep Mister Parnell away for more than 20 minutes. Half an hour at the most."

"As you wish, My Lady."

"Thank you, Mister Hodges. Then I shall see Mister Parnell at 2.30 outside on the lawn. It is such a nice sunny day. Ideal for nature and horticulture."

"Bernadette" by the Four Tops came over the radio.

Once Philippa was out of the kitchen and away from earshot Rebecca scowled.

The wise and wily figure of Mister Hodges had second guessed her thoughts.

"Mister Parnell. When you 'elp Lady Philippa in the garden, you make sure you acts like a total gentleman."

"Don't know what ya means, Mister Hodges," Jim sardonically remarked.

After the lunch dishes from both the staff and the family had been washed and cleared away, Rebecca watched as Parnell, over at the far end of the kitchen near to the back door that staff used as an entrance, seemed to be dabbling with a some of sections of photographic and electrical equipment, not easily distinguishable from a distance.

Philippa walked into the folly. Jim Parnell was already semi naked and appeared to be both irritated and startled as she entered.

"Ya shouldn't showed me up, My Lady. Not in front of the others."

"Then you should not be so disrespectful to me. In front of the others."

"Ya never said that when you wuz heavin' and sighin' underneath me"

"Mister Parnell. Yes, I think you are groovy and a nice piece of male flesh. But let's be clear, you are a gardener working for my father. The Earl of Wye. It is best that you are always aware of that truism."

Jim shook his long blond locks.

"Ya've said that already miss. Ya either wants me or ya doesn't."

"Alright. Get your pants off and let's get onto the couch."

"Is that all, M' Lady?"

"I'm afraid so. Either get on the couch or I'm going. What did you expect?"

"A bit more closeness. Perhaps w'could go out. Somewhere quiet but out together."

"Sorry. That's just not possible. Not at all. You're a noble savage. A nice guy and a great fuck, but you have little above the neck. As I said, a bit of rough to have as a change, sorry."

The voice of Steve Winwood, lead singer of Traffic was heard as their new hit, "Paper Sun" played on a radio somewhere in the garden.

"Ok M' Lady. Best do as ye wishes," Parnell grunted disconsolately.

"Philippa, darling," Louise called over. She was at the bay window that led from the lounge onto the garden. It was fortuitous that her daughter had pulled up her tights and straightened herself out. Otherwise many an awkward question could have been unambiguously posed.

"Yes, Mama."

"On the second post, a letter from Julian. This time you must send an immediate reply. Ask for his telephone number and ring him. He will be missing you."

"I'll read it later, Mama." Philippa took the envelope. She skipped passed her mother then went to her room. "I'm sure it will contain nothing new."

The 18-year-old young woman switched on her gramophone. She placed "The Happening" by the Supremes on the turntable. She then began to read her letter from James and another from Fred Byatt. Fred was apologising for being such a fool and wanting to meet up again.

"Maybe," she whispered to herself, feeling a tad guilty about involving the gardener, "But why should I?" Philippa self-debated. "Fred gave me the brush off, so I needed to have my heat cooled down and Parnell happened to be there. Nothing has been permanently damaged, but Fred will have to grovel to me. I need him to be serious before Julian the sphincter returns. Now, let's have a look at James' letter. It sounds like he's having a real ball out there in the desert."

DANESH AND KELLY

"Hi Prof! Are you in?" Keely called out then entered the lounge with Garside. Inside were their parallel universe counterparts, Kelly and Professor Gideon, looking over a pile of large sheets resembling maps of the galaxies.

"Keely!" Kelly jumped away from the mass of paper and hugged her doppelganger. Garside made towards where Gideon was deeply entrenched in paperwork.

"Keely, I understood that you and David were too absorbed in research to conduct anymore inter-dimensional trips?

"And how come, Kelly, we always slip on exactly the same attire?" Keely smiled in a childish grin. She then gazed bemusedly at Kelly's tight pink dress, dark stockings and short brown leather jacket. The doppelganger remained confounded by the fact that as per the norm she was apparelled almost identically.

"Great minds, great dress sense. But so far, Keely, you have refrained from responding to my question. Why the pleasure of this visit?"

"The Prof unearthed some spell binding revelations in his work. It's about how many worlds there could be. Why they exist, and a barrel load of other bits they talk about for days on end."

"They always do that." Kelly screwed her face. "Prof," she called over the room.

"Yes, darling," Danesh Gideon and David Garside both looked up from the huge array of charts and documents."

"What are you doing?" Kelly was not amused. Her original plans for the day had seemingly gone out of sync well prior to the appearance of the respective doppelgangers.

Gideon almost offered a brief synopsis of his latest revelations.

"Kelly, this is remarkable," Keely shrieked, "We travelled to your world in TIDPA 2. That was at the moment the Prof had unravelled the formulae. We arrived at the suppositions which you and Danesh were also discussing. Spooky, eh?"

"Which is what?" Kelly was still a tad forlorn

"Kelly," Garside finally elucidated, "We were, are, making the first charts. At least we believe it to be so, of the way through gaps in matter to the alternate worlds.

"And thus far," Danesh assumed the exposition, "Based on our advanced mathematical formulae, we can prove the existence of over 400 PUs. Notwithstanding, the list in theory could be almost infinite."

Garside resumed the clarifying narrative. "We may have the first road atlas, if you like. A comprehensive map that will allow us to travel not merely to go one world, or perhaps two at the most and in one direction. This may be the Rosetta stone that unravels the path to unlimited and unbounded parallel universe navigation."

"Tell me." Kelly turned over in bed as Danesh was deeply engrossed in his work documents. "Yes, darling. "He looked up from behind his spectacles.

"I, should I say we, dipped out on a great day today. We were supposed to go on the river in a houseboat, navigated by others. There we could drink, laugh and enjoy the countryside. Then we would dine at the Jolly Fisherman. At least that was the plan. What occurred was that I ended up chatting to myself, albeit it was to Keely. But I actually bore myself, or should I say Keely, unintentionally of course, bored me. So, what was so pressing my darling man that it could not have waited a day or two?"

"My dear, Doctor Aresti. Professor Garside and I have been checking calculations and complex formulae. And these, together with our work on quantum physics, may give us the road map across the dimensions. A chart void of the problems thus far unearthed. It is akin to enhancing from a "dial up" to a broadband computer. Once all is tested appositely, soon we will have the capacity to navigate to any locus, in any dimension. Just down the road from this it may also include expeditions through time."

"Do you believe in fate?"

"As a supernatural phenomenon. No," Danesh coldly re-joined, "I believe we are all a product of the Theory of Chaos. Interwoven events within an infinite number of pure coincidences which when examined forensically each has their ultimate provenance back in the Big Bang. Why?"

"I want to observe something. From within PADIT 2 of course. Nonetheless, I want to see, double check if you prefer. I am almost sure from observations and experiences to date. I wish to study many of my alter egos in these parallel worlds."

"Why?" Danesh curtly repeated

"Fate. If one does not believe in fate, our alter egos are not exactly the same but very similar, very similar. In fact, identical until the age of 18 when some, according to you, seem to move onto another road. Another path on the journey of life after a seemingly inconsequential change. These could be as trivial as going out with, or not, a particular girl or boy."

"Kelly, that kind of logic is ruminated over by all teenagers. You need not be in possession of a PhD or a high powered computer to deduce such a conclusive inspiration."

"I am cognisant of such erudition. Nonetheless, what I intend to discern is do we all truly follow the same path. If one of us breaks a leg, do the others. If one, God forbid, dies accidentally or otherwise, do the others? Does God cover all universes or just the one we reside in? Prof, I want to go to those that are chronologically ahead of us, you have mentioned the theory many times, and assess what happens to me in that dimension."

"I repeat, Kelly. Why?"

"I want to see if fate really does exist. Whether it is a scientific law or supernatural phenomenon. I want to ascertain whether or not it can, if so willed, be cheated."

EMILY-JUNE 1967

Robinson had noticed that Emily's housemate, Gill, was inside the large detached property. He deemed her to be a potential handicap to his conniving stratagems. Accordingly, he had declined the offer of Chinese food and coffee. He drove off at once back to London.

"Gill," Emily called out, "I'm so glad to be back home. What a day."

"How so?" The housemate poured out a glass of claret and handed it to Emily.

"I worked late. On my way home, I was attacked by three or four thugs. I downed two before my knights in shining armour, Artie Cooper's men, came to my salvation."

"My lord, Emm, you've had a right day. I shall heat up your Chinese in the oven. I waited for two hours before I bought yours. It's not too bad, still moist. How's your head?"

"I never said anything about my head Gill. How did you know?"

"Oh, sorry. When you said you were set on you then rubbed your head. I thought you may have been hurt. It looks a tad dark where you rubbed."

Emily thought for a while then continued. "My bonce is fine. Apparently, the bad guys were given a good pasting by Artie's boys."

"How come Artie's men knew where you were?"

"Gill, too many questions. I'm going to sit down and drink my wine. Then I shall go upstairs into my en suite shower. After that I shall slip into my nightie. Finally, I shall partake in the Chinese food."

Emily sipped her Chianti then bolted up the thickly carpeted staircase.

She turned on the shower and the transistor to Radio Caroline. "A Little Bit Me A Little Bit You" by the Monkees was playing.

She unzipped and took off her dress and removed her blouse, stockings and bra then went to the bedroom door. Emily listened for Gill who could be heard in the kitchen. Gill then went to the phone. Emily lifted her bedroom extension before her lodger could glean the fact from the distinctive click. A number was dialled and then the low tone of the connected signal from the exchange came through the earpiece.

"Yes." A deep sinister sounding voice echoed from the other end. It resonated as if it had originated in a different galaxy rather than just another British town.

"I said before," Gill snapped, "you and your lot failed. She's back. She's upstairs havin' a shower. It was Artie Cooper's boys who stopped your people. She was brought home by that North Eastern cop. Just thought you should know."

"That was always a risk, Gill. Please ensure I am suitably apprised of any further information about Miss Wilkinson you can glean. By fair means or foul. Understood?"

"Of course, I do. But neither do I want to end up in gaol. So, if you plan somethin' in future, get it right. Goodnight."

Gill replaced the telephone upon which Emily whispered, "You fucking devious cow."

Emily's pulse rate began to rise. She drew a breath, listened at the door. The sounds of her housemate pottering around in the kitchen were clearly hearkened. This was the first occasion since moving from the sleepy village of Alvescot that she had deemed it politic to have her bedroom door locked.

After showering and changing into her nightdress and bathrobe, Emily dried her hair. She then sauntered slowly and nonchalantly down the ornate staircase.

"Must act naturally, like Ringo Starr said on that Beatles song," she muttered to herself.

Gill had laid a place for her on the table in the kitchen and refreshed Emily's crystal goblet of wine. Gill then took the various dishes from the oven namely egg fried rice, bean shoots, fried pork balls, sweet and sour sauce and chips.

"Lovely, Gill. What have you been up to tonight?"

"I watched Double Your Money on ITV and Doctor Finlay's Casebook on BBC. They were both great. However, the hour is late, and we both have to be at work tomorrow, so I'll bid you goodnight."

"Goodnight." Emily looked up. She turned on the radio as the television channels had closed down for the day.

"Good evening." the formal voice of the BBC newsreader spoke. "This is the BBC Home Service and the news at midnight is read by Jack de Manio." There was a slight pause.

"The Ministry of Defence has announced that 22 British soldiers have been killed in several incidents across Aden which apparently began with a mutiny of the South Arabian Army followed by the Aden Police in the district of Crater-----."

Emily froze, dropping her glass of wine to the floor.

"Philippa," Emily called down the mouthpiece of the red 700 series telephone.

"Yes, Emm. What is it?"

"Have you seen the news? The news on the television or heard it on the radio."

"No. Is something amiss?" Philippa sounded none too interested.

"Amiss! If you call 22 British soldiers being lost in Aden something amiss then yes there is. Have your parents heard anything?" Emily was unusually brusque.

"Alright Emm. I see now why you're a little uptight. Hold on and I'll double check."

Philippa shot into the lounge where Tom and Louise were still up, listening to Brahms First Symphony on the gramophone.

"Mummy, Daddy. Have you heard the news? Emily is on the phone. She was listening to the late BBC Home Service world news. It said that 22 British soldiers were killed in Aden today. Have you had anyone contact you?"

"No, Philippa." Louise was visibly shocked. Nonetheless, she replied for them both. "It is extremely disconcerting. Papa may be able to ring some friends in the cabinet tomorrow."

"We have a Labour government, daddy has no socialist friends," Philippa was perplexed.

"Trust me, Pip," Tom smiled at his daughter, "the mantels of socialism oft disappear when the trappings of power have been grasped. We would have heard by now if James had been injured or worse, nonetheless, first thing in the morning I shall make some calls, you can tell Emily that and also tell her not to worry."

"Thank you, Daddy," Philippa trotted back to the telephone.

Emily began to work on her latest cases her eyes rarely off her black telephone. When it did eventually ring she excitedly picked it up, "Yes!"

"Miss Wilkinson?" the voice at the other end enquired, which took her a few seconds to recognise.

"Mister Robinson, what can I do for you?"

"Are you alright this morning?"

"I'm fine Mister Robinson, what can I do for you?"

"You sound a little edgy Miss Wilkinson."

"Mister Robinson, in case you have not heard, 22 British soldiers were killed in Aden yesterday, my boyfriend is out there in the Marines so excuse me if I sound a little terse, I repeat, what can I do for you?"

"Sorry, Ma'am, I wasn't aware of your personal situation, in that case I would have liked to chat with you, at lunchtime, but it can wait."

"Alright Detective Sergeant, if I receive no adverse news this morning, I can see you at lunchtime, the Red Lion at one, I trust that is alright?"

"Of course, I hope to see you at one."

The phone rang again, this time it was Philippa.

"Yes, Pip," Emily became anxious once more. .

"Emily, daddy checked with his friends in the Ministry of Defence and although 22 British soldiers were killed in Aden, none of them were from the Royal Marines."

"Are you sure?"

"Daddy says that if James had been hurt we would have heard and his friends in the Civil Service part of the Ministry of Defence were adamant that no Royal Marines had been killed. Three had been slightly wounded some place just outside Aden but none of those were officers. I must go Emm, speak to you soon."

"Bye, Pip."

The pub was not overly busy for a summer week day lunchtime. A surfeit of the male clientele were glued to the curvaceous figure of Emily as she entered in a white blouse, light blue jacket and skirt and blue tights with of course blue shoes, the female punters seemed to morph into an envious complexion of jade. The tall figure of Detective Sergeant John Robinson stood up from a quiet corner of the bar. Gladys Knight and the Pips were on the jukebox singing "Take Me in Your Arms and Love Me" as she sauntered across the carpet of the lounge bar towards the police officer.

"Good to see you Miss Wilkinson," Robinson shook her hand.

"And for me also, Detective Sergeant, now tell me, why did you want to have lunch?"

"I have a sort of business proposition, but before we start, let's order lunch, they do a good carvery here, and some drinks."

DANIEL AND JAMES-JUNE 1967

Daniel led the bulk of his troop tentatively towards the town square . of al-Ittihad.

The midsummer sun was beating mercilessly from the heavens so it was no small respite to walk in the shadows of the tall, mud brick constructed buildings, boasting a majlis wide terrace that straddled the thoroughfare along their route.

The 18-year-old officer was acutely cognisant of the risks and many potential hazards attached to his expedition but nonetheless strode with a poise of such self-assurance and confidence that none would have believed the screaming fear that tore into every facet of his consciousness.

The parched, sandy dust of Aden desiccated his mouth as he tightly gripped the wooden stock and handle of his cocked 7.62 millimetre calibre self-loading rifle while the tube of the 66 millimetre calibre Light Armour Weapon wistfully bounced on the upper side of the ochre hued kidney pouches of his webbing fighting order, irritating but not overly so, his eyes were fully and firmly focused on the russet coloured buildings ahead.

On his left, grim faced, dark haired, Corporal Greenham from Exeter in Devon headed his section of riflemen covering the right flank, studiously watching every door and window for movement and ready bring down rapid fire at the first inkling of any possible threat.

Corporal Ely, the canny south Londoner, was on the right side equally as robust and focused while scanning the opposite aspect of the street. There were three Royal Marines carrying a deadly effective general-purpose machine gun, the renowned GPMG, known to Marines as the Jeep, at the ready in the shoulder position marching level with Daniel at the front of the troop.

To the immediate rear of the gunners, but still with clear arcs of fire were four riflemen, their SLR rifles cocked and were in the alert stance as they cautiously moved forward.

Just behind Daniel, Sergeant Helm advanced with Marine Stephen Dixon, the baby faced, mousy haired troop radio operator bearing on his back the bulky Larkspur series A-41 radio.

Daniel could sense that this day would forever indicate in his young life a critical milestone, the date upon which he first fired shots in anger. Alternatively, this pivotal juncture in his life, if the runes were cast pessimistically, could also easily denote for history the conclusion of his tenure of this world.

"Remember watch and shoot!" Daniel assertively called out.

"Marine Dixon, signal the call signs of Mister Moir, Mister Marchant and Mister Quinn to prepare to open fire the instant they hear repetitive shots!"

"Yes, sir!"

As they came to within seven metres of the town square a dark figure in a white keffiyeh and flowing robe, aiming an AK-47 Soviet made assault rifle popped up from behind the wall of the block of flat roof buildings to the front. Daniel fired. The side of the insurgent's head exploded like a tomato as the SLR round struck home. A second face appeared from behind a flat roof, akin to a target in a fairground shooting gallery and was similarly despatched, his cranium torn apart by the cool and determined marksmanship of the second lieutenant.

"Gunners and support riflemen with me, the rest hold your positions!"

Daniel doubled forward followed closely by his men until he could observe Bowman's troop taking cover from a swathe of gunman positioned on the encircling buildings that constituted the town square. The lieutenant's Marines were nervously crouched behind the statue and parked cars in the immediate area. At least two were wounded.

Once Daniel reached the concrete slab surface of the square many more terrorists appeared on the roof and windows aiming at the British troops forming up below.

"Fire!" Daniel screamed to the gunners and riflemen who began to douse the entire area with a large volume of seven point six two millimetre ordnance. Two more gunmen tried to shoot at the Marines, Daniel killed one, and Corporal Ely, positioned on the exit road brought down the other, smiling as he discharged his weapon.

From a hundred metres back, a wall of sustained support fire from the troops of David, Niall and James was now pouring down onto the battle area.

"Get the fuck out of here!" Daniel screamed at Bowman who nervously and finally ordered his erstwhile pinned down troop to withdraw carrying their wounded covered by Daniel's machine gunners.

In an upper window at the far side of the square the young officer espied two insurgents hurriedly setting up a machine gun onto a tripod. A handful of enemy were able to release un-aimed shots, which mercifully ricocheted safely off the buildings. However, the insurgent's GPMG could have proved to be a veritable menace.

Daniel removed the 66-millimetre M72 Light Armour Weapon from his back. He cocked the piece, screamed, "Loaded! Ready! Fire!" and released the missile within. It burst loudly and devastatingly into the offending casement blowing half the upper wall away, leaving a hollow and rubble-strewn chasm.

He rapidly reloaded his SLR and fired more rounds at the rooftops. This fusillade killed another Arab gunman who fell backwards with flailing arms while the AK 47 dropped unceremoniously onto the dirt below. The instant Daniel had seen the last of Bowman's men run along the thoroughfare towards the Saracens he ordered his men to withdraw.

The second lieutenant was walking backwards alongside his men permitting. They fired back towards the square covering the extraction.

Within two minutes, all weapons had been made safe and Lieutenant Bowman along with his men, including the three wounded were travelling back to the Royal Marines camp in Little Aden on board the Saracen APCs and Ferret scout car, the vehicles in which Daniel's troop had earlier been transported to the operation. From the aerodrome across the colony, the thudding rotors of four Westland Wessex helicopters of 845 Squadron were heard as they flew rapidly in their direction. Two of the Royal Navy choppers hovered to the north of the square collecting Niall Quinn and his boys whilst the others evacuated Daniel and his hot and sweaty, dusty warriors from the access road.

Once the last Marine was on board Daniel nodded to the loadmaster who signalled to the pilot it was safe to take off and in less than two minutes they were landing noisily and in massive plumes of red, sandy dust on the helipad on the parade ground at Little Aden camp.

Major Peter Adams and Captain Lowes ran forward to greet the men.

"Great work, Daniel. I knew you'd extract to text book perfection." Adams grinned then turned to the Dublin born officer. "And to you also Niall. A fine piece of cover fire. Check to make sure all weapons are cleared, and all equipment and ammo are accounted for."

"Yes, sir," Niall and Daniel responded in unison as the major summoned Lieutenant Bowman. "What went wrong?" Adams snapped.

"We could have got out, sir. We followed the sighting of an enemy gunman, sir, followed him-."

"Lieutenant, if you had given those orders in a simulated scenario at the AIB you would never have passed. You did not cover your exit, did not send scouts forward to recce the objective, you were not ready for them."

"Sir, I am confident we did not need the services of the rest of the company--."

"I'm certain you did, Lieutenant Bowman, if you had been the prime target instead of the bait to lure our other troops into a trap you and all your Marines would be dead now, a hefty addition to an already dreadful day. Mister Gibson acted in the way an officer should, was involved personally in not only the fire fight but organising his men. Lucky for you that your troop only suffered slight injuries but Mister Bowman you are on notice!"

The officers of 45 Commando were gathered in the mess, awaiting an address by Lieutenant Colonel Owen, the commanding officer.

"This has been a bad day gentlemen, I know we were in action at al-Ittihad and brought down a few of the wogs but we had but three slightly injured guys who are recovering in the sick bay. Details still sketchy but I shall update as best I can. During the night there were a lot of tribal clashes in the South Arabian Army after three colonels had been suspended and an armoury was plundered. At about 09.00 hours, a convoy of trucks carrying sappers of number 60 Squadron Royal Engineers came under fire and about eight men, most I believe from the Royal Corps of Transport were killed. An officer from the Lancashire Regiment was also killed. There was a lot of shooting around Champion Lines. There was also a State Red in Crater and we know several Royal Northumberland Fusiliers have been killed, ambushed by the Aden Police, and a helicopter was brought down, we're not sure of casualties but one fusilier was badly injured, that we know of. In all, 22 armed forces personnel have been killed and the wogs have control of Crater. The electricity and water supply will soon be shut off. However, as the Argyll and Sutherland Highlanders are replacing the Northumberland Fusiliers on Waterloo Lines, and of course control of Crater, Colonel Colin Mitchell of the Argylls wants to retake Crater ASAP. But his regiment has only an advance party here so far. Accordingly, High Command has asked us, 45 Commando, to allocate men to surround Crater. With which, of course, we shall duly conform. Once in position, we will engage any enemy until such a time that Colonel Mitchell and his men can walk back in to the district. So, gentlemen, we need Crater surrounded, pronto. I shall direct a company to move forthwith to the Main Pass side of Crater. Dinner is served but I want to chat with all company commanders after we've eaten. Carry on!"

James and Daniel were chatting outside X-Ray Company HQ, Sergeants Helm and Diggle stood nearby. Major Adams strode purposefully over to his subalterns who smartly saluted their OC.

"James, I know you got no kills yesterday, but Daniel, I understand you were involved in the melee?" "A little, sir, I think I got one."

At that juncture Sergeant Helm stepped forward to wax lyrical the extolling of his troop leader.

"Beggin' ya pardon, sir," Tony Helm's chest bulged outwards, "I think Mister Gibson is bein' a little modest, sir, 'cause 'e took out at least five terrorists, sir. At least three with his SLR, sir, and two 'e blew away with the 66."

"Thank you, Sergeant Helm." Adams grinned. "Mister Gibson is prone to be modest when recounting his achievements. But all of us had best hone up our marksman skills. Today we're off to surround Crater. Yes, today. We'll take the terrorists head on and beat the crap out of them before the Argylls arrive in force in a few days. Get your men ready. Our company is first on the muster. We want that place full of terrorist corpses before the Scots move in."

PHILIPPA-JULY 1967

Fred Byatt sat opposite Philippa in the Plough Inn at Alvescot and sipped on his lager.

"Have you lost interest, Fred I get the impression your feelings for me have gone on a wander?"

"Oh, of course not my little sugary plum, I have just had a lot transpiring in the old brain cells," Fred smiled convincingly.

"I know I have been away at London a lot attending some fab society balls, but I am getting bored. Mater has me watched to keep me from straying so I rely on you to provide my carnal relaxation."

From the jukebox drifted the relaxing sound of the Johnny Mann Singers crooning away to "Up Up and Away".

"Always here to oblige a lovely filly such as you, Lady Philippa." Fred impishly grinned. The sun from outside the pub was strong, the temperature being well into the 80s Fahrenheit.

"Right, I'm going to powder my nose. You can order me scampi, sauté pots and salad then we can drive to the Vale of White Horse and my pad. There we can indulge in an overabundance of sex." "Lady Philippa," Fred whispered as the music changed to the Marvelettes singing "When You're Young and In Love", "Sometimes I believe you may be a nymphomaniac."

"And the Honourable Frederick Byatt, you may well be right."

"Yeah Mister Biggs," Jim Parnell was chatting in the spacious Wye Hall garage and vehicle workshop to Rebecca's spouse and driver for the family, "The lady almost begs for it. I'm not tellin' ye porkies, it's the god's honest truth."

Biggs, who had been virtually ignoring the gardener until that juncture rapidly came out from under the Model T Bentley and looked up at Parnell and glared in a fractious manner.

"Did I hear ya right? You're tellin' me that Miss Philippa seduced you. She does it all the time an' now ya gonna take photos and record it so ya can sell it to a magazine, or get money from 'er."

"Yeah, Mister Biggs, if you says anythin' I'll deny it but these folks 'ave more money than they need, they won't miss a little, well a little lot."

"You've no idea 'ave ya?" Biggs wiped his grease covered hands down with a rag, "We don't just work for these folks, we're part of a family."

"Ye knows that's rubbish." Parnell lit a cigarette. "They'd never invite ya to any of their posh dos, don't ye think it's strange ya wife's always off to London wi' the master?"

"If ya're suggestin' anythin' untoward Jim, best be ready to back it up less ya block'll get knocked off."

"No, I'm just sayin' that the folks of the 'ouse do whats they want an' we 'ave to follow."

"Do ya get paid?" Biggs glared at Parnell. "Jim, does ya get a wage packet every week?" "Course I does."

"They ask us to do stuff an' we does it, Jim, that's what they pay us for. Now we've cracked long enough, I've work to do."

Once Parnell was back in the garden, Fred Biggs jogged to the kitchen where Rebecca and Mrs Cromer were preparing afternoon tea for the family and guests.

"Ey, darlin.'" He snuggled up to Rebecca. "Not 'ere. We're busy." She shuffled him away.

"Well when 'e gets a minute, I needs a chat with ye regardin' what I've 'eard 'bout Parnell and Miss Philippa." Rebecca immediately halted the task in hand. "Come out to the laundry. Right now. Tell me what you've 'eard."

"You seem to be away so much," Louise sighed as Philippa returned, deliberately too late to partake in afternoon tea, a fact with which her mother was erudite.

"Mama." Philippa cast an over emphasised smile at her mother. "I am off to uni in a few weeks. I spend a lot of time in London socialising with your favourite people. And Julian is still oh so far away in Australia."

"I don't know what's come over you, Philippa; nothing of substance appears to grasp your interest or indeed your short span of concentration."

"Yes, there are, Mama, my degree in medicine which I shall commence in about eight weeks is of huge relevance to me and of course my one and only brother at war in some forgotten part of a rapidly dwindling British Empire from where he may never return is of huge interest to me."

"Lower your tone to your mother, I am entitled to a modicum of respect."

"Mama. What do you want of me? I am mixing with the people you prefer. I rarely go out when at Wye Hall apart from when Emily is home for the week end and I have little to tell James when I write every three or four days. What I am doing that is in contravention of your mental guidelines?"

"I want you to contact Julian, his family is well connected and like us they frequently have Royalty on their guest list. I want you to say that when he returns, in November I believe the date is, you will tell him that an announcement will be made on your joint futures. And I suggest you put your medical studies on hold for the moment."

"Mama, Daddy may allow you to cajole me into taking a suitor of your choosing but even he will not allow you to forgo my further education."

Louise snorted, her nose in the air.

"Perhaps your future husband may have his own thoughts on the matter."

As the telephone at the other end of the line picked up Jim Parnell asked "Witney and West Oxfordshire Gazette?"

"Yes." "My name is Jim Parnell and I works for the Marchant family at Alvescot. I might 'ave something that would make ye a good story."

"What is it?" The gravelly male voice at the other end enquired.

"I understands your owner an' the Earl of Wye aren't best friends."

Parnell gazed around the village through the windows of the public phone box.

"I've no idea what you mean."

"I've got somethin' that would not only be a juicy bit o' gossip 'bout 'is daughter but would also smack one in the eye to the earl." "Tell me more."

Chapter Twelve

NARRATOR

Yes, the famous summer of love, it went on and on. The wondrous season encompassed so much ranging from Hippies to Vietnam to Aden to Sergeant Pepper's Lonely Hearts Club Band to San Francisco to Carnaby Street, David Bailey, the United Kingdom and Ireland applied to join the Common Market. Sandie Shaw won the Eurovision Song Contest with "Puppet on A String" and my Dad was serving overseas. I have heard it mentioned many times, how pivotal era it was, musically, culturally, politically, sexually and fashion wise, especially when I played my own contemporary hits and was told the songs back in the 1960s had soul, passion as well as great lyrics and melodies. Of course my grandparents told me similar comments were made towards them about the popular music of their adolescence.

The Summer of Love may have long since retreated into the deep realms and annals of history but for this narrative there is much yet to unfurl. My guests are eager for more.

DANESH AND KELLY

Danesh tapped more calculations into the desk top computer in his office study.

Kelly gazed at the monitor on the control board of PADIT as she navigated the machine whilst returning from another social and academic visit to the world of Keely and David.

A message sprang up. "Eureka, I think. Are you receiving this? Tell me if you are."

The outside was a mass of dark, yet not dark, light yet not illuminating. It was how Kelly once recalled how a blind man perceived the universe, neither dark nor light. Once in a while there would be a mini super nova, or at least something resembling such a phenomenon as PADIT speeded through the esoteric portals, the subatomic gateways which formed the astonishing conduits between parallel universes. She changed the computer music selection to a version of the Shirelle's classic "Will You Still Love Me Tomorrow" sung by the raunchy London singer Amy Winehouse. Kelly then tapped the letters onto the screen. "Yes, I am receiving text. Must try voice next."

"Will do. Do not use any new controls until tested." The next message sent appeared on the monitor. Kelly did not respond, merely turned the atomic power up and within a minute real time had landed in Gideon's laboratory. She speeded accurately through all the safety and power down functions, leapt from the cockpit and bolted up to the professor's study.

"Yes, Prof. You can contact me whilst inter-dimensional navigating. It was a nice surprise."

"Good, Doctor Aresti, a new development. You said you want to talk about some of the ethical aspects of IDT."

"Yes, but there is time to discuss these matters. What I want to know is that if all dimensions are travelling, how would we know who is whom? Can we be sure that they started of their own volition or were people like you given the knowledge independently, even if it was through telepathy or through subconscious means such as dreams and so on?"

"You always pose such existential, multifaceted, profound enquiries when you return, Kelly," Danesh looked up from his keypad.

"I know but the topics of debate and discussions are infinite," Kelly squirmed, deep in mental contemplation and deliberation. She poured herself a glass of wine and recharged the whiskey glass next to the professor.

"Doctor, bizarre and probing your mental faculties are. In the near future our possibilities are immense as there is a huge swathe of discovery soon to unfurl. However, your questions are as you say infinite. And although much we can achieve, so far at least, I am unable to extend one's life farther than medical science can already manage."

"What are you driving at, Prof?"

"Kelly, you will discover nothing if you try all things from a minor approach. You must boil all your channels of research down to a few of greatest significance and priority."

"Come on," Kelly beckoned, "David and Keely are expecting us in their universe, you tell me the beer in their version of the Fish and Eels, the Eels and Fish, is very good and the food is literally out of this world, pardon the pun."

Kelly lifted her skirt to show the tops of her stockings.

"See Prof, I want you to set PADIT 2 to take half an hour in real Earth time to get to their PU."

"Why's that Doctor? Are there some sights you want to see?"

"No Prof, you're getting old. I wore stockings to make you horny. I want to have sex with you in PADIT 2. I want to have an orgasm in the space between worlds, that nothing zone, between heaven and earth, in and out of time, the Cosmic vacuum that predates the Big Bang. I want to explode like a super nova."

EMILY-JULY 1967

Emily was back dressed in a white blouse, brown stockings and dark blue skirt, despite the intense summer heat. The front door of the Red Lion near her workplace was open as she went to the bar, heard a few suggestive comments from men close by then ordered a gin and tonic and a pint of IPA, paid the barmaid then walked the drinks over to a quiet table by the window of the lounge bar. The 22-two-year-old lawyer could feel the eyes of many of the men on her. All of whom turned away when the tall figure of Detective Sergeant John Robinson entered the bar.

"Miss Wilkinson, I hope you haven't waited long."

"No Sergeant Robinson, I've just arrived and bought the drinks, yours is a Greene King IPA, hope that is alright?"

"That's fine, sorry that our last meeting was ended so quickly."

The couple sat on the long-cushioned wall bench seats next to each other, but Emily maintained a discreet gap between them.

"No need to apologise, I also was remiss having failed to recall an appointment, so I would have needed to offer my excuses prematurely, I have sorted out my diary and can spare you three quarters of an hour, so Sergeant Robinson, what did you want to talk about?"

"I want to know if you wish to widen your experience, not stuff for your CV but worldly experience with a solid compensation."

Emily gazed for a while, ruminating, "Sounds like you want me to be a prostitute."

"Eh no, Miss Wilkinson, that probably did not cross our minds, but you have a great rapport with people, they talk to you, would you like to work for us?"

"For the Metropolitan Commissioner or Director of Public Prosecutions, no, apart from small meat money I have not been long enough in my current post."

"Would you believe it if I told you there was an undercover police unit that reports directly to the Home Secretary, Roy Jenkins?"

"It would be hard but seeing the corrupt cops I've come across it's not beyond the bounds of possibility," Emily responded glaring suspicious at Robinson.

At that juncture two men entered the Red Lion and headed towards Robinson and Emily.

She rapidly ascertained from their demeanour that the men were also police officers.

"Hello," the tall, slim man with brown hair that was now showing a surfeit of "snow on the roof" held his hand towards Emily, "I'm Detective Chief Inspector Lyle."

The other officer eyed Emily up and down then sat next to her on the cushioned bench on the opposite side of John Robinson. He was a little younger looking, shorter and stockier built with black locks.

"Hi. I'm Superintendent Guy Porter, and you are Emily Wilkinson QC. It's very good for a woman to make QC." Porter smirked, "And of course I'm all for women doing well as long as men get first bite." Porter put his hand on Emily's knee and she grabbed it viciously not releasing the offending member.

"Mister Porter, I couldn't give a shit what you think, the fact I probably earn more money than you may irk you but of that I could not give a shit either and if you ever try to touch me again I'll take your arm off."

"Miss Wilkinson.," Lyle wished to rapidly alter the tone. He placed a buff folder on the table, "We want to cast a few ideas around to see if any may be of interest to you."

Emily stared at each one of the three men then sipped her G and T before lighting a cigarette as the Otis Reading and Carla Thomas song "Tramp" came on the jukebox.

"Gentlemen. I'm listening and despite your colleague's cumbersome act, I am aware that I am not here to be chatted up. If I was, you'd be wasting your time. So, tell me the real reason you sought my presence."

DANIEL- JULY 1967

The summer heat was brutal. Even up on the lower slopes of the heights of Jebel Shamsan overlooking the rebel held area of Aden known as Crater. A rare piece of desert land, constructed on the floor of an, hopefully, extinct volcano. No respite was to be had from the heat yet the slight breeze that flowed from the Gulf of Aden offered little relief. The inlet was part of the Indian Ocean which stood over to the right of the lofty, rocky position of 6 Troop, X-Ray Company, 45 Commando, Royal Marines lead by Second Lieutenant Daniel Gibson.

The young man scanned the area though his binoculars and then picked up his telephone style radio transmitting and receiving apparatus plugged into the A-41 radio.

"Hello four alpha two, this is four alpha one over."

"Four alpha two, send, over."

"Four alpha one, I'm fucking bored, how long have we been here?"

"Four alpha two, we've been in this position, sporadically, for nearly two weeks," Second Lieutenant David Moir replied on the radio whilst simultaneously waving from his position one hundred metres to Daniel's right, "And I'm bored too."

"Maintain radio discipline and voice procedure!" The booming voice of Captain Lowes came over the net.

Since the mutiny of the 20th of June, 12 days earlier, that had seen Crater fall into the hands of the insurgent group, the National Liberation Front, the water and electricity supply had been shut down. 45 Commando had encircled Crater from the hills above the residential and business area bringing small arms fire down on any suspected sign of rebel activity no matter how seemingly spurious.

Daniel lit a cigarette and filled in his log.

"Sergeant Helm!" he called out and the stocky, balding old soldier moved up from his defensive sangar 50 feet away.

"Yes, sir." Helm lit a cigarette as he entered the sandbagged area his subaltern occupied.

"Amuse me, Sergeant." Daniel grasped his self-loading rifle, removed the round in the chamber, then the magazine, replaced the round in the magazine, inserted the magazine back into the rifle and applied the safety catch.

"Very good, sir. I see all that officer training at Lympstone's not gone t' waste. Ya can still make your weapon safe. How can I amuse ya sir?"

"When are the Argyll and Sutherland Highlanders moving back into Crater? They seem to have been preparing for it forever. We've been here the best part of a fortnight and shot at anything suspicious. The Jocks are still holding back. If you don't know that then is there any gossip from our Marines? Any with girl problems, something juicy?"

"Not that I know of, sir. Lance Corporal Wilson always has women problems and as far as the Argylls go, this is one fucking ego trip for their CO, Mitchell. He wants to be a hero in the press, restore British pride, sir, and 'e will but it'll just last a few weeks. For the lads that get killed 'cause he pissed more Arabs off than we needed to, they'll be dead forever. And men will die as a result of 'im. Colonel Mitchell really is a mad fucker."

"Hmm." Daniel drew deeply on his cigarette unwilling to comment. "I have no opinion, Sergeant. But it is fucking hot up here."

The high-pitched ping of a ricocheting round was heard behind him as the sound of numerous AK-47 assault rifles firing at his positions echoed across the district.

Daniel grabbed his rifle, cocked the weapon and circumspectly surveyed the area from where he believed the accurate, enemy fire was coming.

"Lance Corporal Wilson!" He called to the troop sniper wielding a telescopic sight Lee Enfield bolt-action rifle. "Sir!" The 25-year-old Wilson ran along the connecting track.

"Locate the source of the enemy fire and put a tracer round on it!"

"Yes, sir!" Wilson crawled up to a small rocky outcrop and scanned Crater below then hollered "Watch my tracer!". He fired a single red illuminating round at the buildings below them.

"Seen!" Daniel screamed and aimed his rifle, "Open fire at the tracer!"

The Marines nearby began shooting at the area of hostile activity.

Totally contrary to his training, the teenaged officer released the safety catch of the rifle with his thumb then commenced to unleash a salvo of 7.62 mm rounds on the conurbation below. Every puff of smoke from enemy weapons Daniel fired at whilst Sergeant Helm watched all through the binoculars.

After a couple of minutes or so the insurgents stopped shooting.

"Cease fire!" Daniel ordered.

"Ye don't need a sniper's rifle, sir." Helm gazed down at his troop officer. "Ya SLR brought down another four of 'em. Great shootin', sir!"

JAMES -JULY 1967

Somewhere drifting across the Little Aden camp of 45 Commando, the sound of Petula Clark singing "Don't Sleep in The Subway" was just audible. An off-duty James was writing one of the three letters he sent twice a week back to the United Kingdom. The note he had received from Philippa seemed to sound more than the normal ramblings of a pre-university teenager, some allusions concerning the gardener. These totally irrelevant additions to her short enough missive were augmented by something about a bloke who was rich, even by James' standards, called Byatt, Fred Byatt James assumed, and how she was dreading the return of Julian from Australia. He could hear the distant sound of gunfire from the area of Crater but chose to ignore such a distraction, shooting in Crater was more commonplace than buses going through Oxford.

Niall Quinn knocked on the officer's accommodation door.

"Hey, lunch? It's only Monday so nothing fancy but worth a gin and tonic."

"OK, Niall. Iwas just going to write letters home but they can wait. I'm not really bothered what's for lunch as long as it's edible."

The steward came over to the second lieutenants and offered them menus, which James thought were a tad superfluous as the only entree on offer was braised liver and onions. Major Adams came into the dining room and took a seat at the table with his troop commanders.

The senior officers were either at Crater, Marine Drive or were in conference having lunch brought to them. This left an almost eerie silence and abstruse atmosphere across the mess.

"Gentlemen." Adams sat down, ordered a whiskey then turned to his two subalterns. "Operation Stirling Castle, the retaking of Crater will take place at dawn tomorrow. The Argyll and Sutherland Highlanders will play some pipe and drum melodies then march back in. They form up and prepare to move this evening. Tuesday the fourth of July 1967 will be, we all hope, a great day in the annals of the British armed forces. You chaps will take your troops and be in reserve in case the operation goes arse up. Get some sleep and have them ready to move by 03.00 as the Jocks march into Crater at 05.45 hours."

"Yes, sir," Niall and James responded in unison.

"Any problems?" the Major asked as he put a serviette on his knee whilst the steward brought his whiskey, "I mean anything I should know about."

"Apart from the terrorists, sir." James grinned uncomfortably. "All is well."

PHILIPPA-JULY 1967

"Fred." Philippa sat up in the bed. "I'm a little sore about being tossed around. I'm not a plastic person, I'm groovy and I want to take a slice of the action."

"Yeah babe, you sure are one groovy chick." Fred drew on the marijuana-laced cigarette then passed it over to Philippa.

"White Rabbit" by Jefferson Airplane came on the radio.

"I want to be wined and dined. I want to be able to hold balls, dance balls not men's balls, without feeling guilty about Julian. I want to do my own thing, have my own scene. Not just get married and be a zombie."

"Oh, dear Philippa, you need a loving caring man. A knight, a real man, a man abounding in both muscles and brains. Someone who just can't keep his lecherous hands off you."

The golden early morning sun cascaded gently into the bedroom; the first days of July were outstanding in rural Oxfordshire.

"I want you, my young Sir Lancelot." Philippa sipped her whiskey and smoked her joint.

"No chance, baby." Fred's eyes were droopy as he inhaled the pungent smoke. "I'm my own master and want no chicks in tow to cramp my style. I'm a wandering spirit babe, born to be free and travel the world. We need to talk, babe."

"Oh, but Fred," Philippa slurred, "You're just what I need. Come on, let's have sex again."

"Lucy In the Sky with Diamonds" from the long-playing record Sergeant Pepper's Lonely Hearts Club Band by the Beatles floated through the transistor speakers. Philippa inhaled the joint.

As the resultant chemicals floated through the sensory nerves of the brain, a revolving cone of golden light swept by her hazed eye lids, soon evaporating back into her imagination.

Jim Parnell walked through the main entrance and to the reception desk of the offices of the Witney and West Oxfordshire Gazette, situated in Osney Mead in Oxford. The gardener had taken the morning off and driven his dilapidated Vauxhall Velox to Oxford from Wye Hall from where he would be expecting positive news.

"Mister Cameron, please," Parnell walked up to the 40 odd years old receptionist. She was garbed in a yellow summer dress with a green flower pattern and noisily slurping tea while puffing on a Capstan Navy Cut cigarette.

"'Ave yer got an appointment?" the large brunette curtly asked.

"Yeah, Mister Cameron says to see 'im today at 11.30."

"What's ya name?"

"Jim, Jim Parnell."

The receptionist picked up her telephone and dialled a three-digit number.

"Mister Cameron, there's a Mister Parnell 'ere, says ya wanted 'im to come this morning."

Something was said in reply through the telephone earpiece, which was not audible enough for Jim to discern.

The Miasmic Mist —Volume One

"Mister Cameron wants ya t' go up to 'is office which is at the top of the stairs behind me," the woman cast the gardener a scornful smirk.

Parnell climbed the uncarpeted flight of steps to the dingy peeling paint door and knocked on the door.

"In," a voice called out and Jim optimistically skipped into the untidy office with an even untidier desk behind which an old, bald man sat puffing on a cigarette. A filthy "Craven A" embossed ashtray on the desk was overflowing with cigarette butts. Numerous yellowing papers were spread over the battered old filing cabinets that hugged the walls. The unwashed windows were jammed closed to prevent the papers blowing around the room even though outside it was 35 degrees centigrade. The gardener almost choked in the heat and the billowing clouds of smoke. These rancid exhalations had stained the décor a lighter shade of russet.

"Mister Cameron I assume," Jim stretched out his hand but the man failed to reciprocate.

"I'm Cameron and I want to know what fucking game you're playin' you little shit!"

"Don't know what ya means, Mister Cameron."

"You told me ya had juicy photos and a tape of you an' Lady Philippa Marchant rolling around in the hay. Details of every piece of 'er body and 'er moanin' as she has an orgasm."

"I did, Mister Cameron. I swears it. I give ya them."

"Here's the reel of tape ya give me." Cameron rolled the tape onto a small Brenner recorder/player then pushed the "play" switch.

The theme music for the "Magic Roundabout" came through the speaker.

"That's not what was on the tape I give ya, Mister Cameron."

"Mister Parnell, that's exactly what was on the tape ya sent now look at the photos ya sent me." Cameron opened the yellow envelope marked "Kodak" and tossed out several pictures of flowers and bushes.

"Don't know what fucking game ya playin' Parnell but you go and make accusations like that ya gonna end up in court. Maybe in gaol. Now fuck off!"

Stephen Grenfell

DANESH AND KELLY

The darkness was with intermittent, sporadic salvoes of light and super novae. The machine finally pulled into its destination. A doppelganger planet within an infinite parallel universe lying inside a separate dimension to that of Danesh Gideon and Kelly Aresti.

"Here we are." Kelly adjusted her clothing before opening the door of PADIT.

The weather was unusually dull and inclement in this PU. Kelly had grown used to permanent warm, sunny days and comfortable evenings during her inter-dimensional sorties.

A forked tongue of lighting, like the contour of some mythological demon, flashed from the direction of the Cotwood Hills over to the northwest.

They walked from the parked ID transporter, looking amazingly and deliberately like the cars of that dimension, and up the path towards the middle-class area in which their alter egos resided.

They knocked on the door upon which Keely answered and shrieked.

"Danesh! Kelly! Come in. We have a couple which we know you'll want to meet!"

Kelly egged on by anticipation almost ran into the lounge where David Garside was standing with a man, almost identical to himself. They both wore tweed jackets with leather anti wear patches on the elbows and cuffs, both sported beards, spectacles and looked every centimetre the regular science professor. They both grasped tumblers of whisky and wore cream check patterned shirts augmented with grey ties neither of which was correctly fastened. It was uncanny that both of these men could have been the twin brothers of Danesh, the only difference he could boast was at that chronological co-ordinate, Professor Gideon of Hartfordshire University was clean shaven. That situation had existed only since the morning when Kelly had complained about stubble burns during their voracious love making the previous night. All three considered themselves six feet tall although their respective partners reckoned them to be 1.8288 metres in height. The person standing next to the new professor was a woman with flowing, flaming locks that Kelly gasped when she saw how alike the three women were.

◆ The Miasmic Mist —Volume One ◆

"Danesh." David Garside turned to his double. "Allow me to introduce you to Professor Dannah Gibbet. Dannah leads scientific research at the University of Headford."

"Pleased to meet you, Professor. I'm Professor Danesh Gideon from the University of Hartfordshire."

"So I understand, Professor. Please meet my better looking other half. My all-round research assistant cum test pilot for TIDAP, transporter inter-dimensional, driven by an accelerator of particles. A mouthful I know, your PADIT is much easier to comprehend. Here is my better half, Doctor Philemon Arestant. She works in the Urology Section of List Hospital in Headforshire."

Danesh almost called the sunburst maned, five feet two inches tall Philemon, "Kelly".

"Doctor Arestant," Danesh shook hands with the pulchritudinous young physician. They were joined immediately by Kelly who deemed Philemon a little younger than her and Keely. The three women could have dressed from the same boutique. All wore white opaque blouses, black bras; tight blue skirts, blue high-heeled shoes and each carried blue leather handbags.

Danesh thought for a second he was drifting across a Salvador Dali landscape of surreal creatures, sights and sounds, walking through a dream, rather drifting.

He could make out a bed. A little girl greeted him as some strange dog or bear walked across his field of vision. The girl resembled the face on a photograph he had seen of Kelly when she was young.

"Professor Gideon, I am Doctor Arestant. Are you feeling alright?"

"Sorry, just a monetary relapse. It is just that to have three of Kelly in the room at one time is a little unsettling."

"Professor." Keely stepped forward. "We have compared notes between all three of our groups-"

"And." Garside opted to take the lead. "There is a pattern."

"We know that." Danesh shook his head slightly impatiently. "There is a pattern to everything in the universes."

"It's the lives of our other selves," Philemon cut in, "As Professor Garside intimated, there is a pattern. We have checked hundreds of doppelgangers from the three PUs we have researched to date and we know there are more, many more."

"And that is?" Kelly was anxious to be enlightened.

"Apart from the time differentials caused by the slight, tiny divergences since the Big Bang, our life paths are identical," Professor Gibbett answered.

"But apart from minor details it appears that we all follow the same path. It is akin to travelling to one town from another but using a slightly different route. The main facets are fixed.

It seems," David expounded.

"But this is all basic data we were aware of and have been for years," Danesh espoused.

"Yes," Garside agreed, "But what we seem to have revealed is that the very concept of destiny. The path we take in life, as described in the work by Jorge Luis Borges, "El Jardin De Senderos Que Se Birfucan" or the "Garden of Forking Paths". It appears that the religious folks and astrologers may have been correct but for totally erroneous rationale. Fate, or what constitutes the trillions to the power trillions of incidents, mainly seemingly trivial, that chart our path through life, is actually written not in the stars but in the very fabric of the Cosmos."

"If a person died before their time in one universe, their doppelganger in another will suffer a similar fate." Keely deigned to contribute. "The question then follows, "can fate be changed?""

EMILY-JULY 1967

In the Red Lion pub, the music changed to "The Boat That I Row" by Lulu. Emily stared resolutely at the three men sat close by her. Superintendent Guy Porter looked at Emily with an uncomfortably expressive grin.

"Miss Wilkinson, we know you killed a grown man when you were but five years old."

"Are you going to charge me for that? I was five years old!"

"Far from it. In fact, the reports show that you saved the Honourable James Marchant by dispensing with the animal that was attacking him. Quite the little heroine who showed courage and fortitude way beyond her years. Just what we need," Porter added.

"Do you have any political views?" Detective Chief Inspector Lyle enquired almost nonchalantly.

"If I had, I would not divulge them." Emily took a cigarette from her case. John Robinson obliged her with a light. "It could be a dangerous thing in this day and age."

"Not really," Sergeant John Robinson smiled, "What do you think of the war in Vietnam?"

"Personally, I think it sucks. Like all wars do," Emily tersely replied.

"Your fiancé is in Aden. Does that cloud your views?" Porter enquired as John went to the bar to collect the drinks.

"He is not my fiancé. And yes, it clouds my view. I believe that young men dying for that place borders on the obscene."

"Yes." Guy nodded in agreement. "I did my national service in Malaya, John did his in Cyprus while Richard lied his age and was at D-Day in the last war. Those wars we actually won. Even the small one in Cyprus. However, the Soviets are working under the radar. They intend to undermine and destabilise our economy. Then undercut the population by attacking the current political system."

"Sounds very farfetched to me." Emily sipped her gin and tonic. "Surely our system is too robust to be got at by the Soviets. And why would that be of interest to me? I'm a lawyer not a secret agent like James Bond."

"You're better looking than Sean Connery and yes the Soviets are moving like a cancer. They are targeting our trade unions, universities and some branches of political parties including the extreme left of the Labour Party." John drank some of his Greene King bitter.

The three men all were silent for a moment and sipped their beer.

"Why did you ask me here?" The scenario was irritating Emily.

"They are also moving huge resources and sympathetic people. People with communist links in the family, some who came from Eastern Europe. The web is enormous and growing by the day. They are moving into organised crime also. Blackmailing and bribing for influence." John looked at Emily.

"I can't help you in any of those. You know it's lawyer client privilege." Emily drew on her Embassy cigarette. "If I became involved in what I think you are driving at, if uncovered, my career would be over in a flash.

All my work inflow and any goodwill would dry up at once. So, if you want me to spy for you the answer is an emphatic "no"."

Chief Inspector Lyle took a photograph from his pocket and placed it on the table next to Emily.

"Do you know who this is?"

"Of course, it's my housemate. She works at my chambers. A good lawyer. Why have you got her photograph?"

"Her name is?" Guy looked at Emily.

"Gill, Gill McMenemy, of course. But you know that already."

Lyle produced more photographs

"Here are some more. These were taken in Budapest in Hungary. Do you recognise the woman in them?"

"That's Gill too. What was she doing in Hungary?"

"The man she is talking to, the middle aged, fat, grey haired bloke, is the head of the Soviet KGB office in Budapest. He's Ilya Rifkind and the woman is one of his agents."

"Why would she be in Hungary? Why would a Russian spy want to talk to her?"

"She's not Gill McMenemy, can't possibly be. No trace can be found of any such person of her age range. However, the National Insurance number she uses we traced back to a Gillian McMenemy from Sunderland in County Durham. This girl was born in 1945 and died in a road traffic accident in 1959. The woman you know as Gill McMenemy is actually called Beati Halmi. Her family lives in Budapest. She was recruited by the KGB after being spotted in the local Communist Party overflowing with zeal and diligence for the cause."

John assumed the narration, "A Russian would be suspected far more than a Hungarian,

especially after the way the Soviets treated the Hungarians when crushing the 1956 uprising."

"Why doesn't she just defect?" Emily had been wary of her colleague but was now flabbergasted by the revelation.

"Two reasons," Lyle responded, "One is that she is too dyed in the wood to turn. The second and far more profound is that if she ever even considered such an option, they would kill her family. Quite an incentive to behave."

"What is her brief?"

Robinson responded for them all. "She is here to infiltrate organised crime and high court judges by blackmail from honeytraps. You've heard of them of course. Using any influence acquired she would expand her operation to, enlist other members of politics and the judiciary. This would be to assist in what they term "the struggle." Her job at the moment is to get criminal gang members into compromising positions, some may not need blackmail, to lend support to the cause. Whatever conflict our troops in Germany are preparing for will probably never happen. The Soviets could never win a shooting war against NATO and the West so instead they are using subterfuge and covert methods to undermine societies across Europe and North America. Groups of Vietnam war demonstrators across the world have been infiltrated already."

"How on earth could I help you?" Emily was attempting to absorb the implications.

"Watch. That's all. Photos would be great. However, nothing to do with your work as a lawyer. Simply your housemate and who she meets with. We'll provide you with a special camera and tape recorder and other gadgets. We want to know as much as you can find out without jeopardising your day job. Someday you may be invited to work abroad and if you are amenable this could be a great grounding," Porter imparted, assuming the senior role in the negotiation, "You will obviously be paid a retainer. All tax and National Insurance will be sorted out so never declare it to anyone. A special government bank account will be opened for such a stipend."

"You want me to watch her and tell you with whom she meets?"

"And if possible who her contacts meet . We are fully aware that you will be very limited in time and opportunity." Guy added as he lit a pipe.

"You will be paid 1,000 pounds a year just for agreeing to this and for relevant information you uncover there will be a substantial additional payment. Are you willing to consider?"

"Sounds like a jolly good laugh. I hope you'll not shoot me if I fail to meet standards."

The men all forced a smile.

→ Stephen Grenfell ←

DANIEL-JULY 1967

The day had gone well. The 1st Battalion Argyll and Sutherland Highlanders had marched at dawn back into the Crater district of Aden with a triumphant swagger. The famous Daily Express reporter, Stephen Harper, had both witnessed and recorded the momentous event.

The men wearing the "crucified moose" cap badge had advanced into the rebel occupied district to the sound of Pipe Major Ken Robson and his bagpipers playing the regimental charge, Monymusk. "A" Company had taken positions close by the armed police barracks and the building of the Chartered Bank had been requisitioned as the battalion HQ.

The impressive construction was renamed "Stirling Castle" although the barracks of the Argylls remained at the location entitled Waterloo Lines.

Daniel's radio operator, a "bunting tosser" in Corps parlance, was Marine Stephen Dixon. Dixon was a strong, fresh faced youth from near his parents' farm in Northumberland. He looked up at his troop officer.

"What is it, Dixon? You look as if you've a carrot stuck up your backside."

"Sorry, sir. Sunray confirms Operation Stirling Castle's been a success."

"Thanks. Keep your ear glued to the net, Dixon. I want to know the minute we can get the hell out of this place," Daniel ordered than snarled under his breath as Tony Helm came up to him.

"I heard, sir. Soon we can get back to Little Aden and 'ave a shower and leave this stink hole to our Scottish friends." Helm smiled grittily.

"Yes, the Jocks operation's a success, Sergeant Helm." Daniel lit a cigarette.

"Sir," Marine Dixon called out.

"Yes, Dixon."

"Message from Sunray, sir. It says, "Acorn says all is well in the Castle. Foxhounds can go for lunch at the seaside.""

"Thank you Dixon. Don't know which arsehole invents this verbal rubbish, Sergeant Helm. But you know as well as I do what it says."

"Means we can pack up and get outta here, sir. For good."

"It does. So, carry on Sergeant."

The Miasmic Mist —Volume One

Blond Scot, Second Lieutenant David Moir was nearby and had received the same communication from his own bunting tosser.

The troop second in command, Sergeant Terry Baker, had moved a little down the line to organise their Marines' withdrawal from the heights above Crater. David turned to his senior section leader, Corporal Eddie McGrath.

"Between you and me and not to be repeated, I'm sorry they didn't give you the extra stripe, Corporal. I thought it was in the bag," David spoke quietly and empathetically.

"Thank you, sir. Seems like someone did nay want me in the sergeants' mess."

"I have no idea, Corporal. I am but a subaltern with no influence at all. Otherwise I would have made my choice. Alas that is not the way politics in Her Majesty's Royal Marines works. Now time for us to get back to Little Aden as I want a shower and a cooked meal."

Daniel enjoyed the hot flowing streams, loosening and removing the sand and grit from his body, the water and white soapsuds cascading in therapeutic torrents down his strapping, bronzed frame. He showered with total repose while being both conscious of and within touching distance from both his loaded SLR and Browning pistol. Once cleansed to his satisfaction, he stepped into clean attire before enjoying a cigarette inside his quarters. Inside he enjoyed effective shade from the intense potent glare of the Aden summer sun.

After four days of virtual total sleep deprivation, James was still on his bunk loudly snoozing away. Accordingly, Daniel decided to be remain as silent as was possible or practical.

From the direction of the NAAFI he could make out the recent Monkees hit, "Alternate Title" followed by The Supremes singing "The Happening".

He had spent the last two days with his troop engaging terrorists in Crater as they impatiently waited for the Scots to retake the rebel held district.

The official death toll of insurgents in that part of the colony to date numbered about 19 since the Armed Police mutiny of the 20th of June. Daniel merely recalled the purported words of Disraeli; "There are lies, damned lies and there are statistics" as he knew his troop alone had brought down more than that. However, whether they were all rebels or terrorists remained a matter of extreme conjecture.

The young Northumbrian opened the second letter of the week received from his mother.

Coquet Farm
Warkworth
Northumberland
25th June 1967

Dear Danny,

Your dad has been worried sick after he saw on the TV news all those soldiers killed in Aden, a lot from the Northumberland Fusiliers, we hear that lads from Bedlington and Ashington were killed. I know you said we would be told at once if anything happened to you so we are happy as you must be alright.

Your dad is busy and Little Jackie will be leaving school next year so he can help your dad. Debbie has changed, I think for the better. Debbie will soon be at the Duchess School. She wants to be something she calls an atomic physicist a scientist. I've no idea what it is but she's so brainy it makes me shudder. Weather is good, a little rain but I bet it's hotter where you are. Mrs. Green says she's excited about you and Carol getting married in 1972. You never sound that keen but that's lads for you.

It must be good being an officer, having folks to look after you and getting good food. Your dad wants to buy a new car, hasn't made his mind up yet what he wants. He says he'll get a new Cortina and keep it for you to use when you're home on leave.

Love
Mam

Daniel then scanned the letter from Carol. This one was even pithier than her normal literary efforts.

24th June 1967
The Butts
Warkworth

Dearest, Sweetest, Horny, Danny,

I am so horny; I desperately need your cock inside me. Keep away from the bad men and come home quickly.

Your wet, juicy, frustrated, desperate, nympho.
Carol.

The man simply smiled.

JAMES –JULY 1967

Daniel nudged the still snoring James at the same instant that David entered their accommodation.

"Second Lieutenant Lord Marchant is still gonking away, sleeping like a baby," The Scot commented as he took a chair near Daniel's bed.

"Yes, he is." Daniel smiled and threw an Embassy cigarette to David. "We were up on those dratted heights waiting for your countrymen to move into Crater. It took them forever."

"It did," David conceded then lit his smoke, "Wake up, Lord Marchant. It's your turn to buy the wets in the mess."

James opened his eyes, rubbed them, yawned then stretched.

"The friggin' Scots and Geordies are in town," he semi consciously muttered, "Have you had a letter from Lady Caroline?"

"I get one every day," Daniel answered winking at David.

"Yes. And Emily tells me how much she loves me and how hopeless you are at sex," the young Scot bantered.

"I know the Geordie gets letters from his lady. He wanks over them.

I just wondered if Lady Caroline was still as hot for you." James yawned, sat up then stretched.

"Well Lord Jimmy--," David began.

"Don't call me Jimmy, my name is James--."

"Fuck you, Jimmy." David continued. "You're not Lord Snooty here. We're the same rank so less the patronising of the proletariat. Now get yourself out of your pit and let's get to the mess and enjoy the pink gins you're going to pay for."

Daniel anticipated some measure of an intellectually charged riposte. But James was in no mood for even a mild exchange. He sat up, lit a cigarette then stared through half shut eyes at his fellows.

"Ok Jock, are you and Lady Caroline still hot?"

"Of course, Jimmy. She says she is moist all the time thinking about when we all get out of this boiling shit pit and return to civilisation. Then we can be together."

"Good. It's just that Philippa wasn't sure. Caroline has not been going to the summer balls, even the local ones never mind the London scene." James poured water into a bowl and splashed it over his face.

"Right, I'll just have a quick pee then we can ambulate over to the mess."

The three young officers ordered their cocktails.

"What's Emily up to? Got sick of you yet?" Daniel lifted his pink gin as he, David and James sat at a table at far end of the officers' mess, away from the senior officers and company commanders. It was their first social get together since withdrawing from the edge of Crater. Accordingly, on this occasion they wanted to talk as teenagers and young men rather than hob knob with the brass.

"She's doing fantastically well. The youngest QC in the country. She's brought in tons of work for the chambers. Now she has some kind of part time job as well. Sounds like she's now working alongside the police although she was a little vague on detail. I'm so lucky to have a lady like her," James replied then turned to David. "So, Jock the Scot. What about Lady Caroline? Is she anxiously awaiting the warrior's return from the fray?"

"She's waxing great vibrations about us." David smiled. "And Danny

Boy, is your lady love still keen? Or has she cooled, not like the barren rocks of Aden though, more like a summer in Northumberland."

"She's hot and randy. Now let's drink to us all being back with our ladies, unscathed and whole and as fast as God can speed us." Daniel toasted upon which they all raised their glasses.

PHILIPPA-JULY 1967

Jim Parnell walked into the expansive kitchen of Wye Hall radiating an air of nonchalance.

"I want to see ya," Rebecca called over to the gardener.

"What d'ya want?" Parnell sounded totally apathetic.

Rebecca threw a set of photographic negatives and a reel of recording tape on the table.

"This disgusting thing you tried to do t' Lady Philippa," Rebecca snarled viciously.

"Where did ya get 'em?"

"I knows what ye was up to, Jim Parnell. After all this family's done for you, you repay them this way."

"She asked for it! She pushed! Not me!"

"Lady Philippa's just a kid, only 18, Jim Parnell, you're 27. Ye should 'ave known better."

"I told ye, she led me on! I 'ad no choice," Parnell inanely protested.

"Yeah, bullshit as they say! But even if ye is tellin' the truth, ye tried to sell 'er reputation to a paper most people would not even wipe their backsides on."

"I was only makin' a few quid. Did ye change the photos and tapes?"

Rebecca nodded as Mister Hodges and Mrs Cromer entered the kitchen.

"Course I did. Lady Philippa's been my charge since she was a baby. D' ya think I would let ye profit at 'her expense?"

"Jim, here you are." Hodges handed Parnell a wage packet and a P45 end of employment form.

"Ya sackin' me?"

"We 'ave no choice, Jim. Just go quietly and nothin' will be said. A job is ready for ya, with lodgings, at Didcot. All arranged." Hodges turned solemn. "But if ye decides to challenge, then instead of a week's pay in lieu, new job and good references ye'll get nothin'! It's up to ya. Think yerself lucky we did that! This family's been good to ya."

"Mister Hodges did a lot t' get ya a new position, Jim." Becky glared. "But ye mention anything 'bout my Lady Philippa and ye'll end up in court. Or worse. Now go, they're expectin' ya at Didcot. Mister Hodges'll give ye directions."

The clock had moved on less than half an hour from Parnell's departure when the Countess of Wye entered the kitchen. She was wearing a stylish blue knee length day dress with brown stockings and bore an expression that exhibited no small measure of disquiet.

"Hodges," she called out.

"Yes, My Lady."

"Have you set eyes upon my daughter? Her car is parked way out at the rear of the hall although we have not set eyes upon her within the last few hours."

"No, My Lady. I have not seen the Lady Philippa. Shall I say My Lady is wishing her presence should the Lady Philippa be seen by any of the staff?"

"Please do, Hodges. Thank you." Louise Marchant turned back into the main area of Wye Hall.

"What was that about Mister 'odges?" Mrs. Cromer was interested whilst Rebecca was as anxious and intrigued as the countess.

"We shall 'ave to watch out for Lady Philippa," Hodges uneasily responded.

"She'll be nearby," Rebecca suggested, "I'll go out and see Mister Hodges."

Rebecca was thankful that it was a hot summer's day and there had been no rain for a week.

She stepped down to the folly, found it empty then began traversing the wooded knolls that formed a semi-circle around Wye Hall. She could hear a radio playing The Small Faces latest single "Here Come the Nice" and followed the sound of Steve Marriott's distinct vocals.

Philippa was spotted on a bed of dried pine needles. The debutante was attired in black trousers and a white blouse. The unmistakable glowing auburn hair flowed loosely on the woodland floor as she journeyed through the canyons of a deep slumber.

"Lady Philippa." Rebecca gently shook the sleeping figure. The music on Radio Caroline changed to another new single, "She'd Rather Be with Me" by the Turtles.

"Ugh." The young woman moaned then looked up at Rebecca. "Becky, it's so groovy. I've been tripping, cool. I love you Becky. Come trip with me."

"My God. She's either drunk or been takin' drugs. Stand up, Lady Philippa. We'll 'have to get ya to the kitchen. Can't 'ave her Ladyship seein' ya like this. We'll never 'ear the end of it."

Using the knoll to cover her from view at the back of Wye Hall, she ran into the kitchen.

"Mister Hodges, 'elp me please. Lady Philippa isn't well. She needs our help. Now."

EMILY-JULY 1967

The Crown Court in the town of Croydon in Surrey seemed to be extra sultry on that blistering July day. The old wooden benches, musty smell and the dubious odours from many within s produced an atmosphere that appeared to combine a Jane Austen style cottage, a pop concert and a public convenience. The horse hair wig merely added to the depth of the humidity and radiating high temperature within the court. It was an uncompromising mistress that mercilessly held sway as the defence made its final summation to the 12-good people and true.

The young QC was thankful that she still wore a conservative length of skirt at work. Just on the knee, which allowed her to slip into stockings thus permitting cooling air to circulate and prevent heating to excess.

In this trial, Thomas Neville, a 40-year-old, plump, bald man from Waddon in Surrey had been accused of handling stolen goods. Emily had been assisted by one of her team, the somewhat rotund and overweight graduate, Roy Friarhouse.

Emily was acutely aware that following the successful defence of Artie Cooper, all police officers involved in the prosecution of cases concerning the south London and north Surrey areas, in which Emily was the defence barrister had been briefed in depth. This was mainly to concentrate on her methods but included refining articulation and personal skills whilst giving evidence from the witness box. The young QC was acutely conscious of this tactic. Consequently, she employed her assistants, Roy as well as Gill and William Potter, to conduct the initial cross examination. Once she had sussed out the modus operandi that the police and prosecution were utilising, she would take over in the final bout of questioning. These cases would normally conclude by ushering in the culmination of "My Lord, this case is without corpus delicti." The jury returned after a mere hour and a half of deliberating.

"What say you, guilty or not guilty?" The Clerk of the Court asked the jury foreman.

"Not guilty, My Lord."

Emily made for the nearby East Croydon station and jumped on the London bound train heading for Victoria. The flabby figure of Roy sat opposite her in the musty, uncleaned carriage. He was trying to look up her skirt without her noticing. Naturally she did.

"Miss Wilkinson--."

"Call me Emily, Roy," she interrupted him, "I'm the same age as you. It makes me feel like an old maid when you call me Miss Wilkinson."

"Very well, Emily. How do you do it? How do you get so many people acquitted when they are obviously guilty?"

"Roy, we do not look for guilt or innocence. It is the job of the defence to get the client acquitted. Something you have the education to do with relative ease. We place a reasonable doubt in the minds of the jury. Perhaps you think I'm sitting there sleeping whilst you are cross-examining witnesses. I can assure you I'm not. Now when we get to Victoria I have to shoot off for half an hour on business. Can you ensure Mister Crawley is fully briefed?"

"He has another cheque for 1,000 pounds, Emily. I doubt if he'll be too upset."

"No, he won't be upset but we have to cover all our cases. We don't want a backlog. You'll be back in court tomorrow. Are you fully conversant with the evidence presented?"

"Yes, I've been watching you Emily. Your tactics in court I mean. We can't lose."

"Good, Roy. Then let's have a result!"

Emily caught the London Underground to Liverpool Street then went into a pub just outside the entrance to the station, The Railway Inn. John Robinson was sat in a corner; his much-mellowed North Eastern inflection warmly greeted her. "Miss Wilkinson. How did you do in court today?"

"Good afternoon. I did very well, thank you, Detective Sergeant. May I buy you a drink?"

"No. I'm still old fashioned so I'll buy the drinks." Robinson began to walk to the bar.

"As long as it is clear, with no ambiguity at all, Sergeant, that our relationship will always be professional. Nothing else."

"I understand, counsellor. I can assure you that this operation is far too complex, for me not for you, to be muddied by personal relationships with those involved. No matter what one's personal thoughts are."

"Good, I'll have a vodka and lime. Just a single and if they do sandwiches or pies I'll have one or the other also with a packet of ready salted crisps."

After John Robinson had returned with drinks and snacks they touched glasses.

"Cheers. Now did you photograph all items of interest on that mini camera I gave you?"

"I did. Papers, letters and books," Emily replied, "And here is the film containing it all. I removed it precisely as instructed."

"Good. What result did you get today?"

"I spared another upright member of society from being sent to gaol. Why?"

"Who is your colleague working with? What is the name of her latest client?"

"Colin Todd. A bit of a weird man arrested on suspicion of theft. I've only seen him, never actually had a word."

"Who allocated Todd to Miss McMenemy?"

Emily took out her cigarette case, lifted a Benson and Hedges before Robinson lit it for her.

"She chose it from a batch of cases we had received."

The detective took a photograph from his pocket. "Is this your client?"

"Yes. Don't tell me he's another Hungarian spy?" Emily was clearly a little perturbed.

"We thought it was him. No, he's not Hungarian. But he is a fully paid up member of the CPGB, The Communist Party of Great Britain. What specifically is he up for?"

"Alleged theft of a Willem de Kooning painting, "Seated Woman," " Emily quietly replied.

"I know some of his work, abstract expressionist, also called action paintings. One of the most coveted artists as he is still alive. Unlike his contemporary, Jackson Pollock."

"Sergeant Robinson. I had no idea you were so cultured. I'm impressed."

"Miss Wilkinson. I may be a copper but I have a BA in Fine Arts from Durham University. But enough of that. Could you find out all the info you can on him? You have a legitimate pretext.

I mean you can enquire within your chambers, nothing out of the ordinary. Anything that seems unusual let me know? Of course I need not tell you to take care. No one must know of our arrangement including your Royal Marine boyfriend. Todd and his associates are very dangerous. Their people will kill you without any compunction. As would some sections of the British security apparatus if you get in their way. So far, our force is hitting a brick wall. We have to negotiate a hazardous road in this game. Trust no one, Miss Wilkinson. In fact if you want to resign, no one would blame you."

"Detective Sergeant, you have whetted my appetite for more."

He skilfully handed her an envelope ensuring no one was watching.

"Great." The North Easterner smiled. "In there is your first cheque. Deposit only at the relevant branch and new bank account we have set up for you. Also included with this are a set of instructions in a code. It may sound slightly theatrical but read, digest, then burn them. Now I have to go."

The meeting did not go unobserved.

PHILIPPA-JULY 1967

"Ugh, where am I?" Philippa lifted her head above the pillow. It took her a while to realise she was lying on the spare cot in the servants' quarters.

Rebecca sat her up. "Here, Lady Philippa. You 'ave a drink of coffee. You've had a little sleep. Ya seemed pretty off colour to me."

Philippa then vomited into the bucket by the bed.

"You get yerself sorted, Lady Philippa. Her Ladyship's been askin' for you." Rebecca was dressed in her black hued maid's dress and white pinafore as she left the tiny bedroom. It was only a few seconds of brisk striding that saw her back in the kitchen.

"Mister Hodges," Rebecca called out, "I think Lady Philippa 'll soon be alright. We can tell Her Ladyship she was sleepin' out in the woods near Wye Hall."

"That's top drawer, Rebecca. I was startin' to worry just a little." Hodges was obviously uneasy. Rebecca deemed he looked more than usual like a penguin. Dressed in his tails and bow tie, the face appeared to change, momentarily, to that of a pale, balding man. Perhaps it was merely his expression or more likely the manifestation of an emotionally charged imagination.

The figure of Philippa appeared. She was still dressed in her black bell-bottom trousers, white blouse and black high-heeled shoes. Her dishevelled auburn locks glowed with prominence in the afternoon sunshine. The sound of Nancy Sinatra singing the James Bond movie theme, "You Only Live Twice" drifted gently across the large kitchen area. The teenager sat down at the expansive table. Rebecca took a seat beside her.

"I'm so ugly Becky. Fred jilted me. He said I should be happy with Julian. I must be so, so ugly." Philippa began to cry and wrapped her arms around Rebecca's neck.

"Nonsense, Lady Philippa. You is a beauty, a real beauty and I ain't just sayin' that. Anyone can see. That's why you're always in the magazines. They knows how beautiful you is. Ignore those stupid boys, follow ya own dreams."

"I can't Becky. I must accept my place. I'll write to Julian and tell him that as long as I can stay at university I will consent to be his wife, I'm too tired. I have maniac depression, like Jimi

Hendrix and can't fight it anymore. It'll make Mama, Daddy and my friends happy. Especially Caroline, Kinsey and Elmira. It's what they all want."

"Is it what you want?" Rebecca poured her a cup of strong coffee.

"No. But I have to keep the family reputation intact. A good match is essential." Philippa looked up, took a Balkan Sobrani cigarette from its black packet and used her lighter.

"Sounds like you're talking about breedin' horses." Rebecca smiled.

"A much higher level but the same idea. It's a bit plastic I know. I want to hang out and live. Have fun and a slice of the action but I have a duty to the family."

The Earl of Wye knocked on the kitchen door and entered. Philippa noticed he was in his usual afternoon dress of tweed jacket, white shirt and corduroy trousers. The servants all stood up.

"Pip, you're here. We were a smidgy bit worried about you." Tom Marchant sat next to his daughter. "You appear to be a little upset. Anything you wish to mention?"

"No." Philippa looked up at Rebecca as she put her arms around her father's neck.

"She just had a little nap in the woods. It's very sunny, My Lord." Rebecca smiled at Tom.

"Pip. Mama has been a little perturbed."

"You can tell Mama I'll go along with her and marry that Julian," Philippa promptly imparted leaving her father was monetarily silenced.

"I suggest." Tom looked at Rebecca who gave a slight nod of approval. "That before we formally announce such an item to your mother, you have a very long, hard think. We have to make sure that that's what you truly wish for."

Rebecca grinned at Tom, blushed then quickly looked away.

Chapter Thirteen

DANESH AND KELLY

Danesh looked pleased with himself as the phone rang. It was Kelly. She was half way through her exhausting shift at the Department of Urology.

"Yes, Doctor Aresti. Are you tired of sticking your index finger up the backsides of middle aged men?"

"No. I was just on a break so thought I would give you a bell. Anything up?"

"I received a huge cheque for progress to date on my research into PU travel. We can afford to go to Mesopotamia or somewhere else as exotic for a few weeks' break."

"That money is to fund research, not to pay for holidays." Kelly teasingly laughed. "And anyway, you old goat, you're so full of bullshit you could almost drown in it."

"I can still get an erection without Cialis and that's not BS. I'll book the trip this afternoon, to the luxury resort of Basra in the south of Mesopotamia. After that we could possibly take a luxury cruise on the River Euphrats north to the ancient land of Babylonia."

"How much did HM Department of Scientific Research pay you?"

"Kelly, you're such a woman."

"100 percent female, Professor, as you well know. And yes, I want a cut to shop for clothes if we are going away. It'll make a change to travel to somewhere on our planet in our Universe, instead of a parallel one, I would like to see Mesopotamia and the temples of Babylon."

"Go and buy clothes for a hot dry climate. I'll cover the cost from my latest research stipend. I never asked, Doctor, can you get the time off?"

"Professor, I booked the next two weeks, starting Friday night, as leave whether or not we were travelling abroad. I would have gone to the American state of Canadia and travelled the Rockies had you not come with me."

"No need, delicious doctor. Although I am old enough to be your father--."

"Actually, even if all parents conducted themselves within the law, you are easily old enough to be my grandfather."

"Enough of this pointless theorising, Doctor Aresti. Go and buy yourself some sexy stuff but also bear in mind that Mesopotamia is an Islamic state. You and I will both have to dress modestly when away from the hotel. But inside the complex you can be whatever you wish."

Kelly was silent for a second. "I have enough on my credit card, Prof. Nonetheless, I am owed a generous refund from you. A junior doctor does not earn much, so I shall accept your gracious offer to fund my new wardrobe."

The British and Commonwealth Airlines VC 10 touched down on the runway at Basra International Airport, in the south of Mesopotamia. It slowly taxied to the non-domestic docking area. Danesh and Kelly cleared border control and had collected their considerable array of luggage when they made haste for the terminal exit. Just exterior to the glass door, a man stood bearing a placard bearing the inscription "Professor Danish Gideon" scrawled very untidily on the cardboard surface.

"Professor Hussein." Danesh stepped forward towards the figure. He was dark skinned with a thick black moustache, medium height and about 30 years old. He was garbed in a worn, crumpled grey suit, dirty white shirt and loosened white tie.

"I am he, sir," Hussein responded.

"I am Professor Gideon of the University of Hartfordshire in England. I believe you are the expert to guide us around the ancient ruins of Babylon."

"And much more!" Hussein enthusiastically smiled. "Come. I have a taxi waiting. There is much for us to see and discuss."

DANIEL/JAMES/DAVID-SEPTEMBER 1967

The day was typical. An intense, potent sun was dispassionately and ruthlessly pummelling down from the blinding welkin. It was blistering and singeing all that came unprepared.

Second Lieutenant Gibson and his troop had been ordered to the edge of the suburb of Al Mansura, where it bordered the open land towards al-Ittihad and Little Aden. The Royal Marines were tasked with rendering support fire to a company from 1st Battalion Parachute Regiment. Two ruthless and fanatical terrorist organisations were squaring each other up in anticipation of an imminent British withdrawal. Nonetheless, the National Liberation Front had declared a jihad, holy war, on the Paratroopers. For this endeavour the NLF had received some support, although limited, from their uneasy allies and soon to be opponents, the Front for the Liberation of Occupied South Yemen, known as FLOSY.

Lieutenant Colonel Michael Walsh, commanding officer of 1 Para, was aware that the Arab insurgents would fight the British despite the outcome of any political negotiations and in the true spirit of his regiment would robustly return any aggression visited upon his men.

The remaining regiments deployed within the crown colony included Lieutenant Colonel Colin Mitchell and his 1st Battalion Argyll and Sutherland Highlanders who were successfully holding Crater from their bases in "Stirling Castle" and Waterloo lines. In Ma'alla district the historical 1st Battalion South Wales Borderers commanded by Lieutenant Colonel Nick Somerville also retained control. The regiment made famous in books and movies for their historical defence of Rorke's Drift during the Zulu War of 1879.

On the flat roof of a low, single storey mud brick structure a section of Daniel's soldiers were down in the prone position. The Royal Marines' green berets were reversed on their heads forming a peak at the front. This minor alteration in rigging was authorised to shield their eyes from the relentless glare of the sun as they brought down 7.62-millimetre fire onto insurgent positions in support of the Paratroopers beyond. A British Broadcasting Corporation news camera crew was hovering around annoying Daniel as he attempted to prosecute a battle with the NLF. The

BBC had filmed the men on the roof and had now moved to the street. It was from behind cover in this position where that the rest of the engaging the enemy with rifles and light machine guns.

"Sir," Marine Dixon called from his radio set.

"Enemy to the front!" Sergeant Helm loudly bellowed. Daniel at once fired several rifle rounds at gunmen moving between scrub bushes a hundred yards from the troop position. The flawless marksmanship brought down several insurgents who fell onto the billowing and rustic, sandy dust.

"Lieutenant." A fresh faced, sandy haired man approached. He carried a microphone and followed immediately by two other individuals with sound and vision recording equipment. Daniel assumed the associates to be a cameraman and a sound engineer. "I'm Brian Barron of the BBC. Can we have a quick word?"

Daniel snarled at the young man holding the microphone a second before a bullet projectile hit the nearby wall. This nearby shot ricocheted, hit and killed a terrified dog darting past. The luckless canine jerked into the air then lay still in a twitching mess of blood, fur and entrails.

"Keep down!" Daniel screamed at the television film crew who were now nervously unsure of where to move. "On the deck or it'll be your last interview!"

"Mister Gibson, Sir!" Marine Dixon called out once more.

Daniel opened fire along with several of his men as more enemy moved towards the Paratroopers' positions. After the subaltern had discharged seven more rounds, he reloaded his SLR before walking over to where Dixon was speaking on his radio. A few more small arms shots hit the wall to his rear. This incoming ordnance kept the BBC staff extremely tight to the ground as Saracen armoured personnel carriers were seen encroaching on positions to their north well inside Sheikh Othman. The APCs were simultaneously firing 30 calibre Browning machine guns at the same locations as the Marines. Soon, the seemingly continuous shooting by the insurgents at Daniel's position ceased.

"Yes, Dixon! What is it?"

"From Sunray, sir. Foxhounds to return home, sir."

"Very well, Dixon. Signal Pronto to give us a lift. I don't fancy yomping back to Little Aden." "Yes, sir," the signaller crisply responded then went back on his A41.

"Mister Barron and your BBC men!" Daniel called almost facetiously to the figures rigidly prostrate on the sand surfeited ground. The reporter looked up at Daniel. Barron was certainly not outwardly betraying any sign of nervousness as the young troop commander hastily added. "We're moving back to our base at Little Aden. Now! If you want an interview, you'll have to do it this instant."

He then turned to the extremely suntanned figure of Tony Helm. "Sergeant. Pronto is coming. Get Corporal Foster's section down from the roof. Get the other guys to prepare to move. The OC, or perhaps it's the CO, wants us back at the camp. Soonest."

"Yes, sir," Helm nodded then screamed out, "Corporal Foster! Bring your section down! Corporal Greenham! Corporal Ely! Have ya men prepare t' move! Pronto's on the way! Pronto's transport case you thick fuckers 'ave forgot. It's on the way!"

David Moir had completed his active service for the day, so he thought. He was moving towards the mess for a welcome drink when Terry Baker called over from the briefing room.

"Beg your pardon, Mister Moir. Major Adams says all the officers and senior NCOs 'ave to meet in the officers' mess, sir."

"Very good, sergeant," David responded in his lilting Edinburgh intonation, "I thought I would at least have a drink first."

"Later, sir. I'm sure the CO'll not be long. Have a smoke."

"Crikey. Cheap Royal Navy" blue liners", Sergeant. I normally wouldn't but as you're offering and they're less than a halfpenny each, I'll take one."

While Terry Baker was lighting David's cigarette, James and Sergeant Diggle appeared. A few moments later a whining column of Saracen APCs roared through the main gate in swirls of choking dust. These armoured vehicles were ferrying Daniel and his fatigued men. The area before the briefing room suddenly seemed to be replete with officers, warrant officers, colour sergeants and sergeants. Within a few minutes the dust caked figure of Daniel appeared, shadowed by Sergeant Helm and Marine Dixon.

"Davy, what's up? I was having great fun zapping the wogs in Al Mansura. We had to end it rapidly for a bloody lecture."

"Danny Boy, you're so gung ho. Relax and have a smoke. Dismiss your signaller and just enjoy our CO chatting," David advised as they all marched into the hall.

The tall figure of Lieutenant Colonel John Owen was just inside the entrance as the three young officers and their respective sergeants entered the expansive wooden structure.

"The three musketeers you guys are called. A trio I interviewed at the AIB almost a year ago. Of course, you may not recall," Owen imperiously proclaimed.

David, James and Daniel each cast a nervous smile.

"Mister Gibson, a quick word please."

Daniel sidled over to the commanding officer.

"Mister Gibson. I understand you were interviewed by Brian Barron of the BBC today."

"That is correct, sir."

"Yes. What did he ask you?"

"He asked who I was and how long I had been in the colony. But most searching and deep was "If I was killed before the British withdrawal what would I have died for?" Not too cerebrally challenging, sir."

The lanky Owen stroked his chin briefly in thought before posing the inevitable question.

"And how did you respond?"

"It was very easy, sir." Daniel assuredly smiled. "I informed the reporter from the British Broadcasting Corporation that I would have died for our country and the Corps. If he wanted a political answer he ought to consult our Prime Minister, Harold Wilson, or Defence Secretary, Denis Healey. I'm an officer in the Royal Marines and not a politician."

"Well done. young Gibson. Very diplomatic. And Mike Walsh sends his personal thanks. Your troop helped 1 Para 's cherry berries a lot today. They appreciated the accurate fire support. Are you on a short service stint?"

"Yes, sir, I'm off to university in October 1969."

"Well, you could do worse than consider a permanent commission. Still, I must give my talk. Well done, again."

"Thank you, sir," Daniel replied as the CO gathered his audience.

The Miasmic Mist —Volume One

PHILIPPA-SEPTEMBER 1967

"That's absolutely top hole, darling. When will be the most appropriate date for it to be formalised? It shall of course require an announcement in The Times. The engagement of our only daughter to such a prestigious suitor must be made known to all."

"Mama, no one says top hole anymore. That's 1930s not 1960s speak." Philippa smiled a little. "I'm sure when Julian returns he will have his own opinions on such matters."

"I'm sure." Louise adjusted a few flowers in a nearby vase. "He is so assertive and so right for you."

"Mama. My ambition to become a doctor will not a subject of negotiation. We all agreed to that. Especially Daddy."

"You're young Philippa. You will soon discover that there is no need for a woman to acquire a university degree. Except of course to be able to discourse intelligently with their husband's guests when they sit down for dinner. To qualify as a doctor will take many years. Are you sure you will want to study for that long? Especially with a husband."

"Mama, we have ploughed this field many times. I will marry this favourite of yours. But only if I am able to complete my studies and practice as a doctor for a number of years."

"Louise." Tom Marchant could feel the groundswell of an argument approaching. "You have your wish so allow Philippa hers."

"I'm sure Julian will work on her. I doubt if she will get to study medicine let alone be a doctor. It's superfluous, but time will tell." The countess nodded. She was happy that finally events were moving along her desired path.

The sound of the Beatles and George Martin's orchestra performing "All You Need Is Love" was playing on the Dansette in Elmira's boudoir. Within were she, Caroline, Kinsey and Philippa all dressed only in their underwear. The girls were chatting, trying on new clothes and smoking. In between such activities they were drinking Babychams that were laced with a little brandy.

"Philippa. It's taken you two months." Elmira tried on some lipstick. "Were you unsure?"

"I was initially. But now I am sure. I believe that Julian will make an exemplary husband. I have rung up Woman's Own and Cosmopolitan to tell them there will be a story, probably in mid-December. I am now getting quite used to the idea of marrying Julian."

Kinsey changed the record to "Itchycoo Park" by The Small Faces.

"I prefer tough men. Like James and especially that young officer that was here a few months back." Kinsey sensually inhaled.

"Me too." Caroline expressively smiled.

"Oh yes. The red-hot Lady Caroline Feversham. She likes tough Marines. Especially between the sheets and especially one from Scotland called David." Kinsey chuckled followed by the others.

"I don't mind Julian. But he is a bit of a wimp. Also has a temper," Caroline remarked.

"He's fine. I'll be able to tame him," Philippa expounded with some conviction.

"Of course, you will." Elmira glared deprecatingly at Caroline. "You'll be perfect together." "When is David back from Aden?" Kinsey looked at Caroline.

"I'm not sure. When he writes he says it may be late January. However, the BBC and ITV news said it could be before the end of the year. Whichever, the sooner the better."

"Kinsey wants to know when Daniel is coming back." Philippa lit a cigarette as the song changed to "Let's Go To San Francisco" by the Flowerpot Men.

"I think Daniel would be perfect for Philippa," Caroline intimated, "He's easy going but can be very assertive when he wants. Neither is he threatened by decisive women."

"I need a man for life," Philippa proclaimed, "Tough army officers are alright for fun but what do they do after they leave the Army or get too old? Julian is a career man. He'll be rich from his own endeavours, as well as his father's fortune. Daniel is sweet but will never be in the same league as Julian."

"Is Julian rich? I heard not. However, Miss gorgeous red head, you are still officially single," Kinsey impishly interjected, "Enjoy tonight's ball and if any young lovely boys take your fancy, that's the way the cookie crumbles."

"I think we all should." Elmira smirked.

"I shall attend. But I am keeping myself for David. When the warrior returns from battle he shall be exposed to all the pent up, frustration of a tidal wave of sensual cravings. They shall manifest themselves in a torrid night of hot sex." Caroline was almost delirious at the erotic fantasy she had conjured up.

"Come ladies." Elmira beckoned. "Let us select our ball gowns. Then apply the requisite war paint needed for our mating rituals. We have but three hours to prepare."

EMILY-SEPTEMBER 1967

"Emily," Gerald Crawley called from his office. His star lawyer entered through the front entrance even earlier than her usual 7.30.

"Yes, Mister Crawley?"

"Come through. It seems you are becoming quite the celebrity."

Emily shuffled her way into Gerald's luxuriant office.

"Cosmopolitan approached me. They wanted to ask my permission for you to write an article every month for them. The subject matter would encompass swinging London and how young professionals, live, work and play. Her words not mine. Helen what's her name?"

"It's Helen Gurley Brown," Emily answered for him.

"Yes, her. Plus, Independent Television News and the BBC want an interview. And Woman's Own want an article accompanied by a photograph of you. This is due to the fact that your boyfriend is both in Aden and he is the brother of their current social scene flavour of the year. The famous socialite and debutante, Lady Philippa Marchant. Apparently, Lady Philippa appears in some way, shape or form in the magazine every week."

Emily was monetarily lost for words. "It seems you have a great grasp of the current happenings, sir."

"Not at all, Emily. And in private you can call me Gerald. It's been a long time since I held my commission in the Army. During the War in fact. No. I have no idea at all about current happenings as you put it. It is my daughters who update me on such current "in the scene' matters. To the matters in hand. Providing you give the chambers a free plug in these projects I have no objection. In fact, would encourage them."

"Thank you, er, Gerald." Emily nodded politely.

"The only caveat I have is that we ensure all current cases are dealt with. Do you have enough staff? The workload has gone totally through the roof since Artie Cooper became our unofficial sponsor."

"I have, Gerald. I know we could do with more clerical back up. I am aware that Artie's daughter is in the sixth form and wants to help at weekends. She wants to be a lawyer it would be great experience. Just to file and so on."

"Great idea." Crawley beamed. "Perhaps I could get my eldest daughter in also. She is taking "A" level Law right now."

"That would be wonderful." Emily showed genuine appreciation.

"So, arrange your diary. Work out when we can bring them in. And see if Mark could do with help also. I'm sure we could all use extra hands."

"Miss Wilkinson, I'm Geoff Hill, editor of "News at Ten"." The middle aged, tall, dark haired, distinguished figure came towards Emily. She was waiting in the reception lounge of Independent Television at 200 Grays Inn Road, a short distance from her chambers.

"Pleased to meet you, Mister Hill." Emily stood up and they cordially shook hands.

"The pleasure is all mine, I can assure you. You will have a seven-minute slot on tonight's programme, Miss Wilkinson. All I require is that when asked a question, within obvious time constraints, you give as broad a reply as possible. The public wants to know all about this famous, successful, beautiful, hip, groovy chick who is also a brilliant and renowned QC."

"I understand, Mister Hill. I talk for a living." Emily enthusiastically nodded.

"Great. George Ffitch, an old hand at the business will interview you. Has the fee been sorted? I believe 300 pounds was agreed?"

"It has. A veritable fortune. Especially for a few minutes. ."

"Trust me, Miss Wilkinson. We expect three million additional viewers, merely because of your appearance. Companies have been vying for space in the commercial break and at the end of the programme. Your fee will be repaid to many times over in advertising income."

"Dean." Emily kissed Sinclair on the cheek. "I understand you have a photo shoot arranged for me in London. This will be to augment the article or articles I shall be writing for your magazine over the next month or so."

"You look more beautiful each time I see you, Emily. Come with me to the USA. You'd be able to retire with a massive fortune by the time you're 35."

"Dean, I'm always in the same wardrobe when you see me. And no, that is not a veiled invitation. A pinstripe skirt and jacket, white blouse, black shoes and dark brown hose. Nothing changes. And no, I am not attracted to the thought of working in your land"

"Your make up and your hair. They've changed." the American offered Emily a Marlboro which she accepted. He lit her cigarette as "Gin House Blues" by Amen Corner came on a radio. It was from somewhere in the background of the bulky warehouse looking studio.

"Ok, they've changed. I'm in a rush Dean. Can you get your photographers and whatever sorted?"

"So sexy and assertive and blonde. Helen would love you. Are you sure you'll not come Stateside with me?"

She looked at the hippie style, flaming orange hued outfit that the man from New York was wearing. The style of hair was becoming much longer. Emily could barely believe the fashion transition that was evolving. The colours were flamboyant and loud, deafeningly so. They complemented the prominent tone of his voice.

"You never know, Dean. But don't hold your breath. Now can we move please?"

"Detective Sergeant Robinson, people will talk."
"I hope not, Miss Wilkinson. In your dark glasses it would be harder to immediately recognise you. Nonetheless, we must be careful. That's why I picked this quiet pub. I got you a gin and tonic. Hope that's alright and I put some music on the juke box to masque our conversation."

"I was Made to Love Her" by Stevie Wonder was the first of his selection to play.

"That's fine, Sergeant, a gin is great. I've had a busy morning, interviews with ITN and the BBC as well as Woman's Own and a photograph session with Cosmopolitan. I'm well behind so what can I do for you?" "Only a catch up. The boss wants to know if you have any info."

"I have to be careful. Even if I have a legitimate reason to look. But there is an address. I have no idea if it has anything to do with what you are after. However, it appeared in separate documents belonging to my colleague and underlined in her notes. They seemed to be tenuously connected to that man you wanted watching."

"Colin Todd. Where is it?" Robinson circumspectly glanced around the lounge of the Blue Monkey.

"Chingford Road, Walthamstow. They are business premises near the greyhound stadium, it may or may not be of value but I'm sure you have people who can check it out."

Tom Jones singing, "I'll Never Fall in Love Again" came on the jukebox next.

"I can. It's good. Whatever you can find out may help."

"I have a name. I don't know if it's real, but it appears scribbled on her notes. It may be a ruse or something innocent."

"It may not, Miss Wilkinson. I'll take it and the number of the property on Chingford Road."

"I have no number, Sergeant, just a name. Parkers. That's all I know about the property. And the name of the mentioned person is Aaron Iveson. I'm sure it could well be an alias. However, she said she'll meet up with him this Friday. And there'll also be a follow up in November, at Sadler's Wells. I repeat I would certainly be recognised so I can't follow her. She'd guess at once what's up."

"No. We'll do it. Good stuff. You'll have a payment in your special account on Friday and more if this information comes good. Thanks, Miss Wilkinson."

DANIEL, JAMES, DAVID-SEPTEMBER 1967

The tall and imposing figure of Lieutenant Colonel John Owen addressed his officers and senior NCOs in 45 Commando briefing hall.

"Gentlemen. An update of important info for you to share with your men. Something that has been ongoing since May." Owen looked across the room. "And to be frank, I have no idea why it was not completed long before as it's now the ninth of September. The last of the service families will be out of the colony before the end of this month. The date for final withdrawal may be this year. Late December or thereabouts. I'll keep you posted."

Owen lit a cigarette then turned again to the Royal Marines before him.

"45 is leaving Little Aden before the end of the month. We are moving into flats in Tawahi vacated by the service families. Once we leave Aden, 45 will finally be going to Blighty for the first time. Our initial UK base will be Stonehouse Barracks in Plymouth. The British Petroleum oil refinery in Little Aden will stay. Hopefully it will not be attacked. The Prince of Wales' Own will be leaving Tawahi for home in October. They will be replaced by Lieutenant Colonel Dai Morgan and his 42 Commando RM who'll act as our reinforcement as we hold the line for the withdrawal. Before that, we have work to do here. I know the Jocks are imposing "Argyll Law" in Crater. They're also suffering fatalities. I know we must act in the full spirit and ethos of the Corps and never shirk our duty. But be extra vigilant. It's been reported that the NLF and FLOSY are now fighting each other. We have to keep out of it. It's not our fight and I don't want more of our chaps in Silent Valley., I want you all to get home safely."

The officers, warrant officers and sergeants listened intently.

"From next weekend, we'll not be conducting anymore offensive operations. We shall only return fire that is targeted directly at us, Defensive actions only. I'll let you know ASAP the minutia of the final withdrawal including the RN task force coming here. But the main points you need to know are that we are leaving Little Aden within two weeks and moving to the flats at Tawahi. We keep out of the fight between the NLF and FLOSY. One other very relevant detail. We must no longer refer to the Arabs as "wogs". The unofficial sobriquet, nickname to those not so well educated, for Arabs is "gollies". But you did not hear that from me. All other important news I 'll impart as soon as I hear it myself. That's all gents."

David, Sergeant Baker, James, Sergeant Diggle and Daniel had congregated in a circle outside the wooden briefing hall waiting for

Sergeant Helm to return from the camp office with the day's English football results. The subdued Helm returned to the group with the news. He unrolled a sheet of foolscap paper like a mediaeval harbinger and turned to Dave Diggle, "You're an Argyle supporter too. Ain't ya? Sergeant Diggle."

"That Oy am," Diggle cagily responded.

"Well the final soccer scores 'ave just come through on the BBC World Service. At 16.00 hours Zulu Time on Saturday the ninth of September 1967. We, Plymouth Argyle, lost nil one at home to Rotherham United."

"I'm a rugby union man, Bath is my club." James cheekily grinned. "But as Daniel is a Sunderland supporter I'll root for their rivals, Newcastle United. How did they do?"

"Well, sir, they lost four nil away to Nottingham Forest. No need to smile, Mister Gibson. Sunderland lost five one at home to West Ham United."

"Sergeant Helm, you're supposed to uplift me and not bring me gloomy news."

"I'm just the messenger Second Lieutenant Gibson. Don't shoot the messenger, sir." Helm almost laughed

"That's English fitball," David Moir protested in his lowland inflection, "I'm from Edinburgh, Sergeant. How did Heart of Midlothian do?"

"Bad news for you as well, sir. Hearts lost four one at home to Hibernian. Your Edinburgh arch rivals. I believe."

"Yes, they are. Let's have a drink before dinner," David suggested, "My wee throat is parched."

"Hey Davy." Daniel handed over a pink gin. "We may be home before Christmas. Will you be getting down on one knee for Lady Caroline when we get back?"

"Aye, I just may. I want to spend the rest of my life with her. She's one foxy lady."

DANESH AND KELLY

Kelly looked at the wide Euphrats valley as the hire car sped north. The cooling breeze flowing through the open top two-seater diesel.

"Where are we going, Professor?"

"We are going to a town called Najaf. It's about 100 kilometres distant. Just south west of the ancient site of Babylon. That's where we"ll spend the night."

"It's such a long way away. Such a beautiful country this Mesopotamia. I'm so glad President Bushell kept the country from going to war with President Assad over Persia. It could have destroyed this exquisite landscape."

"The politics are complex," the professor solemnly responded, "Accordingly; you will forgive me if I refrain from such a discussion. We are heading north to an area known as the Fertile Crescent. In ancient times it stretched from the Gulf of Persia to Turikaye to Jerusalem. We shall look over the ruins of Babylon and other areas of Babylonia. Hopefully, with other academics like Professor Hussein."

"Look, Prof. A sandstorm over to the east." Kelly pointed to a swirling oval cloud of sand and dust some distance over to the west. In the radiant, open sunlight seemed to be a cone of luminescent gold. The young doctor was attired in summer pink and white culottes and shirt sleeved collarless jacket, white training shoes, dark glasses and white brimmed hat. She was absorbing each moment of the northerly ride from Basra. Kelly was more than grateful for the respite from work and the chance to visit a Mid Terra country.

"Just a dust devil. It'll probably either burn out or change direction." Danesh sounded sanguine and ceased looking at the spinning apparition.

An hour or so later and he turned off the main highway between Basra and the capital Bagahad. Within a short period, he was stopping outside the entrance of the Hotel Babylon near Najaf.

A bellboy ran out to collect their bags while the concierge showed them to the reception desk. Once they had checked in, the couple made their way to the room on the first floor.

Danesh generously tipped the bellboy, before Kelly undressed to take a shower.

"It's a great view Prof," she called from the balcony in her bathrobe and towel wrapped around her head, "You can feel what it would have been like around here 3500 years ago. Why did we come here? I hope you're not a secret psychopath. I mean someone who would lure an innocent maiden into the desert then bury her in the sand. Later on, dig her up and turn her into a walking mummy. Just like in the Brendan Frasier blockbuster."

"Yes. I bring you all the way to Mesopotamia to murder you when I could have done it in Nazeing while enjoying total privacy anytime over the last few years. The people I wish to meet studied at my university. It was almost the same time I was an undergraduate. From the small amount of information I was able to deduce, there may be a connection to our project somewhere here. Of course, there may not but whether we'll find a thread of propinquity to our work or the converse it is still a great country to visit. I have directions for tomorrow."

"It's beautiful here, Prof. Let's go down to the restaurant and enjoy a lavish dinner. Have an early night and watch a sexy movie then have sex. Lots of sex." Kelly cast an inviting expression s she drank her coffee.

The next day, in the cool of the early morning and after a hearty, healthy breakfast, the couple checked out. Kelly assumed the driving role. She steered along the highway that ran adjacent to the River Euphrats towards the town of Karbala.

Danesh checked his notes and viewed the scenery of the remarkable Biblical terrain juxtaposed to the thoroughfare. "There's another of those dust devils." He pointed to the west an hour or so into their journey. "Looks like it's actually following us," Kelly commented, and half laughed, "I'll put my foot down just like Lewis Hamilton."

"It's moving away. They're just air currents."

"I know, Prof. But in Arab countries they are called fasset el 'afreet or "ghosts' wind". In Mesopotamia and Persia, they are referred to as the djin, or "devil", genie in English. The genie of the lamp was not really a nice creature. Nothing at all like Aladdin and those other pantomime tales."

"You sound well versed on such matters, Kelly." Danesh looked up from his notes.

"Prof, I've always had an interest in the supernatural. But I must confess I cheated a bit on that one. I looked for it on my laptop. I searched it on Gowgle last night after that one came near during the day."

"You're so resourceful, Doctor Aresti. Now, according to directions given me, we turn off at this next lay by. It has facilities, so we can take a natural break. We can enjoy a snack of pita bread, humus, cheese and coffee before we move on. I'm expecting to see a Professor Gidron at this spot. Hopefully soon. I intend to discuss a variety of topics of mutual interest. Professor Hussein said it would be here, he's supposed to be present also. I hope he was accurate. This rest area truly is in the middle of nowhere."

Kelly turned the car off the dusty main highway into a totally vacant lay-by boasting several dozen parking spaces and a toilet block.

"Prof, I'm off to spend a penny. You can stay with the car. We must be close to the site of Babylon."

"We are." Danesh studiously checked the map. "You go and powder your nose. Then I'll go when you get back. Then we'll have a light picnic lunch. This exactly the spot that Hussein gave me the map reference to."

"You unpack what you want," she suggested. Her light green two piece and large hat flowing in the restless wind wafting restlessly from the direction of Saud Arabia. "However, I would love humus, pitta bread, olives, cheese and coffee. Not that Turkish shit, European freeze dried, with brown sugar and cream."

A few minutes later as Kelly returned from the ladies' toilets; another dust devil ascended from the desert floor. It moved towards the car seemingly on a fixed bearing. Ostensibly beckoned by invisible puppet strings or an imperceptible master of ceremonies the mass continued its advance. The churning, eddying mass halted some ten metres from their vehicle. It appeared to transform into an amorphous, swirling mist like ether. The apparition slowed and commenced solidification until it adopted an outline. A silhouette that both instantly recognised.

"Kelly. From that uncanny mist, that billowing sprite of the desert, see. It's PADIT. Our PADIT." "Not quite Prof. Almost. But see the door, the opening catch on our PADIT is on the left. That one is on the right."

It was the unmistakable sleek pointed shape of PADIT 2. Shaped like a large smooth cucumber, in deep metallic blue with very narrow blackened windows, the wheels for use only in emergency and the whirring sound as the craft came to a halt. Kelly and Danesh were held speechless for some moments. The entrance hatch flew backwards. From out of the machine a tall man appeared. He had dark, greying hair, long and flowing, blown by the gusts of the Sharqi. The figure was bedecked in white twisting robes and apart from the long beard, Danesh thought, the figure could be mistaken for him. The similarity was uncanny. The individual was clearly a doppelganger of his ilk. Nonetheless, there was much dissimilar between this man and the others he had been in association with thus far.

"Professor Gideon." The voice of the man reminded Danesh of the Shakespearean actor, Simon Callow, playing in Hamlet. "I'm Professor Danelaw Gidron. You wanted to talk. Jump into my transporter. You already are conversant with the craft. And bring your delightful assistant."

"I'm sorry, I can't leave the car. It's hired."

"You will be back here within 30 seconds in real time. I'm not travelling inter-dimensionally," Gidron announced.

"Then where?" Kelly took a sharp breath of incredulity.

"50,000 years back into the depths of history. Come. We can parley on the way."

PHILIPPA-SEPTEMBER 1967

The ball was humming with the buzz of the guests and the sound of the group called "The Ace of Spades" playing the Bee Gees song "Massachusetts". The ensemble was from well-placed families not only of Oxfordshire but also of much of the south of England and even further afield. The next song was the Jefferson Airplane psychedelic classic, "White Rabbit".

Caroline in a dark, long evening gown was true to her word. She listened intently to the music and sipped on Bucks Fizz as the music changed to the Herd song, "From the Underworld".

She mouthed along to the chorus harmonies.

"Caroline." Philippa appeared and sat next to her friend. "Don't you want to dance?"

The radiant blonde looked up and smiled. "Of course, I want to dance, Pip. But only with David. When he comes home from Aden then I'll dance all night."

"I hope that soldier boy knows how much you think about him."

"Of course. I write every other day, and he writes to me. Do you not write to Julian?"

Philippa was in a shimmering bottle green gown with her dark red hair tied up. She nonchalantly grinned. "My God, no. I drop a succinct missive every other month. Mama insists. But no. I would never be, could never be, romantic with Julian in the same way that you are with David."

"You sound like an old maid, Pip." Caroline looked up and sipped her drink.

"So different for you. I was the same with Miles, you know Miles in the group who died? So groovy, so cool, so young but he died."

"It was sad, Philippa. But if you're in love with Julian you should write hot letters, pulsating with sexy vibrations. Tell him you're the sole theme of every erotic fantasy that unravels in the deep recesses of your teenage hormonal thoughts. He's the only man that will ever make you tremble at the knees, moist in the nether regions and make your heart thunder."

"Crikey Caroline, you should get a job writing rhymes, risqué ones, for greetings cards," Philippa beamed as the music changed to a version of the Box Tops hit "The Letter".

A tall, slim, young man in dinner jacket approached Philippa.

"Perry." She looked up then kissed him on the cheek. "What are you up to?"

"Unlike your valiant brother, fighting the foe in foreign lands, I'm working at a bank in the City of London. All very boring stuff but the remuneration is super."

"Do you know Lady Caroline Feversham?"

"Of course, but not been formally introduced. Hi, I'm Peregrine Walker-Thorpe. Perry to my friends."

"Nice to meet you, Perry." Caroline shook his hand then listened to the music as the Ace of Spades announced they would now play the Monkees song "Pleasant Valley Sunday".

"When is James home?" Perry asked as he offered Philippa a cigarette from his silver case.

"He doesn't know," she replied as he lit her Rothmans King Size then his own, "But he thinks it will be either late December or early January. The government has said that the British will leave Aden no later than the spring of 1968."

"Dashed lot of trouble. The quicker we sneak out of the place and leave it to the fuzzies the better." Perry drew on his cigarette. "But listen, Pip. I've got a splendid bottle of Chateau Lagrange port and two glasses. So, if you possess some inclination to grab a few atoms of the proverbial fresh air and want to meander a touch in the rustic surroundings of the mansion's horticultural masterpieces, I'm your dude."

"You want to walk me out?" Philippa looked at Caroline who passed an assenting nod.

"Er, yes, I suppose I do. Any probs with such an undertaking?"

"Perry, you are a breath of fresh air. I think the music here is so righteous, but the guys are so uncool, a lot of spaz. Am I your choice? Let's find a scene."

"I guess so. Let's go outside. We can still hear the vibrations. It's nearly autumn but still warm."

They walked beyond the gardens and into the meadow beyond. The argentine moonlight cascaded down on the bucolic nocturnal landscape, the air just betraying the initial sting of the encroaching winter.

The couple sat down whereupon Perry poured from the bottle into one of the glasses.

"I thought you were outta sight with some dude in Australia. Hitched or at least on the way to formalising getting hitched." Perry handed over a glass. "Try this port, it's a bit rich on the palate but I love it, it's cool, righteous even."

"You know Mama has been scheming for me to marry Julian."

"Julian Lee Fartface." Perry laughed out loud. "He's been on the scene for years!"

"Mama is determined I marry someone of our background."

"Shit, Philippa. The dude is an intelligent retard. About as interesting as watching paint dry. Does your Mama know they're lots of cool dudes on the scene? Is she permanently blitzed?"

"Unfortunately, not. She set her sights on him for me years ago. I conceded. A bit cowardly I know but I have a quiet life and he may make a good husband."

"Oops, what was that? I just saw a pig fly. Pip, James would not allow it if he were here, I'm sure. All I can say is if you get spliced to that chop, that bummer, the male skag, you'll spend your life wishing you'd run a mile."

Philippa rolled up her skirt and removed her tights and briefs.

"Climb on Perry, lets, have a ball. Then get blitzed and stoned. So, no more talk about Julian. I'm not engaged to him. Yet."

Perry kissed her passionately and eased her onto the grass. They proceeded to make loud, athletic, passionate love.

EMILY-SEPTEMBER 1967

The petite, bubbly, 35-year old secretary was typing away merrily. Emily purposefully walked towards her followed by two nervous looking teenage girls.

"Karen." Emily sincerely smiled. "We have two young ladies here. Both of whom embrace a wish to become a lawyer."

"Oh, very good." Karen was suitably impressed.

"This young lady is Miss Dorothy Cooper." Emily pointed at the more diminutive of the girls. "And the other young person is Miss Claire Crawley. The daughter of our head of chambers."

"Wonderful. What can I do for the girls, Miss Wilkinson?"

"There must be numerous tasks. Basic. Yet nonetheless important so accuracy is essential. Some duties that they can assist you with. Or even take off your hands for a few days or so."

"Filing, invoices, writing new labels, something like that. There's nothing technical I can give them." "Sounds just the job. I'll leave them with you if you don't mind. I'll call back later to see how things are." Emily nodded then turned to the young females. "Karen is secretary to the head of chambers. She'll will sort you out basic tasks. But remember, as always, although speed can be important at times, with these duties accuracy is king. Double check everything."

At lunchtime Emily returned to assess the progress of her protégés. The young women were enjoying a coffee and sandwich in the kitchen.

"Hi." She watchfully entered.

"Emily. I'll make ya a tea or would ya prefer coffee?" Dorothy stood up, looking very adult and trendy in her apricot shaded Quant miniskirt and white lace blouse.

"Coffee thanks. How are you girls doing?"

"Groovy," Claire piped up. She also wore a miniskirt, hers was blue. Along with white shirt and white tights and short "Twiggy" style hair.

"But more to the point, Miss Wilkinson. We've been going through your Cosmopolitan photos and column you wrote. So hip. What a gas."

"Yeah," Dorothy shouted over as she put ground coffee in the percolator, "I loved the contrast between you in your work gear, pinstripe skirt, down to the knee, and jacket suit, white blouse with brown tights, and your party rags. So cool and hip."

"Brown stockings actually, much cooler in court." Emily smiled at Dot.

"Ok. But the contrast between your work kit and your glad rags for painting the town. A mini, mini skirt that barely covered your arse, frilly top and white tights."

"And that brilliant article you wrote. About the aspirations and realistic ambitions of the new breed of professional women in a male dominated economy. It was simply a gas." Claire was obviously enthused.

"Thanks for the panegyric. An encomium if you want a synonym to impress a lecturer or examiner. I have to go. I hope to see you two tomorrow. Don't forget, the pay will not be much, about five pounds a week. The experience will be worth a fortune. If you exploit it!"

Emily gave instructions to Karen, Roy Friarhouse and William Potter about current cases. She exchanged notes with Mark Carlisle and then collected her brief case and headed for the Tube station. She had been more than a little economic with the truth. Withholding from all, except Sergeant Robinson, the true designation for her early departure.

"It was something in the tone of her voice, always so sober, contained. This time she was a little aggravated," Emily had said to Robinson some time earlier during a telephone booth call, "There were copious notes made which were not in her case. They are probably still in her stuff.

I shall leave work early under a pretext and snoop through it before she returns to the house."

"Take care, these people miss no detail. Ensure all things touched are replaced exactly, I mean exactly, where they were. Take a photograph with the Polaroid before you snoop then use it to ensure total precision."

"I will, Detective Sergeant," Emily reassured him, "Now I must go."

The train from Liverpool Street pulled into Broxbourne station. Emily leapt onto the platform and skipped up the stairway towards the exit before darting at speed along the pavement that ran adjacent to the New River. She sprinted into her seven-bedroom house along the prestigious Mill Lane area of Broxbourne, one of the more desirable areas in the green and leafy county of Hertfordshire. Emily scanned around to ensure no one was hovering nearby. She jogged around to her substantial property and entered by the side door. The athletic young woman bolted upstairs, dropping her cream Gucci bag onto her bed and removing her pink Oscar de la Renta coat. She then unhurriedly and charily tip toed into Gill's bedroom. There Emily stood over the cluttered desk top and photographed it with her SX 70 model Polaroid self-developing camera.

Once she had the picture and had checked to ensure which items went where unlocked the drawers of the desk. For this she utilised a spare key Gill was unaware she held. Emily photographed each drawer before carefully inspecting the myriad of papers and notes inside.

Within ten minutes there was a huge amount of data which she deemed worthy of further investigation. Notwithstanding, the piece de resistance lay at the very bottom of the right-hand draw. She read the front of the cream envelope "To John Gollan/ Aaron Iveson, The Communist Party of Great Britain, PO Box 928 London W1". The young lawyer gave the communiqué a cursory glance digesting the final two lines, "From Abdullah al Asnag, Front for The Liberation of Occupied South Yemen (FLOSY) and the Aden Trades Union Congress and Salim Rubai Ali of the National Liberation Front (NLF)."

"Christ. I have to get this to Sergeant Robinson."

DAVID -SEPTEMBER 1967

David yawned and scratched his head before arising from his canvas bed. The awakening subaltern grabbed the dull green bag that contained his washing and shaving kit. He was about to make for the company officers' heads in their soon to be abandoned camp when his colleague grunted.

"Ya Scottish git. Can ya not make less noise?" A petulant Niall growled in a thick Dublin brogue while desperately attempting to catch up on sleep. This much needed rest was being even more hampered by the Bee Gees "Massachusetts" clearly audible from the proximate NAAFI.

"Yes, Second Lieutenant Niall Quinn, otherwise known as a grumpy Irishman. I shall endeavour to preserve your beauty gonking," David light-heartedly replied.

There was no small measure of irony in his voice and hummed away a Scottish melody as he energetically strutted away to his ablutions.

Once showered and shaved, he had barely dressed before Sergeant Baker called. Baker was nicknamed the "geriatric" as he was now at the ripe old age of 30. A span regarded as ancient by most of the Corps.

"Sir." The sergeant knocked. "The company 2IC wishes to see you and your men and Mister Marchant and his troop ASAP. Sir."

"Wonder what Mister Lowes wants. Where's Major Adams?"

"Don't know, sir. I think he may be in confab with the CO. It just sounded urgent."

"It always does, Sergeant." David failed to masque his sardonicism, "Are the section commanders and their men prepared to move?"

"Of course, sir. Corporals McGrath, Wake and Rayson are awaiting orders."

"Then let's crack on. You check out the men. I'll be over ASAP."

When David entered the briefing hall the moustached figure of Captain Lowes was already chatting to Lieutenant Bowman and James.

"Mister Moir, I'll not be long. I know Mister Gibson and Mister Quinn are having a much needed gonk after just returning from long sorties. Bravo Zulu to those two so to prevent them from being dipped, you subalterns can spin them when they wake up. Major Adams is otherwise engaged so I shall have to gen you up on a couple of items."

Lowes stopped to light an Embassy tipped.

"Right, first thing. This is all restricted. For us guys only, at the moment." Lowes drew deeply on his cigarette. "We all know we are abandoning the barracks here in Little Aden in just over two weeks. It has been reported that in the parleys with the leaders of FLOSY and the NLF, the Aden governor, Sir Humphrey Trevelyan, requested that "as the British were leaving could they please stop killing our soldiers?" His words not mine. To which Salim Rubai Ali of the NLF responded, and I quote, "Sayedy, we not only have to drive you from our land, we have to be seen to drive you out. We can only stop killing your soldiers when the last one of them has left our soil and only those now in your Christian paradise, sleeping in your military graveyards, may remain." Sir Humphrey contacted the Foreign Secretary, Mister George Brown who duly informed the Prime Minister, Harold Wilson, who contacted the Secretary of State for Defence Denis Healy and they were not amused by the comments."

"Not surprised, sir," David commented, "Can we give the gollies a duffing up? Zap a few or a lot. Just one for the road before we chop chop out of here?"

"I'm coming to you Mister Moir." Lowes smirked at David. "I have something jacked up for you and Mister Marchant. However, I want you all in one piece to see your divs. Following the commitment by the gollies to keep killing us, Mister Wilson has thrown in the towel. We'll be leaving this honking shit hole on Wednesday the 29th of November, this year, 1967. It's Tuesday the 12th of September today. Only 78 days left. There'll be no independence parade or lowering of the Union Flag and no bands playing the new and old anthems. Just a rapid bug out and off to Blighty. We'll be back home before Christmas. To Stonehouse Barracks, Plymouth. So, take care. Stay alive and ensure you get back. Now, Mister Moir, Mister Marchant. I have a mission for you both so have your pens and papers ready."

DANESH AND KELLY

The strange PADIT like vessel came to a halt. It landed on the flat roof of a very lofty building. Danesh and Kelly attempted to peer through the darkened windows. The tall, white robed and flowing locked figure of Professor Danelaw Gidron stood up from the controls and turned to them. "Come, Professor. Come and see the ancient city of Walika, Babylon to you. Although your Babylon will not come from this moment in the annals of history for another 45,000 years."

Danesh and Kelly followed Gidron out of the transporter and onto an impeccably clean surface. Upon closer inspection they perceived a brightly coloured mosaic showing battles, buildings and wild animals. The fauna represented on the melange of brightly coloured tiles included lions, tigers and woolly mammoth.

Danesh gazed with awe into the distance, stunned by the sheer beauty around him.

The massive stepped stone buildings that dominated the immediate area for as far as the eye could see and were constructed from pale meleke limestone. The soaring edifices reached up to about 100 metres in height and 500 metres in length. Most of the impressive constructs boasted a flat roof upon which were growing extremely ornate gardens. Others were used to store vessels and vehicles of some description. On the lower ground towards the river, sweeping away from their locus, were much slighter, more modest, wood and clay structures. Danesh deduced they were most likely a style of factory or workshop. A vibrant and scorching sun stood high in the firmament.

The slopes nearby shone with a golden glow whilst the land beyond the city, near the banks of the river, was lush and fecund. An emerald green brilliance of dense vegetation in which numerous animals grazed. The beasts looked like cattle but were much too hefty in stature to be any breed he had ever seen. Aurochs, Danesh thought, then immediately dismissed the notion. On the roads moved vehicles that resembled SUVs and were devoid of any animal propulsion, but they did house what seemed like a large mirror on the roof.

A strange flying machine that vaguely resembled Da Vinci's blueprint of a helicopter flew overhead.

"It is called a gyrocopter. That's the name in English," Professor Hussein elucidated as he joined Gidron to welcome the guests. Danesh was overflowing with incredulity.

"Professor Hussein. Where are we.? I am stunned beyond words. What dimension is this? Where is this world?"

"Professor Gideon. I must apologise for my slight subterfuge. I dearly wished for you to join us but believed, somewhat correctly, that you may have been slightly reluctant to travel in our world. It may have entailed days of superfluous negotiations. But fear not, Professor, you and your assistant will not lose out on your vacation. We shall return you to your motor vehicle, as promised, a mere 30 seconds in real time after you departed." Hussein smiled through his black moustache. The white suit gone, replaced by flowing cream and yellow robes.

"Where is this place?" Danelaw Gidron looked at Kelly and Danesh then answered, "In a three-dimensional world, we are about 10 miles, 16 kilometres, from where we picked you up."

"Is this the same dimension as ours?" Danesh was overwhelmed with rigorous cerebral activity.

"Yes." Hussein replied for his colleague, "Precisely. The landscape over yonder is indeed where we met up a short while ago. Of course, the river has changed position many times. In your epoch it has been totally destroyed. By that I mean there is no trace of our great city in your time. It appears in no historical or archaeological chronicles."

"But where are we?"

"I told you Professor. We are 50,000 years back in time from the point where we collected you," Gidron imparted almost blasé at his own rejoinder.

"That's impossible!" Kelly spoke up.

"How?" Gidron was still smiling, totally unmoved.

"There were no civilisations 50,000 years ago. For whom do you work?"

"Professor. You are an eminent scientist. Your work is based on hard facts or provable hypotheses. Ergo, why does your rationale gainsay the notion that advanced civilisations existed long before your own history had any trace or affirmation thereof. Even should they fail to receive a mention in any archaeological evidence or written archives?"

"There is no evidence of anything more advanced than primitive hunter/gatherers before about 6000 years ago; your claims are without foundation."

Hussein maintained his smile. "Let us partake in food and drink. Then we shall convoy you to the forests, mountains and wildernesses far beyond the city. The flora and fauna therein may tilt your estimation. We shall bring great elucidation to enhance your great erudition as we enlighten you on our time in our world."

"How do you know English? You could not have spoken it as a first language?"

"Of course not, Professor Gideon. Our native tongue is Walikan," Danelaw illuminated, "It would sound like a mixture of Arabic, Aramaic and Hebrew. A mishmash. And of course, these languages evolved from Walikan and sister vernaculars from nearby kingdoms. I learned

English from an Englishman. Several English people in fact together with Americans and Australians. The English language itself is an evolving tongue. I invited my tutors to visit me here in Walika. Naturally I travelled to England, the United States and Australia where I became totally fluent. My sources claimed to have been abducted by aliens. No one took them seriously. Poor souls. Since those early days we have developed the e-Rosetta. A complex computer that from first use can translate in about five minutes all languages after being spoken at for 30 seconds to a minute. Once it has been used for 20 minutes, translation is immediate. Our names have been altered from Walikan to be more acceptable in later periods of time. However, we will now always be known as Danelaw and Hussein. They roll off the tongue more easily. No need to confuse matters by imparting our original moniker. Now let us pack refreshments. We have honey wine, fruits, flat bread, dates and cheese. Once stores are on board, we shall travel to the Untamed Regions. There is a wealth of the magic of Mother Nature for you to discover."

PHILIPPA-SEPTEMBER 1967

Philippa made her way shakily down stairs. It was almost 11.30 in the morning, yet she was still in her dressing gown. Somewhere the current hit song, "The House That Jack Built" by the Alan Price Set was playing. She picked up the letter on the salver. It was clearly from James.

"Good morning, my little precious." Tom Marchant kissed his daughter on the cheek. He placed on his trilby then with Fred Biggs following stepped out to the Daimler.

"Morning, Daddy," Philippa groaned then continued to negotiate her way to the kitchen.

She sloped warily into the dining area of the kitchen. The preparation of the luncheon menu was approaching its conclusion.

"Lady Philippa." Rebecca immediately came forward. "Ya seems to 'ave 'ad a rough night, My Lady. Would you like a spot of lunch?"

"Ye gods, no," came the nauseated response.

"I'll get ya some orange juice and coffee. Maybe a little fruit or cereal."

"Grapefruit juice and black coffee with one sugar will be wonderful. Thanks, Becky."

The Woman's Own current cause celebre did not feel like the flavour of the month, or months that precise moment. Following a night of brandy and Babychams tailed by heavy Dom Perignon consumption, Philippa's head felt more than a little on the tender side. She slowly opened the letter, which had come from British Forces Post Office, BFPO Number 69, The Crown Colony of Aden. Becky brought over her coffee as she read the precious missive from her brother.

"James will be home before Christmas!"

"That's marvellous, Lady Philippa. Does he say when?" Rebecca perked up somewhat as did Mrs Cromer and Mister Hodges.

"He only said they'll be moving from their current barracks, in Little Aden. Then to a district on the main peninsula called Tawahi. I have no idea of the correct pronunciation. He estimates that at the beginning of December they'll all be withdrawn. Forever that is. And that he should be back at Wye Hall on Christmas leave on or around the 15th of December."

"Beggin' your pardon Lady Philippa," the 69 year old Mister Hodges interjected.

"Yes, Mister Hodges." Philippa looked up. She sipped her fruit juice then lit a cigarette.

"Well they told us in the First War, back in 1918, that that would be the war that would end all wars. But we've 'ad plenty since. I just want young Lord Marchant back 'ere. I think the sooner we leave that place the better."

"I agree, Mister Hodges," Philippa drew on her Balkan Sobrani; "James will be home soon, must mean all the fighting is over. I shall have to tell Lady Caroline the good news."

After her mainly liquid breakfast Philippa wandered up into the study to find her mother reading The Times whilst smoking a Craven cork tipped. The matriarch bedecked in a white blouse, stretch trousers and flat-bottomed patent leather sneakers.

"Darling. You are still attired in your dressing robe. Once you are married you shall have to behave in a more structured manner."

"Yes, Mama. But I'm not married yet. Julian is back in early December. Did you receive a letter from James?"

"No. However, we did notice that you did. Is there any news? Apart from complaints about the heat, the smells and the locals."

"James will return from Aden before Christmas. Isn't that simply splendid, Mama? He and Emily can celebrate my engagement with me."

"Yes. Well I'm sure you can wait until the New Year before you throw your engagement party."

"Whenever it is, Mama, I shall ensure that James, plus a few of his fellow officers, and Emily, are present. Caroline will be there with her beau David. I know that Kinsey and Elmira and many others love the broad shoulders and rippling biceps of Royal Marines' soldier types."

"I can understand that. It seems to be the fashion now for men to be not slim but outright thin. Girls too. I'm glad you have kept your figure."

"Many say I'm fat. These days you're supposed to be able to see a girl's ribs. Otherwise she's overweight."

"You're not fat at all. In fact, just right. I hope you are being faithful to Julian," Louise authoritatively commented.

Philippa looked up at her mother.

"I'm still single. He's going out with women in Australia. He told me."

"He's a man and that's what men do. So, let's have no scandals that could come back to bite us once you are husband and wife."

"As I have said, Mama. Provided I am permitted to complete my studies. Qualify and practice, as a doctor, I shall be the perfect obedient, dutiful wife."

Louise Marchant endeavoured no response.

"You had so much to drink last night, Pip. That Henry Baxter, he was gasping to get you alone, so much testosterone." Elmira applied a little make up. The others obsequiously nodded.

"You have that rebuking tone on your voice, Elmira. You sound like dear mater lady."

"Yes, I know. You are the star of that lovely magazine. Your photo seems to be in it every other week. You are the toast of the ball and party circuit."

"Sorry, ladies," Philippa suddenly piped up, "I need to get back home. Now. I feel ghastly."

The young debutante drove swiftly back to Wye Hall. She dashed straight upstairs to her private bathroom where she loudly vomited. "Shit," Philippa cursed. Once composed, she took a rapid shower then ambled to her bedchamber. She tuned her Bush transistor to the soon to be defunct Radio Caroline and listened to listen to the new release by The Move called "Flowers in The Rain". The room appeared to vibrate and a whirling mass, like a thick oily fog materialised from the ether.

"Are you Philippa?" A voice came from the inside the formless mass.

"You again! You know damn fine who I am. Quit playing grotty games!" she snapped, "I've never seen you for years and you choose to visit when I feel like and look like crap. Not very cool at all. Are you a ghost? Do you still want to marry me? Either give me some answers or get lost. I'm not in the mood?"

"You are such a strong woman, Philippa." the dark hued amorphous nebulosity seemed to throb like a heartbeat.

Philippa was unmoved. She lit a cigarette as the music on the radio changed to Diana Ross and the Supremes performing "Reflections."

"Are you a ghost? A demon? Why do you not come out from behind that blob of smoke you seem to live in?"

"Supernatural beings exist only in the minds of people. All things must adhere to the laws of the Universe. Even should not all of those edicts have yet been revealed."

"I'm bored. I feel a little fragile from an excess intake of alcohol. Either explain or piss off!"

There was a momentary silence when only the voice of Diana Ross could be heard. The entity from the mist spoke again.

"I shall impart all portentous and perilous complots for which you require elucidation."

EMILY-SEPTEMBER 1967

"Gill." Emily greeted her housemate as she came into the kitchen. "Do have some claret. I bought an Indian takeaway. Chicken Madras curry, poppadoms, nan bread, onion bhaji, rice and potato bhaji. There's plenty for us both."

"Sounds absolutely delightful," the woman she knew as Gill replied, "I shall just go upstairs, have a quick shower and change and be back down. I'm starving."

"Some great cases we've got," Emily commented as Gill returned in a bathrobe drying her hair with a towel.

"Yes. So much work."

"So much income." Emily proffered a mild rebuke.

"Yes, of course. A steady income is essential and thanks to you we have that."

"Not just me. I see you have some meaty cases. One of a young Arab who seems to be involved with a shady piece of London underworld."

"Yes. He fled the Middle East as the place became unstable and looked for work here. He was vulnerable and some members of an East End gang coerced him into doing odd jobs for him. He was a getaway driver in an armed robbery. He was caught"

"Where did that case come from? It doesn't sound like one Mister Cooper would have referred to us?" Emily tucked into a portion of curry and rice.

The BBC 7.30 News on the television with Robert Dougal headlined on the referendum in Gibraltar. The electorate had voted to remain British by an incredible 12,000 for to 44 against. Emily waited for any items relating to Aden. When none arose, she turned back to Gill.

"Sorry. I did not hear where we got this case from."

"I believe it was a postal application following a phone call from a local solicitor. Some friends had approached the solicitors and it ended with us."

Gill poured herself a glass of claret then continued.

"Something that may be of interest to you. He's the brother of Abdullah al Asnag, the leader of the freedom fighters in Aden. Sorry, some refer to them as terrorists. He's called Ali al Asnag."

"What's he doing here?" Emily was intrigued.

"Originally he came as a student. He applied to the London School of Economics. As Aden is still a UK possession, he has a British Colony of Aden passport. So, there was no problem with immigration."

"Only for a month or so. FLOSY is now locked in a power struggle with the NLF and the NLF is winning says the BBC News. In between fighting our troops of course."

"I guess so. I had heard his life was in danger but no proof. Somehow, he got involved with the Thompson gang," Gill replied then helped herself to some food.

"Will you win the case?" Emily bluntly posed.

"I think so. No real evidence from the DPP. I don't even know how they deemed it in the public interest to continue with the prosecution. I'm really pleased to have all this sharp end work. It's stuff men normally always do."

"Well Gill, only in our chambers under our boss. Anywhere else, and I think you know it, it would be men only on the cases. Women doing the filing and phoning."

"It's about time the whole shitty system was changed," Gill grunted, "Do you know that 10 per cent of the people hold 90 percent of the wealth? Men hold almost every position of real authority. That is apart from the Queen."

"I do. And I don't care. Politics is not my scene. I leave it to the politicians. I didn't know you were a communist, Gill?"

"I'm not. I'm a Labour supporter. But I do believe in equal rights. Do you not?"

Emily thought for a while before she responded.

"I believe in equal opportunities. Getting a job because of your abilities and not because you are a man or woman and not because of who you know."

Emily checked to ensure she was not followed. After scanning the street, she carefully entered "The George" pub on Liverpool Street.

The entrance of a beautiful woman by herself had many heads turning. That was until she sat next to the equally as handsome Detective Sergeant Robinson. He already had a gin and tonic waiting for her. "You have things to tell me, Miss Wilkinson. Fire away. I'm all ears."

DANIEL/DAVID/JAMES-SEPTEMBER 1967

Daniel tossed and turned in his bunk. The through current of less sultry atmosphere brought some measure of relief from the burning late summer temperature index although not the disturbing visions lodged firmly in the farthest realms of his unconscious dreamscape. He could see figures calling. Distant yet clear They were imploring him to act, to run, to love and leave. A multitude of ethereal supplications were offered up as he wandered through the topography of some unknown world, a landscape lying deep within the recesses among the innards of his very psyche. The faces seemed proverbial although not immediately identifiable. At least in his conscious being and Daniel in turn called out to one such visage somewhere far away before a chilling feeling drew him from the place in which he had wandered.

"Shit!" He sat up in his bed, stretched a little. The young man lit a "Benson and Hedges" cigarette then went outside the accommodation. There he found the stoic and patient Tony Helm stood to attention.

"Sergeant. You worry me," Daniel petulantly groaned, "You always seem to be near when I have a gonk and wake up."

In the light and his barely awake vision, Helm looked somewhat different. He seemed smaller. The receding hairline was higher than usual, and a sickly grin was etched on the pallid countenance. It was the diametric converse of his normally tanned and healthy outlook. In a split second he returned to his poised normal self. Daniel deemed the illusion to be a product of the intense light and lack of sleep.

"Part of my job, sir. It's just coincidence. I was passing but my job's t' keep an eye on the men as well as the young officer that leads us. That's you, sir. Don't worry, Oy'm not stalking ye. But ye young officers 'ave a lot on yer minds right now. My job is t' help ya, sir."

Daniel remained unconvinced. As he looked up, a strange mental black cloud circumnavigated his brain. It was followed by a seeming swirling bright incandescence that caused unsettlement. He was left in a nigh state of panic until the calming vision of a gentle expression briefly followed the hallucination.

"Has there been any shooting since we got back, Sergeant?"

"No sir. But all patrols is on even 'igher alert as FLOSY and the NLF 'ave a short ceasefire. They reckon it's so's they can attacks our boys, sir."

"Who's gone out today?"

"From our company, sir, only two troops at the moment. Four and Five. Mister Moir and Mister Marchant, sir. Their mission's to probe the outer borders where the roads from the Causeway, Al Mansura and Al Ittihad meet up. Intel says the' Arabs is about to start another shindig like they did in June near there, sir. We 'ave those two troops and the army also 'as a few platoons workin' on it, sir. We needs to find out if and where the gollies are gonna zap us then blast 'em.

Mister Moir and Mister Marchant 'ave the South Wales Borderers to the east and One Para on their north side. They should be fine, sir."

Daniel looked at the pug nosed, flat faced, 26-year-old. The senior NCO was well built with a balding head that was now burnt almost black from the merciless Aden sun.

"Yes. Of course, they will. I must have had a bad dream. I thought something had gone wrong." "We can call on Hawkeye as well, sir. The RAF Hunters at Khormaksar, 84 Squadron with their FGA9 aircraft. They're dyin' to 'ave a crack at the gollies before we leaves this place, sir."

The force of Royal Marines arrived with some speed at Observation Post Bravo. This concrete structure was on the dividing line at the end of the Causeway between Aden, Al Mansura and Little Aden. It was manned by soldiers from the 1st Battalion of the Parachute Regiment.

James walked over to David, marching with a purpose at the head of his troop.

"Well, Davy boy. One of our troops must move over there and probe for the bad guys while the other must remain in reserve. They'll provide firepower and or reinforcements if needed along with the cherry berry Paras."

David sardonically smiled. "Jimmy, you're such a Sassenach arsehole at times. I heard the orders, do ye think I'm deaf? The captain was wrong to let us choose ourselves. Ye English halfwit. I'll go ahead. Ye stay here."

"No. Sorry. You Scottish numbskull. My troop will go. You hold your guys in reserve."

"For fucks sake, Jimmy. The gollies are ready t' do mischief and we're gabbing on! I'll toss a coin! I'll have heads!"

David took an Aden fils coin from his top pocket and threw it into the air. "There ye go Jimmy, it's heads. 4 Troop goes! Ye stay here with ya boys and cover me. Especially with the GPMG."

David then turned to his second in command. "Sergeant Baker. We've drawn the short straw. Our troop is point. We'll draw the gollies out. March in arrowhead until we reach the road. Then you go into all round defence wi' Corporals Wake and Rayson. Corporal McGrath and me are both from Edinburgh. So, we'll move forward with his section and check the buildings nearest the roundabout. Any questions?"

"No, sir!"

"Davy." James looked up at his friend. "You and your guys be careful. The gollies are after a showdown."

"Ye just stay here, Lord James. Have 5 Troop ready to give me some big bangs fire support and reinforcements. If necessary. Have your gunners in position from now!"

"Alright, Second Lieutenant Moir. I await your instructions," James mordantly replied.

DANESH AND KELLY

The lunch having been eaten, Professor Gidron and Professor Hussein escorted Danesh and Kelly back to the PADIT like machine.

"Is it time to travel back to our era?" Danesh looked suspiciously at Gidron.

"No. We still have much to show you." The robed figure smiled at them both.

"This machine can travel through time, dimensions and space. We are setting it merely to fly. Not through time but across the continent. I wish to show you the landscape of that which you term the Upper Palaeolithic period. 50,000 years before your epoch. We will show you where you are compared to your own Earth, it is very different. We have stored warm clothing for us all as we'll land, and you can see the Earth of the Ice Age. Yes, it is temperate, nay warm here. But the ice sheet covers almost all the northern part of the Northern Hemisphere," Hussein enlightened the couple.

"Unlike in your century, once one ventures outside the cities the world is very, very wild," Gidron stated, "I am carrying a laser gun and a rifle. The potential predators are not all on four legs. The Neanderthal man is still in northern Europe. They will eventually disappear. That I discovered on my time travels. It will not be by death but simply their assimilation into Homo sapiens. That occurrence will be relatively soon, within a few thousand years. They live in caves and basic villages and do not take kindly to strangers. That includes those who can understand their primitive language. However, I know one settlement we can view as I have a rapport with the leader. Nevertheless, outside the city is never truly safe."

"We shall give you due warning. But of course, inside PADIT there is no danger at all. That is unless the power cells die on us and they have enough energy for a hundred years." Hussein smiled as the transporter door slid back. The small black tinted viewing slits were expanded and clarified into large observation windows.

"Come. This is a picnic in the Ice Age. Take a window seat." Gidron showed them into the craft then sat in the pilot's chair.

The doors closed. He flicked several levers and switches, spoke into what Danesh assumed to be a microphone. In an instant their PADIT shot into the air giving Kelly a brilliant view of the predominantly stone built city. The machine turned, and with the early morning sun on their starboard side, burst into supersonic speed.

"This will become what you call the Black Sea." Gidron pointed to a massive body of water below. He banked to port before descending to 300 metres above sea level.

Kelly was gripped by the viridescent surface beneath. She also took in the features of the internal facets of PADIT. This version had two comfortable seats in the cone shaped cockpit area, covered in what appeared to be soft leather. The cylindrical rear of the accommodation area boasted four luxury chairs in two rows facing each other. There were small tables set in between the comfortable, benches and arm rests. The décor was in pale green and the extensive light walnut cabinets with glass doors were stocked with foods and wines of such lofty eminence. As the journey progressed both Kelly and Danesh became aware of the paucity, in fact nigh zero, external noise level that allowed them all to converse with ease.

"The island of Cyprus is below." Hussein pointed towards the taupe area underneath the craft. "But as you can see, it is merely the much higher area of land. The small sea down there will become part of the Mediterranean. After many thousands of years."

"It is nearly all terra firma." Danesh was aghast with wonder. "The Med I mean. This will all become water?"

"Yes." Gidron nodded. "The islands of Cyprus, Malta, Sicily, Corsica and Sardinia, as you call them, are coming up soon. We have no name for these although the locals do. They exist not except as uplands and hill ranges. You can see to the west there is another massive salt water lake which will also form part of the Mediterranean."

"It's amazing," Kelly was awestruck.

"Below we call Ibatara, you call it Hispana." Danelaw learnedly pointed. "Presently we shall be in Gaul. You label the land, Franc."

The machine flew above a white blanket that seemed to go north forever.

"That is the southern border of the ice sheet," Hussein imparted, "We shall move west. The land of Britannia is completely covered by the ice and of course there is no North Sea. Even centuries after the end of the Ice Age there is land where the North Sea and English Channel will eventually be formed."

"What's down there?" Kelly was buzzing with excitement.

"The land of the Neanderthal man," Hussein responded, "We shall land soon well away from their denser populations. This area will become Gaul many thousands of years in the future." The PADIT hovered over a densely forested, mountainous area.

"Look." Danelaw handed Kelly a pair of electronic binoculars.

"What at?" "Over there. Beneath the trees on that proximate slope." Hussein pointed.

"Mammoth!" Kelly exclaimed, "Are they really mammoth?"

"They are. Mammuthus primigenius. Now look towards the valley, next to those ancient oaks."

"It's huge. What is it?" Kelly gasped at another giant creature.

"A megatherium, "Danesh replied for his colleague, "For those who are not palaeontologists, it is known as the giant sloth."

"Jeepers. It's like being in that Speilberger dinosaur movie except we are really there instead of seeing cloned versions of them," Danesh enthusiastically commented.

They raced southerly over vast plains before more immense, evergreen forests came across their vista.

"Sabre tooth cats! Woolly rhinoceros!" Kelly scanned the ground far underneath with her ultra-powerful binoculars. A huge feline growled, and another massive furry herbivore snorted as if rebuking the craft for having the audacity to disturb its lunch.

"Not far from here is a herd of the largest land mammal ever to walk the Earth." Danelaw turned PADIT and accelerated. Within minutes they came upon a large forest glade.

In this primeval, deciduous woodland a herd of truly gargantuan animals grazed quietly. They seemed to disregard the flying machine just above their heads.

"Baluchitherium. A massive hornless rhino which is four times the weight of the African elephants in your epoch. This is northern Gaul, Franc, or will be. They have roamed the planet since the days of the dinosaur and will continue to until man makes them extinct in 35,000 years," Hussein sombrely narrated, "You can see species of deer. The giant version of the armadillo you have in your era called the Glyptodon. The cave lion which is 25 percent larger than African lions. And cave bear. There are close relatives of the elephant that your scientists refer to as the Mastodon. This epoch, known to you as the Pleistocene, spans from 2,500,000 years back in time to 35,000 years in the future. Our future of course. Not yours."

"Can we find somewhere to stop and have lunch?" Danesh suggested. "I would like at least to walk on the ground. Even if it is but a few metres from the PADIT. And also, Professors, I want to know why you brought us here."

"I shall touch down near a Neanderthal settlement. I know the head man. It is safe from big predators, although I shall carry my weapons. There we can eat, admire the countryside and talk. We'll need to don warm clothing though," Gidron advised.

PHILIPPA-SEPTEMBER 1967

The nebulous, enigmatic and conversing haze remained before Philippa.

"Do you have the capacity to come from behind that rather obnoxious, repugnant mist? It is both unsettling and annoying. I am still fragile from overindulgence in the juice of Bacchus and want to sleep. You have a choice. Either come out into my space or leave it!"

The static cloud swiftly dissipated revealing the blue metallic tone of a machine, which spanned from one end of her substantive bedroom to the other. The strange craft was rounded at the rear. The front, or at least Philippa assumed it was the fore, was pointed with black small window like slits. One thing that the young woman immediately noticed was that the strange vehicle was not on her bedroom carpet but hovering a few inches above the expensive shag pile.

She put the record "Itchycoo Park" by the Small Faces on her Dansette record player.

A large opening, a doorway, instantly appeared like a dark chasm on the starboard side of the craft. A man appeared. He was tall, slim and in clothing that although not current fashion could easily have been sometime in the recent past. She was at a loss however to be able to pinpoint as to when. Or where. The gear consisted of a pair of chinos, brown patterned shoes, a tartan flannel shirt, green tie and a tweed jacket with leather patches both on the elbows and the end of the sleeves. It was certainly not the garb she would have expected from an alien that had sporadically visited her since she was five years old. Philippa estimated the person to be good looking, in his mid-50s with long greying hair and beard and seemingly in good physical condition for someone of those years.

She opened a bottle of Coca Cola and poured some into a glass.

"Hi." She held out her hand. "I'm Philippa. What shall I call you?"

"Please, just refer to me as Professor. I see you have developed into a beautiful woman."

"You look vaguely familiar. You told me when I was five that we would be married. I think you are sharp, good looking I mean, like a Paul Newman or Gene Hackman. Perhaps a tad older than them. Nonetheless, Professor, you are far too old for me to marry. Why did you say you would?"

Philippa poured out a glass of whiskey and handed it to her unusual guest then lit a cigarette. "You'll stop those in a few years' time," he haughtily imparted.

"Don't bore me or lay it on me, brother. I got loaded last night and still feel like shit. Enlighten me. Why did you say we would get married when we are most certainly will not?"

"Yes, I know. I thought I was travelling through time until through my experience and research, yes, good old-fashioned nose to the grindstone stuff, put me straight. I discovered that our worlds are about 40 years apart.

We all have doppelgangers in all PUs. These people are virtually identical people to us living in all of them. The person you met was me but I came from the future of my world to this day of yours, upon which I saw you. You were grown up, so I travelled back in time to when you were young. Not just to see you but also to get data. I just wanted something to say something, so I said we'd get married. Sorry."

"Oh, my whole life has been one of waiting to see you and marry you."

"Please. I have not conveyed my story adequately. You will marry my doppelganger in this world. I thought when you were five it would be me for some obscure reason. I shall give you a photograph."

The professor handed a plastic looking thin grey box.

"In there is a photograph of me taken when I was 20. In a year's time, precisely to the second, it will unlock. Do not try to open it before then. The picture of the man you will eventually marry shall be revealed. He is a younger version of me."

"It's very confusing and a tad spooky." Philippa took the container as the record changed to the psychedelic "We Love You" by the Rolling Stones.

"Yes, I know. Do you want to be acquainted with all the salient points and more? As well as a greater insight into me and my world. Or would you rather we left it as it is?"

"You remind me of that man in the programme, Doctor Who, on the TV. He's played by Patrick Troughton. It's all about flying through space, time and dimensions."

"Yes, that TV series will still be popular 40 years from now."

"Professor, how did you know you were in a parallel universe?"

"You look as if you need to rest."

"I do. Can you set your machine to return here at 9.30 tomorrow night?"

Philippa was anxious reach the conclusion of the revelations during a return visit of the mysterious professor.

"Certainly." "Good, then I shall expect you at that hour. I shall arrange snacks and drinks and will want to know everything you are able to divulge."

"Philippa, as your Doctor Who would know, for someone who travels through time there is never an excuse to be unpunctual."

"Then I shall see you, here, tomorrow at 9.30 pm."

The Professor kissed the back of her right hand and sauntered back into his hovering machine. Within seconds both he and the enigmatic craft had seemingly evaporated into the ether.

Philippa leisurely bathed, changed into her nightclothes then went to her bed where she slept. Very soundly. As she slumbered she was transported to another place in which a malevolent apparition approached. The phantasmagorical being was not drifting in via some celestial mechanics rather in a cascade of chilling, golden beams. It was as the portentous and execrative presence was reaching Philippa that she abruptly awoke.

EMILY-SEPTEMBER 1967

"What have you got for me?" John Robinson enquired as Emily sipped her gin and tonic.

"The Soviet Economics Attaché in their London embassy is to meet up with an Aden national. Aden is still a British colony at the moment of course. The Aden national is the brother of the leader of the Front for The Liberation of Occupied South Yemen. Known more widely as FLOSY."

"When and who else will be involved?" Robinson straightened up.

"I was getting to that, Sergeant." Emily cast a rebuking glance. "Al Asnag, the trade union man from Aden, is to meet with members of the British Communist Party. This gathering will include Colin Todd, militant trades union officials, the left-wing students' union and trusted student activists. They want to create an umbrella action group to coordinate dissent, grooming and nurturing it until social unrest follows. From that embryonic stance, they wish to progress onto a full-blown revolution. From what I can deduce, they are already well on course."

"The sort of stuff we have had wind of for years. What's new about this?"

"The two bent coppers I embarrassed at the trial of Artie Cooper are in it up to their necks. They are the middlemen with the criminal underworld who think they are playing along with the lefties to exploit them for egocentric gains. Conversely, the left wingers think something similar about the criminals. Nonetheless, they are in an unholy alliance. The Soviets will lavish them with funds and tutor them in insurgency and civil dissent. I believe these tactics are in play or at least on the cusp of moving. The British leave Aden before Christmas. Once that happens the Soviets will flood into that country and then the green light will be on to use their operatives in Aden and the UK. Sergeant, this is massive. If the numbers quoted are anywhere within the same ball park of accuracy, then we may soon have a revolution. It could transpire within hours. Much, much faster than the armed forces and police can be effectively mobilised. The nearest firm date I can glean for commencement of civil disobedience is the spring of next year."

"Miss Wilkinson. What can we do?"

"I can't be your eyes and ears. It would be just too obvious. A bona fide agent would be more flexible than I can be. All these disparate groups are meeting at a Labour Party building in Croydon, Surrey, on October 26th and then again on the 15th of January next year. The heads of all the strands of this ambitious operation and their criminal allies will be under one roof. I must add that the Labour Party is not involved. They hire rooms out to many organisations at this building. It's on Park Hill Road."

"Do you have all the names of people who will be present?"

"I have all those to date, Sergeant. I'm not going to tell you how to do your job. But I suggest you tentatively approach Artie Cooper and see if he knows anything about this."

"I may do that. And thanks for this. There will be money in your special account. Soon."

"Thanks Detective Sergeant. I have written all details down in the code we agreed. See you later." Emily put on her sunglasses as she left the pub and made her way to Liverpool Street Tube station.

Within half an hour she was back at her office. Whilst snooping around Emily noticed a long list of new cases and walked passed Fiona at her reception desk. She cast a polite smile and "Hello", before pacing into the work area to where Karen Finch was busily attacking a mound of paperwork. "Karen, what on earth is all this?

"Miss Wilkinson." The small 35-year-old brunette looked up from behind her thick 1950s style spectacles. "I adore you for doing that Cosmopolitan interview. It's bringing in so much extra work that we'll have to recruit more staff. That I love. But there's so much to get through.

Mister Crawley tells me I can claim overtime. With the extra dough I can buy a new outfit next pay day."

"Karen, that's great. But use our young trainees. They must be able to assist with rudimentary stuff. We only have them for a week or so and like all good potential female employees they can at least type."

"They are good, Miss Wilkinson. Fiona has been a big help also. However, it is mainly detailed stuff. Anyway, I forgot. Mister Crawley wants to see his high flying blue-eyed girl as soon as she appears."

Emily was slightly taken aback for a split second before Karen adjusted her glasses and punched a button on the intercom. Momentarily she appeared to assume a different countenance.

"Miss Wilkinson is here, Mister Crawley."

"Thanks, Karen." The voice from the box crackled. "Send her straight through."

She walked into to find Gerald Crawley in a chipper mood. He wore no jacket but donned a waistcoat and white shirt, black tie and matching trousers. Emily esteemed him to be the archetype of a head of legal chambers.

"You're going to work in New York for two weeks." There was a slight hint of prevarication.

"Sir. Do I have a say?"

"No, well yes. I was so sure you would accept I accepted on your behalf."

"And this project is--?" Emily squirmed.

Gerald looked long and hard at her. "Can you sing?"

"Yes. Is that the position? A singer in New York."

"No. Of course not. Not yet anyway. You are such a virtuoso it would not have surprised me, but I am in the real world and I know I will lose your services. Very soon I fear."

"Why do you say that, sir? I am extremely happy working here."

"Emily, you are extremely ambitious, talented, beautiful, articulate and intelligent. That scares your average male of the 60s. In "In Crowd" of London pop stars, one from The Who, artists, footballers, that long-haired guy from Belfast in Northern Ireland is one, all want to date you. Of course, you refuse. I have had dozens of enquiries bribing me to let you go. You're a QC and will certainly follow Rose Heilbron to become a female High Court judge. Now, to add to your numerous radio and TV interviews, Cosmopolitan want you to view and write about the New York scene. They want you appearing once again in the magazine only this time you will do it in the Big Apple. It will be for two weeks only. Although I suspect they are seeking your services full time." "Then why did you accept?"

"6000 dollars are why. And that is only what they are paying the chambers in compensation. It's enough to pay for three lawyers, not QCs of course, but three LLBs for a year. That does not even include what you'll be paid. A stipend plus first class airfare and five-star hotels. Besides, I would not stand in your way."

Emily was disoriented, dwelling in a rare state of reticence.

"Two weeks in the Big Apple sounds exciting. I shall contact Dean. But I have no plans at all to move on," she quietly imparted

"That's good. So how are Miss Cooper and my daughter faring in their work experience?"

"They are bright, intelligent young women and will both make good lawyers. Now, if you'll excuse me, I have to contact Dean."

DAVID, JAMES, -SEPTEMBER 1967

The blond figure of Second Lieutenant David Alexander Moir marched at the head of his troop with a sanguine and grim determination. The Royal Marines were advancing in arrowhead formation towards the Al Mansura district from where the causeway met the highway to Little Aden. The day seemed to be both auspicious and portentous. A peccable sensation swirled about.

David moved with acute wariness. His radio operator from Liverpool, Ray Rooney, emulated his caution as he paced but a few feet to the rear. The strapping 17-year-old bore the bulky A41 Larkspur Series radio and harness on his back. The signaller walked fastidiously near his subaltern with ear phones on his head and a microphone grasped in one hand and a loaded nine-millimetre Stirling sub machine gun in the other. The dust, flies and badly uneven, grimy surface bothered David much less than the battered row of vermeil mud brick and wood building buildings that lay ahead.

According to military intelligence, these constructs may well be the location and cover for a determined force of NLF and possibly FLOSY fighters. The insurgents were apparently itching for a grand finale showdown as a fitting culmination to 131 years of British imperial rule.

James and his men took firing positions some 100 metres from the two-story structures towards which David was leading his troop. One of several edifices capable of affording good cover to many hostile gunmen should they be hidden within.

David held up his hand. This signal brought the column to a halt upon before a shallow drainage ditch adjacent to the intersection. He called over Sergeant Baker.

"Sir." The senior NCO stepped forward. His green beret just managing to remain on his pate of thick black hair after a sand imbued gust of wind blew from the Gulf of Aden immediately to the south. "Sergeant. You stay here behind this conduit with Corporal Wake and Corporal Rayson's sections. Set up the gun groups and riflemen to bring down immediate rapid fire. Have the radio operators keep in comms with Mister Marchant."

"Yes, sir."

"I'll move forward with Corporal McGrath and his guys. I hope you see the gollies before they get a chance to open up. The fire control orders are "watch and shoot". Accordingly, if you see any rebels open fire at once. Don't wait for my order to fire. Let 'em have it wi' both barrels and radio Mister Marchant to give fire support too. Questions?"

"No, sir," Baker resolutely inhaled.

"Good. Corporal McGrath, let's go!"

David cautiously advanced with McGrath immediately to his rear, binoculars in one hand, self-loading rifle in the other.

A well camouflaged NLF sniper was crouched on a roof. Watching. He was alongside many others as he patiently aimed his AK-47 and fired. David felt a stinging ball of fire in his shoulder. The pain rapidly evolved into agony as he dropped his rifle and binos. The Scot tumbled surreally into the ochre hued dust.

"Mister Moir!" Corporal McGrath screamed and ran towards his officer. A sniper's bullet sliced open the NCO's head in a cloud of blood red mist and grey fluid. The lethal impact being clearly visible from where Sergeant Baker and the other Royals were positioned. At once the skyline seemed to explode with ordnance. Multiple bursts and projectiles were landing at twice the speed of sound, turning the dust and sand into a macabre and pinging staccato. McGrath's section hit the ground and took what scant cover they could find.

"Fire!" Baker screamed bringing his two sections to life with the double taps of the GPMG machine guns and crack and thump of the SLR rifles.

James surveyed the outline for a second. In his adrenaline replete mode, he saw numerous heads of insurgents appear from behind the rooftops. He aimed his weapon and yelled, "Open fire!"

DANESH AND KELLY

"The air is so fresh. It is making me light headed," Danesh commented as they alighted from the craft.

"There is a much greater percentage of oxygen in the atmosphere." Danelaw walked across the dense wiry grass towards a pine forest. They were on the slopes of a range of hills about 200 kilometres to the south of the commencement of the ice sheet in a land which would eventually be named Gaul. And much later, Franc. A wide valley sloped away to the north. There was a powerful, chilling breeze dancing from the cold regions. Kelly was dressed in a borrowed thick fox fur coat. She ran energetically to catch up with the others.

Hussein carried a large basket whilst Professor Danelaw lugged a box in which several clay bottles of ancient white wines were sealed.

"Sorry I nearly got left behind," Kelly panted, "I was looking at the marvellous flora and a herd of mastodon moving across the valley."

At that juncture a figure headed towards the small group. He was small, short limbed and very hirsute. Boasting a large head and chiselled face, broad chin and nose, the man was wrapped in a deerskin cloak. He carried in his right hand a stone pointed spear. The head was tied to the primitive wooden shaft by cord cut from animal hide. Seconds later several more of these diminutives, by their standards, converged on Danesh, Kelly, Danelaw and Hussein. Danelaw raised his right arm. The lead

Neanderthal stopped and lifted the same mitt with an unintelligible grunt. The two figures conversed in a tongue that Danesh deemed to be similar to that of his sons when they were in their early teenage years.

Danelaw turned to the others and smiled. "This is Grathyst. He is the chief of this arm of the tribe of these mountains, the Manitranta. They deem me to be a god. However, I did not make the mistake, as in that movie you had in your time "The Man Who Would Be King" and have them think gods do not bleed. I told Grathyst that we are gods but have borrowed our bodies so we can bleed. He will escort us to his camp. Nearby, we shall eat. Not his fare of course. A dish of cold fat, bones and berries is not to my palate. After that we shall view the varied herds of fauna that inhabit the huge valley. then see the herds in the valley."

"Why not tell him the truth?" Kelly seemed marginally irked.

"Doctor Aresti." Danelaw shook his head condescendingly. "It is dangerous enough to tell my own people what we do, what we can do. These are truly delightful folk, void of the scheming and plotting, fanaticism and ambition that will envelope our world, this world, in 1,000 years. I do not want to interfere with their lifestyle or habits be they religious or otherwise. It would be dangerous for us, but far more perilous for them."

Danelaw tugged his beard and looked up at Grathyst. He continued with his narrative. "If they knew the people to their south, what they are capable of. The fate these ostensibly civilised people intend for his race, they would move south and attack. Naturally they would be annihilated. As things stand, as long as the status quo remains intact, they still have 15,000 years. That is much more than many races in your time have left."

No more words were uttered as the Neanderthal chieftain led the group over a hill, down a goat track and into a simple village in a forest clearing, which stood at the foot of a sandstone cliff where several caves were honeycombed onto the face.

Grathyst edged Danelaw over to a simple animal hide shelter. To the immediate exterior, a female was slicing chunks of meat from the carcass of a wild goat. Danesh thought back to his college days studying Ice Age palaeontology and deemed the unfortunate animal to be the Caucasian Tur. The woman was pale skinned, thick set, round faced and large jawed. She had thick straggly hair and a wide nose being dressed in a pungent skin robe. Grathyst grunted at the female whereupon she stood up to her full height, rather less than the chieftain's 1.62 metres.

"Professor," Danesh called over. He was feeling slightly chilled even in his borrowed fur coat. "What does the head honcho want?"

Danelaw looked up, his thick beard flowing in the wintry north wind.

"He wants to exchange." The man from 50 millennia past smiled at Danesh then winked at Kelly.

"What does he want to trade?" Danesh was a tad discomforted.

"He wants Doctor Aresti. In exchange for his woman he calls Fodle. It translates in English to

"body like a stream"." Professor Gidron almost laughed.

"Tell him he can fuck off!" Kelly was in no mood for ladylike pleasantries.

"It's alright, Doctor. I told him you were betrothed to the chief of our tribe and it was a union sanctioned by the gods. That was good enough for him."

"How do they trust you?" Kelly enquired as the group followed Grathyst. He was moving down the valley to where a herd of the elephant like mastodon were grazing. They were ignoring the sabre tooth cat. This giant feline seemed wary of the group of humans encroaching on its territory.

"I stole an idea from Sir Henry Haggard. I read a book from near your time, "The Great Mines of King Solomon". The hero, Alan Quartermain, knew when an eclipse of the moon would happen as he used an Askham almanac. Accordingly, Quartermain fooled the African tribe into believing he had caused the eclipse himself. Once I had a grasp of the very basic Neanderthal language, I told Grathyst that I was more powerful than the moon goddess, Hechla. When I knew the lunar eclipse was imminent I merely proclaimed that I would temporarily banish Hechla. When the actual eclipse occurred, he fell totally under my dominion."

They moved further into the valley. Below some trees, adjacent to a babbling stream, they unrolled thick blankets on the rough grass and sat on them. Once they were in some modicum of comfort, lunch was unpacked. Deer ran across the archaic landscape, some chased by big cats. A mile or so away, through the binoculars, huge bears could be seen next to a winding river. Grathyst grunted a semi smile and returned to his settlement; a mere

400 metres further up the slopes. At that moment Danelaw and Hussein produced ornate wooden plates upon which were placed servings of rich, grainy bread, cheese, boiled eggs, a gritty humus and massive olives.

These dishes were handed to Danesh and Kelly followed by carved opulent goblets of a sweet white wine.

"A toast." Professor Gideon proposed. "To our endeavours."

"To our endeavours!" The others repeated.

"Then." Danesh added. "Perhaps Professor Gidron will reveal the reason why we have been swept back in time to join them for a delicious lunch in the most beautiful venue one could ever imagine."

"We must keep an eye on the hourglass, but all shall be revealed. I give my word."

PHILIPPA-SEPTEMBER 1967

"Time Seller", the current top 30 hit for the Spencer Davis Group played across the hall. Philippa, Kinsey, Elmira and Caroline sat around a coffee table in the lounge as the ball went on nearby. They attacked their bottles of Dom Perignon, smoked and giggled.

"What would you think?" Philippa almost spilt champagne down her silver Paco Rabanne miniskirt. "If I told you I had a visit from a man who knows me. In fact, sleeps with me. Another me. A doppelganger. But in a parallel universe?"

"I'd say you had been partaking in a Lucy in the sky with diamonds type trip." Elmira, in her dark red Mary Quant mini giggled. "Have you been inviting strangers to your boudoir on Les Liaisons Dangereuses?"

"Are you imagining things?" Caroline enquired, rather more sombrely than Elmira. She looked stunning yet uneasy garbed in a blue Quant creation. "I imagine David is with me. However, the last time I had such thoughts, a frightening shiver moved across my soul."

A quartet of young men staggered to where the girls were chatting. They all had obviously well imbibed with bow ties undone.

"Hi ladies, some s--exy, groovy men t--o embolden your night with vibrations from be--yond the pale," the figure of Nigel Doncaster managed to slur out.

"Go away or I'll have you thrown out!" Elmira shrieked.

"Good God," Doncaster responded, his three friends mute with alcohol or nerves or both, "I knew th---at Pip was out o---f bounds, Julian told us, and he's a bad a—ss.

But I thought you---u would be a blast, maybes cop a feel. Julian would thump us b---ut Elmira, Ki—nsey and Carol---ine should be easy, out for a blast."

Elmira threw a glass of water over Doncaster, champagne would not be wasted in such a way. He took the hint and all four moved on.

"Such skanky anal sphincters," Elmira grunted after the retreating and dejected young men. She then lit a Benson and Hedges from her silver cigarette case.

"I want to hear more of this ethereal visitor." Kinsey re-entered the chatting then sipped her glass of bubbly.

"We all do." Elmira scowled at her friend. "Come on, Philippa. Let's have the entire dream sequence."

"He came two days ago. His time travelling craft landed in my bedroom and he was enveloped in a thick mist."

"Wow," Caroline exclaimed, ignoring the squirm from Elmira, "Was he dishy?"

"As dishy as a middle aged to old man can be. Like an older version of Dustin Hoffman or Warren Beatty," Philippa nonchalantly replied then also lit a cigarette, "He was very groovy. Not plastic like most old people. He had a familiar face. Can't place it though. But he did say that in his universe he and I get married."

"That sounds great, Pip. Were you dreaming.?" Elmira sounded unconvinced.

"Hey. Who knows? What is reality? Why do I exist? Why do I feel like this? No reason, no reason at all. But I was dreaming, I think, when a bad ass spectre wanted to hurt me. He really was spooky. Like a demon from the astral plane or the like."

"Did your spectral visitor return? The nice one." Kinsey displayed veritable interest.

"He did. Yesterday he returned and was bang on time. We shared food and wine and he spoke for ages. He was telling me all about the mathematical concept of parallel universes. And a crap load of very heavy, not very cool, chin wagging which left me brain dead. I'll never make a scientist. The stranger told me I needed to follow my heart and be a doctor. He also said, and this was more than a little scary, that some ogre of the Cosmos is a danger to me. This thing could pursue me and my doppelgangers across the entire Cosmos. It sounded pretty down beat and a real drag. However, I shall put my entire mind into my medical studies."

"Pip, you start university in two weeks. I'll bet my substantial inheritance, baby, that as soon as Julian, your intended, comes back from down under, you'll drop out of studies before Christmas."

"Elmira. That will not happen. And as I said, my spirit cum spaceman cum time traveller or whatever told me to keep up my studies."

"He's a spectre, product of acid or whatever, Julian is real." Kinsey smiled. "I'm sure Elmira is spot on, I'm more than convinced Julian will have you out of university. Possibly before Halloween. I think you should keep off the Lucy in the sky."

"I'm not tripping. I'm sure this figure, the man from the mist, this man is real. Very real."

The Rolling Stones record of "Dandelion" began to play.

"I believe you," Caroline sensitively spoke, "I felt such a presence in my room."

"The pair of you need to make an appointment with a shrink," Elmira opined as John Lloyd, her tall, elderly butler came towards the table.

"Yes, Lloyd," she curtly snapped.

"Begging your pardon, My Lady. But there was a telephone call for Lady Caroline. The countess requests Lady Caroline returns home. She said immediately, My Lady."

EMILY-SEPTEMBER 1967

The Boeing 707 landed smoothly at John F Kennedy airport in the Queens borough of New York. Until recent times it had been known as Idlewild. The British Overseas Aircraft Corporation first class flight had been excellent. Emily had fixatedly viewed the forest of skyscrapers on Manhattan as the enthralling descent neared its conclusion. She was now listening to the sound system for announcements while airport staff conveyed the portable staircase up to the airliner.

All she knew about her two weeks in New York City was that she would meet a very feisty brunette, aged 45. Emily had been told that the woman held radical views on the role of women and ran Cosmopolitan magazine. She was married to David Brown whom Emily understood to be a producer in the movie industry.

She briefly checked her bag, once again, for her black United Kingdom of Great Britain and Northern Ireland passport and BOAC plane ticket. The young lawyer looked stunning in her blue Mary Quant mini skirt, calf length leather boots, white tights, primrose blouse and short black leather jacket and cap.

She descended the passenger steps and boarded the waiting shuttle bus.

Once her passport had been stamped, she cleared immigration. After her luggage had appeared on the reclaim carousel she briskly walked through the United States of America Customs hall.

This transit was comfortable and without incident following which she stepped enthusiastically into the arrivals area. There the sound of the familiar intonation of Dean echoed across the expansive structure.

"Emily! Here!" He enthusiastically called out.

The assertive, dark haired, fashionably attired young American kissed her on the cheek, grabbed her luggage trolley and excitedly exclaimed, "So cool to have you this side of the Pond. We weren't sure if you'd accept. Helen is dying to chat, wants to check out your vibes. She wants to take you to dinner. Tonight."

Dean pushed the cart in the direction of the JFK parking lot. "I'm gonna drive you to Park Avenue in Manhattan to the Waldorf Astoria. Nothing but the best. You can have a quick shower and change. Then I'll collect you at about three and take you to the magazine offices on West 57th Street near Central Park. You're gonna love being here and working with us. We'll all have a ball."

Emily was still a little disoriented. "Where to Dean? It's only 11 in the morning here but my body tells me it's four in the afternoon. I need to adapt."

The room was sumptuous beyond her wildest dreams. The Waldorf Astoria was lavish and luxurious even for a successful, wealthy barrister with her own home in the stockbroker belt of Hertfordshire. The of the expansive double room boasted an incredible selection of the finest beers, wines and spirits. Emily chose a mini bottles of best Moet and Chandon.

She undressed and ran a bath of hot bubbly water. After tying up her long blonde hair, the young lawyer poured a glass of the bubbly and eased her way into the hot steaming whiteness. The radio was playing the Beatles song "All You Need Is Love" as she was enveloped in the mist.

The young woman had barely slid into the welcoming heat when the telephone rang.

"Shit," Emily muttered. She grabbed a towel and strutted through to the bedroom and picked up the hand piece. "Emily Wilkinson speaking," she calmly replied, wishing not to sound officious.

"Emily." The voice at the other end was authoritative without the propensity of being overbearing. "Yes."

"This is Helen, Helen Gurley Brown. I have a busy schedule for you this fortnight. Not too busy to have a blast at night. But if you can, I'd like to see you at the office in, let's say, about an hour."

"Fine, I know Dean is coming at three to collect me."

"That's fine. He'll be over to bring you here in an hour. I look forward to meeting you. Bye."

"Bye." Within minutes she was dressed in an Yves Saint Laurent Africa bush style dress, with a safari mode hat and matching bag with brown calf length boots. She had checked and was aware that these items were the height of fashion for September 1967.

Precisely on time, Dean had collected her from the Waldorf. He drove into the parking area beneath the Hearst Tower at 300 West 57th. The headquarters of many publications notably Cosmopolitan.

"This is mind blowing!" Emily was fully energised. "So much. So much of everything. I need to come back from my non-acid trip. It's so groovy."

"This is just the start." Dean escorted her to the lift where they went up several floors. "Helen is determined to have you on the payroll. But this is the USA. Very few women are captains of industry and there'll be a lot of folk who'll not see eye to eye with you. However, Helen sees you as a bulwark in her cause."

"Dean, I'm only here for two weeks. And that is mainly due to the substantial bribe Helen gave my employer."

"Right on. Maybe this time. But I've a hunch that once you've been blitzed and got into the cool Big Apple scene and felt all the good vibrations, you'll want to hang around a while."

They exited the elevator and made their way through a vibrantly active office where everyone seemed to have their head facing their desks in seemingly unbroken activity. The two walked by several suites until they came to the personal assistant, a pretty brunette, feverishly tapping the keys of the latest IBM Model D electric typewriter.

"Betty." Dean looked down. "I have Miss Wilkinson here. Can we go in?"

The young PA looked up at Emily, smiled, and said in a thick Brooklyn nasal intonation,

"Hi, Miss Wilkinson. The beautiful Limey lady lawyer. I'm Betty Lutz. You're as pretty as Dean described. Sure, Dean. Go in. Helen's expecting you both."

Dean knocked. They entered a spacious office, surrounded by bookshelves and photographs of famous, beautiful people. The large stained oak desk protruded well into the office floor space and on a majestic executive armchair a woman was speaking firmly to someone on the phone. "I don't care how, Jimmy. I want that interview on my desk tomorrow!" She slammed down the hand piece. Another man who was slightly built and dark skinned, stood near the obviously self-confident woman. She was brunette. Her hair was in an early 60s backcombed style. The woman was nonetheless attractive. She stood up from behind her desk and walked inquisitively over to Emily while casting attentive glances all over the exquisite frame and visage.

"Miss Wilkinson, I'm Helen, Helen Gurley Brown. And Dean, you're so right. She is even more spectacular in the flesh than on Kodak. May I call you Emily?"

The young barrister knew a little about Helen Marie Gurley Brown. 45 years old, originally from Arkansas, married in 1959 to film producer David Brown and author of the book "Sex and The Single Girl". A staunch advocate of women's rights and now editor in chief of the prestigious magazine "Cosmopolitan".

"As long as I may call you Helen," Emily promptly responded.

"Oh my, she looks so divine. An angel walking the Earth." the effeminate sounding male approached the young lawyer.

The man was slim, mixed race, medium height and in a shirt and sleeveless pullover. He wore trousers with turn ups and 50s style swept back oiled hair and glasses. He enthusiastically eyed over Emily, abounding with admiration he almost sang, "My, oh my. You are such a catch. And my, my you'll be turning the boys' heads, and some of the girls too I'll wager."

"Emily. You sound like my kinda girl. Let me introduce you to my other assistant, Andy Downs. You may need to worry about a lot of guys lusting after your exquisite torso. But not Andy. Although in your country being homosexual has been legal since July, not quite so here. We still must be a tad discreet. Andy will come with us when we go out. Trust me, he'll show you a good time."

"Yes," Dean added, "But Helen we have a way to go, even today. There's an interview with Pete Jennings on ABC News. Later we have to arrange with Ruth Meyer a radio interview on WMCA."

"Dean. That's Andy's area," Helen firmly interjected, "You go and sort out the New York Times interview with Harold Denny. Andy will take care of radio and TV appearances."

"Emily." Helen turned to her guest. "I have a very busy and structured time table for you but mainly I want you to reach out to young women. I want you to talk to them in their own vibrations. On TV, radio, in newspapers and in our magazine. Girls and young women aged from about 17 to mid-20s and above. Your views on professional women. The challenges in an almost total male environment. What does your boyfriend feel about your job? And as you have a boyfriend serving in the British military overseas and facing danger you can empathise with those who have sweethearts, brothers, cousins, and in some cases sons, serving in our very controversial war in Vietnam."

"And I want a chance to sort out your hair and wardrobe." Andy sounded excited. "And show you to the nightlife of the town."

"Sounds like I'll have a lot to do." Emily smiled.

"Yes. And 5000 dollars, tax free, plus first-class travel and hotels I'm sure will ease the hardship some." Helen passed a mild rebuke.

"I love hard work but I'm starving." Emily pointed at her stomach area.

"We have reservations for the Empire Steak House for seven, but we can bring them forward. I'm more than a little hungry too. Andy will sort out the food. You and I shall go to the bar downstairs and get to know each other. Andy will join us for dinner."

"Sounds marvellous," the lawyer keenly responded.

"Then let's go!"

"I'll see you at five at the Empire and Emily." Andy was beaming as he clasped his hands. "I'm so, so excited to work with you. Even for a short haul. And I want to take you shopping before tomorrow night."

JAMES-SEPTEMBER 1967

The mêlée was in hot, deadly progress near a row of buildings proximate to the Causeway.

James estimated the force of NLF and FLOSY fighters shooting at them could easily number more than 200. The Royal Marines under David's command were returning fire as best they could, as were his own men augmented by two Paratroopers on a general-purpose machine gun from Observation Post Bravo.

James' throat became ultra-dry. It was burnt like the harsh terrain around him, as rounds in dense lethal swathes ricocheted, emitting a high pitch whine, from the rocks behind his troop. One sliced open the arm of a rifleman who yelled and fell backwards. He dropped his SLR and rolled onto the harsh, lapidary surface from where his trenchant screaming continued unabated.

"Sir!" yelled James' radio operator, Marine Teddy Roland. An 18-year-old from Carlisle in Cumberland.

"Yes!" James responded while loosing off two rounds. He was aiming only at the billowing smoke and flying dust surrounding the enemy position.

"Mister Moir's operator says they are pinned down. Two Marines are wounded. Sergeant Baker thinks Corporal McGrath's dead and Mister Moir is still alive. Just!" Roland called out.

"Sergeant Diggle! We need more men. We can't possibly win this fire fight without a fucking shed load more rifles!"

The small projectile of a rifle round created a minor tornado as it landed near to the tall figure of Andy Diggle.

"Sir! For fucks sake! Sir!" the NCO bellowed out in a tone of severe vituperation, "Call in fuckin' Hawkeye now! Sir! We're gonna be fuckin' wiped out here!"

James grabbed his rifle and rolled across the rocky floor a few feet to where Roland was taking cover from the incessant fusillades splattering in the area.

"Hand set!" he called to the baby-faced signaller who immediately passed over the telephone like accoutrement.

James grabbed it as a well-aimed shot smashed the left leg of the nearby gunner.

"Number two! Take over!" Diggle yelled at the Marine next to the wounded GPMG specialist.

The second man rolled next to the general-purpose machine gun and commenced firing treble taps of 7.62-millimetre ordnance at the NLF position. Another soldier placed a field dressing on the gunner's wounded limb.

The cacophony of death continued unceasingly along with the screams of wounded. Hostile rounds mercilessly scraped just above James' brain as he spoke into the mouthpiece.

"Hello Hawkeye. This is Sunray Charlie Two. Request an immediate air strike at—wait one." James checked the co-ordinates on his map. "At one, zero, six, two five, niner, I say again, one, zero, six, two, five, niner. Confirm over."

"Roger Sunray Charlie Two. Strike at one, zero, six, two, five, niner. Wilco. Out!" The Royal Air Force operator signed off. The dream of two pilots from Number 43 Squadron at nearby at RAF Khormaksar finally became a reality. On this sole occasion, they were to take an active role in the final stages of the South Arabian campaign.

As the AK 47 and Lee Enfield bolt action rifle fire continued to rain down mercilessly onto the outnumbered X-Ray Company, the distinct sound of two jets taking off from across the colony was clearly perceptible.

It was audible even above the numerous and continuous cracks of assault rifles intermingled with the odd grenade and two-inch mortar explosions.

A shower of blood flew in all directions as a bullet ripped flesh from the shoulder of a rifleman. The Marine let out an initial scream then lay under whatever cover he could improvise before dressing his wound. James fired twice more towards the structures. The buildings smouldered with intense, strident and deadly rifle fire. He spoke again into the mouthpiece of the radio handset. "Hello Charlie. This is Charlie Two!"

"Charlie. Send. Over."

"Charlie Two. Contact. Contact. We have contact at Oscar Papa Bravo. Several down. Sunray Charlie Three down. Have requested Hawkeye to assist. Need Starlight. I say again, need Starlight soonest with several vehicles at Bravo. Soonest. Like now!"

"Charlie. Wilco Charlie Two. Roger and out." The operator at Little Aden responded just as two Hawker Hunter FGA 9 jets banked over the Gulf of Aden then turned towards the Causeway.

The Arabs on the roofs and the windows were too busy pumping AK 47 rounds at the beleaguered British troops to notice the two silver shapes on the skyline, approaching from the Gulf of Aden.

Flight Lieutenant Jeremy Parr was on a mission. He and his fellow jet jockey, Flying Officer Sammy North, both of 43 Squadron Royal Air Force were on a mission.

They had been the pilots on standby duty in the mess of RAF Khormaksar when the scramble bell had gone off. The two young men were given the relevant co-ordinates by radio once strapped into the ejector seat and flying helmets were on and secured.

Their Hawker Hunters, fighter/ ground attack aircraft, had, within moments, been revved into life and were speedily taxiing onto the runway with the incessant roar of the Rolls Royce Avon 203 engines.

"Red Leader One. Hawkeye Two. Clear to go". The control tower gave permission to take off and seconds later, in a thundering acceleration, the brace of jets was airborne.

Parr's father had been a Spitfire pilot with 610 Squadron Fighter Command operating from Biggin Hill in Kent during the Battle of Britain. Parr senior had eleven Luftwaffe kills to his credit plus one he had shared with the squadron CO.

Stephen Grenfell

North's old man had flown on many sorties with 85 Squadron RAF from Croydon aerodrome in Surrey. Unfortunately, and despite his valiant efforts, he had completed his service with no confirmed enemy aircraft destroyed to his name.

Jeremy and Sammy had a grasp of Royal Air Force history and both knew that the junior service had not been involved in air to air combat since the ill-fated intervention in Suez 11 years earlier.

They were also totally conversant with the fact that during all other British operations abroad, air cover had been principally provided by ship borne jets from the strike carriers of the Royal Navy's Fleet Air Arm.

The two pilots had only arrived from the United Kingdom a week before. This solitary action that a beset young Royal Marines' officer had requested whilst under heavy fire, was in all probability the one and only opportunity they would experience in their lives of anything even remotely close to that which could be veritably defined as "combat".

"Red Leader." Sammy pulled on the controls, maintaining air speed at 300 knots. "Best make this count. Our last chance for glory!"

Through the "mush" of the radio and engine firing Jeremy replied, "Roger that. We'll turn now over the ocean, starboard. Down to 500 feet and then run at the target at 300 hundred knots."

"Roger, Red Leader. All bombed and ready to strike!"

The two peninsulae of Aden and Little Aden, the Causeway, Aden port, Steamer Point and the Radfan Mountains beyond were clearly visible as Jeremy flicked up the safety cover of his weapons system control. The vibration of the Hunter and the crackle of his radio conducting every aspect of the environment in which he sat. After checking the oncoming target location against the artificial horizon on his instrument panel, the young pilot clicked his R/T microphone to send. "Sunray Charlie Two. This is Red Leader One. Coming in with Hawkeye Two onto reference one, zero, six, two, five, niner. Advise take cover. Soonest!"

"Roger Red Leader One. Wilco!" The voice of James came through his earphones.

The smoke of the weapons firing from the Arab position next to Oscar Papa Bravo was clearly visible as the Hunters' four aptly named 30-millimetre Aden cannon burst out spraying the row of concrete and brick constructions. This action left rubble and other detritus flying in all directions. The Marines and others below had to dodge a sudden downpour of large empty brass cannon cases cascading down from the firmament.

Jeremy and Sammy then flew past, banked, headed towards the target once more unleashing from beneath each swept back wing eight, three-inch, high explosive rockets. It was well before a single second had elapsed when a massive, dull, yet ear torturing vibration was felt.

The very instant the missiles exploded on their targets a mere 100 metres from where David's Marines were pinned down, the sides of the buildings disintegrated. The structures were instantly transformed into a macabre mass of smoke, dust and gory chunks of human body parts.

Jeremy and Sammy flew the short distant back to the RAF base. The intense battle had ceased in a microsecond.

"Tower. This is Red Leader One. Mission accomplished. Returning to base. Out."

As the two Hawker Hunter pilots flew back to Khormaksar aerodrome where they would soon be in the officers' mess knocking back wallops and wanks, several thousand feet beneath their aircraft, James ordered his troop of Royal Marines to move forward at the double.

DANESH AND KELLY

A chilly airstream began to twist a dismaying path from the direction of the ice sheet.

"Great wine." Danesh drank a wooden goblet of the rich, clear green draft. "It's like Liebfraumilch."

"That Teutonic swill from your era would not grace the same table as this great vintage," Danelaw was defensive, "if we had time, I would show you the entire Earth, and all that walks upon it including the great Walikan vineyards and the wine makers of the Euphrats."

"Giant Irish elk!" Kelly bubbled with excitement as she concentrated on the valley through her binoculars.

"Megaloceros giganteus." Hussein stood up. He identified the fast-moving creatures by their future Latin name. "As you have said, your people will know them as the Irish elk. That is simply due to the best specimen of them being found in a peat bog in Ireland. A country that is at the moment buried well beneath the huge ice sheet is only one place these deer will inhabit. But they shall not survive to see your civilisation rise."

"So many species are now extinct in my time. You enjoy an abundance of the same creatures in this valley alone. How much in the rest of the planet?" Professor Gideon commented poignantly then took more bread, cheese and humus, "How come there was, or is, an advanced civilisation on our planet 50,000 years before us. It's simply not possible."

Another herd of mammoth crossed the enormous expanse of the valley.

"That hypothesis is anchored purely on erroneous speculation. It has no basis in fact. Where do you think you are now? In a dream?"

Danelaw sipped his wine then added, "You have a book in your epoch. The decades you have lived through, Professor, called "Chariot of the Gods". Is that veritable?"

"Erik Von Daniken." Danesh nodded to his nigh double. "I have no idea where I am. Perhaps a version of "Jurassic Parkland" as in the movie. A form of advanced technology. Von Daniken was as outlandish as this experience. As best I can recall all his theories discredited."

"They were indeed bar one proposition he offered," Danelaw replied as Kelly was still taking an odd nibble of food then feverishly breathing in the Wurm Pleistocene period world to which they had apparently and been mysteriously transported.

"Which is?" Danesh oozed cynicism.

"How long do you deem Man to have walked this planet. By Man I mean Cro-Magnon, Neanderthals and any other subdivisions of our species that existed but your epoch has not yet discovered? The subject we touched on briefly."

"1,000,000 years," Danelaw speculated based on readings he had managed while at university.

"There seems to be a group of men in skins, unlike Grathyst and his people, over by that yonder forest," Kelly interjected whilst immersed in the amazing clarity of the views her borrowed electronic binoculars afforded.

"Try 2,500, 000 years." Danelaw smiled. "Your people and any in your future will probably never find most traces of these beings. The vast majority lie beneath the bed of what you now call the Sea of the North. How far back in your history was the oldest recorded civilisation?"

"It's here in Mesopotamia. It could be as much as 9,000 years old," Danesh responded, now intrigued.

"We know beyond uncertainty that such examples from China, India and parts of South America are much, much, older. Nonetheless, it is a lot less than 2,500, 000 years. Von Daniken speculated that within that time frame many civilisations could, and did, rise and fall. There was more than suffice of a chronological frame for this to occur. In that facet, the author was somewhat on the money as you say. Trust me, Professor, when we return to my city, I shall give you artefacts, in new, mint condition as you would say, that you have in museums which could not possibly have been manufactured in the modern era. The tools or stone have gone. You travel into other universes. There no aliens and never have been any. The distances too great. There are no ghosts, no little green men from Mars. But as you well are aware, there are men, and women, who can travel from equally, if not more so, mysterious realms of the Cosmos. I have only brought you back in time."

Danesh almost swayed as he poured more of the white sack wine. "Why did you collect us from our time? I also forgot my iphone to take a pictorial testimony of this ancient history. It's in the car!"

Danelaw smiled and looked at Kelly who was drinking in every second of her ice age experience. He took from his pocket what seemed like just a thin black rock or piece of bakelite.

Danelaw walked over to her, tapped her on the shoulder and handed her the jet hued object. A massive stampede way across the immense river basin seemed to be of bison and horse.

"That is all you need. It is a movie and still camera. Look through the aperture and press on the small switch here, Doctor. This is a zoom as well so take moving pictures now of all you survey. Just speak at the device and it shall do exactly as you command. The camera can even understand your somewhat advanced, erratic and rather complex tongue."

"Thank you, Professor. I shall indulge. May I use it back in my time?" Kelly was excited.

"Of course. Professor Hussein will advise should you need it."

"Why did you collect us from our chronological period?" Danesh persisted.

"You will suffer similarly although in a somewhat disparate manner."

"What?"

"There is a problem that natural philosophers, now called scientists, have and have had throughout history. It is a recurring theme across the entire Cosmos. The dilemma is that those who trust in the supernatural, the clerics, have referred to us as vassals of Mammon. In your time the entity is usually referred to as The Devil. The influence of those who deny our learnings is growing vastly. They are now calling for all our equipment to be destroyed. Some even are petitioning for every natural philosopher to be put to death."

Danelaw stepped around a few paces.

"There is a movement fermenting already in Walika and that is why we did not go there. A law has been submitted to the Ruling Chamber to outlaw us. The court will legalise it today. The more we explain about the Universe with facts and evidence, the more we are endangered by fanatics who have no such data. They refer only to burbled writings from many centuries ago. We hear rumours of the being or person fostering and expounding such notions. He or it is extremely perfidious and evil. Hussein and I will soon be murdered by our people, unless--."

"Why us?"

"We, Professor Hussein and I, we need safe havens in time and other universes. However, these refuges must lie at a juncture in the Cosmos where the data indicates a high level of personal security. And of course, only with like-minded people. You are not merely my doppelganger in time, but the calculations indicate your world and time offers us the optimum level of safety. We would only need sanctuary for a short period. We already have access to several such safe lodgings, but we need more. There will be of course some recompense involved."

"What guise will such material or services take?"

"Knowledge. I shall impart all that I know including many mathematical formulae that have remained elusive to you. I shall bequeath you equipment and also I can save a life."

"Mine?"

"No, Professor. You are in no danger other than the normal tribulations of life."

Danelaw gazed over towards prone the figure gazing through the binoculars. "A malevolence hunts across the Cosmos. He seeks one singular species of female. One day I may be able to salvage the life of someone very close to you."

A spear brazenly landed right in the centre of the spread of food and wine. From a mere 50 feet, a large band of skin clad warriors charged. The time travelling scientist grabbed his Lee Enfield rifle and fired over their heads. The assailants instantly halted. The noise momentarily stunning the party of ice age insurgents. "Let's run!" Danelaw yelled, "This was not on the plan! This set of cavemen wants us for supper!"

PHILIPPA-SEPTEMBER 1967

"Becky." Philippa poured herself another cup of tea. Concurrently, she was being served with chocolate brownies and salmon with cucumber sandwiches. The debutante not caring a jot that such a level of indiscriminate ingestion would ruin her luncheon.

"Yes, My Lady." Rebecca looked up from the large bowl she was stirring.

"In less than two weeks I shall be at university studying medicine. I shall not be around to annoy you so much. I trust I shall be missed. At least a little."

"Lady Philippa, of course ye'll be missed. And you're no annoyance, not in th' least. It's a pleasure to 'ave such a lady as yourself visiting us 'ere in the kitchen."

"I need to start packing stuff to take with me to Oxford. It's such a drag. Could you help me, Becky?"

"Of course, Lady Philippa. You just say when. Between three and five afternoons is best."

"That's cool, Becky." Philippa smiled as the strains of Anita Harris singing the romantic melody "Just Loving You" came on the radio. "Now I have to start getting ready for my Medical Sciences course at Oxford. See you later."

Tom Marchant was in the lounge reading the Daily Telegraph when his daughter vibrantly made an appearance.

"Daddy," she called, "Becky is going to help me pack for Oxford. I told her it was such a drag. She'll do it all. And you can do the unpacking when you drop me off."

"You are such a minx, Pip." the earl smiled affectionately at his daughter.

"Philippa, you should do it yourself. Not rely on servants. Even worse asking Daddy," Louise uttered an overt chide.

"Becky is more than a servant, Mama."

"Whatever. But we both know that Julian is home from Australia in two months' time and I know he is not exultant with your rather stubborn decision to go to university. He will be your husband and should be able to dictate how you demean yourself from now on."

"Mummy, this is getting to be such a drag. And I'm bummed out on the whole scene."

"I wish you would speak English, instead of that hippie vernacular," Louise moaned.

"Darling, she's 18. A young woman. Emphasis on the young. Allow her a modicum of independence."

"Tom, you always side with her," the countess snapped.

"No," he began to protest as Mister Hodges knocked and entered.

"Sorry to disturb you, My Lord." "Yes, Mister Hodges?" The earl enquired.

"My Lord. There is a telephone call for Lady Philippa from Lady Caroline. The lady sounded very distressed, My Lord."

EMILY-SEPTEMBER 1967

"Emily, do you not think you are endangering the family? Surely women should not have careers, but take care of their husbands?" Peter Jennings asked.

The young British QC was being interviewed on ABC television. It was by the anchor of the New York TV news programme, "Pete Jennings With the News".

"Do men really feel that insecure, Mister Jennings?" Emily cutely smiled at her interviewer. "Surely a man who is self-confident would feel no threat by a working wife? By the way I am not married--."

"But you are engaged. Your fiancé is fighting in Aden. Many young American girls will identify with that."

"I'm sure they will. But alas my boyfriend has not yet gone down on one knee so in every sense of the word I am single. But even if I was married he would support my stance. It makes complete sense for a woman to be well educated and have work experience."

"Why?" The interviewer probed more.

"Mister Jennings, you surprise me. What happens if she is left a widow? And the insurance payments, if any, do not cover all living expenses. In such circumstances she can only be considered for a decent position with a living salary if she has a good education and some work experience. Even for couples who want a family, the extra income of a working wife, if saved and invested well, will be invaluable when the children come along."

"And your boyfriend is an officer in the Royal Marines?" Jennings changed the topic.

"He is. He's serving in Aden right now. I feel at one with the hundreds of thousands of girlfriends, sisters, wives and mothers who have their loved ones fighting in Vietnam. I wish them all the best and pray for their men to come home unscathed."

"And you are in New York for two weeks only?"

"That is correct." Emily beamed as Jennings winked at her out of camera shot. "I am doing a few radio shows to discuss young people and their problems. I am also writing some articles for Helen Gurley Brown for her magazine, Cosmopolitan."

"Miss Emily Wilkinson, the youngest Queen's Counsel. From Oxford in England. Thank you."

The second the camera was off her, Dean and Andy were there to whisk her off to the next appointment. This one was more pleasurable. It entailed visiting the renowned stores Bloomingdales, Brooks Brothers and Macey's with Andy Downs to view the latest fashion lines. Then onto WMCA radio for an interview with Ruth Meyer. It had been a hectic ten days for the young woman in a strange yet vibrant city. She had visited the best restaurants, famous museums and of course the Empire State Building. Emily had walked by the site of ground being cleared where two massive towers called the World Trade Center were scheduled to be erected over the next few years.

The Statue of Liberty and Ellis Island, reached from Battery Park, resonated with great interest as were the seemingly endless numbers of yellow taxicabs in the city.

The British QC had met Andy Warhol and received advances from film and music stars. To all she made her apologies and gave her reasons for declination always as "I have an urgent dinner date which Helen insists I attend". A line used so frequently some even began to believe it.

"Shit," she exclaimed to Andy after the penultimate day was finally over, "I'm being hit on by gorgeous guys. Famous guys with bodies to die for. I'm desperate for a fuck and I turn them all down. Why?"

"Simple, my delightful young lawyer. You love your valiant warrior fighting the Queen's enemies and don't wish to hurt him."

"Is that right?" Emily was taken aback; and unsure. She had put it down to seeking an uncomplicated existence, especially while in New York.

"Could not be righter, Miss QC. He's a very lucky man to have a woman determined to stay his woman. You're so right to send those poseurs on their way. Those stars, if I can bring myself to describe them so erroneously. All inane and talent less. They only wanted to date you, to bed you, then add it to their resume by leaking it to the press. Now my lovely lady, I have to be away as we've a long final day tomorrow. We're all shopped out, eaten and drunk out. I'm a queer so I can't help you with your carnal desires. My humble advice to you would be, bath, have a final Scotch and cigarette than slope into your bed. You're one cool, foxy, tough chick. Have a ball when you get back to little ole England. You 've enough bread to buy your man his own dukeship or whatever you call them."

"He's already in line to inherit an earldom. But I'll certainly have a ball when I see him." Emily kissed Andy on the cheek. "You're one cool dude. I love chatting to you. Thanks for today. It was a blast."

"My pleasure." Andy's girlish visage beamed before he strode over to the door and left.

Emily undressed. She slipped into her pink, flannel, dressing robe then a bath. A dull knock came from the hotel room door.

"Andy," she groaningly muttered, "What on earth have you forgotten?" She stubbed out her cigarette, turned down the radio that was playing "Ode to Billie Joe" by Bobbie Gentry and walked to the polished oak ingress.

Once opened, a six-foot-tall figure stood before her. He was dressed in a conservative grey suit, white shirt, swept back hair with a flat face that seemed very eastern European. The intruder forced his way in and slammed the door shut.

"What the fuck do you want?" she asked.

"You bin looking where y' should not. My boss says you've to be put out of action."

He took a long cord from his jacket pocket. "Don't worry, it'll soon be over."

Emily did not prevaricate. Her left leg flew out so rapidly that the would-be assassin did not perceive it. He merely felt the excruciating sensation and gross discomfort as her foot contacted with the scrotum and ruptured a testicle. In less than the blink of an eye the powerfully athletic QC had grabbed a lamp stand and smashed it venomously on the figure's pate. He groaned then leapt back to his feet only to have a full bottle of wine demolished to smithereens on his skull. Blood and the 1946 vintage merging as the figure fell back onto the luxuriant carpet and lay still.

Seconds later, seemingly void of the need for a door key, Andy dashed into the room. In his right hand he grasped a black Browning 45 calibre M1911 automatic pistol.

"Sweet Jesus, I thank you," he sighed looking at the prostrate, bloody figure on the Waldorf hotel room carpet, "I thought I was just a smidgeon too late!"

DANIEL/JAMES-SEPTEMBER 1967

The dust from the floor of the area nearby to James was picking up. It was like little sprites, taunting and teasing the young officer as he dashed forward now safe in the knowledge that those who had escaped the wrath of the Royal Air Force had run for their lives.

"Sergeant Diggle!" he screamed back at his troop number two, "Starlight is on the way, you check our wounded, make sure they're patched up til the blood's stopped, I'm going to see to Mister Moir! Keep Corporal Pierce and his section with you!"

"Yes, sir!" Diggle responded. The sergeant removed a dressing from the fighting order of a wounded Marine, took it from the sealed, waterproof outer wrapping then placed it over the lesion on his leg.

James doubled ahead to the location of the now dead Corporal McGrath and seriously wounded David Moir. The energetic subaltern had his rifle cocked and the safety catch in the off position as he hastily negotiated the uneven ground towards where the two casualties lay on the sandy, grime ridden surface. Teddy Roland, despite carrying a cumbersome A41 radio, kept up with his troop leader as they passed the position held by Sergeant Baker applying "first field" wound dressings to injured soldiers.

"Sergeant Baker!" James yelled, "Starlight is on the way! Take your able-bodied guys forward. Corporal O'Connor and Corporal Wright's sections! Clear the demolished buildings. Take any papers from dead or wounded gollies. Make sure it's clear! Keep alert! Have the gun groups ready to give covering fire."

"Yes, sir!" Baker affirmed then bellowed to the sections required.

"With me!" James shouted at his young signaller then bounded the few yards to the subaltern. The body of Eddie McGrath lay face down in the filth. The arms were spread-eagled as an amalgam of blood and grey cerebral mush oozed from his open skull where bone and hair mingled with the gore.

"David." James squatted next to his wounded colleague, raising the limp head to the level of his knee. The Scot's eyes seemed to disappear upwards then return. The lips were dry, and his shoulder was a sanguineous mess with bone, muscle and veins protruding through the crimson pool that was the upper section of his shirt. James removed David's field dressing from his fighting order straps, ripped off the outer covering and applied the bandage onto the gaping wound.

"Jimmy," the wounded man painfully gasped, "Glad t' see ye, but you're late, Jimmy. Too late."

"Shut your face, you Scottish prick." James' banter was accentuated by a choking sensation in his voice. "Starlight's on the way. You hang in there! The ambulances are coming."

"Ah canna feel a thing, Jimmy, Ah'm goin'. Like that Scottish Soldier song by Andy Stewart, ah'm goin', Jimmy."

"Fuck you! Don't you dare die on me Davy! Don't you dare die on me! Hang in there!"

"Aye Jimmy. You're a great guy. Tell Caroline I love 'er. Tell my Mum and Dad too."

"Tell them yourself! You're gonna be fine, Second Lieutenant Moir! You're going to be fine! Tell me about Edinburgh! Tell me about Hearts!"

"Great city. Great team." David smiled as two medics dashed over and eased him onto a stretcher. "Get him treatment at once!" James bawled at the bearers.

"Yes, sir," a Royal Army Medical Corps member, replied, "We'll take him to the British Military Hospital at Steamer Point. He'll receive the best treatment in Aden."

"Doesn't sound reassuring," Sergeant Diggle grunted as he caught up with James.

The swell of emotion gripped James for a few moments. He fought back a deluge of tears then with equal rapidity composed himself.

Lieutenant Colonel John Ivor Headon Owen, the CO of 45 Commando Royal Marines, stood on a review platform on the parade ground at Little Aden RM base. The tall figure faced the men under his command. All were present apart from those on guard, chefs in the galleys, a few medics and those either in the sick bay or at the British Military Hospital at Steamer Point.

The sullen and ashen faces of Daniel and James betrayed an even greater level of trauma than the other congregated Royal Marines.

"Gentlemen." Owen began to speak, his voice swaying with melancholy.

"Gentlemen." He composed his demeanour. "Today has been a bad day for both 45 and the Corps as a whole. In an heroic engagement with NLF fighters an exemplary NCO, Corporal Edward McGrath was killed and a very competent and promising young officer, Second Lieutenant David Moir was badly wounded. Both Corporal McGrath and Mister

Moir are from Edinburgh. I have since heard from the BMH at Steamer Point that Mister Moir succumbed to his wounds and passed away two hours ago."

The uttering of sheer disbelief was clearly audible even in the open air of the barracks. The commanding officer continued. "Six Royal Marines were also wounded. Two are in the sick bay here in Little Aden; the other four have been kept in for observation at Steamer Point. It is a bad day. We have lost. But we shall, as in the spirit of the Corps, do our duty until we leave this place to the Arabs. And of course, the Soviets. Have a couple of wets tonight and celebrate the lives of our comrades who made the ultimate sacrifice. Remember our lads as we should then catch some zeds. Be ready and fit for duty at reveille. Carry on!"

Daniel glanced briefly at James. He had he faraway look oft seen in Aden. Veterans of multiple campaigns had christened such a manifestation "the 1,000-yard stare."

"What we going to do?" Daniel's voice verged on being indistinct.

"We're going to down a few for David. And when we get home, we're going to down one helluva lot more," James robustly asserted. Daniel nodded in approval.

The sombre location, flat and surrounded by jagged bare rocky peaks, had been called Silent Valley by British colonists in the first half of the 20th Century. The title had been credited to the rumour, or otherwise, that radio signals could not be picked up in that area of desert just off the Little Aden peninsular. The weather was the norm. A gentle breeze blew in from the north but not with suffice potency to cool the area from the brutal sun. The heat was preponderant in all areas of the Middle East at that time of year although in the temperate zone of the Northern Hemisphere autumn was on the way. Not so in Aden.

The bearers, mourners and rifle party were suffering sheer discomfort both physical and psychological as they roasted in the dry heat. However, the punishing elements did not allow the Marines to detract their attention one iota from the service to their fallen.

Lieutenant Colonel Owen recited the Ode of Remembrance-

"They went with songs to the battle. They were young.
Straight of limb, true of eyes, steady and aglow.

They were staunch to the end against odds uncounted.
They fell with their faces to the foe."
"They shall not grow old as we that are left grow old.
Age shall not weary them, nor the years condemn.
At the going down of the sun and in the morning
We will remember them."
"We will remember them." The assembled ranks repeated.

The bugler played the Last Post. A stern looking rifle party fired three rounds each into the air. The draping Union Flags were deferentially removed from the coffins of Second Lieutenant David Alexander Moir RM and Corporal Edward McGrath RM before being lowered into their graves. As they strode towards the transport wagons that would return the Marines to Little Aden camp, Daniel looked back. He gazed at the wilderness sepulchres where their fallen friend and his sergeant would now lie until the final gasp of the Cosmos. He then cast a glance at James.

"We were at the AIB together. Then Deal and Lympstone. We fought together through this poxy, degenerate anal sphincter of place. I thought we'd be a team at least until the end of my service. Now Davy is going to spend eternity in this shithole."

"True. Three of us came and at least one will not return. For Davy, we'll have to make sure we get home. One of us playing a harp is more than enough," James gloomily replied.

"Yes." Daniel nodded philosophically. "My heart must go out to Caroline. How the hell will she cope?" "Not well I fear."

DANESH AND KELLY

"Run!" Danelaw cried as the mass of Palaeolithic marauders rapidly gained ground.

Kelly, by far the youngest and most athletic, easily made the wooded and grassy crest of the rise above the valley floor. It was only 50 metres to where the black PADIT like flight craft was hypnotically hovering less than a metre above the ground.

Grathyst, Fodle and the remainder of the Neanderthal group had frenetically taken flight from the caves. They had melted deep into the dense primordial forest that stood alongside a proximate section of the wide gulch.

"Come!" Kelly screamed at the three men who were panting and puffing some distance behind.

Danelaw stopped and fired the Lee Enfield again. The round hitting a tree just to the side of the Cro Magnon pursuers.

Hussein ran past Kelly as she frantically urged on the others. The prehistoric nomads grunted at the professor as he re-cocked his rifle. They all seemed to be bearded, short, filthy and adorned in animal skins. One of the group had peeled off from the others and was executing a personal pincer manoeuvre. Hussein had stopped to impatiently await the others when a stone-headed lance tossed by the lone Cro Magnon pierced the muscle on the small of his back. The primeval scream he emitted seemed to have the capacity to curdle the fabric of the soul.

Danelaw had now lost patience. He removed the powerful laser pistol from his belt, aimed and rapidly downed three of the primitive humans in as many beams.

The dazed figures lay on the rough grass and moss. Their fellow attackers grunting at them in disbelief while touching their unmoving bodies.

"Move!" Danelaw urged. "Those cavemen are not dead. Just stunned."

"You forgot your friend," Danesh picked up the groaning Hussein and carried him with ease to the transporter. Fortuitously the spear shaft and point fell from the wound after a few paces.

Danelaw leapt into the pilot's seat whilst Danesh laid Hussein face down on the floor at the rear of the PADIT.

"First aid box!" Kelly called out as soon as she was inside. The doors closed.

"That orange box with a star on it," Danelaw yelled back. Within seconds they were airborne. Flying 1000 metres above the picturesque valley and its ice age fauna.

Blood was cascading in torrents out of the gouge in Hussein's back and flowing onto the thick carpet of the accommodation area.

"That is agony," Hussein groaned as Kelly cut away the dark crimson stained clothing.

"Is this all you have?" Kelly called out.

"It's a first aid box. Not an emergency operating theatre." Danelaw banked starboard, ascended and turned the throttle to full.

Kelly banged a syringe of morphine into the back of the disconsolate figure. She was thankful that the label was printed both in some ancient language as well as in characters and words that closely resembled seventeenth century English. It abated any requirement for a prolonged curative discussion with the pilot.

"The pain's subsided Doctor," Hussein whispered as Kelly rammed bandages into the gaping chasm in his torso.

"I know, Professor Hussein. I've given you a pain killer we call morphine."

"How is he?" Danelaw shouted from the cockpit area. He increased the airspeed to beyond that of sound.

"I can stem the blood a little. I've given him a strong analgesic, but we must get him to an emergency operating theatre. Quickly!"

"I would not dare take him to a public hospital. Even if they agreed to treat him it would not be wise."

"Then he may not survive!" Kelly was in no mood for niceties.

"I have a fully functioning operating theatre in my house." Danelaw turned around. "You will have access to all the surgical instruments, drugs, blood, plasma, and equipment you require."

"Who will be my assistant and my anaesthetist?" Kelly called out.

"I have loyal staff that will perform both functions. I shall radio ahead. The doctor is Hussein himself. Consequently, Doctor Aresti, it will be up to you to perform the actual emergency surgery."

Danelaw's PADIT flew at beyond Mach 3. In under three quarters of an hour, the versatile craft was landing on the roof of Danelaw's mansion in the suburbs of Walika. The sunlight on the majestic Euphrats River was shimmering and dancing in the late afternoon hours. On the roof two women stood next to a hospital gurney. They were dressed in what Kelly imagined 19th or early 20th Century nurses in Britannia may have been bedecked.

Long black dresses, with white-bibbed fronts and white nurses' hats on the top of the head. Hussein was placed on the trolley. One of the women called to Kelly, "Doctor, with me. You'll need to scrub up and change." In a second the young physician was sprinting after the nurse to the prep room.

Two hours later Kelly made an appearance in the lounge where Danesh and Danelaw were eagerly anticipating news.

"Tariq Hussein will live," she sighed and poured herself a goblet of wine, "I've cleaned the wound, sewn him up, bandaged him and administered blood and a sedative. He'll be hurting for a while. But it will diminish over the next week. And painkillers will make it bearable. Your nurse can remove the stitches in a week."

"Doctor, you have been a saint. Someday I may be able to return the good deed." Danelaw smiled in gratitude.

"Forget it, Prof. Just give us a lift back to our own time. I've had enough excitement for one day let alone 50,000 years before I'll be born."

"Stay here. Dinner will be along soon then you can sleep. And first thing in the morning I will return you to your car. It will be in exactly the same spot. A mere 30 seconds after you left it."

"Kelly," Danesh interrupted with a non-sequitur, "Did you know that the legend of Sodom and Gomorrah is factual. Or in this phase of recurring history is, it was caused, will be caused, by a nuclear war?"

"Professors. I've had far more incidents to cerebrally absorb today than I am capable of. You will forgive me if I refrain from debating that hypothesis until another day."

Kelly's main assistant in the theatre, a Walikan woman, entered via the main double doors. "Lady and Gentleman. Dinner is served. And Doctor, I did not cook it, I merely announce it."

"Professor Gideon." Kelly sounded extremely formal. "We will accept the invitation to dine and rest here. We will take our leave first thing in the morning. I trust Professor Gidron, your doppelganger in this amazing epoch, hath no further escapades in store for us."

"Nothing planned, Doctor Aresti. At first light I shall transport you back 50,000 years to your epoch to the precise time and location that we vacated. Rest assured though, our paths shall cross again." Danelaw stoically nodded.

The Miasmic Mist — Volume One

PHILIPPA-SEPTEMBER 1967

Philippa turned her Morris Mini onto the minor country road that ran from Aston to the tiny hamlet of Shifford. Already fearing the worst, the debutante was chain smoking. She uttered, "No, they've just broken up".

Lady Caroline Feversham had left her parents' home and made for her private retreat in the beautiful remoteness of central Oxfordshire.

"I sincerely hope that this is not a Dear John letter," she griped loudly, smoking a Rothmans King Size while listening on the Philips car radio to Dave Davies and his solo song "Death of a Clown". "After all that you've put me through. And your parents. It better not be just a Dear John. But then on second thoughts, I hope it is just a Dear John!"

Philippa had deliberately not listened to the news either on television or radio and had totally evaded even glancing at any newspapers. She worried for her brother. And her friend whose lover was serving in some far-off land that Philippa would have been totally incapable of pointing to on a map. Nonetheless, British soldiers were involved in that place and some were losing their lives.

The tiny settlement of Shifford boasted a population of about 30.

Lady Caroline owned a property about half a mile from the church. The house was bought as a gift for her 17th birthday. Philippa took a mere five minutes to cover the short distance to the rustic estate.

On this early autumn afternoon, the place was silent but for the odd chirp of some wild birds. Golden sunlight was cascading gently through the canopy of the woodland that straddled the 18th Century construction. Philippa brought the car a halt, applied the hand brake and switched off the engine. She slowly slipped from the car, locked it then gazed at the impressive obverse of the building. The solar light reflected from the glass of the upper floor lattice windows. For a startling moment the young socialite deemed she saw the unsightly ashen face of a balding man, grinning evilly at her. Terrified, the 18-year-old looked away, returning her glance several seconds hence. Mercifully the obnoxious visage had gone. An impish trick of the gloaming radiance she concluded. Philippa inhaled deeply then marched without announcement through the ajar, bulky oak door and into the house.

The interior was even more silent. A scenario that was totally unexpected. The young woman tentatively strode into the ample red brick kitchen that lay deserted. There had been a vague anticipation of seeing Elmira, Kinsey and the others of their current "In Crowd" reassuring Caroline. Telling her empathetically that her officer boyfriend was just a ship that passed in the night and that she would soon meet a far superior suitor to replace him. The reality was dissimilar. Instead, an eerie, almost ghostly, silence hung around like a preternatural mist. Engendering a stillness that only the grave afforded.

"Caroline," Philippa called out. She moved nervously and with no small measure of apprehension into the dining room and then the lounge. Both of these reception rooms were empty as were the larger utility room, downstairs cloakroom and even the garage.

"Not funny," she muttered. The memory of the chilling optical illusion was still lying fresh on her consciousness. It heralded an atmosphere resembling a thread from the plot of a Washington Irving, Nathaniel Hawthorne, Edgar Allen Poe or Dennis Wheatley novel. Philippa had lately read works by all those authors and her imagination was now in overdrive. She had recently watched the movie "The Innocents" based on the novel "The Turn of the Screw" by Henry James. It had terrified her, something the young woman was now rapidly becoming. Although it was still light, the haunting outlines of dusk were commencing their shadowy, cloaking descent over the county.

Philippa was now in two minds whether to cut and run or check upstairs.

"You silly bitch." She called herself. "Panicked by a dark house when you've been visited by strange things since you were tiny. Get a hold and find Caroline."

The carpeted staircase was cleared in seconds. The bathroom was void of anything bar some soap and a crumpled towel.

Philippa walked slowly into the expansive master bedroom where she could espy the blonde head of Caroline. The young woman was sat on the luxurious double bed, gaping emptily at her forlorn reflection in the ornate dressing table mirror. The black mascara had been swept down her face by the shedding of a river of pain that was leaving amorphous dark lines, akin to bruises, sloping down her pale cheeks.

She was still crying. Dirgeful. Swaying slightly to and fro, sniffing and choking on the sheer volume of tears. There was no effort required in concluding that this was not merely a simple Dear John missive.

The few feet to where Caroline sat were circumspectly negotiated in what seemed like torturous epochs until Philippa nervously inhaled. She saw that her friend held a sharp scalpel type knife tightly in her right hand which was pressed onto her left wrist. Fortuitously it had not yet sliced open the skin. The young debutante did not speak but quietly and calmly sat next to Caroline. No resistance was offered as she warily coaxed the blade from her grip and placing it well away on the dressing table. The distraught woman did not even look up as Philippa put her arm around the shoulders.

"It's alright, Carol. I'm here. I'm here for you. Tell me."

Caroline turned, pressed her head into Philippa's shoulder and upper chest area and began to wail loudly. She sobbed for some while before unsteadily divulging, "He's dead, Pip. David. My valiant Royal Marines' officer is dead. Dying heroically in Aden, his mother said. But he's dead. He's never coming home."

"I'm so, so sorry Carol. Should you not be at home with your parents?" Philippa stroked the golden locks.

"No." Caroline sniffed then cried and spoke simultaneously. "This is where I last saw him. We slept together here. Fucked here. I can still smell him around me. This is where I want to be."

"That's alright. You can be wherever you want. Have you some wine?"

Caroline pointed at a bottle of Merlot on a table in the corner of the bedroom that surprisingly appeared to be almost full. Philippa unhurriedly stood up and collected two flutes from a glass cabinet. She placed them, the wine and an ashtray on the dressing table to their front. Two cigarettes were lit, and one handed to Caroline who accepted without response. The stare being an amalgam of shock and a glazed unreality. For Philippa, bizarrely, and monetarily, it was the same look she imagined a zombie may possess. Two glasses were filled almost to the brim, one offered to Caroline who accepted it once more without acknowledgement.

"You know I saw him, Pip. I swear to God I saw David."

"Tell me about it." Philippa wanted her friend to talk. She was not concerned as to the subject matter. Merely to keep her conversing.

"I could hear music. A song that I'd never heard before. No radio was on."

"Tell me about it," Philippa softly repeated herself.

"I could hear a song. I think a Scottish song but I'm guessing. It was something about picking wild mountain something or other. It had a nice tune. And in this mirror, the one in front of me, David appeared. He was in his number one blue uniform with cap. He smiled and mouthed "I'll always love you". Then he walked into a strange distance until I could no longer see him."

Philippa took a long draught of her glass and smiled at her friend in the mirror as she began to sob again.

"He came to tell you how he feels. On his way to Heaven; you're such a lucky girl to have that."

"Fuck that. I want him here, not in fucking Heaven. You mean a place where stupid little angels fly around and someone with a big beard says whether you go to the penthouse or drop to the basement. It's shit. I want him here. He's gone, taken from me! Whatever short time I had with my Adonis, I would rather have had those few hours with him than live 1,000 years and never know such warmth and belonging. Such a man. Such a lover. Such a father he would have been. I've been making a list of things that David will never now get to do."

Caroline picked up a piece of foolscap paper which was covered in scrawl.

"David will never walk me back down the aisle. David will never eat haggis and chips with me on the way to Edinburgh castle. David will never see our child born. He'll never see their first day at school, be there at their first date, their prom, their wedding. He'll never see his grandchildren. David will never walk me at dusk through the Cairngorms. He'll never be there when I graduate. David will never hear the charts on the new Radio One. He'll never see his beloved Heart of Midlothian play again and will never see the port of Leith or Edinburgh Zoo. We'll never honeymoon in---."

Caroline burst out again into loud lamentation.

"I know." Philippa poured more Merlot then hugged her friend. "I know what it's like. I lost someone close that I loved too."

"Did you know he was coming home in two months' time?" Caroline wept into her glass. The tears were flowing in torrents down her mascara darkened cheeks. She picked up her cigarette and inhaled deeply. "Two months and he would have been home. Now he'll be in that disgusting place forever. They buried him out there yesterday. At least you went to the funeral of your love. My man went to fight in a horrible place and died for what? I wish someone could tell me. I'm going all transcendental. All existential. All this hippie shit about going to the astral plane on a groovy cloud. His lights were turned out. It's shit, total shit; he'd just turned 19 years old and died for nothing! Nothing! absolutely nothing! You need to go for the man you want. Not what others want for you, Pip."

"I know, life's not fair." Philippa's words radiated an assuaging timbre. "Whatever you want Carol, I'm here for you."

"There'll be a memorial service in Edinburgh. In early December or late November. David's mother has asked me to attend. I'd like you to come with me."

"Of course." Philippa stroked Caroline's golden tresses." I'll take a couple of days off university. I'll drive us up there."

"Pip, I'd like you to stay with me here tonight. I want to get totally blitzed. I need to get pissed out of my mind. And bore you to death talking about David."

"Do you not want Elmira, Kinsey and the others to join us?"

"No. They are not what I need right now. You are beautiful, Pip."

"OK, let's get blitzed. Come on downstairs. To the wine cellar and we'll get drunk. Have you food in the house?"

"Tons of tinned and some in the freezer. Plus, fresh bread and milk." Caroline was still trembling as she replied.

"Get out of this morgue of a bedroom. Carol. We'll get you showered and into clean clothes. Downstairs, put on music starting with "Even the Bad Times Are Good," by the Tremolos. Get out a ton of cheese, crisps, peanuts, garlic bread and any other junk you have, to go with the champers and a crate of Via Colla Dolcetto d'Alba Langhe. I'll listen to you cry all night about David. Pay homage to his glorious memory. I'll embrace eulogies in his praise 'til dawn comes over yon horizon. I'll wipe your tears when they flood down from you as they will. I'll stand here to be with you. To catch you when you fall. Whatever it takes. But it's time to get blitzed!"

DANESH AND KELLY

Kelly had washed and packed away all her clothes from the holiday in Mesopotamia.

Danesh had returned his laboratory to scan through an absolute plethora of formulae, calculations and hypotheses bequeathed by Danelaw. The young physician knew she would see little of the gifted professor before the following evening so decided to cut short her leave and return to work at the Hartford County Hospital.

"Doctor Aresti, I was not expecting you." Tim Lane, the A and E consultant approached her, slow and almost hesitant. Lane was 40 years old and tall. He wore trendy spectacles, was dark haired and dressed in a white shirt, dark suit, navy blue tie. Kelly thought of him as being quite handsome.

"Yes, Mister Lane. I'm actually still on leave today but I was getting bored. My partner has gone AWOL into his lab so I'm here to help. I'm sure you could use it and the paperwork will take all of two minutes to amend."

Kelly was soon changed and into her blue two-piece blue scrubs and checking through notes for patients awaiting diagnosis.

"Doctor Aresti." Jean Mackay approached. She was a 40-year-old ward sister and the stalwart of Kelly's Accident and Emergency.

"Yes, Sister Mackay." Kelly smiled

"We have a man in casualty with a few injuries. They do not appear too urgent but need examining. The patient may need psychiatric help."

"Sister. We get drunks and nut jobs through here every day. What's different about this one?"

"Normally the psychologically flawed talk drivel, incoherent garbage, this one is different.

He says he is from somewhere, another universe, another time, and actually sounds persuasive.

At least to me he does. A word of warning, he needs a shower."

"Give me his notes and let's have a look at him." Kelly was pleased to be back into the relative security of her work routine. She drew the curtain back, looked at the paperwork relating to the man on the couch.

"Doctor!" A small filthy man sprang from the lying to upright position in a second. The individual had a sallow complexion, dark hair that was rapidly being lost was unkempt, and unshaven. His eyes seemed to burn through Kelly. He as remotely familiar but she could not recall how or from where.

"Doctor, you should be dead. I'm from a sister dimension, one of an infinite quantity of such parallel universes. And in that you are dead. Get away, Doctor. I've seen your future. You should be dead! Run! Grab your scientific people and get away! You'll die if you don't!"

EMILY-SEPTEMBER 1967

"Andy. What the hell are you doing with that gun?" Emily exclaimed. She attempted to reconcile the anomalous image of the effeminate, gay man with the large pistol in his right hand.

"I'm amazed. That's a top Soviet assassin, my dear. You should be in the hereafter. Ironically,

he looks as if he's singing with the angels now."

"I'm just a little rusty. Nonetheless, I burst his balls then smashed a lamp over his head. When that was not suffice I wasted that lovely gift of yours, the 1946 Californian Cabernet Sauvignon. I regret but I cracked it over his skull. Anyway, I'm in shock Andy. You didn't tell me why you look so manly. Like Mike Connors in that new TV show we watched, "Mannix". I'm so impressed. But why the gun?" Andy did not reply, instead he went to the hotel room door and looked in both directions down the corridor.

"Get me three vodka miniatures from the mini bar, darling," he requested, sounding far less machismo than his determined entrance had indicated.

Emily opened three small bottles and handed them to him. Andy poured one of the bottles into the throat of the deceased assailant. The other two were scattered liberally over his clothing and down the front of his shirt.

"He was seen drinking heavily in the hotel bar. He probably was but these men from Moscow can down vodka the way we can water. He may have been feigning inebriation. He had booked a room in this place. I hope the lousy Soviet KGB budget stretches this far. I'm sure it must.

This Soviet agent had received a signal from their office in London. His orders were to kill or kidnap you. Now, before I respond to your inevitable questions, give me a hand with him."

Emily and Andy frogmarched the dead man to the linen chute, opened the hatch and tossed the corpse into it.

"Nothing at the bottom to cushion his fall. He'll look like he fell accidentally."

They furtively moved back to Emily's room where she instantly returned to her enquiry.

"Who are you Andy. Besides a big boy. You must offer a clue as tomorrow I'm back to England. I want to know?"

"My darling sexy, foxy Emily Wilkinson QC. You have friends in very high places."

"What do you mean?"

"Like you, I actually have a day job. I work for Helen. But I also moonlight for the State Department. Of course, I'll never admit that salient fact. In the same way that you moonlight for MI5 and MI6 back in the old country."

"Andy. I'm flabbergasted."

"Your Foreign Secretary, George Brown, contacted our Secretary of State, Dean Rusk. He told him that Moscow wanted you to be neutralised. Rusk said that would not happen on his watch. So, they made sure someone was close, very close. I could not get much closer so I was given the job."

Chapter Fourteen

NARRATOR

Yes, the Summer of Love closed and the music that vibrates within the electric impulses which constitute my consciousness, the iconic sounds were not only the hippie, underground and pop songs but also a Scottish air from the very floor of the Highlands. My father was a young man during that period and as the famous summer slipped nonchalantly away from a seemingly unyielding present into a crackly, distorted past, that Scottish melody always made his eyes well with melancholy. It was connected to the passing of his friend from that wonderful country north of the border.

My mother was always up to something. Something of great import so my doting grandparents often told me. But they never elaborated on such a vague assertion.

The adventures and the danger subsided, momentarily, whilst my father and his friends served out their tour of duty and missed their ladies, some more than others, waiting for them back at home. Of course, this is an important juncture within the aegis of this account. The proceedings, music, fashion, art and politics were all ground breaking and trend setting but the main events are yet to unravel. Daddy looks up proudly, he always maintains that guise. Accordingly, I am assuming that he is pleased thus far and feels not too much discomfort and embarrassment at my revelations. I shall proceed while all runs smoothly.

Stephen Grenfell

DANESH AND KELLY

For Kelly, the experience of travelling though the inter-dimensional portals was altering. Navigating through a separate fabric of the overwhelming dimensions of space and time was transforming as an understanding. The eternity of parallel universes that she had venerated and yearned for, now seemed to be manifesting into a somewhat mundane and stale experience.

The very expedition to beyond that which was deemed unattainable to many and within her own thought processes lacked the farrago of surreal light shows and displays she normally would perceive. Could it be that she was taking less note of the cosmic fireworks? Even such indicators that many agnostics deemed as the evidentiary power. The proof of a Divine Entity. Were they now becoming contemptible with a growing familiarity?

PADIT 2 stopped near the house where Doctor Keely Marston resided. Kelly pressed the alter button and the vehicle morphed, assuming the shape of a normal car. She carried her laptop and a bag up to the door where she pressed the bell button.

"Kelly." Keely was always almost identical in dress. Today the choice was red shirt, blue jeans, white fleece and pink slippers. The only differences were that Kelly was in a blue shirt and wore black patent leather high-heeled shoes. The flaming red locks of both were up in a trendy bun at the crown of the head. Keely kissed her cosmic twin on the cheek. "Come in. So nice to see you. What brings you here?"

"A social call of course. But I do have some pictures I'm dying to show you. Plus a few more questions."

The large house was far too expensive to be afforded on the salary of a young E and A doctor. Kelly was all too aware of such a situation. The mortgage repayments were made by the much older and exceedingly more affluent Professor Garside as were most of the luxuriant interior furniture, fixtures and fittings. The night was falling in that PU and Keely was anxious to be the perfect host.

"Have you eaten?" Keely enquired of her guest.

"No. I just leapt into PADIT and took off."

"Are things alright between you and Danesh?"

"As far as I know they are fine. He's been immersed in his work for a week."

"I'll open a bottle of Riesling. Or would you prefer a red?"

"Riesling is fine. Keely. Can you order a take away? I have pictures to show you."

"I know you like Indian, so I'll ring the local restaurant. Anything special you'd like?"

"No thanks. Second thoughts, I'll try chicken tikka masala and brown rice," Kelly replied setting up her laptop as Keely handed over a glass of wine.

Within minutes the food had arrived, Keely spread it across the coffee table and the women ate as Kelly pressed the "go" switch.

The video had only been running for a few minutes when Keely cried out,

"What the hell is this? Some fancy dress wildlife park with a few computer produced scenes thrown in. Nice commentary. You even have guys dressed up as cavemen?"

"I wanted to ask if you had been on this trip. Obviously not. It took us back 50,000 years."

"We have. Just checking to see if it's bona fide, Kelly. Where did you meet the guy who took you?"

"Danesh and I went to a country called Mesopotamia. We met him there. It's near the Middle East."

"Yes. We call it Mespotia. Same difference. Was this dude called Danelaw?"

"Yes, precisely. He was called Danelaw, Danelaw Gidron. A professor from 50,000 years ago. He was, is, Danesh and David's doppelganger only fifty thousand years older. And unlike Danesh, David and their numerous other cosmic twins, there seems to be only one Danelaw Gidron. Which universe boasts his authentic provenance? Well no one seems to possess such erudition."

Keely went to her laptop and within a few moments the screen was illuminating with similar Ice Age vistas.

"My photographs from the same sojourn. It now seems like 50,000 years ago. We moved close to Neanderthals, Cro-Magnon, woolly mammoth, sabre tooth cats and all the other residents of that era. It came as somewhat of a surprise to learn that there were advanced civilisations 50 millennia back. And one at least that can, could, travel not only to its future but to other universes."

"It came as a huge shock to me., Keely. I had to snap photographs galore and take samples before I believed it was not just one highly complex ruse. I guessed you would have gone there also, we seem to follow identical paths. But that's not why I'm here," Kelly confessed.

"Then why?"

"It's probably me being a little too gullible after all the nigh miracles I have come across these last few years," Kelly imparted then took a sip of wine, "But as you do in your universe, in my accident and emergency department we get all types of fruit cakes and nutters."

"Tell me about it. Our hospital is full of them. Especially at weekends," Keely empathetically smiled

"Well I'm scared. I had one patient in yesterday who not only knew me, knew about Danesh but could describe where we had been and how."

"You get some very clever mental patients." Keely was intrigued.

"This one knew far more than he could have even if he had broken into our house. He claimed to be from a parallel universe and said my life is in danger."

"Yes. Part of the job. I'm sure there is a lot of it he researched and filled in the blanks by creative thought. Kelly. I had one like that about ten years ago, may be less. He told me exactly the same thing. He was a tramp, a homeless guy, or so I thought. And he told me, or shrieked at me should I say, about how I travelled places I should not frequent and that my life was in danger. It was written in the rings of the Cosmos."

"Yes. He told me without prompting that I would come here, and you would tell me about him. Who is he?"

"Kelly. I don't know. An apparition? A ghost from the past or future?"

"Ghosts don't exist." Kelly stood up and looked at the screen on Keely's laptop. "Fuck! That's him! He's a fucking caveman from 50,000 years ago and dressed in gear not too unlike our modern hippie stuff. Not Danelaw's prehistoric clobber."

"Shit, Kelly! I never noticed that before. At first glance I thought he was just a caveman. I never looked closely at them. But when you do, you can make it out. You're right, it is modern gear he has on. Ironically not unlike caveman stuff, but modern nonetheless."

"Keely. I think we need to get info from as many parallel universes as we can. Methinks this tramp, caveman, knows a lot more than we do and we need to find all we can about this person. And rapidly. I think this being is a very dangerous individual. Or thing!"

PHILIPPA-NOVEMBER 1967

The undergraduate medical student skipped along to the John Radcliffe. She had now advanced six weeks into her university studies. The young red headed scholar intended this learning to lead to a Medicinae Baccalaureus, Baccalaureus Chirurgiae, BM BCh degree, a Bachelor of Medicine and Surgery. She felt energised in her black 1920s gangster moll style hat, a pink and grey long polo neck jumper, black short skirt and navy blue woollen tights.

"Miss Marchant," a student ran to catch up.

"Hi, Lizzie. Please call me Philippa or Pip. We're both female undergraduates so we have to stick together." Her fellow student was Elizabeth Perkins, Lizzie. Lizzie hailed from south Yorkshire and possessed a cheery disposition. She stood five feet tall and was a tad more on the plumper side than Lizzie herself would have preferred.

"That's lovely." Lizzie warmly smiled.

It was a bright autumn morning. The pathways were already partially covered by the detritus of fallen leaves and small branches. Lizzie donned spectacles, a long brown coat, blue tights and a pair of calf length leather boots. A couple of male students whistled at Philippa who overtly ignored them. A further pair of young men from their class altered direction to saunter behind the girls. One ran forward and nearly thrust his face into the young woman on the right.

"Lady Philippa Marchant. Will you take cocktails in my rooms tonight?"

"Mister Nigel Fenton," the debutante responded with no lack of insincerity.

The tall, handsome, slim figure before her strikingly reminded

Philippa of the former Manfred Mann singer, Paul Jones. Nonetheless she remained cool and aloof.

"Yes." Fenton almost panted with anticipation.

"I have been absent away from my domicile for a full two months now. I am so blatantly obviously craving for the delectations of your amazing physique. But alas my religion forbids such depraved acts of fornication. However, the gorgeous Miss Perkins is not hamstrung by such Biblical constraints and impediments. And even though she be a maid of the highest standing, she may entertain your invitation."

"Er, not at the moment. Come on Philippa. What's the harm in a little nocturnal relaxation? A little music, a little wine--," Fenton was stopped in mid flow by a determined riposte.

"You should have refrained from betting with the male undergrads you would bed me soon." Philippa coquettishly touched his chin. Very lightly and only momentarily. "As I said, Lizzie is available. Invite her, and I may come. Sorry, but no I won't. But you can still invite my friend."

The other undergraduate flashed a brief smile at Lizzie then immediately removed it when Fenton turned around. He was much shorter and stockier than his colleague with thin mousy hair that was combed forward. "Come on Puddy, let's go, these tarts aren't worth the effort."

The other student was Peter "Puddy" Edmonson. A thickset 18-year-old who did not consider himself to be good looking. Upon Fenton's request, he followed obsequiously along towards the main building of the university college.

"You're so confident with boys, Pip," Lizzie deferentially remarked, "I can't even get them to look at me. You toss them back like an angler with a small fish."

"You should be more self-assured, Miss Perkins." Philippa locked arms with Lizzie. "Even to get here. For any girl to get to this college is no mean feat. I can tell you now, Puddy fancies you but boys are not as mature as us girls. They're still at school. We've moved on. He'll only make a move when that cretin Nigel is not hovering and Nigel needs him for support."

"I never noticed." Lizzie looked up at the beaming face of her new friend.

"I did. And I shall try to sort you out with a date. Then it's down to you."

Radio One, the new station, was playing gently nearby. The song being The Foundations singing "Baby Now That I've Found You". As the girls neared the college office complex a stringy middle-aged administrator stepped out onto the walkway. The woman donned a wardrobe which would not have felt out of place in the 1930s. "Lady Philippa Marchant," the administrator called.

"That's me."

"Lady Philippa. There is a telephone call for you, it's in the office, I'll show you."

"Thank you. Lizzie, I'll catch you up. Unless you want to wait."

"I'll wait for you."

Philippa marched with purpose following the blandly attired woman.

They walked through reception and into a general office where she pointed to a telephone that was off the hook.

"Philippa Marchant speaking."

"Pip, it's Caroline. I hope it is not inconvenient." The voice at the other end of the line sounded distant.

"Of course not, Carol. I'm just on the way to a lecture. I have a few minutes to spare."

"You know you said you would drive me to David's memorial service in Edinburgh."

"I do recall. And will, if you still want me to."

"Pip, I know it's short notice but it's this Saturday. It's alright if you think I'm being beastly and inconsiderate."

"Not on the least, Carol. I'll just clear it with my lecturer. I'll drive up tonight."

"You're an angel. A real angel. See you tonight."

"Of course, Miss Marchant. I shall ensure we have time for a catch up session." Max Silver nodded in agreement. The short, slim and bald professor of preclinical medicine was more than willing to assist his most famous and adept student.

"Thank you, Professor Silver. I shall see you and the class on Tuesday morning." Philippa smiled and skipped off.

Stephen Grenfell

EMILY-NOVEMBER 1967

The pinstripe suited figure of Sir Philip Allen, Permanent Under Secretary at the Home Office, knocked and entered the plush and lavish décor endowed suite of the secretary of state.

"You asked to see me, Home Secretary." The short and grey haired 55-year-old civil service mandarin approached his political master.

The man in the chair was a nomad. A political nomad. The latest and soon to be former holder of one of the four high offices of state. There was to be a shuffle. "Or was it a reshuffle," Allen silently pondered. After which the current occupant would join a list of numerous professional politicians he had seen come and go as Home Secretary since he commenced his vocation in the mother of parliaments back in 1934. Such great days then, Allen thought. When Britannia truly ruled the waves and such a small nation controlled an empire that covered a quarter of the entire landmass of the globe. Much less so now. It was a mere residue. The territories now under the rule of the Crown were negligible when set against that formerly great domain. And yet, in only two weeks' time it would diminish to an even greater level of insignificance and attenuation when the ignoble withdrawal from the Crown Colony of Aden was completed.

"Yes, Sir Philip." the Home Secretary, the Right Honourable Roy Jenkins, sat in a leather bound armchair and puffed on a cigar. "I did. I received this report from MI5 who were given it from the Department of State in the USA. It appears veritable that the Americans know more about our security measures than we do."

"I take it, Home Secretary, that we are referring to an agent we code name Miss X?"

"Miss X! How truly old hat and very palpable for a code name. Who concocts such cognomen? Sir Philip." Jenkins spoke in a rich educated accent. Allen found it difficult to believe at times that the Home Secretary was a socialist. A champagne socialist was one uncomplimentary description used by opponents, referring to his attendance at Cardiff University and Balliol College, Oxford.

"Yes, Home Secretary."

"You and I are both aware that once the Aden withdrawal is out of the way there'll be a cabinet reshuffle. The old political Bradford Barn dance, or musical chairs if one prefers, will come into play. Accordingly, Jim Callaghan, I have been informed, will take over here and I'll be Chancellor."

"I have heard such speculation, Home Secretary."

"The Civil Service will forever retain that esoteric idiom that takes most a lifetime to decipher," Jenkins drew on his Cuban.

"Merely acting with some modicum of discretion, Home Secretary. And as you were operational at Bletchley Park for a while, you would break little perspiration in translation thereof."

Allen smiled and nodded.

"Yes, well. I don't want this to land cold on Jim's lap. Firstly, how secure is this?"

"No one, and I mean no one, apart from you, me, the Head of MI5 and MI6, the Prime Minister of course and some uppermost agents are even remotely cognisant of her very existence."

"How did we recruit such a talent? I'm surprised a QC would jeopardise her career by working for the intelligence services."

"According to the MI5 agents, who themselves masquerade as police officers, are actually police officers and MI5 personnel combined, Miss X is not sentient to the fact that she is employed by MI5. The lady in question deems herself merely a small-time observer. She thinks her job is solely to pass on minor snippets, minutia of intelligence, very clandestinely, to trusted police officers."

"How can we operate such deception? According to this report, which incidentally we only received thanks to our American cousins, in September she, a girl, killed a top Soviet spy.

The now deceased undercover agent was not some green, wet behind the ears recruit but from the highest level the KGB has. And this agent of ours slew the Russian with her bare hands. Certainly without a weapon. What can you tell me about this amazing lady? How did the Yanks know?"

"They have operatives called "moonlighters", Home Secretary. These are agents who do not go under cover as such but retain their own veritable identities and careers. However, when chance arises they will impart information to the secret service or be personally influential. I am reliably informed, Home Secretary, that the American operative is a trained assassin and was supposed to eliminate the Soviet spy before he accessed

Miss X. However, our daring British agent had already liquidated the Soviet asset by the time he arrived on the scene. One up for Her Majesty's Government. The American State Department was very impressed, very. She also brought information to the fore that was crucial in detecting and arresting Warsaw Pact, Communist and militant trade union activity in London set on disrupting the UK economy. And that was only a week ago. A very competent young woman."

Jenkins stood up and gazed across Whitehall. "Give me a brief resume of this lady, Miss X. Then tell me how impressed LBJ and his administration were with her. She gives the impression of one with no small measure of savoir faire, I can attest to being at the zenith of amazement."

"Glad to have you back Emily." Gerald Crawley entered Emily's new private office aside the meeting room of the chambers. He seemed bereft of any formalities such as asking her new secretary, Hazel Brown, whether or not she was available,

"All hell seems to have erupted onto the scene."

"How so, sir? I was only taking a long week end back home." Emily looked up from the pile of envelope folders. Each one contained details of a new case.

"We had a bit of a disaster. Gill was arrested on Friday night. Maybe under the new Criminal Law Act just given the Royal Assent. The very one upon which the ink has barely dried on the Queen's signature.

"Good grief. I was about to tell you what a great time I had with my parents in Oxfordshire. I come back after a break of five days to a new office, a new secretary and one of our lawyers has been arrested. Specifically. What are the charges?"

"The police say she could also be charged under the Espionage Act of 1911. Mark is trying to see her. It seems as if there were a fair number of trade unionists, Russians, and left-wing activists somewhere. Allegedly plotting something. She lodged with you. Did you notice anything?"

"No, of course not." Emily lied convincingly.

Crawley shuffled around for a while, blatantly uncomfortable, fidgeting yet anxious to impart some momentous herald.

"Sir. Is there something else?" Emily was becoming unsettled by his gesticulations.

"I would like to have dinner with you. After work. A proper dinner."

"Sir, we can have dinner or lunch anytime providing it is to do with the business of the chambers."

"I had thought of something a little more exclusive. A quiet restaurant in a less well frequented part of the West End."

Emily looked up at her boss. Although he was in good condition aesthetically, and seemed so physically, he was nonetheless 47 years old.

"Mister Crawley---."

"Please call me, Gerry."

"Gerry, I am so flattered. I was approached by men in New York. And back here. I am filled with regret to decline. But I must. That is not to convey anything is amiss with you. There is absolutely not. I am staying faithful to James. And please do not think badly of my declination. I have turned down pop stars, film stars, artists, journalists and even budding politicians and I would rather have gone out with you than any of them."

"I am flattered." Crawley smiled. "And if you change your mind--."

"Of course. However, James is due back from Aden in a few weeks' time."

The telephone rang, she picked up the handset.

"Is that Miss Emily Wilkinson?"

"Andy!" She exclaimed. Immediately recognising the New York tonal vibrations at the other end.

Gerald smiled uncomfortably and left.

"Hi, Miss Wilkinson. I know you've just got back from a weekend with the folks. But my second boss, apart from God, you know who I'm talkin' about, and he wants us to meet up. Just briefly. As I'm coming to London to view a fashion show for Helen."

"I'll see you soon, Big Boy," Emily joked, something that Crawley, hovering nearby heard also.

The phone rang again, this time it was John Robinson.

"Sergeant. You have a mountain of explaining to do."

DANIEL-NOVEMBER 1967

"What would you like for luncheon, sir?" The young steward asked Daniel as he and James took seats on a table together.

"I'll have a cold beer and fish and chips," Daniel wearily replied.

"I'll have the same." James nodded at the steward.

"Shit, James. We've been in this hole of a place five months. It seems more like five years."

"It's alright, Daniel. Just another three weeks and we can kiss goodbye to it forever."

The surroundings of the temporary officers' mess in Tawahi were somewhat sparse. In fact, it was merely a large tent with several tables and chairs, suffice to seat the 40 or so officers of the commando. Lieutenant Bowman entered the mess,

"Marchant and Gibson. Got nothing better to do than to lounge in the mess?"

"Yes, Lieutenant. Such a pastime we plucked from your routine."

"Speak with some decorum to a senior officer," Anthony Bowman snarled at the same moment Major Peter Adams walked into the mess.

The steward marched from the bar area with two glasses of lager beer and placed them on coasters in front of the two junior subalterns.

"Mister Gibson, Mister Marchant. The CO wants to see you. He's having some scran right now. Make it in fifteen minutes. Tops." Adams then marched off.

Once the two young men had demolished their lunches they replaced their green berets over their short-cropped hair and set off at pace.

The adjutant, 27-year-old Captain Ben Vickery, was outside Owen's room reading some papers as the two briskly entered.

"Sir!" they both came to attention. "Our OC, Major Adams, informs us that Lieutenant Colonel Owen wished to see us."

"I know who your OC is Mister Gibson. Just knock and the CO should bid you entry." Vickery pointed at the cheap looking green wooden door with a small opaque glass window on the upper part.

James duly tapped and a voice from within boomed, "Come!"

They entered, came to a halt then brought their feet down to attention.

"Sir. Second Lieutenant Gibson and Second Lieutenant Marchant to see you. Sir!"

"Relax, Daniel. You too, James. It's not a bollocking. You're not in the rattle," the 45-year-old imposing figure quietly revealed, "I've good news for you. You're both being jacked up to full lieutenant. Effective immediately. The paperwork has gone through.

I was told you two and the late Mister Moir were called the "Three Musketeers". I'm sure you were wingers, very close. But death is an occupational hazard in the Corps. Otherwise few of us would have joined. Mister Moir would also have been made up by the extra pip. All three of you have acquitted yourselves in the most exemplary fashion, in the true ethos and spirit of the Corps. The extra salary, paid before Christmas, will at least be enough to buy a round of drinks in honour of those two great men now in Silent Valley."

"Thank you, sir," the young men responded in complete synchronisation.

"Now buzz off, I have to arrange our withdrawal from this God forsaken place!"

Outside Captain Vickery watched the newly promoted officers emerge, "Congratulations gentlemen! However, that's as senior as you'll get Lieutenant Gibson as you're on a short service commission. On the other hand, Lieutenant Marchant being a 12-year man will certainly make at least Captain. Mister Gibson, are you having second thoughts?"

"No, sir, three years in the Corps then university. A short service commission is perfect."

"You still have almost two years to serve. That's plenty of time for a change of heart. And although it makes Fanny Adams difference to us, the National Liberation Front have finally defeated the Front for The Liberation of Occupied South Yemen. It was announced on the seventh of November. I'm glad we kept well out of their little internal squabble. It seems an independent Aden will be ruled by the NLF, not FLOSY. Plus, the Soviets."

"Sir." Daniel approached Vickery.

"Yes, Lieutenant Gibson?"

"Sir. Any chance we could do a sortie over to Silent Valley before we bug out?"

"Not a hope," the adjutant responded with forethought, "The gollies have control of the entire colony bar the Aden peninsula and Sheikh Othman. We couldn't risk it even if they would allow us in. Lieutenant, we've all lost wingers, close wingers. Make a pledge to Mister Moir's memory, an undertaking to make a pilgrimage back here with your children or grandchildren, once all this shit has blown over. You can do it in 30 years or so."

As Daniel and James neared the former family flat that served as their accommodation, Sergeant Helm approached.

"Post for Mister Gibson. A letter from a lady back home for the young second lieutenant."

"It's Lieutenant Gibson now, Sergeant. And thank you for delivering mail."

"No problem, sir. And congratulations on your well-deserved promotion."

"I might as well write a letter to Emily, not much for us to do here," James muttered. He was looking over Tawahi at the distinctive jungle green uniforms of Royal Marines from 42 Commando who were patrolling the streets.

At that point, and well above the subalterns, two Sea Vixen fighters with their unmistakable twin booms flew with an ear-splitting clamour. The aircraft were part of the Royal Navy's 899 Squadron, based on the nearby carrier HMS Eagle. An element of the reinforcements allocated to oversee the withdrawal.

"We've done our bit, and a lot more," Daniel talked over the afterburner noise of the jets, "You write to Emily. I'll read this masterpiece from Carol and we can discuss our options once we get out of this place."

"We gotta get out of this place!" they both crooned the chorus of the summer of 1965 hit for The Animals.

DANESH AND KELLY

Kelly landed PADIT in its usual spot in the large garage of Danesh's Nazeing property. A picturesque location down a remote lane in the glen that straddled the Lea Navigation waterway.

She was irritated, anxious, depressed and uncomfortable. These sentiments were exacerbated by the veracity that she needed to uncover more, so much more and with, or without, her doppelganger, or doppelgangers. It was an acute, nigh existential, conundrum which required hasty resolution.

The young physician burst unceremoniously into the secluded, laboratory void of a single inkling to announce her entrance.

Danesh had been noticeable by his prolonged absence of late. On sudden appearance he was tapping calculations into his laptop and making manual notes on a pad.

"Prof. We, I, need to do some rapid research," she blurted out then began to weep a little.

"Hey, Doc." Danesh came to his feet. "What's up?"

She recounted the anecdote about the man in the A and E who warned her of death. And who also appeared as a caveman on Keely's Ice Age video.

It was not to the best timing and taste that Danesh was listening to Luke Kelly singing "The Unquiet Grave."

"Switch that shit off!" Kelly growled which he instantly obliged.

"Prof. You have a lot of loose ends. I want to know more, more about other PUs."

"Calm down." He handed her a glass of whiskey.

"Now, Doctor Aresti. Let me know what irks thee. Surely it cannot be the video of a caveman who looks like a patient you treated."

"Fate is fixed! I'm scared. I don't know what to do. It's like the spectre of death has played a macabre round of dice for my soul and I came second."

"I think both of us need to sit back take a breath and focus. After all you see and hear in the course of your work, this seems a tad akin to hyperbole. Let's discuss."

Kelly walked from her car towards her door. A relatively inexpensive flat in the village of Stanstead Abbot. An exclusive area in Hartfordshire where she could secrete away from the world. Including and especially from Danesh.

"Doctor Aresti." The figure in the shadows approached. "You are disquieted and acutely so."

She recognised the voice of her recent patient prior to distinguishing the features. "What the fuck do you want? I have a pepper spray. I'll call the police!"

"Doctor. I have no impairment or mischief aforethought. I too am in a maelstrom of obfuscated cynicism. I have travelled a mysterious path and am still on the journey. I pray you afford me a small portion of your extraordinarily valuable moments."

"Keep your distance! Keep at least 20 feet away from me. Stand back. A long way, and I'll let you in. But I'm ringing 999 if you come anywhere near to me. Understand?"

Kelly could sense an odour, something sweet and putrid. It reminded her of a bloodstained shirt that has not related to soap or water for countless months. Penurious. Yet captivating some charismatic, atypical attribute.

"Of course. I hold a requirement to converse with thee. We share a requirement for edification in such aberrant matters. Those that dwell awkwardly betwixt and between the light of rationality and the dark of the subterranean caverns between existence and that which lies beyond reality."

"Are you a ghoul? A zombie? A ghost?" Kelly's agitation ebbed by a diminutive notch.

"Nay, perhaps yeah. I am solicitous to extrude much and many arcane, esoteric details to you and your kindred throughout the infinite web my peripatetic existence hath cast my way. I beg thee dear lady, permit me counsel."

"Shit. You're not from around here with a vocabulary like that. I'll open the door and walk inside and then I'll turn on the lights. When I call, you will enter and sit precisely where I say. I shall call the police immediately you do not conform. Am I clear?"

"You could nay be further lucid," the balding, bearded, pallid man responded.

PHILIPPA-NOVEMBER 1967

The Mini turned off the road from Hitchin in Hertfordshire and onto the A1 near Stevenage.

"Pip, we'll have to stay overnight somewhere. We'll never make Edinburgh by tonight." Caroline looked out of the car window at the exterior crisp autumn scenery bestriding the highway that connected the capitals of Scotland and England.

"Whatever you want." Philippa handed Caroline a packet of Dunhill cigarettes. "Light us both one."

Once onto the main carriageway, Philippa pressed down the accelerator then tuned the car wireless to Radio One. It was playing the Troggs with their gentle hit song "Love Is All Around."

"This will be a traumatic ordeal for you, Carol. Are you prepared for such a bummer?"

Caroline smiled at her friend. "You're such a beautiful person, Pip. I'll never be prepared for this, but I'll cope much better with you beside me."

"You're far too kind. And we don't need to scrimp on the hotel. Daddy, always Daddy, gave me 100 pounds to cover all and any expenses."

"Crikey, Pip. We could buy an actual hotel for that. What does the earl think we are going to get up to?"

"Daddy always says it is better to take more money than you need and bring some back than find you are financially embarrassed." Philippa slowed down as the traffic flow became more congested ahead of them.

Simon Dee, the DJ on the radio announced that the next song would be "San Franciscan Nights" by Eric Burdon and the Animals.

"It's 12.30 pm." Caroline looked at her wrist watch. "It's about 370 miles, probably more, to Edinburgh from Hertfordshire. It'll be dark well before five o'clock. Perhaps we can stay overnight in York?"

"We go where you want," Philippa lightly responded, "We'll eat somewhere first. Unless you would prefer the packed meal that Becky made up for us. I can't drink alcohol until tonight. Daddy says that this new breathalyser law, put in by that dreaded transport minister, has scuppered all that."

"Barbara Castle." Caroline jogged Philippa's memory.

"Yes, her. Well Daddy says not to drink when driving. Even a glass of champers."

"Pip, that's fine. I'll not drink either. And personally, I would much prefer Becky's homemade delights to a pub lunch. She's a wizard cook."

The next morning they viewed the façade of the Grand Hotel in central York. Caroline seemed to have descended into a cavernous, sombre disposition. She stared emptily at the outer walls of the Georgian period stone construction.

"Hey." Philippa hugged her. "It's going to be fine. Get into the car. It's at least four hours to Edinburgh and I hope you know where to go."

Caroline was silent for a few seconds, chewed briefly on her long blonde locks then gave her friend a forced smile. "I have directions. We need to keep on the A1 road though."

"Hop in. I'll have to get petrol at the first garage we come to. Let's go. The service is tomorrow so we'll have to depart now, or we'll not get there in time."

Philippa turned on the radio to Donovan singing "There Is A Mountain", checked to ensure no cars were near, turned on the engine, put the Mini into first gear and they were off.

All the way up through Yorkshire, Durham and Northumberland the A1 highway boasted magnificent views. Apart from the requirement of absolute concentration as Philippa negotiated the transit across Gateshead and Newcastle across the magnificent Tyne Bridge.

The city centre traffic was kind to them and within 20 minutes the green countryside of Northumberland opened out.

"It's really groovy," Caroline commented on the landscape whilst singing along to the Dave Clarke Five performing "Everybody Knows."

"Hey, light up a ciggie for both of us, Carol."

Caroline pressed in the car lighter then removed two Rothmans King Size from her silver cigarette case. She lit one and handed it to Philippa then another for herself.

"Do you know Daniel? James' friend." Caroline asked as she turned up the radio to the song "Autumn Almanac" by the Kinks.

"Of course." Philippa sounded insulted that such an obvious query had even been posed.

"Why?"

"Just a thought, he lives half way up Northumberland, on the way back we can drop into his farm, visit his parents," Caroline cast Philippa a conniving smile.

"You mean check him out?"

"Yes. But I know you don't fancy him. Sorry. A bummer of an idea. I'm kinda freaky right now and hacked off with all the aggro. Sorry."

"Carol, space out. It's cool and a groovy idea and so bad. I don't mind Daniel. In fact, I like him a lot and perhaps if my future was not already determined things may be different."

"Pip. One thing you gotta do, being one bright wholesome chick. You gotta do your own scene. Not what you think it should be but what you want. No one else. It's your life."

"Ok." Philippa listened for a few seconds as the next release by the Beatles, due out in a fortnight from then, "Hello Goodbye", was played on the radio. "Just one hitch in your romantic scheming stratagems. Which is before you ask. According to James he has a woman and they are very serious. Almost hitched."

"Get real Pip. How many times have we heard that over the last few years? Whatever. Let's just pop in and introduce ourselves. We'll see how together Daniel and his love really are."

"Great idea. You're one wholesome chick yourself. We'll drop in on the way home. Now where do we have to go?"

"Follow the A1 right into Edinburgh. It's a way to go. As yet we haven't even reached Alnwick. But once we get to Edinburgh city centre on the A1 we turn onto the A7. We stay there as far as Melville Drive on the A700 and we head for an area called Marchmont. Their house is 24, Warrender Park Road."

"Best let me know nearer the time." Philippa mused contemplatively.

EMILY NOVEMBER 1967

"That is one amazing woman, and so young," Roy Jenkins commented after Sir Philip Allen had completed a short biograph. He next looked at the photograph that had appeared in Cosmopolitan. "And such a good looking young filly."

"Home Secretary." Sir Philip continued. "Miss X is an asset for investment. A clandestine weapon to unleash as and when the occasion demands. But her very existence must be held within the highest level of classification, even more surreptitious than the United Kingdom's nuclear code. She is capable, ultra-capable. An infinite scope for utilisation."

"Quite so, Sir Philip, quite so."

"Mark." Emily walked into the office of her colleague. "What's up with Gill? What charges have been brought?"

"Espionage under the 1911 act. I spoke with her in Holloway Prison. The police and MI5, I think, swooped on a place that was being used for a meeting, they say, of people involved in subversive activities. Apparently plotting against the state and a host of other allegations."

"Anything I can do?"

"Not really, Emily. But thanks for the offer, we are already compiling the defence case. John and Paul have covered most of the nitty gritty."

Emily checked with her own team. Luckily it seemed that for the next two days only minor cases were being heard.

It was back in her office when her secretary rang to say that a Mister Downs was on the phone.

"Yes, Andy." She almost giggled down the telephone.

"Emily. I hope you can make dinner tonight. I've booked a table for us in Leicester Square and we can see a show if you want."

"Dinner is fine, Andy. Early if possible. I want to catch up on some sleep. We have a lot of new cases coming in. Shall we say that you collect me from the chambers at seven?"

"You're some woman. See you at seven. I'll collect you and pay for a taxi to run you to wherever you live." "No need for that. But to Liverpool Street Station will be a godsend."

"You're on, honey."

In the quiet pub Emily was none too amused.

"Sergeant Robinson. Can you tell me what the fuck is going on? I thought you, me, were going to observe Gill. Not arrest her?"

In her normal pinstripe skirt and jacket and blonde hair up at the back, Robinson thought she looked even more foreboding. Conversely more alluring.

"Look at me, Sergeant, not at my chest. I'm not some dolly bird WPC you can smack on the arse when you feel a tad horny or grope in the stationery cupboard. I may be a blonde, and in a lot of guy's eyes that is a synonym for stupid, but best you don't make that mistake. At least not with me!"

Robinson was dumbstruck. Women, including those highly educated such as the young QC, were rarely so feisty. At least not with a police officer. "I never took you as an idiot, Miss Wilkinson. We did as you suggested."

"Which was?"

"We sent an agent into the meeting and it was not good." Robinson quietly unfolded. "The situation was way advanced. Your colleague, Beata Halmi or you would know her as Gill McMenemy, had already processed extreme activists to infiltrate trade unions. And worse the Soviets had well advanced plans to radicalise students across the country. Do you know anything about the war in Vietnam?"

"Not much about the military strategy or politics but it's becoming one faux pas. I know it's growing in unpopularity."

"It's probably too late to prevent as Soviet and North Vietnamese agents are either in, or about to be embedded in the UK students' unions. Besides that, they are targeting our military and security establishments for intelligence. The Viet Cong can never defeat the Americans militarily. But if they turn the heat on with demos and civil unrest to a massive crescendo across the world, President Johnson will have no option but to withdraw. Even perhaps with some shallow face-saving option and ultimate loss of the presidential election next year.

The North Vietnamese want to win the war and the Soviets want to humiliate the United States. The ramifications of which could resound for 20 years, or much more. We found a load of activists at their second meeting. We knew what they were up to and had to move. We brought trusted cops, agents and troops then poured in and arrested them. Although, apart from your workmate, it's a bit of "after the horse has bolted" syndrome. Wilson slapped "D" notices on all newspapers to stop them reporting the raid. But we'll have to charge them with something. Perhaps exchange a few with the Ruskies. Our prime minister will not openly back the Yanks in Vietnam but in private he'll support them with all but direct military involvement. He refused to partake in the war last year. I could not tell you earlier. Even though you have friends in very high places, this op had to be kept secret. And still is. We're still checking on Al Asnag, former leader of FLOSY in Aden who is now operating in London. His brother is in prison here now. You came across that info for us. There you know all now."

"What do mean I have friends in high places?"

"Nothing. Just bear it in mind that you have a lot of support. There are many battles to be waged and we are symbiotic with other agencies. Keep low for a while. I mean just stick to your normal day job. I shall contact you in due course."

Emily took her leave from the police officer and left the pub whilst being totally cognisant of the fact that someone was watching her. She dispassionately moved on.

DANIEL/JAMES-NOVEMBER 1967

17, The Butts
Warkworth
Morpeth
Northumberland
England
Wednesday, 1ˢᵗ November 1967

Dear Daniel,

I'm at university now and it's not cool to have a soldier as a boyfriend. So I'm sorry, all has changed, we're over. I hope you do not think me beastly. Well if you do it's too bad.

Carol

"The bitch," Daniel called out.

"What's up?" James looked up from his composing of yet another epistle of adoration to Emily.

"Nothing." His colleague jumped up and lit a cigarette. He grabbed his rifle before placing on his green beret before storming out of the flat that was their barracks.

The view from Tawahi was much more urban than that of Little Aden. And although no shooting had been heard for a few days, the clinical and ebullient patrols of Royal Marines from 42 Commando still doggedly marched through the dusty, detritus strewn streets. They were counting down the hours until the final withdrawal.

"Release Me" by Engelbert Humperdinck was heard from somewhere just as a Hawker Hunter flew passed in a deafening, thundering cacophony. Out in the Gulf of Aden there had been a steady build-up of the Soviet fleet in anticipation of the British leaving. Although for now they remained for now well outside the colony's territorial waters.

"Fuck," Daniel muttered as Sergeant Helm approached. Somewhere, not too distant from where he stood, soldiers of the 1st Battalion Argyll and Sutherland Highlanders were canorously singing a stirring refrain from their homeland as they worked away, their spirits obviously lifted by the nearing departure.

"Ye look steeped in melancholy, sir," Helm observed. As always, his uniform was immaculate. The green beret stood on his head. Straight. The cap badge perfectly positioned directly above the left eye as if ordained by divine preference. "Is it the Jocks singing, sir. They actually sound quite harmonious. Not like when they've had a dram or two. Nice song, sir."

"It is, Sergeant Helm. It's called "Wild Mountain Thyme"." Daniel looked up and drank in the scenery and the pleasant voices. "It was written by an Irish Scot called Francis McPeake but based on an old Scottish folk song called "The Braes of Balquhither". Now that you are suitably educated, Sergeant, what can I do for you?"

"The men await orders, sir. Rooms, rifles, kit, cleaned many times over. Are we due out on patrol?"

"I doubt it. The CO wants no more of 45 in Silent Valley. Tomorrow we'll take up safe defensive positions near the airport. To cover other units as they depart. The Argylls are being evacuated three days before us. Other are leaving sooner. We have to cover the Crater to RAF Khormaksar road. It should be a change at least."

"I still think our troop officer is unsettled, sir."

"Sergeant, you are either very perceptive or just downright nosy. But yes. I did get a Dear John letter from my long-time girlfriend. It seems it's not cool for girls at university to go out with military guys of any service."

Helm screwed his face a little then smirked.

"You must send an apt riposte, as you young officers would say, sir. Wait a moment if you would be so kind, sir. I'll be back in a jiffy."

The straight figure of the senior NCO marched down the pathway of the block of flats. Used until the September just gone by families of married soldiers.

The balding, erect figure marched faultlessly and directly into a large, smoke filled lounge utilised by the men of his troop for relaxation and listening to music. The Traffic song "Hole in My Shoe" was playing.

"Ten-hun!" Corporal Ely called out and all the loafing Marines jumped to their feet.

"Men," Helm called out in his powerful, commanding tones, "Two things then you can return to ya wanking and smoking. First, tomorrow we're off to cover the road from Crater to the airport. Just watching, no shooting. Second. One of my buddies 'as 'ad a Dear John letter. So, I'd be grateful, and won't forget the sentiment, if any of ya can give me any spare photos ya might 'ave of girlfriends, wives or lovers."

Within minutes Sergeant Helm had returned to Daniel. The new lieutenant was deeply inhaling smoke from a cigarette and gazing over the bay from outside the officers' quarters.

"Here, sir." Helm handed Daniel a wad of about 20 snapshots. They were without exception poses of pretty girls in attire that ranged from fully clothed through various levels of dishabille to nigh on naked. The subaltern looked through them with obvious interest.

"What are these for, Sergeant?"

"The best reply to a Dear John, sir. Boys get 'em every week. Ya put these photos in a letter which says, sir, "Dear", whatever ya ex lady's name is, "thanks for your letter of such and such but I've no fucking idea who you are. Please identify from the enclosed snapshots". It won't get 'er back, sir, but it'll really piss her off."

"Thanks, Sergeant. I'll do that. Thank you."

"I can't do such a thing." Daniel had had a change of heart. "Would you do that to Emily?"

"She would never have sent me a shit note like. Certainly not whilst I was away fighting. But if she had, sure. I would send her a load of photos of strange, unclothed women. Sergeant Helm is a very astute man, send them, today. With a covering letter and then let's have a couple in the mess."

"James. What gripe has Bowman got with you?"

"A long story. I went to school with the dipstick. Gave him a couple of bloody noses. Papa helped out his dad and the father of Philippa's intended. I guess he resents that."

A knock came to the door. A baby faced, dark haired and slim second lieutenant sheepishly entered.

"Who the fuck are you?" James harshly growled.

"Sorry, sir. I'm Second Lieutenant Matthew Field. Just passed out of Lympstone. I'm replacing a casualty. I'm told here's where the action is."

"You're three months late, Second Lieutenant!" Daniel angrily snapped. "There's spare room in the next cabin. And you're not replacing a casualty, it was a man! An officer! A brilliant officer! A fucking great officer and man! We've enough gash and gobshites. We don't need any more wet behind the ears yoyos!"

"Yes, sir. Sorry, sir." Field rapidly retreated from the verbal onslaught

DANESH AND KELLY

The small, dishevelled, balding, unkempt figure nervously followed Kelly into the kitchen of her flat. Once she had motioned, he took a seat on a wooden chair.

The man was almost shaking with apprehension. However, a stirring inkling inside her indicated that his demeanour was simply theatrics. At that juncture, a gleam of pity descended from the young physician.

"Have you eaten? Would you like some food?"

"A crust of bread and a glass of water would be appreciated, Doctor, thank you."

"I'm hungry so I'll make a fry up of egg, sausage, chips, beans and fresh bread. Firstly, I'll put the kettle on."

Once they had eaten Kelly opened a bottle of beer and handed it to her enigmatic guest,

"Now, who are you, and why do you keep popping up?"

"My name is Professor Grant Woburn. At least that's how I am known to most. I worked in a particle collider, the Hadron Machine in Swissland in the earlier civilisation. The society that you know as being of Tariq Hussein and Danelaw Gidron. It lies on the chronology highway about 50,000 years back from this era. And there was even another even antecedent to that."

"How do you know so much about Danelaw and Tariq?" Kelly glared at Woburn.

"We worked on a parallel project. I worked the same undertaking with your own lover. But in another dimension."

"You look like a bag of shit tied up in the middle. What's your story? So far it sounds a little, more than a little, concocted from the realms of Douglas Adams or Arthur C. Clarke." Kelly maintained a piercing glower on her guest. "All scientists can waffle on and embellish. At least all the ones I have encountered in this world and other universes. What's so different about you? Professor."

"The Large Hadron Collider in Swissland. That is the divergence. Doctor."

"I've heard of the LHD. You say there was one 50,000 years ago?"

"Indeed, there was. Doctor Aresti. However, I ventured over proximate to the proton beams in full acceleration. Being engrossed in my work, too engrossed, I slipped accidentally but directly into their path. It transpired to be a mere microsecond before it was boosted to full power. I was blasted by, protons, anti-matter and what you have called the Higgs boson particle."

Kelly looked again at the pitiful specimen before her. "What on earth happened?"

"I wander in a scientific version of Purgatory. Doctor. My body matter modified. Although I am not a supernatural entity as I bow to the Laws of the Universe, nonetheless, someone such as you requires a PADIT to voyage to another universe. Using the faculties and powers inherited from my impact with the LHD, I can convoy by thought process or other command. I can travel through space, time and objects. I have observed all peoples in all universes from the dawn to dusk of time., I am with sapience of all the secrets of the Cosmos. In some planets of certain universes, I am worshipped as a deity. Whereas amongst other commonwealths I am feared and detested. The Collider bequeathed me powers beyond comprehension. I can cure, kill, disappear, fly, transform. That is how I can tell you the date of your death. Doctor. You are strongly counselled to exercise the ultimate in vigilance. Dire peril stalks each petite step you make in all universes. I may be with the capacity to offer relief to your unholy predicament."

PHILIPPA-NOVEMBER 1967

The sound of Felice Taylor singing "I Feel Love Coming On" came from the car radio. The accelerator pedal was pressed well down as the Mini moved hastily. Philippa was driving along the A1 main road through the Scottish county of East Lothian. Caroline had fallen asleep on the front passenger side. Philippa decided against waking her as perhaps she may have enjoyed too few trips of late to the Land of Morpheus. The medical undergraduate admired the stunning scenery as the town of Musselburgh was sign posted. She knew that the capital of Scotland lay just beyond that locality. It took less than three quarters of an hour to reach their destination. Philippa was pleased with her navigation skills as the car stopped outside the magnificent and massive, stone-built town house that was 24 Warrender Park Road. A property within the desirable Marchmont area of Edinburgh. She switched off Gene Pitney singing "Something's Gotta Hold of My Heart", before killing the engine.

Philippa quietly removed their suitcases from the boot of the red Austin Mini as Caroline woke up. "Pip!" The slumbering passenger jolted back into consciousness. "Are we here?"

Yes. Today you meet Mr and Mrs Moir. This will be a somewhat atypical initial encounter."

"Pip. I'm scared."

"I know, Carol. Let's just go as the Bard said, "Once more to the breach". All will be well."

The two girls, suitcases in hand, moved slowly up the path to the large oak front door of the imposing construction.

Philippa pressed the bell button and within a few moments the door opened.

A woman stood just within the entrance. She was about 45 years old, round faced with brown that betrayed a hint of grey. She was stout without being overweight and dressed in conservative blouse, cardigan and Maroon tartan skirt.

"Come." She beckoned upon which Philippa and Caroline nervously acquiesced.

"I'm Maura Moir. My husband will be present shortly." The soft Scottish accent reminded Caroline immediately of David.

"I'm Caroline--," was all that was managed before the young woman burst into tears and threw her arms around the older woman who happily reciprocated.

"My, my me wee lamb. I know who you are and you're just as pretty as David said. It's sad for all of us, my wee lassie. Let's get ye sorted out first. We can chat more in a moment. I'll show ye to your room."

"I'm Philippa Marchant." Pip held out her hand, which was accepted by Maura Moir. "James' sister. David was very close to him and another young officer from Northumberland, Daniel."

As Philippa affirmed this simple fact she perceived written on the kind face the understandable stress and despondency of recent weeks.

"Yes. Yes. James and Daniel. That's right. Now let me show you to your room"

They walked up the stairs. The décor of wood panelling, thick carpets, exquisite and unusual ornaments and bright paintings was impressive. Notwithstanding, the atmosphere was laden with melancholy.

"The guest bathroom be over here. Ladies. Freshen up and we'll have afternoon tea in half an hour. We need to go over tomorrow's arrangements."

EMILY-NOVEMBER 1967

The "Groovy Scene" restaurant was a totally new 60s happening in London. It was also the venue for Andy and Emily's first meeting since she had left New York.

"What can I get for you?" The young waitress buoyantly enquired. She was bedecked in a mock Guards tunic with a small representation of a bearskin hat, black miniskirt and calf length boots.

"A gin and tonic to start with. I'll only be a short while." Emily smiled at Andy.

"Why the rush my azure eyed Limey lady?" Andy was bemused and a tad disappointed.

"Surprise." She winked at him, her blue eyes smiling. "Now, Andy. Tell me about this Soviet agent we bumped off in New York. Who was he?"

"Vladimir Gerasimov. A top assassin from the KGB and you eliminated him all by yourself. Our mole in the KGB tells us that the Soviets believe that a top US assassin ambushed him. That was after you had lured him to your room. The mole told them our version, the correct one. He claimed he had intercepted a CIA coded despatch. He informed the KGB, but they did not buy it. Even Communists can't believe a woman could be capable of killing a top assassin. Let alone without a weapon. Naturally huge and thanks have showered from President Johnson. I say again lady, you have friends in high places. This has thrown the proverbial cat among the pigeons as far as Kremlin agents in the US goes. They're all shit scared."

Emily stood up and looked around the establishment.

"Andy. We shall chat much tomorrow. I am going to make a couple of phone calls. Order yourself a drink and another G and T."

Two minutes later Emily had returned. Before Andy had even had the opportunity to continue his discourse, the tall, dark haired, suited figure of Mark Carlisle walked into the restaurant.

Emily walked over to Andy whilst Mark nervously waited in the entrance forum. She whispered to him,

"A friend from the chambers. I have to go. But don't forget, Andy, if you two hit it off it's legal here now. Providing that you are both over 21, consenting and discreet. He knows nothing about yours or my moonlighting. He's a QC."

"Mark." Emily strode over to her colleague and kissed him on the cheek. "Come and meet Andy, Andy Downs from the New York office of Cosmopolitan. Andy, this is Mark. I must shoot off, but I think Mark, being an intelligent man, will provide you with top class entertainment. Goodnight darlings. Have fun."

She checked around the street and almost sprinted to her car. The distance to Broxbourne from her workplace measured no more than 24 miles. Nonetheless, in the morning, it was far less aggravation to walk to the station for the early train to Liverpool Street than drive. However, on this day, perhaps it was the arrival of Andy, Emily was in a mood to be immodest. She had driven her new Triumph TR4 Sports car from her home and parked the shining red, two-seater convertible in her personal spot nearby the chambers.

"Might as well do something with the money I earned in New York. And this baby can move." She playfully muttered whilst opening the door and almost leaping into the front seat.

The radio played "Light My Fire" by the Doors. She prevaricated a while. The map was checked by torchlight, as she planned her route. Within a minute the barrister took off. Emily was barely pressing on the accelerator as the sports car almost flew along High Holborn before turning north. A set of headlights seemed to be on her tail at every turning, roundabout and set of traffic lights. She smiled and listened to an old Rolling Stones' song, "Under My Thumb" from the 1966 Aftermath album.

Emily checked her rear-view mirror as the vehicle kept up its pursuit.

"Don't know who you are but you'd better be fast." She smiled at the opaque outline behind the headlights.

Almost keeping within the legal speed limits, Emily joined the A10 near Tottenham. She monetarily debated with herself before resolving to negotiate a scenic detour around the narrow back roads of rural Hertfordshire. She esteemed somewhat cannily that the vehicle on her tail was also of high performance.

Accordingly, circumspection was deemed to be of paramount import.

DANIEL/JAMES-NOVEMBER 1967

The order had been given. "Only equipment that can be carried will be taken. The rest will be left to rot in the sands of the soon to be former British colony."

Daniel was irritated. He commanded a guard detail comprised of some of his troop. As he stood with his men he was aware that time was not moving with suffice rapidity. His impatience was growing. The mission of the British forces in that part of the Middle East was almost complete.

Now all he wished for now was to remain alive until he and his men finally withdrew from Aden. That operation was planned for lunchtime on the following Wednesday, the 29th of November. He smoked a cigarette. Daniel was anxiously awaiting the return of his section size force from their final mandatory patrol. This duty was executed on the streets of Tawahi alongside Royal Marines of 42 Commando. The SLR rifle felt uneasy in his grip and he scanned the horizon from the small, concrete observation post he shared with Marine Stephen Dixon.

The dull sound of approaching footsteps was clearly perceived. The perpetrator masked by an RM Land Rover parked nearby.

"Waqqif willa ootliq an-naar!" Daniel had his rifle in the firing stance. The safety catch was off.

"Sir! Nice bit of Arabic, sir. I've halted as ya asked so don't shoot. Please. Sir."

"Sergeant Helm." Daniel was visibly relieved. "I'm a bit jumpy."

"Sir. Take the Rover back t' the base. I'll watch here. Our guys are comin' back now."

Daniel ruminated for a few moments. The last few weeks had been nothing short of nerve demolishing and an hour's respite would be welcome.

"Fine. All is quiet, Sergeant. I'll be back in an hour."

Daniel marched into the officers' mess to find James and Niall were having a coffee, reading newspapers and smoking cheap Royal Navy "blue line" duty free cigarettes.

"Dan," Niall called out in his Dublin brogue, "All quiet on the Western Front?"

"Like a mausoleum," Daniel responded and ordered coffee from the steward, "Too much so. I just want to get out of here."

"Only another week. The Arabs won't try anything again with all the firepower we have in town." James grinned. "That new yoyo, Field. He's out on foot patrol with Ser'nt Baker."

"The sergeant will take care of him." Daniel nodded. "The last thing we need is a yoyo officer fresh out of Lympstone to get killed with just a week to go."

"Do you two fancy coming to stay for a few days just before Christmas?" James looked over at his friends. "Mister Field said he would. We have to get logistics and accommodation sorted out at our new base at Plymouth. Visit after that."

"Stonehouse Barracks." Niall filled in James' knowledge hiatus.

"Yes. Well we'll have that all sorted about eight days before Christmas. Come to my place for a few days before you set off for your own pads."

"Nice of you to offer, James," Niall responded first, "But I 've a lovely Irish colleen to meet in Dublin 12 the second I get back to the Emerald Isle."

"You, Dan? Your woman gave you the bum's rush. You may have luck at my place."

"Who is there James? It's fine for you. You have a gorgeous blonde lady. I'm lady less."

"Do you fancy my sister?" James tried to read Daniel's expression.

"Of course. Who wouldn't? She's beautiful. But when we were at one of those parties she ignored me. I took it personally."

"Dan, she ignores everyone. That is except for her close friends and our father. She's a snob."

"She's soon to be engaged?" Daniel remained totally bemused.

"More chance of me flying to the Moon than Philippa marrying that sphincter. Nonetheless, even if she is not available there'll be others," James enthusiastically commented, "And to be honest, Dan. After what we've been through here I'd rather have a fellow Royal Marine with me when I have to face the hordes of plastic civilians. Need moral support."

"Lieutenant Marchant. You sound as if you have a sensitive side. I'd love to go to your chateau but only until the 22nd of December. I'll have to do Christmas shopping the next day and I'll try to take a young lady off your hands."

"Not my hands but the sentiment is appreciated, Daniel. All we must do now is to get out of this poxy cloaca maxima and its barren rocks. The crap house of the Middle East."

DANESH AND KELLY

Kelly recounted to Keely the perplexing tale of the man who called himself Grant Woburn. They were sat alongside their recently uncovered doppelganger, Philemon Arestant.

"This is so weird." Philemon looked at Kelly. "It's like looking in a mirror. We even keep the same length hair and styles. Blue denim shirts, jeans, leather jackets, black tights and black heels. And we all have red hair. Put up."

"Yes. Always happens. It's no surprise anymore. Phil." Keely poured coffee from her percolator. "Phil. This is weirder. Have you seen this guy from Babylonia?"

She pointed at the picture of Woburn taken back in the Ice Age.

"Yes. Of course. Dannah and I went on a trip, not to Babylonia, it was in Judea or the Holy Land. There was something Woburn deemed important about that place. Very important I think. It was a year or so back and Woburn chatted with us for ages. Dannah loved talking. This dude seemed to know everything, I mean everything. Like you two, I'm a surgeon. We have to know a lot. This guy knew more than a lot."

"Did you see him 50,000 years ago. On a time travel cruise to where Babylonia is, was, was to be?" Kelly was growing in anxiety. Keely opened her laptop screen and showed the video of the person called Grant Woburn.

"Yes!" Philemon shrieked as another section of her memory was activated. "Not 50,000 years ago. That was a mind-blowing trip with one of Dannah's really mad scientist friend. Not mad like Dannah. Really out of this universe. No, this man came to visit me at home. That was after he had appeared in my Emergency and Accident room. About two years ago. He told me all sorts of frightening things. He scared me, a lot. The guy claimed to be able to travel through time and dimensions by thought."

"He's scared the crap out of me." Kelly announced. She slurped down her coffee and immediately headed for the door. "I'm returning to my universe. I have to talk about this to Danesh."

She kissed Keely and Philemon on the cheek and was away.

Once PADIT was parked in the area outside the laboratory, Kelly strode through the door to where Danesh was tapping data into a desktop computer.

"What's up?"

"Do you know a guy called Grant Woburn. Perhaps is or was a professor?"

Danesh looked up, startled. "Why?"

"This man has no doppelganger. He claims. But for millennia has had unnatural aptitudes. He claims. He says that he has been travelling through dimensions, through time and space. He purports to enjoy unlimited access to every quarter of every Cosmos. What do you know about him?"

"I know he's not to be trifled with. He's not human. Well not in the same way that you and I are. Danelaw has a much greater understanding of this entity. Danelaw told me that he and Tariq will be here in about a week."

"Professor. I need to know about this figure. He has already decided, or fate has and it's impossible to know for sure. But somehow me and all my doppelgangers are in mortal danger."

PHILIPPA-NOVEMBER 1967

The two girls tautly paced downstairs. They walked into the lounge where a fresh pot of tea, salmon with cucumber sandwiches and an assortment of cakes were waiting for them.

A middle-aged man had joined Maura Moir. Philippa, upon observing a distinct family similitude immediately took to be David's father. He was tallish, slim while in the process of adding a few pounds and was smoking a pipe. The man had thinning light brown hair. He was wearing a white shirt, a blue woollen waistcoat and a pair of corduroy trousers. The eyes were sunken and brimming with sadness.

"Lady Caroline, Lady Philippa." Maura took the man by the arm and walked him towards the young women., "This is my husband. David's father. Alexander Moir."

"Pleased to meet you." Caroline and Philippa shook hands then Maura pointed to the florally patterned sofa. "Ladies. Please sit."

Both were dressed conservatively to show respect not only to the circumstances but also to their hosts. Caroline was in a very loose fitting, navy blue, knee length dress, with a very large and droopy cardigan and blue stockings. She carried a large handbag which matched her black, patent leather high heeled shoes.Philippa was wearing a much closer fitting, nonetheless conservative, black dress, black tights and black polo neck jumper.

Maura handed them a cup of tea and an ornate China plate each.

The Moirs could not have been described as sybaritic but they did seem to appreciate a comfortable lifestyle.

"My husband is an advocate. He works for the Procurator Fiscal of Edinburgh. You young ladies are aware that Scottish law is different to that of England. Please, help yourselves to refreshments."

"Thank you." Caroline tried to remain calm. "I do. I wish we could have met under enhanced circumstances."

"Yes." Alexander Moir sipped his tea. "Our son spoke about you. Significantly."

"Aye, he did that. And such a pretty wee thing you are." Maura poignantly added.

"He had no brothers or sisters." Mister Moir swallowed. A maelstrom of emotions seemed to simmer just below the surface.

"Aye. We've nothing left of him except a few clothes, most he took to the Marines with him," Maura sniffed, "nothing at all left of our wee boy."

"Perhaps there is." Caroline stood up and removed her large, loose fitting woollen cardigan. The definite outline of a pregnancy bump was unmistakeable. Philippa was wordless with incredulity. Maura and Alexander were similarly dumbstruck.

"Yes. I know it's a huge shock to you. But you're to be grandparents. The father of the child is David, your David. He or she is due in January."

"My wee lamb. That's such great news. What'll ye do?" Maura was hemmed between the outermost of grief and the ultimate in elation.

"No one need know ye were not wed. Of course, David's name will be on the birth certificate. Won't he?" Alexander was more pleading than enquiring.

"Yes. No scandal. Ye can stay here and go to university. We'll take care of the bairn during the day." Mrs. Moir suggested.

"Aye. No one need ever know ye were never married." Alexander added.

"Crikey, this is a bombshell and a half, Carol." Philippa had to concentrate to prevent herself from uttering an inappropriate expletive. "I didn't even suspect."

"Sorry, Pip. I thought it was proper I should tell David's parents first. We can goss about it all the way home." Caroline then turned to Alexander and Maura, placed her hand inside her bag and removed a document from within.

The second the young woman began to unfold the paper, the white background with dark writing of a Scottish marriage certificate was to be seen. Caroline raised the document into the air.

"Yet another surprise for you. David and I were married."

The three onlookers were driven into a further state of disbelief.

"When? How?" Maura exclaimed.

"I was scared before David was deployed to Aden. Very scared. I'd had nightmares, dreamt he was not coming home. A self-fulfilling prophecy as it turned out. So, I begged him to marry me and he did." Caroline stood up and walked to where the Moirs were standing.

The large left hand of Alexander was clasped by her left hand and the right of Maura held by Caroline's same.

"The plan was to placate me and marry before he left. Once he had returned from abroad we would have a large religious ceremony in which all the families would have been invited. You know of course, David told me, that you can marry in Scotland without your parents' consent. If you are over the age of 15. We travelled to Jedburgh and using someone Mister Moir knew, there we were married in a registry office on Saturday the 15th of April, legally under Scottish law." Caroline smiled at her in laws.

"And another thing. Not only were your son and I married but your grandchild was conceived in wedlock. David wanted us to keep it quiet as all sides would have made a fuss. At the end of January, you will be grandparents and you'll be amazing grandparents. So, you'll have something of David left in this world, something real and tangible that is partly made from him. I know not yet what my plans are. My parents, whom I informed first, and you second, also want to look after their grandchild whilst I finish my studies."

"We'd just like t' help," Maura looked at Caroline.

"I know. And you will. Trust me. Grandparents are essential to children. I may accept your offer, but it will have to be from next September. When the baby will be about seven months old. Now I want to request that the programme for tomorrow be altered, just a little. So, I may be squeezed into it and say a few words."

"That'd be just fine," Andrew managed a smile, his eyes a tad moist.

EMILY-NOVEMBER 1967

At the Hertfordshire town of Cheshunt, Emily turned her TR4 west off the A10 and drove along a lesser road in the direction of Potters Bar. The same outline had turned in her direction of travel as "I Can See for Miles" by The Who blared out of the car radio.

"Right you weasel," she muttered, "Let's see how competent behind the wheel you are."

The sports car powered through Goff's Oak and then Cuffley turning north easterly along the B156. The lights did not falter in remaining fixed to her tail. Just before the B157 she swung north towards the hamlet of Newgate Street with the pursuing lights still clearly in her rear-view mirror. Moving increasingly frenetically through the gears, she accelerated along the very narrow, barely tarred and gritted side road until she turned west approaching Appleby Street.

The chasing car was closing the gap between her TR4 and its front bumper when she accelerated to an even greater speed. A risky manoeuvre for these roads but her shadowing pursuer remained merely yards from her vehicle.

Emily now pushed the car to almost 90 miles an hour, still the beams on her rear held their pace. She accelerated the hyper two-seater to an even greater rapidity.

At the precise spot she had reckoned, Emily swerved on an extremely acute bend, leaving tyres and brakes screeching. A black tarmac surface heated under the frictional atom stretching of her Michelins whilst she altered axis. The car behind saw the diversion but it was already too late and crashed through a wooden five bar and careered down a precipitous, slimy mud and grass slope. Along this incline the vehicle collided with massive old oak tree at great speed and with a loud report it exploded. Within seconds the vehicle had transformed into a huge fireball.

"Come in, Sergeant Robinson. Drink?"

"No thanks Miss Wilkinson. You did well."

"Who were they?"

"Not sure. Not 100 per cent. Although we should know tomorrow after the boffins have done their stuff. You did very well. A pretty hair-raising exercise all around. Miss Wilkinson. Like I said, you were remarkable."

"Sergeant. Yes, I did. I drove very fast and pushed my brand-new car to the limit. That's all. The fact that I knew they were following me, well anyone with even less than legally blind would have known. Do you want a drink?"

"I'd love a night cap. Even later than a night cap. Breakfast?"

"Not on your life, Detective Sergeant."

"Is there some problem, are you--?"

"Sergeant. Yes, there is a problem. I don't like being chatted up. I have a guy who is away fighting for this ungrateful country. I keep myself for him. And no, I'm not a lesbian. And that,

Sergeant Robinson, is the one and only time we'll ever have this conversation."

"Sorry. I was out of order."

"Yes, you were. But more than your ill manners, I'm more concerned with as to who was cooking in that car after they'd followed me from London. It was very good of you to tell me where some delinquents had removed the black and white chevron sign of that extremely sharp bend. Fortuitously, Sergeant, I drove along there last week end so easily knew how to find it."

Emily poured Robinson a whiskey and turned on her record player starting with "Black Velvet Band" by the Dubliners.

"I'll ring you at work once we have info as to the ID of the occupants." Robinson was clearly more than a little discomfited.

DANIEL/JAMES-NOVEMBER 1967

"Move along!" Sergeant Helm bellowed as the last elements of 45 Commando Royal Marines advanced towards the throbbing engines of Wessex helicopters belonging to the Royal Navy's 848 Squadron. One Royal Marine from 9 Troop of Zulu Company had adopted a black Labrador dog. He was determined the bemused creature would escort him all the way back to Stonehouse Barracks.

The company commander of Zulu, Major Bailey, was not amused with the inclusion of the pawing, slavering canine but turned a blind eye when he learned that the troop officer gave his blessing. To justify his decision, the subaltern had cited the image it would give the Corps when the commando arrived for the first time in Blighty, service parlance for the United Kingdom.

Daniel waited back as the choppers ferried waiting troops out to ships on the bay.

"Sergeant." Daniel clasped his rifle and looked at Tony Helm. The troop sergeant was shepherding the last of X-Ray Company to the landing zone to await the next flight. "It's Wednesday, the 29th of November 1967.

We can claim to be part of history. We were here on the last day the British had a presence in Aden."

"Yes, sir." Helm squirmed disdainfully. "And to be honest, the gollies can 'ave the place. It's a shit hole. And in a few years no fucker, except a few 'istorians and veterans like us that was 'ere, will fucking know anythink about this place, sir."

"True, Sergeant Helm. The last place British soldiers will ever fight. At least it could be."

"I doubts it, sir. They'll always be sendin' us Booties off t' war. We was the first in this place in 1839. Now we're the last out."

The approaching green RM helicopters indiscriminately cast about the all too familiar thick choking clouds of sandy, ruddy dust.

"Sergeant, this colony was always ephemeral. Nonetheless, we're running out of this place like thieves in the night. Even the lowering of the flag will be out at sea on HMS Fearless. Don't you think that's a bit un-British?"

"Sir, to be honest and excuse the vernacular, I couldn't give a fuck. I just want to get 'ome. 45's never been 'ome, sir. Never since we was formed. Plymouth 'ere we come."

The barren and rocky Radfan Mountains began to fade into the distance. They were seemingly welded to the peninsula of Aden and her sister Little Aden.

Daniel and James looked over the guardrail across the waters of the Gulf of Aden. They were on board an oil tanker steaming north. The vessel was ostensibly from Saudi Arabia. The sunlight bounced from the waves of the Indian Ocean as the last Royal Navy ship left territorial waters and vessels from the Soviet Union then procured the recently vacated docking areas in the port of Aden.

"Are you sad to leave?" James enquired. He handed Daniel a cheap Royal Navy "blue line" cigarette.

"In 20 years, perhaps. Who knows? But right now, I want to be as far away from it as possible. The last man to leave, I heard, was Lieutenant Colonel Dai Morgan, CO of 42. He was dropped from Tawahi onto Albion at about 15.00 hours."

"Couldn't even be a 45 man. However, we did our bit Danny. We fought, won, lost a great friend and we can forever bore our grandchildren to death with our heroic exploits."

"I'd rather keep quiet about this shit. It's hardly the same as our parents in World War Two."

"It is Daniel. You're right. It's not good when we breathe and others do not. Fuck this place. We've left it forever. Let's concentrate on our cabins at Stonehouse and then I want you to come for a few days to my pad in Oxfordshire. We'll shiters, but only after I have my wicked way with Emily. About 30 times. And you can cheer up my sister or one of her friends. According to the letters she's sent, she bloody well needs it."

DANESH AND KELLY

"This person, or being, was not in Ice Age Europe when we travelled there with Danelaw. Was he?" Under duress, Danesh had finally deigned to listen to Kelly voice her concerns

"I would not have noticed but for Keely the last time I visited. She picked him out in a video I had taken. It was that chase. Away from the belligerent Cro Magnon. I was actually recording the event."

The scientist walked across his laboratory. "Come Kelly. I am with exigency to enjoy a little respite. Frankly, I'm stuck. So, let's go into the house and discuss this as it is clearly a matter of major concern to you. And your immediate doppelgangers."

They moved hastily from the work building to the accommodation section. Danesh ran upstairs to a quick shower and change of garments. Even the genius professor could sense the redolence acquired by omitting to change clothes at least once every two or three days. Kelly sauntered into the kitchen. She added ground coffee beans and water to the percolator and she waited for it to boil. Whilst lingering, she unpacked her laptop and was setting it up as Danesh returned. He was both aesthetically and fragrantly enhanced.

"You look and smell a lot better, Prof. Now this guy, Grant Woburn. Have you seen him?"

She showed the video of Woburn that Keely had taken way back in the Pleistocene. It was from an age at least 40,000 years back from their time.

"I've heard the name. Somewhere in my travels. Danelaw and Hussein are coming tomorrow for a few days as arranged. He's so exact with times, perhaps we can ask him. After all, he's been around a lot longer than we have. Should I say he's been travelling a lot longer than we have."

Danelaw and Hussein arrived punctually. So much so that a clock could have been set by the hour of their appearance.

"Professor Gidron!" Kelly exclaimed as the two exited their version of PADIT carrying large leather bags and flasks. "It is so wonderful to see you again."

She kissed him on the cheek then did likewise with Hussein.

"Doctor Aresti. I can assure you the pleasure is mine. Tariq and I have brought fruits, honey, nuts, spices, cheeses, bread and wine to augment your fine larder."

"Danelaw." Danesh strode into the landing area adjacent to his lab. "It is a pleasure to see you. We have much to discuss, I have studied the data you bequeathed me back in Walika, there is much clarification I shall request apposite to such statistics and annotations."

"We shall discourse on such topics, Danesh, I must confess to being in possession of a healthy appetite so let us break bread and sup of the grape."

"There is food prepared in the kitchen." Danesh ushered them gently through into the large dining area. Large dishes of salads, fruit, nuts, cheese, pickles and wines were placed on the extensive kitchen. They were followed by large Willow pattern plates, cutlery and cotton napkins.

"Tuck in." Kelly invited whilst pouring wine into glass and silver goblets.

"Thank you." Hussein spoke for the first time.

"Yes. Danelaw and Hussein. Kelly wished to know if you had erudition relating to a character that seems to travel far and widely through time and other dimensions."

"And this person is so called?" Danelaw enquired.

"Professor. I have been to see other doppelgangers of mine. They too talk of the individual. There are legends about him spanning centuries. So, they maintain."

"Doctor Aresti. What name does this person adopt in your universe?"

"Professor Gidron. I saw him first at the hospital. Then he came to my house. He called himself Grant Woburn. Professor Grant Woburn. Do you know of him? Professor. Hussein."

Danelaw's jaw dropped whilst Hussein spilt some of his wine.

"Ye Gods. Our assumptions remain veritable. We have long anticipated his return. The beast seeks our spoor again." Danelaw quaffed a long draught of wine. "I had mentioned him to you briefly some time ago. Notwithstanding, we earnestly believed he had abandoned his quest. Hussein we must be judicious and prepare accordingly."

"Danelaw. Who is this person?" Danesh was startled by their portentous response.

"At the same time that Hussein and I, and many others, were developing the Hadron Collider there was an ambitious one of us. The name he entitled himself then was Professor Diabalo Derbish. Despite his seeming veracity, I esteemed even that to be but an alias. However, this person held untold theories about gods, demons and the like. He asserted a seemingly provable connection between those mythical entities and bona fide science." The professor hesitated. "He was a good friend of ours although we never discovered his true name," Hussein stated, "And one day when the collider was on full power he deliberately exposed himself to its utmost intensity and force."

"What happened?" Kelly was becoming unsettled.

"He simply disintegrated." Danelaw assumed the narrative. "Well he gave the impression he had. Following the initial expose. Then, amazingly, he reconstituted before our eyes. Derbish was enveloped in luminosity. He was an exploding radiance which immediately dissipated. We have searched for him and have heard legends of his exploits over the centuries. Famous and infamous. It was he who turned our people against us. He appears to boast unusual attributes, powers, abilities. One could be forgiven for believing this thing is good, he is not. To those he requires services from he can appear charitable nay benevolent. Derbish, aka Woburn is extremely dangerous. Not merely to us in this room but to every person in every universe. He intends to usurp dominion over all epochs and worlds. He has the power to at least, at the very least, cause monumental catastrophic and irreversible damage to the fabric of space and time. He needs a strain of human blessed with a special variation of DNA to feed on. They are known throughout the Cosmos as the Aphrodite Sisters. The potency within these individuals is suffice to prolong his murky existence until he finally prevails. The creature may only be slain by another race of humans with equally unique genes and chromosomes. They are entitled the Hercules Strand. One thing is certain, the beast is awake once more. It appears that he is hunting again!"

PHILIPPA-NOVEMBER 1967

The two young women were suitably dressed for such a sombre occasion. Both donned black dresses, black coats and of course identically hued hats. Caroline was proudly wearing her gold wedding band.

They walked slowly down into the lounge where Maura and Alexander stood nervously treading the carpet. Mrs Moir saw them and walked up to Caroline carrying 33 rpm long playing album. "This record was performed by a folk group called The Corries. David only liked the one song on it. He was more into The Rolling Stones, as you know. But the third track on the record is a song he would have played to you. When you visited with him. That's what he planned." Maura began to get upset.

"Put it on, the track you mentioned," Caroline gently implored, "I'd love to hear it."

"Aye, we've plenty of time."

Maura removed the disc from its sleeve and dust cover then placed it on the record player, lifted the needle arm and placed it on the black vinyl. A few bars of acoustic guitar led into the lilting vocals "Oh the summer time is come---" then to the chorus "And we'll all go together to pull wild mountain thyme---."

"That's the song." Caroline wept. "I saw David in the mirror. The day I learnt he was gone. That song was coming from somewhere. I swear to God it was."

"Nae one doubts ye, my lamb." Mrs. Moir hugged Caroline whilst Alexander looked on totally at a loss as to how he should react. "The record's for ye to keep. David would want ye to.

Are ye in fine fettle to speak? It's at the Church of Scotland kirk. Saint Giles on Marchmont Street. There'll be a lot of folk there?"

"I shall repel all mournful manifestations and lamentations." Caroline smiled.

"Ye can tell ye's well educated using big words like those." Alexander managed a short grin.

The trip to the church in a black Vauxhall Cresta saloon taxi took only a few moments as Saint Giles stood at the beginning of Kilgraston Road. The minister of the church, the Reverend Doctor Hamesh Ferguson, stepped forward to welcome the party. "Mister and Mrs. Moir. So nice to see you on this very sad time for your family. If you need anything. Earthly or spiritual. Please let me know. Both of you, I shall do my best to accommodate all."

"Thank you, Reverend," Alexander then pointed to Caroline, All in black. Tear flowing in torrents down her cheeks. It was paradoxical that these sombre streams appeared colourful and majestic in the autumn sunshine of the beautiful city of Edinburgh.

"This young lassie, my apologies, this young lady, Reverend, was very, very special to our David. She wants to say a few words, I trust ye can fit her somewhere into the programme." Maura had a supplicatory countenance as she looked at Doctor Ferguson for both affirmation and approval.

"Of course, Mrs Moir, this is a memorial service for David. Whatever ye wish."

"Thank you, Reverend. Then she'll speak as soon as you've done your opening talk and we've sung the first hymn." Alexander seemed pleased.

The massive photograph of David stood on an easel in the centre of the aisle. It was between the north and south transepts at the area of the nave nearest to the altar. He was wearing his number one uniform, blues, and the shot had been taken just after he had passed out from officers' training at Lympstone. The Reverend Ferguson had made his opening address and the first hymn, "Abide with Me", had been sung. The minister stood facing the sizable congregation. Most were sitting rigidly, and many were openly weeping.

"Ladies and gentlemen. An unexpected yet much appreciated addition to the programme. Something I believe that David would certainly have approved."

Caroline stepped forward to the lectern and faced the mass of surprised and interested faces. They were totally focused on what this young English woman would have to add to the already substantial service of remembrance. The hat was positioned perfectly, the coat buttoned up and the black hose and shoes a perfect match for such an occasion.

She coughed gently and then spoke into the protruding microphone.

EMILY-NOVEMBER 1967

It was almost the crack of dawn when the young lawyer had set off for work. She arrived at 7.00 am was expecting to find the offices still empty.

"Hi," Mark called over to her, "That was a great favour you did for me. Emm."

"Which was?" Emily was desperately trying to ascertain what her colleague was mumbling on about. "Oh, the date with Andy. How did it go?"

"Marvellous. You're such a diamond. Emm. I owe you one."

"We have a mountain of cases. How's your team doing?"

"Up to date. Well as well as we can be. I need to see Gill today. She's in Holloway on remand." "Mark. I'd like to have a chat with her. Would you mind?"

"Not at all. Emm. I don't relish going to Islington to see Camden Castle anyway."

"Give me your notes and I'll have a word. There must be something we can do."

The phone rang in her private office. Emily was burrowing through mountains of paper. Her eyes were straining. She had already conjectured that reading spectacles would be necessary by the time she was 30. Perhaps even before.

"Emily Wilkinson speaking," she spoke into the mouthpiece.

"Emily, You beautiful chick. What a great move of yours to match me up with Mark."

"Andy. You big masculine hulk. I tend to suspect that Mark enjoyed the night as much as you. I'll transfer you to him."

"Before that, Emily. I need to see you. Word has it that you eliminated two more bad guys last night. Men with a shady employer. Someone that is somewhere between the Martians, the Red Indians and sons of Mekon."

"It's the first I've heard."

"I'll ring later. Now, babe. You can transfer me to the delectable Mark."

Her Majesty's Prison Holloway was not given the sobriquet of Camden Castle for nothing. The gaol looked positively mediaeval from a long way away to close up.

The lawyer walked up to the outer gate. The prison warder on duty was obviously a former guardsman by the way his shirt was perfectly pressed, and the cap rested uniformly and authoritatively on his head. It almost entirely covered his eyes.

He humourlessly telephoned the office to ensure she had a bona fide reason for her visit.

Emily was ushered through a further two locked gates until she gained access to the interior of the complex. The thick and concentrated atmosphere of sweat, soap, urine and faeces attacked her senses and hung like an immobile stagnant cloud on the senses.

A second guard was a woman and not so obviously ex-military as the others. She showed the young QC to a room in which a table was placed with two chairs on opposite sides.

The warder stood at the back as the prisoner known as Gill McMenemy was escorted in. She was dressed in grey blue jacket and white blouse with a matching knee length skirt. Gill went to hug Emily until the guard shouted "No contact! Sit!"

The prisoner sat and the lawyer cast a reassuring smile while removing notes from her bag.

"Gill. What the hell's going on? What are you doing here? I go to New York for two weeks and when I get back you're banged away in prison."

"It's a stitch up, Emily. Have you any fags? They're like gold dust here?"

Emily took two packets of Benson and Hedges and a box of Swan Vestas from her handbag. She handed them to Gill who rapidly removed the cellophane covering, took out a cigarette, lit it and inhaled deeply.

"I want to check them!" The female guard growled.

Once she was satisfied they were only tobacco, Gill handed the warder a couple. The woman accepted the offering without any response and returned to the back of the room.

"That's like the nectar of the gods. Thanks Emily. But where's Mark?"

"He was snowed under, so I volunteered. Now, Gill. If we are to stand any chance of getting you out of this rancid place, you'll have to be honest, truly honest with me. Let's start. What actual evidence have they got which could incriminate you?"

DANIEL/JAMES DECEMBER 1967

The accommodation quarters for single officers were built in limestone and dated back to the 18th Century. They were more than adequate for Daniel, James, Niall and the others following their return from Aden and were situated in the N and E blocks on Durnford Street. A thoroughfare within the military leaning city.

They had been disembarked by Wessex helicopters during the hasty withdrawal from Aden. The ship that they were initially taken to had taken them to Saudi Arabia. The complement had next been transported by wagon overland to the capital Riyadh. A BOAC airliner had flown the three companies of Royal Marines to London Heathrow airport where coaches awaited. They were finally driven the 180 miles or so to Devon. Namely Stonehouse Barracks, the Royal Navy base and other complexes around the city of Plymouth.

Daniel and James were dressed in their Lovat number two uniforms. That afternoon the CO, for at least a month or so, Lieutenant Colonel John Ivor Headon Owen, would present them with the General Service Medal. A round silver hued decoration with the legend "Southern Arabia" etched upon the bar like clasp. It was accompanied by a stylish purplish blue and green ribbon.

The extra rank pip, medal and the green lid of the Royal Marines' Commando meant that Daniel, James and Niall had come of age within the Corps. No longer would senior NCOs glare disparagingly at them. They had fought the fight, slain the enemy, suffered and returned home from the fray. Daniel and Niall were but 19 years of age. James had barely turned 23 yet now they were men of the world. Veterans of war. The one perquisite deigned them by the CO was to room together. That came after they were also allowed first choice of the cabins. Second Lieutenant Matthew Field knocked and entered.

"Sir." He approached Daniel.

"Yes, Mister Field. And cut the "sir" crap. We're all lieutenants."

"Thank you, Mister Gibson, I've been given two different hours for the presentation of medals. what time were you told?"

"Mister Field." Daniel empathetically smiled. "You are now an old man. A veteran of battle. You should know that you take your instructions from the most recent order. Provided that the officer was senior in rank to you. But being a second, all officers are senior to you."

"Ignore him," James intervened, "It's at 14.30 hours. Straight after lunch."

"Thank you, sir, sorry, Mister Marchant."

"Mister Field." Daniel looked just slightly remorseful. "We were a little too hard on you in Aden. It was a bad time."

"I understand Mister Gibson. It never crossed my mind that you were even a little harsh."

The afternoon in Stonehouse Barracks saw decorations handed out. Some of the new "old sweats" officers with a General Service Medal ribbon had personally thanked their NCOs and men before marching with an assured air back to the mess. Daniel, Niall and James found themselves first at the bar.

"I'll be generous and put the first round on my tab," Daniel lordly proclaimed.

"Hear that Jimmy?" Niall grinned. "The last time Danny boy flashed the smokes I put it in the Globe and Buster. Mine's a Guinness. A pint. I need a change from pink gins and gin and tonics."

"Two whiskey and gingers, please," Daniel called over to the bar steward. The Marine had a job title which was naturally prone to mispronunciation. "And a pint of Guinness."

Niall offered his case of cigarettes. The two others accepted. Daniel was signing the bar bill while James busily and rapidly reading a letter from back home.

"Shit!" James exclaimed at the same time Tony Bowman and Matthew

Field entered the mess. Matthew was a tad dejected. The junior subaltern had fallen just short of the thirty continuous active days service necessary to qualify for the coveted General Service Medal.

"What's up?" Daniel lit his cigarette, "Has Emily given you the boot?"

"If she has Jimmy, maybe she'd like a real man. An Irishman?"

"Hey, Lieutenant Bowman, Mister Field, the first round's on Mister Gibson's bill," Niall smirked in a puerile manner.

"Two G and Ts, Mister Gibson, please," Bowman seemed to reply for them both.

Daniel called the steward.

"Hey, Jimmy," Niall was even more juvenile in his tone.

"Mister Quinn. You hold the Queen's commission. Please address me fucking well correctly."

"Mister Marchant. Jimmy. Why the expletive? It's not like a toff like ye t' swear?"

"God sakes James. What's the crack? Tell us or we'll have to tolerate Irish phrases all afternoon?" Daniel impatiently urged.

"My sister has, or should I say my parents have, announced her engagement to the Honourable Julian Lee-Watersby in The Times."

"He sounds a right sphincter," Niall muttered whilst quaffing his stout.

"He likes debating in front of crowds." James sounded a tad juvenile.

"He's a mass debater. Get it?" Niall guffawed. "A wanker!" Daniel offered some input.

"Actually. Julian is a good egg. From the best type," Bowman interjected.

"If you say so. I am more inclined to concur with Dan and Niall. In fact, I am positive they are correct," James affirmed.

In the microsecond between one remark and a blazing row Major Adams and Captain Lowes approached the group of subalterns.

"Sir." Niall stood erect whilst their company commander and second in command took a place at the bar. "Lieutenant Gibson is buying the first round."

"Thank you, Mister Quinn. I'll have a Scotch, neat, and Mister Lowes' tipple is a brandy." Daniel called the steward and dutifully added the drinks to his tab.

"Cheers everyone. Now, a few things." Major Adams sipped his drink.

Fortuitously I have all my troop leaders here. One of course did not make it, but life goes on."

"What is it, sir?" Niall made a grasp at maturity.

"In January, Mister Gibson is going to Israel for five weeks exchange. When he returns in March, we, X-Ray Company, we're off to reinforce 42 in the Far East! We'll be on board HMS Albion. It could be South Korea. Some speculate, although personally I doubt it, that it may even be Vietnam."

PHILIPPA-NOVEMBER 1967

Caroline looked beautiful yet of suitable attire and demeanour for the sombre occasion. Her normally flowing golden locks were all covered by a wide brimmed black hat, on her jet hued coat were attached both a red poppy and a golden cap badge of the Royal Marines. She looked briefly at the photograph of David perched nearby and swallowed.

The people of the congregation were still bemused. Caroline took a few moments to collect herself and just as the minister was about to offer assistance, she came up to the microphone.

As she momentarily gazed across the breadth of the kirk, for a second Caroline deemed she could see a golden, swirling cone of unnatural light. This was followed rapidly by the sudden appearance of a sallow faced man, seated alone, in rear aisle with deep red lips and a head of black receding hair. She was convinced it was a deception of the autumn sun as when she looked up again the seat was empty. The young aristocrat then addressed the congregation.

"My name is Lady Caroline Feversham-Moir. My father is the Earl of Bamburgh. I am proud beyond words and honoured beyond the capacity of the English language to express to be the widow of that marvellous man, Second Lieutenant David Alexander Moir. A Scottish hero who gave his life in Aden on September the 12th of this year."

Loud gasps echoed around the stone kirk. Many of the women began to wipe away flowing eyes.

"We were married on the 15th of April in Jedburgh and following that a child was conceived. He or she will be born in two months' time." Even more gasps, smiles and tears followed from the pews.

"Aye, ye surprised a few folks. It was a beautiful speech. An exquisite eulogy. The folks love ye. They're all so pleased for Alex and me as we'll have a grandchild in the New Year. They all said what a bright, bonnie lass ye are." Maura handed Caroline a cup of tea before attending to other guests for the post service refreshments.

Maura returned a few minutes later. "I'm not going to push ye. And ye can think about it. But Alexander and I would be more than happy t' look after the bairn so ye can go and study. He's got connections. If ye want, we can get ye into Saint Andrews."

"Mrs Moir."

"Call me Maura. We're family. You're my daughter in law."

"Indeed I am. So, Maura. I shall return home. Mummy and Daddy will invite you to visit. This they've already indicated. And studying in Scotland does appeal to me. I shall certainly need assistance with child minding. I shall need help with a baby full stop."

"Philippa and ye'll stay the night?"

"Of course, Maura. But we'll need to be off early. It's s a long way to Oxfordshire."

"Aye, it is wee lamb. Give me your ma's number and I'll telephone her before Alex and I travel down. We may use the train."

After a hearty Scottish breakfast followed by a sustained period of snapping photographs and wishing each other fond farewells, Caroline and Philippa took off. Philippa was driving. She deftly negotiated the streets of Edinburgh during the early morning hours.

The Mini car was soon back on the A1 and travelling south at speed.

"Are you going to uni up here?" Philippa enquired. Caroline stared towards the gey North Sea. The young widow was relieved to be back into maternity casual hipster trousers, blouse and leather jacket.

"I may. I really need to get to know them better before I commit. It's too early."

"You sure do girl. I know it's early days and you're still in mourning but someday you'll have to think about another guy in your life."

"Not for a long time," Caroline confidently affirmed.

"I guess. But James has officer types visiting all the time."

"No way, Pip. Never another soldier. I couldn't live through that again."

"You know, Carol. There is a type of dude you need. That is when you're in the right place for someone."

"That would be?"

"Someone not so cool. Someone not thought of as groovy. Someone not in the "In Crowd". They would be intelligent, loving, caring, well-educated and with great prospects."

"Yeah. But like I say, we'll talk about it in the future. Going out with another man now would seem like I was committing adultery. We'll chat later."

Philippa handed her cigarette case to Caroline. "Light me one up and for you."

"I'm stopping. As from today, Pip. I want to set a good example to my baby. I've been cutting down for months. But I'll light you one up. Shall we pop in on Daniel's family in Northumberland?"

"Of course. That's why we left so early."

EMILY-NOVEMBER 1967

The unmistakable pipe was billowing from the armchair as the Cabinet Secretary, Sir Laurence Helsby, approached.

"Prime Minister, sir."

"Yes, Sir Laurence."

"You wanted to be kept personally updated on the progress of the agent known as Miss X?"

"Sounds like a brand of washing powder. In a television advertisement. Was it for Daz? Anyway. Yes, I did request such updates. As did the Home Secretary, so update me Sir Laurence."

"Mister Callaghan has been briefed by Sir Philip Allen, Prime Minster. I shall impart all that I have gleaned. Which veritably, sir, is somewhat partial."

"Come on, Cabinet Secretary. I want to know. We have a female. Very attractive, I am told. A woman James Bond who is working for us and she is not cognisant whom her authentic paymaster is."

Helsby opened a copy of Cosmopolitan and showed an article and accompanying photograph to the PM.

"That is Miss X, Prime Minister. She is well educated. With a bright future in American television when she finally acquiesces. The lady is also a very young but capable QC and an expert in unarmed combat and martial arts. Judo and karate."

The 59-year-old head of the Civil Service and former university lecturer was content with his knowledge of the top secret and highly classified security operative.

"She's smokin' hot." Harold Wilson noted in his distinct Huddersfield accent.

"She is indeed a very pulchritudinous young lady, sir. A request has come down from her via the classified undercover police anti espionage unit. It was done via a coded message. The matter can only be progressed with your total approval and authorisation."

"The kind of things our new Chancellor of the Exchequer must have relished delving into? What do you need my personal nod on?"

"That I shall impart to you now, Prime Minister."

The day had so far been a plethora of challenging ordeals and mind crunching tribulations.

The silver linings had been restricted to a letter from James to inform Emily that he was safely back in the United Kingdom and would be home on leave on the 17th of December. The other being the assistance of blonde Claire Crawley and raven-haired Dot Cooper lending a hand in the chambers whilst on Christmas holiday from their sixth form schooling.

"Emily." Gerald Crawley stepped into the general office. The QC and her staff were attending with some no small measure of energy and application to the large volume of outstanding cases and ancillary work.

"I shall assume at least one of the current court workloads. I have a pressing requirement to keep my hand in with such cases. Which one would you recommend?" Crawley offered.

"Mister Crawley. You could handle any with ease. But should you have a yearning for something of substance. Meatier. Then there is the one of a Peckham man charged with stealing cars and GBH. It seems like the police were turning a blind eye, for a commission. Until he stopped paying."

"Sounds tickety-boo. Where are you today?"

"Guilford Crown Court. I'll take the train and use the occasion to meet up with other potential clients."

Emily had successfully defended another individual. Once the not guilty verdict had been relayed from the foreman of the jury to His Honour, her assistant, the plump Roy Friarhouse had taken the train to Victoria Station. His manager had detoured to the Starr Inn on Quarry Street.

Emily, in her typical work attire of black pinstripe skirt and jacket, had walked the short distance to the hostelry from Guildford Law Courts on Mary Road.

Andy was sat at a window table. He was dressed in jeans and thick reindeer replete Yuletide pullover and matching Alpine woollen hat, enjoying a port and lemon. There was a gin and tonic already on the table awaiting his guest.

"My lovely QC. How goes the day for my English rose. The golden-haired goddess of the courtroom?"

"You're such a flirt, Andy. I can't believe you're a homo. By the way, love the sweater and hat. So Christmassy and you all the way." Emily kissed him on the cheek.

"Thank you. And alas, much as I love thee pretty damsel, thine bed can never be mine."

"I'm spoken for. Now gorgeous Andy. What do you want?"

He looked furtively over his shoulder then back at Emily.

"Fool on The Hill" from the Beatles "Magical Mystery Tour" EP came on the jukebox.

"My people tell me two Soviets, with possible links to British unions and students, were killed in an unfortunate accident at a place called Appleby Street. Rather sad?"

"It certainly sounds rather poignant and melancholic." Emily smiled. She sipped her drink then lit a cigarette.

"It's not a nice game you're embracing, my gorgeous Limey lady. It's full of assholes who wouldn't think twice about killing a lady. Even one as sweet as you."

"I can look after myself. Even a lady like me."

"I know you can, my little English beauty, my sweetheart, and sincere apologies for my asinine inference about the fair sex. However, for the times judo and karate may not quite be enough to repel the bad men, take this."

He handed over the box of a REMCO Okinawa cap pistol.

"It's a toy."

"The box says it is, Emily. The piece inside is the real McCoy. It's a 32 calibre Walther PPK automatic pistol. With a magazine, cleaning kit and a couple of hundred rounds of ammo. James Bond's favourite shooter. You keep that baby stashed safely on you for the times when you can't fight your way out or I'm not close."

Emily smiled and put the toy box in a Carnaby Street carrier bag as The Small Faces song "Tin Soldier" came across the pub.

"Are you seeing Mark again?"

"You bet." Andy beamed. "Every night for the time I'll be in good old London town."

PHILIPPA-NOVEMBER 1967

"Turn off next left." Caroline pointed at a minor road branching off the A1 while reading the road atlas. "Make for a hamlet called Brainshaugh on the River Coquet. Then head towards another hamlet called Guyzance. Go through that and follow the road down. You'll see the main road branch left. We go straight on, across a railway bridge then keep driving. The farm house is down a bank. On the right."

"Christ, Caroline. These roads are not wide enough for two vehicles to pass each other."

"Just have to hope it's a quiet day, Pip. Sunday should be."

The Mini traversed the hump-backed bridge. Beneath the stone structure, an Edinburgh to London Inter-City British Rail express was thundering south. A long and straight stretch of road followed after which came a gentle curve to the left. There was a dense pine woodland standing on the opposite facet and more open farmland before the road turned down a steep bank. This gradient revealed a concentration of agricultural buildings reaching away from the large farmhouse with lawns and a kitchen garden. Beyond this, more arable fields and verdant meadows were bustling with sheep and cattle. The sign clearly said, "Coquet Farm".

"I always thought Daniel was from a family of manual workers." Caroline commented as Philippa parked the car on a grass verge opposite the entrance to the farmhouse.

"Many farmers are, by and large, manual workers. Of sorts. However, they can tend to be very wealthy land owners as well," Philippa responded while turning off the engine.

The two girls, in almost matching outfits of hipster trousers, white frilly blouses, brown leather coats and brown boots, walked to the green painted wooden entrance door. It was set in a high brick wall that kept the garden secluded. Philippa opened it. Then they walked inside. There they came upon 20 feet by 10 feet brick and glass extension to the main property. The young women halted at the half open stable style door and rang the bell.

A man dressed in jeans, thick working brogues, a flannel shirt and cardigan came from the main house and into the porch. "Aye, lassies, what can Ah do for you?"

"Mister Gibson?" Philippa ventured.

"Aye, that's me. And ye are?"

"Sorry, I should have said, I'm Philippa. My brother, James, is a friend of Daniel. We saw you briefly at the officers' passing out parade at Lympstone last April."

"And I'm Caroline Moir. I'm the widow of David Moir."

"Aye. I can remember Lympstone. A helluva train journey. Ye just look like a wee bairn. Ye are not auld enough to be a widow. Poor little thing. Come in. We're about to have Sunday lunch. Are ye hungry?"

"If it's no trouble. Mister Gibson," Philippa replied. She and Caroline were salivating from the savoury aroma of roast lamb strongly emanating from the kitchen.

"It's nay bother, lassie. Call me Jackie. Daisy. We've got two guests for dinner!"

The kitchen was large, not massive like Wye Hall but suffice for the needs of the Gibson family. Daisy Gibson, in a blue pinafore worn over a pink cardigan and a worn blue skirt, fumbled nervously with her hair. "Come in lassies. Debbie. Fetch a couple of chairs from the back room for the lasses to sit on."

The Miasmic Mist —Volume One

The 11-year-old gawped as the two women entered. "You're both so beautiful."

"So are you." Philippa smiled radiantly at Debbie who rapidly carried two chairs through from the front room. "Little" Jackie Gibson could not keep his eyes off the beautiful guests.

"Mum has made a huge amount of roast lamb. As well as Yorkshire puds, roast and mashed potatoes, spuds, peas, carrots and broccoli. And her fabulous gravy. Plus, homemade apple pie and custard for afters."

"Sounds like heaven." Caroline sat as Jackie senior pointed at the chairs.

Little Jackie briefly gaped at the girls. "Do ya know our Daniel?"

"Yes, we do," Philippa happily replied.

After lunch was over, Philippa and Caroline offered to wash up. An offer immediately declined by Daisy. "Guests never wash up in this house."

"Well thank you. That was truly gorgeous, Mrs. Gibson." Caroline was amazed by the high culinary standard of the lunch.

"Call me Daisy, lass. And I'm glad you liked it. Can ye stop for tea?"

"Sadly, we have to move on. We just wanted to call in and pay our respects. Your son Daniel is a splendid man."

"Aye, 'e can be a right pain when 'e wants. But I'm pleased e's home from Aden. Ah got a letter the day afore yesterday. He's gettin' married in a few years' time to a village lass, Carol. They've been together for years. Isn't that right, Jackie?"

"Is it?" Jack Gibson looked up from glancing at the Sunday Sun newspaper.

"Mother. Ah think Carol's goin' out with someone else at university. She wrote to Dan," Little Jackie interjected. It seemed to unsettle Daisy.

"Wey Mrs. Green said Carol and Danny were still gettin' married."

"Mother. Mrs. Green's talkin' out of her backside---."

"John Gibson, don't ye use such language," Daisy growled at her younger son as Debbie dried the dishes and put them back into the spacious eye level cupboards.

"Daisy, Jack, Jackie, Debbie. It was so nice to meet you all. We must set off. But thank you so much for Sunday lunch." Philippa was genuinely appreciative.

The two young women shook everyone's hand then they skipped to the Mini. Philipp soon made it to the A1 and quickly headed south.

"Amazing." Caroline gazed at the verdant landscape while Philippa pressed down on the accelerator.

"Beautiful. Unpretentious. A slight erring away from our backgrounds."

"Philippa. You've turned into Kinsey and Elmira and that bunch. This is the 60s. A brave new world. Marry that dip stick Julian if you wish. I like a more earthy man. With some brains of course."

"Carol. You've changed, a lot. Is that good?"

"You heard Jackie. Daniel's brother. He said that Daniel is single again. He's available for female consumption, and you're dithering over Julian."

"I think my path with Julian is irreversible, it is my destiny. I have to marry into a family of standing. It keeps the stock pure. Or so I am perpetually being told."

"That. My dear Pip. Is just sheer balderdash. You're such a lotus eater and you know it's a load of the smelly stuff as well."

EMILY-NOVEMBER 1967

Detective Sergeant John Robinson had finally managed to scrape a meeting with his favourite QC. This time it was in The Croham pub, South Croydon, Surrey.

"Miss Wilkinson." He pointed to the chair as Emily entered. She placed down her brief case before removing her long, fur collared Kremlin style coat.

"Sergeant. You said it was important on the phone."

"I think it is. It shows how much influence you have. Good looks, being a QC--."

"Cut the crap, Sergeant. I liked to listen to flattery when I was 14 but I've moved along since then. What have you got?"

"Very well, Miss Wilkinson but I wasn't flattering you. I was merely pointing out a fact. You should learn to be a tad less volatile."

"I apologise Sergeant. It's been a rough day. But please, say what you have to."

"Your suggestion to have Miss McMenemy released as the evidence has more holes than a colander. Which you found out already when you went to see her. It has been given the green light by the highest echelons in Westminster."

"How high?" Emily was curious

"The highest I was informed. Whether it was true or not I doubt. But they did say that Harold Wilson himself signed off on your idea."

"What's the drill?"

"You visit her in prison. You tell her she is being released then when you are walking out with her, our guys will re-arrest her and take her away. She'll then be asked if she wants to come over to us."

"Ham fisted crap, Sergeant. It's something you could have done months ago."

"Yes. But the time to strike was not right until now. And also, Miss Wilkinson, we need to keep your involvement away from her in case she can still contact Moscow or Budapest. She can't know you work for us and you must ensure there is no reason, no reason at all, for her to even slightly suspect that we have engineered the situations."

"I want a chat with her in Camden Castle. I prefer that appellation. A very artistic nomenclature for Holloway nick don't you think, Sergeant? Anyway, I'll have a chat with her. After that I'll tell you whether you should arrest her. It may be better for her to confide in me."

"Whatever you think best, you've got friends in high places."

Emily had gone through all the necessary security checks. She was sat in the same legal representative's briefing room when Gill was brought through still wearing her prion uniform.

"Emily, I didn't expect to see you."

"Sit down Gill, "Emily placed a packet of Embassy king size and a lighter on the table. "Have a smoke."

"Thanks." The woman known to most as Gill McMenemy lit a cigarette then inhaled deeply.

"I'm a good QC. Do you agree?"

"Of course, you are Emily. The best." Gill acknowledged while remaining calm.

"You claimed at our last meeting you knew nothing about the charges levied against you. You were adamant."

"I don't."

"I have scrutinised the Crown's case against you and it is full of discrepancies," Emily stated, took a cigarette from the packet and flicked on the lighter.

"Gill. I may, may, just may be able to get you off the charges. But you'll have to divulge everything. I mean everything."

"There's no more to tell you."

Emily turned to the tall, middle-aged female guard. "Leave us please. If you have any concerns I shall take them up with the governor forthwith."

Once they were alone Emily turned on Gill.

"You're not talking to a filing clerk in the chambers. Do not take me for a fool. At your peril you'll do that!"

"What are you talking about?" Gill nervously responded.

"I have found enough holes in the Crown's evidence to deem that there is no real case to answer. It is all based on suspicion, circumstance and coincidence. Most police believe coincidence does not exist." Emily paced around the room. "They have something. I have no idea what, but you are not only on their radar, you're in their sights."

"I still don't know what you are talking about."

"Gill, I don't know how well your knowledge of English law is. But I can tell you that the Sydney Silverman act of two years ago only abolished the death penalty for murder."

"I never killed anyone. It's all made up as I'm a Labour supporter and have left wing friends."

"That did not appear anywhere. The fact you vote Labour. Hey, want to know a secret? So does the Prime Minister. That is irrelevant. Gill. So, do not fuck about with me. I'm trying to help you, but I have to know. It's bad, very bad. They want to try you under the 1795 Treason Act. The penalty for which if convicted is death by hanging!"

Chapter Fifteen

DANESH AND KELLY

Danelaw cast a cursory glance over the Danesh calculations.

"You're well versed on the Euler's formula. And I see you have also combined your own data with the Lattice Effective Field Theory, you are well on the way."

Kelly, Keely and Philemon entered the room. "Professor Gidron." Kelly looked up at Danelaw. "We are very nervous. We feel very threatened by the man you refer to as Diabolo Derbish. As we've not seen him for a long time, is there any chance he may not re-appear? If he does how can we fight him?"

"Doctor Aresti. Ladies. I really have no inkling as to the whereabouts of the man. Or being. He spans time and dimensions. All dimensions. As far as neutralising the creature, I only have ancient writings with which to refer. They maintain this is not a supernatural phenomenon but one subject to the laws of science. The instrument that what will repel him is pure iron extracted from a meteor. The agent of his demise, or at least reduce the atoms of his body to energy, is a hot spike or spear made of the same metal. This is sadly conjecture. As are his whereabouts at any one time. We simply are to state explicitly. Despite the allusion of his name, he is not a devil or other creature from the Pit. It is merely a sobriquet that has been handed down over centuries. He is written about in ancient scrolls. They can be viewed in the National Museum."

"Then we should find meteor iron. But first, Professor. I would like you to take us back to the Middle Ages." Kelly asked. The others nodded.

"Why?"

"We. Keely, Philemon and me, are intrigued. All of us, in our respective universes have a church in the county of Northumbria, or Northumberland, or Northernhumbria depending on which PU is your provenance. The priests of the parish wrote about a legend. The folktale tells of a man that appeared from nowhere. He literally materialised from the ether. This person claimed to be a man called Granby Woburn. To others he was Diabolo. To some he was the Beast or Ha-Satan. The date is specific in the Gregorian calendar. Although when it replaced the Julian calendar in 1582, ten days were lost. Accordingly, we have accounted for that."

"And what do you intend to do? If and when you find whom you seek." Danesh looked solemnly at Kelly.

"We wish to know his intentions. Consequently, we must visit the Castle of Wark, and the Church, in Northernhumberland on All Saints Day's Eve, in 1127 ACE. There it is written he comes and speaks to the villagers and exorcises their woes and sins. Our objective is to slay the monster if we can."

"Professor." Keely stepped forward. "If you are to gainsay this, please speak. We are all cursed by this being. We each share a burning exigency to confront him. You hold the sole means of conveyance back through the epochs."

"If your menfolk grant me leave to conduct such an expedition." Danelaw smiled.

"Sorry, Professor," Kelly curtly reacted. "We require not to enlist the dispensation of men. Whether they share our beds or not. We are not goods or chattels. Either you shall transport us, or we shall seek your doppelganger and request such convoy from him."

"I have no doppelganger. In the vein of Diabolo Derbish I exist only in mine own universe in a single chronological time frame. Your lovers are the nearest to such an entity. However, I have no hindrance in conveying you to where you ask. I beg to submit my earnest regrets for my transgression and beg the charity of your sufferance. However, should we journey our presence should not stand too divergent from the norm. In 12th Century England that could be exceedingly dangerous. It will be laden with suffice peril. I will need to search through my onboard computer files. You ladies may assist. We need to ascertain precisely the dress, language, customs, religion and politics of that time. We may speak to Derbish. We may not.

We may even slay him although that is problematic to the nth degree. Whatever transpires we will need a thoroughly structured stratagem. We cannot. I repeat, cannot, cause any major alterations to the known course of history."

"Professor we are forever in your debt." Kelly smiled and kissed the robed figure on the cheek.

"Doctor. Trust me, it is as much for mine own self-seeking pretexts that we shall journey back to the 12th Century."

PHILIPPA-DECEMBER 1967

"Philippa. You need to choose a gown for your engagement ball. I understand from the Duchess that Julian wants it to take place over Christmas."

"Sorry, Mama. It's not going to happen. It will be early in the New Year when my brother can attend. I'm not going ahead without James."

"James will be on leave soon, poppet," the earl interjected, "He said he'll be here by the 17th. He'll stay overnight on the 16th in either Plymouth or Exeter. James will then travel up with two friends who will stay until just before Christmas."

"Who's coming?" Philippa's ears suddenly pricked up.

"That is of no concern to you Philippa." Louise emphasised. "You have a fiancé with whom to devote your time and efforts."

"Lieutenant Gibson and a new officer called Field." Tom Marchant winked at his daughter. "They'll be up from Devon about lunchtime on Sunday. They'll arrive at Didcot. We may be all able to have a quick beer at The Plough before lunch back here at the hall."

"Daniel is coming?" Philippa barely concealed her interest.

"Why should that be of significance to you?" Louise admonishingly scowled.

"On the way home from Edinburgh, Caroline and I popped into his parents' farm in Northumberland. They're lovely folk. His sister is a sweetheart."

Rebecca knocked and entered. She was carrying a large silver tray of assorted deluxe sandwiches and rich cream cakes for afternoon tea. Andy Shearer followed. He was negotiating a trolley of best China cups, saucers, teapots, sugar bowls and milk jug. Mister Hodges was present to supervise matters.

"Becky." Philippa jumped from the sofa. "I'll come with you to the kitchen. I need to learn more recipes now that I'm betrothed."

"Go on, Pip." Tom smiled at the 19-year-old before Louise was able to intervene.

The music playing down in the kitchen was "Thank U Very Much" by the Scaffold. Philippa made her way to the massive table and took a seat.

Rebecca sat opposite pouring flour into a huge mixing bowl.

"James and two officer friends will be here Sunday, Becky. Daniel is one of them."

"Yer likes that gentleman, Lady Philippa." Becky added sugar to her blend. "But now that yer engaged, all such thoughts 'ave got to be kept out of yer 'ead."

"You're married Becky and you still look at other men. Like my Dad. You've always had a crush on him and that's all it is. The same as me. I can look at James' friends but that's all it will be."

Rebecca had turned momentarily red as the radio music changed to "Daydream Believer" by The Monkees.

"Of course, yer can look, Lady Philippa." Rebecca nodded then began to stir her bowl.

Mrs Cromer pottered around very slowly. Almost all the kitchen duties were now being performed by Andy Shearer and Rebecca. A new maid had been appointed for general house duties. Betty Ainsworth was 15-year-old, dark and spotty faced and slightly plump.

"Betty," Philippa called. The teenager was bringing supplies from the extensive larder.

"Yes, My Lady," Betty nervously replied.

"Who do you deem to be the most handsome. Stevie Winwood, Steve Marriot or Robin Gibb?"

"Oy likes Scott Walker, My Lady. The ones you said are all good lookin' boys, but Scott is a real man. Oy likes real men."

"Me too. It's a big day on Sunday. We have some real men coming for lunch and dinner. I have dinner with my betrothed. So, I shall enjoy lunch."

↠ The Miasmic Mist —Volume One ↞

EMILY-DECEMBER 1967

The woman known as Gill McMenemy energetically paced from her chambers in Lincolns Inn Fields towards the London Underground station at Holborn.

"Very good." She smiled to herself. "You think you're such a star. Such a celebrity. But you'll never outmatch me."

As she purposefully strode along Remnant Street, a black Ford Cortina pulled alongside her. Three strapping men in dark suits dashed from the car and dragged her screaming onto the back seat before noisily accelerating away.

"I have been illegally snatched," Gill growled. She grimaced at the captors standing before her. The room was semi dark room and was furnished with a basic table and a few plastic chairs.

"I was released by a judge for insufficient evidence."

John Robinson glared at her. "It was the QC acumen of Emily Wilkinson that got you released. She was determined to have you set free. Unfortunately for you, she has no idea that we exist. Accordingly, we have a few points to make."

He crashed his fist on the table, Gill startled backwards.

"Te egy hazug, mondd meg az igazat!"

"I don't understand." She shook with terror. "I have no idea of what you are saying."

"Come on, Gill, or is it Betty, or Beata in your own language?"

"I have no idea what you are saying."

Robinson took a photograph from a file.

"Recognise this? You betrayed the top man of all top men!"

"I have no idea what you are talking about. All you have is a photograph of a person that resembles me." Gill persisted.

"Trust me, Miss Halmi." Robinson handed Gill a cigarette. "The British are stiff upper lipped men. And some women. They play the game like it is cricket. But in our world, the dark recesses of subterfuge and espionage, no such rules exist. We can be just as brutal as your own Allamvedelmi Hatosag or the Russian Komitet Gosudarstvennoy

Bezopasnosti. You know them as the AVH or KGB, and we have been watching you for a long time."

"I do not know what you are talking about." Gill remained defiant.

Robinson brought the back of his hand across her face with such force it knocked the woman backwards and onto the floor. The cigarette disintegrating in mid-air.

The two other men in the room helped her to her feet. Gill wiped the blood away from the side of her mouth.

"Let's make this easy." Robinson lit a cigarette and handed it to Gill. "I know who you are. You know that I know who you are. You think that this is a civilised country? Well by I guess and large we probably are. We have no death penalty. Wrong! I have men in my team who'll get you to talk. Yes, they will, and once that information has been wrung out of you, you'll finally go on trial for treason. The judge will have the capacity, should he wish, and he will wish, to have you hanged. You have two choices. Be tortured and die on the gallows from whence you will be carried to the very jaws of Hell. Or join us. It's up to you. But the cold morning in the death cell is not a happy place. And that will be after my men have finished interrogating you!"

"I have no idea what you are talking about!"

Emily had driven Andy along the A4 to Heathrow Airport in her Triumph TR4 sports car.

The New Yorker had hugged her at the entrance to Terminal One.

"You take care, my lovely blonde Limey beauty."

"I shall. Have you Mark's details?"

"Naturally. He and I shall keep in touch. That was a great ploy of yours. I'll get you a man sometime in the Big Apple."

"My man is home from war in a few days. Then it'll be wall to wall sex."

"Enjoy it. And keep your focus. Don't trust anyone too much. It's a mad, bad world you are flirting with. No good guys. Just ones that are less bad. And of course regarding our day jobs, Helen still wants you over at the other side of the Pond."

"Thanks, Andy. Have a great flight home."

↣ The Miasmic Mist —Volume One ↢

Emily drove back to Lincolns Inn Field to complete her any outstanding jobs.

The receptionist, Fiona Derby, rang through to her extension.

"Emily Wilkinson speaking."

"Miss Wilkinson. It's Detective Sergeant Robinson here. I need a few words."

"OK, Sergeant. Where am I going?"

"I'll give you the address. But make sure you're not tailed."

Emily picked up the file on Gill. She drove to the East End address Robinson had given her. It was a long row of empty warehouses. Robinson came out from one of the buildings and greeted her.

"Miss Wilkinson. Come. I have need of your services."

"This had better be good, Sergeant. I have a lot of work to do."

"It is." Robinson grinned and ushered forwards. He opened a door, pointed to the inside. "Your friend's in there. She wants a word with you."

Without warning he rammed his shoulder into Emily. She flew forward and almost landed on Gill. Sitting, shivering, on the floor. She was black eyed and terrified.

Robinson was now holding a Browning nine-millimetre pistol. He was pointing the weapon directly at Emily. "There's been a change of plan. Miss Wilkinson."

DANIEL AND JAMES-DECEMBER 1967

The train from Plymouth had arrived on time at Oxford from where the connection had left punctually for Didcot. The three young officers were all a little fragile from the previous eve's solid revelry.

Niall Quinn and Tony Bowman had made tracks separately earlier in the day. James, Daniel and Matthew took their seats in the first-class smoking compartment. In what seemed no time, the engine braked as it pulled into Didcot station. The young subalterns collected their RM issue suitcases and bags of gifts and wine. The trio energetically alighted onto the wet platform and purposefully strode out onto the parking area.

"James!" Philippa ran forward and tightly hugged and kissed her brother.

"So wonderful to have you back. I trust you're well."

"I'm alive, Pip. That's as well as you can be. Thanks for asking though. You know Daniel, I mean Lieutenant Gibson." Philippa froze. For a few moments she was enraptured by his presence and aura She then deigned to give him a small hug.

"Pip. This is Second Lieutenant Matthew Field."

"Pleased to meet you." Philippa smiled before turning her glances back to Daniel.

"Come." She beckoned. "I drove the Bentley down as Mister Biggs had other duties to do. Mummy and Daddy are so excited you're home. And before you start giving me a lot of grief about what you went through, I have been comforting David's widow--."

"Widow?" James exclaimed.

"Yes, widow, David and Caroline were married in April. Just before he was sent to Aden, she's very pregnant, the baby's due next month. A lot you didn't know. I'll fill you in. But it's so good to see you home and safe."

"Daniel is off to Israel for a few weeks. When he returns our company is being sent to the Far East. To reinforce 42 Commando. It may be a little hairy."

"Christ. Keep that from Mummy and Daddy. At least until you are about to go. Not sure if mater lady could take you being off at war again."

"Where's Emily?"

"She's not back from London. You'll have to ring her parents."

DANESH AND KELLY

"You have to understand," Danelaw explained, measuredly and in detail, "The language we know as English did not properly develop until the time of the Great Bard, Shakespeare. In the 16th and early 17th Centuries.

"Right, Professor," Kelly stated, "You have a computer which translates our English into 12th Century Middle English. Set it up. Then we can use videos you took as you travelled through that century to know what to wear."

"You'll need at least one man to go with you." Danesh added.

"Like hell do we!" Kelly almost spat the words out.

"Sorry. But not only is it nine centuries back but it is a full nine centuries behind in culture. Women then were not permitted to talk back to men. They were simply the property of their fathers or husbands. They had to adhere strictly to instructions issued by these men and others.

Indeed. Back then husbands used a device called a Scold's Bridle and for many centuries afterwards. This was placed on the head of a disobedient wife to humiliate and silence. You could be severely punished for the most minor of transgressions. Rather like going to some modern countries nowadays and wearing a bikini in public.

I'm not being a male chauvinist. I'm merely being practical. If you wish to have some modicum of success in your adventure you must compromise. A little."

"I guess that makes sense." Keely conceded, "I suppose we'll need our partners. I think."

"I don't think so." Kelly vehemently disagreed. "They stay here. Or they'll try and take over. Danelaw will be our token man. Do you have a woman?"

"Of course. Doctor Aresti. My wife. You met her back in Walika." Danelaw smiled. "And. You'll all need to wear different clothes and cover much of your faces. The fact that you are almost identical may set off superstitious folk. They may deem you witches or some other Satanic entity. It'll be like the computer generation meeting the ignorance of the Dark Ages."

"I think we have all the food and other essentials we'll need. Your PADIT has a large shower room and two toilets." Kelly was double-checking her list of items.

"PADIT carries enough supplies to last six people a month. We will all need to be aware of the location where it will be parked. The craft will have need to be secreted in woodland which we will search out while still travelling through time, albeit slowly," Danelaw informed the women, "That way, we shall be invisible to people below us and once we have sought a landing zone, we can drop down and make plans."

The women kissed farewell to their companions.

"We'll be back in about two minutes real time." Danelaw smiled reassuringly at the stunned figures.

He was attired in a medieval outfit of a blue long outer tunic called a bliaut. A full skirt that became trumpet shaped; red leggings hose called chausses, and underneath the top of his dress was a shirt called a chainse. The women wore also wore red bliaut with long dangling sleeves that reached to the ground. Their undergarments were linen chemise and each of them giggled a little as they fitted their brown leather belts, known as cinctures, and placed metal tags at the end. The girls had braided hair covered by a veil. This style was to accord with the custom for married women, of whom they would assume the guise. Danelaw cast a brief glance over them.

"On board ladies. To the 12th Century. And remember, you're my daughters. Widowed by war."

PHILIPPA-DECEMBER 1967

Philippa brought the Bentley up the long gravel driveway that led to Wye Hall.

As she pulled onto the paving set before the main entrance, Fred Biggs came out to meet her.

"If you wish, I'll park the car, My Lady. That should allow you to see to his Lordship and the guests."

"Thank you, Mister Biggs. That would be nice."

The three Royal Marines officers collected their suitcases and other baggage. With James leading they made for the house. Philippa ran and caught up with Daniel then walked alongside him.

"Caroline and I visited your family." She smiled nervously. "Your mother and sister had prepared a simply scrumptious Sunday lunch."

"Northumbrians are very hospitable, and mother is a grand cook. You should visit me sometime up there."

Philippa offered no response. She turned red and swiftly looked away.

Mister Hodges, Rebecca, Andy Shearer, Mrs. Cromer and Betty were all in the entrance hall. The lounge door was open. Tom and Louise stepped forward.

The countess hugged her son. "I'm so pleased to see you home. It has been rather an alarming period that we have been through. Papa and I are so relieved to have you back home. I'm so, so sorry about David. Philippa drove Caroline up to Edinburgh."

"I know, Mum." James smiled. Louise was briefly startled by her new form of address. "Father. You're looking well."

"So are you, young man." Tom shook hands with his son then turned to the two guests. "Daniel. It's nice to see you again. My daughter tells me that your mother is a wonderful cook. Give your parents my regards when you get home."

"I will, sir," Daniel cheerfully affirmed.

"Tom Marchant. Second Lieutenant. Your name is?"

"Field, sir, Matthew Field."

"Well. Now that formalities are over, Philippa is going out with her fiancé and friends. It's a gangster and molls night. James. I have not heard from Emily," Louise dryly imparted.

"She works in London. She'll not be long. I'll take the guys for a few wets at the Plough after dinner. In civvies. It'll be nice to socialise in mufti."

Julian Lee-Watersby was fresh from his assignment with the Australian Department of Defence. He sat in The Angel pub on Witney Street in the Oxfordshire town of Burford.

Near him in a select area of the lounge bar were a number of well-known eligible ladies and debutantes from the upper reaches of British fashionable society.

The current high-flying movie starring Warren Beatty and Faye Dunaway, "Bonnie And Clyde", had spurred them all to wear attire that seemed to replicate the 1920s. Julian was wearing a gangster hat, double-breasted suit with Oxford bag trousers, a white shirt, black tie, patent leather shoes with white spats. To his left Elmira sat. She was smoking a cigarette in a long holder and eying up all around before commenting to Kinsey.

As with all the young women, raven haired Lady Elmira Bernard was dressed in 1920s "flapper" style. She was donned in a black, knee length pearled Charleston dress with black head band, brown stockings and shoes relevant to that decade. On the right of the Honourable Julian was Kinsey. She also smoked from a long cigarette holder. Kinsey wore a red flapper dress, red shoes, crimson stockings with the tops visible held up by a matching coloured garter belt. She also carried with a matching red handbag wore a red cloche hat. The other women in the area were either dressed like gangster molls or in very chic Coco Chanel designs of the period. Caroline was noticeable by her absence although most had been aware for a while she was protruding from the belly region.

"Where's Philippa?" Julian knocked a whiskey back then lit a Senior Service cigarette.

"She loves you, Julian. But between you and me, that chick needs a big dude to sort her. She needs a bit of masculine discipline to bring her into line." Elmira smirked.

"You can do that, Julian," Timothy Walden looked up. The mousy haired crony was in a trilby, white shirt with black trousers and black braces. He augmented those with a black fake moustache. "Philippa is a great looking chick, but she's too used to making her own scene. She needs bringing into line."

"Yeah, yeah." Echoed the sycophants sat across from the sofa bench seats.

"It's not that she needs a firm attitude, I think she wants it." Kinsey smirked.

"She's been mixing well. If you get my drift." Elmira winked at Julian. "My God, Kinsey, look at that dress. It's so yesterday. She must have been to a pawn shop!"

The women giggled as the music changed to "La Derniere Valse" by Mireille Mathieu. The original version of the current Engelbert Humperdinck hit, "The Last Waltz."

Julian knocked another whiskey back as Philippa came into the lounge. She was in a stunning Charleston dress, headband and huge feather together with a long necklace of pearls, belt, bag and long cigarette holder. Elmira, Kinsey and other woman leapt from their seats to kiss Philippa on the cheek.

"Hi darlings. Sorry I'm a bit past early but I had to get ready for Julian. Didn't I dear?"

She kissed lightly on the lips then took a seat next to him.

"Oh, Pip. You've not missed much. A few candy asses. It's going to be a bummer happening. Lots of ditzes and dipsticks. I hope we get some studs in although you've got your bad ass dude," Elmira commented as Timothy brought over some drinks.

"Philippa. We need to talk. A few points require some clarification before we reach our nuptials."

"And they are?"

"I think we need a few moments outside in private, let's go outside for a second."

"It's freezing out there."

"Come on, outside. I'm telling you."

Philippa looked venomously at Julian then acquiesced. The couple went outside of the Tudor looking pub just as the Georgie Fame hit, "The Ballad of Bonnie and Clyde" came over the speakers.

"What is it, Julian?"

"You've been unfaithful to me."

"Yes. We agreed prior to our engagement you were going out with other chicks and I could date other dudes. Now I've agreed to marry you, of course that will be no more."

"I want you to stop university. Now!" "Julian, that's not going to happen, we agreed!"

"I've changed the agreement! You're a slut and you'll do as you're told!"

"Fuck you, Julian! I'm off!"

Philippa was knocked to the ground with the painful crashing of a fist into her face. Several times.

NARRATOR

The path bends precariously along the banks, the very shores of the river of time. Or times. You have by now realised that my tale lives on two separate levels of the all-encompassing Cosmos. That aegis in which all matters atomic, sub atomic, past, present and future, living and departed, all reside in some awkward conglomeration of reality and existence. Another milestone is attained within this tale. As in all legends and chronicles there must be a destination, a turmoil and conflict, love, tragedy, re-evaluation, erratic turns, recovery onto the axis of spearhead. Most of all a struggle between those who deem morals low or superfluous and the amazing heroes who will lay down their very existence to uphold the noble ethos of a civilised, well evolved being.

My mother was always caught in some strand of ongoing and chronic havoc. Although my father nearly always complied with her sensual petitions. He was the muscle and intelligence; she was the soft mannered professional albeit a scorpion. Harmless until vexed.

The sea crashes onto the sand filled expanse as there is an alloying of compounds within the missive. Am I but a harbinger transferring others' words? A lay line of extraordinary depth and wisdom. Whatever, my captive audience is still awake, even attentive, so I shall continue.

EMILY-DECEMBER 1967

"Sergeant Robinson. What the hell is going on?" Emily growled. The Browning pistol was pointed directly at her.

"Sorry, Miss Wilkinson. Things have changed. You're a liability now."

"And how do you think you'll get away with this?"

"You'll never be found. Neither will that turn coat!" Robinson snarled at Gill.

"I think you're the turncoat. See, I know what the score is. As you would say. Sergeant."

Robinson's face morphed fleetingly into a pasty visage surrounded by the golden yet iniquitous rays of some bizarre candescence.

The charged microsecond was broken by the grating sound of a car moving rapidly in the direction of the warehouse. This minor distraction initiated Robinson to turn momentarily. A costly error. He would never see the withdrawal of a Walther PPK pistol at lightning speed from Emily's blouse. She fired instantly. An ear pounding, deafening report followed. The right side of Robinson's head exploded into a red mire before he dropped lifelessly to the floor. A dark ethereal mist seemed to rise from the corpse. The noise attracted one of the co-conspirators to nonchalantly enter the room. His existence was concluded with the same sanguine immediacy as a second shot echoed and a further cadaver slumped to the concrete.

Emily walked out of the room into an adjacent area. The third double agent went for his weapon never to know that he was light years unpunctual. The PPK cracked again. An erstwhile captor slumped to the filthy ground. Dead.

Billy Parkins burst in with two others of Artie's "employees". Each of them was holding a Smith and Wesson pistol.

"Miss Wilkinson. Are ya alright?"

"Billy! How did you know where I was?"

"We 'ad ya followed, Miss. Orders from Artie. Never let ya out of our sight. We got held up. Only seconds behind ya. Sorry. Ah sees you've 'ad a spot o' bovver."

"Billy, I'm going to Scotland Yard. Can you take Gill to Artie's until I get back?"

"Ah'll be behind ya. My two geezers will take the lady to Artie's pad."

"Very well. But best put your gun out of sight. And when we get to the Yard, you wait outside for me. If I'm not back in thirty minutes, ring the Daily Mirror. Tell them that rogue MI5 agents working as London cops murdered three of their own. Make sure the Commissioner knows. Artie will have a line to him."

Emily pushed open the door and walked to the reception desk of Scotland Yard.

"Yes, Madam," the constable asked in a seemingly facetious manner. His eyes moving up and down her physique.

"Please pick up your telephone and ring Detective Chief Inspector Lyle. Tell him it's Emily Wilkinson and I have a matter of the utmost urgency to discuss with him."

"Not sure if I can do that, Madam."

"Constable. I'm not one of Mister Lyle's bits on the side. I have to see him urgently!"

"Calm down, you must be near the time of the month---."

Emily was about bypass the deskman when Richard Lyle and Guy Porter appeared.

"It's fine, Constable." Lyle marched towards the livid figure. "We know Miss Wilkinson. Come with us. Emily. Please."

"Not on your life. I'm going nowhere with either of you!"

"There's nothing to worry about. All will be well." Porter attempted some modicum of reassurance.

"I'm not going anywhere with you lot, I certainly don't trust you."

"What would it take for you to trust us, Emily?"

"Nothing! You're a two-faced set of charlatans!"

"Would a chat with the prime minister reassure you? We're on your side."

"Only if I can take my colleague Arthur Cooper and his men with me. There's the only ones I would trust."

"Mister Wilson will speak to you. Alone. But if you feel more secure with Artie and his boys, so be it," Lyle conceded, "I'll just make a call. Take a seat. Constable. Get Miss Wilkinson a cup of tea. And do it now!"

DANIEL/ JAMES-DECEMBER 1967

The current hit and ballad by the Bee Gees, "World", was playing on the jukebox as the three young Royal Marines' officers, now in trendy civilian order, were on their third pint of the night.

"Where the hell is Emily?" James was shuffling uncomfortable in his seat in the lounge bar as Fred entered the establishment and made towards James.

"Lord Marchant, sir."

"Yes, Mister Biggs."

"His Lordship got a call from Lady Philippa, sir. He sent me to pick her up from The Angel in Burford, sir. The earl said you may want to come with me. She sounds in a bad way, sir."

"What's happened, Biggs?"

"Don't know any details, sir. But it sounds like Lady Philippa and The Honourable Julian 'ave had a disagreement, sir. I think she may be bruised, sir. Badly bruised."

James leapt to his feet. "If that person has laid a finger on my sister, I'll put him in hospital."

"James," Daniel calmly called out, "Collect your sister first. Make sure she's alright then we can discuss any retribution. But not while you're seething. Let's get her safely home."

"Very well. Let's go Mister Biggs. It's not far to Burford."

"She's at a call box on the outskirts, sir."

"Let's move!"

On a public bench near the red phone box, a figure was whimpering. The face covered in her hands. Darkness covered much but she was obviously in some discomfort.

"Pip," James called out. Philippa stood up, covering her face then wrapped her arms around her brother. She was sobbing. Loudly.

"It's ok. It's alright. Let's get you home."

The Bentley pulled onto the drive outside the entrance of Wye Hall. The instant Fred Biggs had applied the handbrake; Philippa jumped from the car and ran around the back of the stately home.

"Where's she gone?" Daniel was a tad perturbed.

"She's gone to talk to Becky. Our former nanny and one of the cooks. She tells Becky everything. I want to know what that scoundrel did. I'll swing for him."

James strode angrily into the house heading for the lounge. He was followed by Daniel and Matthew. Both of whom felt ill at ease.

"What's up? What the hell is going on?"

"James. Please tone down your language." Louise was fidgeting. The possible ramifications of the incident were slowly descending on her.

"Mother, I've just come back from a war. A small one but still a war. Now my little sister is in tears. Has Julian hit her?"

"I don't know," Tom confessed. He poured whisky from a decanter into four glasses then handed one to each of the men. Rebecca knocked and entered then approached the earl.

"My Lord. I think you should come."

"What's up?" Louise was incensed.

"I'll see to it, darling." Tom walked out of the room with Rebecca.

"What is it?" he asked as they were on the way to the kitchen.

"That gentleman. If Oy can calls him that, sir. He's raised his fists and struck your daughter. She's badly cut and bruised and will need to see a doctor. Oy'll go and bash 'im meself, sir. Harming a poor little mite like my Lady Philippa."

"I think one of the three Royal Marines officers currently in Wye Hall may just alleviate you of that task, Becky. Let's see her."

A tear laden Philippa was sat at the kitchen table. Mrs Cromer was trying to ease the pain on the black eyes and cuts. She ran up to her father and threw her arms around his waist.

"He punched me Daddy. He knocked me out. Just because I wouldn't stop uni. I'm not marrying him--."

James and Louise entered the kitchen. Both were shocked by Philippa's injuries.

"W—What happened, darling?" Louise was visibly shaken.

James saw the condition of his sister with the benefit of good illumination.

"Pip. Did that man do that to you?"

There was no answer merely a sobbing nod.

"Mother! Are you still expecting Philippa to marry that animal?"

"Lower your voice James. I'm not one of your Marines. Of course, if Philippa wishes to call off the engagement we should discuss the matter with the family first," Louise meekly suggested.

"The only discourse I'll be having with the Honourable Julian will be when I ram my fist down his cowardly throat."

"No, James," Daniel diplomatically interjected, "You're seething. In a red mist of anger. Understandably so. It is clouding your judgement. Considerably. You and I and Matthew should drive to the pub and I shall ask the gentleman a couple of pertinent questions."

DANESH AND KELLY

Kelly, Keely and Philemon climbed carefully into Danelaw's PADIT. They meticulously lifted their long bliaut skirts as entered the passenger area and sat back in the comfortable armchairs within. Danelaw joined them soon afterwards and punched several characters and digits into the keyboard of the vessel's computer.

"Ladies." Danesh called to the rear of his transporter. "I remain a little befuddled as to the precise objective of your voyage to this period in history. I assume it is to neutralise the creature Derbish. Accordingly, allow me to briefly lay down a few ground rules. These are essential when in a time period completely dissimilar to that in which you ladies normally reside."

"Whatever you ask we shall accede. Within reason of course," Keely spoke first.

"Thank you. Doctor Marston. I am relieved. Nonetheless, I still have a personal requirement to impart my instructions for when we disembark. This in real time I calculate to be no more than 20 minutes."

The view outside PADIT altered from seemingly natural light to that which secretes away outside the spectrum of human comprehension, creating a whirlpool of the outermost bizarre shades. Flashing images that may or may not have represented tangible subjects flew by in a nanosecond.

Incandescent visions of a surreal and unearthly aspect rolled by the portholes of the machine as it whirred, vibrating only slightly from the huge power of the sub atomic thrusters on its chronological adventure. The pyrotechnics from the exterior dissipated as the setting transformed to one of the shorelines of a sea. Obviously of the Earth. Then came an estuary and a slow flowing river. Very tentatively, and still on an accelerated time drive he decelerated his passage through history. This was maintained to prevent being seen. Danelaw steered the vessel along the course of the waterway for a mile. On the bend of the river stood a settlement of cottages and houses. They were all wood and brush built but some boasted sandstone walls around the exterior for additional support. Nevertheless, the constructions appeared somewhat rickety to the three young women as they viewed the early medieval landscape.

The pilot of the atypical vessel did not even discern the outlook. Danelaw was more concerned with seeking an appropriate site in which to deposit PADIT. The craft would require concealment for the duration of their stay in the settlement of Wark.

A wood and stone fort was constructed on the apex of the steep hill that overlooked the hamlet down below. On the battlements stood two extremely bored looking men. They were probably soldiers of some variety although no armour or weapons were perceived.

Thick deciduous and evergreen woodland lay beyond the crest of the rise. Steering like any skilled aviator, Danelaw slowly brought PADIT to a buoyant hover above a bower, a glade in the thick forest that swept back from the river and encompassed most of the bucolic surroundings. Danelaw switched off the controls once the machine was static. It was suspended a foot above the mud encrusted and leaf carpeted surface. A security procedure was keyed into the pad upon which the large hatch gently slid sideways.

The aroma was one of earth and decomposing foliage alloyed with a distant stench of urine, faeces, burning logs and cooking cabbage.

"Come." Danelaw motioned. He picked up four metre length wooden rods from pile aside a cottage. "Let us hasten to the locus you wish to be. It is down the hill in the settlement. This is the county of Northernhumberland and this is Wark village. It is approaching the night of All Saints Day and the year is 1127 Anno Domini."

Through the oak and beech woods several people ambled. Each carried garlands and were festooned with flowers, twigs and leaves.

"Professor. Shall we follow these people? They seem to be heading where we wish to be."

"Yes, Doctor Aresti. PADIT is camouflaged by the forest. The cold wind we feel this day shall not affect her. But it is of the utmost import that we commit to memory her precise location, should we need to take flight from this awesome locus."

Danelaw, Kelly, Keely and Philemon were all attired in similar style and colour clothing. They deftly circumvented the hill fortress by marching along the soft path that twisted its way down to the river in the valley below. A few of the dirt encrusted locals viewed them with deference and some females even curtsied to the women.

"We are bedecked in the apparel of the nobility," Danelaw elucidated as they reached the foot of the slope away from hilltop citadel. At that juncture a sizable gathering of plainly dressed people was amassed. Kelly adjudged that the local inhabitants reeked. Although one would merely need to have been in possession of a mediocre sense of smell to discern that indisputable truism. They were smaller than one would have seen in their century. The filth on their bodies was not just superficial. Much of it was engrained deep into the epidermis. It was apparent to the visitors that these folks rarely felt the balmy, soothing trickle of water on their skin.

The standard of clothes varied from untidy to rags and it became evident that garments were laundered even less regularly than their bodies.

"Ye folk. My ladies. Ye grand and noble sisters times threefold."

The Miasmic Mist —Volume One

An old yet sagacious looking woman circumspectly stepped forward. She was in attire that had witnessed many summers. The crone was a figure for whom it was nigh impossible to gauge the measure of her years.

"She's probably only 40." Danelaw turned to the three women as the beldam moved closer. The woman appeared to edify the penurious life styles of the local populace.

"My little ladies. I be Guyzanc. Ah sees 'e in my pot. The incubus from the effulgent shape. The man from the light. The creature of the mist. Ah sees 'im and he be not to thine betterment wee ladies of standing."

The original tint of the dye that had been absorbed by her wool and linen garments had long since become indistinguishable. They hung from her body as if part of her total being.

The attires seemed dirt brown but may have been mauve and covered a lean, cadaverous outline.

Her long spider like hands were an ochre hue from the sun and intrinsic clay. The hair was matted. It appeared greasy and filthy, possibly uncombed for years. The face was a deep brown. The mouth seemed a void as almost all her teeth were missing. Those that were present, so black it was problematical to even catch a glimpse of them. She was very small by 21st Century standards, standing at no more than one and a half metres. Yet the virago was brimming with spirit. She looked at each of the women in turn, giving them each a small, grunting curtsey. Afterwards, Guyzanc moved up close to their faces and glared at them. The dark, penetrating eyes seemed to meliorate through to the dark chambers where the soul is reputed to inhabit.

The halitosis thick air stuck to the nostrils even several metres from the woman.

The malodorous, unkempt figure walked away a few paces. Guyzanc then suddenly turned back on Kelly. "Tis, thee. Tis thee. Thou shalt lie in a grave. An unquiet tomb, that huddles bestride an ancient oak in yon great forest. That be thy bourne. The Devil cometh. He cometh this day. Cometh on the eve, All Hallows' Eve. He shall trail thee as his prey and return with thee to his lair. In Hell."

"Madam, I know not that to which you imply. I am but a lady. A widow of war. I travel with my father and sisters."

"Diabalo of Woburn knoweth better, My Lady." The harridan cast a chilling smile. "Accept these points of a lance. They be forged with iron from a distant silver star. Attach to a long shaft. Thou shalt then possess a spear with capacity to combat the being."

She handed Kelly two metal points. They had been cast from some strange coloured metal or alloy. Upon finger contact, a tingling sensation was felt.

"He cometh, the man cometh!" Voices echoed from near the wooden church of Saint Lawrence.

"Let's go ladies. The issue of thine expedition approaches." Danelaw cautiously advanced. He also accepted two outlandish metal tips. They were then rammed with great force onto wooden shafts.

PHILIPPA-DECEMBER 1967

It was somewhat fortuitous that Peregrine Marchant had called in on his way to London. He was able to administer treatment on her cuts and bruises.

"You'll be alright Philippa." Peregrine packed his medical accoutrements back into his bag, "Whatever caused them, if it was a male--."

"It was. Uncle Perry. And three officers of Her Majesty's Royal Marines are currently en route to have a tête-à-tête with the person responsible. I shall leave it at that."

"Very well. I am sure that the matter is in hand. I'll be off now. May see you in London?"

"You may see me. Uncle Perry. And you for your help."

"My pleasure," Peregrine kissed his niece on the cheek then strode off. Rebecca hovered close by. Although silent, she was raging internally. Caroline came into the kitchen.

"Pip. Becky rang me. What the hell is going on? Your face is a mess!"

"I know but it's in hand, you should not be getting overly excited in your heavily pregnant state, I believe I have no real friends, not true friends," Philippa smiled sheepishly and despondently at Caroline.

"You do have true friends." the young woman negotiated herself onto a chair next to Philippa. Rebecca brought over more tea and cakes.

"Becky." Caroline smiled appreciatively. "I'm fat enough as it is. But I can never resist your absolutely dreamy cakes."

"It's baby weight. Lady Caroline. You'll lose it once the little un's born."

"I hope you're right, Becky. Because at this instant I feel like an elephant."

"Who are my true friends?" Philippa changed the subject.

"Me, Judith, Christine and Pat to name but four. And of course, Becky. She loves you were her daughter."

"Pat, Christine and Judith will never speak to me again," Philippa quietly moaned

"Of course they will."

"How do you know?"

"Because I hear things. Pip. All you have to do is to pick up the phone and grovel. Something that is alien to both of us. Show some humility. Then apologise before bribing them with claret, cigarettes and chocolate."

"I'm not too good at saying sorry," Philippa confessed.

"Come. Let's go to the telephone. I'll dial the number then all you have to do is speak." Caroline pointed. They walked into the foyer whereupon Caroline dialled some numbers on the rotary phone. "Hello," the voice of Pat Laidlaw was distinct.

Caroline hand the handset to Philippa. "Pat, it's Philippa."

"What do you want?" The tone was not one of deep enamour.

"Pat, I---I know I've been a bitch. And a real dipstick."

"You certainly have."

"What I want to know is. How much grovelling, apologising and bribery I need to offer in order that I may win back your friendship, and that of Judith and Christine?"

There was a long, heavy, uncomforting pause. What's brought this on?"

"Pat. You were right all along about Julian. He's a swine. He hit me." Philippa began to sob.

"I knew all along he was a total Barclays Banker. And no need to cry, Pip. But rekindling of our most trusted and valuable friendship will cost you."

"How much?"

"We come around now. You lavish us with your best wine, cigarettes and chocolate. And we may. Just may. Consider thinking about granting you some measure of forgiveness."

"It's a deal." Philippa smiled with satisfaction.

Stephen Grenfell

EMILY-DECEMBER 1967

Artie Cooper was extremely wary when police officers had called for him. They had claimed that Emily Wilkinson QC urgently required his services. A car had taken the semi reformed criminal to Scotland Yard where she was anxiously awaiting him.

"What's up? Miss Wilkinson."

"Artie. I don't trust anyone anymore. Except you. I want you to come with me. Bring the boys too. I'm told safe passage is guaranteed."

"That's ok. Miss. Me an' the boys 'll stay wiv ya all the way."

"Thank you. You're such a gent."

The party travelled in two limousines supplied by the Home Office. The tall presence of Detective Chief Inspector Lyle and the chunkier figure of Superintendent Porter accompanied them as they made the short drive. They steered onto Whitehall followed by a right turn into the world famous Downing Street. They stopped outside door Number 10. The official residence of the Prime Minister of the United Kingdom of Great Britain and Northern Ireland and First Lord of the Treasury. Emily almost bounded out of the car.

A uniformed police officer stepped forward and ushered Emily through the world-famous door.

Artie, his three men and the two plain clothes officers followed.

In the reception hall a woman, aged about 35, stepped down the staircase and approached Emily. She was dressed in a conservative brown matching knee length skirt and jacket, brown shoes and matching hose.

"Miss Wilkinson. I'm Marcia Williams. I'm the private secretary to the prime minister. Would you care to follow me? Please."

Emily looked at Artie who nodded. Then the young woman followed Williams up a staircase adorned with portraits of all former prime ministers, the most recent being Sir Alec Douglas Hume, voted out of office three years earlier. They stepped along a corridor and then into an office where the familiar round face of Harold Wilson sat behind a desk. His pipe was emitting clouds of tobacco smoke into the upper reaches of the spacious room.

"Prime Minister. Miss Emily Wilkinson QC." Marcia announced then promptly exited. Emily stood nervously before Wilson.

"Miss Wilkinson, I've heard a lot about you. And you look every bit as nice as I've heard. If you don't mind me saying so?"

"Prime Minister. I must tell you. Should anything untoward become of me, every newspaper, radio and television station will be informed at once. I'm privileged to be here but I would like to have a few answers to some burning riddles."

"You seem to be at a loss as to whom you should trust?" Wilson smiled reassuringly at her.

"I most certainly am at a loss. Prime Minister."

"You have been an exemplary asset to our country, Miss Wilkinson. You have defended her from three known spies cum assassins who are now playing harps or whatever. And despatched a group of traitors who had only just been turned by the Soviets."

"I thought Sergeant Robinson was untouchable. A man of utmost honesty and integrity."

"He certainly seemed to be," the leader of the United Kingdom government commented, "But it came to light when information only five people were privy to was found to have been leaked. Leaked to the Soviets here in London."

"Why did he change?"

"No one knows for sure. By deduction we narrowed the leak to three police officers working for MI5. We knew only one could be guilty. You solved the puzzle for us and now three enemy agents are no longer of this world. I shall not ask how you acquired the weapon utilised. My guess it was from the USA. Thank you for what you have done. You are a very capable and extra-ordinary woman. Would you care to work full time for us?"

"That is such an offer, Prime Minister, sir, However, in the short term at least I have too much I need to focus on with my law career. There are not enough hours in the day."

"You have saved the careers of several senior civil servants. I know there is a clandestine bank account from which we recompense you for work done. Here is a Christmas bonus with the thanks of a grateful nation. You turned Beata Halmi over to us also. Congratulations."

Wilson handed her a brown envelope. "It's five thousand pounds. In cash. And properly recorded in HM Accounts. Your fiancé is an officer in the Royal Marines. He's just returned from Aden and is currently on leave. Treat him to a wild holiday. Cancun in Mexico or somewhere equally as exotic."

"Thank you, Prime Minister. But I'm in London and he's home. I shall need to rush to get to Oxfordshire. I'm already extremely unpunctual."

"Relax, Miss Wilkinson." Harold picked up the phone. "Send me the ministerial chopper. Tell the pilot he's going to Alvescot in Oxfordshire."

"I know you are in great demand. From the legal profession, from the United States and a plethora of other derivations. However, should you experience a modification to your current opinion, then let me, Mrs Williams or Mister Callaghan know."

"I certainly shall, Prime Minister." Emily smiled as the chugging sound of helicopter rotors became audible.

"Mrs. Williams will escort you to the helicopter. After you've wished your friends a fond farewell. The pilot will drop you at the nearest open ground to your house. I'm sure you can furnish any meddlesome neighbours with an apt cover story explaining as to how the Royal Air Force gave you a lift."

DANIEL AND JAMES-DECEMBER 1967

Fred Biggs turned the Daimler into the car park of The Angel pub in Burford. He stopped the vehicle and applied the handbrake.

"May I come with you, Lord James, sir?"

"Yes, Mister Biggs. You may indeed."

"It's just that my wife, Rebecca, she's always bin protective 'bout you and especially her Lady Philippa. As she calls her ladyship. She wants me to be ready to help if needed. Sir."

"That's fine, Mister Biggs. Your wife has been a saint to us. I understand."

Daniel, Matthew and James together with Fred walked vigorously into the pub. Outside the entrance to the lounge, they could see through the small oval window on the bar entrance door that the 1920s themed party was in full swing.

"He's the one with greased back hair. Third from the left. He's dressed like a gangster. Maybe I should belt him--."

"James. Stay here! You, Matthew and Mister Biggs wait here. Only come in if I'm set on by a horde, and I mean a horde of them. Not just two or three. That number I can easily handle."

Daniel strode confidently into the lounge as "In and Out of Love" by Diana Ross and the Supremes was playing. He marched up to where Julian was seated and menacingly glared at him.

"Can I help you?" The civil servant sounded imperious and condescending yet a tad unsettled.

"Yes!" Daniel spoke doughtily with absolute equanimity and loudly so all in the room could hear, even above the strains of Diana Ross. "I understand that you have a propensity to hit women. A bit cowardly I know. Accordingly, if you ever elevate yourself to the level whereby you deem yourself competent suffice to assail a member of the male gender, I shall be more than happy to accommodate you."

Julian was silent. The room nervously awaited his imminent riposte.

Daniel turned to walk away but on the parameters of his field of vision he could see his antagonist charging, a bottle in his hand.

The 19-year-old Royal Marine moved slightly to one side. He grabbed the arm bearing the offending object and threw Julian over his shoulder. There was a loud thud and grunt as he hit the floor. Daniel next grabbed his assailant by the neck. The head was savagely thrust to make violent contact several times with the wall. As he lay in pain on the floor, Daniel grabbed him by the hair and sent a clenched fist flying into Julian's nose. This had the effect of sending blood and mucous in all directions. The clientele was silenced. Some briefly cheered.

Whilst his friend lay groaning in agony, Timothy Walden jumped up and faced Daniel. Walden tried to emulate some movie hero. His arms were raised in some martial arts pose.

"I'm an expert in karate." Walden claimed. "I'll break you in two."

"Come on!" He taunted Daniel.

In a split second, an open hand flew out and knocked Walden flying backwards. He fell groaning, ignominiously, onto the aptly coloured maroon carpet of the lounge.

"Don't play with the big boys until you've practised. Practised for a hell of a long time!" Daniel snarled threateningly. "By my reckoning, you've about ten years work to do before you're even in the same ball park as a Royal Marine."

Once outside Daniel said to James and Fred. "He's hurt. Let's return to Wye Hall."

DANESH AND KELLY

Danelaw led the three women across the muddy market square of the settlement. A grimy area that stood before the stone walls of the consecrated grounds of the Church of Saint Lawrence.

The villagers had snot ridden faces. Their clothing was filthy attire and they enjoyed a life expectancy not more than 40. Yet they were beaming in adulation. It was mystifying. No agent or condition was immediately apparent as to account for the source of their flowing rapture.

"There be it!" Guyzanc, the putative sorceress pointed. It was at a cone, a golden tornado that whirled above the ground. It hovered on the church periphery. "He be here soon! The golden light. That be his guiding lantern from the other side."

The crowd were now praying and calling out to the heavens. A tunnel of luminosity rose up in a whirlwind of radiance with millions of tiny sparks emitted. Within the minor aurora there gradually materialised a short figure. This manifestation was attired in a red cloak and long, wide brimmed ochre hat with a crimson shirt, sky blue trousers and knee length ebony shaded leather boots.

"People! I visit you all again! I bring great news of your ultimate salvation! From the Almighty himself!"

The entire gathering fell to their knees. All bar Danelaw, Kelly, Keely, Philemon, Guyzanc and another person. He was covered from head to toe in a mantle of black leather.

"Strangers! Strangers! They be not mine associate! Nor yours.!"

"Strangers! Not associates!" The crowd repeated. The chant drew down a macabre sensation. A curtain of unadulterated fear that enveloped the bedraggled situate.

It was obvious within seconds that the figure from the light was Grant Woburn. The deranged being was stirring superstition and mayhem into the gullible, pediculous people. Kelly was shocked. It was but no time since he had sat so benignly before her.

"I bring you all news. The good King Henry shall march on the Scots!"

"Derbish! Woburn!" Danelaw called. "Whatever sobriquet you have elected to adopt. Be off with you and leave these good folks. Henry marched on the Scots many years ago. You are even more unhinged than I expected."

"Professor Gidron. I have warned you many times. Alas, you have not the predisposition to comprehend. Thou art light years without your time and depth!"

An atmospheric maelstrom came towards the Danelaw.

"My. My. You are even dressed in the correct attire. You and your doomed ladies."

Three of the villagers were drawn into the auburn funnel. They screamed until within the rotating materialisation then there was silence.

"Sin! Sin! They sinned! You have all sinned, so a penalty was levied. The price of sin is death! Now the ladies shall come with me! Are you prepared for your final journey?"

"My clothes are the wrong colour." the ingenuous non sequitur came from Kelly.

"I drew you here! Worship the True One!"

"We will exalt thee!" The crowd called out.

Woburn ran at the women. He was blocked by the mere sight of the man in the black leather cloak. The enigmatic warrior lifted a lance and powerfully hurled the shaft at Woburn.

This brawny figure watched as the javelin flew at a velocity that made it almost imperceptible to the eye.

"Daniy of Wark," Derbish taunted, "Return to thine hovel and hone thy skills. Thou shalt never be equal to mine own aptitudes." The young man in black released another spear. This effort sliced the clothing of the creature, drawing a small amount of odd coloured fluid.

"I still hold mine tenure of this world. Two spears Daniy. Thine competencies require some seasoning!"

Whilst the being known as Derbish continued his mocking of Daniy, Danelaw lifted a similar lance. With an almost inhuman force, he thrust the wood and metal implement towards the balding, dwarf like apparition.

The point flew onto and seemingly through the figure. In a normal human being the area would be described as around the left scapula.

"Ah!" Diabolo shrieked. A torturous clamour that scraped painfully across the eardrums of the assembled crowd. He raced back, howling in agony and at immense speed back into the vent of his personal shimmering storm. The vision immediately evaporated into the ether.

"The day must be mine. I must be with greater alacrity to kill the beast or did I perchance slay the fiend?" The cloaked figure muttered. Instantly, the crowd of people were unaffected. They were acting as if nothing at all had just transpired. No confusion or bewilderment.

"Sir," Keely called out to the young man. He had thick chestnut hair was robed in a chain mail tunic. The warrior also wore linen trousers and leather boots and a leather cloak. This was now drawn back to reveal his face. "What be thy name?"

"Lady Kielty. All of thee be Lady Kielty. How be such a thing? Did God make three of you to supplant those who fallen in the struggle?"

The non-plus crowd were now totally disinterested. They sloped off to their mundane businesses.

"Sir. What be thy name?" Kelly enquired this time.

"I be Daniy of Wark. My father be a tenant of land up over yon hill. But like such simple folk we fight when needed. I have hunted the Diabolo since a child. He took my mother. Now, I, along with the old knight, hath slain him! He be expeditious. Speedier than the launched arrow at noonday."

"Daniy." This time it was Philemon speaking. "We travelled from afar. Is the creature that hunts us now in the land of the afterlife? Or be he licking his wounds in some dark recess of the Cosmos?"

"He shall return," Guyzanc cackled in a blood curdling pitch, "Daniy of Wark merely scratched the demon. The old knight may have dealt him a mortal blow. But mine bones would surely whisper their dreadful missive should he now lie in Purgatory. Or beyond. In Hell!"

Danelaw stepped back to where the women were standing. "Ladies. I fear the hag doth speak with some measure of veracity. Grant Woburn may well have perished. At the lowest expectation he is impaired, but it is premature for jubilation. We cannot rest. For the time being best we remain alert. And always vigilant."

Daniy then offered more counsel. "Travel with utmost circumspection when I am not with presence. And you Lady Kielty, all three of you, do not return presently to this place. It be abundant with grave peril. If you do he shall take you., He would already hold you in his hellish dungeon but for my lance and that of the old knight. If he is still granted life, never seek to confront the beast. He maintains to these simple folk that he needs to save souls. But those that he seeks most, the souls he hunts like a ghostly carnivore, are those of every Lady Kielty in Middle Earth."

Danelaw had seen and heard enough. "Daniy. I offer my gratitude. I am in concurrence with you. I truly believe that this place and this time are very dangerous for the ladies. We shall go."

"I would return to thine lands with haste. I know not how long Diabolo of Woburn will be absent if still outside Purgatory. But I implore thee, all three, depart with haste! His design be to eliminate. The creature needs to eliminate all of you, all Lady Kieltys. That is before he can prevail and take dominion of all in the heavens and the Earth. I beseech thee go. And go now!"

"Sir. May our paths cross again?" Kelly was intoxicated by the very demeanour of her new champion.

"Lady Kielty. Shalt thou to travel this road another time, thou shalt find me at the farm. The farm across the ford over the river on the road going west. Now go. For pity's sake. Ladies. Leave, Diabolo may return. Only the passing of many days will divulge the mystery whether he live or lie in the land beyond Middle Earth. He may return and take you!"

Danelaw intervened. "We have to go. As the man says. It brims with peril in this place at this pivotal digit on the celestial chronometer."

PHILIPPA-DECEMBER 1967

Philippa had called on every favour she had in her favour bank. She had managed to stock up with several boxes of extremely expensive Harrods handmade chocolate truffles as well as several bottles of 1960 vintage Amarone della Valpolicella singular Italian red wine.

The stash had also included several very costly examples of the pink packet embracing a painting of a smoking cavalier, the coveted WD and HO Wills' Passing Clouds upmarket cigarettes. Despite the December cold, Caroline was out on the balcony of Philippa's bedchamber breathing in the late night air.

"A car is coming, Pip. You wait here, and I'll go down and show them up."

"Thank U Very Much" by the Scaffold was playing on the Dansette record player.

In her flowing blue maternity dress, Caroline walked down the wood panelled staircase.

The young widow reached the foot only to discover it was not Philippa's three friends who were making an entry but James, Matthew and Daniel. They were awaiting Fred Biggs who was parking the car. Caroline stared at James, the unhealed emotional trauma reopened as her lower jaw began to tremble and in a howl of agony she commenced wailing.

James placed his arms around her and tenderly spoke into her ear.

"It's alright, Caroline. It's alright. You have a good cry."

She looked up at the tall figure holding her.

"James, I miss him. I miss him so much it hurts. It hurts badly. Very badly."

"We all miss him." James brushed the hair from her eyes. "We always will miss him. His last words were, "tell Caroline I love her"."

The words invoked and unlocked even more suffering from deep within the young woman as James added. "You have to be strong. For the baby. That's what David would want of you."

She smiled. "Thank you, James. Emily is such a lucky girl."

At that juncture the music changed to Gene Pitney singing "Somethings Gotten Hold of My Heart" and the doorknocker rapped again.

Caroline sniffed and smiled, then moved slowly away from James to greet the old friends Judith Parkhouse, Patricia Laidlaw and Christine Vickers.

The three women were in flared trouser suits and frilly blouses.

"Caroline!" Pat hugged her. "What is that conspicuous bump on your belly?"

"I'll tell you when you're old enough. Upstairs. Philippa broke all records to accede to your requests. She really wants to make it up."

"Perhaps." Judith nodded. "Let's go and meet the old girl and see what she has to say!"

The four of them pranced at speed up to Philippa's bedroom.

"I'm so, so sorry," Philippa sobbed. She hugged all of them including and especially Caroline.

The bruising on her face was both painful and impossible to disregard.

"Jeez, Pip," Judith exclaimed, "That's one hell of a shiner that arsehole Julian gave you. You have obviously called off the engagement. Haven't you?"

"Of course, I have. James and Daniel were going to have a word with him."

"I had a phone call just as I was coming out." Pat revelled in being the harbinger of hot gossip.

"I understand it was more than a word. I heard that some dishy bloke went into the Angel pub and warned Julian. As this Adonis was about to walk away, that Barclays Banker Julian tried to hit him with a bottle. Julian had his head bashed off the wall and his nose broken."

"Also," Judith energetically interjected, "That puff Walden tried to attack this dude. He must be one of James' officer Marines types, and he ended up, Walden I mean, on the floor. It must have been so groovy."

"Where is out booty, Pip?" Christine finally emerged from her mute state. "I am told that we have wines worthy of the most esteemed connoisseur, hand crafted chocolates of the ultimate in eminence and those elegant oval cigarettes that oft grace the House of Lords."

"I have all that, am I forgiven?"

The three newcomers remained silent for a few seconds then Pat spoke for all of them.

"Hand over copious quantities of our tribute and we agree to put you on probation. So long as we can try on all your new outfits. And you allow us first refusal on all dishy single officer types James invites here. All that being so, it is very conceivable we may forgive."

Philippa handed over a bottle of Valpolicella, a corkscrew and some glasses.

"However." Philippa qualified the latter remark. "The one called Daniel I have first refusal on. There is another who is quite dishy though. He's called Matthew."

Stephen Grenfell

EMILY-DECEMBER 1967

Flying Officer Don Rampton delicately manoeuvred the Westland Wessex HC.2. He was landing the helicopter onto the unlit meadow adjacent to the house of Emily's parents.

The thundering rotations of the powerful Rolls Royce Gnome engines made conversation impossible without the wearing of earphones. The chubby shape of loadmaster, Warrant Officer Mike Powell, beckoned to Emily. "You can get out here. Miss. Just toss your earphones on the seat before ya go and slide out."

"Thank you." she smiled. "And thank you mister pilot. You've both been wonderful."

The young woman dropped gently from the platform of the helicopter and into the raucous, swirling whirlwind within the downdraft of the rotors. In a second she was sprinting across the paddock to the fence that separated the pasture from the bungalow beyond.

Powell spoke into his intercom and the helicopter rose from the bucolic pad up into the darkness.

She hitched up her skirt and cleared the fence in a single bound then ran to the side door and into the kitchen.

"I'm home. Mum!"

"Come in here. Emm," Mary Wilkinson called out from the front room.

She dashed in, kissed her mother on the cheek then hugged Harvey Wilkinson, beaming at the arrival home of his daughter.

"You're watching colour TV!" Emily exclaimed.

"There's a full colour service now on BBC 2." Mary was ecstatic at their latest acquisition. "We're watching "Horizon". It's great in colour. A bit too brainy stuff for me but Oy likes seein' stuff in colour."

"It's lovely. Dad, can I put something in your strong box please."

"Course ye can." Harvey jumped up and strolled into the study room. There he moved a picture to expose the door of a combination safe. The dial was turned several times upon which the steel door opened. Emily handed him a brown envelope which he placed on a shelf separate away from the other packages and documentation.

"Thanks Dad. You're brilliant." Harvey just smiled.

"Dad," she called out again.

"Yes, sweetness."

"Do you think I could be a real pain and borrow the car? I have to get to James' place and I left mine in London?"

"Did ye come by train?" Mary was up and turned the tap on to fill the kettle. "There was a loud noise outside. It must have been a helicopter from Brize Norton."

"That was me, Mum. I caught a lift with the RAF."

"Really. You just asked 'arold Wilson and 'e called ye a helicopter?"

"No, Dad. I knew a couple of RAF pilots who were flying this way and they offered to give me a lift. Providing I mentioned them in the Cosmopolitan the next time I write an article." Emily was convincingly economical with the truth. "So, Dad. Can I borrow the car please?"

"Course ye can, me dear," Harvey tossed a bunch of keys to Emily who cleanly caught them. "I'll just have a quick bath and change. Then I'll put on some war paint and be off."

The Ford Cortina turned into the drive leading to Wye Hall. Within moments it pulled up just to the side of the main entrance. The large oak double doors opened and James stood below the imposing lintels.

"Darling! "He ran out as Emily threw herself at him. James caught her in mid-flight. They swung around several times while they passionately kissing.

The couple marched unceremoniously into the house where Rebecca, Daniel and Mark stood.

"Miss Emily. So nice to see you. May I fetch you something?"

"No thank you, Becky. I'm here to see my fiancé just back from the war. He's surging with primitive emotions from the battlefield."

"You know Daniel," James pointed. He stepped forward.

"Nice to see you again, Emily." he gave the QC a quick kiss in the cheek.

"And this is Matthew, Matthew Field. He joined us in Aden for the last part of the tour." James completed the formalities.

"Pleased to meet you."

Emily and Matthew shook hands then she turned to her lover and drew him into the lounge.

"Upstairs. To your bedroom. I've had numerous men attempt to seduce me. Now you're here, you can both seduce me and fuck me. At least four times in a row!"

James smiled. They ran at once through the lounge and up the side stairs to his bedroom.

Emily was unbuttoning her blouse as they walked and once in the room she kicked off her shoes, unzipped her gold lame miniskirt and allowed it to drop to the floor upon which she took care to place it over the back of an armchair. The following manoeuvre was the rapid removal of her tights, briefs and bra upon completion of which she impatiently threw back the covers and leapt into bed.

James was still fumbling through his shoelaces. She jumped up, undid the buttons on his shirt, unhooked his trousers and slipped into the welcoming large double bed.

Within seconds they were both completely naked and Emily was sitting on top of James. For the next hour they continued their loud, athletic lovemaking.

"Shit, Emm." James panted. "I'm worn out. You sure were one randy chick."

He lit two cigarettes and handed one to her. She was still gasping and glowing with perspiration.

"I've waited six months for those five fucks. Lord Marchant. Don't ever leave me for that long again. My fanny starts to take over my brain. I get randy attacks. Erotic dreams and I start gagging for it in strange places. Like a lift, the Yanks call them elevators, in New York. Now, fill me in on all the gossip."

"I take it you still love me?"

She tenderly stroked his chin. "Dearest James. You have no idea just how many pop stars, film stars, TV folk, and even my boss at the chambers, I've turned down to be faithful to you. Of course, I love you. I would never have subjected myself to the voluntary torture of complete abstinence until I got you back in bed if I didn't love you a huge amount, now tell me the gossip."

The Miasmic Mist —Volume One

PHILIPPA/DANIEL-DECEMBER 1967

The breakfast table was humming although little was said. The wireless was tuned to the new Radio Four station; the programme being broadcast was "Today" featuring Jack de Manio.

"The Duke of Surrey is not amused." Tom Marchant looked over his "The Times" towards his son. "I'm sure he's not. But he must bear some responsibility for rearing such an ugly specimen as Julian," James nonchalantly responded.

"He says he'll get the police onto the "thug", his words not mine, who injured his son."

James ignored his father and walked to the serving table to grab another sausage and rasher of bacon.

"Becky is such a great cook. And Papa, if the Duke does call in the law, we'll call them in for his assault on Pip. Such a cowardly act. This person did not attack Julian. Julian tried to hit him with a bottle while his back was turned."

"I'm not criticising, James. I would have thumped him, but Daniel did a much more professional job."

"I know you would, Papa."

"The only caveat I will introduce into our discourse is that the Duke is very wealthy. In addition to the influence gained thereof, he wields a massive amount of power and sway in the political and financial spheres of the country. It is not beyond the bounds of possibility, following the shame of the break up after so much publicity, that he may seek to cause me some monetary or other impairment. Or you. Or indeed anyone in fact he takes some disdain to."

"Papa." James filled the breakfast cups of Daniel and Matthew with fresh coffee. "You're a peer of the realm. Not without a shilling or two. And friends in lofty towers in the corridors of power and banking. I'm sure you can take care of yourself. Whatever. It is worth the monetary cost to keep that animal away from Philippa."

"You're so optimistic these days. James. Are you and your chums being deployed elsewhere?"

At that hiatus Philippa sauntered into the room. She was bleary eyed and in her rose-coloured silk dressing gown. She kissed her father on the cheek.

"Daddy, where's Mummy?"

"Out. Shooting or shopping. Not sure which," Tom replied, "Are your friends still asleep?"

"Yes, Daddy. They downed a few glasses of wine and are still snoring away like puppies. James, may I have a word, please, in private?"

He followed his sister out into the lounge.

"What is it, Pip? You're not having second thoughts about breaking up with Julian. Are you?"

"Christ no!"

"Then what has arisen that requires a private chinwag?"

"It's Daniel."

"What's he done?" James sounded extremely defensive about his friend.

"Does he fancy me? Or even like me? I know he brought swift and true retribution against that pig yesterday eve, but he never looks, or smiles, at me?"

James quietly chortled.

"Daniel fancies you like mad. But he's a straight forward Northumbrian."

"So, what?"

"He's shy. Even though he flirted with you recently, you ignored him once at a party when he was trying to get your attention. He took that as a permanent snub. He's not like your usual crowd who'll keep chasing you even though you knock them back. Listen, Pip. If you want him that badly you'll have to be the proactive one. Because if you wait for him you'll be an old woman before he comes to you."

"What should I do?"

"Get one of your friends to take Matthew to the pub. You catch Dan by himself and ask him. He'll almost certainly say "yes". Then go for a pub lunch and take him to your pad. But you'll have to be quick. He's travelling home to Northumberland to see his parents for Christmas. First thing in the morning. Might I suggest you move with some haste. Now I want to finish eating my breakfast."

Somehow Daniel had wandered into the library. He was checking out the enormous collection of volumes and novels housed in the massive, lavish area.

Breakfast had been excellent, far better than even the finest served in the officers' mess.

Nonetheless, nagging and conflicting sentiments and emotion were flowing with some acerbity through the channels of his life force. He was opening a few pages when Philippa slowly, silently and nervously entered the tome brimming chamber.

"Hello." She smiled.

"Hello," Daniel looked up.

"I wanted to thank you for upholding mine honour."

"It was no problem. He was a big man but the bigger they are the harder they fall. And he fell very hard."

"I'm not doing anything today. Would you like to come with me for a pub lunch? Then a drive out? I know my black eye looks bad. Sorry."

"No need to apologise in any way shape or form and I could think of nothing I'd like better than to have lunch with you."

She broke into a huge smile. He gently took hold of her right hand and drew her to him. They open mouthed kissed her for some time.

"I've wanted to do that since I first saw you, Lady Philippa Marchant."

"Please. Just call me Pip. Lieutenant Gibson. And later there could be a lot more kisses."

"I look forward to it. As long as you call me Dan."

"I will, Dan. I have to bathe and get changed. It'll take two hours, So I'll see you outside the main entrance door at 11.00 this morning. Is that alright?" "That will be splendidly fine."

She ran out of the door leaving Daniel more upbeat than he had felt in months. He speculated that the ghosts of a previous relationship were probably well and truly laid to rest.

Daniel's innermost thoughts were on a journey of self-analysis and speculation. It was no arduous task for him to promptly discern that the pub lunch was akin to all such procreation rituals. One of those mandatory rites in the mating game.

He muttered away within his own mind, "It is like asking a woman if she wants a drink when one truly means "can I have sex with you?" Or "shall we sleep together?" which are basically the same. Unless you are dating the enigmatic Lady Philippa Marchant. I think anyway there are such a superfluity of mysteries within that beautiful head to unravel. A veritable plethora of personal attributes and character traits to encounter and appreciate. This will be a fine expedition into the soul. We can dance under the moonlight. Sing our life's tales beneath the shimmering stars and read poetry enveloped within a blanket of passion and desire."

"Did you enjoy lunch? The Plough Inn is a nice pub."

"It was very nice, thank you, Pip. I really liked the place."

"I know I pressed you a little, but we are short of time. You go home tomorrow."

"Yes, back to Northumberland. I'd love to stay here but I promised mother I'd be home before Christmas. She suffered enough while I was in Aden. So, I have to keep my word."

"Don't worry. I have plenty of booze and food at my place. I want to introduce you to my private retreat."

The car drove through the small village of Goosey. It lay in Berkshire but straddled the border with Oxfordshire in the picturesque Vale of White Horse. They arrived at a very impressive brick built detached cottage. Philippa turned into the gravel drive.

"Here. My personal pad. Let's have a drink and that snog you promised me."

"I'm in favour of that." Daniel was still mesmerised and staggered by the whirlwind of an experience.

Several hours later, in the middle of the night, a naked Philippa walked across the floor. Her clothing was covering much of it like very expensive, discarded detritus. She sat in the armchair facing the large double bed. The young woman looked over at the sleeping Daniel, half covered by the bedclothes. She lit a cigarette and gazed passionately again at the dozing figure before her.

Through the impure light of the early hours of the new day, Daniel appeared angelic, celestial and divine. A pleasurable glow emanated across her body. Principally the nether regions as she recalled with warmth, physical longing and deep carnal intimacy, the five occasions the young

Marine officer had brought her on to climax. Such demands on her life force had never felt so natural and serendipitous. So exciting and pleasing. Their bodies and souls, she believed, were forever meant to interlock.

"Lieutenant," Philippa whispered to the slumbering outline, "I like you. I like you a lot. A very lot. I think this is an unanticipated occasion, perhaps our futures may well be entwined."

NARRATOR

There lies in the shady breach between the fastidious writings and the amazing revelations of the saga contained therein. The spirit of chronicles yet to be divulged. I have reached a hiatus in the tale. Ergo I must take my leave albeit not permanently. There are many more chapters of love, loss, war, peace, tragedy and singular travel to impart. The audience remains attentive, they eagerly await my return.

END OF VOLUME ONE

Acknowledgements

To all my friends and family over the years who have imparted their experiences to augment mine own especially all my masters at the Duke's Grammar School, Alnwick, Northumberland. Now sadly gone. And those in formerly in uniform who helped fill gaps. Namely Pete Smallridge, once in 45 Commando Royal Marines, Aden 1967, and John "Jock" Lithgow formerly of 1st Battalion Argyll and Sutherland Highlanders, Aden 1967. Also, Chris Stokes, formerly of 1st Battalion the Wessex (TA) Regiment who helped enormously with detail. My mother for some historical background information and the Hoddesdon Library and Wikipedia for verifying dates, mainly of hit songs and movies.

About the Author

Steve Grenfell was born in West Hartlepool, county Durham, England. He went to school at Amble in Northumberland. Then to the Duke's Grammar School in Alnwick, Northumberland. A town about 40 miles south of the England/ Scotland border.

Once out of college he went into industry management within several companies where he further honed writing skills. He has served in both the British Territoral Army (Reserves) and Royal Marines (Reserves).

Steve has a grown family living in England. He now lives in the United States, (Burbank, California) with his wife Brenda. They travel extensively including regular visits to the United Kingdom to see friends and relatives.

Printed in the United States
By Bookmasters